Homecoming

Cynthia Voigt was born, raised and educated in New England. Then she moved to Maryland, where she lived for over twenty years. She taught for most of that time, everything from beginner reading to senior English, and she also wrote, eventually succeeding in getting her work published. She now lives in Maine with her husband; her two children are grown up and have moved on into their own lives.

Homecoming was her first published book. It grew into the Tillerman series, seven books long. Besides this, she has written several other books, of various kinds for various ages, and one other completed series, the Kingdom books, as well as the unfinished Bad Girls stories.

Cynthia continues to write because it satisfies two basic needs: the need to have something interesting to think about, and the need to be doing something. She continues to miss teaching, but enjoys all the time now free for reading, tennis, movie-going and just hanging around with friends.

Collins Modern Classics

Homecoming

by

Cynthia Voigt

Illustrated by Sharon Scotland

Collins

An imprint of HarperCollins*Publishers*

First published in the USA by Atheneum Publishers 1981
First published in Great Britain by Collins 1984
First published as a Collins Modern Classic 1999

7 9 10 8 6

Collins Modern Classics is an imprint of
HarperCollins*Publishers* Ltd, 77–85 Fulham Palace Road,
Hammersmith, London W6 8JB.

The HarperCollins website address is
www.**fire**and**water**.com

Copyright © Cynthia Voigt 1981
Illustration copyright © Sharon Scotland 1999
Postscript copyright © Cynthia Voigt 1999

ISBN 0 00 675427-9

Printed and bound in Great Britain by
Omnia Books Limited, Glasgow

CONTENTS

To Jessica & Walter

Part One

Chapter One

THE WOMAN PUT her sad moon-face in at the window of the car. "You be good," she said. "You hear me? You little ones, mind what Dicey tells you. You hear?"

"Yes, Momma," they said.

"That's all right then." She slung her purse over her shoulder and walked away, her stride made uneven by broken sandal thongs, thin elbows showing through holes in the oversized sweater, her jeans faded and baggy. When she had disappeared into the crowd of Saturday morning shoppers entering the side doors of the mall, the three younger children leaned forward on to the front seat. Dicey sat in front. She was thirteen and she read the maps.

"Why'd we stop?" asked James. "We're not there yet. We've got food. There's no reason to stop." James was ten and wanted everything to have a reason. "Dicey?"

"I dunno. You heard everything she said, same as I did. You tell me."

"All she said was, *We gotta stop here.* She didn't say why. She never says why, you know that. Are we out of gas?"

"I didn't look." Dicey wanted some quiet for thinking. There was something odd about this whole trip. She couldn't put her finger on it, not yet. "Why don't you tell them a story?"

"What story?"

"Cripes, James, you're the one with the famous brain."

"Yeah, well, I can't think of any stories right now."

"Tell them anything. Tell them Hansel and Gretel."

"I want HanselnGretel. And the witch. And the candy house with peppermint sticks," Sammy said, from the back seat. James gave in without a quarrel. It was easier to give in to Sammy than to fight him. Dicey turned around to look at them. Maybeth sat hunched in a corner, big-eyed. Dicey smiled at her and Maybeth smiled back. "Once upon a time," James began. Maybeth turned to him.

Dicey closed her eyes and leaned her head back. She put her feet on the dashboard. She was tired. She'd had to stay awake and read maps, to find roads without tolls. She'd been up since three in the morning. But Dicey couldn't go to sleep. She gnawed away at what was bothering her.

For one thing, they never took trips. Momma always said the car couldn't run more than ten miles at a stretch. And here they were in Connecticut, heading down to Bridgeport. For one thing.

Chapter One

But that might make sense. All her life, Dicey had been hearing about Momma's Aunt Cilla and her big house in Bridgeport that Momma had never seen, and her rich husband who died. Aunt Cilla sent Christmas cards year after year, with pictures of baby Jesus on them and long notes inside, on paper so thin it could have been tissue paper. Only Momma could decipher the lacy handwriting with its long, tall letters all bunched together and the lines running into one another because of the long-tailed, fancy z's and f's and g's. Aunt Cilla kept in touch. So it made sense for Momma to go to her for help.

But driving off like that in the middle of the night didn't make sense. That was the second thing. Momma woke them all up and told them to pack paper bags of clothing while she made sandwiches. She got them all into the old car and headed for Bridgeport.

For a third — things had been happening, all at once. Things were always bad with them, but lately worse than ever. Momma lost her checker's job. Maybeth's teacher had wanted a meeting with Momma that Momma wouldn't go to. Maybeth would be held back another year. Momma said she didn't want to hear about it, and she had ripped up every note, without reading any of them. Maybeth didn't worry her family, but she worried her teachers. She was nine and still in the second grade. She never said much, that was the trouble, so everybody thought she was stupid. Dicey knew she wasn't. Sometimes she'd come out and say something that showed she'd been watching and listening and taking things in. Dicey knew her sister could read and do sums, but Maybeth always sat quiet around strangers. For Maybeth, everyone in the world was a stranger, except Momma and Dicey and James and Sammy.

Momma herself was the fourth thing. Lately she'd go to the store for bread and come back with a can of tuna and just put her hands over her face, sitting at the table. Sometimes she'd be gone for a couple of hours and then she wouldn't say where she had been, with her face blank as if she couldn't say. As if she didn't know. Momma didn't talk to them any more, not even to scold, or sing, or make up games the way she used to. Except Sammy. She talked to Sammy, but even then they sounded like two six-year-olds talking, not one six-year-old and his mother.

Dicey kept her feet on the dash, and her body slouched down. She looked out through the windscreen, over the rows of parked cars, to where the sky hung like a bleached-out sheet over the top of the mall buildings. Bugs were spattered all over the windscreen and the sky promised a heavy, hot day. Dicey slid still further down on the seat. Her skin stuck to the blue plastic seat covers.

James was describing the witch's house, listing the kinds of candy used for various parts of the building. This was the part James liked best in Hansel and Gretel, and he always did it a little differently from the time before. Picturing the almond Hershey bar roof and the shutters made of cinnamon liquorice sticks, Dicey did fall asleep.

She woke covered with sweat from the hot sun pouring

in through the windscreen. She woke hungry. Maybeth was singing softly, one of Momma's songs, about making her love a baby with no crying. "I fell asleep," Dicey said. "What time's it?"

"I dunno," James said. "You've been asleep a long time. I'm hungry."

"Where's Momma?"

"I dunno. I'm hungry."

"You're always hungry. Go and ask someone what time it is, OK?"

James climbed out of the car. He crossed to the walkway and stopped a man in a business suit. "Twelve-thirty," James reported.

"But that means I slept for more than two hours," Dicey protested.

"I'm going to eat," Sammy announced from the back seat. He opened the bag of food and pulled out a sandwich before Dicey could say anything.

"What do you want me to do?" James asked, looking into Dicey's face. His narrow little face wore a worried expression. "Want me to go look for her?"

"No," Dicey said. (*Now* what had Momma gone and done?) "Sammy, give Maybeth a sandwich too. Let her choose for herself. Then pass the bag up here."

When everyone had a sandwich, and James had two, Dicey reached a decision. "We have to wait here for a while more," she said. "Then we'll do something. I'm going to take a walk and see if I can find her."

"Don't you go away too," Maybeth said softly.

"I'll be right where you can see me," Dicey said. "I'll stay on the pavement – see? – just like a path in front of the stores. Then maybe later we can all go into the mall and look in the stores. You'd like that, wouldn't you?" Maybeth smiled and nodded her golden head.

Dicey did her best thinking when she walked. On this warm June afternoon, she walked so fast and thought so hard, she didn't even see the people going past her. If Momma went past she'd say something, so Dicey wasn't worried about that.

She was worried that Momma had wandered off. And would not come back.

("You always look for the worst," Momma had often told her. – "I like to be ready," Dicey answered.)

If Momma was gone… But that wasn't possible. Was it? But if she was, what could they do? Ask for help, probably from a policeman. (Would he put them in homes or orphanages? Wouldn't that be just what the police or some social worker would do?) Go back to Provincetown, they could go back home. (Momma hadn't paid the rent, not for weeks, and it was almost summertime, when even their old cabin, set off alone in the dunes, could bring in a lot of money. Mr Martinez wasn't sympathetic, not when it came to money, not when it came to giving something away for free. He'd never let them stay there to wait for Momma.) They could go on to Bridgeport. Dicey had never seen Aunt Cilla – Great-Aunt Cilla. She knew the name and address, because

Chapter One

Momma had made her write it down four times, on each paper bag, in case something happened: Mrs Cilla Logan, 1724 Ocean Drive, Bridgeport, Connecticut. Aunt Cilla was family, the only family Dicey knew about.

The sun beat down on the car park and heated up the air so even in the shaded walkway Dicey was hot. The kids must be hot too, she thought, and turned to get them.

Momma must have gone away on purpose. (But she loved them, loved them all.) Why else the addresses on the bags? Why else tell them to mind Dicey? (Mothers didn't do things like going off. It was crazy. Was Momma crazy?) How did she expect Dicey to take care of them? What did she expect Dicey to do? Take them to Bridgeport, of course. (Dump it all on Dicey, that was what Momma did, she always did, because Dicey was the determined sort. "It's in your blood," Momma said, and then wouldn't explain.)

Anger welled up in Dicey, flooded her eyes with tears, and now she was swept away with the determination to get the kids to Bridgeport. Well, she'd do it somehow, if she had to.

Momma wasn't at the car when Dicey returned, so Dicey said they'd wait for her until the next morning.

"Where'll we sleep?" Sammy asked.

"Right here — and no complaints," Dicey said.

"Then Momma will come back and we'll go on tomorrow?" Sammy asked.

Dicey nodded.

"Where is Momma? Why's she taking so long?" James asked.

"I dunno, James," Dicey answered. Maybeth was silent, staring.

After a few minutes, Dicey hustled them all out of the car and trailed after them as they entered the mall.

The mall was built like a fortress around a huge, two-storey enclosed street, where store succeeded store, as far as you could see. At one end of the central section was a cage of live birds in a little park of plastic trees and shrubs. The floor of their cage was littered with pieces of popcorn and gum wrappers. At the other end, the builders had made a waterfall through which shone different coloured lights. Outside, beyond the covered pavement that ran like a moat around the huge building, lay the huge, grey car park, a no-man's land of empty cars.

But here inside was a fairyland of colours and sounds, crowded with people on this Saturday afternoon, artificially lit and planted. Inside was a miniature city where endless diversions from the work-day world offered everything delightful. If you had money, of course. And even without money, you could still stare and be amazed.

They spent a long time wandering through stores, looking at toys and records and pianos and birthday cards. They were drawn to restaurants that exuded the smell of spaghetti and pizza or fried chicken, bakeries with trays of golden doughnuts lined up behind glass windows, candy stores, where the countertop was crowded with large jars of jelly beans and sourballs and little foil-covered chocolates and peppermints dipped in crunchy white icing; cheese shops (they each had two free samples), where the rich smell of aged cheeses mingled with freshly-ground coffee, and hot-dog stands, where they stood back in a silent row. After this, they sat on a backless bench before the waterfall, tired and hungry. Altogether, they had eleven dollars and fifty cents, more than any one of them had ever had at one time before, even Dicey who contributed all of her babysitting money, seven dollars.

They spent almost four dollars on supper at the mall, and none of them had dessert. They had hamburgers and french fries and, after Dicey thought it over, milkshakes. At that rate, they could have one more meal before they ran out of money, or maybe two more. It was still light when they returned to the car. The little ones horsed around in the back, teasing, wrestling, tickling, quarrelling and laughing, while Dicey studied the map. People walked by their car, vehicles came and went, and nobody paid any attention to them. In car parks, it's not unusual to see a car full of kids waiting.

At half-past eight, Dicey herded everybody back into the mall, to use the bathrooms they had found earlier. Later, Sammy and Maybeth fell asleep easily, curled up along the back seat. James moved up to the front with Dicey. Dicey couldn't see how they were both to sleep in the front seat, but she supposed they would manage it. James sat stiffly, gripping the wheel. James had a narrow head and sharp features, a nose that pointed out, pencil-thin eyebrows, a narrow chin. Dicey studied him in the darkening car. They were parked so far from the nearest lamppost that they were in deep shadows.

With her brothers and sister near, with the two youngest asleep in the back seat, sitting as they were in a cocoon of darkness, she should feel safe. But she didn't. Though it was standing still, the car seemed to be flying down a highway, going too fast. Even the dark inside it was not deep enough to hide them. Faces might appear in the windows at any time, asking angry questions.

"Where's Momma gone?" James asked, looking out at the night.

"I just don't know," Dicey said. "Here's what I think, I think if she isn't back by morning we ought to go on to Bridgeport."

"On our own?"

"Yes."

"How'll we get there? You can't drive. Momma took the keys."

"We could take a bus, if we have enough money. If we don't, we'll walk."

James stared at her. Finally he spoke. "Dicey? I'm scared. I feel all jiggly in my stomach. Why doesn't Momma come back?"

"If I knew, James, I'd know what to do."

"Do you know the way?"

"To Bridgeport? I can read a map. Once we get there, we can ask directions to Aunt Cilla's house."

James nodded. "Do you think she's been killed? Or kidnapped?"

"Rich people get kidnapped; not Momma. I'm not going

to think about what might have happened to her, and I don't think you should, either."

"I can't help thinking about it," James said in a small voice.

"Don't tell Sammy or Maybeth," Dicey warned.

"I wouldn't. I know better. You should know I'd know better than that."

Dicey reached out and patted him on the shoulder. "I do know," she said.

James grabbed her hand. "Dicey? Do you think Momma meant to leave us here?"

"I think Momma meant to take us to Bridgeport, but—".

"Is Momma crazy?"

Dicey turned her head to look at him.

"The kids said so, at school. And the way the teachers looked at me and loaned me their own books and talked to me. And Maybeth. Craziness can run in families."

Dicey felt a great weight settle on her shoulders. She tried to shrug it off, but it wouldn't move.

"Dicey?"

"She loves us," Dicey muttered.

"But that's the only reason I can think of that might be true."

"There's nothing wrong with Maybeth. You know that."

"It runs in families. Hereditary craziness."

"Well, you don't have to worry about it, do you? You're the smart one, with A's in school and the science projects that get entered in the state contest."

"Yeah," James said. He settled his head back on the seat.

"Listen, I'm going to go to a phone and see where the bus station is and call them up to find out how much tickets cost. You lay low."

"Why?"

Dicey decided to tell him the truth. "Just in case. I mean, three kids in a car in a car park at night… See, James, I think we've got to get to Bridgeport and I just don't know what would happen if a policeman saw us. Foster homes or something, I dunno. I don't want to risk it. But one kid…and I'm pretty old, so it doesn't look funny."

"OK. That sounds OK."

"We've got to get to Bridgeport."

James thought about that, then nodded his head. "I never listened much to Momma's talk about her. What will she be like, Aunt Cilla?"

"Rich," Dicey said.

"It would be a long walk," James said.

"Long enough," Dicey agreed. She got out of the car fast.

It was full dark, an overcast night. The car park was nearly empty; only two cars besides theirs remained. Dicey wondered how many cars were left in the other three car parks that spread out from the other side of the building. It felt as empty as all of space must be. She hoped there were cars in each lot. The more cars there were, the safer their car was for them.

Dicey headed confidently for the walkway, as if she had every right to be where she was, as if she had an important errand to run, as if she knew just where she was going. She remembered a telephone at the far end of the building. It wasn't a real phone booth, but a kind of cubicle hung up on the wall, with an open shelf underneath to hold the directory. James could probably see her from the car, if he looked for her. From that distance, she would look small.

The walkway was lit up, and the store windows were lit, so she moved through patches of sharp light. At the phone, she took out the directory to look up bus companies in the yellow pages. She ran her finger down the names, selected one that sounded local and reached into her pocket for change.

She heard footsteps. A man approached her, in a uniform like a policeman's, but tan not blue, and without the badge. He took his time getting to her, as if he was sure she'd wait, sure of his own strength to hold her, even at that distance. He moved like he thought she was afraid of him, too afraid to run.

"Hey," the man said. His shirt had the word "Security" sewn onto it. Where his belly sagged, the shirt hung out over his pants. He carried a long-handled flashlight. He wore a pistol at his belt.

Dicey didn't answer, but she didn't look away.

"Hey, kid," he said, as if she had shown signs of running and he needed to halt her. He was heavy, out of shape. He had a pig-person face, a coarse skin that sagged at the jowls, little blue eyes and pale eyebrows, and a fat, pushed-back nose. When he came up next to her, Dicey stepped back a pace, but kept her finger on the number in the book.

"You lost?"

"Naw. I'm making a phone call."

"Where do you live?"

"Just over there," Dicey said, pointing vaguely with her free hand."

"Go home and call from there. Run along now. If you were a girl, I'd walk you over, but—"

"Our phone's broken," Dicey said. "That's why my mom sent me here."

The guard shifted his flashlight, holding it like a club. "Phones don't break. How's a phone break?"

"We've got this dog that chews things up. Slippers, papers, you know. He chewed the phone. The cord, actually, but it's all the same – the phone's broken."

"Are you bulling me?"

"I wish I was."

"What's your name, kid?"

"Danny."

She felt funny, strange, making up lies as quickly and smoothly as if she'd been doing it all her life.

The man took a piece of gum out of his pocket, unwrapped it, folded it in half and stuck it into his mouth, chewing on it a couple of times.

"Danny what?"

"Tillerman." Dicey couldn't make up a new last name, except Smith and nobody would believe that even if it was true.

"You don't look more than ten. Isn't it late to be out?"

Dicey shrugged.

The guard grew suspicious. "Who're you calling?"

"The bus company. My sisters and me are going down to Bridgeport some time soon, to stay with my aunt."

He chewed and thought. "Sometime soon wouldn't send you out after ten at night to phone. What's the rush?"

"My mom just got back from the clinic and she's gonna have her baby, any day now the doctor said, and my aunt needs to know what time the buses arrive so she can meet us on Monday. So's we can take a bus it's good for her to meet. My mom asked me to come find out so's she can call first thing in the morning, before my aunt goes to church. It's hard for my mom to get around now — you know."

"Where's your father?"

"Gone."

"Gone where?"

"Dunno. He just up and went, way back, last winter."

The guard nodded. He reached in his pocket and pulled out the pack of gum. He offered a piece to Dicey, but she shook her head.

"Can I call now, mister?"

"Sure thing," he said. "I wouldn't have bothered you except that there've been some windows broken around here. We think it's kids. I'm the security guard. I've got to be careful."

Dicey nodded. She inserted the coins and slowly dialled the numbers, hoping he'd go away. But he stood there and listened. Behind him lay the car park, a vast open space where occasional clumps of planted bushes spread long shadows over the ground.

An impersonal voice answered. Dicey asked about tickets to Bridgeport, how much they cost.

"From where to Bridgeport."

Dicey grabbed at a name. "Peewauket." That was what the map said. She pronounced it Pee-Walk-It. The guard listening narrowed his eyes.

"From Peewauket?" the voice asked, saying it Pwuk-it.

"Yeah."

"Two dollars and forty-five cents a person."

"What's the rate for children?"

"The same. The charge is for the seat. Unless you've got a child under two."

"What time do buses run?"

"Every other hour, from eight to eight."

Dicey thanked the voice and hung up the phone. She stood with her arms hanging down at her sides, waiting for the guard to leave.

He was studying her with his little piggy eyes. He held his flashlight now in one hand and slapped it into the palm of the other. "You better get back now," he said and then added, "You didn't write anything down."

"I've got a good memory."

"Yeah? I'll give you a test." His body blocked the way to the safe darkness of the car park. "You don't remember anything about broken windows in the mall, do you? For instance, just one for instance, at Record City."

Chapter One

"I don't know what you're talking about."

"I wonder about that. I really wonder, Danny. You said Danny, didn't you? Tillerman, wasn't it? You see, we figure it was probably kids did it, account of nothing's been stolen. Or maybe just one kid did it, that's what I'm thinking."

Dicey glared at him. "I said I don't know anything about that."

He put one arm out to bar her in, resting his hand against the side of the phone. "I can't think of why I should believe you. Nope, now I come to think of it, I don't think I do believe you. The only question in my mind is, what do I do with you?"

Dicey thought fast, then acted just as fast. She lifted her right knee as if to hit him in the groin where she knew it would hurt bad. He lowered his arm and stepped back, to protect himself. In that one second while he was off balance, Dicey took off. She sprinted into the darkness of the car park. As soon as she was in the cover of the shadows, she turned left around the corner of the building, away from their car. He thundered after her.

Dicey ran smoothly. She was used to running on beaches, where the sand gave way under your feet and each thrust of your legs was hindered. Running over asphalt was easier. Dicey pulled away from her pursuer. His steps were heavy and his breathing was heavy. He was out of shape and too fat to catch up with her. She had time to crouch behind one of the little islands of green that decorated the car park. She had on a dark shirt and jeans, her face was tanned and her hair brown; she was confident nothing would give her away.

He stopped by the front entrance, shining his flashlight out over the car park, like one bright eye. Dicey watched him. He listened, but his chest was heaving so much that she was sure he couldn't hear anything but the blood pounding in his ears. She smiled to herself.

"You haven't got a chance," he called. "You better come out now, kid. You're only making it worse."

Dicey covered her mouth with her hand.

"I know you now. We'll find you out," he said. He turned quickly away from the car park and looked further along the front of the mall. He hunched behind the flashlight. He used the beam like a giant eye, to peer into the shadows. "There you are! I can see you!" he cried.

But he was looking the wrong way. Dicey giggled, and the sound escaped her even though she bit on her hand to stop it.

He turned back to the car park, listening. Then he swore. His light swooped over the darkness, trying to search out her hiding place. "Danny? I'm gonna find you."

Dicey moved softly away on soundless sneakers through the covering shadows. He continued to call: "I'll remember your face, you hear? You hear me? Hear me?"

From halfway across the car park, safe in her own speed and in shadows, Dicey stopped. Her heart swelled in victory. "I hear you," she called softly back, as she ran towards the empty road and the patch of woods beyond.

Much later, when she returned to the car, James awoke

Chapter One

briefly. "Everything's OK," Dicey whispered, curling down on to the cold seat to sleep.

Chapter Two

DICEY AWOKE AT the first light. A chilly dew beaded the windshield. James's body leaning against her side was the only warmth in the car. He still slept, so she didn't move, even though her stiff muscles ached to be stretched. She watched the sun rise into a cold grey sky that turned warmer and brighter as the first peach-coloured beams of light grew golden, then yellow, then white. Surrounded by sleepers, Dicey sat content. The car was a cave within which they were safe. It held them together; and it protected them from outside forces, the cold, the damp, people.

At last James stirred, and his eyes opened. All four of them had the same hazel eyes, although Dicey and James had their father's dark hair, not the yellow hair their mother had passed on to Maybeth and Sammy.

James's hazel eyes looked at Dicey for a minute before he

spoke. "It's still true." His voice was hollow and sad. Their momma was really gone.

Dicey nodded. Sammy surged over from the back seat. "I gotta go to the bathroom. Bad."

Dicey turned her head and a muscle protested all the way down her back. "Maybeth? You awake?"

Maybeth was awake.

"OK, then. Let's take our clothes bags and change. And the food bag too, if you'd like to eat breakfast outside." Dicey took the map of Connecticut and jammed it into her clothes bag.

It was Sunday and nothing moved in the car park, the same few cars stood empty. The air was clear, clean, lucid, lying lightly upon the world that morning. The children scrambled out of the car and Dicey led them across the highway to the woodsy patch where she had hidden the night before. She led them into the thickest clustering of trees, then they separated to go to the bathroom.

They ate the last peanut butter sandwiches sitting on a low stone wall, listening to a few birds and watching the sunlight fall in bright, moving patterns on to the leafy floor of the woods. The air grew warmer.

Dicey finished her sandwich and crumpled the wax paper up. She tossed it into the food bag. Then she stripped down to her underpants and put on a pair of cutoff jeans and a T-shirt. She also put on a pair of socks. The others changed too. Dicey insisted that they wear socks.

"Why?" James asked. "It's hotter with socks on."

"If we're going to walk they'll keep us from getting blisters."

"Is that true?" James demanded. "I never had a blister."

"Of course, it's true," Dicey answered. "Now let me look at the map and think, all of you."

The little ones explored the little patch of woods while Dicey studied the map. Route 1 was the road they'd been driving on. They could follow it for a while, then they'd have to go on the Turnpike to get over the Thames River, to New London. After that, they'd have to switch to a road that followed the coastline, because Route 1 turned into the Turnpike for a long while. There was the Connecticut River to cross, then Route 1 again, or maybe they could take a coastal road, to New Haven. After New Haven, the map showed a yellow patch connecting the cities, all the way down to Bridgeport. That meant heavily populated areas. But Route 1 ran the whole distance.

Dicey looked at the map. Maybe two or three days, she judged. They had about seven dollars, so they could spend about two dollars a day on food. Half what they'd spent on one meal yesterday. But that was OK, because you didn't starve in two or three days. You could get awfully hungry, but you wouldn't starve.

"James?" she called. "Maybeth. Sammy. Come here now."

They ran up and sat in a circle around the map. Dicey showed them where Bridgeport was and about where they were. Then she made her announcement: "We're going to walk down to Bridgeport." The idea was so factual in her mind that she was unprepared for questions.

"What about Momma?" Sammy asked.

"I don't know where she's got to," Dicey said.

"We can wait for her here," Sammy said. His mouth puckered up.

"No, we can't," Dicey said, and she told them about the guard. "Momma will know we went on to Aunt Cilla's," Dicey said. Sammy's mouth set in a firm line. "We can't go back," Dicey said, "and we've got to go somewhere."

"That's all right," James spoke, "but why don't we take the bus?"

"Because we don't have enough money. Each ticket is two forty-five. That makes nine dollars and eighty cents all together and we've only got seven dollars."

"If we hadn't had supper last night," James said.

Dicey had already been over that in her own mind. "But we did," she cut him off. "So it's no good thinking, if we didn't. We're going to have to walk. Maybeth?"

Maybeth looked up from a pile of stones she was making into a long circle around herself. "That's fine, Dicey," she said. No questions, no worries in her round hazel eyes, just *that's fine*. Dicey felt like hugging her.

"How far is it?" James asked.

"I don't know for sure," Dicey said.

"How far can we walk in a day?" James asked.

"There's only one way to find out, isn't there?" Dicey asked. Only Sammy didn't smile in return.

"It'll be hard," she added. "We have to carry as little as

possible. Just one bag for all of us."

They sorted through their bags. Sammy refused to speak
or help, just sat cross-legged with his jaw set, picking at the
dirt with his finger. Dicey took out two changes of
underwear and two clean shirts for each, then she added a
pair of extra socks and one comb. Toothbrushes they could
get at Aunt Cilla's. There was about half a bag full when she
was through. It felt light enough in the cool morning, but she
knew that it would get heavier as the day went on. She
inhaled the sun-sweetened air and looked around her.

"I'm not going," Sammy said. He glared up at Dicey.

"What'll you do?" James asked him, perfectly reasonably.

"Wait here for Momma. Not here exactly, in the car."

"Sammy, you've got to come with us," Dicey said. "First
we're going to stash these other three bags in the car, then we
start walking. So get up."

Sammy shook his head.

"Don't you understand?" Dicey asked. "Momma's not
coming back, not here."

Sammy didn't answer her. Sammy's stubbornness was
beyond measure. When he made his mind up, there was
nothing you could do to move him. Threats didn't work. He
didn't mind being spanked or slapped. Explaining was no
good; it was as if he didn't even hear what you were saying to
him. Even Momma couldn't bully him into doing
something. Even James couldn't trick him into it.

But you couldn't go off and leave a six-year-old alone, in
the woods, in a strange place.

Chapter Two

Dicey crouched down beside him. The other two stood silent behind her. "Sammy? Momma's not coming back here. That's what I think. I think she's forgotten."

"Momma wouldn't forget me."

"No, she wouldn't. But she's forgotten where we are, I think. So if we go to Aunt Cilla's, that's where she'll probably be. We have to go find her."

"I don't want to," Sammy said. But he was thinking about what she'd said.

"I don't want to, either," Dicey said. "But we have to."

"No, we don't," Sammy said.

Dicey stood up in frustration and stamped her foot on the ground. "Then I'll carry you," she announced.

"I'll kick you." He stood up.

Maybeth stepped forward. "No, you won't," she said to Sammy. "Momma said to do as Dicey tells us. You heard her."

The two stared at one another. They were both sturdy little blonde figures, with round bellies. Sammy, shorter than Maybeth, but almost as heavy.

"Please, Sammy," Maybeth said.

"OK," Sammy said.

At the edge of the woods, where the grassy roadside banked above the macadam, they stopped to wait for an opening in the traffic. It was Sunday morning. People were driving to church, or to the beach. The children could look back and see their own car, green and lonely, in the middle of the car park.

It was kind of like a home, the car, Dicey thought. She understood why Sammy wanted to stay there.

They crossed the road, but stopped at the edge of the car park. A blue police car was driving around the lot. It stopped by their car. A policeman got out and opened the door. He stuck his head in. He opened the glove compartment and went through the maps, as if he was looking for something. He walked all around the car. He wrote something down in a little notebook. Then he looked towards the mall.

"Walk." Dicey gave the order. She took Sammy's hand. "Don't anybody look at our car."

They walked on, away from the mall and the car park and the car. Dicey led them back to Route 1. There, they turned south. They dumped the three grocery bags in the first rubbish bin they saw. Nobody said a word.

Route 1 was mostly garages and small shopping centres and discount stores and quick food places. There were no green patches and few sidewalks. They walked along concrete or asphalt, or on roadside gravel. Soon, their feet hurt. Dicey walked at half her normal speed, because of Sammy's short legs. Trucks roared by and the sun grew hotter. The air smelled of oil and gas and nothing else. After an hour and a half, Sammy began to complain. It was the first time any of them had spoken.

At the next McDonald's that had outside tables, Dicey let them sit down. One at a time, they went inside to the bathroom. They had to go through a room that smelled of hamburgers and french fries, and they all became aware of how hungry they were. Dicey ordered two large Cokes which they, all four, shared.

Chapter Two

That refreshed them. Sitting still also refreshed them.

"How much longer is it?" Sammy asked.

"A long way," Dicey said. "We'll have to sleep outside tonight."

"Good-o," Sammy said. "Can we have a fire?"

"I don't know. It depends on where we get to. This road is awful."

"That's for sure," James agreed. "Dicey? When do we get lunch?"

"I've been thinking," she answered. "If we walk for a while, then rest a little, that's the best way. So we'll walk another hour or so and I'll go into a supermarket. We should have fruit every day, and maybe some doughnuts and milk. I'll see what they have. We've got to make our money last."

It was hard to start off again. Sammy lagged back on Dicey's hand and she snapped at him, time and again, to keep up. He didn't like being snapped at, so he pulled back a little more, while pretending to be hurrying as fast as he could. Dicey turned her head and saw Maybeth and James trudging along. Traffic passed them, roaring and honking. They passed building after building, and an occasional vacant stretch, where wispy trees looked like weeds grown up. Dicey's fingers cramped from holding on to the bag, so she moved it under her armpit, holding it by a hand across the base.

The minutes stretched out. Dicey checked the time at every garage they passed. At noon, she began looking for a place to buy lunch, and at the next shopping centre they turned off the highway and walked to the front of a supermarket that was open for business on Sundays. Dicey left the little ones with James, sitting on a kerb off around to one side, and entered the market alone.

The electric eye door swung open before her. Dicey headed for the produce aisle, not even bothering to take a trolley. If she could spend just fifty cents for lunch, they'd have a dollar fifty for dinner. She picked out four apples, then searched for the kind of rack they have in every supermarket, a place where they offered items that were damaged or old. She found it back by the meat department. She stood before it a minute, selecting a box of doughnuts at half price. That would be three doughnuts and an apple apiece.

It cost eighty-eight cents.

They ate sitting on the kerb, with the sun hot overhead. Sammy couldn't eat his third doughnut but he didn't want to give it away, so Dicey put it into their bag. They trooped in pairs into the market, first James and Sammy, then Dicey and Maybeth, to drink water from the fountain and use the toilets. The pair waiting outside watched the bag, while the other pair was inside.

"Now we rest," Dicey said.

"How much longer is it?" asked Sammy.

"I told you. More than today."

"Where are we going to camp?" he asked.

"I'll tell you when we get there," she said.

"I haven't seen any place that looks good for sleeping," James said.

Chapter Two

"I figure we'll have to get off this road to find something, otherwise the cars would keep us awake. I figure we'll turn off the road and see what we find. There was that wood, this morning. That would have been all right. So there are bound to be others. Don't you think?"

"Walking is no fun," Sammy said.

"Think about the soldiers who had to march everywhere," Dicey said.

"We could pretend to be soldiers," James said. His eyes lit up. "You could be the general and I could be the major, and Sammy and Maybeth could be the army. And we could sing songs while we walk, so it would be like marching, and maybe give drill orders. We could be Revolutionary soldiers, going to Concord."

Dicey didn't say that wouldn't make any difference, they'd still be walking. She agreed to go along with it.

"Everybody who talks to you has to say sir." James elaborated on the plan. "And you two have to say sir to me. We should have a drum."

When they set off again, they sang a song about marching to Pretoria and pretty Peggy-o running down the stairs, letting down her golden hair. It was a song Momma sang. It even had a line in it, "What will your Momma think," because in the song pretty Peggy-o ran away with the captain.

The afternoon wore on, wore away. Each rest period got shorter. At mid-afternoon they lay back in an overgrown lot next to two tiny houses, the only houses they'd seen that afternoon.

"I wouldn't want to live on this road, would you?" Dicey said, to nobody in particular.

"I bet it wasn't always like this," James answered. "It might have been a nice road once. A country road. And these people might be old people, or poor people, who can't afford to move. Like us."

"Yeah, but our house was out in the dunes. We had the ocean. Our house was nicer than the ones other people wanted."

"The bathtub was in the kitchen," James reminded her. "It was small, even smaller than these houses."

"So what?"

"Nobody else would have lived in it. Only us. Some of the kids said their parents thought it should be torn down."

"What do I care what people say?" Dicey asked.

"They called it a shack," James went on.

"*I* liked it," Dicey said. "The ocean's better than fancy bathrooms, any day."

In the little one-storey house next door, a door slammed. They turned their heads to watch as an energetic old woman came out, waving a broom over her head and shouting something.

She was shouting at them. Dicey couldn't hear the words, but she understood the expression of fierce anger on the woman's face. As she came closer, they could hear her voice. "Get out of here, get out. Go on, get out! I'm counting to ten and then I'm calling the police. I've had it with you kids, hanging around and taking down clean laundry and dumping it in the dirt, and tossing your trash and bottles into my lawn, and throwing rocks at my door and your cars and your noise. One — " She shrieked, her chin wagging up and down.

The four children sprang to their feet. "Here we go," Dicey said.

"I can't," Sammy said. "I'm tired."

"You've got to," James said.

"No, I can't."

Dicey tried to persuade him. "We're soldiers, remember?"

"No, we're not. That's just pretend. You have to carry me. Piggyback."

Dicey also was tired. "I'll just leave you here," she said.

"OK." Sammy sat down.

The old woman shrieked anew.

"I've got to carry the bag," Dicey pleaded.

His eyes regarded her calmly.

"OK, OK." She gave in. James took the paper bag. Sammy jumped up on to Dicey's back. They set off, to the accompaniment of the old woman's voice: "And don't come back. Ever!"

"We won't," Dicey muttered. "Don't worry."

The afternoon was bleached hot white, hotter and whiter for Dicey with Sammy on her back. The air tasted bad in her mouth, as she gasped for breath. The raucous cars roared past, unheeding. Dicey forced her feet to move, and her legs, and her hands to hold tight on to Sammy's feet, and her back to stay straight, because in the long run that would hurt less.

It was only four when they stopped at a light, waiting for

it to turn green, so they could cross the road. "Off," Dicey said
to Sammy. He slid down.

There were at least three more hours of daylight. But
Dicey could go no further. She turned around and saw
Maybeth's eyes big with unshed tears.

The light changed and they crossed. Dicey stopped on the
other side. "OK," she said. "The next grocery store, I'll get
food. Then, we'll have to get off this road to find a place to
sleep. It'll be hard, because it's got to be private enough."

Three faces nodded at her, eyes blank with exhaustion.

It was a small market where Dicey stopped next. Again,
she went in alone. She bought bananas (they were cheapest
by pound) and a package of hot dogs and a loaf of bread (you
could wrap a slice of bread around a hot dog, like a roll) and
a half-gallon of milk (it was a little cheaper that way). It cost
almost three dollars, but she couldn't think of what to do
about the expense. They were running out of money.

When a narrow road ran off of Route 1, marked by a sign
that said: PHILLIP'S BEACH 6 MILES, Dicey led them across the
four-lane highway and on to it. She chose the road because
of the Dead End sign, which, she reasoned, meant that there
wouldn't be many cars on the road. It turned out to have
been good thinking. The road twisted through a wooded
area, like a river, and soon the sound of the highway had
faded away behind them.

The road made two sweeping curves before Dicey saw a
ramshackle house, with a "For Sale" sign in front of it. The
house had such a small front lawn, it sat almost on the road.

It looked abandoned, its clapboard siding faded to splintery grey. "Stay here," Dicey said.

She walked across the front of the house, where tall grass on the short driveway told her no car had driven, not for a long time. She walked around to the back, alert to run should a face appear in the empty windows.

The yard, overgrown and long neglected, stretched out behind the house to a large tree, and beyond that, to woods. The quiet stretched out, over the long grass and distant trees. An unscreened porch opened along the back of the worn house. That meant they could have some shelter.

Dicey trotted back and called her family to join her.

The yard was like a private park, without swings of course, but green, and scattered with trees. Dicey sat down in the middle of it between two brown bags, one holding clothes, one food. The others sat facing her.

"Feels good, doesn't it?" James asked, but didn't wait for an answer. "Maybe we should just stay here and live here. It wouldn't be too bad. I bet we can find a way into the house."

"That's trespassing," Dicey said severely.

"It's empty," Sammy pointed out.

"I'm just daydreaming," James said. He lay back on the long grass and spread out his arms and legs. He closed his eyes. A lazy smile floated over his narrow face. "It's a bed. Better than a bed. A cloud."

They all fell asleep. When they woke, long bars of sunlight lay across the lawn. Sammy woke up first and roused the rest of them by calling back from the far end of the yard, "Hey!

There's a brook back here! James! Wake up and come see."
Dicey, her back too stiff to jump up as the others had, stayed
put and rolled over on her stomach to watch them run to
join Sammy. They'd be OK for a while. She didn't have to
worry about water. They could all swim, and they had good
sense about water. Living next to the ocean, they had to.

She wondered what time it was, and how much daylight
was left. The sun was still above the horizon. Maybe seven?
That seemed about right. But she wanted to look at her map
to see where they were before the light got bad, and they
would need to gather some wood. She listened to the
splashing and calls while she traced her finger down the map.

One day should put them about halfway there. She started
at a dot named Madison and began moving her finger
backwards. She saw no marking for Phillip's Beach.

She called to James. He had noticed a sign saying they
were near Stonington. "What?" she called back. He spelled it
for her.

But Stonington was almost next to Peewauket and they
hadn't gone any distance at all. She called to James again. He
was quite sure. Stonington. Then, they had travelled maybe –
Dicey measured with her finger from the legend at the
bottom corner of the map – eight miles? Maybe ten. At that
rate – she walked off sections of road with her fingers – it
would be days. More than a week. Two weeks.

They'd have to conserve money, and food. Quickly she
calculated a way to eat only half of the food tonight and the
rest for their next dinner. No more Cokes, either; they'd cost

sixty cents. No more small markets; they were more expensive. They could fish in Long Island Sound or the rivers (string and a hook, they'd have to buy those), and why didn't she have a knife? None of them did, not even a jackknife.

They hadn't planned this properly. They hadn't planned it at all. Dicey couldn't see how they'd make it to Bridgeport, and a cold panic settled in her stomach. There was nothing for it though, was there? Just going ahead. People might give them food. She might be able to earn food or money, somehow. She couldn't think how they'd manage it. But they would have to manage it, somehow. Then she didn't think any more about it. She couldn't.

They gathered wood, some twigs, and handfuls of dried leaves. Accustomed to building fires on the beach, they found it easy to light the small starting pile of leaves and twigs, with the matches Dicey had taken from the counter in the store. They skewered hot dogs on green sticks, and when they were cooked, wrapped them in slices of bread. They passed the milk container around and around. Each had half a banana for dessert, and a quarter of Sammy's doughnut. The fire, fed with bigger branches, burned brightly in the darkening air. Dicey wanted them to sleep on the porch. "It's more hidden away," she explained.

"I'm going to sleep by the fire where it's warm," Sammy said.

"We're not going to put any more wood on the fire," Dicey told him.

"Why not?"

"Dangerous. It could spread. It could burn you."

"I'd wake up first," Sammy said. "It couldn't burn me."

"Well, I'm not going to take a chance," Dicey said.

"Well, I'm going to sleep here anyway," Sammy said. He lay on his stomach facing the fire, with the light drifting over his stubborn face.

"We've gotta sleep together," Dicey said.

"I don't see why," he answered and yawned.

"We've gotta stick together," she repeated.

"Momma didn't," he said.

"Well, we have to," Dicey said.

"Well, I don't care," he said. He refused to speak again and was soon asleep.

Maybeth curled up next to Dicey, resting her head against her sister's thigh. "It's all right, Dicey," she said. "I'm going to sing. Doesn't the fire make you feel like singing?"

Dicey would have said no, but after Maybeth had sung through one verse of Momma's song about the cherry that had no stone, she joined in, and James did too. The song put Maybeth to sleep.

"You tired?" Dicey asked James.

"Yeah, but not tired enough to sleep yet," he said.

"We'll let the fire go out, then carry them to the porch."

"If you say so, but I don't see why," James said.

"It'll be safer out of sight."

The fire crackled and spat. Its light made a hemisphere of warmth across which Dicey looked to see her small sleeping

Chapter Two

brother. "James? Do you remember Sammy at the beach?"

James grinned. "I do. That was some fun, wasn't it?"

They gathered up the two sleepers and carried them back to the porch. Sammy half-awoke, to protest, but slept again. He was too tired even to quarrel. Poor kid, Dicey thought. James lay down with them, but Dicey returned to the dying fire, to be sure it burned out entirely.

…Sammy at the beach, when he was only a year and a half old, and running. Summer days, eight-year-old Dicey was responsible for taking them all down to the beach. Sammy wore an old bathing suit of James's over his diapers. The first thing he'd do, every time, was take off his clothes. Then he'd turn to see their expressions and laugh and clap his hands together, with a smile spread all over his face. He had a little noise he made, to go with the clapping… "Aaayy." He'd learned that from them, because they would applaud his mistakes and his learnings and cry, "Yeaayy," as they clapped.

Dicey could still remember his short, plump little body, sturdy legs and round blonde head, and his tiny penis that bobbled up and down as he ran. He had a game he played with the waves, of going down to them, then turning to run back. Usually he tripped and fell, and the tip of the wave would wet him, as it washed up the beach. He would raise a dripping face and laugh, then elevate his backside, put his feet under him, and totter erect again. He would clap and cry, "Aaayy," and they all giggled and clapped back at him.

Sammy had been such a cheerful baby. He had been able to bring laughter even to Momma's face. They would watch him move around and explore, the way other people watched television. When had Sammy changed?

His first words were "hot" (he would grab out for anything) and "no" ("Doe," he would cry, waving his arms, his face dreadfully earnest). He emptied cupboards and drawers, he unmade his bed, he grabbed homework papers and ran away, laughing. He was naughty, but not mean. Not selfish. And he was stubborn, even then when he was a baby. Dicey had watched him learn to turn around in a circle, patiently practising, tumbling over his own feet, falling in a heap, sitting down in surprise. It took him days to do it, but he learned.

He was no less stubborn now, no less determined to have his own way – but what had happened to that happiness? Could anyone change that much? It must have been gradual, or they would have noticed. Dicey tried to remember the last time she heard Sammy laugh, and that had been laughing at Maybeth, because a doll she made out of sea grass had been washed away by a wave. But Dicey also remembered Sammy's merry eyes, and his mouth with only ten teeth, opened wide in the kind of laughter that took over his whole body and made him stumble and fall down laughing.

The fire was out. She stamped on it, just to be safe, and retired to the porch.

Chapter Three

DICEY WOKE FROM a dream about a big white house that faced the ocean. Aunt Cilla's house.

The sun was rising over the trees behind the brook, rising in waves of molten pink. James lay sprawled on his back. Sammy was curled up into a ball, and Maybeth had thrown one of her arms over him. Dicey tiptoed off the porch and down to the brook for a quiet wash.

Maybeth and James woke up immediately when she spoke their names. "It's still true then," James said.

Sammy moaned and turned away, burying his head under his arms. "It's time to get up, Sammy," Dicey said.

"'Tisn't," he answered, squinching his eyes closed.

"You all go down and wash now. I'm going to check the map. We'll eat when you're ready."

Dicey tried to look at the map realistically. She considered the lines that were roads, the green patches that were parks, and the flat blue of the sound, so different from the tumultuous, grey-faced ocean where she had grown up.

They ate half a banana each and finished the milk. Afterwards, prepared to set out but reluctant to leave their sanctuary, they sat in a row on the porch.

"There's a park, maybe two or three days down the road. We'll stay there for a couple of nights," Dicey offered. She showed them where it was marked on the map, Rockland State Park, with a tent to show there was camping. "It'll have a beach. We've got three dollars and eighty cents left. We're gonna have to think up some ways of getting money."

"Maybe we can find some on the ground," James suggested. "If we look."

"Anyway, we've already got dinner for tonight."

James studied the map. "Where were we yesterday?" he asked. Dicey showed him. "Only there? We'll never get to Bridgeport."

"Yes, we will. We've just got to keep moving, that's all."

"Why?" James asked.

"Because that's where Aunt Cilla is," Dicey said. "And Momma might be there too."

"What if she's not there?" James asked.

"She will be," Sammy said. "Don't say that. She knows we're going there."

"That's how much you know," James said.

Sammy attacked James. He hurled his little body at his brother, using his feet to kick as fast as his hands pummelled.

Chapter Three

Dicey pulled him off.

"Cut that out, Sammy. You hear me? Do that again and I'll whip you for sure."

Sammy stood, sullen and silent.

Maybeth had watched this. "Momma said to do what Dicey tells us," she reminded Sammy.

"Anyway, it's time to go," Dicey said. She took Sammy's hand and pulled him, none too gently, after her. In her other hand she carried the grocery bag that held their clothes and food.

It was another hot day. The white sidewalk of Route 1 shimmered in the heat and in the fumes, from gas and oil. The noise of traffic pounded in Dicey's ears. Her feet marched beneath her, step, step, step, plodding. As repetitive, as relentless, her mind marched over the same problems: money, food, distance, where to sleep, Momma: step, step, step.

They marched, rested, marched, lunched on water and a box of stale doughnuts, walked, rested, and once again on the final lap, Dicey carried Sammy on her back.

They were more tired at the end of the second day than they had been the day before. They had spoken little all day. Once again, Dicey led them off Route 1 towards the water to find a place to sleep. This second night they sheltered in a small stand of pines, a few yards from the road, and within sight of a big brick house. They couldn't risk a fire, so they ate the hot dogs, uncooked.

The one bright spot in the day had occurred in the afternoon, when Sammy spied a dime, on the sidewalk outside the supermarket where Dicey bought the doughnuts. Added to the two pennies Maybeth and James had picked up earlier, Dicey figured that they were only twenty-one cents out of pocket for food. That left her with three dollars and fifty-nine cents. Still enough.

On the morning of the third day, the sky was overcast. James awoke with his usual observation, "It's still true." He was the only one with the energy to speak. The others were too hungry and thirsty. They assembled themselves quickly to return to Route 1.

A breakfast of milk and bananas (fifty cents) gave them energy. As they came closer to New London and the busy Thames River, Route 1 became increasingly cluttered with restaurants, bars, quick food chains and shopping plazas. Sammy found a quarter on the roadside.

"I'm tired of doughnuts," Sammy said, as they approached a supermarket.

"What do you want then?" Dicey asked. "Doughnuts are cheap, that's why I get them."

"I want a hamburger and french fries. I want a Coke."

"Not possible," Dicey said. "How about peanut butter sandwiches? We could spread the peanut butter with our fingers. And if I get a whole loaf of bread, we could have them again for dinner, so that would be OK."

The younger children agreed, without enthusiasm. She found a loaf of bread on sale for fifteen cents and a jar of peanut butter for seventy-one cents. That totalled eighty-six cents, for lunch and dinner. That would leave them with two dollars and forty-eight cents. Still enough?

Dicey didn't say to herself, *enough for what*. She couldn't have. Neither could she have said what amount of money would not be enough.

Before going to the checkout queue, Dicey drifted by the meat counter. Hamburgers were expensive. Chicken, on the other hand, wasn't too expensive, not by the pound. But would they be able to cook it? She lingered by a package of chicken wings, which, at twenty-nine cents a pound, held some interest for her. Then she wandered over to the fruit and vegetable counter and discovered potatoes. Potatoes were cheap. You could eat all of a potato. If they could just build a fire.

That night, it was in an unfinished house in a new development that they slept. Dicey picked out the house, but would not let them go into it until dark. Until then, they wandered around the maze of roads in the development, watching the children at evening play. At last it was dark and Dicey let them return to the half-built house. Only the joists had been put in for walls, but the rough floors were down. They lay on plywood. Dicey gave Sammy and Maybeth the extra clothes from the bag, to make pillows. Dicey lay on her back and looked up, past the roof frame to the sky. Low clouds reflected light from the ground, which blurred softly as she fell asleep.

Fear of being caught woke Dicey before dawn. She knew that construction work began early in the day. It was one thing to be seen camping in the woods; that might be kids having a night out with their parents' permission. But four kids sleeping in an unfinished house – that would be police business.

She woke them all at the first grey light. "It's still true," James said. But he seemed to expect no response.

After a skimpy breakfast of milk, they started out and soon were crossing the River Thames on a bridge that arched like a rainbow, high enough to allow huge cargo ships to travel under it. The river, seen from the height of the bridge, seemed blue and sparkling clean. They knew better, because they had seen it close up. But the look of it refreshed Dicey. It reminded her of the sea, and it reminded her that they were heading for the water.

Sammy, cranky since the time he'd got up, had to be dragged away from the railing of the bridge. He had to be scolded every few steps to keep up. He never answered, just kept his eyes fixed to the ground. His jaw muscles worked. Dicey ground her teeth and stamped her feet in anger, still walking.

Step, step, step, on hard concrete sidewalks that made their feet hurt. Stop at the lights, then start again. Horns blared. Engines roared.

They ate lunch sitting on a bench at a bus stop on Route 1, finishing the bread and peanut butter, scooping it out with their fingers and licking it off. It was not really enough for lunch, none of them was satisfied, but Dicey pushed them on, to get out of the city.

When the smaller, quieter Beach Road turned off Route

1, she told them to go on it. Immediately, even though James protested and Maybeth's eyes glistened, even though Sammy lagged behind and her voice was hoarse with nagging at him, Dicey felt better. They were heading towards the water.

At a small supermarket, she purchased two pounds of chicken wings and four potatoes. Instead of starting right off, she pulled out her map and showed the younger children where they were. "It'll be less populated," she pointed out. "We'll be able to have a fire and—"

Rain began to fall, in fat drops that slapped the ground.

Dicey's heart sank. You couldn't build a fire outside in the rain. She hoped maybe the rain would stop, but she didn't think it would. She had never eaten a raw potato. She couldn't imagine eating uncooked chicken. She didn't know what to do.

So she urged them up and on.

"It's raining," Sammy said.

"I know that," Dicey said.

"It's like a bath," James said. "It'll clean us off."

"It's cold," Sammy said.

"Not that bad," Dicey answered.

"I'm not going anywhere," Sammy said. "And you can't make me any more. You can't."

Dicey's patience was at an end. She spoke bitterly. "No, I can't. And maybe I don't even want to. You've been a pill all day. I'll tell you what, you don't think I'll leave you, but I will. I'll be glad to leave you behind."

"I know." Sammy's voice was low. "So go ahead. Go on,

because nobody cares about me except Momma, and Momma will come and find me but she won't find you, so go ahead."

"All right, I will. Come on, you two." Dicey stood up and strode off. James followed hesitantly. Maybeth waited.

"He's been holding us up all day long," Dicey called back. "And now he's doing it again. It's not fair to the rest of us."

She saw Sammy bend over and pick up something. She saw Maybeth go back to Sammy and hold out her hand to the little boy. Sammy put his hand in hers and came trudging after.

Dicey walked ahead of the others through a rain that resolved itself into drifting mist. It was grey, cool, chilling. She clutched a grocery bag in each hand and then, as the brown paper grew sodden, under each arm. She didn't allow an afternoon rest, just kept moving ahead.

They came to marshlands, tall grasses and cat-tails, shadowy in the grey afternoon. They passed bigger houses that had larger lawns. Then Dicey saw water on the right, a large inland pond. You couldn't sleep near it though; it was surrounded by sharp-edged marsh grass that grew only on muddy ground. However, opposite it a sign pointed to a dirt road running off into sparse, piney woods. PUBLIC BEACH, the sign said.

Dicey turned and waited for the others to catch up with her. Rain had plastered their hair down over their foreheads. Beads of moisture hung from their eyelashes, and their faces glimmered with water.

"Let's go there," she said.

Chapter Three

"How far is it?" James asked.

"I don't know," Dicey answered. "But it's sure to be deserted, isn't it?"

The growth of pines was not thick enough to do more than interfere with the rain, and the needle-carpeted ground underfoot was damp. Their feet squished in their sneakers.

The beach at the end of this road was backed by low, rolling dunes, which flattened out to a narrow belt of sand before giving way to the placid grey water. The four children stood atop the dunes and looked down over the empty sand. Three picnic shelters had been erected for the pleasure of the people of Noank, three open-sided structures with shingled roofs, tables, and in each shelter a stone fireplace for cooking.

"It's going to be all right here," Dicey said softly.

"Look," Sammy said, coming up beside her. "Look what I found, all together. Somebody must have had a hole in their pocket." He held out a little square hand to show Dicey a cluster of pennies and nickels.

"Good for you, Sammy," she said. Her relief at finding shelter and a way to build a fire had washed away the anger of the day. She smiled down at him. "And look what I have for us."

She pulled gently at the top of the smaller grocery bag. The bag split, but she caught it from the bottom. "Chicken. And potatoes."

All together they ran down towards the nearest shelter, through the gentle rain. Halfway down the incline, Sammy tripped. He rolled the rest of the way, not trying to stop himself. When he came to join them under the roof of the picnic shelter, he was a sight. Dicey giggled. Then she laughed helplessly. Sand coated his wet hair and face and clothing. He looked like a biscuit, rolled in sugar.

At first she thought Sammy was going to get angry. Even so, she couldn't stop laughing; and James and Maybeth joined in with her. But instead, Sammy smiled, threw up his arms and executed a stiff little jig, joining in their laughter. For just that moment he was again the little boy Dicey remembered, who loved to wrestle and tickle and never asked you to stop, who made games out of everything and anything.

The younger children scoured the beach for pieces of wood. Dicey went back to the woods to get needles and dry branches of quick-burning pine.

When the fire had burned down to coals, Dicey spread the potatoes out on the grate. Then they all went back down the beach to find more driftwood. They returned with arms laden, and Dicey turned the potatoes, rinsed in rain drops, over and then arranged the chicken wings near to the edge of the fire so they wouldn't scorch. Rain padded softly on the beach and water. The fire spat when chicken fat dripped into it. The smell of cooking chicken rose faintly on the air. The four children stood watching, by the stone hearth. Their skin dried, then their hair and finally their clothing.

They tried to pull one of the tables over nearer to the fire, but it was bolted to the cement floor, as was every bench, so they ate in the chilly air beyond the fire's heat. The food was hot enough to warm them from within.

Chapter Three

They ate without speaking, first wolfing it down, then savouring each bite, chewing on the narrow bones, eating every scrap of potato. There was more than enough chicken. Everyone was stuffed full by the time the food was gone, even James.

"I wish we had some butter," Sammy said.

"Or salt," Dicey added.

"Barbecue sauce is what I want," James said, "and some corn on the cob and some watermelon for dessert or a sundae, a chocolate sundae. I wish we had that."

"I wish we had Momma," Maybeth said.

Silence fell again.

Dicey got up and put two fat pieces of wood on the fire. She sat down in front of it. James gathered up the bones, put them into the rubbish bin and came to sit with her. Sammy and Maybeth followed him. The fire glowed feverish on their faces. While the early evening light was still adequate, Dicey spread her map out.

"We'll go there tomorrow," she decided quickly, pointing her finger at a green square labelled "State Park". "It's the one I told you about. We'll rest a day there. How does that sound to you? We've been walking for four days now."

"It sounds great," James said. His finger traced the red Thruway markings down to Bridgeport. "It's a long way," he said. "Why is it all yellow there?"

"Densely populated area," Dicey said.

"Like yesterday?"

"Yeah."

"Where'll we sleep?"

"How should I know, James? We'll just have to worry about that when we come to it."

Dicey put her hand in her pocket and took out her money. She asked Sammy to give her the money he'd shown her. He didn't want to but she insisted, and he retreated to a sulky silence. They had one dollar and fifty-six cents left now. Still enough.

Dicey folded up the map and put it on top of the table. She went down to the water's edge and came back with a heavy rock, which she dried on her shirt and then placed on top of the map. Over the water, the air turned purple with twilight. She rejoined the others before the fire, sitting between Maybeth and Sammy. Maybeth moved closer to her and began to hum.

"I know an old lady who swallowed a fly," Dicey sang.

"I don't know why she swallowed a fly," James answered her.

Dicey leant over towards Sammy. She pointed her finger at him.

"Perhaps she'll die," he sang out, his eyes lighting up.

They sang the whole song through until Dicey spoke the last line. She waited, just long enough, before saying, in a solemn voice, "She died, of course."

Contentment blanketed them. Full stomachs, the warm crackling fire, the rain pattering on the roof and falling gently on the sand pulled them together and held them close.

"Sometimes," Dicey remarked, "I feel as if we could do

just about anything. Because we're the Tillermans."

"And I am too," Sammy said.

"Yes, you are," Dicey answered.

James spoke quietly. "Dicey? Do you know where Momma is? For sure?"

"No."

"Why did she go?"

Maybeth spoke when Dicey didn't. "Momma's got lost. That's what I think."

"How could she get lost?" Sammy asked. "She knew where we were."

"Not lost from us," Maybeth said.

"Lost from who?" Sammy asked.

"Not lost from anyone," Maybeth said. "Just lost. But we have Dicey to take care of us."

"Dicey's not our Momma," Sammy said.

"Lucky for us she isn't," James remarked.

Sammy turned on him. "Don't you say that. That's not nice."

"But it's true," James insisted. "Dicey wouldn't ever go off and leave us. You wouldn't, would you, Dicey?"

"No," Dicey said.

"See?" James asked Sammy.

"Momma loves me," Sammy said.

"You know what?" James asked. "We're the kind that people go off from. First our father and now Momma. I never thought of that before. Whadda you think, Dicey? Is there something wrong about us?"

"I don't know and I don't care."

"No, but think about it. We were always alone out there in our house; nobody came to see us. And Momma talked different from other people, sort of more slow. I can't think of anybody else like us in Provincetown. Did Momma ever talk to you about our father? Did she say where he went?"

"No," Dicey said.

"Do you remember him?" James insisted.

"A little."

"Tell," Maybeth asked.

Dicey gathered together her few memories, like scattered marbles. "He was tall and dark-haired, with hazel eyes like Momma's. We all have eyes like theirs. James reminds me of him, and I guess I do too. You little ones look more like Momma. He had a skinny head, like James and me. He had a big, loud laugh. He built our beds for us."

"I know that," James said.

"I remember him picking me up and sitting me on his shoulders. He'd call me his little only. I don't know why." This was vivid to her, the masculine voice crooning, "*the little only, only in the world, only only.*" "He could pick Momma up too, when he was excited, and swing her round in a circle. They'd sing, sometimes, when just the two of them were home. But most of the time he had friends who'd come to see him, and Momma would take us to the beach – me and James and Maybeth. Once he bought Momma a bright red sweater and I saw her kiss him."

Dicey stared into the fire, trying to piece together

something whole from her few vague memories.

"He knew about cars. During the summer, he'd work as a bartender. They had fights sometimes. Real fights."

"Is that why he left us?" James asked. "I don't blame him if it was, because Momma sometimes was – you know."

"Sometimes what?"

"Sometimes so drifty and moony she could drive you crazy."

"I don't think that's why. I don't know why he left. I remember when he did and Momma trying to explain something and crying." But she remembered more than that, she remembered that Momma was pregnant with Sammy and that made her father angry. Then, sometime, after he'd gone but before Sammy was born, two policemen had come into their house and didn't sit down but asked Momma questions, and Momma just said, "*I don't know, I didn't know,*" over and over, when they asked her. One of them had knelt down to ask Dicey something, but Dicey wouldn't talk to him, just looked up at Momma and held her hand tight. So, the older Dicey reasoned, her father had probably broken the law. What law? How could she know? And then he'd run away.

"I never had a father," Sammy declared.

"You did so," James answered. "Everybody has a mother and father."

"Not me," Sammy said. "I never want to have one."

"Well, you can't do anything about it," James answered.

"We all have the same father," Maybeth said.

"And I don't even know his name," James said. "Dicey, do you remember his name?"

"No."

"But it wasn't Tillerman," James said. "That's Momma's own name, not his. You know what that means, don't you?"

"What?"

"We're bastards."

"I am not!" Sammy cried, leaping to his feet. "I'll fight you if you say that. I'll make your nose bleed."

"Don't you remember?" Dicey asked James, who held Sammy at arm's length.

"Remember what?"

"When Maybeth was little, still a baby. There was a big party at our house. Momma wore her yellow dress with the flounces, and she had flowers in her hair. They got married, right outside. There was a man in a blue suit, and they stood together in front of him and said the words. Don't you remember?"

James struggled to find the memory in his mind. "No, no I don't."

How could he, Dicey thought, since she was making it up.

"Somebody had a guitar and Momma danced with you and everybody watched and applauded."

"Maybe," James said. His eyebrows were squeezed together with the effort. "But why *do* we still have Momma's name and not his?"

"Because it's the best name," Dicey said. "It's a good, strong name. Momma said."

"Is that real?" Sammy asked. Dicey nodded. "And we can let the fire burn all night?"

"Sure. It'll be safe here."

Sammy lay down and put his head on his forearms. "I'm going to sleep now," he announced.

Soon Maybeth too was asleep, her head in Dicey's lap.

James emerged from a reverie. "I didn't know they got married," he said.

"You never asked."

"I won't say it again in front of Sammy, but I don't blame him for going. Now I won't mind as much."

"What does it matter?" Dicey asked.

"It wouldn't matter to you. You always knew how to fight. You'd fight anyone who said anything to you – like Sammy does. But I can't fight. And the kids... said things about Momma, bad things, about not being married."

"Nobody ever did to me."

"They wouldn't dare."

That was true, and the thought made Dicey proud.

"Would they say things to Sammy?" she asked.

"Yeah. Especially after Maybeth. I think Sammy really got it at school."

Dicey fell asleep before the fire that evening, thinking of Sammy and how he must have hated to go to school every morning and then come home, and if Momma was there she would talk to him – but less and less like a mother, and if she wasn't there he would wonder. That could change a person.

Chapter Four

SOMETIME DURING THE night the rain stopped. They awoke
to a sun already risen in the sky. They awoke to the last traces
of mist floating above the water. They awoke to thirst. "It's still
true," James said.

One by one, the little ones first, they went off behind the
dunes to go to the bathroom. Waiting her turn, Dicey stared
at the water. It seemed to stretch off endlessly, in shallow blue
wavelets. The waves here didn't crash on the shore with a
steady sound like muted thunder the way they did in
Provincetown. Here the little waves murmured and gurgled,
like contented children. A light breeze came off the water,
smelling of salt and marshlands.

They set off eagerly, to find something to drink, and in the
knowledge that they would have to walk only a few miles to
the park. They could wait to eat, after last night's dinner.

Chapter Four

"What's the name of this park?" James said.

"Rockland," Dicey said. They were walking abreast on the untravelled road.

"Why?" asked James. "What do you think? Named after somebody called Rockland? or because the land is rocky there?"

"How should I know?" Dicey said.

"Most of the land so far has been flat down by the water," James continued. Dicey stopped listening.

They drank from a water hose at a gas station. The attendant, busy and incurious, barely looked at them, so they walked off, Dicey turning to look over her shoulder.

"He's not watching us," Maybeth said to Dicey.

"I don't want anyone to know who we are, or that we're alone."

"We're not alone," Maybeth answered.

"She means without adults," James said.

"But he let us drink the water. He didn't seem to notice us much."

"You can't tell," Dicey said. "You can't tell who to trust."

"Yes I can," Maybeth said, but not to quarrel. She said it simply, as if it was her name.

Dicey smiled at her and took her hand. "Well, I can't," she said.

The road wound between occasional houses. It was hedged in low stone fences and went up hills and down hills and around hills. They saw few cars and no stores. Trees were in full leaf, the bright green of early summer. The sun warmed them, the shadows of trees cooled them. The houses they passed had smooth green lawns and long white stone drives. Just before the road into the park, there was a small general store, its one plate glass window cluttered with signs for circuses, garage sales, and church suppers. Dicey went in alone.

Inside was a young man with red hair that sprang up all over his head in spurts. He had freckles and wore overalls over a plaid shirt. Dicey wandered over to the fresh produce counter. He came to watch her.

She picked out four potatoes and a bag of apples. She put these down on the counter by the cash register. Then, she got a half-gallon of milk. She went to the hardware shelves and looked at the knives, pans, fishing rods and nets.

"Can I get you something?" the young man asked.

"How much are hooks?" Dicey asked.

"You going fishing?"

Dicey nodded.

"There's not much to catch around here. The clamming's better. You ever been clamming?"

Dicey shook her head.

"You take one of these" – he pulled down a long-handled, claw-fingered rake – "and drag in the sandbars for clams. The clams dig in, just below the sand, and you can see their air holes. Or you can dig for them with your fingers. The rake is more efficient."

"But how much are hooks?"

"Ten cents each."

Chapter Four

"I'll take one please. Do you have any fishing line?"

He offered her a spool, for $1.50. Dicey shook her head. They'd unravel some clothes, or something.

"What're you doing, anyway?" he asked as he rang up her purchases.

"We're going to the park, my brothers and sister and me. We're going to cook out. And fish. And maybe dig some clams."

"Your folks with you?"

"Naw. We're going on our own."

He looked at her. "Sounds like fun. Look" – he unrolled a long piece of fishing line from the spool, cut it off, wound it around three fingers to make a tight coil – "you'll need this if you want to try fishing. You got a map of the park?"

"Is there one? We just found the park on a state map and decided to come over and see what it's like."

He reached under the counter and pulled out a small folded brown map. "You'll have it pretty much to yourselves. People only come on weekends, this time of year. Take care now," he said, ringing up her money.

"We will. Thanks an awful lot."

"If you like the service, you come back." He smiled. Dicey hefted the bag and left quickly. They had twenty-six cents left. Not enough for anything.

Just inside the entrance to the park, the road turned to dirt. Woods grew up on both sides, pines and hardwoods, with none of the stone fences the children had come to expect. They walked down the entrance road a way, then

Dicey led them off into the trees, out of sight of the road. They sat down and she gave each an apple to munch while she studied the map of the park.

Rockland State Park was the same general shape as the state of Connecticut, except in miniature. The two long sides of the rectangle were a little over three miles. The short sides measured a mile and a half. The eastern length ran along the Sound in an uneven line. One large cove made what the map called LONG BEACH. There was also a small cove further north, called just BEACH. The rest of the shore front seemed to be headlands and rocky promontories. The high land began at the southwest corner of the park and ran down to the water, which it met up with about halfway along the length of waterfront. In the southeast section the map showed marshlands, labelled BIRD SANCTUARY.

"It's four and a half square miles," James said. "Can I have another apple? Is this all there is for lunch?"

"I thought we'd fish," Dicey said.

The road they were on led through the centre of the park until it branched apart about halfway through and went as two roads to the two different beaches. The map showed picnic areas and a playground off to the left, near the inland border. Opposite that, a small campground lay in the highlands on a path that branched off to the right. A larger campground, with six camping sites marked on it, was on a road that turned off the left fork. This campground lay on the headlands that overlooked the water, near the small beach. The picnic area had "Facilities" marked on it. "What do you

Chapter Four

think that means?" Dicey asked, pointing.

"Toilets, I guess," James answered. "Do you think they have showers too?"

Dicey had been hoping for a kitchen house of some sort, with pans and a stove. Where you could make a soup. James didn't think that was likely.

"OK," Dicey announced. "I say we walk down to here" – she pointed to the large campground – "and put our stuff at this site." The site nearest to the water. That would feel more like their own home. "Then we better get down to the shore and see if we can find some clams. When we've solved the food problem for the day, we can take it easy."

Once again they set off, walking four abreast. Perhaps it was the deep silence around them, perhaps the salty wind off the water, perhaps the sense of forest and solitude; for whatever reason, this walk was a pleasure. Dicey's legs swung out and she began to sing the song about pretty Peggy-o. The others joined in. They sang softly, though, so that their music would contribute to the quiet, not destroy it.

They passed the playground area to their left. It had tennis courts, car parks and a children's section with swings and slide and sandbox and seesaws.

They continued past to the campsites, which had fireplaces, water taps and flat dirt spaces, where a tent could be pitched or a car pulled in. They put the two bags down and looked about them. It was high land, and trees soared above them. Hulking grey rocks broke through the earth at irregular intervals, some so large you could climb to the top and sit looking down. A faint path led off to the east. One behind the other, they followed the path. Soon they were standing on top of a rocky bluff, looking down to shallow water. The path ran on for several more yards along the front of the bluff, then descended to a small beach. The children ran down that section of path, slipping, tumbling, jumping from rock to rock.

The beach was nestled into the rocks, as if after hundreds of years of work the waves had succeeded in making themselves a little room to rest in. It was high tide. Dicey knew that by the closeness of the waves to the line of seaweed that etched the sand. There would be no clams for lunch – you clammed at low tide, on the sandbars. There would be no lunch then, and they'd just have to stand it. They could drink some milk.

She explained this to the others and they did not complain. Sammy took off his sneakers and waded in the water, which he reported as cold. "Not as cold as ours, but too cold for swimming." Maybeth gathered the fragments of shells that nestled among the grassy seaweed. James went off to climb the rocks at the water's edge. Dicey stood, looking out over the water.

You could see no land across the Sound, just unending, restless dark water. A couple of white sails skimmed along in the distance, bellied out in the wind. The sun toasted her face. She breathed deeply.

Somehow, they had to get some more money. Maybe she could go back to that store and offer to work. She could sweep and straighten out shelves. She could fetch things. But then she'd have to think up stories to tell the young red-headed man, and she was tired of making up stories, tired.

James called out, then came running back. "Dicey? There're mussels on the rocks." He held out two of the black, bearded molluscs. "You can eat mussels, can't you?"

"We sure can," Dicey said. "We can eat them right here."

Dicey and James pulled mussels from the rocks and washed them off in the water, while Maybeth and Sammy climbed back up the hill for twigs and larger pieces of wood. Soon they had a large mound of mussels waiting beside a crackling fire. Dicey gathered an armload of damp seaweed from the water's edge. When the fire was ready, she placed a layer of wet seaweed right on top of it. Steam hissed its way up through to the air. quickly, Sammy dropped the mussels onto this bed, and Dicey covered them with another layer of seaweed.

"It's like a pie," she said.

"Or a sandwich," James said.

"It looks awful," Sammy said, poking at the fire with a stick.

"But they'll taste good," James answered. "Anything would taste good. It's funny, you know? When I thought there wasn't anything for lunch I wasn't that hungry. But now—"

"Now I'm staaaarr-ving!" Sammy shrieked. He jumped up, did two cartwheels, which took him to the water's edge, and landed on his feet with his arms out. "And we're gonna eat!"

They ate the rich, meaty mussels for lunch. That evening, when the tide was low and the muddy sandbars appeared among puddles of water, as far as a hundred yards out, they gathered clams. These they steamed as they had the mussels. With supper, they drank part of the milk and had an apple apiece. They buried the fire in sand and tossed the shells into the water. Then they climbed back up the steep hill, to hurl apple cores into the woods and go to bed.

They slept behind the campsite rather than in it, in the woods nearer the water. Dicey couldn't relax. When she saw that the others were all soundly sleeping, she quietly got up and went back down to the little beach. For a while she just sat in the sand, hearing and seeing the dark waters. Then she walked back and forth along the water's edge. The stars burned high overhead. Silence and solitude: she might have been alone in the world.

If she had been sitting when the voices approached, she would have kept still and tried to remain unnoticed. But she was standing by the water, clearly silhouetted there, and she could hear a woman's voice saying, "There's someone here."

Two figures approached, descending the hill cautiously, hand in hand.

"Hey, man," the man called.

Warily, Dicey nodded to him.

"Don't be afraid of us, we're harmless," the woman said. Only she was a girl, really. They were both young, in their teens.

"So am I," Dicey answered.

"Are your folks camping here?" the boy asked.

"No," Dicey said.

"We are," the girl said. She looked up at the boy's face. "We've been here for two weeks already, haven't we? Was that your fire we saw earlier?"

"Probably," Dicey said. "I had some clams."

"You live near here?" the boy asked.

"Yeah," Dicey said. Well, right now they were living about fifty yards from where she stood.

"We always come to this beach," the girl said. "It feels like our own private beach by now. Doesn't it, Lou? It does to me. Except for weekends, it's empty. You're the first person we've met on it during the week."

Dicey made a grunting noise in answer.

"What's your name, kid?" the boy asked.

"Danny."

"Danny what?"

"Don't pry, Lou. Leave him be," the girl interrupted. "I'm Edie. This is Lou, short for Louis. You'll scare him," she said to the boy.

"Naw I won't. Will I?"

"I dunno," Dicey said.

"I know about him and it's OK," Lou said. Dicey looked up in alarm. She couldn't see his face clearly. "You ran away, didn't you? It all got to be too much for you, and you cut out. Isn't that about it?"

"So what?" Dicey asked.

"So we're in the same boat, on the same trip. So you

haven't got any reason to worry about us squealing on you, or laying a heavy go-home message on you. So, relax."

Dicey grinned. "OK," she said.

"Are you alone?"

"Not exactly."

"That's relaxed? I've seen people who thought they were about to be mugged more relaxed. OK, I won't bug you. We'll all enjoy the scenery together here and talk about cabbages and kings."

"I gotta go now."

"If you stick around here," the girl said, "we'll see you again. I'd like that, Danny. We're easy to find, at the small campground. We'll be there, or at the playground, or down here."

"OK," Dicey said. "Well – see you."

They had forgotten her by the time she reached the top of the bluff. They stood where she had left them, their arms around each other, facing out over the water. She returned quickly to her family and fell asleep easily.

First thing the next morning, while they munched apples and passed the milk carton around, Dicey told the others about her encounter of the night before. "I told them I was a boy," she said. "Named Danny. Can you remember that?" They nodded. "Maybeth? You too."

"But why?" James asked. "What does it matter?"

"It's safer to be a boy than a girl," Dicey said. "People leave boys alone more. Anyway, if we meet them again don't tell our last name. I told them I was a runaway. We'll all be runaways."

"Are we runaways?" Sammy asked.

"Sort of," Dicey said.

"We were running away with Momma." James worked it out. "But then Momma ran away from us. And now we're running away from everybody. But we're running to Aunt Cilla's house, and that makes it different. And Momma may be there. That's another difference. We're runaways *to*, not just runaways."

Dicey gave her orders for the morning. James and Sammy were to fish, while she and Maybeth washed out the clothes they had been wearing. They wouldn't wash the shorts, just the underwear and socks and shirts. She had seen a film at school once, where the village women washed out the clothes and dried them in the sun.

Dicey carried the clothes down to the beach. James and Sammy came down later with some worms they had dug. The boys sat out on a rock surrounded by water, while the girls stood knee-deep in the waves, dipping and rubbing the clothing.

Half an hour later, James waded out to stand beside Dicey. "There are no fish here," he said.

"The map said there was fishing. That means there must be fish."

"Well, nothing's happening."

"Go back and wait."

"Why? Sammy's there."

"Sammy is only six years old. How do you know he'll know what to do if he gets a bite?"

"He won't get a bite."

"James, do as I say," Dicey ordered sternly. He shuffled off, picking up stones and throwing them out into the water, loitering by the base of the bluff, and finally Dicey saw him climb back up by Sammy.

In another few minutes he was back where Dicey and Maybeth were spreading clothes out on the sand.

"It's no use," James said. "Why are you putting them out here? They'll get sandy."

"That'll blow away once they're dry."

"I don't want sand in my underpants," James said.

"Our job is laundry, yours is fishing," Dicey said, and she sent him back.

He was beside her again in another few minutes. "It's boring," he said.

"We've got to eat," Dicey muttered.

"We can eat mussels and clams."

"I need to know if there are fish."

"I know that already — there aren't."

"All right," she cried, exasperated. "Never mind. Just stop pestering me. I don't care what you do, but let me get on with my work."

James wandered to the far end of the beach. He scratched at the rocks with his nails. Dicey looked to be sure Sammy was all right. The little boy sat patiently, the line hanging down from his finger into the water.

When all the clothes had been soaked and scrubbed, then wrung out and laid on the sand, Dicey waded out to the rock where Sammy sat. She scrambled up to sit with him. "Hey, Sammy," she said, "catch anything?"

Sammy shook his head. His mouth was set in a stubborn line. He glared down at the water.

"Tide's almost high," Dicey observed.

Sammy nodded.

"Maybe you should give up."

"Hush up, Dicey." Sammy spoke in a whisper. "Fish don't like noise."

"But James says there aren't any fish here," Dicey whispered.

"James is wrong. Look." He pulled up the string and showed Dicey a half-eaten worm still impaled on the hook. "I've lost two other worms. Something is down there eating them. I'll catch it."

Dicey left him there and went back to the beach. She started a small fire, more to let Sammy know she had faith in him than because she thought he would actually catch anything. Then she skipped stones across the water.

Maybeth stood swaying in a half-dance by the water's edge, singing to herself. James was climbing up among the big rocks that had tumbled down to the water. Dicey watched him scramble to the top of a rounded boulder and stand up. He saw her watching and waved his arm at her. Then, in a continuation of that motion, he began to fall over.

Dicey didn't see James fall, because when he lost his balance she had taken off down the beach. She didn't know what she would do when she got there, but she would be as close as possible in case there was something she could do. She climbed over the small boulders at the bottom of the pile before she looked for James. He had disappeared – except for one foot, which stuck up over a rock above her head.

Dicey found James cradled in among rocks. His eyes were closed. His face looked pale. "James?"

He didn't answer.

Was he dead? That couldn't happen, could it? And why not, considering the other things that had happened.

James's eyes fluttered and opened. He stared around as if he couldn't see her. "Dicey? What happened?" he asked. He hunkered his body up.

So, she thought, no bones were broken.

"You fell," she said. "Are you OK?"

"I fell?"

"You were waving and you fell off the rock."

"Oh. Let me think. I don't—" he said. "My foot slipped, I remember. I shouldn't have been climbing with wet sneakers."

"But are you OK?" Maybeth was standing at the bottom of the rocks, looking up. "It's OK," Dicey yelled down. Sammy still concentrated on the water below the rock. He hadn't seen James fall. "Are you?" Dicey asked James.

"I think so." James moved his arms first, then his legs. "I guess my back's not broken," he remarked.

"How do you know?"

"If you move someone with a broken back, the spine separates and the person dies, right away," James stated. "Boy, was that scary." He sat up beside Dicey. "Oooh…" He bent his head and covered the back of it with his hands. "Dizzy. I must have banged my head."

Dicey helped James make his slow, sliding way back down over the rocks. He leant against her as they walked back to the fire. She sat him down beside the little blaze and examined the back of his head. "There's no blood, but it's swelling." She pushed the place. "Here."

"Don't, Dicey!" James cried. "That hurts!"

Maybeth brought James a T-shirt soaked in the cool water. Dicey wrapped that around his head and told him to lie down. James said it felt better when he was sitting up and he thought he might have concussion. Dicey asked him what that was and he told her the symptoms. "And I do have a headache," he said hopefully.

"Bad?"

"Pretty bad, not terrible," he said. "But if I fall asleep within about half an hour, you better call an ambulance. The danger is lapsing into a coma."

Sammy pushed through the shallow water to them, his hands behind his back. "Look!" he called, holding out three small fish. "I told you. Is something the matter with James?"

"I dunno," Dicey answered. "He fell off those rocks."

Sammy wasn't interested. While James sat aside, silent, they roasted the fish as they had the hotdogs and peeled off the hot meat with their fingers. James refused any. "It makes me sick to look at them," he said.

Dicey studied him while she chewed. He looked sort of

bad. He was the one who knew what the symptoms of concussion were, so he could fake it. But she couldn't imagine James faking nausea and missing a meal. Should she take him to a doctor? How could she explain their situation to a doctor? How could she pay a doctor?

"Just as well you're not hungry," she commented. "There wouldn't be enough to go around."

James didn't respond.

They cleaned up the bones and innards and tossed them into the water. Dicey praised Sammy absentmindedly for catching the fish. Then they gathered up the sunbaked clothes and shook the sand from them. "Let's get back to the campsite," Dicey said. "James should be out of the sun. Don't you think, James?" James nodded, but cut the movement short, as if it hurt his head to move it.

Back at their camp they all sat around and stared at James. Dicey was pretty sure more than a half-hour had passed. Sammy wandered around, tossing stones, hitting bushes with sticks. "What can we do?" he finally demanded.

"Nothing," Dicey said.

Sammy kicked at some stones. "Why not?"

"You could take them to the playground," James told Dicey. "My headache's not that bad, if I don't move. I'm not sleepy. If I could just sit quiet. You know?"

"Are you sure I can leave you alone?" Dicey asked. "What about concussions, how long do they last?"

"You're supposed to keep the patient quiet for a few days, until the headaches stop," James told her.

"So we can't travel tomorrow," Dicey said.

James started to shake his head, but winced.

"Or until you get better," Dicey continued.

"That's probably right," James said. "I'm sorry."

Dicey swallowed back her crossness and impatience. "It's OK, I guess. I mean, it'll have to be, won't it?"

She scratched with her finger in the dirt. How long would they have to stay? Days and days?

"I'm sorry," James repeated. "I'll tell you when it stops, Dicey."

"OK," she said. "Then we *will* go over to the playground. You won't go wandering off, will you?"

"What do you think?" James asked. He was leaning back against a rock, his face still pale.

"Then we're off. First stop the bathrooms. James, don't you have to go to the bathroom?"

"No," he said. "All I want is some quiet."

They cut through the woods rather than going down the road. Dicey picked up a long stick and swung it at tree trunks, trying to work things out. They would have to stay another day, at least. She would have to keep an eye on James too, to be sure he was all right. But she wanted to get going tomorrow morning. She broke her stick against a trunk and picked up another one. But she couldn't get going because it wouldn't be safe for James.

The longer they stayed in a place, the greater their danger of being noticed.

As they emerged from the woods, Dicey saw the boy and

the girl who had talked to her on the beach. Louis and Edie. They looked at her. "Remember," she whispered to Sammy and Maybeth, "I'm Danny. Remember."

"Yes, Dicey," they said.

The boy and girl were even younger than they had seemed at night, maybe even sixteen. Edie had long heavy brown hair and protruding brown eyes. Louis had wildly curling brown hair and wore heavy-rimmed glasses, which he continually pushed up on his nose. His teeth were crooked, which made him look friendly.

"Hi, Danny," Edie called.

"Hi," Dicey answered, approaching them. "Meet Maybeth and Sammy."

"I want to swing," Sammy said.

"First the bathrooms, then you can play."

"You coming with me?" Sammy asked.

"Of course," Dicey said, then remembered who she was, or, rather, who she wasn't. Sammy just grinned.

The men's bathroom was like a girls' except there were three urinals in a row, and only one toilet. The toilet had no door on it. It wasn't so bad. All the same, she hurried and her heart was beating fast when she pulled the clumsy wooden door closed behind her. Sammy was inside washing his hands and face, giggling, but Dicey didn't want to risk hanging around any longer than she had to.

Louis and Edie were standing around Maybeth when Dicey came out. She sent Maybeth and Sammy over to the swings.

"Not exactly alone," Louis said, facing Dicey.

"Not exactly."

"And there's another one," Louis said. "Maybeth shook her head when I asked was this all of you."

Dicey nodded.

"He's not with you now," Louis observed.

Dicey sighed. "He had a fall so he's resting."

"Is he all right?" Edie sounded worried. "What happened?"

"He fell," Dicey said. "He says he's OK."

"So – where you heading?" Louis asked.

"Up to Provincetown, on the Cape," Dicey told him. "We used to have some family there. It's a neat place in summer."

"Edie, want to go with them?" Louis asked. "It would be good cover, in case your old man has the cops out."

Edie shook her head. She looked at Dicey with frightened eyes.

"Provincetown's a good place, from all I've heard," Louis went on. "Some jobs. Lots of people. Cops don't look too close."

"You said we'd stay here until our money ran out," Edie said.

"You scared?" Louis challenged her.

"You know I'm not. I proved it, didn't I?"

"Sure. You got hold of the money just fine. You can relax, Edie – Danny here isn't about to tell anybody anything. Are you, kid?"

Dicey just stared at him.

"It's not as if she really robbed him," Louis went on explaining. He was talking to Dicey, but he was watching the effect of his words on Edie. "I mean, *I* wrote the cheques. She just took the chequebook. Besides, the way I figure, I'm saving him a lot of money – on her college education. So he should be grateful to me. Right, Edie?"

"Sure."

"So – whaddayou say? Want to travel with these kids?"

Edie shook her head. "I like it here," she said.

"And if I decide I don't?" Louis asked.

Edie looked up at him. Her eyes had tears in them. "Hey," Louis said. He threw his arm around her. "Hey, I'm just kidding. Can't you take a joke?"

Dicey sidled away from them and went to the swings. Let it go on being a joke, she thought. She didn't know what to do if Louis and Edie tried to go with them.

She couldn't wait there long for worry about James, and for worry about when they'd be able to get moving again. Sammy complained, but she hurried the two little ones back to their campsite. James greeted them in his normal voice. His head, he said, was better now. His appetite, he said, was huge – he'd missed lunch, after all. They all went down to the little cove. James moved his body slowly and cautiously, as if he was afraid it might break.

They gathered clams for dinner while James watched the fire. Dicey wrapped the potatoes in seaweed, too, and baked them in the fire. They had brought the milk carton down with them. They picnicked in tired solitude, eating as much as they wanted. Behind them, the sun went quietly down. Twilight crept over the water towards them, dainty as a mouse.

Chapter Five

DICEY AWOKE TO the beginning of a bright day. She lay still for a long time, looking at the cloudless sky through the branches and leaves of green maples and sycamores. The leaves made designs on the background of the sky, intricate patterns that shifted with any slightest breeze. She heard James stir and rolled over on her side to watch him.

James's eyes opened. He yawned and stretched. Dicey waited for him to say what he always said first thing, about it still being true. Then everything would be back to normal.

He caught her eye. "I wish I'd seen you going into the boy's bathroom," he said. "I thought I'd split when Sammy told me."

"I noticed," Dicey said. "How's your head?"

James rolled it back and forth. "Almost OK," he said.

"What do you mean, almost? Does it hurt?"

James thought. "It feels tender. As if it could hurt. It doesn't exactly *hurt*, but it feels like it will."

Dicey sat up. "We can't go until James is better," she said sternly to herself, "that's the most important thing." So, they'd have to wait another day.

They had only apples left in their food supply, and Dicey wanted to save them, in case. So they went down to the little beach, leaving James behind. Three or four families already crowded the beach, and the Tillermans had to eat the apples for breakfast after all.

"It's a weekend," James explained. "That means a lot of people around, especially on beaches, I bet."

"But what'll we do?" Dicey asked him. She answered herself. "We'll try fishing in the marsh. You'll have to stay here alone," she cautioned James.

"Danny?" a voice called from the road. "Is that you?" It was Edie, and Dicey stood up to show the girl where they were. Louis was with her. They had come, they said, to see how the third brother was and to warn the children that it was a weekend, so lots of people would be in the park.

Edie was carrying something bulky, an instrument. She sat down beside James and played on it a little, leaning it back against her shoulder. The sound was part banjo, part harp. "You like that?" she asked James.

"What is it?"

"An autoharp. Here," she said, and sang a song for them about a girl who wanted to follow her boyfriend to war.

"I like that," Maybeth said, when Edie finished.

"I do too, honey," Edie said. "Do you know any songs you'd like me to sing?"

Maybeth shook her head.

Dicey looked at Edie over James's head and asked, "Do you know Pretty Peggy-o?"

"Sure," Edie said. She bent her head over the autoharp and her long hair fell down like a curtain. She strummed a couple of chords, then raised her face. But this wasn't their song. This song was about William the false lover and how he tricked pretty Peggy-o into running away with him but then murdered her. Edie sang the song quick and cruel, with sharp metallic sounds from her instrument.

"You're a good singer," James said.

"I thought we were going," Sammy said.

"Going where?" Edie asked.

"Fishing," Dicey told her.

"Do you have the hook and line?" James asked. Dicey nodded. "And worms?" She hadn't thought of bait. Count on James to think things through, Dicey thought, and forgave him for his lack of persistence the day before and for being careless and falling.

"Shall we stay with James?" Edie asked. Dicey didn't object.

When they had gone out of earshot of the campsite, Sammy said he wasn't going fishing with them, he was going to the playground. He didn't want to walk any more, ever. He didn't want to explore. He wouldn't get into any trouble. He didn't mind being left alone. And he would not go with

Chapter Five

them, no matter what Dicey said or did.

Dicey decided she could probably leave him safely at the playground. She instructed him to go back to the campsite if he got bored, not to go wandering about. "And don't talk to anyone."

"Why not?" Sammy demanded.

"Well, you know, don't talk about us."

"I wouldn't do that. I'm not stupid."

Maybeth and Dicey crossed the dirt road from the playground and found the path to the small campground. Another path led to a bluff overlooking the marshes. They walked without speaking through the warm morning. The only sounds were the rustling of the leaves above them and the rustling of their feet on the leafy ground. They emerged from the woods on top of a low bluff that marked the border of the marshlands. Below, the heavy grasses swayed. Narrow canals of water moved gently. The scene could have been painted in watercolours, so pale was the green of the grass, so subdued was the blue of the water.

They climbed down a short path and stood on the muddy ground of the lowlands. A heron looked up at them, curious but not afraid, before he flew to a more secluded spot. Clusters of gnats hovered in the air.

"It's so quiet," Dicey said. Maybeth nodded. "Think there are any fish?" Dicey asked, feeling her hunger. Maybeth didn't answer. Dicey walked out along the mudflat until she found a spot she liked. There she baited the hook with a worm from her pocket, put it into the water, and waited.

Maybeth sat beside her, braiding sea grass into long and useless lines. Dicey caught a fish almost right away, six or seven inches long. She rebaited the hook and caught another, even larger. She couldn't believe her luck. Every few minutes she could feel the tentative, jerking nibble on the end of her line.

When she had enough, Dicey took off her shirt and piled her catch into it. As long as they could fish, they wouldn't go hungry. She smiled at Maybeth. "Let's go back and eat," she said. It would be OK. They could wait for James to get well.

They stopped by the playground to pick up Sammy, but he wasn't there. Dicey hurried back to their camp. James sat alone, scratching at the ground with a stick. Fear clutched at Dicey's stomach. "Sammy?" she called. She shouldn't have left him alone for so long. "James, have you seen Sammy?"

Sammy stepped out from behind a boulder. Dicey let out a little snort of relief.

"Look." Dicey held up the fish she had caught. "Anybody hungry?"

"Why were you hiding?" Maybeth asked Sammy.

"We heard somebody coming. I didn't know who it was." His hazel eyes searched out Dicey's face. "I found something."

"What? Bring it over. We need some wood, too, to cook the fish."

Sammy went behind the boulder and came out holding a big grocery bag, which he set down before the fireplace. "Look at this," he said.

Egg salad sandwiches, a bag of potato chips, ham

sandwiches, pieces of celery stuffed with peanut butter, a bag of cookies, paper plates, paper cups, paper napkins.

James sat silent, watching. "Where'd you find it?" Dicey asked.

"Left in the woods behind the bathrooms," Sammy said. "And some people gave me a hot dog too, but I ate it with them. They had catsup. I was so hungry," he said.

"Sammy," Dicey spoke slowly. "This looks like somebody's picnic."

"They might have forgotten it," Sammy said.

"That's not the truth," Dicey said.

"Is too," Sammy said.

"What's it matter?" James asked. "I mean, we're the hungry ones. They could probably go back to the store and buy food, whoever this belonged to. Or just go home and eat. We need it."

Dicey couldn't entirely disagree with him. "But it's stealing," she said.

"Just food," James argued. "Louis said it should be a natural right for everybody to have enough food."

"Does Louis know?"

"No. Sammy wasn't back."

"Sammy? Tell the truth," Dicey said.

"They left it on one of those tables. I don't know who they were. They left two bags on the table and I could see there was nobody watching, so I took one. I wanted you all to have something to eat. Dicey?" He made himself look straight at her. "I wanted to help out."

Dicey understood. "Well, you surely did that. But stealing – we don't steal." Not unless they had to, not unless they were starving, and then it should be Dicey herself to do it. Not a little boy six years old.

"I think it was pretty smart of him," James said. "And brave."

"I ran," Sammy boasted, "I ran so fast – it's hard to run with a big bag. Nobody caught me."

"I'm glad of that," Dicey said, reaching to pat his tangled hair. "I don't know how we would have got you back if you'd been caught."

"Would you get me back?" Sammy asked.

"Of course. What do you think?"

"I don't know," Sammy said.

"We're all together, aren't we?" Dicey asked him. "We'd just have to get you back. But it would be hard, really hard – so I'm glad."

They ate the celery and the egg salad sandwiches right away, because mayonnaise could spoil. The rest of Sammy's food they put away for some other time. Meanwhile, they built a fire and roasted Dicey's fish over it. Even James was full when they finished. They stayed put for the rest of that long, early summer afternoon, but when the evening cool came into the air and the families on the beach left, the Tillermans went down by the water. James sat quietly by the water's edge, while the rest played tag until dark. James wanted quiet; the heat had given him a headache. But he told Dicey she didn't have to worry about him.

When they returned to the campsite, Louis and Edie were waiting for them. "James? We got you something," Edie said. "It's convalescent food." She handed him a small grocery bag. It held two oranges.

"Thanks," James said. "They look terrific." He peeled an orange and ate it.

Dicey grabbed the other one from him, peeled it and split it in half. She gave half to Maybeth and half to Sammy. James looked like he wanted to say something to her, but he didn't.

"Guess what?" Edie said. Her voice came out of the dark.

"What?"

"When we went to get the oranges, there was some man in there buying food, who said his lunch had been stolen."

Louis took over the story. "He was a big, fat guy. Asking what the country was coming to when a family's picnic lunch was stolen in a public park. He said it was probably dope addicts. He was all for calling in the police. But the guy who runs the store said it was probably somebody's idea of a joke. The big guy said that if he could get his hands on the joker, he'd show him what he thought of it. He reminded me of your father, didn't he, Edie? Isn't that just what your father would do? Then, he pulls out a wallet a foot thick, crammed with bills. He peels off a couple and goes out, still complaining about his bad luck. I say good luck to whoever walked off with his lunch."

"Why?" James asked.

"Big guys like that, with thick bankrolls — they've got so much that they don't know what to do with it. And they're always the first ones to call in the police on little guys. Like us. Like you."

Dicey went over to the rubbish bin to throw away the orange peel. Edie went with her. "Danny? I wondered if you kids had taken it."

"No," Dicey said. "No, how could we? We were fishing at the marsh."

"I thought – you know – if you were hungry enough," Edie said.

"We're not hungry," Dicey said. "We've got plenty."

"If you say so," Edie said.

Louis called over: "Hey, Danny, James says you caught a mess of fish."

Glad at the change of subject, Dicey told him about the marsh and how easy it was to catch fish there. Louis said it was illegal to fish in the marsh, because that area was a game sanctuary. "So you better be careful. You don't want to get caught at it."

How were they supposed to eat then, Dicey asked herself. By buying food, she answered. The whole world was arranged for people who had money – for *adults* who had money. The whole world was arranged against kids. Well, she could handle it. Somehow.

"If you were caught," Louis said. "Kids have no legal rights at all. That's one reason I took off. What about you kids, Danny? How come you're on the road?"

"Huh?" Dicey asked, pretending she hadn't been listening.

"You're about the most secretive bunch I've ever met,"

Louis said. "I don't even know where you're from. Where are you from?"

"Nowhere special," Dicey said.

"You don't trust me." Louis's voice hovered in the darkness. He waited for an answer.

"Don't tease him, Lou."

"I don't trust anyone," Dicey said. "It's what you said, kids have no rights. So we have to be extra careful."

"Why don't kids have any rights?" James asked.

"Because parents own them," Louis answered quickly. "Your parents can beat you, steal your money, decide not to take you to a doctor — anything they want."

"There's a law I have to go to school," James said. "That's a right, isn't it?"

"If you look at it that way."

"They couldn't kill me," James continued. "That would be murder."

"If it could be proved."

James thought about this. "Then the only person who will look out for me is myself."

"You got it. And you better learn how to do that, learn quick and learn good. Look out for yourself and let the rest go hang — because they're out to hang you, you can be sure of it."

"What about love?" Edie asked.

"You tell us all about it, tell us all about your old man; and then talk about love," Louis said. "Danny here knows what's what — he doesn't trust anyone."

"What do you two do when you're not camping here?" Dicey asked them.

She saw the two heads turn towards one another, and the look they exchanged.

"I can't remember," Edie said, in a soft voice. "Nothing before now seems real to me any more. Nothing before is worth remembering."

"So I guess you'd say we didn't do anything. And now we do something – we pluck the lotus. Right, honey?"

Then they got up to leave. Edie said she'd come by tomorrow and bring James some soup. "That sounds good," James said. The two young people stole silently away. Dicey was listening, but she couldn't hear their footsteps. For a little while she wondered if they were hanging around, to overhear something.

The next morning, Sunday morning, dawned warm. Morning spread a haze of golden heat over the trees and boulders. James said it wasn't a good day for him to travel, it was too hot, it was too far, he just wasn't feeling right. So Dicey took her family across the top of the highland to the long beach. She guessed, correctly as it turned out, that that beach would be a favourite spot, that it would be crowded on this hot Sunday. She planned for the Tillermans to lose themselves among the mob of people there. James protested, saying he wanted to wait for Edie, but Dicey told him he had to come with them. The sun would give him a headache, he said. She said she thought he could stand that. "How much longer are we going to have to wait, anyway?" she demanded.

"I don't know. I told you, I'll say when I feel OK again," James said. "It's not my fault I'm ill."

Dicey didn't answer.

The long beach was a flat crescent that marked the edge of a shallow cove. Children straddled the water's edge and a few bolder ones were actually swimming. Towels crowded the sand, like bright pieces of confetti. On the towels lay people in bathing suits, surrounded by picnic baskets, paper bags, canvas totes, blaring radios and coolers full of ice and drinks.

The Tillermans walked about, unnoticed, and later returned to their camp for a quick lunch of ham sandwiches and potato chips, which finished off the food in Sammy's bag. Then they went back to the long beach. Dicey was glad not to meet Louis and Edie.

Later in the afternoon, when the beach began to empty, Dicey looked around, to gather James and Maybeth and Sammy together. They could leave tomorrow: she had watched James and she was pretty sure he was fine. Sammy was nowhere to be seen. Neither James nor Maybeth had spoken with him, not for a long time.

Dicey looked out over the low sandbars, not yet covered by the incoming tide. She knew she didn't have to worry about Sammy having drowned. She decided to wait for a few minutes. He might, after all, just have slipped away to the woods to pee.

Sure enough, within ten minutes, she saw his sturdy body trudging down the path from the highlands. They went to meet him. As they walked along the cliff that fronted the

Sound, Dicey asked him where he'd been. Sammy turned his head to look behind them, and then announced with swelling pride, "I got us another one."

"Another what?"

"Another food bag. It was all the leftovers a family couldn't finish. I watched them eat, then pack up the bag. Then they all went down to rinse off sand in the water, and I grabbed the bag, and I ran. It's at the camp."

"Good job, Sammy," James said.

"No, it isn't," Dicey said. She knelt down in front of him. "And Sammy knows that," she said, looking straight in his eyes. His mouth grew stubborn and he would not look at her. "Stealing isn't right," Dicey said.

"Not even if you're hungry?" Sammy argued.

"You're not hungry, not really hungry," Dicey said. "We never stole things. Tillermans don't have to steal."

"Well, maybe we should," James interrupted. "It's like a war, isn't it? Us against everyone so we can get to Bridgeport. Otherwise, you'd have asked a policeman for help right away, when there was one hanging around our car. Remember?" Dicey remembered. "So if it's like that, what's wrong with Sammy taking somebody's leftovers?"

"And more too," Sammy grinned up at James. "There's money. A wallet."

"Oh, no." Dicey groaned. "Sammy, you can't take a wallet the way you can food. You just can't get away with that. We have to take it back."

"No!" Sammy cried.

"Yes," Dicey said firmly. "And on the double. I'm right, aren't I, James?"

Even James agreed.

Dicey sent James and Maybeth on to gather mussels and clams and firewood. She hurried Sammy back to the camp, and he showed her where he'd hidden the stolen bag. "But they're gone home," he protested. "Their towel was gone when I came back."

Worse and worse. Dicey thought hard and fast. She took the wallet out of the bag – it was a man's wallet, brown leather – and grabbing Sammy by the hand, ran back to the long beach. She wanted to make him give it back himself and apologize. But she couldn't, not at the risk.

The long beach was empty under shadows that fell from the cliff out towards the water. But Dicey heard voices coming from somewhere. She stood halfway down the steep hill and made Sammy point to where he had found the bag. She lifted her arm and hurled the wallet at that spot. She didn't wait to see where it landed, but turned and ran back laboriously, uphill. She didn't wait for Sammy.

Safe again under cover of the trees, Sammy spoke sullenly, "It had almost twenty dollars in it."

Dicey didn't answer. She couldn't think of what to say. Finally she said, "You have got to do what I tell you. What *I* tell you, not anybody else."

Sammy nodded as if he understood.

They had a fire on the beach that evening and steamed mussels so hot and chewy they burned their tongues on the tawny meat. The smell of damp seaweed, richer than the smell of wet wood, rose with the smoke from the fire and lingered over their faces. They were salty after the day at the water. They were together. The light dimmed, melting into early twilight. Stars became visible, pinpricks of light on the silken sky. If they hadn't known better, they would have thought that when the fire died out and the moon shone bright in the sky, they could turn and trudge slowly up over familiar dunes to their own home. Where Momma would look up absentmindedly to greet them and ask if they had a good day.

Sammy dug wells for the water to run into. Maybeth arranged shells and water-polished stones into an intricate design. James skimmed rocks out over the water.

"We'll get going again tomorrow," Dicey said.

"I'm not sure, Dicey," James protested. "I don't think I should, yet." Dicey looked at him. He looked like he meant what he said.

"We could stay here," Sammy added. "It's OK here."

Dicey sat down beside the fire, her knees drawn up under her chin, poking at the blaze with a long stick and thinking. They had to go. But what if James wasn't better and it hurt him? Should she wait another day?

Louis and Edie came up silently behind her and surprised her with some chords on the autoharp. Dicey welcomed the music, but she had wanted to avoid any further contact with them.

Edie played and sang. Louis took Maybeth by the hand and led her in a galloping dance up and down the beach.

Chapter Five

Sammy trailed them in a jig of his own, while James clapped time energetically. Dicey watched him – some brother! He was no more sick than she was. They were leaving tomorrow, if she had to drag them out of the park herself.

The dance over, they all relaxed around the fire while Edie continued to sing. Louis held Maybeth at his side. Sammy curled up against Dicey. The sky turned black velvet. Deep satin water curled against the sand.

"We gotta go to sleep," Dicey said, after a while.

"Don't go yet, Danny," Edie said, putting down the autoharp. "I don't know when I've had a better time."

Dicey stood up and dusted sand from her behind. Barely awake, Sammy waited beside her. James stayed seated, his eyes reproachful.

"Maybeth?" Dicey spoke gently.

Maybeth came over.

"Goodnight, honey," Louis said.

Maybeth didn't answer.

"Doesn't she ever say anything?" Louis asked.

"Sure. Sometimes."

"Wait," Edie said, "we'll come with you."

They climbed up the steep path. At the top of the hill, Dicey turned to say good night, so they would go away, but Louis was holding on to Edie's arm and pointing.

Between the trees they saw a bright light that rhythmically flashed red.

"What is it?" Dicey said.

"Shut up," Louis said. "Move it, Edie." They slipped away

into the darkness.

He was right, Dicey realized. It was a police car going along the road that ran past the campsites. She pulled her family into the bushes and told them to lie down.

"It's a police car," James said quietly. "Heading towards our camp."

"I dumped the bag in the trash," Dicey said.

"That's where they'll look," James said.

"I can't see what's going on," Dicey said. "Lie quiet, everyone."

Darkness rustled through the trees. Faintly, the water lapped at the shore. Dicey thought. "We're going up to the woods past the playground, long way round," she said. "We'll sleep there and get out of here at first morning."

"But…" James said.

Dicey felt Maybeth's small hand on her arm. "But nothing. You've been fine all day today, and you know it. Don't lie to me, not any more. I won't believe you."

They waited a long time, then began a silent journey across the dark park. They made a wide circle around their campsite. They saw nothing, they heard nothing, only the insects and the noise of the wind. Dicey was sure of her direction, but she wasn't sure just where they were until she saw the pale emptiness of the playground before her. They were so tired by then that they just stumbled into the woods beyond and slept there, slept uneasily.

Chapter Six

THEY AWOKE IN pale, predawn light. Mist lay in patches along the ground. The wet, black trunks of trees loomed out of the foggy half-light.

"It's still true," James said.

It was damp, and their clothes were sodden. Dicey wanted to get moving, right away. "Ready? Let's use the bathrooms and then get out of here."

Dawn gilded the sky when they arrived at the park entrance. The fear, which had stayed beside them since the night before, retreated at the promise of a bright morning. The sound of a car motor gave Dicey warning. She drew her family back into the cover of the woods.

"Why?" James asked.

"Shut *up*," Dicey whispered fiercely. "Lie down. Lie still. I don't know, but I don't want anyone to see us."

A police car, followed by another police car, roared along the main road. Both slowed down and turned onto the dirt road. They stopped, just inside the gates, one behind the other. Leaving his engine running, a policeman got out of the first car and walked to the car behind him. His leather boots shone. He wore dark glasses and had a gun at his belt. He leant into the window by the driver's side and unfolded a map that Dicey recognized as a map of the park. He pointed to parts of it.

Dicey strained to hear what they were saying, but the engines drowned out their voices.

The policeman nodded his head sharply, twice, and strode back to his own car. The flashing lights on top of the police cars were turned on. The two cars roared down the road.

"Let's go," Dicey said. "On the double."

They hurried down the road.

"What was it?" James said.

"I don't know," Dicey said.

"Were they after us?" James asked.

"I don't know," Dicey said.

"Or Louis and Edie," James said. "Nobody knew we were there. People knew Louis and Edie were there – they bought food every day."

"We bought food, too."

"Only that first day. How long ago was that?"

"I can't remember. But we did take those lunches."

"Sammy did that. That wasn't us."

Dicey thought aloud: "Louis and Edie are runaways; and

maybe more. Anyway, we got away in time."

The children walked the long morning through. Conditioned by the earlier hard days, refreshed by the days at the park, both their muscles and spirits were in good tone. The road wound south, following the coastline.

At noon, they rested by the roadside, leaning back against one of the low stone fences that ran all over this countryside.

"I'm hungry," James said. "Aren't you?"

"We haven't passed a store of any kind since that one town," Dicey answered. "And no garages." Then, like a black fist punching at her head, she realized: "My map! I don't even know where we are. How could I forget the map?"

"Should we turn around?" James asked. "That town had a grocery store."

"That was miles back. Besides, you might as well know. We don't have much money left, just twenty-six cents. I was going to try to get work at the store by the park, but I was afraid we'd get too conspicuous when we had to stay. So now, we have to keep going," Dicey said. "We've seen railroad tracks, right? That means there must be more towns ahead."

"But what'll we eat?" James asked.

"For now, nothing. We can't. We'll just have to keep going and see what happens. If I had my map I could see where the water is and we could fish or clam or find mussels. I need a map."

They were tired when they stood up, more tired than when they had sat down. The folds of the hills and the symmetry of the trees no longer had the power to please them. They walked more slowly than before. The feeling that she did not know what to expect, or when to expect it, made Dicey jumpy.

In an hour they passed a sign marking the limits of a town called Sound View. Dicey felt better. Soon the houses sat closer together and the welcome sight of a small shopping centre placed on two sides of a crossroads greeted them. Shopping centres on this road were quite different from those on Route 1. These were small, fancier. They had no huge car parks, just a row of parking places right up against the sidewalk. Instead of large glass windows plastered with sale signs, these stores had small panes, like house windows. Everything looked clean.

Dicey instructed the other three to stay where they were, while she crossed the street and went into a Texaco station. The office was occupied by one man with a fringe of hair round his shiny head who was dozing with his feet up on a wooden desk. He snored gently.

His head snapped up as Dicey closed the door loudly. His blue eyes studied her. "What can I do for you?"

"I'd like a map, please, of Connecticut."

He pulled out a drawer and selected one map from several file folders there. "That'll be fifty cents," he said.

"But I don't have any money," Dicey said.

"OK," he said. He replaced the map in its folder, closed the drawer, and once again raised his feet to the top of the desk.

"I have to have a map," Dicey said.

"Paper's expensive, kid. We don't give maps away any more."

"Who does?"

"Nobody." He closed his eyes.

Dicey stood, chewing on her lip. Money, money, money, always money. And she couldn't get into the drawer, find the right map, and get out the door — not fast enough to make it. "Mister?" He opened his eyes. "I really want one."

"That's tough on you, kid. I'm sorry."

"Could I work for one?"

"Doing what?"

"I dunno. There must be some chore — something. Sweeping? Washing? Are the bathrooms clean?"

"My bathrooms are always sparkling clean," he said. He closed his eyes. Dicey stood thinking. She wondered if she could pump gas. It didn't look hard.

"That window," the man said. The office had a large plate glass window that faced the pumps and the street. "That window needs washing. You know how to use a squeegee?"

Dicey didn't even know what a squeegee was. "Sure," she said.

"I didn't get to it yesterday," the man said, lumbering into a closet and pulling out a bucket, a rag and a long-armed utensil that had to be the squeegee.

"Inside and out," he said.

Dicey nodded.

"All over and no streaks."

Dicey nodded. If he would just let her get to work on it.

"I'll give you the map and a quarter too. Fair enough?"

"Fair enough."

Dicey began on the outside of the window. She signalled her family to wait, and James nodded to show he understood. The three sat down on the kerb, facing Dicey. Dicey filled the bucket, added some cleanser from a bottle she found in it, sloshed the mixture together and began spreading the water over the window. She did it in four sections, wetting the glass, pulling the squeegee down over it firmly, squeezing the squeegee out and repeating the last step twice. The glass gleamed. Then she went inside and did the same thing. A few cars pulled in, were filled with gas and pulled out again. Every time a car pulled away, Dicey looked to be sure her three were still there.

She finished, emptied the bucket and put it away. The man came in from filling a car. He handed her a map and a quarter. "You got an audience," he said.

"They're friends."

"Well, that's a good job. If you're around later in the week…"

"Thanks, mister," Dicey said.

"You earned it, kid."

Dicey returned to her family, the map in her hand.

"You were hours," James said. "I'm so hungry my stomach hurts."

"The map cost fifty cents, so I washed the window. And got a quarter more, too."

"Let's eat," Sammy said.

Chapter Six

They walked along the front of the first section of the shopping centre, but saw only a restaurant and some clothing stores. They crossed the street and entered a small market filled with speciality goods, delicatessen items and huge, fancy pieces of fruit. Everything on the shelves cost much more than fifty-one cents. The people who worked in the store stared at the Tillermans suspiciously, and Dicey hurried them out.

"But I want to eat," Sammy protested. "I'll die if I don't eat."

Dicey pulled him firmly out the door. "Hush up – you don't know what people will think," she whispered fiercely in his ear. He snuffled. "Look, you won't die, not in one day. Starvation takes days and days."

A small bakery, its windows filled with decorated cakes and layered pastries, also did business in the second part of the shopping centre. Dicey would not let them linger before its windows, but she sat them down around her on the kerb just beyond it. Their knees were up against the bumpers of a blue Cadillac car.

"OK," Dicey said. "We've got to do this smart."

"What do you mean?" asked James.

"We've only got fifty-one cents, and around here that won't buy enough to feed even one of us. This is a ritzy area. So – we want some bakery goods, because they're cheapest, but not at full price. So, we've got to make that lady in there feel like giving us a lot for our money. So, we've got to make her feel sorry for us."

James nodded.

"I'll go and tell her how hungry I am," Sammy volunteered.

"No, you won't and have her start asking questions," Dicey snapped. Her own stomach was taut within her, and she was having trouble thinking well. "It's got to be done right. By the right person."

"That's you, isn't it?" James asked.

"Not this time, it isn't. Nor you, either. People don't take to us the right way, not at first. Maybeth would be the best one."

Maybeth shook her head mutely. Her eyes grew large and stared at Dicey.

"I know." Dicey sighed. "So Sammy, it's you, after all."

"Good-o," Sammy said. "Give me the money."

"Not so fast. If she asks you, we're staying in a summer house — where?" Dicey searched her memory. "In Old Lyme and we went for a walk and got lost, and there's nobody home this afternoon to come and get us in the car. Do you have that? And we're hungry. That's if she asks you."

"What if she doesn't?"

"We need enough food for lunch, and maybe dinner too. For just fifty-one cents. So, unless she'll give you two loaves of bread for it, sort of hem and haw. Say that's too much. Tell her you've only got fifty-one cents. Ask her if this road will get us home. Be sort of brave and pitiful — do you know what I mean, Sammy? But whatever happens, don't tell her the truth."

Chapter Six

He stood up, his legs sturdy and brown. He held out a dirty hand and Dicey put the money into it.

"Can you do it, Sammy?"

"I think so."

"If there isn't anything right to buy, don't buy anything."

"Dicey — I wouldn't do that."

No, he wouldn't. He couldn't be bullied. They watched him walk back and enter the bakery. They heard a jingle of bells as he closed the door. Then they waited, silently, for what seemed a very long time, studying the front of the big car. It stared back at them with empty glass eyes.

Dicey turned her head when she heard the shop door open with a jingling of bells. Sammy had a big white bakery bag in one hand. In the other, he had a round cookie, half-eaten. His eyes met Dicey's, and he quickly shoved the rest of the cookie into his mouth.

"It's fine," he said. "She had a couple of old doughnuts, and some rolls and a pie she said she couldn't sell after two days. She said she'd call our parents, but I said I didn't remember the phone number yet. She said maybe my sister would. So I said I'd come out and you'd tell her the number after you ate because I thought you were pretty hungry."

Dicey jumped to her feet. "Good job, Sammy," she said. "OK, let's go. I don't want to answer any more questions. We'll eat as soon as we're out of sight. We'll eat the pie — that's worth waiting a little for, isn't it?"

They trotted down the road and around a corner. Once out of sight, they sat on the grass to eat, breaking pieces of apple pie off with their fingers and licking all the sticky sauce before seizing another portion. They were too hungry to save much for later; only two rolls were left in the white bag when Dicey put her map into it, rolled down the top and led them off again. She wanted to get to a creek she had seen on the map. It was a little creek that fed into the mouth of the Connecticut River. There might be fish in it. If they could fish, then they could have breakfast before they set off. And then it wouldn't matter so much that they didn't have any money left.

They didn't have one penny left. Not one.

Four miles up the road they found the creek. Dicey led them up it, away from the road. The creek was bordered with marshes, but if you went a few yards back the land got higher, dryer. It was posted: NO HUNTING. NO FISHING. NO TRESPASSING. But Dicey figured they had to risk it. A small fire, during daylight hours, that wouldn't be so noticeable.

She set James and Sammy fishing down by the creek and took Maybeth back into the trees. Together they cleared a place for a fire, surrounded it with stones, then gathered twigs, leaves and branches to burn, plus four slim branches on which they could thread the fish.

For all their patient waiting, James and Sammy caught only two fish. Those Dicey cooked and shared out among them, dividing the fish and the two rolls evenly. It was not enough, not after a long day's walk. They went silent to sleep hungry, thirsty, huddled together to keep warm.

Dicey woke early and dug up some worms. She took the

Chapter Six

line and hook down to the creek and tried to catch breakfast.
Fish bit in the early morning. The fishing boats that went out
from Provincetown went out when night was still dark, so
that as the first light brought out the fish they could be there,
nets down and ready.

Birds awoke. The sun came up, although you couldn't see
it through overhanging clouds. The water gurgled quietly at
Dicey's feet. She heard an occasional motor boat, far off, but
no cars. However, off in the distance there was a humming
that suggested heavy traffic. This noise was carried to her on
a steady wind that blew from off the land towards the water.

No fish were biting. Not that morning.

She heard James calling her with panic in his voice.
Slowly, she trudged back to her family.

"I told you," Sammy said to James, "because the fishing
line was gone."

"I didn't know where you were," James said. "Why didn't
you say where you were going?"

"You were asleep," Dicey answered. "Let's get going."

She did not say a word about eating. They did not ask her.

It was a subdued four children who returned to the road,
walked over the little bridge and through a tiny town that
didn't even have its own post office building, just one section
of the laundromat set aside, and a small flag flying outside to
show where the post office was. They walked through town
and on, north along the Connecticut River. It was a low, grey
morning, and Dicey thought someday soon it would rain
again. She didn't have the energy to care about that. Besides,

you could drink rain water.

By noon they were at the town of Old Lyme and Dicey had identified the distant rumble, grown louder now, as the Thruway. Here Route 1 joined the Thruway to cross over the broad river.

They passed the Thruway entry ramp and a shopping centre backed up again the fast-moving highway. They cut through to the river's bank and stood looking up at the soaring metal that arched overhead to cross the river.

When Dicey realized that the bridge had no walkway, she stared out over the river. It wasn't terribly broad, but it was much too broad to swim.

If there was no walkway, they would have to walk on the shoulder of the road. Someone would be sure to stop them. If they didn't get run over first. Cars and trucks and buses — all hurtled over that bridge as if the devil himself was chasing them. He'd be chasing them from both directions then, Dicey thought; he'd catch you either way.

Dicey crouched down where she was and buried her face in her knees. How could they go forward from here? The railroad bridge downriver had a draw section in the middle that was raised up. They couldn't cross there. It was miles and miles upriver to the next bridge. Tears welled up behind her eyes and the corners of her mouth pulled sharply down.

You don't cry, she said to herself. Not you.

No money, no food, no way to go forward. The silence behind her told her that her brothers and sister were watching her. Maybe they could just all stay right here, without moving, and turn to stone. Then her troubles would be over. Dicey opened her eyes and studied the darkness of her knees. There was nothing more she could do. Nothing. She had done her best and that wasn't good enough and now she could do no more. That was it. The end.

She sighed and felt a small hand on her shoulder. Maybeth. She raised her head to look out again over the impassable river.

At least it was beautiful, with curves and marshy islands and yachts moored along the edges. At least the trees that crowded up to the top of the bluff spread above them, proud and growing. A solitary, two-masted sailboat glided down the river. She watched it.

"Dicey?" Maybeth said.

"Yes, Maybeth," Dicey answered, without turning her head. Food, money, a way forward. They had none.

"What's wrong?"

Dicey almost laughed. "What's right?" is what she wanted to answer, but she didn't speak. Never mind even the way forward, you couldn't get food without money and they had none.

Kids just couldn't earn money.

She had, yesterday. She had earned seventy-five cents in all. They could eat something today, if they had seventy-five cents now.

James asked, "What're we going to do now?"

"I dunno," Dicey said. So, she had to earn some money. But how? There was that shopping centre. It had a big car park, and a supermarket. She pictured it carefully, and then pictured herself coming out of the market with two big bags filled with groceries after she had earned money somehow, bags filled with fruit and meat and breads and cans of vegetables and a pan to cook things in. And a can opener; it would be just her luck to forget the can opener.

In her daydream, the Dicey she saw walking out of the store with enough food for her family to eat for days, with her eyes smiling and a big grin stretching her mouth, that Dicey tripped and fell. The food scattered over the ground. The wheels of cars squashed the scattered oranges and bananas. A dog took the package of hamburger meat and ran away with it. The people around went off on their own ways, carrying their own heavy bags of groceries.

Was this how Momma felt? Was this why Momma ran away? Because she couldn't think of anything more to do and couldn't stand any more to try to take care of her children.

Dicey said to herself, I'm getting as bad as Momma. Imagination doesn't do any good. Then her mind flicked back to the people with their heavy bags.

That might be a way. If they all did it. They might earn something.

She turned her head and ran fingers through her hair. They had to look neat or people wouldn't trust them.

"Listen, we could carry groceries to cars out at that shopping centre. People might tip us."

"I wanna eat first," Sammy said.

"We can't." Dicey looked directly into his eyes. "We don't

have any money left, you know that. All we've got is this," and she held up the white bag in which she was carrying the map.

"Dicey? Is everything going to be all right?" Sammy looked scared.

Momma always reassured him, whenever he was afraid or when she'd been angry because she was worried. She always smiled at him and said everything would be all right. And somehow, it always was.

"I hope so," Dicey said. "I don't know. I'll tell you, if this idea works and we can earn some money, the first thing we'll do is buy a quart of milk. The first forty cents we have. That's a promise."

The fear stayed in Sammy's eyes, but he nodded his head. Dicey tidied them up as much as possible. She had not noticed how dirty they'd become. Maybeth's hair was a tangled mess. James's hands were brown with dirt and his nails were black. And Sammy looked — well, Sammy looked like most six-year-olds, so that might be OK. Her own shorts were grubby, her knees stained. But her dark hair was always kept short, so that must look all right. They'd just have to try it.

They stationed themselves outside of the entrance doors, where the paper bags were brought out on a rolling belt. Maybeth looked at the people going in and coming out and shook her head. Her eyes grew big and pleading. Dicey understood. She told Maybeth to sit quiet at the far end of the belt. Maybeth nodded and ran off. She sat and didn't move a muscle, just sat quiet as if she was waiting for her mother to come and take her home.

Most of the people the children approached said, "No, thank you," with a kind of puzzled look, as if it didn't often happen that someone offered to carry their grocery bags. Some, especially ladies with babies, said yes, with a grateful look, and Dicey or James or Sammy would carry huge bags out to large station wagons. The people would give them a dime, or some nickels.

True to her word, at the end of the first half-hour, when they had forty cents, Dicey went inside to buy milk. They ducked around the corner of the building to drink it, careful not to spill any as they poured it into their mouths. The cool, rich liquid flowed down Dicey's throat and settled gently into her stomach. The carton was soon empty. "Better?" Dicey asked. "Better," they said. They returned to work.

All afternoon they went up to strangers and asked if they would like their bags carried. Dicey learned to read the no or yes in people's eyes before they spoke it. Then, unexpectedly, the way good luck always surprises you, they had a piece of very good luck.

An older man and a little girl came out of the busy store. They stood waiting for their bags to emerge from the metal doors the rolling belt used.

Soon, the man moved to a group of three grocery bags. The little girl followed beside him. Dicey stepped up to him. "Would you like me to carry those bags?"

He looked at her. "We've got three," he said, hesitantly.

"My brother could help too," Dicey said.

Chapter Six

"The car is across the car park, by the restaurant," he said.

"That's OK," Dicey said.

The man waited, hesitating, maybe, for her to say more, to ask again. When she didn't speak, that seemed to decide him and his eyes twinkled at her. "Why not?" he said to the little girl. "Sure," he said to Dicey, "you and your brother carry these two and I'll take the third. Be careful – there are some eggs in there somewhere. We did remember the eggs, didn't we?"

"Grandpa," the girl spoke. "You keep asking that. Stop teasing. But Grandpa," – her mouth puffed out sulkily – "you said I could carry a bag. You said."

He shook his head at her.

"You said I could because I'm your helper on the boat."

He ignored her. Dicey ignored her too, not liking the tone of her voice.

"But I'm bigger than him," the little girl said, pointing at Sammy. "It's not fair."

They walked along to the car. Sammy carried the lightest bag. The man and Dicey carried the heavier ones. The little girl trailed behind. To make conversation, the man asked Dicey how much money they'd earned, and she answered that they hadn't counted yet. He asked her how long they'd been at it, and when she answered all afternoon he said she must like working. Dicey shrugged. He said he himself liked working, but he wasn't sure if he didn't like it because it made vacations so much more pleasant.

Dicey smiled at this.

"So you're all in it together," the man said. He didn't say it nosey, but as if he was really interested in her, Dicey.

Dicey wanted to answer, even though she couldn't tell him the truth. "We want to get our mother a birthday present," she said.

"What are you thinking of getting her?" he asked.

"She needs a new ironing board," Dicey answered.

"Your father can help you out a little, can't he?" the man said. Dicey knew that was the way this man would do it.

"He's not around," she said shortly.

The man just nodded. They had come to the car. It had Pennsylvania licence plates. He held the rear door open while she and Sammy put the bags inside, and then he put his own bag in. He put his hand in his pocket. "How many of you are there?" he asked.

"Four," Dicey said.

He took out his wallet and gave her two dollars. "That's fifty cents apiece," he said.

"It's too much," Dicey protested. She would not take the money.

He folded the bills and stuffed them into the pocket of her shorts. "That, young lady, is for me to say. Now scoot, and good luck to you."

Dicey thanked him and turned to go. By then the little girl had scuffed her way to the car. She stood up on tiptoe to speak to her grandfather, and he lifted her firmly into the car, talking to her. He was angry with her, but not rough. He plunked her down on the seat by the steering wheel.

Chapter Six

Dicey and Sammy walked away. "How much did he give you?" Sammy asked, as soon as they were out of earshot.

Before Dicey could answer, she heard running feet and the little girl caught at her arm. "Wait," she said. She held another dollar in her hand. "This is from me. Grandpa said I could. Mommy gave it to me to buy her a present while I was spending the night with Grandpa on his boat, but everything was plastic and she doesn't like plastic. She says it's tack-y. She'd rather I wrote her a story anyway, and I can do that tonight. Grandpa got me some paper and crayons. To keep me quiet, that's what he said. I talk a lot. Maybe I'll write her a poem because that would be shorter. So this is for your mother. I'm sorry I got mad."

Dicey hesitated again. "Take it, Dicey," Sammy urged.

"Please take it." The little girl smiled. "I want you to, I do. Mommy likes my poems better than anything. She says they're stu-pendous. I'm going to write one about fish, because we're on a boat. Do you think fish would eat flowers, because I write good poems about flowers."

Dicey could barely keep up with the stream of chatter. She grinned and took the dollar. "OK," she said.

"OK," the little girl said, happily. She ran back to the car where her grandfather waited. Dicey did not watch them drive away.

"Good-o," was all Sammy said, but he strutted back to his post by the supermarket doors.

Shortly thereafter, Dicey called James and Sammy together, and they counted the money they had earned. Five dollars and fifteen cents. Dicey nodded in satisfaction.

"That sure is an improvement," she said. She went inside to buy peanut butter, bread and milk. She still had $3.84 when she came out. "And we got a good heavy bag too."

They returned to their wooded post looking over the winding river. They could see only two houses, one on each side of where they sat, both built low to the bluff and designed to face out over the river, both with those walls of windows that modern houses have. After they had eaten, Dicey explained the next difficulty, that they couldn't walk over the river on the bridge. She no longer felt so hopeless, so she could say it without sounding defeated. They had earned money, more than enough money. And that grandfather and the little girl – Dicey didn't know why they had made her feel better, but they had, even though it wasn't going to get any easier.

The Tillermans sat in a row and looked down at the river flowing below. They looked at boats moored close together in marinas, or alone at the ends of long docks. Overhead, cars roared across the bridge.

"We could go upriver to the next bridge," James suggested.

"That'll take days," Dicey said. "But we may have to." She was reluctant to journey away from the water; she didn't want to go far from the Sound that was part of the sea.

"Does the river get narrow enough to swim across?"

"I don't know," Dicey said. "It would be too risky to light a fire, wouldn't it? I feel like sitting by a fire, don't you?"

Chapter Six

Maybeth snuggled up to Dicey and hummed tunelessly. Dicey sat looking down, not thinking or worrying, just feeling her full belly and her sister's warm body, watching the river water shimmer in the sun, remembering with pride how James and Sammy had worked that afternoon, wondering which boat the little girl was sleeping on and thinking those two would remember her. A melody came into her head and she sang one of Momma's old, sad songs: "'The water is wide, I cannot get o'er. Neither have I wings to fly.'"

The melody floated out over the water, where she could not go.

"'Give me a boat that will carry two, and two shall row — my love and I.'"

The setting sun floated gold along the surface of the water.

"'Oh, love is bonny, when it is young,'" Dicey sang. "'Fair as a flower when first it is new.'" Then she stopped. "We'll take a boat," she said.

"Good-o," Sammy said.

"Where will we get a boat?" asked James. "Where could we get a boat?"

"All these yachts have little dinghys that go with them, so the people on the yachts can get to and from their moorings. We'll take a dinghy and row across and tie it up on the other side. I can row and so can you, James, if you have to."

She led them down the steep bluff, clutching the bag with leftover food and the map in it. She wouldn't leave food or map behind again, no matter what. They slid most of the way down, bouncing on their behinds, giggling. At the foot of the bluff, Dicey turned upriver.

They found a rowing boat easily. It was upended on the ground beside a long private dock. Waiting for dark, they watched nervously up the cliff to the house whose lighted windows looked out over the silver river. When full dark came, somebody inside pulled curtains over the long windows. Then the children stealthily approached the boat.

James and Dicey carried it down to the end of the dock and lowered it noiselessly into the water. James held the painter while Dicey went back for the bag, the oars and Maybeth and Sammy. They were accustomed to boats, so they had no trouble getting into it quietly. Maybeth sat at the bow, Sammy and James at the stern. Dicey shipped the oars and James pushed off. The boat slid away from the dock.

Dicey lifted the oars in their rowlocks. She brought them down cautiously, unused to their weight. The oars bit into the black water, and the boat shot ahead.

The current carried them slightly downstream, Dicey's strokes carried them across, the smooth water eased their passage. The bridge loomed overhead. Its thick pilings caused races in the current that could trap a small boat and maybe even overturn it. Dicey knew enough to simply follow these races until the boat had floated out of their currents. Then she dipped the oars once again into the dark water.

The sky was dark. The air was dark, so dark that they could barely make out one another's faces. The water flowed beneath them, black and bottomless.

Dicey headed for the lights on the opposite shore. It felt good to stretch the muscles in her back and arms, to lean back and then pull forward against the oars.

In the middle of the river the current eased and the boat shot straight ahead. Then, as they drew near the far bank, Dicey felt the twists and eddies begin again. James directed her to a huge marina, where lights burned in many buildings and in many of the small windows of the boats tied in rows along the docks. It looked sort of like a car park. They pulled up beside a boat that was dark and empty and tied their dinghy to its stern. Dicey thought that if she left the dinghy there it had a good chance of being claimed or returned.

They had come down close to the mouth of the river, where its water flowed out into the Sound. A small town lay on the low flatlands. They walked through the town, to the south. It was late at night and the houses became fewer, but there was no safe place to sleep. After an hour, they were all tired, and Sammy stumbled with every third step. Dicey put him on her back, giving James the grocery bag. She discovered then how much the long rowing had strained her muscles.

They came to a church, shining white in the dark air. Behind it stretched a graveyard, with groves of trees planted among the tombstones. Dicey turned towards the graveyard.

Behind her, James drew in his breath.

At the first grove of trees, Dicey put Sammy down. He was already half-asleep and just curled up on the ground.

Maybeth settled beside him without a word. Dicey stood, looking at James.

"It's a graveyard, Dicey," James said.

"I know," she said. "But we're tired."

"Do you believe in ghosts?" he asked.

"I never saw one," Dicey said. She sat down. James sat down right beside her. They could see tombstones placed in neat rows. Some of them had statues on top.

"I don't believe in ghosts," James said. "All the same, I don't like this place. It's — too quiet."

Indeed, the silence was thick as fog around them. The silence vibrated, as if with things beneath it struggling to break through.

Dicey yawned. She was too tired, the day had been too long, for this kind of worrying. "I like quiet."

James flicked his eyes over the cemetery. "We're all gonna die, you know."

Dicey nodded. "Not for a long time."

"Do you think Momma's dead?"

"I don't know. How could I know that?"

"No matter what, we're all gonna die," James remarked. "So it doesn't matter what we do, does it?"

Dicey was thinking about other things, about maps and food. She didn't answer.

"Unless there's a Hell, to punish us. But I don't think there is. I really don't. Or Heaven. Or anything. Dicey?"

"Yeah?"

"You know the only thing you can count on, the only

thing that's always true? It's the speed of light. Louis told me Einstein figured it out, 186,000 miles per second. That's the only sure thing. Everything else — changes. I was proud of Sammy for stealing that food, you know that?"

"So was I."

"You were? You sure didn't act it. You acted angry."

"Well, I was."

"Dicey, that doesn't make sense."

"I'm too tired to make sense, James. I'm trying to figure out where we might be. We came way downriver. We'll have sandwiches for breakfast and finish the food up so we don't have to carry it." Dicey let her mind wander. "Did you ever hear Momma talk about her father, James? We had to have a grandfather, you know."

"Probably dead," James said. "Everyone's either dead or dying."

"Go to *sleep*, James," Dicey said. "That's just morbid. You'll make yourself crazy."

"I make myself crazy when I try to figure out a good reason why I *shouldn't* be morbid," James answered.

"Go to sleep."

"I don't want to."

"Go to sleep, please. You're not crazy. You'll never be crazy. You're just too smart for your own good. Anyone who stays awake so he can have ideas like that…well, he ought to be going to sleep."

Dicey lay back and closed her eyes resolutely. James sighed.

Chapter Seven

MORNING BROKE LOW and cloudy. Streaks of smudged grey clouds covered the sky. "It's still true," James said. He looked out over the cemetery, where bright green grass contrasted with the faded marble of tombstones, and the tombstones reflected the cold grey of the sky.

"Some of them are bent over," James said. "I bet they're old, really old. Hundreds of years."

After breakfast, while Dicey gathered together their litter and packed it into the paper bag to be discarded at the first rubbish bin they saw, the little ones explored the graveyard. Sammy stayed with James, because James could read everything to him. Maybeth wandered among the rows, studying the statues of angels and lambs.

Dicey had a sudden fear that she had forgotten where they were going, so she recited Aunt Cilla's address to herself.

Chapter Seven

Mrs Cilla Logan, 1724 Ocean Drive, Bridgeport. She ought to make the others memorize it. She made a mental note to do that as they walked that day.

Then she studied the map and admitted that they would have to go back to Route 1. She didn't want to. She wanted to stay among big houses and tall trees, on the shore road that would keep her close to the water. But Route 1 was the shorter way, even though it looped up north of the Thruway before entering New Haven.

Those decisions made, Dicey went to call the others. They had to start. They had money and a map, their stomachs were full – it wasn't a bad way to begin.

While she waited for Maybeth to return and for James and Sammy to finish out what was written on a cracked stone that slanted back towards the earth, Dicey looked at the gravestones about her. She read an inscription: *Home is the hunter, home from the hill, and the sailor home from the sea.*

What a thing to put on a grave.

As if to say that being dead was home. Home, for Dicey, was their house in Provincetown, where the wind made the boards creak in a way that was almost music. Or Aunt Cilla's big white house that faced over the water, the one she had dreamed about. Being dead wasn't home, was it? Unless – and she remembered what James had been saying last night – home was the place where you finally stayed, for ever and ever. Then this person *was* home, and nobody would be truly home until he, or she, died. It was an awful thought.

Only living people had homes. That was the difference.

(If Momma was dead, where was her grave? What was written on it? Nobody would even know her name or who she was or when she was born.)

If you took home to mean where you rested content and never wanted to go anywhere else, then Dicey had never had a home. The ocean always made her restless; so even Provincetown, even their own remembered kitchen, wasn't home. That was why Dicey ran along the sand beside the ocean, as if she had to race the waves. The ocean wasn't home, then, and neither was anywhere else. Nobody could be home, really, until he was in his grave. Nobody could rest, really, until then.

It was a cold, hard thought written on that cold, hard stone. But maybe true.

If Dicey died, she supposed she wouldn't mind having this poem on her tombstone, now that she thought about it. She was the hunter and the sailor, and she supposed dead people did lie quietly in their graves.

"James," she said when he came back. "You know what you were saying last night?"

"Yeah?"

"You're pretty smart," Dicey said.

"I know," he said.

A pale sun showed behind the clouds. It looked like there were two layers of clouds now, one layer lower, like a grey veil spread before the other. Where the veil broke, you could see silvery islands of clouds on which tall angels might stand. Not cute little Christmas angels, but high, stern angels in white robes, whose faces were sad and serious from being near God all day and hearing His decisions about the world. Dicey was hypnotized by the molten silver of the cloudy islands and not until the veil of fuzzy grey blew across it again did she begin their march of the day.

Route 1 had not changed in their absence. Stores, shopping centres, garages, furniture outlets, restaurants, quick-food stands: the cement procession marched on, broken only by traffic lights dangling from heavy wires over the roadway. Traffic was heavier, and the exhaust and the diesel fumes could not rise into the sky on that first grey day, but hung over everything. Their faces and hands felt grimy all the time. Day by day, their money dwindled away.

When she thought back on this part of their journey, Dicey found that she could remember very little of it, that it all blurred together in her memory, all the long days, all the strange nights. They spent a night on a shaly beach, with no shelter and no fire. They spent a night in a grove of pines that stood at the entrance to an estate, where Dicey woke frequently with the fear that they would be discovered by the owners of the big stone house that lay at the end of the drive. They spent a night by the entrance to another state park. As Route 1 looped north, they crossed under the Thruway and spent a miserable night huddled at the back of a shopping centre. They slept sitting together on the concrete walkway, against the concrete wall. As they approached the large city of New Haven, the buildings were closer together and there were no more open spaces.

In all these days, the sun had come out only twice, once for an hour early in the morning, and once late in the evening to give them a fine sunset. Slowly, rain had been building. The rain finally began to fall during the night they spent in a tiny playground beside the Branford River. The next day they spent the last of their money, standing in the rain to eat cold doughnuts. The rain continued, steady and gentle, all that day. Dicey led them under the shelter of an empty car wash for that night and roused them early so they would be gone before anybody arrived to open the business or to wash a car. She roused them early even though nobody in his right mind would wash his car on a rainy day. You couldn't expect people to act as if they were in their right minds. Dicey was taking no chances.

They approached New Haven and Dicey took out the map, which she carried under her shirt, where the cloth and her arm would protect it. She planned their way through the city. She wanted to get across it before dark. She didn't like cities and didn't want to have to spend the night in one.

That they had nothing to eat and no money to buy food with, these facts she refused to think of. They would cross the city first, and then get some money. They would cross the city hungry because they had to.

James, Maybeth and Sammy greeted this announcement without a change in expression. They did not speak or sing any more, just followed Dicey meekly. If she had food to give them, they ate it. If there was no food, then they said nothing. Dicey thought she might prefer to have them complain, but that was another worry she would not deal with until they had crossed the city. That was a worry that went along with the limp James had developed from a hole worn into the sole of his left sneaker; with the grey under Maybeth's eyes and not having heard her voice for days; with Sammy's new habit of clinging to her hand and doing whatever she told him, right away, not even the start of a quarrel.

James, Maybeth and Sammy listened quietly while she recited the streets they would take to cross the city. "We have to get off Route One to cross the rivers," she said. "So we'll follow the train tracks for a while, then walk a couple of blocks on a street named Quinnipiac, up to Ferry Street. That will take us over one branch of the river. When Ferry meets with Chapel Street, we'll turn left and start walking across the city. We'll go over a river, then by a big college. There, we'll be about halfway. OK?"

They nodded, three pale faces.

"Then, we're going to have to get back to Route One, so we'll turn left on to a cross-street to meet up with it. It doesn't matter which street we take. We can follow Route One the rest of the way out of the city."

They nodded, six blank eyes.

"So let's go. Or we won't get across before dark."

Dicey walked with Maybeth and James took Sammy's hand. At first, most of the buildings were low, four or five storeys of soiled brick. They walked beside the railroad tracks and saw only the backs of buildings, houses with no grass in the yards, ripped curtains in dirty windows, fences that looked like some giant rat had been gnawing at them. The empty windows of factories stared down. Rain fell steadily. Sometimes, they would glimpse a face through an open window. Most often, except for the people looking out of train windows, they saw no one.

They crossed a small river, walking on a narrow, fenced-over walkway that was built to run beside the road. Rain showered down and made miniature puddles on the turgid river water. Green and oily slime floated on the river and gathered in stringy islands by its banks.

Chapel Street was wide, lined with stores. Groceries, five-and-dimes, an occasional cinema, army-navy surplus stores, off-licences with metal gates across the windows. The street passed a small park before it crossed another river. On the other side of the river, tall modern buildings, with whole walls of windows, lifted up out above the squat brick constructions.

The Tillermans walked on, over the Thruway. They passed hotels, clothing stores, jewellers and bookstores; then old brick churches, with signs out front saying what sermon would be given the next Sunday, and a few large old city homes. As evening thickened and lights were turned on, you could see inside where large mirrors hung on ivory-white walls and long curtains framed polished wood tables.

Dicey did not look in the store windows as the others did, or in the windows of the houses. She looked at the unsmiling faces of the people walking past her.

Night, hurrying down upon them, was not in their

favour, nor was the rain, falling steadily. But they were all past hunger, she thought – she knew she wasn't hungry any more. Just tired.

It was after ten when they came to the college and the square park that lay at the centre of the city, bordered by the college on one side, a chapel on the opposite and the city on the others.

Dicey finally admitted that they would have to sleep the night in the city. This park would have to do, even though it was too open. She chose a cluster of bushes far from any street lamp. "Look, you all go in there," she pointed to a kind of nest made by the low branches of the piny bushes. "You curl up here, as covered as you can. I'll stay out here and keep watch."

Without a word, they obeyed.

The rain pattered down. People hurried across the park, their heads bent. Dicey sat on a bench near her family's hiding place and looked across the park to a long wall of college dormitories. Some of the windows had lights in them. One had someone sitting in it.

Dicey sat and stared into the night without seeing, without thinking. Lights shone all around her. The streetlight cast puddles of light on the wet sidewalks. The raindrops caught the light from the lamps and glowed, falling, like yellow pebbles. Bright red neon light shone hazily on top of a building in the distance. The arch-topped windows of the dormitories showed like yellow cutouts. The water on the roads and sidewalks reflected light with silvery sheen.

Dicey sat and kept the watch. Three little children, alone

in a city: she couldn't sleep.

How many more days until Bridgeport? And Aunt Cilla's big white house.

How would they get money? Why had she thrown away the twenty dollars Sammy found? How would they eat all those days until Bridgeport?

How was she going to see to it that they got there, when she didn't even know where it was?

Dicey thought the rain had grown warm, until a stuffiness in her nose and an ache in her throat (like she was trying to swallow an apple whole) told her she was crying. But she never cried! And now she couldn't stop.

She heard footsteps approaching, the first in a long time. Just one person. She bowed her chin down and folded her arms across her chest, trying to look as if she was asleep. She held her breath against a sob that was swelling in her throat. But she kept an eye out. If she needed to, she could break and run, away from the bushes where her family slept. They all knew Aunt Cilla's address.

Somebody – a man she guessed from his trouser legs and loafers – sat down at the other end of her bench. His trouser legs were wet, as if he had been walking for a long time. They clung against his calves. Dicey didn't move.

But the sob moved. It swelled up and broke through her clenched teeth. Dicey's panicked eyes moved to the face of the person beside her.

He had turned to look at her. He was young. He wore a yellow raincoat and his hands were jammed into the pockets.

Chapter Seven

In the dim light, his eyes were dark and serious. His hair was plastered down over his forehead.

When he spoke, his voice was flat. "You looked like a girl crying. I thought you were a girl crying. Can I help?"

Dicey bit her lip and shook her head.

"You lost?"

Dicey shook her head again.

"OK." He seemed to believe her. "Can you walk home from here?"

This made Dicey feel like smiling, but not from laughter. She shook her head.

"Cat got your tongue?"

"Nope."

"OK. I'll tell you what I think. I think you don't have a place to sleep, you're probably hungry, you're frightened and worried, and you don't want to tell me anything. So far, am I right?"

"Yeah."

He shifted on the bench and turned to face Dicey. "OK. Now. You don't have to believe this, but you can trust me. I've been in your kind of jam myself, more than once. If it helps, I'm studying at the college, if that tells you anything about me."

"Schools are closed in summer."

"Not colleges. They have summer session. I'm taking a geology course because I flunked it this year and I have to pass it to graduate. I want to graduate next June."

"You don't sound stupid," Dicey said.

"Oh, I'm not. I just didn't work at it, so it's my own fault. Look, I have an idea for you."

"Yeah?"

"Yeah. Don't say no right away. OK? OK. Why don't you come with me and get some food and camp out in my rooms tonight? It's better than the Green — it's dry, at least. I've got a roommate so you won't have to worry about being alone with me."

"I've got roommates too," Dicey said.

He smiled.

"No, three — over there."

He looked at her carefully. "OK then, we'll all go. All your age?"

"No. Younger. They're my brothers and sister."

His jaw fell a little, and then he pulled it up sharply. His eyebrows twitched, as if he were keeping them from shooting up in surprise. "Will wonders never cease?" he asked. He stood up briskly. "Let's see the worst. I've made up my mind anyway and I guess four kids can sleep on our floor. You've made up your mind to trust me, haven't you?"

"I'm afraid so," Dicey said. That made him laugh, but she didn't know why. "Wait here," she said.

He stood absolutely still, as if to show that he would do exactly what she told him, and a smile played around his lips. He wasn't serious. He was teasing her. Dicey looked up at him through the rainy light, still trying to decide. He made his mouth still, and then she nodded at him. "OK," she said. "But we don't have any money."

"I do," he said.

Dicey roused her family. They woke easily, even Sammy, who usually slept deeply.

They rose up out of the bushes, Maybeth first, then James, then Sammy. Their eyes were surprised, but they didn't question her. She felt suddenly very sorry for them. She wondered if she had done the right thing, when she began this whole journey. Was she doing the right thing now?

With one arm round Maybeth's shoulders, holding Sammy's hand tight, Dicey led her family back to where the young man stood waiting. James tagged behind, limping slightly.

The smile went out of the young man's eyes when he saw them. Dicey was briefly worried, but he crouched down on his heels, ignoring the puddles, and looked up at them all.

"You don't have to feel sorry for us," Dicey said. "You can back out."

"Not on your life. That's not it. I'm curious – intensely curious – about you. What are your names? Mine's Windy…well, Windy's what they call me here because they say I talk too much. How did you get here? Where are your parents? Are you hungry?"

"Yes," Sammy said fiercely.

"When's the last time you ate?"

"Yesterday, I think," Dicey said.

"Then what are we hanging around here for?" the young man asked. He stood up and took James's hand. James was too tired to protest at this extraordinary gesture. "I know just the place," Windy said. He led them to one of the city sides of the Green and into a small diner that had a long counter and four booths. The clock read 1.30. Windy herded them into a booth, then brought over menus. He called the waitress before they had even opened the menus and ordered each of them a large glass of milk. He asked for a cup of coffee for himself.

Dicey could barely see the words and prices. Food smells filled the diner, and she was out of the rain. It was warm and bright. The words on the menu swam before her eyes. She looked at their rescuer.

He sat with James beside him. He had dark curly hair and a black moustache and black eyebrows that moved up and down or wrinkled as if they had a life all of their own.

"Who'd believe this?" he asked, meeting Dicey's eyes. "I ask you."

The waitress put his coffee down before him and gave each child a tall glass of milk. "Y'want straws?"

Dicey shook her head and grabbed for the glass. They drank, in large gulps at first, and then, when their stomachs had welcomed the first eager swallows, more slowly. All four glasses were empty when the children put them down.

"What can I getcha?" the waitress asked.

Windy looked at them. They had forgotten the menus. He grinned. "Four hamburgers. No, make that eight. Four large orders of fries. That's all for now, but we'll probably have dessert. Do you have any apple pie?"

"Yeah."

"Give me a piece of pie now, please," he said. "And save four pieces for the kids."

She shuffled away, writing on her order pad. "Is that OK?" Windy asked Dicey. "We can change it if it's not OK. It wouldn't be any trouble. But I thought maybe it would be hard for you to decide, and the little one doesn't look old enough to read yet."

"I can too," Sammy said.

"Apologies for insulting you," Windy said, and his eyebrows waggled, as if they were laughing.

"I wanted hamburgers," Sammy said. "Anyway. And french fries. That's what I wanted."

"Ah," Windy said. "And what is your name?"

Sammy looked at Dicey. She nodded.

"Sammy," he said.

"How old are you?"

"Six. How old are you?"

"Twenty-one. Really very old."

Dicey remembered her manners. It was easier to remember manners with milk in her stomach and food on the way. "I'm Dicey and this is Maybeth and that's James." She answered the question in his eyes before he asked it: "I'm thirteen, Maybeth is nine, James is ten."

His dark eyes studied her. "I once ran away, when I was James's age," he said. He told them a long story about running away one morning when he was afraid to go to school because he was short and skinny and somebody was waiting there to beat him up. In the middle of the story their food was set before them. Dicey stopped listening. Windy could eat and talk at the same time. But the Tillermans ate in absolute silence, in huge bites, barely tasting what they chewed before they swallowed it. They all had apple pie for dessert. Throughout the meal, Windy's voice blew over them, smooth and steady. It didn't matter what he was saying.

Windy paid the bill and left a dollar on the table for the waitress. Dicey, warmed from within, tried to thank him, but he shrugged it off. He took them back to the Green, saying he wished he could stop the rain because he, for one, had had enough of it and he suspected they had too. He led them across the Green to the long dormitory building. There, the halls were narrow and brown, like tunnels. They climbed up four flights of stairs, twisting past closed doors. Finally, Windy threw open a door and ushered them into a room.

It was a mess. Ashtrays overflowed with cigarette ashes and butts. A newspaper had been left scattered on the floor around one armchair. Books were piled on the three desks and on the low table before the sofa and along the mantelpiece. Beer cans lay around a wastebasket that was so full it looked as if it wanted to erupt like a volcano and spew trash all over the room. It was warm and messy and comfortable, and filled with yellow light. Outside, dark rain fell. But they were inside.

Windy went through a door and turned on a light in the next room. Dicey caught a glimpse of bunk beds and dressers. He returned with an armload of clothing, mostly T-shirts and sweatshirts. "The bathroom's through that door." He pointed to the door beside the one they'd entered through. "Go get off your wet clothes and put some of these on. I guess you might want to go to the bathroom too."

"I do," Sammy said, so definitely that Dicey smiled.

"Meanwhile, I'll see if anyone's around."

When they had gone to the bathroom, they covered themselves with Windy's dry shirts which, if none too fresh, were dry and warm. They hung their own clothes on the towel racks to dry. Dicey washed out all of their underwear, using the cake of soap on the sink. They returned to the living-room. Windy waited there and another young man was with him.

"Stewart," Windy said, "let me introduce my findings." He remembered all of their names and ages. "This is Stewart, my roommate," he said.

Stewart smoked on his pipe and looked at them. He was tall, taller than Windy, and skinny like Windy. He had blond hair, so pale it was almost white, hanging fine and straight down to his ears. He had a strong, square jaw and a moustache as blond as the hair on his head. His eyes, as he looked at the Tillermans, might have been grey or blue, Dicey couldn't decide which. It was as if his eyes changed back and forth between grey and blue, but she wasn't sure if that was possible.

"What's going on?" he asked Windy.

"I found them, as I said. Dicey first, and then the others. They need a place to sleep and it's raining cats and dogs, and mice and pterodactyls, and God knows what else out there –

so I thought to myself, why not here with us?"

Stewart smiled quietly. "Why not indeed? I'll come in with you and they can have my bunks."

James grinned at Dicey. Real beds.

Stewart took them into his room. He cleared books and papers off the top bunk, and James climbed up onto it. Sammy and Maybeth lay down on opposite ends of the bottom bunk. Dicey thought they looked like two little dolls in a dollhouse, lying there. James was half-asleep before she turned out the light and closed the door behind her.

She thought she would go back and sleep on the floor in that room, but Windy said she should take the sofa in the living-room for her bed. He brought a pillow and blanket from his own room. "What do I need those for?" Dicey asked. "You keep them. I'll be fine."

Windy passed her the armload of linen. "Go ahead. Live it up. I can do without for one night."

"*You* can do without," Stewart said. "Listen, he took them off the bed where I'm going to sleep. And if you really don't want them, I'd be glad to have them." Dicey passed them over.

"Can we talk a little before you go to sleep, Dicey?" Windy asked. "Are you too tired?"

Dicey was so comfortable that she would have been glad to talk all night. She didn't want to go to sleep, because then she wouldn't be able to enjoy being comfortable. But she wasn't sure she wanted to answer any questions. She was too brain-tired to be as careful as she ought.

Chapter Seven

They all sat down. Dicey sat alone in the middle of the sofa, and the young men took two armchairs.

Stewart started. "Windy says you're not lost."

"No. I know where we are."

"A fundamentalist," Windy said to Stewart. His eyebrows moved. He asked Dicey, "What about your family? Do they know where you are?"

Dicey shook her head. "But that doesn't matter."

"Why not?" Windy asked. Dicey didn't answer that.

"Are you in trouble?" Windy asked.

"I don't think so," Dicey said. "I hope not."

"OK," Windy said. He leant forward and rested his chin on his hands. His eyebrows were temporarily still. "What *will* you tell us? We'd like to help if we can. Do you believe that?"

"Yeah," Dicey said. "Yeah, I do." She thought. "I mean, you already did, didn't you?"

"How about your parents?" Stewart asked. He was resting his head against the back of the chair, looking at her.

It wasn't that she couldn't lie to him. She could lie to anyone and make it good, if she had to — she'd certainly discovered that. But she didn't want to, not to him or to Windy. She wasn't going to lie to them, she decided.

"We don't have parents. We're on our own," she said. Stewart's eyes did not change, but waited, quiet as water.

"Wait a minute," Dicey said. "Let me think a minute, OK?" He nodded. "We come from Provincetown, in Massachusetts. On the Cape." He nodded his head, just a little. She heard Windy swallow back a question. "My father walked out on us when I was about seven. Just before Sammy was born. We were OK until lately, when things happened wrong. My mother lost her job. And things. So she told us we were going to Bridgeport, where she has an aunt, and we all packed into our car."

Stewart held her eyes with his.

"We were in Peewauket and she left us to wait in the car while she went into a big mall. But she didn't come out, and we couldn't find her. So I decided that we should go ahead to Bridgeport and hope she'll meet us there."

Stewart asked, "How long did you wait for her?"

"All day and all night," Dicey said. "We waited in the car. She didn't come back. I'm hoping…I don't know. The only place I know she might be is Bridgeport."

"What if she isn't there?" Windy asked.

"There's this Aunt Cilla," Dicey explained.

"Do you know her?" Stewart asked.

"No. But she sends us cards every Christmas."

"You didn't ask anyone for help?" Stewart asked. "The police?"

Dicey shook her head firmly. "I don't know for sure what they would do. They might send us to a foster home. Or split us up. I don't know what Momma – she didn't say anything, she just disappeared…I have no idea what happened. No idea. I couldn't risk telling the police. And that's all true," Dicey said.

"How long ago was this?" Windy asked.

"In June. Maybe two weeks, maybe three."

"And you've been walking from Peewauket all this time?"

"We stayed at a park once. The little kids can't go very fast."

"Is that all you want to tell?" Windy asked.

"Please," Dicey answered.

He nodded his head and his eyebrows arched as he smiled at her. "Then I say we get some sleep. What do you say, Stew?"

"Just thinking about all that walking makes me tired," Stewart said.

"You OK here, Dicey?" Windy asked.

Dicey nodded. She hoped she hadn't made a mistake in telling them.

Windy turned off the lights and Dicey stretched out on the sofa. She didn't even hear the door close behind them.

Chapter Eight

DICEY OPENED HER eyes to the grey ceiling of the living-room. She opened her ears to city noises floating in on warm air that came through open windows. She sat up, alarmed at finding herself alone. Then the events of the night before came back to her, and she relaxed, stretched, bounced on the sofa and smiled to herself. She went to the window and looked out.

The rain had been swept away with the darkness. Everything on the Green below sparkled in the early morning air. It even smelled fresh outside.

Dicey remembered that in the bathroom she had seen a stall shower. She went in quietly. She folded up their clothes hanging on the rack, except for her own, and put them in a pile on the sofa. Then she went back and turned on the hot water, so it would be hot when she had gone to the

Chapter Eight

bathroom. When she was ready, she stripped off Windy's T-shirt and stepped into the warm water, pulling the curtain closed behind her. The warm water beat down on her back and her chest and her hips and her arms. She revolved slowly, her eyes closed, like a wind-up toy that was running down. She had forgotten just how it felt to take a bath or a shower. It felt gentle and warm, like somebody's arms around you.

Dicey took a cake of soap and washed herself, head to foot, hair and ears, toes and fingers, face, torso. The soap slid on to the floor. She bent over to pick it up and the water tattooed on her behind.

She took one last slow turn under the water that turned into five last slow turns. Then she turned both handles off and stepped out.

As she rubbed herself dry and dressed, she thought: I can do anything. Anything. We're going to be all right. It's all going to be all right.

She squeezed some toothpaste on to her finger and brushed her teeth. Her teeth squeaked and her mouth tasted minty. She grinned at herself in the mirror and ran her fingers through her damp hair.

She opened wide the door of the bathroom and saw, not only her brothers and sister, sleep still in their dazed eyes, but also wild-haired Windy, and Stewart. Maybeth came to take Dicey's hand.

Dicey asked Windy if they could all have showers. She turned on the water for Maybeth and returned to the living-room.

"So. What's next?" Windy was asking. Stewart had sat down in the same chair he occupied the last night. He looked around, but didn't speak. His face looked fuzzy and confused, not quite awake. Windy answered himself:

"Breakfast is next. And then we have to see about getting these kids to Bridgeport."

"Really?" Dicey asked.

"Really," Windy said. "Stew has a car and it's only – an hour from here? You'll do it, won't you, Stew?"

The grey-blue eyes rested on Dicey. "I've got an eleven o'clock class."

"Then after the class," Windy said.

"OK. Sure. Do you mind waiting?" Stewart asked Dicey.

Dicey shook her head at his foolishness. "Do you know how long it would take us to walk it? Three days. Maybe four. I'd be a jerk to mind waiting a couple of hours," she said.

"And you're not a jerk," Windy said. He was leaning against the mantelpiece, looking down at her.

"Nope," Dicey said. Maybe she should have been more polite, but she felt too happy for that. "Other things. Bossy. And I lie and I fight, but I'm not a jerk."

Windy looked amused. He exchanged a glance with Stewart.

The little children paraded in and out of the bathroom, putting their clothes on in their bedroom. At last, everybody was dressed.

"Can you lend me some cash?" Windy asked. "Stewart?"

Chapter Eight

"I've got a twenty," Stewart said. He went into his bedroom.

The living-room was filled with warm air and sunlight from the windows. The Tillermans were all fresh and clean and not starving. They would have breakfast. They would get a ride to Bridgeport.

It was almost over.

Stewart stood in the doorway of his room. Dicey looked at him and smiled, but he did not smile back at her. He waited there, silent, and looked over the small group of people standing between the sofa and the fireplace. His eyes were grey now, a distant wintry grey. "I can't find it," he said. He looked at Windy over the heads of the children.

"You sure?" Windy asked. "It's not like you to keep good track of your money." His eyebrows made dark arches over his eyes.

"I'm sure this time," Stewart said, still not looking at the children. "I just cashed the cheque yesterday and put the money in my wallet. I didn't spend any. My wallet was in the top drawer."

Despite the warmth of the day and the brightness of the room, Dicey felt a chill spread out from her stomach and everything grew shades darker, as if a big black cloud had just covered the sun. She looked at Sammy.

Sammy shook his head, decisively.

James's eyes were on the floor and his hands were clenched in his pockets. "James," Dicey said.

"Whyn'cha ask Sammy?" James said. His eyes were hot and angry.

"Sammy said he didn't," Dicey answered. She held on to her temper.

"Then neither did I," James said.

Dicey looked at Stewart, who still stood in the doorway to his room where the little kids had slept last night. He looked back at her and she was ashamed.

"Give it to me, James," she said quietly.

James pulled one hand out of his pocket and opened it wide. A crumpled bill fell to the floor. "Get it yourself."

Dicey exploded. "I told you we don't steal and you just go ahead and do it. And then you try to lie to me about it. I could kill you, James. You hear me? You're so smart, but you can't even figure out—" She was so angry the words got jammed up in her throat. "Look what you've done!"

James stood with his head bowed. Silence filled the room, a cold silence.

The crumpled bill lay there on the floor. Dicey couldn't look at the faces of the young men.

"You've ruined everything," she said. She strode to the window and looked out, pounding with her fist on the windowsill. She tried to find something to say to James that would make him fall down on to the floor, that would knock him over and hurt him.

Finally James spoke. "You didn't yell at Sammy, you didn't say you wished he was dead."

"Sammy's six!" Dicey turned around. "And Sammy didn't take money, he took food. And Sammy didn't take it from someone who'd helped us. Even you can see the difference."

Chapter Eight

"He" – James kept his eyes on the floor but he jerked his head towards Stewart – "doesn't need the money like we do. He's got sweaters and guitars."

"So what!" Dicey hissed. "And who are you to say, anyhow? All I asked you was to do what I say, only that – and now—"

Maybeth went to James and looked up at him for a minute. Then she took hold of the hand he had out of his pocket.

"You're a thief," Dicey spat the words at James. His hazel eyes flicked up to hers. "You steal."

"Big deal," James answered, from deep within his own anger. "It doesn't matter."

"OK," Dicey matched anger to anger. "OK, if that's the way you want it. But until we get to Aunt Cilla's you will do exactly what I say to do – or I'll leave you behind. Do you understand?" James nodded. "Then we better get out of here."

James nodded.

"Apologize, James," Dicey ordered.

He had to obey her, so he apologized, looking into the empty fireplace. "I'm sorry."

"OK. Let's go," Dicey said to her family. She felt sick inside.

"Why?" Windy unexpectedly spoke. He bent down and picked up the bill, smoothed it with his fingers and held it out to Stewart, who came forward to take it. "As far as I'm concerned, we found Stew's money. Right, Stew?"

"No," Stewart said. "But you did want to borrow it, didn't you?" He handed it back to Windy.

Dicey wished they were out of the room and on their way again, on their own.

"Dicey?" Stewart said her name. She looked at him. "What did Sammy steal?"

"Some lunchbags at a park," Dicey said. "Two. It was different. We needed food, sort of. He thought we did, anyway. He doesn't understand. He did it to help. There was a wallet in one bag, but we took that back. Sort of. Not just because it was stealing money, though. Really because we didn't want to have police coming in. I guess James doesn't understand either. He's not bad."

Stewart looked at her and she looked right back at him. James was her brother and she would have to stick by him; and she wanted to stick by him. How could Stewart know James? He couldn't, but Dicey could.

"It does matter, James," said Stewart.

"Why? We all die anyway," James said.

"Sure, but you can see to it that you like yourself when you die," Stewart answered. "You can be sure you don't hurt anybody while you're alive. Especially, you can be sure you don't hurt yourself. Are you a thief?"

James shook his head.

"But you stole," Stewart said. "Who did you hurt? You're right about me, I'm not rich but I can go to the bank and take out another twenty. So you didn't hurt me very much. You hurt yourself. More than anyone you hurt yourself."

"That doesn't make sense. Nothing matters. There's nothing you can count on – except the speed of light. And dying," James said.

"So that's what it is," Stewart said. He studied James's face. "Well, that may be true, but it's not a big enough truth to contain me. I plan to be a man when I get through. Not only a man, I plan to be a good man."

"Why?" James asked.

"Because I owe it to myself," Stewart said.

"Is that all?"

"No," Stewart said, but he didn't add anything to it.

"I don't understand," James said.

Stewart didn't answer him.

"Can I learn to understand?"

"Maybe," Stewart said.

"I'm smart," James said. "Will that help?"

"Maybe," Stewart said. "Maybe not."

James nodded.

Dicey waited for the conversation to continue, but it didn't, and James just stood there looking at Stewart as if Stewart were a mountain or something terribly large. So she began to move towards the door, pulling Sammy with her.

"Hold it," Windy said. "Where are you going? Dicey? We've got breakfast to get and then Stew's going to drive you to Bridgeport. That's right, isn't it, Stew?" His eyebrows moved as he spoke, emphasizing the words.

"Of course," Stewart answered. "Get me some doughnuts and coffee, will you?"

Windy took the Tillermans to the diner they had eaten at the night before. Dicey followed along, as quiet as Maybeth. She felt as if she was no longer in charge. In a way, she was relieved to let somebody else give directions and make decisions. In another way she was angry at these young men for taking over their lives, for telling them when and where to eat, for leaving her out of the conversation with James.

In the diner, which looked dingy by daylight, Dicey had fried eggs, while the others had pancakes. She had time now to enjoy the taste of her food. When she had eaten both eggs, she took one piece of toast and mopped up some yolk on to it.

Never had she enjoyed a meal more. She said so to Windy and he told her she looked like she'd like to climb on to the plate and roll around in the eggs. Dicey giggled and said she guessed she might. Windy finished his own breakfast and Maybeth's. Dicey took part of Sammy's pancakes and gave the rest to James, who was never full. They all drank milk.

When they returned to the room and Windy had given Stewart his coffee and doughnuts, he said goodbye to the Tillermans. "I've got a lab this morning and you'll probably be gone when I return," he said, shaking hands solemnly with each of them.

They thanked him, but he waved the words aside. "Any time," he said. "It was fun." He grinned at them and his eyebrows arched.

Stewart quickly wolfed down the four doughnuts and while he was sipping coffee he pulled out a guitar and played.

Chapter Eight

The Tillermans sat quietly and listened.

His was not an ordinary guitar, although it looked like one; it had a belly and neck and six strings like ordinary guitars, but instead of cradling it against his arm, Stewart laid it on his lap. He held a metal bar to the strings of the neck and plucked the strings over the belly. The sound this odd guitar made was metallic and round and slidy. When he reached over for his coffee cup, Dicey asked him what it was.

"A Dobro," he answered. He explained how it was made and how he played it. Then he played a slow, mournful melody on it, concentrating hard, biting his lip, leaning over the instrument and moving his shoulders with the rhythm.

Maybeth stood beside him and watched. "That's 'Greensleeves'," she said.

Stewart nodded. "Do you know it? You want to sing it?"

Maybeth sang the old song in her clear voice. "'Alas, my love, you do me wrong, to cast me off discourteously.'"

At the conclusion, Stewart smiled at her. "You do know it."

"Momma sang to us," Maybeth said. "We know a lot of songs."

"What else do you sing?" Stewart asked. He looked around at all of them.

"Play something you like," Dicey answered him.

"I play blue grass," Stewart said. "You know what that is?"

They didn't, so he played a song about a miner's child who dreamed her daddy would die if he went to the mines that day, but he went anyway.

"That's silly," Maybeth said, when he had finished.

"OK, then, what about this?" Stewart asked. "'Oft I sing for my friends'," he sang. His voice was soft as clouds and clear as the sky could be. "'When death's dark form I see. When I reach my journey's end, who will sing for me?'"

It was a short song, and Maybeth asked him to sing it again, and she joined in with him.

When that was finished, he looked at them. "Do you all sing? Like that?"

Dicey nodded.

Then Stewart put down the Dobro and said he had to go to class, but as soon as he got back he'd take them to Bridgeport. He went into his room and came back with a guitar case, out of which he took a regular guitar. "You can mess around on these if you like," he said. Even after he left, the room was filled with the harmony they had made, and the singing.

James picked up the Dobro and plucked at it with his fingers. "Dicey? I'm sorry. Really. I won't ever do anything like that again."

"I know," Dicey said. Her anger was entirely forgotten. "I didn't mean most of what I said."

"You think Stewart is smarter than Louis?" James asked. "I do," he said.

"How should I know that?" Dicey asked. "I like him a lot better. I like Windy too. Maybeth?"

Maybeth nodded. She was looking at a book of pictures. "Sammy?"

Sammy stared out the window. "How long do you think it'll be? Until we get there?"

"Not long. They said an hour."

"What's it like there?"

"I dunno, Sammy. Why?"

"Will Momma be there?"

Dicey looked at the back of his round little head, where the yellow hair stood out at crazy angles. *No*, her heart said inside her. "I dunno, Sammy," she said aloud. He didn't answer, just stood looking out.

Stewart's car was a battered old black VW beetle. The three little ones sat in the back seat, crowded together. James sat in the middle because he could see out easiest. Dicey was in the front seat. "It's a good thing you don't have luggage," Stewart said. "We'd never fit it in."

The day had grown hot and muggy. City smells hung heavy on the air. The little car clattered, like a giant sewing machine.

They made their way on to the Thruway and joined the cars hurtling along there. Stewart stayed in the middle lane. Cars passed them on both sides.

"I left my map," Dicey said.

"We'll get another," Stewart answered her, without moving his eyes from the road. "I don't know Bridgeport at all. Do you?"

"How could we?"

They drove with the windows open. The air roared in their ears. Things went by so fast when you were in a car, you could barely look at anything before it was gone. But this area, all concrete and sad little houses, was the kind you liked to pass by quickly.

Dicey leant over and said loudly: "I don't know where we would have slept along this road."

"Where'd you sleep when you came to New Haven?" Stewart glanced quickly in the rear-view mirror.

"Behind some stores. In a little park. Once in a carwash," Dicey told him.

"Then you'd have found somewhere along here," Stewart said.

They went through a toll booth where Stewart paid a quarter, and then after a while saw signs saying: BRIDGEPORT. Stewart kept to the middle lane.

"Aren't we going to get off?" Dicey asked.

"Not yet. I'm hungry, aren't you?"

"Yes," Dicey said, "but—"

"I thought we'd go down to Fairfield – it's only ten or twenty miles on – and eat at a McDonald's there. I know where that is, and I like going somewhere that I know where it is. We can pick up a map of Bridgeport too, so we can see how to get there, to your aunt's house."

Ten or twenty miles, two days' walk. Four days there and back. Dicey just nodded. "If you want to," she said.

"What I don't want to do is drive into a strange city without a map," Stewart said. He studied the traffic behind him in the rear-view mirror and turned on his signal blinker. "Besides, Fairfield's pretty."

Chapter Eight

"Do you live there?" Dicey asked.

He shook his head. They pulled off the Thruway and on to a four-lane road lined with low buildings, hung over with stop-lights, bleached white by the heat.

"This is Route One," Dicey said.

"You know it?"

"We've been on it most of the time."

"That's too bad."

Stewart stopped at a petrol station and came back with a map. He pulled into the nearby McDonald's and they all ordered lunch. He carried their tray to a big table back in a corner. Dicey handed out the wrapped hamburgers and the parcels of french fries. She jammed straws into the Cokes.

Stewart had ordered two Big Macs. He ate them as if he were starving. When Dicey told him this, he said he felt like he was starving, most of the time. "But I'll outgrow it," he said. "It used to be worse. I used to eat much more – a whole large pizza – and still not be full. Now I'm sometimes full. When I was in high school, I felt like I could eat all day long and never fill up."

James nodded at him, chewing.

After they had cleared the table and thrown out the wrapping papers, Stewart unfolded his map. Dicey told him the address and he found the street easily. It was one of many little streets running across the map of the city.

"But it's not near the water," Dicey said.

"Why should it be?"

"It's called Ocean Drive. I thought it would be near the

water. A big white house."

"Ocean Drive runs through the heart of town, a few blocks from the downtown section. But the street goes down to a main street that ends up at the harbour," Stewart pointed out. Dicey was unreasonably disappointed. "Maybe it was a joke," he suggested.

"Some joke."

"You like being near the water."

"In Provincetown, we were right next to it. Behind the dunes, but next to it. I'm used to it. Yeah, I like it. I don't feel right unless I'm near the ocean."

"You feel that way and you're going to Bridgeport? You're in trouble," Stewart said. "Listen, are you in a big hurry? Do you want to go to a beach for a while before you go to your aunt's?"

"Yes," James and Dicey said.

"No," Sammy said. "I want to see Momma. Right away."

"We don't even know whether she's there, Sammy," James argued. "You can wait an hour, can't you?"

"I don't want to wait any more," Sammy said. "Dicey?"

"Just for an hour, Sammy. Please?" she said. His face grew stubborn. "I've decided," Dicey said. "For an hour. No more."

Once they got off Route 1 in Fairfield, everything was clean and neat. The houses all looked freshly painted. The lawns all looked freshly mown. The cars all looked just washed. It was the kind of place where all the door handles shone with polishing.

They drove through a little village and then down by

Chapter Eight

some big houses around some curves – and then Dicey could see the water. At first she only glimpsed it in the spaces between the large trees that grew around the houses; then she could see a long narrow beach ahead, with marshlands on the other side of the road.

Sammy wanted to stay in the car, but Dicey insisted that he come out with them at least to begin with. "Then you can go back and wait in the car if you want," she said. "That's fair, isn't it?"

They spent an hour at the beach, no more. Sammy kept track of the time on Stewart's watch. They waded and dug. The children wandered up and down while Stewart and Dicey sat watching the little waves that meandered up on to the smooth sand. Dicey stared out over the quiet blue water, knowing that although the surface was calm, the great tides were moving underneath. She listened to the rippling waves mingled with the voices of the other people at the beach. They didn't talk much. Stewart didn't seem to be a talkative person, and Dicey didn't mind. He only asked her one question:

"What'll you do if things don't work out at your aunt's?"

He could have been reading Dicey's mind. She turned quickly to look at his face, but he was looking out over the water, his grey-blue eyes glinting in its reflections.

"I don't expect Momma to be there, you know," she said. He nodded. "Aunt Cilla must be pretty old now. She's really Momma's aunt, not ours. So she might not want a mess of kids. Is that what you mean?" He nodded. "I don't know what I'll do. Or if she's not even there. I guess I'll have to go to the police then, won't I? Or somebody. For help." He nodded. "What do you think I should do if——"

His eyes turned to her. "I honestly don't know. Except stick together, all of you. That's the most important thing."

Dicey agreed.

"If you can," he said. "If you are able to. You might not be able to."

"You and Windy — you were a big help to us," Dicey said.

"That's OK," Stewart said.

"Especially Windy."

"Windy had a good time. You brightened up his life."

"Especially you, too."

"I didn't do anything. Sang you a couple of songs. Got you some bad hamburgers."

"And took us to the beach, don't forget that."

They found 1724 Ocean Drive without any trouble. It was one of a long row of houses that stretched down treeless streets. It was a small house, shingled with grey asphalt. Three concrete steps led up to the plain front door. On one side of the door, two windows faced the street. There were thin curtains on the windows and you couldn't see in. The house looked flat-faced and empty. Dicey sat in the car and studied it before she got out. Was this going to be their home?

They clambered out of the car and said goodbye to Stewart. He left the engine running while he climbed out himself to shake hands with each one of them, James last, and wish them good luck.

Chapter Eight

Then he drove off, down the street, away, the little black car clattering busily. Dicey waved to him, but he must not have seen her because he didn't wave back. She turned to the closed door. She was nervous, but not in any way she had been nervous before. She looked at James and Maybeth and Sammy standing in a silent row and tried to smile at them. Then she went up the steps, hoping she looked more confident than she felt. At least they were all freshly washed. Dicey knocked on the door.

Chapter Nine

NOBODY ANSWERED DICEY'S knock. She could hear the echoes of her knockings inside, so she knew that she would have heard footsteps if someone had been hurrying to answer the door.

She knocked again, louder. While she waited, to be sure no one was at home, she studied the brown paint on the door. It was a thick reddish-brown colour and in the inset panels you could see brush strokes.

Nobody was there. Dicey swallowed, as much in relief as in disappointment, and turned to face her family. "I guess we wait," she said. She sat on the bottom step. They sat behind her and beside her.

They had nothing other than what they wore. Even Dicey's map, rain-soaked and ripped, had been lost. Stewart had taken his with him.

"I thought Aunt Cilla was rich," James said. "This isn't a rich person's house."

"I must have been wrong about that," Dicey said.

"Momma said she was," James insisted.

"Then Momma was wrong."

"Do you think Momma's here?" Sammy asked. "If she's here, why isn't she here?"

"I dunno," Dicey said. "It's Thursday, a working day, isn't it? So if she's got a job she'd be there, wouldn't she?"

"What about Aunt Cilla? Is she too old to work?" James asked.

"I don't know anything about her except what she wrote in her letters — and that wasn't true."

"Why would she lie?" James asked.

"I dunno," Dicey said.

"Dicey?"

"Yeah, Maybeth."

"Why did Momma go?"

Dicey looked at Maybeth's round and worried face. She looked down the quiet street, where no cars were parked, where all the houses were the same and had the same closed and empty faces.

"I don't know, Maybeth, but I can tell you what I think." Maybeth waited.

"I think she got so worried about so many things, about money and us, about what she could do to take care of us, about not being able to do anything to make things better — I think it all piled up inside her so that she just quit. She felt so sad and sorry then, and lost – remember how she'd go out and not come back for hours? I think she got lost outside those times, the way she was lost inside."

"Amnesia," James suggested.

"Maybe. So she decided that she'd ask Aunt Cilla to help us, because she couldn't help us any more. And maybe, when she went off into the Mall, maybe she'd run out of money and she couldn't take us any farther and all the things that had piled up inside her head sort of exploded there. And she just forgot us. Like amnesia, where you forget everything, even who you are. She couldn't stand to think and worry any more. Everything she thought of, every place she went to, it all looked so sad and hopeless and she couldn't do anything about it – so it all exploded and left her brain empty." Empty. That was the way Momma had looked those last months. As if she were far away from them.

"Will she be better now?" Sammy asked. "Do you think?"

"Maybe she's not even here," James said.

"She has to be," Sammy said.

"Why?" James asked. Dicey thought of stopping the conversation, but decided not to.

"Because," Sammy said.

"Because is no reason," James said.

"Because if she isn't here, then I don't know where she is. And she doesn't know where I am. And how can she find me?"

"Maybe she doesn't want to find you, or any of us," James

said. "That's what Dicey said, that she had to get away from us."

"Momma loves me," Sammy said. His chin stuck out in the stubborn way.

"Yes, she does," Dicey said. "And so do I."

Because she did, she loved all of them. That had kind of sneaked up on her over their journey.

"See?" Sammy said to James, "I told you."

"But that doesn't prove anything," James protested.

Sammy didn't pay any attention to him.

The sun moved slowly across a white sky. At the end of the long summer afternoon, or at the beginning of the long summer evening, the street gradually filled up with traffic, and the sidewalk became crowded with people. One after another, buses stopped at the corner and a short parade of men and women climbed off. Some carried briefcases, some grocery bags. They walked on, down the street or up the street. Some went up the stoops of the grey houses, pulled out keys, unlocked doors and went in. Others walked on, around corners, out of sight. No children lived on these streets.

The Tillermans silently watched the people move to and fro past them. Most of the men and women walked with their eyes towards the ground, or fixed blankly ahead. Sammy moved closer to Dicey and held on to her forearm with his small, tense hand. He did not say a word, but his eyes flicked back and forth. He was looking for Momma.

Dicey just watched the people, with no particular thought in her mind. She could not do any more. From now on, things would happen to them.

She saw men in workshirts with tired shoulders, carrying plain black lunchboxes. She saw women in brightly flowered summer dresses, the dresses wilted by the heat as if they were real flowers, the women's faces sagging after the work day.

A short round woman wearing high-heeled shoes walked towards the steps where they sat. She actually looked at them and seemed surprised, but she walked on past them. A man in a green khaki suit, carrying a scuffed briefcase, stared at them for a minute before he let himself into the house next door.

A few minutes later, a woman of the same age as the man, about fifty, Dicey guessed, struggled up the steps to the next-door house, carrying two huge bags of groceries. She noticed the Tillermans just as she pulled the door closed behind her and her eyes widened.

The little round woman in high heels walked past again, from the opposite direction and on the opposite side of the street. She stared at them. She was wearing a plain black cotton dress and had short grey hair that was permed into sausage-like curls that bounced and jiggled on her round head. She walked as if her feet hurt her, as if she had been standing and walking in the high-heeled shoes all day long. Dicey wondered where she was going.

The people coming home from work had filled the street for a while; now they thinned out, melted away into houses, out of sight. All the sounds were faint ones from distant traffic or from the humming of air-conditioners up and down the block. A solitary man wearing shorts and sneakers walked his dog on the opposite side of the street.

The round woman came towards them again. This time, as at first, she was on their side of the street and looking at the ground. She held her purse in both hands, protectively close against her side. Dicey thought she must be old.

She stopped about three feet away and looked at them. At first only Dicey was looking back at her, into pale blue eyes that blinked behind plastic-framed glasses sitting high up on her nose. She wasn't that old after all, close up.

"What do you want?" the woman asked. "What are you doing here? What do you want here?" Her voice was high and a little scared. Her lips pursed.

Dicey stood up. "We're the Tillermans," she said. She named them all. The woman's expression did not change.

Dicey knew then that Momma was not here.

Dicey kept on talking. "I'm hoping you're our aunt, our great-aunt, Mrs Cilla Logan."

Then the woman's expression did change. A little half-smile, a silly helpless smile, fluttered her mouth. "That is Mother," she said. "Not me. I'm her daughter. That is, I was her daughter." She fumbled around in her purse and took out keys. "Mother passed on this last March," she said. Dicey had a sinking feeling in her stomach. "But do come in. There's no need to stand talking on the front stoop."

The woman unlocked the door and stepped inside. The Tillermans followed. It was dark and stuffy after the summer evening light. They entered a narrow hallway that led to the rear of the house, passed a room with thin curtains, passed a narrow dark staircase going up and went into a kitchen.

The kitchen was large enough for all five of them, but not big. Sunlight made it brighter than the rest of the house. It was shiny clean. The grey linoleum floor gleamed, the refrigerator shone, the windows, looking over a tiny yard, were polished. There was a Formica-topped table in the centre of the room, and the woman told the Tillermans to sit at the four chairs that surrounded it. She opened the windows and the back door, then fetched herself a chair from the front room, putting it beside Maybeth. Before she sat down, she put some water into a kettle, put the kettle on the stove and took a mug out of a cupboard. As she did all this, she spoke to them in starts and stops. "Yes, Mother passed away. You couldn't have known. It was her heart. Her heart was always weak, but we never knew. She wouldn't complain, you see. She was only in her seventies. Seventy-two. A wonderful person – everybody said how wonderful she was. It was a shock to me. I found her, when I came back from work. Sitting in her chair by the window. A Wednesday, it was. We had a high mass for her." She sighed, the kettle whistled, and she poured water into her mug. She dunked a teabag, in and out, in and out. "I have been – not quite the same since Mother went away. People have said that to me. It has been hard for me."

She turned to face them, and Dicey saw little tears gathering in her little eyes. She took off her glasses and polished them on a paper towel.

The Tillermans sat silent, their mouths clamped shut, not

knowing what to say. The woman sat down at the table with them. She sipped at her tea. James looked at Dicey and raised and lowered his eyebrows, as Windy had. Dicey smothered a giggle.

"And then, of course, to see four children on my doorstep. Well, I had no idea. You don't mind, do you? You aren't offended? I was afraid. You hear of such strange things happening these days. Especially to women who live alone now. I hoped you would go away. If Mother were here, of course..." Her voice drifted off, her eyes drifted away from them and out to the windows.

Nobody spoke.

Finally, the woman gathered herself together with a kind of shake over her whole body. "But what am I thinking of? Are you thirsty? I don't know what I have for children to drink. Living alone, I don't keep much food in the house."

"Please," Maybeth said, "I would like a glass of water."

The woman looked at her. She smiled at Maybeth and said, "Of course, you all would like a drink of water, wouldn't you? What a pretty child you are. Really, like an angel. I was a pretty child too. Everyone said so – and we have photographs."

She got them each a little jelly glass full of water. They drank quickly and then Dicey refilled them once, twice, three times. The woman smiled absently.

"What are you doing here?" the woman asked, as if the question had just occurred to her. "Where are your parents? Who did you say you were?"

"We are the Tillermans," Dicey said again. She announced all of their names again, "James, Maybeth, Sammy, and I'm Dicey."

The woman repeated their names softly to herself. "My mother's maiden name was Hackett," she said.

"Our mother," Dicey began. She looked sharply at Sammy in case he might be about to interrupt, "is your mother's niece. We used to get a card and letter from your mother every Christmas, and Momma would read it to us. That's how we knew about Aunt Cilla, and her address. But I don't even know your name."

"Eunice Logan," the woman said. "Miss Eunice Logan. That makes us cousins, you know."

"Does it?"

"Yes, because your grandmother was my mother's sister. That means your mother and I are first cousins. Does that make us second cousins?"

"I don't know," Dicey said.

"Your grandmother would be Abigail Tillerman. Abigail Hackett she was before she married. Priscilla Hackett was my mother, you see. Before she married."

"Do we have a grandmother?" Dicey asked.

"Of course. Everyone does. But where are your parents? Are they visiting in Bridgeport?"

Dicey found herself ready to lie again. She could say they were visiting and the children had come to meet Aunt Cilla, and then later the Tillermans could go off and – and do what? If she lied, then she would get herself into a box. They had come such a long way. They had to have some kind of help from this cousin she'd never even heard of before. (That was strange too, that Aunt Cilla had never mentioned a daughter.) If Cousin Eunice didn't help them, they would have to go to the police. Dicey had to tell the truth.

But first she had to say it to Sammy. Say it out loud. "Momma's not here, Sammy," Dicey said.

He nodded, and tears welled up in his eyes. Dicey reached over and put her hand on top of his. He laid his forehead on her hand and closed his eyes.

"You don't know where your mother is?"

"No," Dicey said. "She ran away, I think. Anyway, she disappeared. We were on our way here to find Aunt Cilla, so we just came along. We hoped she'd be here."

"Where's your father?"

"He's been gone for years," James said, his voice sharp.

"You're alone?" Cousin Eunice asked. They nodded. "Oh dear. Oh dear, oh dear. You poor sweet little things. I don't know what to think. I have to ask advice. Will you excuse me to make a phone call? You're absolutely alone? I don't know what should be done."

She hurried out of the room, swinging the door closed behind her. Sammy raised his head and Dicey retrieved her hand, now a little wet. "I don't understand," Sammy said.

"Neither do I," Dicey answered. "She'd never heard of us, you know that? And we'd never heard of her. But Momma answered those letters, every year."

"What should we do?" James asked.

"Tell the truth and see what happens," Dicey said. "We can't do anything else. Can we? James?"

"We could take off again, and look out for ourselves until—"

"Until what?" Dicey asked.

"Until we grow up?"

"We could," Dicey agreed. "We always might do that and we'd figure a way out, I guess. But for now I think we shouldn't, unless we have to. We don't have any idea where Momma is, and I want to find out. Maybe this Cousin Eunice will take care of us — I could work later and pay her back. That's what I'm hoping will happen. Just so we're together."

"Is Momma gone for always?" Maybeth asked.

"I don't know," Dicey said. "She might as well be."

"Don't say that!" Sammy cried. "Don't you ever!"

Cousin Eunice returned. "My friend — he's an advisor really, he's my spiritual counsellor — he'll be by after supper. We have to get some more food — I have only two dinners in the freezer. Dicey? Can you go to a store and get three TV dinners? I don't know what kind you children prefer. Is that all right?"

"Of course," Dicey said. She flushed and said, "We don't have any money."

"None?"

"None. I'm sorry."

"Don't be sorry — I feel so sorry for you — I don't understand what has happened—"

"Neither do we," Dicey answered.

Chapter Nine

"How could you? You're only children." She reached for her purse and took out ten dollars. "This will be enough. You must want milk, children should drink milk. And fruit? Can you decide what you need? Will this be enough?"

Dicey nodded.

"The grocer is two blocks away, just around a corner. You go up the street, turn right, and you'll see it. But don't talk to strangers."

Dicey nodded, lowering her head to hide her smile.

"And you should call me 'Eunice'. Cousin Eunice. Because we're cousins. And could you pick out a cake from the frozen foods? Something light, perhaps lemon; something that will sit well with tea."

Dicey walked to the store, not thinking about anything in particular, just taking it slow. There was a kind of pool of sadness in her heart, she thought, and she wondered why it should be so. Not only for Momma, because she had not expected to find Momma here. She didn't ever expect to see Momma again, she realized. The sadness was for themselves, even though they were much better off now than they had been, say, just last night at this time. Dicey picked out three chicken TV dinners and went to the fruit counter.

Once again, everything had changed on them. Perhaps it was all this changing that made her sad. Or perhaps the disappointment, after finally arriving at Aunt Cilla's house, and finding only Eunice there, whom they had never heard of. A stranger. Who pitied them.

Probably, they could never go back to New Haven. She

wished they could have stayed there longer. She wished she knew something more about those two young men. She didn't even know their last names. Or phone numbers. Or address. Stewart hadn't even stayed to find out if the Tillermans would be all right. The Tillermans had just drifted through his life, touch in, touch out, and gone without a thought.

Dicey paid for her purchases and walked slowly back to the little grey house. Maybe it was just that she was away from the ocean, the salt water with its tides and turbulence, that made her sad.

Father Joseph, Cousin Eunice's friend, was a priest, a slender, restless man with thick grey hair and deep lines in his forehead. He had cool, thoughtful, light-brown eyes, deep set, and a thin mouth. He wore shiny black trousers and jacket, a black shirt-front, and the band of white, crisp and stiff, around his neck. Cousin Eunice introduced him and fluttered nervously around him on her high-heeled shoes, bringing him a cup of tea and offering him a tray with china pitcher of milk and a little china bowl of sugar cubes.

Father Joseph did not show pity for the Tillermans as Eunice had. They sat together in the living-room, on the chairs and the floor. He asked them about their home in Provincetown and their school, about Momma, about living in a summer resort area, about the fishing fleet and about books. After a while, he suggested that the younger children go to bed, while he and Cousin Eunice and Dicey made some plans.

Chapter Nine

"But they have no nightclothes," Cousin Eunice said.

"We can sleep in our underwear," Dicey said. "We washed everything out last night."

The priest remarked. "You did? You do seem to have managed well."

Dicey took the younger ones upstairs. James protested, but she told him: "We're guests. We're strangers here. She didn't even know we existed, and she's trying to help us. Let's just do as we're told, OK?"

James and Sammy were to sleep in the small back bedroom that looked out over the yard, in a double bed. Maybeth would sleep in the other twin bed in Cousin Eunice's room. Maybeth looked small lying there, her curls spread behind her on the pillow, her hands folded over the clean sheets. "You OK, Maybeth?" Dicey asked.

The little girl nodded.

"I think I liked it better when we all slept in the same place," Dicey said, smiling at her. "Like that first night."

Maybeth nodded.

"I expect I'll be sleeping in with James and Sammy, on the floor, or downstairs on the sofa," Dicey said. "If you want me."

"It's OK, Dicey," Maybeth said. "I won't be lonely."

"Lonely? All cramped together here in this little house? Why, I'll hear you if you roll over. I'll hear you if you sneeze – and come running."

Maybeth smiled at Dicey and closed her hazel eyes.

Dicey went back downstairs, where the adults awaited her in the living-room, which was cluttered with the kinds of things collected over a lifetime, pictures and little china figurines and pillows stuffed with pine needles.

Father Joseph greeted her. "Sit down, Dicey, we have to get to business now. That's an odd name, Dicey. What is your real name?"

Dicey sat cross-legged on the floor, between the two in their chairs, looking up at them. "Dicey's my name," she said. "I don't have another one."

"You just don't know it," the priest assured her. Dicey didn't argue. After all, maybe he was right.

He studied her, as if he wanted to see her thoughts. He made her uncomfortable.

"Your cousin has agreed to make you welcome here, until we can make inquiries about your mother, and your father."

Dicey looked at Cousin Eunice, who smiled foolishly at her and said, "It must be temporary, I'm afraid, but—"

"Your cousin has – certain plans, of which she may tell you later," Father Joseph said. He smiled at Cousin Eunice across the top of Dicey's head, and she blushed like a little girl. "However, the Church has summer activities in which your younger siblings can participate. A day camp for the little boy and the young girl. James will attend a school-camp. Will he object to that?"

"He likes school," Dicey said. "He's awfully smart."

"I thought so," Father Joseph said. "I'm one of the teachers there, so I can see that he gets into the proper classes. And of course there will be more active things to do in the afternoon."

"That sounds fine," Dicey said. "Thank you. Thank you both. I know we've just sort of fallen on you," she said to Cousin Eunice. "I'm sorry."

"Oh, don't be sorry," Cousin Eunice said, leaning forward, pushing her glasses back up her nose. "We are family, aren't we? And when I think of you, all alone — abandoned — like myself really, in a way. Why, I couldn't do anything else, could I? Only, I work, you see, so I have to be gone all day, and there will be so much to do with four children in the house. Cleaning and shopping, laundry."

"But I can do that, can't I?" Dicey asked her.

"That is what we hoped," Father Joseph said. "And the Church, Eunice, can give you clothing, as well as all the support we can offer, and counsel. Have the children no other relatives?"

"None that I know of," Dicey said. She knew she had interrupted, but she didn't like him talking about them as if she weren't there.

"Mother had just one sister," Cousin Eunice said. "Abigail. She would be their grandmother. But I don't know much about her. She was much younger than Mother, twelve years, and then they never were close. I've never met her. They might have had a falling out. I did write to her when Mother passed away, but I received no answer."

"Was the letter returned to you?"

"No."

"So it must have been received. By someone."

Dicey was listening hard.

Cousin Eunice waved her little hands. "Let me see. Abigail married a man named John Tillerman."

"Where does she live?" Father Joseph asked.

"In Maryland, down south, on the Eastern Shore. A town called Crisfield. I don't know anything about it. It is where Mother lived as a girl."

Father Joseph nodded.

"This John Tillerman farmed, I think I remember." Cousin Eunice wrinkled her brows with the effort. "They had children." Dicey nodded her head. "I don't know how many but one daughter would be Dicey's mother. I don't know where they are now."

Crisfield, Eastern Shore, Maryland, Dicey said to herself, to fix it in her memory.

"By that time, Mother had been in the north for years and married to Father, and they lived here. Mother didn't like her sister. She didn't like to be reminded of her family. I don't know – she wouldn't speak of them. She became a part of Father's family. These are the first Hackett relations I've met. I'll try to remember more, Father Joseph. We have photograph albums."

"That would be most helpful. I myself will see what I can find out about the Tillerman family. Sometimes the Church can make the more sensitive personal inquiries that the police authorities can't." He turned to Dicey. "What is your religion?"

"I don't know," Dicey said. "We never went to church." He frowned slightly.

Chapter Nine

"There is another question which I'm afraid I have to ask. The matter of your name. Tillerman. That would be your mother's name. Your parents were not married?"

Dicey shook her head. "I don't think so," she said. Cousin Eunice sucked in a noisy breath. Dicey did not look at her. She pulled at the laces of her sneakers, as if she had just noticed they were coming loose.

"Had you the same father, all of you? Would you know that?"

"Yes," Dicey said. Her head snapped up and her eyes met his. He did not seem surprised at her anger. "Sammy and Maybeth look like Momma, but James and me, we look like our father. I remember him, a little. Because I'm the oldest."

"Yes, yes," the priest said, smiling a little. "I'm sure you're right." He didn't sound sure.

"No, you're not," Dicey said, "but I am. And I know. Aren't there birth certificates? There have to be, don't there? We were all born in Provincetown — why don't you call the hospital there? They'll tell you. Momma wasn't—" She couldn't find the polite word. "She didn't have boyfriends, she didn't even go out on dates. She's nice. She's good. She loves us — and you probably don't believe that either, but she does. We'd know and you wouldn't."

He held up his hands. A smile lifted the corners of his mouth. Cousin Eunice fluttered in the background making little protests to tell Dicey she shouldn't talk like that to a priest.

"No, no, Eunice. The child is probably right. She would

know better than we."

"Then why did she abandon them?" Eunice asked. "Oh, I'm sorry, I didn't mean to say that," she apologized to Dicey. Dicey didn't respond.

"That is what we'll try to find out," Father Joseph said. "I think, Dicey, if you can, I'd like you to speak to the Missing Persons Department."

"The police?" Dicey asked.

"The police."

Dicey thought. She didn't want to talk to the police. But how else could they find where Momma went? And what if something bad had happened to Momma and the police could help her? And if by not talking to them Dicey could hurt her? She had a sudden memory of Momma's sad moonface and her sad moon smile in the car window; and then of Momma running to comfort Sammy when he had fallen off a chair and was frightened, pulling the little boy on to her knees and wrapping her arms around him, saying crooning comforting things. The two round yellow heads bent towards each other, and Momma's strong hands cradled the back of Sammy's little head.

"OK," Dicey said. "They can't put us into foster homes when we're here with Cousin Eunice, can they? We're not runaways, are we? I don't want us to be separated," she explained to the priest.

"Neither do we, if it can be helped," he answered. "I'll contact the police and someone will come here to see you. Shall I come with him?"

Chapter Nine

"OK," Dicey said again. She was thinking furiously, trying to see if there was a trap in this, or danger.

"You really have no choice," the priest said.

Dicey nodded, with her eyes on his, but she was reciting to herself: *Crisfield. Eastern Shore. Maryland.*

Father Joseph left, then, and Cousin Eunice brought Dicey a camp-bed that she kept in the cellar. Dicey put it into the last of the floor space in the boys' bedroom. Cousin Eunice wanted to object to having Dicey in with the boys, but she didn't want her own room to be crowded, so she didn't say much.

Dicey looked in on the sleeping Maybeth before she made her final stop in the bathroom and lay down on her camp-bed. She could hear James breathing softly. Sammy turned and rustled in the sheets.

Dicey lay on her back with her arms under her head, staring at the blank, black ceiling. They had come here, had come here safely. If this was to be their home, then she could learn to get along here. She would have to. Stewart was right, they had to stay together. That was the only important thing.

She was lulled to sleep by the words repeating in her head: *Crisfield, Eastern Shore, Maryland.*

Chapter Ten

A SHARP KNOCK on the door woke Dicey. She opened her
eyes wide. The window was dark. Dicey had slept and
awakened in so many unknown places that she never had
that first, morning feeling of being lost, or not knowing
where she was. She knew where she was, or rather, where
she wasn't.

The knock came again. Dicey jumped off the camp-bed
and squeezed around the corner of the bed where her
brothers slept to open the door.

Cousin Eunice stood there, wearing the same black
cotton dress, or its twin sister, and the same high-heeled
shoes. "I am about to leave," she whispered. "Can you come
downstairs for a word before I go?"

Dicey nodded. She closed the door and searched through
the darkness for her shorts and her shirt.

Chapter Ten

A rustling noise in the bed made her turn her head as she was about to leave. James sat up. "It's still true," he said.

"Go back to sleep, James," Dicey said. He lay down obediently, and his eyes closed.

Dicey found Cousin Eunice in the kitchen, drinking a cup of tea. Beside her on the table lay a black purse, black gloves, and a little round black hat with a brim that tilted up.

"Good morning," Dicey said.

"I'm sorry to wake you so early," Cousin Eunice said. Her face was pale above all the black around her. "But I am going to six-thirty mass. I always do that," she said. "I get breakfast on my way to work. There's a diner on the way, quite clean. Mother didn't like making breakfast. And I've always gone to early mass."

Dicey nodded. She sat down facing her cousin.

"I pray for Mother, and for myself, and for the world," Cousin Eunice said. "This morning, I shall pray for you, and for your poor mother."

Dicey felt uncomfortable. "Thank you," she said. Was that what you were supposed to say to somebody who was praying for you?

"I thought of staying home today," Cousin Eunice went on. She talked without looking at Dicey. "But I've never missed a day of work, not for any reason. Not in twenty-one years. Somehow, I didn't want to miss today."

Dicey nodded.

"Father Joseph said he would come by this morning and bring some clothing for you. He will register the younger children at camp, so that they can begin right away. So you must be sure to be here when he arrives."

"We will."

"But there is shopping that needs to be done, and usually on Thursday evenings I clean the living-room, dust and vacuum, wash the windows, damp mop the floors. I couldn't get that done last night."

"I can do that," Dicey said.

"Do be careful not to break anything," Cousin Eunice urged.

"I will," Dicey said.

"Here is some money. Try not to spend it all." Cousin Eunice handed her twenty dollars. "We'll need something for supper, I suppose. Can you cook?"

Dicey nodded.

"It has to be fish," Cousin Eunice said. "Today is Friday."

"I've cooked fish," Dicey said. Well, that was true. She had just never cooked fish on a stove, in a pan. What did Friday have to do with fish?

"I get home at five-forty. Will you be all right?"

"We'll be all right," Dicey said. "You don't need to worry about us."

"I don't know how you've managed it," Cousin Eunice said. "You must be a very resourceful child."

Dicey didn't know what to say.

"But you're here now, and I'll take care of you," Cousin Eunice said.

"That's awfully nice of you," Dicey answered. It sounded

so flat. But she felt flat, flat and – she admitted it to herself – disappointed.

"How could a Christian do less?" Cousin Eunice asked. Then she got up and put her hat on her head. She drew her gloves on over her plump hands and picked up her purse. "Until this evening, then. You're sure you'll be all right?" Dicey nodded. "Don't forget Father Joseph."

"I won't."

"And the living-room."

"I won't. I mean, I'll do it."

"And the shopping."

Dicey nodded.

"Fish, remember. Why don't we have a tuna casserole?"

Dicey nodded. She hoped she could find a cookbook in this neat and tidy kitchen, maybe behind a cupboard door.

Cousin Eunice left, drawing the door quietly closed behind her. Dicey breathed a sigh of relief, but the door opened immediately. "Don't leave the house empty," Cousin Eunice said. "There must be someone home, at all times. Thieves come, even in broad daylight these days."

"All right," Dicey said.

"It's not as if I have anything valuable," Cousin Eunice said. "But they steal anything. And murder – and other things – I don't know – the world has gone crazy. I'll have a key made for you, just one. Until then, don't leave the house unlocked."

"I won't," Dicey said. "Don't worry about us. We'll be fine."

"How can I help worrying?" Cousin Eunice asked. She did not give Dicey time to answer.

Dicey looked at the clock hanging on the kitchen wall. It was shaped like a cat, with a long, curled tail that twitched the seconds. Six-fifteen. Dicey familiarized herself with the kitchen, cupboards (no cookbook), drawers, refrigerator and freezer. She took a dustcloth and the vacuum and went into the living-room.

The room was cluttered, but not messy. Dicey didn't think it needed cleaning, but if Cousin Eunice wanted it cleaned then she would clean it. She dusted the wooden-backed chairs, the table tops, the windowsills, the one bookcase which held a Bible and two rows of photograph albums. Dicey thought she should ask permission before she looked through the albums. She dusted the pictures on the walls, of Jesus and Mary, like the ones that she used to see on Aunt Cilla's Christmas cards, of Jesus being crucified, and photographs, of a round-faced man standing beside a round-winged car, of a sharp-eyed woman with a fur round her neck, of a little girl with curly hair and a flouncy white dress and bouquet of flowers held in her white-gloved hands. Dicey dusted the row of china cats on top of the bookcase. She dusted the lamps and the door handles. Then she ran the vacuum over the pale blue rug, careful to clean under tables and chairs.

When she finished, it was seven-thirty. She set out bowls and spoons and glasses of milk. Cousin Eunice had two kinds of cold cereal, cornflakes with sugar frosting, and a fruit cereal which said it had fifteen flavours in its different-coloured little balls. Dicey put both boxes in the middle of the table. She wished she could find some flowers to put in a glass in the middle, but there were none in the back yard. Nothing grew there except a straggly, neglected cover of grass.

Dicey enjoyed getting ready for this meal. The morning sun brightened the living-room beyond. Light made things cheerful.

They ate a quick breakfast and then Dicey washed and dried the bowls and glasses and spoons. Maybeth helped her put them away. Sammy and Maybeth went out to the back yard. Dicey took James upstairs and made him help her make their beds. Cousin Eunice had made her own.

She left James in charge while she went to the store. There she purchased bread and milk and fruit, tuna fish and noodles and (after reading the instructions on the back of the bag of noodles) a can of mushroom soup, peanut butter, jam. She also bought a dozen eggs, a box of pancake mix, a jar of syrup and a cheap red rubber ball (because if Sammy was going to spend most of the day waiting around, he'd need something to play with).

Returning, unpacking the groceries, piling the dollars and change beside the toaster, washing the apples before putting them in the refrigerator, Dicey heard herself humming the song about Peggy-o. It was like playing house.

James wandered in and took an apple. "There aren't any books in the house. Are we going to stay here?"

"I don't think we can do anything else," Dicey said. "So

we've got to please Cousin Eunice, you know? And that Father Joseph too, I suppose. We've got to be on best behaviour all the time. Can you do that, James?"

"Sure," he said. "But it's an awful small house for four kids."

"Bigger than ours was."

"Yeah, but there we had the dunes and the beach."

Dicey went out into the tiny yard and called Sammy and Maybeth to her. To them she repeated what she had just said to James. They nodded solemnly to her, then she pulled out her hand from behind her back and tossed the red ball to Sammy.

He grabbed for it, missed, ran after it and caught it in two hands. He bounced it high. He turned and grinned at Dicey. Then he ran up to her and nearly knocked her over, hugging her. He called Maybeth to play catch.

Dicey watched them playing, proud that she had thought to get the ball. Glad in her heart that she had been able to give it to them.

They had finished lunch and washed and dried the plates and glasses by the time Father Joseph arrived. He carried two large shopping bags, which he passed to Dicey. "Clothes," he told her.

He gathered up the younger children and walked off down the street with them. James walked beside him. Sammy ran ahead. Maybeth trotted behind.

Dicey was alone in the house. It felt strange to be alone. Being alone inside was very different from being alone outside. Inside, there was nothing to do. And she felt full of energy.

She wanted to take a walk but she couldn't leave the house empty. So she sorted through the bags of clothes.

The clothes were worn, but clean and pressed. Their own clothes were worn out, but that was somehow different. Other people's old clothes – Dicey quelled the thought. She must remember to be grateful. For Dicey and Maybeth there were dresses, for the boys, shirts and trousers. Dicey didn't like dresses. There was no underwear. No blue jeans. Two pairs of shoes, heavy leather shoes that tied with laces. She would have to tell Father Joseph what they needed. Or maybe Cousin Eunice could give them the money for shoes and underwear.

In an hour, Father Joseph returned. The children were not with him, but another man was. He wore a business suit of olive green and had a round face and yellow-brown eyes that protruded. Goggle eyes. He had round fat fingers, and he jingled the money in his pocket. He peered at Dicey.

They all went to sit at the kitchen table. "The children are staying at camp for the afternoon," Father Joseph said to Dicey. "You and I will go pick them up, so that you can learn the way. Is that all right?"

Dicey nodded. She wondered if she should have changed into one of the dresses.

"This is Sergeant Gordo. He works with the Missing Persons Bureau of the Police Department, and he is also a personal friend of mine."

"How do you do," Dicey said.

"How do. Hot enough for you?" Sergeant Gordo asked. He laughed at his own joke. "Well. I understand you've got a missing mother."

Dicey nodded.

He took a pad out of his rear trouser pocket and prepared to write with a ball-point pen. "Give me her particulars," he said.

Dicey didn't understand.

"Name, age, weight, description, any distinguishing marks, last seen."

"Liza Tillerman, thirty-six," Dicey said. "I don't know how much she weighs."

"How'd she built? Fat? Thin?"

"She's regular," Dicey said. "Sort of thin, I guess, but she has a regular shape."

"Height?"

"Two or three inches taller than I am."

"How tall are you?"

"I don't know."

"Stand up, will you?" His eyes measured her. "She'd be about five-six or seven. Any scars or moles?"

"She's got a big mole on her chin, and one at the back of her neck, under her hair. There are more, but those are the big ones. She's got blonde hair, long blonde hair. Hazel eyes, like mine. A round face, with high cheekbones."

"What was she wearing when she took off?"

"Blue jeans. A sweater − a big, red, man's sweater, with holes in the elbows. Sandals. A purse over her shoulder."

Chapter Ten

"Rings? Watch?"

Dicey shook her head. Momma didn't have jewellery.

"Wedding ring?"

Dicey shook her head. The two men exchanged a glance.

"When did you last see her?"

"I'm not exactly sure. It was early in June."

"Where was it?"

Dicey told him about the mall in Peewauket. She told him about the car and how they had left it there.

He snapped his notebook shut. "I'll see what I can do for you," he said.

Dicey swallowed. "Do you think she's dead?"

He pursed his lips. "I can't say that, not now. If she is, we'll find out soon enough. Dead bodies stink, so we find them."

Dicey nodded. She didn't trust herself to speak.

Father Joseph seemed to understand that and he changed the subject. "I've put in a call to the church in Maryland."

"Crisfield," Dicey said. His eyes studied her briefly.

"Yes. The priest there will see what he can find out. Your people aren't Catholic."

"No," Dicey said. "We aren't anything. At least, I don't think we are."

His eyebrows went up. "Your Cousin Eunice is a devout Catholic," he said. "She was raised in the Church. But of course it was her father who was a Catholic – her mother converted when they married. She herself is very traditional in her devotion – she still chooses to keep meatless Fridays, for example."

But none of this interested Dicey. Her attention remained with the officer.

"How long will it take you?" she asked Sergeant Gordo.

"I can't say now, can I? Maybe a day. Maybe a year."

"No, I mean if she's dead."

"That'll take less time. If there's any possibilities I'll show you some pictures – oh, within a week."

"So if you don't tell me anything in a week—"

"Then we can be reasonably sure she's alive. Father Joseph tells me you don't have any idea what made her leave you."

"She didn't say," Dicey said. She looked at him. She didn't like him, but he could help her. "Do you want to know what I think?"

He took out his pad again. "Anything might be useful."

"I think she ran out of money and didn't know what to do, so she just – forgot about us. Her mind just erased us. Because she was so worried about us. Does that make sense?"

"The kind of people we deal with? Anything makes sense. Was she worried about anything in particular?"

"Everything. Always. She lost her job. That was why we were coming to Aunt Cilla's house – here."

"What about welfare? Or unemployment compensation?"

Dicey shook her head. "Momma said she couldn't do that. She wouldn't even talk to anyone. She said charity was not for the Tillermans."

"I wish more people felt that way," Sergeant Gordo said. He folded his notebook and put it away again. "Well, I've got work to do."

Father Joseph stood up too. "And we have some children to pick up."

"But I can't leave the house. Cousin Eunice said not to leave the house empty and unlocked, and I don't have a key. Can't you get James first and then the other two? James can show me the way on Monday morning."

Father Joseph looked doubtful.

"James will remember all right. He's smart."

"Oh yes, that's very clear. I suppose we can do it that way."

Dicey saw them out, and when they had gone she sat waiting on the hall staircase for her family to return to her. It seemed like a long time, waiting there in the dim, silent hallway.

At last they were at the door, James thin and thoughtful, Maybeth who hurried up to take Dicey's hand, and Sammy, who stood grinning by the door. Dicey thanked Father Joseph and said goodbye to him. She took her family out to the kitchen. She gave them fruit and then they all went out to the back yard. Sammy wanted to play catch with Dicey, but she wanted to talk.

"What did you do? What was it like?"

"I talked with the teachers," James said. "It's a school building and they have arts and crafts and games in the afternoons. All the teachers are priests," he said, taking a huge bit of banana and chewing it. "They've got a library just for the school and labs with Bunsen burners and chemicals in cupboards. I knew almost all the answers to their questions," he reported proudly. "I think I'll like it."

Dicey was glad to hear that.

"They talked to me as if I was a high school student," James added.

"What about you Sammy? What did you do?"

"Played."

"Played what?"

"Blocks, sandbox. We had running races and I came in second. Some of the boys I beat were much older than me."

"What about the girls?"

"No girls in my camp. All the girls are in one, all the boys in another."

"So yours was all girls?" Dicey asked Maybeth. She nodded. "What did you play?" Maybeth didn't answer. "Did you stand with the teacher all the time?" Dicey guessed.

"Yes," Maybeth said in a small voice, with a small smile.

Dicey rumpled her hair. She wanted to know more about what they had been doing. Each of them had had an entirely separate afternoon. "Did anybody look friendly?" she asked.

"I didn't see any of the guys," James said. "They were figuring out what classes to put me in. They asked me what prayers I knew, and what about the Gospels and the saints. I don't know anything about any of those. Catechism," he pronounced the new word. "They'll teach me."

"You sound glad about going to school."

"Boy, am I." James smiled at her, his hazel eyes smiling too. "These fathers, they're all so smart. Really smart. I never had a teacher like that, not even one. These guys know so much. And they really want to teach me what they know. You can tell that. Yeah, I think I am glad. So would you be."

"I doubt it," Dicey said. "It takes different things to make me glad."

"Like what?"

"Like knowing we've got food."

"Be serious, Dicey."

"The ocean," Dicey said. "And lots of room outdoors. But mostly the ocean. And the food too, that was serious."

"Father Joseph said to tell you we're all enrolled. He said you should take us on Monday."

"What was it like where Sammy and Maybeth were?"

James shrugged. "Playgrounds mostly, next to schools. Paved. Lots of jungle gyms and swings. The teachers for the girls, where Maybeth is, are nuns."

"Did you like the nuns?" Dicey asked Maybeth.

Maybeth didn't answer.

"All the other girls were wearing dresses," James reported.

"We have some dresses," Dicey said to Maybeth. "Father Joseph brought them today. Do you want to go and try them on? And see how they look?"

Maybeth nodded. Dicey took her upstairs and she tried on the dresses. Cousin Eunice had come home before they got back downstairs.

Dicey found Cousin Eunice sitting again in the kitchen, waiting for the kettle to come to a boil. The little woman looked tired. She had taken off her glasses and was resting her forehead on her hands, rubbing her eyes. Dicey sent the children outside to play in the back yard and cautioned James to keep them out there. She sat down facing Cousin Eunice. "Are you tired? Can I get you something?"

At that moment the kettle whistled. "I'll make the tea," Dicey said, hopping up. She poured the water and dipped the tea bag in.

"Thanks," Cousin Eunice said. "Yes, I am tired. And I have an instruction class tonight—"

"An instruction class?"

"Religious instruction. I am studying to…I am studying. But my feet hurt so, I don't know if I can go tonight. Well, of course I can, but—"

"What kind of work do you do?" Dicey asked. The woman was almost curled over on to the tabletop. Her face was pale and her eyes lacked expression. Dicey couldn't imagine what kind of work would make a person look like that.

"I'm a junior foreman. We attach the lace insets to lingerie, my girls and I. You know, on slips and nighties there are lace panels, or the cups of brassieres." Dicey didn't know, but she nodded anyway. "I've been quite successful in my work. There are only half a dozen junior foremen who are women, and only one senior foreman. But it's tiring – the supervising and the sewing and the quality control. It's a responsibility. You wouldn't believe some of the pieces of lace they expect us to set. We have to mend some of the pieces before we can even baste them in. And I'm on my feet most of the day, what with one thing and another. When Mother was here, she knew how tired I was." Her small, high voice droned on. "She'd always have a cup of hot tea waiting for me when I came in the door. And dinner on the table at six. I do get so hungry."

"Do you always get home at the same time?"

"Oh yes, at twenty to six, precisely." Dicey made a mental note. "But I have to begin dinner if we're to eat before my class." Cousin Eunice replaced her glasses and pushed herself up from the table, tottering a little in her high heels. She put a pot of water on to boil. She opened the can of tuna and the can of soup. Dicey tried to help, but she felt clumsy – as if she was interfering, not helping. So she set the table and found the noodles for Cousin Eunice.

"And did you get the living-room done?"

"Yes I did."

"Good. You washed the windows?"

"Oh no. I forgot that. I'll do it in the morning."

"Oh dear, in the morning we'll do the upstairs. And take the sheets and towels to the laundromat. And do our personal laundry. I think we'll have to let the windows go until next week. Although they get so dirty."

"I'll do them," Dicey assured her.

"And the floor. Did you damp mop?"

"No, no I'm sorry, I didn't. I didn't know what you meant by that."

"We'll have to do the living-room as well, tomorrow. Somehow."

"I'll do it, don't you worry about it."

Cousin Eunice poured the noodles into the boiling water. "But Cousin Eunice?"

"Yes, Dicey."

"You know that Father Joseph brought us some clothes."

"That's nice."

"Yes, it was nice. We are grateful. You'll tell him, won't you?"

"Yes, I will."

"But – we need underwear, and there wasn't any. And blue jeans or shorts, just one more each, so that when we play we won't ruin good clothes. And sneakers. At least, the others need sneakers. I can still wear mine for a long time. I guess I don't have to have a second pair of shorts."

"Oh, dear."

Dicey pushed the forks around on the table, as if she was still setting it.

"So we'll have to go shopping tomorrow too," Cousin Eunice said.

"Thank you," Dicey said.

"I don't know how much things for children cost."

"Neither do I. I'm sorry," Dicey said. "Maybe I could get work?"

"I don't think so," Cousin Eunice said. She was stirring the noodles with a long-handled fork. "I was talking with my girls and they said someone your age could only get babysitting jobs. I don't know anybody who has small children. We might advertise in the paper, I suppose, but who would take care of the housework then? The girls said – you know how silly some people are — that I was a saint to take you in, that anybody else would turn you over to social services. But I said, I can't do that, they're my own flesh and blood. Which in a way you are, you know."

"Yes," Dicey said. Then she added, because she knew it was true even though she didn't feel that it was true, "You are being awfully kind to us."

Cousin Eunice nodded and smiled her foolish smile.

"James is excited about school," Dicey told her. "Maybeth and Sammy are enrolled in day camp."

"That's nice. And you dusted?"

"Yes. Everything." Dicey was glad to be able to answer yes to one of the cleaning chores. "Are those your photograph albums in the bookcase?"

Cousin Eunice nodded as she put a colander in the sink.

"May I look through them?" Dicey asked.

"I suppose so," Cousin Eunice said. "I didn't keep the albums. They're Mother's work. Some of the pictures are very, very old. You'll be careful, won't you?"

"Yes," Dicey said. "Will you be late coming home tonight?"

"After ten. There's no need for you to wait up. Mother never did. I expect you'll all be in bed by the time I return. There's a television in my bedroom you can watch. As long as you don't play in there. Children like watching television, don't they?"

Dicey answered with more enthusiasm than she felt.

"And tomorrow we'll have to remember to have a key

made for you." Cousin Eunice sighed and drained the noodles.

Chapter Eleven

SOMETHING ABOUT AUNT Cilla's house (even though she knew it belonged to Cousin Eunice, Dicey still thought of it as Aunt Cilla's house, and still regretted her lost dream of it) made Dicey's brain slow down. Maybe it was trying so hard to please Cousin Eunice that had that effect on her. Maybe it was the routine of every day, with meals, cleaning, times to drop off the little children and pick them up, shopping, mending and ironing, having the cup of tea ready for Cousin Eunice at precisely twenty to six. Maybe it was just fatigue after her long journey there. Or maybe it was that nothing seemed to happen, except the same thing happening over and over again.

Even that was not precisely true. Sergeant Gordo called up one morning when Dicey was alone in the house. He asked her to come down to the police station, and gave her careful instructions for getting there on the bus. She took just enough change for her fare from shopping money and took a bus down to the old stone building, with bars on the windows of the second and third storeys. There she sat in the midst of a large, busy room to look at some pictures of women who might be Momma. None of them were. All of them, Sergeant Gordo told her, were dead and unidentified. They had found the Tillermans' car, he told her, and the Peewauket police could sell it and send the money to Dicey. He didn't expect she would get very much for it, he said.

"Does that mean Momma's not dead?" Dicey asked.

"I think we can assume that," Sergeant Gordo said. "Now, I'll start checking hospitals. Part of the problem is that we don't know where to look. If you'd reported her missing right away, we'd have had a better chance."

"I'm sorry," Dicey said.

"Fat lot of good that does now," he answered. His phone rang then, and he waved her away. "I'll be in touch if anything turns up."

Dicey didn't have much time for thinking about her family. James, she knew, was perfectly happy. He studied at night and went through the heavy wooden doors into the school at a run, every morning. Now and then he would report some amazing fact to Dicey. One time he told her about Alaric's treasure, that disappeared long ago when Rome ruled the world and America wasn't even discovered. Nobody had ever found the treasure because Alaric hid it so well. He diverted a river, then buried the treasure in the river bed, then rerouted the river back to its old path. The treasure was somewhere there, in Italy. Only Alaric had known where. He even killed all the men who had worked to hide it, so they couldn't tell. James pored over the maps in his history book, trying to think out where the treasure might be. James was always willing to tell Dicey what he was learning, even though he seemed to have no interest in discussing other things with her.

Sammy, on the other hand, demanded more and more of her attention. He ran up to her every afternoon, grabbed her hand and pulled her away from the gate where she waited with Maybeth silent beside her. "Let's go," he said. "Let's play ball. Will you play catch with me? Can we race on the sidewalk?" He wanted to wrestle with her after dinner and needed her to tuck him in every night.

Maybeth was Maybeth. Silent and peaceful, she went off to church with Cousin Eunice on Sundays dressed in a frilly pink dress Cousin Eunice had bought her, wearing a little straw hat with flowers on the brim and white gloves. She even had a little white purse. Cousin Eunice had taken a great liking to Maybeth.

Dicey wondered if she was losing touch with her family.

Dicey had looked through Aunt Cilla's photograph albums. She didn't know what it was she was looking for, just something. There were only two pictures of Aunt Cilla's childhood, before she met and married Mr Logan and lived in Bridgeport.

The first picture was a posed photographer's picture, badly

yellowed, of a man with a long beard and a woman with long hair piled on top of her head. The woman held a baby on her lap. Beside her stood a girl with curling blonde hair and a silly smile. Underneath this picture Aunt Cilla had written in her lacy handwriting: *Mother, Father, Abigail and myself.* Dicey thought Abigail must be the baby, since Cousin Eunice said Aunt Cilla was twelve years older than her sister.

The other picture must have been taken at a birthday party, because there was a cake with candles at the centre of the picture. A pretty young woman in a white summer dress held a knife to cut the cake. Beside her, on one side, stood her parents, the man's beard turning white and the woman grown fat. On the other side stood a girl with wildly curly dark hair and a sour expression. The three adults were looking at the photographer and smiling. The little girl scowled down at the cake. Her hands were behind her back. Dicey would have bet that her fists were clenched.

Dicey recognized the oldest daughter as Aunt Cilla. The younger girl was Abigail. The sour one. Her grandmother.

One afternoon Dicey went early to meet James. She went early on purpose and entered the school building rather than going around to the playground to where James usually waited for her. She found Father Joseph in a small office, sitting behind a wooden desk correcting papers.

"We're very pleased with James," he said to her. "Sit down." He pulled out a chair. "How is everything going for you? You've been with your cousin for about two weeks now, haven't you?"

Chapter Eleven

"Yes," Dicey said.

"Is something wrong?" he asked her. Then he seemed to recall something that had slipped his mind. "I've been wanting to talk with you anyway and haven't got round to it. I'm glad you came in. Shall we deal with your business first, and then get on to mine?"

"But you said you were pleased with James," Dicey said. She was alarmed. "He's happy here. Awfully happy."

"James is fine, fine," Father Joseph said. He closed up his grade book, folded his hands and looked at her. "What brought you to see me?"

"I wondered if you had heard from your church in Crisfield," Dicey said. Her mind was working furiously. Was something wrong about Maybeth? Or Sammy? Or both of them? She knew something was wrong with Sammy at camp, she'd known that all along.

"What do you know about your mother's family?" Father Joseph asked.

"Nothing. Momma never talked about them, never at all. Except Aunt Cilla. And that wasn't the truth – but Momma didn't know that. I found a picture of my grandmother in Aunt Cilla's albums, but she was only a girl, Maybeth's age. Cousin Eunice doesn't know anything. Did you find out something?"

"A little. The family is not Catholic, you know."

Dicey nodded. He kept bringing that up.

"So they aren't parishioners. If they were parishioners, then we would know a great deal about them. But – your grandmother. Her name is Abigail Tillerman."

"I knew that. There were names under one of the pictures."

"She lives alone on a small farm, outside Crisfield. She lives absolutely alone there. Her husband died some years ago."

So Dicey didn't have a grandfather.

"They weren't Catholics, but Crisfield is a small town, where everybody knows everybody else. So – the priest asked some questions of his older parishioners. They had known the Tillermans. None of them had been friends – the Tillermans didn't seem to have friends – but they knew about them. He told me there were three children in the family. A boy, John, named after his father. People say he is in California. Nobody has heard from him for years, not his mother, nobody – twenty years or more. A second son died in Vietnam. Do you know about the war in Vietnam?"

Dicey nodded. Well, she had heard of it, and James would be able to tell her about it.

"Then the daughter, your mother. She ran off when she was twenty-one, they say, to join a merchant mariner she had somehow met, a man named Francis Verricker."

"My father?" The man who had swung her to his shoulder and named her his little only.

Father Joseph rubbed his hand over his eyes. "Yes. At least, that is the name on the birth certificates from Provincetown. I have no reason to think he was not everyone's father. The police are trying to trace him for me. They had searched for him some years ago. He seemed to have disappeared."

"I don't mind," Dicey said.

"I do." Father Joseph's voice was sharp and angry. That surprised Dicey, and, sensing his concern, she was grateful to him, for the first time in all the time in Bridgeport, truly grateful.

"Do you mind hearing unpleasant truths, Dicey?"

"Yes. But I'd rather know the truth than not, if that's what you mean."

"I thought so. The Tillerman home – it must have been unhappy. Do you know what that can mean?"

"I think so," Dicey said. "I mean, we were happy. We were – whether you believe it or not…"

"Oddly enough, I do believe it."

Dicey smiled at him. "You see, there were kids at school – they hated their parents or they hated other people so much that you knew – it wasn't just being angry, it was hating. I can't explain what I mean, but I could feel the unhappiness."

"I see that James doesn't have all the brains in the family," Father Joseph said.

Dicey was flattered. "He's the clever one. I'm just – practical."

"Well, the Tillermans seem to have had that kind of unhappiness. The priest – or his informants – seem to blame her parents, especially the father. Remember, this is conjecture, not fact. It may just be gossip, you know. This is just what someone told him and he told me. Your grandfather seems to have been a stern man. An unbending man. Over-

HOMECOMING

righteous perhaps. Perhaps cruel. Nobody knows anything certain. Your grandmother always let him have his way. Nobody can say what she thought. She never spoke of it. He had his boys do a man's work, from the time they were eight. He used a whip for disobedience, a real whip. He did not tolerate disobedience of any sort. He quarrelled with his neighbours. He was angry – probably hate-filled too. She – your grandmother – was apparently the kind of woman who sticks to her husband's rule. She may have thought he was right. Or something else."

"It doesn't really matter which, does it?"

"In effect, no. You *are* practical."

"I haven't had much choice."

"Speaking practically then, your other uncle is dead, your mother has disappeared, and I don't think your Uncle John wants to be found. Which leaves your Cousin Eunice."

What was wrong with her grandmother? Dicey didn't ask aloud. She sat silent for a while. "What a family," she finally said.

"You shouldn't judge unless you've been there and known what actually went on," Father Joseph said.

"Come on," Dicey protested. "And Momma's – but she gave us a good home in Provincetown. She took good care of us, as good as she could."

"Yes, I think so, in some ways. One wonders," he said carefully, his light brown eyes resting on Dicey's face, "if there isn't a strain of – mental weakness."

Was he reading her mind?

"Your grandmother's isolation — she has no phone, so the priest drove out from Crisfield to talk with her. She wouldn't let him into the house. She apparently screamed aloud so that she wouldn't hear what he was saying."

Dicey remembered Momma's strangeness and James's idea that craziness was inherited.

"I mention this to you because I want to tell you that, if it can be inherited, you have probably *not* inherited it. In my opinion," Father Joseph said.

"Are you sure?"

"No, of course not. But remember, you've already been through more trials than most people endure in a lifetime. You and James, you two at least, seem to have the strength and resilience to go on. Isn't that what sanity is?"

"I don't know," Dicey said. She rose to go, her mind filled with what he had said.

"But we *are* concerned about your sister. She is — so far behind her age group. She doesn't speak. She can't read or work with numbers."

This again.

"She can." Dicey sat down again. "She can do all that. She isn't — she doesn't in front of strangers. Her teachers always said she couldn't do things, but at home, with me or James, she could. You don't believe me."

"No, I don't."

"You didn't believe me about our father being the same," Dicey reminded him.

"That's true."

"You just have to give Maybeth time."

"How much time? There's Sammy, too. The brothers report that he is not mixing in well. He is hostile to his peers and hard to direct and control. He plays alone, because the other boys avoid him."

Dicey sighed. "It was hardest on Sammy when Momma left us. And before it was hardest because she paid so much attention to him. James told me on our way here that in Provincetown Sammy had it hardest of anyone. Because of coming after Maybeth. And the things people said about Momma."

"How did you and James manage?" Father Joseph asked.

"James is clever. He'd think his own thoughts and ignore people. I suppose I just fought back too hard for people to want to tease me. But Sammy wouldn't. I mean, he'd fight, but he's not as fierce as I am." Father Joseph smiled. "When he was a baby, he was always happy and friendly. That's the way he really is. He can still be that way. Sometimes, on the way here, you could see it, you could see him getting to be more like himself."

"Sammy is a difficult child," Father Joseph said. "But I suppose his hostility isn't surprising when you think of causes. He needs a warm, loving home."

So do we all, Dicey thought. She looked quickly at Father Joseph. "I love Sammy," she said.

"Of course you do. You must consider, however, the effect of these burdens on your own life. I think you must. I think you must give some thought to adoption and foster homes.

Chapter Eleven

Sammy, despite his behaviour, may prove the easiest to find a home for. It will be hard to place Maybeth. A retarded child—"

"She's not!"

"She has the symptoms," Father Joseph answered gently. "And you, an older child. You also would be hard to place. Your cousin – I don't know what her plans are now."

Dicey had no idea what he was talking about. She shrugged her shoulders.

"James also is old for adoption, but he would easily find a permanent home here at the school, or he might stay with one of our families. His academic promise makes him most desirable."

Dicey could think of nothing to say.

"You should think of these things," Father Joseph said, still gently. "I know you don't want to, but you must think them through and be ready. Think of yourself also. You are still a child yourself."

A child? Dicey felt a hundred years old. Or more.

"I'm not asking you to decide. Just to open your mind to other possibilities."

Dicey nodded. She knew she should thank him, but she couldn't. So she just walked out of the room, without a word.

That afternoon, in the mail, Dicey received a cheque from the Police Department of Peewauket, for fifty-seven dollars. The receipt with it said "Profits from the sale of one 1963 Chevrolet sedan, less costs." Dicey looked at the cheque and smiled, for the first time in days, it felt. She could give it to Cousin Eunice and that would make her cousin feel better about taking the Tillermans in. Or she could buy some blue jeans for herself and Maybeth, which would make them feel better. Or she could hide the money away, for what purpose she didn't know.

Dicey knew what she should do. She should give the money to Cousin Eunice. Instead, she cashed the cheque at the grocer's, where the man knew her, and put the money into the box Maybeth's church shoes had come in.

Having money made a difference. It woke Dicey up. She began to think of how she could earn more during the day when everybody was gone. She could easily spend less time on housework if she pushed herself to be faster and more efficient. If she did that she could have some time for earning. Dicey felt like her old self again.

Because she was young, Dicey couldn't get a regular job. Over the next few days, she thought hard about what she could do to earn money. She could wash windows, she knew how, she'd done it. She decided to try that. If that didn't work, she would try something else.

The first place Dicey asked for work was the grocer's. The manager-owner, Mr Platernis, liked her, so she figured she'd try him first.

Dicey suggested to Mr Platernis that she wash his windows three times a week, for two dollars each time. He studied her.

"I've only got two windows," he said.

Chapter Eleven

"They're plate glass, and big. I'd do them inside and out, and then I'd restack the canned goods and dog food," Dicey countered.

"You'd need some special equipment," he said. "A long-handled washer, a bucket, cleanser."

"If I knew I'd be using them I'd buy them," Dicey said.

He considered this. Dicey enjoyed the bargaining. He enjoyed it too. "I'd buy them here," Dicey added. "I'd buy all my supplies here too."

"You going into the business?"

"I might be."

He thought some more. "Two dollars is a lot of money."

"A shop with clean windows is more attractive to customers. Especially a grocer's shop. More people would come to shop here."

"I can do the windows myself."

"Three times a week? They get pretty dirty."

"I know, oh, I know. How about a trial period of a week?"

"Two weeks," Dicey said. "It'll cost me that much to get the equipment."

He laughed at her. "All right, two weeks. And I'll call some other people who might be interested, some other store owners in this area. We'll see if they would like to employ your services."

"Would you, Mr Platernis? You won't be sorry." Dicey grinned at him.

By bargaining this way, before she knew it, Dicey had six regular jobs, washing the city grime off the windows of neighbourhood stores. She had two grocery stores, one hardware store, one shoe store, one pawn shop and one dress store. The dress store was her best job – they had four big windows they wanted washed three times a week, so she earned twelve dollars a week from there. That, added to the six dollars weekly from Mr Platernis and four apiece from the other three stores, made a total income of thirty dollars a week. Her supplies, once she had made the original purchase of bucket and long-handled squeegee, cost her five dollars a week. Mr Platernis let her store her equipment in the cupboard with his own cleaning equipment and supplies, just to keep an eye on her, he said. He didn't need to worry – Dicey liked her work, she liked making money. The money in the shoebox began to mount up. Dicey's spirits mounted with it.

She was working hard, but she seemed to have more energy than before. The July heat thickened and deepened, but Dicey wasn't slowed down by that. Mr Platernis couldn't get over her high spirits. "You must have been raised in the tropics," he said, mopping at his face with a cloth handkerchief. He often stood outside and talked to Dicey while she worked. He would help her replace the soup cans and bags of dogfood she had to move before she could wash the inside windows.

"I like having something to do," Dicey said.

"I'd think you have enough to do keeping house for Miss Logan and your family. Since you arrived I haven't seen her, except passing by. You're doing all her shopping, and the rest of it too, I'm guessing."

Chapter Eleven

"That's not the same," Dicey said.

"You don't like housework," Mr Platernis concluded.

Dicey didn't contradict him, though she knew that wasn't it. She didn't mind housework. She'd always kept house in Provincetown, although Momma wasn't nearly as fussy as Cousin Eunice. But it wasn't the same when you always had to remember to feel grateful.

Dicey bought herself three maps: one of Connecticut, one of New York and New Jersey, one of Maryland and Delaware. She found Crisfield easily enough, way down at the end of Maryland, facing the Chesapeake Bay.

One night at dinner Dicey tried to find out something about her grandmother. "Did you ever visit your mother's family?" she asked.

Cousin Eunice looked up in surprise. "Of course not. Mother said she didn't want to go back, and she wouldn't have me going near the place. Sammy! What are you doing? Sit up! Don't lie on the table! Bring the fork to your face, not your face to the fork." Her eyes, sulking behind the glasses, went back to Dicey. "I don't know why you children can't work on your manners yourselves, instead of worrying me with them. Don't you think I have enough to do?"

Dicey cast a quick eye around the table. Maybeth put her left hand into her lap and straightened her back. Then she met Dicey's glance with a silly smile, half worried, half apologetic.

"I have enough to do," Cousin Eunice went on. "And added to—" she hesitated and seemed to remember something. "Sammy? Is that a cut on your hand?"

Sammy chewed and nodded.

"How did that happen?" Cousin Eunice asked.

Sammy stuck his jaw out. He did not answer.

"Answer me," Cousin Eunice said.

"I don't remember," Sammy muttered.

"That is a lie."

"How do you know?"

"I know because I heard about how you got cut, that's how I know."

"Then why did you ask me?" Sammy demanded.

Maybeth bowed her head lower over her plate. Dicey looked at Sammy, trying to will him to be cooperative. Or at least quiet.

Cousin Eunice spoke through stiff lips. "Don't be fresh. Don't you ever be fresh with me. You hear? The reason I asked you is because — because — because I wanted to hear what you would say," she finished lamely.

"I didn't say nothing," Sammy said.

"What was the fight about?" Cousin Eunice asked.

"Nothing," Sammy said.

"Sammy?" Dicey interrupted. "Cousin Eunice wants to hear your side."

"I can't remember what it was about," Sammy said stubbornly. Dicey could have picked him up and shaken him.

"Who won?" James asked.

"James!" cried Cousin Eunice.

Sammy lifted his head. "Me, I did."

Chapter Eleven

"That has nothing to do with it," Cousin Eunice said.

Yes it does, Dicey said to herself. It does to Sammy.

"I don't want you to fight any more," Cousin Eunice announced. "I want you to promise me that you won't."

Sammy chewed silently. He kept his eyes on his plate. At least, Dicey thought, his mouth was closed.

"Sammy—" Cousin Eunice warned him.

He shook his head.

"Then you will go to your room. Right now." Cousin Eunice's voice sounded angry, and tired. "And you will stay there for the rest of the night. You tell lies. You won't promise not to fight. I won't have you at my table."

Sammy got down from his chair and trudged out of the room. They heard his slow footsteps going up the uncarpeted stairs. They heard the door slam behind him.

"I don't know. I just don't know," Cousin Eunice said. She shook her head and the sausage curls on it bounced. "At least I hear some fine things about James. James seems to be making quite a good impression." She smiled at him.

James wavered between saying something rude and being flattered. Dicey watched him nervously. "James is smart," she said, trying to tip the scales.

"It's not only that," Cousin Eunice said. "James conducts himself well, too. He is a credit."

"It's a good school," James finally said. Dicey let out her breath. James looked across at her, waggled his eyebrows the way Windy had, and kept on talking. "When you think of all there is to learn, in order to understand things. Like history and science – there's so much to learn. The fathers say that part of man's purpose is to increase his knowledge, so that he can understand better how great is God's work. A lot of people think knowledge is dangerous. But they're wrong. Did you ever think of that, Cousin Eunice?"

"Yes, of course," Cousin Eunice said. "God wants children to study hard and behave well in school."

James answered slowly. "I suppose you could say that. But that's not the way the fathers talk about it, about learning. They don't treat it like a duty. They treat it like a gift. Like grace."

"I don't think you can be right about that," Cousin Eunice said. "Not grace. That's not what the Gospels say, is it? Nobody's ever told me the Gospels say that. I've always understood that duty is the most important, even the best."

James shrugged. "Maybe learning's just that way for me. Lucky for me, isn't it?"

Cousin Eunice smiled at him. The tension was gone from the table. But Sammy hadn't had much dinner and he was up in his room. Dicey tried not to think about that. It was his own fault anyway, for being so stubborn. But Dicey had never talked about her fights when she got home – you just didn't do that. That was squealing. Momma never asked about them. Why did Cousin Eunice have to ask?

After the dishes were done and Sammy was asleep and Maybeth was tucked into her bed and James was settled down to homework in the living-room, Cousin Eunice called to Dicey to join her in the kitchen. Dicey saw that a cup of tea had been made for her, and for some reason that made her nervous.

"Sit down, Dicey," Cousin Eunice greeted her. She was wearing another one of her black dresses. Dicey had never seen her wearing colours. Her eyes looked out at Dicey from behind polished glasses. "I was talking with Father Joseph today."

"I didn't know that," Dicey said. She wondered what was wrong now.

"He took me to lunch," Cousin Eunice said. "Well, I was surprised when he asked me. I wasn't sure it was right – but he insisted that it was. We didn't go to a real restaurant, but it was a very nice cafeteria, everything as clean as you could want. I had a fruit salad. There's something I haven't ever told you, you see, and Father Joseph thinks I should."

"What is that?" Dicey asked.

"Before you came, you and your family, I had certain – ambitions," Cousin Eunice said. Her voice was very soft and she stirred her tea thoughtfully. "Father Joseph knows of these, of course. He approved of them, with certain reservations. And since he had approved, I was sure it was the right thing."

"What was?"

"To enter a sisterhood. To become a nun. I was going to be a nun before...and Father Joseph had made the preliminary arrangements for me. It's a useful life. I have a substantial savings account, which would make up my dowry, that and the house. So you see, I could have managed well."

"It sounds—" Dicey tried to think of what she should say "—nice. You'd make a good nun."

"Do you think so? I had hoped so. However, that is out of the question now." Cousin Eunice's eyes filmed with tears, and she shook her head. "Because of you children. You need me more, Father Joseph says. It is God's work, just as much, caring for abandoned children." As she spoke, she looked over Dicey's shoulder at something Dicey couldn't see, something Dicey suspected wasn't there at all, and her eyes shone. "That is my duty. You will be my family now." Her soft voice vibrated with the pleasure of resolution and sacrifice.

"Are you sure?" Dicey asked.

"It is God's will," Cousin Eunice said, bowing her head.

Dicey sipped tea, which she had never liked, and thought about this. "That's awfully kind of you."

Cousin Eunice smiled at Dicey.

"You're giving up something you want," Dicey said.

"You are not to speak of that," Cousin Eunice said. "I wasn't going to tell you at all, but Father Joseph said that you and I especially must understand one another. So that if sometimes I grow sad…you will know why and sympathize with me rather than feeling you've done something wrong. Perhaps Maybeth is meant to be a nun, perhaps she has a vocation, and it will be my place to guide her to it. Perhaps she will be my purpose in life."

Dicey wanted to get up and run, but she made herself sit still.

Chapter Eleven

"Father Joseph suggested that I adopt you, so that I will be the legal guardian."

"What if Momma comes back?"

"Surely she has shown herself unfit to raise children?" Cousin Eunice answered. Her lips pursed.

Dicey couldn't answer that.

"However, Dicey, you and I must deal with Sammy. He's causing some trouble at camp. Not just today – constantly. Father Joseph said he had spoken to you about this. Sammy has to be brought into line. I couldn't adopt a child who will bring nothing but trouble. Could I? You saw how he behaved at supper. Sammy has to understand that his behaviour is unacceptable."

"But—" Dicey said, and then changed her mind. "How would you do that?"

"I'll talk with Father Joseph. He's not sure that my house is the best place for Sammy, but he feels we should try it for a while, to see if we can keep your family together. He's concerned about Maybeth, too, he told me, but I could assure him that we would do well, Maybeth and I. But Sammy – I don't know. I'll see. Father Joseph knows about disciplining boys. James, fortunately, is biddable. Sammy has to be brought into line, so he doesn't shame me."

Dicey stayed absolutely still. She didn't even blink. She didn't trust herself to speak.

"I *do* feel better, now that we've talked. Don't you?" Cousin Eunice looked happy. Her curls bounced on her head. "You will be like a family of my own. If I'd had a daughter, she might be just your age. You'll grow up and have children of your own. So that when I'm older, I won't be alone. Just as Mother wasn't alone. In a way, I'm glad about this. Aren't you? And you children will have a good mother."

We already have a good mother, Dicey said angrily to herself. Hold on, she said to herself. This was what Father Joseph had decided. It might be for the best. The Tillermans would be able to stay together – maybe. They would have a home. Dicey knew she should feel grateful to Cousin Eunice. But she didn't. She felt like crying.

Chapter Twelve

AUGUST CHOKED THE city. The morning sun had to burn its red path through low-hanging hazes and clouds of industrial smoke. The streets steamed, as concrete reflected heavy sunlight. The temperature climbed until one in the afternoon, and then continued climbing. When it rained, fat grey drops plopped down upon the roads, then bounced up, as if in a half-hearted effort to escape. At evening, darkness gradually smothered the sun, until night fell upon the city.

Dicey rose early every morning, cooked the breakfasts, cleaned the kitchen, walked her family to their daily activities and hurried back to pick up her equipment and wash whatever store windows were on her schedule for the day. Then she completed whatever housekeeping chores Cousin Eunice had assigned before she went to fetch her family, played briefly with them, prepared dinner and made Cousin Eunice's cup of tea.

Weekends were a little different. For those two afternoons, the Tillermans could go off to a park or a public beach after they had completed the morning chores, or after Maybeth had returned from church with Cousin Eunice.

Sometimes it was more convenient for Dicey to meet Maybeth at the church, if they were going to picnic at the park, or if Cousin Eunice had friends she wanted to visit. Dicey would wait outside the big brick building, waiting for the heavy doors to be opened from within. The steeple stretched tall up into the sky. There was a gold cross on top of the steeple, and from below it looked as though the tip of the cross scratched the bottom of the sky.

When the doors opened, Dicey watched carefully for her sister. Lots of children went to church with their parents, all of them dressed up. The girls wore organdy dresses and party shoes and ribbons in their hair, or hats. The boys wore real suits and ties. Cousin Eunice always walked out slowly, surrounded by a group of women who could have been her sisters. They dressed alike. They all wore those high-heeled shoes. They all had curled their hair into sausages.

These women made a pet out of Maybeth. She would stand in the middle and they would tell her how pretty she was, how lucky she was to have naturally curly hair and what a sweet, quiet girl she was. "You're going to break some hearts for sure," they said, giggling.

Maybeth listened to this and smiled foolishly.

Chapter Twelve

"An angel like you – nobody will be good enough for you. She's a treasure, Eunice," they said.

"Don't I know it?" Cousin Eunice answered, smugly.

"A doll, a perfect doll."

Dicey put her hands behind her back and clenched her fists, waiting for Cousin Eunice to see her.

When Cousin Eunice called her, the women stepped back and smiled primly at her. Maybeth put out her hand for Dicey to take. Her eyes were wide as she looked at Dicey, wide and pleased with the attention. The silly smile stayed.

On Sunday afternoons the Tillermans chose to go to a small park nearby because on summer weekends it was less crowded than the beach. There were trees there, and grass. Several times Dicey saw Mr Platernis in the park, who greeted her warmly with: "How's my go-getter today?" Nobody commented on this, except James, but Dicey abruptly changed the subject.

She found a time, soon after her talk with Cousin Eunice, to try to explain the situation to Sammy.

"You've got to be cooperative at camp," Dicey said.

"I don't like them," Sammy said.

"Don't like who? The boys? Or the teachers?"

"Don't like any of them."

"Why not?"

"They're all bossy."

That was all he would say. His little jaw stuck out, and he pulled at blades of grass as they sat by the sandbox.

"We've got a problem, Sammy," Dicey said. "We have to

please Cousin Eunice. The way for you to help is to cooperate at camp. Act more friendly."

"Why?" Sammy asked.

"So we can all stay together with Cousin Eunice," Dicey said.

"When Momma comes we won't have to. And I don't want to anyway."

Dicey sighed. She didn't much want to herself. She daydreamed about Crisfield and a farm; but she had learnt her lesson about believing in daydreams, learnt it from Cousin Eunice and her house that wasn't a big white house by the ocean.

"Would you do it for James and Maybeth and me?" Dicey asked him. "Would you try, for us? I know it's hard. I know you get angry. But we need you to try. When we were on our own, you stopped quarrelling and helped. Remember?"

Sammy nodded.

"You liked that, didn't you?"

Sammy nodded.

"All I want you to do is be more that way at camp. Can you try?"

Sammy nodded. "You sound like Momma," he said.

"What do you mean?"

"Well, you do. When she'd ask me to be gooder, that was the way she'd talk."

He ran off to join Maybeth on the swings. Dicey watched him catch a flying swing and leap on to it, then pump furiously with his sturdy little legs. When he caught up with Maybeth, he cheered for himself.

Day succeeded day in slow procession. Cousin Eunice treated Dicey differently since their talk. She wanted to sit with Dicey in the kitchen every night, with cups of tea which Dicey could never completely drink, and talk about religion and serving God and how when she was a girl she had wanted to be a nun. But her mother said she wasn't strong enough in spirit, didn't have a real calling, should wait to see if she got married.

Dicey listened. She began to feel sorry for Cousin Eunice, who had lived all her life in this city, who had gone off to work every morning along the same grey city streets. Dicey didn't like the sound of Aunt Cilla. She had lied to Momma in her letters. It seemed to Dicey that Aunt Cilla had tried to keep Cousin Eunice all for herself. And then, Dicey thought to herself as the soft voice droned on about service and prayer, just when Cousin Eunice was about to do what she'd always wanted, the Tillermans turned up to tie her down again. Poor Cousin Eunice.

If that had happened to Dicey, she'd be angry. Cousin Eunice wasn't angry at all, just sad sometimes. As if this was the way her whole life had to be, not getting what she wanted, always giving it up for the sake of someone else.

Maybe she enjoyed giving things up for the sake of someone else. Some people liked that feeling. But even if that was the case, Dicey knew her cousin would rather have been a nun. That was what she really wanted.

It wasn't very much to want, and she didn't have even that.

The money in Dicey's shoebox increased slowly, day by day. Sixty-five, seventy, which, with the fifty dollars she had left from the car, made one hundred and twenty, then one hundred and forty dollars, one hundred and fifty.

Maybeth came home from camp with a note addressed to Miss Tillerman. The note requested Dicey to come to camp the next afternoon at two, an hour before the children went home. Somebody named Sister Berenice wanted to talk to her.

Dicey didn't want to go. She knew what the sister would say. She read the note and reread it. She considered throwing it away and pretending she had never got it, as Momma had done. She ripped it up into little pieces and dropped them into the wastepaper basket. She didn't want to hear whatever the sister had to say, about Maybeth being retarded and needing a special school.

James was no help. He seemed convinced that the fathers, and the nuns too, couldn't make a mistake. "Go and talk to her. Maybe she knows something we don't. Maybe she knows something that can help Maybeth. Just plan to learn from her, about whatever she has to say. You've got to keep an open mind, Dicey. You've got to leave a door open so understanding can get in. That's one thing I've learnt."

"It's not just minds," Dicey said. "You all think it's just smartness that counts. But Stewart didn't think that. And I don't think I do, either. I don't want to go."

"Suit yourself," James said. "I'd go."

"I'm not you," Dicey said.

Chapter Twelve

But she kept the appointment, wearing one of the second-hand dresses that made her feel stiff and awkward because they never fitted properly. She wore sneakers, because they were the only shoes she had. She held her chin high and a little angry – she knew Maybeth and this woman didn't.

Sister Berenice waited for Dicey in one of the classrooms next to the camp playground. It was a room for very small children. All the chairs were small. The tables didn't even come up to Dicey's knees.

Sister Berenice rose from her desk when Dicey came into the long room. The sister was very tall and very thin. She wore a black suit with a longish skirt, and her face was framed by the cowl she wore. She had pale blue eyes and her mouth looked stern. When she pulled up one of the little chairs for Dicey to sit on, Dicey saw with surprise that she wore a silver wedding ring on her right hand.

"You're a child," she said. Dicey nodded. "I asked Maybeth," Sister Berenice said, sounding cross, "I asked her who her guardian was and she said Dicey, her sister. I asked if you were married and Maybeth said no. Well, actually, she just shook her head. It is the longest conversation we have had. I didn't think to ask Father Joseph how old you were. Who is the person legally responsible for Maybeth?"

"Our Cousin Eunice, I suppose," Dicey said. "Until they find our mother."

"Miss Logan," Sister Berenice murmured, in apparent disbelief.

"She took us in. She didn't have to do that," Dicey said.

"She'd never even heard of us." She wanted Sister Berenice to appreciate what Cousin Eunice had done. She wanted to appreciate it herself.

"How old are you?" she asked Dicey.

Dicey's temper flared. "I'm thirteen. How old are you?"

A smile bent the corners of Sister Berenice's pale mouth. "Fifty-three, old enough to recognize spirit when I meet it. Tell me about your sister, Dicey."

Dicey stared at her in surprise. For a minute she couldn't think of anything to say. Usually, people told her about Maybeth, and she tried to explain that they were wrong. Nobody had ever asked her, first.

"She's shy," Dicey said. "She almost never speaks to strangers. And people always want to speak to her, because she's pretty. Usually, she stays stiff and quiet and stares, with big eyes. She doesn't even talk to us much. But when she does, it's always the right thing to say. Not right–polite, right-true."

Sister Berenice sat listening, with folded hands. So Dicey went on.

"I don't know why Maybeth is the way she is. But she's always been that way. From the time she started school, her teachers thought she was stupid. I suppose I can understand that. She would be so quiet that you'd think she didn't know anything. She stayed back one year, in first grade. Then the teacher wanted to keep her back this year, or at least that's what I think. Momma never opened those notes."

"You said she almost never speaks to strangers. That means

she sometimes does. Who did she speak to?"

Dicey told her how Maybeth had talked to Stewart and sung with him. "She sings – it's lovely when she sings. She learns songs fast, music and words. She couldn't be retarded and do that, could she?"

Sister Berenice just smiled.

"And she *can* read," Dicey said. "Not like James, but as well as Sammy. She used to read to me at home when I asked her to. And she *can* add and subtract." Dicey thought. "She's not quick, but she can work the problems out. It just takes her a longer time to learn school things, and she's too shy to say what she knows. When she plays, she builds gardens and castles and makes up stories about them." Dicey had never before defined so exactly just what Maybeth could and could not do. "I suppose she's slow at school, but I don't think she's retarded. Or anything like that."

"Would you go and look out of the window at the children?" Sister Berenice asked Dicey. Puzzled, Dicey obeyed.

The playground was surrounded by a tall fence. Little groups of children were gathered about, playing or reading or listening to one of several nuns who were out there with them. Dicey's eyes searched for Maybeth among the many little girls.

She found her, sitting in a circle around a nun with a guitar. Maybeth sat behind the group. Her dress, like Dicey's, was long and dark. Her face was round and sad. All the other little girls were singing and clapping their hands, but Maybeth was staring at the nun's hands as they clapped on the instrument. She was not singing. She was not clapping.

The nun stopped playing and said something, at which all the little girls jumped up and ran to different parts of the playground. Maybeth didn't move. The nun bent to speak to her and she looked up.

"But she looks frightened," Dicey said. "Why does she look frightened?" She heard the rude, demanding tone of her own voice.

Sister Berenice didn't answer.

"I see what you mean," Dicey said. Maybeth did look different from all the other little girls. Dicey watched her sister walk slowly over to the swings. She stood there. Several girls were swinging energetically. There were some unoccupied swings, but Maybeth didn't get on to one. The other girls paid no attention to her.

It was as if Maybeth wasn't even there, not even to herself. What was wrong with her? She looked – empty.

"But she isn't that way," Dicey started to say.

"I wonder," Sister Berenice said in a voice that suggested doubt. Sister Berenice didn't believe Dicey. Why should she?

"Father Joseph said that you were unusual," Sister Berenice said to Dicey.

"He did?"

"Yes." The rich voice assured Dicey that this was the truth. "To keep your family together, and fed. But I wonder if you have faced the truth about Maybeth. I think you may be fooling yourself." This, too, Dicey recognized, was the truth.

Maybe she was, maybe…

"Do you know the kind of special schooling available to a child like Maybeth? Not through us, of course, but the state maintains excellent facilities for disabled children. There is much they can learn and do, such children, if they are properly taught. Is it fair to Maybeth to deny her the opportunity, just because you don't want to face the facts?"

"No," Dicey said. The word burst from her.

"I didn't think you wanted to do that to Maybeth."

"No," Dicey said again. "Those aren't the facts."

"Oh, now," the nun said. She sounded disappointed in Dicey.

Dicey sighed. "I'm sorry," she said. "I don't mean to be rude."

"Are you thinking of Maybeth or of yourself?" Sister Berenice asked quietly.

Dicey didn't know, and she didn't care; she was too tired and discouraged to think of an answer. This nun had already made up her mind anyway. Dicey didn't want to think about Maybeth any more. She was arguing more from habit than conviction. "You just don't know," she repeated.

"I think I probably know better than you do."

Dicey was finished arguing. She just wanted to get out of there and take Maybeth with her. "Can Maybeth come with me now? It's almost time."

The nun stared at her for a long time. Finally she answered, "Yes, of course." But her voice said more, it told Dicey that the sister was sorry she had asked Dicey to come in. Well, Dicey was sorry too. She nodded, and left the room.

Dicey entered the playground through the tall iron gates. She started to walk over to where Maybeth was, but a young nun came and asked her what she was doing there. She sounded important, as though she was accustomed to being obeyed without question. Dicey explained who she was. She said that she had been meeting with Sister Berenice and had permission to take Maybeth home. The young nun looked back at the windows behind them and stood aside.

Maybeth had seen Dicey. She smiled at her, but did not come running as Sammy would have. Dicey smiled back and hoped the way she was feeling didn't show in her face. "Let's go and get Sammy," she said, holding out her hand.

Sammy had a cut on his forehead that someone had covered with a big plaster. His lip was swollen. "Oh, Sammy." Dicey could not keep the worry out of her voice. "You said you'd try."

"I did."

"You were in a fight," Dicey said. "And a pretty bad one."

"He said—"

"Who? Who said?"

"Johnny. I don't know his last name. And I don't care. He's a big kid. He's in fourth grade. I made him cry and I didn't cry."

"What did he say?"

"He said I was going to a foster home because nobody here likes me. He said he heard the fathers saying it. It's not true, is it Dicey? So I fought him."

"What did the fathers say?"

"Johnny's the one that heard them. He said they didn't know he could hear."

"No, no. I mean when they stopped the fight. They did stop it, didn't they?"

Sammy nodded. They were walking to James's school. Dicey held one hand of each of the little ones. There was too much bad news in this day.

"They didn't say nothing. We didn't tell 'em nothing."

"So they think it's all your fault, don't they?"

Sammy nodded. "I have to stay inside alone tomorrow. All day."

"Oh, Sammy. Why didn't you tell them what Johnny said?"

"Because they try to find out everything. What's a foster home?"

"You didn't know? And you fought about it?"

"It's not good, is it? I could tell that. From how he said it."

Dicey sighed. "A foster home is where somebody not your own family takes you into their home to live. And somebody gives them an allowance, to pay for you."

"You wouldn't let them do that, would you, Dicey? I told Johnny and he said you couldn't stop them."

Dicey felt helpless, absolutely helpless, with the two little ones holding her hands. She knew how Sammy felt. She wanted to fight somebody herself. Or to run, fast, not waiting for lights to change. But she had the two little ones holding on to her.

"There's James now," she said to Sammy. Sammy ran to meet his brother. James was walking quickly, a huge smile on his face. At least one of us is happy, Dicey thought.

Dicey called the bus station and found out that it cost twenty-six dollars to get to Crisfield. Fifty-two dollars there and back. She would still have some money, so she wouldn't be dependent. She would stay in a hotel or something, for a couple of days. It was only for a couple of days, until she took a look at this grandmother, to see for herself.

She purchased a small overnight case at the Goodwill store. She located the bus station in Bridgeport. There, she picked up a bus schedule and found out that if she left Bridgeport at ten o'clock in the morning, she would have to change at New York for Wilmington. At Wilmington, she decided by looking at a map, she could get a bus to take her down to Easton, then Salisbury, then Crisfield. Easton and Salisbury were yellow on the map so they were big towns. There would be sure to be buses.

This was on a Thursday. She thought she would go the next Monday, so that the little ones would be in camp during the day while she was away. James could take charge, for four days. That was all she'd be gone for. They would just have to get along without her for four days. There was no way she could take them with her. Just as there was no way she could tell Cousin Eunice she was going.

That evening, Cousin Eunice came home late from work carrying a bakery bag. "Father Joseph called me at work. He is bringing a friend by after supper, after the children are in bed," she said. "I got a cake on my way home. Did you get the living-room done today? It's Thursday."

Dicey nodded.

"Father Joseph said you have already met this man, a policeman. I have not. Did you wash the windows?"

Dicey had forgotten that. She lied. Well, it wasn't an entire lie, since she had washed windows that day. She just hadn't washed the windows Cousin Eunice meant.

"And a good vacuuming? I don't know – the house gets so dirty with all you children. I don't know how you manage to collect so much dirt and bring it inside." She fluttered about the kitchen, fussing over one thing and another, looking in the icebox for lemons, in the cupboard to be sure her good teapot was clean and there was sugar in the sugar bowl.

It could not be good news they brought. Dicey knew that ahead of time. If it had been good news, the sergeant would have called her up right away, or Momma would have called her up, or Momma would have appeared at the house.

Father Joseph and Sergeant Gordo arrived late. The two men and Cousin Eunice sat in all the chairs there were in the living-room. After she had passed around the teacups, milk, sugar, lemon and cake, Dicey sat on the floor. She was wearing one of the stiff dresses Father Joseph had brought. Cousin Eunice twittered as she poured tea, then fell silent.

"We have located your mother," Sergeant Gordo said. He held a teacup in one hand and a plate with cake in the other. He could neither eat nor drink, because he had no free hand.

He looked around for a table to set the plate on. Cousin Eunice made a little *Oh* sound at this news.

"I thought so," Dicey said.

"I don't have anything good to tell you," Sergeant Gordo said.

"I didn't think so," Dicey said. She made her face expressionless.

"You're a smart kid," the sergeant said. "Your mother is in a state hospital in Massachusetts. She was found in Boston. She— Do you know the term catatonic?"

Dicey shook her head.

"It means the patient won't respond to anything. Your mother – well, she doesn't do anything, doesn't speak, won't move at all, not even to go to the bathroom. When they found out about her family, the doctors tried talking to her about you. No response. No response at all. Nothing. They think she's incurable."

Dicey nodded. "Are you sure it's Momma?"

"Her fingerprints match the ones the hospital took when you children were born."

"Why did they do that?" Dicey asked. She didn't know why she asked. She didn't care what he answered.

"So the mothers and babies can be sure they go together. They do the baby's feet. So nobody gets mixed up."

"Oh."

"And I've got a picture."

Dicey took the photograph. She looked at the vacant-faced woman lying in a bed, her hair cut off short and her hazel eyes staring at the camera without any expression, as if the camera and photographer were not there. Her face looked so flat and empty, so far away, as if it hung miles above the earth and could not be bothered by anything happening on the little planet below. "They cut her hair," Dicey said. "Are they sure she's incurable?"

"These head-shrinkers are never sure of anything. But they're as near to sure as they can be."

"I could go and see her," Dicey suggested.

"I wouldn't do that, little girl. They'll get in touch with us if there's any change, and then maybe it might do some good."

"It would be best to forget her," Father Joseph said.

"What if I don't want to?" Dicey demanded, angry.

"I didn't mean that, child. I meant, it is better not to have false hopes."

Dicey clamped her mouth shut.

"Poor Liza," Cousin Eunice said. "She's only five years younger than I am. Do you know that?"

Cousin Eunice poured out more cups of tea, which Dicey passed around. The adults talked around her and above her, about adoption procedures and welfare applications. "Sammy is on trial here," Cousin Eunice said to Father Joseph.

He nodded. "As is Maybeth," he answered. Cousin Eunice shook her head but didn't say anything. Dicey walked out of the room. She heard Cousin Eunice start to call her back and Father Joseph say to let her go.

Maybeth was asleep and so was Sammy. James wasn't.

Dicey undressed and lay down on her camp-bed. Her mind was blank.

"What about Momma?" James whispered.

"How'd you know?"

"That policeman...they came in a police car."

"Momma's gone crazy," Dicey reported in a flat voice, "and they don't think she'll ever get better. She's in a mental hospital. She was in Boston. How do you think she got to Boston?"

James sat up. "What kind of crazy?"

"A kind where you just lie in bed and don't do anything. James, do you think Maybeth's like Momma?"

"Yes."

"Do you think Maybeth could go crazy like that?"

"Yes. If – if she had to. You know? Momma had four kids and no job. Our father walked out on her."

"But we were happy, weren't we? When we were in Provincetown. We were, I know it. Momma wasn't crazy then."

"Maybe. I don't know, Dicey. Does that mean this is our home?"

"Yeah. I suppose so. I don't know, James. Would you like that?"

"It's a good school," James said. "I've never been in a school like this, where the teachers all know so much and they like it when you ask questions and they keep giving you more work. Nothing bothers the fathers, you know? Oh, swearing and things, those. But they're so sure they have the answers, they don't mind you asking questions. In this school, I'm really glad I'm me. I can learn anything – do you know how that feels, Dicey? The fathers show me how and I learn. You better believe I'm happy."

"Should we tell Sammy and Maybeth?"

"About Momma? I suppose so, sometime. Not right now. Or is right away better?"

So they woke the two younger children and told them the bad news. Maybeth just nodded and sat closer to Dicey on the camp-bed.

Sammy stuck his chin out. "She'll still get better maybe," he declared. "How do they know so much anyway? I don't care what they say. I won't believe them."

Dicey grinned at him, unable to stretch her mouth wide enough to let out all the feelings his silly stubbornness let her feel. Then she began to cry. "I'm sorry, Dicey," Maybeth said.

"Me too," Dicey said, burying her face in her sister's hair. "I'm sorry too."

Now she had to go on Monday and find out fast what Crisfield was like. What their grandmother was like. Cousin Eunice would flutter and flitter, and before they knew it the Tillermans would be adopted. Or something worse.

It was not that Dicey was ungrateful. They might end up here. Cousin Eunice's house might be the best place for them. Even for Sammy and Maybeth. It might be the best they could do, even if Sammy and Maybeth had to go somewhere else. But Dicey had to know that for sure.

That weekend she took the family to the beach. She was

especially careful to pay attention to them. She laughed at Sammy's jokes and turned cartwheels on the sand with him and tossed him up over her shoulders into the water until he was exhausted. She built castles with Maybeth, decorating them with bits of shell and coloured stones, telling stories about princesses and giants. She talked with James about history and science, listening with all her brain, so her questions would show that she was really interested.

On Monday morning, she walked them all to camp and school. Sammy hesitated at the gate and said, "I wish it was always the weekend."

Dicey ruffled his hair.

Maybeth let go of Dicey's hand and walked slowly over to where the little girls were gathering. Her dress was too long for her. She looked clumsy.

Dicey asked James to pick up the little children. "I'll leave the door unlocked. I've got something to do," she explained. "Can you get them at the end of the day? And don't be late – Maybeth worries."

James smiled happily over his pile of books. "Sure thing," he said. He ran up the steps to the doorway and turned to wave before he went inside.

Dicey hurried back to the little grey house. She had already told her customers she was taking the week off. She pulled the overnight case out from under her bed, put underwear, toothbrush, clean shirts and shorts into it. She put in the shoebox with her money, the bus schedule and her map of Maryland. She would wear a dress for travelling.

Downstairs, Dicey wrote a hasty note to James, asking him to take charge until she got back, telling him where she was going, saying she was sorry but he would have to tell Cousin Eunice. She put her house key into the envelope and sealed it. She wrote James's name on the front and left it on the kitchen table. Suitcase in hand, Dicey opened the front door.

James sat on the stoop.

"I thought so!" he crowed, laughing at her as she stood, open-mouthed, the suitcase in one hand, the door knob in the other. "You can't fool me!"

"I left you a note," Dicey said. "I've got to hurry or I'll miss the bus."

"The next bus doesn't leave Bridgeport until ten," James answered. "You've got a whole hour." He smirked at her.

"James!" Dicey cried. "You've been snooping in my things."

"And here comes Sammy, right on schedule," James said. "I told him, when I found that money box. Besides, there was that man at the park, the grocer. I'd make a good detective. We're going with you."

"I don't have enough money," Dicey said. "What about Maybeth?"

"You'll think up a way," James said. "Where are we going, anyway?"

"But what about your school?" Dicey asked. "I mean, you're the one who's really happy here. I will come back, you know that."

"How do I know it?" James asked her. "I know you mean to – but what if you can't, or don't?"

"I wouldn't do that!" Dicey protested.

"How do you know? How does anybody know? I don't want you to leave me behind. Besides, school – well, Dicey? Listen. It's me that makes the school so good, my brain. Other kids don't like it as much as I do. So, there are books all over the world, in libraries. The fathers help me, an awful lot – but there must be other schools with good teachers. Even if there aren't, I'll always be me."

"Are you sure, James?"

"I'm sure I want to go with you. And so does Sammy."

Dicey couldn't think clearly. She couldn't think at all.

Sammy marched up to them. "I crossed four streets with lights," he announced. "Hi, Dicey. I didn't believe James, but he was right."

Dicey didn't even try to argue further. They all went back inside. She sent the boys upstairs to get changes of underwear for everyone, and shorts and shirts. She changed into shorts herself. She wrote another note, to Cousin Eunice this time, a note much harder to write. Dicey knew that Cousin Eunice wouldn't understand, no matter what she said.

"We are going to Crisfield," she wrote. "I don't want you to worry about us, because I will take care of everyone. I don't know what will happen there. When we find out, I'll write to you." Dicey chewed on the end of the pencil and tried to think of some way to let Cousin Eunice know that they were grateful to her. "No matter what happens to us, I think you should go ahead and become a nun because it is what you really want to do," she wrote. "Your cousin, Dicey Tillerman." Once again, she put the house key in the envelope and sealed it.

Dicey went alone to fetch Maybeth. The boys waited at the corner, with the suitcase.

Dicey walked right into the playground. Groups of little girls ran around. The young nun approached her. Dicey took a deep breath. "I've come for Maybeth Tillerman," she said. "I'm her sister. Sister Berenice said I should pick her up now," she lied.

The nun hesitated. She squinted her eyes at Dicey.

"You can go and ask Sister Berenice if you like," Dicey said. "But then we'll be late for Maybeth's appointment and she'll be angry."

The nun called Maybeth from the sandbox where she was playing alone. Dicey took the little girl's hand and walked slowly out through the gates. She had to hold herself back from running.

"Where are we going?" Maybeth asked.

"We're going to see the place Momma lived in when she was a little girl," Dicey answered.

"All of us together?"

"All of us together," Dicey said. "That's the only way the Tillermans travel."

Part Two

Chapter One

THE ENGINE RUMBLED like hunger in the belly of the bus. The fumes that floated in through the open windows were swollen with heat. They were on their way. Again.

Dicey leant back in her seat and tried to make herself relax. They had until evening, when Cousin Eunice got home. Unless the camps wondered why all the Tillermans were absent and called Cousin Eunice at work. She didn't think that was likely.

James leant towards Dicey. They were the only people sitting in the back of the bus. Nobody would hear them over the sound of the engine.

"It's like a prison break, isn't it?"

Dicey knew what he meant. Even so, "That's not fair," she said. "Cousin Eunice wasn't a jailer."

James shrugged. "Whadda you think?" he asked out of the

corner of his mouth. "I think, if we can get to New York without being caught – we'll be home free."

Home, Dicey thought. She remembered the inscription on the tombstone: *Home is the sailor, home is the hunter.* Until she died, Dicey wouldn't expect any place to be home. Home was with Momma – and Momma was in a hospital where the doctors said she'd always stay. There could be no home for the Tillermans. Home free – Dicey would settle for a place to stay. Stay free.

Cousin Eunice's house wasn't free; it was expensive. The price was always remembering to be grateful. And there was danger to Sammy and Maybeth of being sent to foster homes or special schools; danger to Dicey and James of forgetting and saying what they thought before wondering if it would sound ungrateful. At Cousin Eunice's house, they were kept busy so they wouldn't be a bother, couldn't get in trouble.

Dicey had lowered her sights. She no longer hoped for a home. Now she wanted only a place where the Tillermans could be themselves and do what was good for them. Home was out of the question. Stay might be possible, if this grandmother could be persuaded...

Dicey stopped thinking. She wanted to keep it simple. Get to Crisfield and see, that was her plan. That was all of it.

"Anyway, they know where we're going," Dicey told James.

"How could they know that?"

"I said so in the note I left."

"Dicey! Why'd you do that?"

Chapter One

"I don't think it would be fair to leave her to worry."

"She'll worry anyway. She likes worrying."

"I can't help that, James. I can't help what she's like. I can only help what I'm like."

"You've ruined it," James went on. "We can't be running away if they know where we're going."

"We're not running away – we never were running away," Dicey said. "We're just going to see."

James shook his head. "I'm running away. Before – we were always the ones who were run away from. This time I want us to do it. What's your plan?"

Dicey didn't answer.

The road flowed under the wheels. They were back on Route 1. Maybe it was her doom, always to get back on Route 1. She squeezed Maybeth's fingers. "Maybeth? What's the matter? You scared?"

Maybeth looked at Dicey and nodded.

"So am I, a little," Dicey said. "We'll just wait and see. That's all we can do."

"I don't want to go back." Maybeth spoke in a small voice.

"I thought you liked it," Dicey said. "The church, the pretty dress you wore there, all the attention."

"I did," Maybeth said.

Dicey decided to tell the truth, now. "We might have to go back. Do you know that?"

Maybeth nodded.

Well, Dicey thought. She had underestimated Maybeth. She'd been fooled, like the nuns were fooled and Maybeth's teachers. She'd been fooled into thinking Maybeth wasn't who she knew Maybeth was.

"Look, Maybeth," Dicey said, "if we do have to go back I'll go with you to church, and we'll both talk to the nuns. To Sister Berenice. I won't leave you alone so much."

Maybeth smiled, a tenuous little smile, and turned back to the window.

Smog made the air seem thick, like light, yellowed fog. In the heavy traffic the bus stopped and started, stopped and started. Buildings soared up higher than Dicey could see out of the window. She twisted her head down to see their tops.

The bus turned on to a new street and headed east. Dicey felt as if they were in a maze and would never make their way out. Cars honked. Lights changed. They travelled down a narrow channel over which other roads crossed on high bridges. All the traffic, all the people, the tall buildings – Dicey felt scared, and exhilarated. There was so much life, all here in one place, teeming, whirling about her. More than at the crowded summer beaches in Provincetown. It was like a pot of vegetable soup boiling on a stove, everything moving. A restlessness and excitement came into Dicey with the air she breathed. Anything can happen, she thought.

At last the bus turned off into a huge warehouse. It followed a ramp, up and around, then fitted itself into a slot before a wall of glass doors. It became one of a row of buses.

The Tillermans stood up. Dicey led them to the front of the bus and down the steps, one after another, on to the sidewalk before the doors. Everyone was hurrying. Everyone

Chapter One

acted as if he or she or they knew exactly where to go.

"What now, Dicey?" asked James.

"An information booth," she answered briskly. "Then bathrooms, and maybe something to eat."

They entered a huge, hollow hall lined with benches and ticket windows. Emptiness hung high over their heads although the room was crowded with people. The information booth was in the centre of this hall. Dicey stationed her family by a water fountain and went up to stand in line.

When her turn finally came, she couldn't think straight. The girl behind the glass window spoke without looking at Dicey: "Next? Little boy?"

Dicey gulped. "When's the next bus to Wilmington, Delaware?"

Without speaking, the girl handed her a schedule.

"Where are the bathrooms?" Dicey asked.

"Lower level, on the street side."

"Where can I buy a ticket?"

"Upper level, any window with a yellow or green light."

Dicey fled, dragging her suitcase.

"She thought I was a boy," she said to James.

"So did Louis and Edie," he answered.

Dicey put the suitcase down and opened the schedule. They had forty minutes to wait. She would play it safe. "OK, listen, James. Take this money" – she gave him a ten dollar bill – "and go get two tickets for Wilmington. That ticket window over there with a green light."

"Why not four?"

"Just in case," Dicey answered. "Two and two is not the same as four."

James looked at her.

"Not in this case," Dicey said. "In this case, it is but it isn't."

"You can say so," James said. "And I'll do it. And I see what you mean. But you're wrong. Two and two is always four."

When they had all four tickets, Dicey started walking along the concourse. She found the escalators leading down. "Now we go to the bathroom."

The women's room could have held Cousin Eunice's house in it and had room to spare. Lines of women waited before each closed door, old, young, medium, some alone, some with friends, some with children, one with a tiny baby that rode in a pouch on her chest. The air smelled of perfume and cleanser. Maybeth and Dicey entered the cubicle together, because Maybeth didn't want to go in alone. Dicey protested, "But you're nine." Maybeth just shook her head.

They took turns, Maybeth first. Dicey set the suitcase on the floor and opened it. She took out shorts and a shirt for Maybeth and her shoebox of money. She put twenty more dollars in her pocket. As they left the room, they tossed Maybeth's rolled-up dress into the trash.

When they emerged from the women's room, Dicey could not see James and Sammy. People hurried past, some carrying suitcases, some shopping bags, some just purses or newspapers. You could get lost here in this crowded station.

Chapter One

You could get swept away. Or grabbed by somebody.

"Maybeth? If we get separated—" Maybeth caught Dicey's free hand. "Just in case," Dicey said. "We'll meet back by that information booth I went to first. Remember it?"

James and Sammy joined them. They had a hot dog apiece, standing up at a counter, and a glass of orange drink. Dicey looked at a clock — only ten minutes until the bus left. The air hummed with voices, distant engines, and the muffled droning of the loudspeaker announcing what buses were leaving for what cities. If they could get on the bus all right, and out of the city, then they were on their way. And they might make it.

James and Sammy went on to the bus first. Dicey dawdled by the gate, with Maybeth beside her. Maybeth went first up into the bus. Dicey followed, pulling their two tickets out of her pocket and handing them to the driver.

He looked at her with a grimace. "What is this, kids' day out?"

Dicey tried to look as if she didn't know what he was talking about.

"Never mind. But I'll tell you what I told them. We've got a long drive and I don't stand any horsing around."

"We won't," she said.

"I know, I know. You're angels from heaven. Go on back."

After a few minutes, the driver closed the door and turned on the engine. He backed out of the parking slot. With every turn of the wheel, Dicey felt her stomach loosen and her muscles relax. By the time the bus entered a tunnel, a smile was beginning to turn up the corners of her mouth. She felt her back relaxing into the back of the seat. Beside her, Maybeth hummed softly. The bus zoomed out of the tunnel and into the light. Dicey stretched, smiled, yawned – and fell asleep.

When Dicey opened her eyes, she saw the sleek, straight lines of the rectangular interior of the bus. Out of the windows, on both sides, lay farmlands. Fields of corn ripened under a bright sun. The corn swayed in the wind, like dancers with scarves.

Dicey wasn't tired any more. She was relaxed inside and out. She felt lazy and unworried. The bus rolled along.

It was as if, during that nap, Dicey had travelled days away from Cousin Eunice's house in Bridgeport. That time now felt like a distant memory, something so far behind them that they didn't have to concern themselves with it, not any more.

She looked past Maybeth's head, out of the window. Fields, farmhouses, trees, sky with clouds; her eyes roamed lazily over them all. Her thoughts roamed lazily too, over memories and ideas. She rode outside time and place.

She thought about Momma, and it seemed to her that she almost understood why all of this had happened to them, to the Tillermans, all this sadness and running away. She thought about the long walk from Peewauket to New Haven, and the grandfather who had tipped them two dollars and Stewart with his blue-grey eyes; then her mind switched to the journey ahead, twisting and turning. What did it matter where they were going, as long as they were going?

Chapter One

Sammy was asleep on James's shoulder. Dicey leant over to ask softly where they were. James told her the last stop had been Trenton.

Dicey took a map out of her suitcase. She unfolded it halfway, to show Wilmington and the Chesapeake Bay. Beneath her, the wheels rumbled on the road.

Sammy woke up. He punched James. James hit him back. Dicey quelled them with a glance and instructed them to play odds-and-evens while she thought. "But I'm hungry," Sammy argued.

"I can't do anything about that," Dicey answered.

"Why not?"

"Because I'm not a hot dog tree," Dicey said.

"Why not?"

"Because if I were, then you'd be one too because you're my brother. Only you'd be a pickle tree," Dicey said, turning back to her map.

"Pickle tree," Sammy repeated, trying to repress his giggles, not wanting to laugh at Dicey's joke.

Dicey studied the map. Just below Wilmington, the Chesapeake Bay drove up like a wedge between two sections of land. The eastern shore of Maryland, where Crisfield was, was on the land between the Bay and the ocean. It looked about two hundred miles from Wilmington to Crisfield. So it might be a lot further. Maybe as much as thirty days of walking. Too far. But there were some cities that must have buses running to them: Salisbury, Cambridge, Easton.

They'd already spent too much on bus tickets. Money was

always the problem. Dicey wanted to have money left over, so they could get back to Bridgeport, if they had to. She figured they'd have to walk part of the way anyway, and she wanted to have some tools for camping. A jackknife, one with a can-opener on it. A pan of some kind. Ponchos, for when it rained. She let her mind wander on briefly to other things, to a backpack and bedrolls, to a portable stove. No, those would be silly; but a fishing line and hooks would be useful. There was a lot of water around, so there must be fishing.

They had another choice: they could go down the western shore, to Baltimore or Annapolis – it would have to be Annapolis because that was near the only bridge over the Bay. That would leave them about half of the distance to Crisfield still to cover. Maybe two weeks of walking.

They would have to get over the bridge if they did that. The map said Toll Bridge, so they probably couldn't walk over it. They might hitch-hike, but Dicey didn't like that idea. She didn't like being in somebody's car and not able to run away. Besides, who would pick up four kids? They might have to take another bus.

Definitely, then, the eastern shore was better. At Wilmington they would get on a bus going south. How far they went would depend on how much it cost. That was easy enough. She folded up the map and returned it to her suitcase.

The bus made its way through Philadelphia and then south through more farmland, some small cities. After another hour, after a bridge like a section of roller coaster, they came into Wilmington.

The Wilmington Bus Depot was a one-storey building, a single room with wooden benches, a lunch counter, lockers where you could store your suitcases, six windows where tickets could be purchased and at its centre an information booth with a clock on top of it. Three forty-five. Dicey told James to stay with Maybeth and Sammy by the door. Only one bus stood waiting, now that the one they had ridden on had gone on to Baltimore. That bus, she saw by the sign above its front window, was going to Annapolis.

Inside, Dicey picked out a schedule from the assortment at the information booth. The first thing she did was to see if Crisfield was there, at the bottom of the list of towns. It was. After Salisbury, Eden and Princess Anne, came Crisfield.

Her eye went back up to the top of the list, found Wilmington and traced the buses leaving for the eastern shore. There were several, but most went no further than Cambridge. Only one went down to Crisfield, a morning bus.

Then Dicey saw that the last afternoon bus heading south to Cambridge left Wilmington at two-thirty. The only bus after that didn't leave until nine at night.

Nine. By nine, Cousin Eunice would have been home for almost three hours. By nine, she could call Father Joseph. By nine, they might be able to trace the Tillermans, and maybe find them, and stop them. She didn't know Dicey had money, did she? She might think the Tillermans were walking. But Dicey couldn't count on that. She couldn't count on anything. She rushed up to the information booth and asked when the bus for Annapolis was leaving. The man put his hand over the microphone and told her, "Five minutes."

Five minutes, how could she think it through in five minutes? Dicey hurried over to a ticket window and bought four tickets to Annapolis. They couldn't just sit around the bus station for five hours, waiting to be recognized. Cousin Eunice would have to do something to find them; she would think it was her responsibility.

Dicey joined her family. "We missed the last bus until nine."

"Tonight? We better stay here," James said.

"No," Dicey said. "We can't. We'll go to Annapolis. It's the only bus."

"But Dicey—"

"Do as I say, James."

She wasn't thinking, she knew that. She wasn't thinking clearly. She hurried her family on to the bus just as the driver was closing the door. They sat at the back. Dicey chewed on her lip.

"Nobody will expect us to go to Annapolis," James said. "It was good luck that we missed the bus."

"I don't know about that," Dicey said.

The bus left Wilmington and headed south. This bus was air-conditioned, and you couldn't open the windows. The windows were smeared with grime, so you couldn't see out. The hour and a half to Baltimore seemed endless. At Baltimore, a lot of dressed-up people got on, commuters, Dicey guessed,

Chapter One

going home from work. The bus grew crowded.

The circuitous route from Baltimore to Annapolis, where they kept getting on and off the same road to stop at little huts by the road to let off passengers, took another hour and a half. Dicey tried to control her impatience by reminding herself that if they had been walking it would have taken days and days. This was slow, but it was faster than walking. They'd be walking soon enough.

At last, the bus turned into a car park before a low brick building. The bus driver turned around and called, "Annapolis. End of the line."

The Tillermans hopped up and joined the few people waiting to get off the bus. Dicey just followed in the direction the majority took, turning left down a sidewalk, away from the bus station. Behind her, the sun lowered, so they were walking on their own shadows, heading east.

"Where we going?"

"We'll find a place to sit down and think," Dicey said. "I'm looking for a park."

They passed a drugstore and a finance company and three banks. They saw bookshops and card stores, clothing stores and a wine-and-cheese store. The road they walked along came up to a roundabout. Cars and trucks whirled round it, circling a church that stood at its centre.

Dicey led them round the roundabout. Streets led off, but none promised to go to a park, although one said it went to the hospital. At the top of one street, Dicey looked down and saw blue water with sails on it. She stood, staring.

It looked like the painted backdrop to a movie, not like anything real. The long main street went downhill and then fetched up at the water. On the blue water, boats sailed or motored as if they were in an entirely different world, and it wasn't clear, in the bright August light, where water ended and sky began.

They headed down the hill to the water, passing stores and shops and more banks. The street was crowded bumper to bumper uphill and the sidewalks were crowded with people. At the foot of the street was another roundabout, around which cars travelled slowly, with a steady chorus of horns and many near collisions. Across this roundabout, a quiet finger of water, hemmed in by concrete, marked the corner of a narrow area where people thronged, eating, talking, sitting and watching one another. Dicey moved through the milling crowd and along beside the water. They passed boats crowded as closely together as the cars in a car park, motor boats, sailboats and old, worn fishing boats.

At the waterfront, beyond a huge car park jammed with cars, they found a public park. It had no grass, just trees in wooden boxes. The ground was covered by wooden flooring. Benches, however, there were in plenty. The benches right at the water were all full, but one beneath a sparsely-leaved young tree was empty. The Tillermans sat on that.

"It's hot," James said. His face was red. Sweat plastered his hair to his neck. The air hung moist and heavy over the park. A slight ripple of a breeze came off the water, but that did little to relieve them. Everybody seemed slowed down by heat. Nobody walked briskly, everybody sauntered. A lot of people were licking ice cream cones. Dicey's mouth watered.

"What time's it?" James asked. Without waiting for an answer, he hopped up and asked the same question of a man moving by, who held his suit jacket over his shoulder. "It's seven-thirty," James reported. "Time for supper."

"How about ice cream for supper?" Dicey asked. She didn't know just how much money she had in her pocket, not enough for a real dinner.

"We passed a hamburger joint," James countered.

"Ice cream," Sammy said.

"Hamburgers," James said.

Sammy stuck his jaw out.

"Ice cream's cheaper," Dicey said. "Double dip?"

"Can I have seconds?" James asked.

"We'll see how hungry you are," Dicey said.

James agreed.

"But first I've got to figure out a couple of things, OK?"

"Like what?" James asked.

"Like where to sleep, and how to find an Army-Navy surplus store. And how to get across the bay."

"Get across the bay? Why?"

Dicey pulled out the map again and showed him where they were. Then she pointed out Crisfield.

"Oh, Dicey. What are we doing on this side?"

"I told you, we missed the last bus."

"Yeah but—" James caught a glimpse of Dicey's face and stopped speaking.

"I know. I know. But if we can just get across, we'll be much nearer."

"How can we do that? OK, we're here. We need a place to sleep tonight, right?"

"I guess. The Army-Navy store will be closed, wherever it is."

"If there is one."

"I'm sorry, James," Dicey said. "I panicked. When I found out we'd missed the last bus—"

"It's OK, Dicey, I just thought you had it all planned."

"I did. For me to go."

"Are you angry at us?" Sammy asked this. It sounded like the beginning of a quarrel.

"No. Well, yes, a little, but that doesn't matter. I'd rather be all together. Really, I would. I'm just confused still because I didn't have any plan for all of us. Can you understand that?"

Sammy didn't answer.

"I was going to come back," Dicey said to him.

He looked at her, with the question in his hazel eyes. "Really?"

"Really. Really and truly. Don't you trust me, Sammy?"

"You said you didn't trust anyone."

"I didn't mean any of us. I didn't mean you. Would you leave me behind? Or James or Maybeth?"

"No!"

"Well, I wouldn't leave you, either. I feel the same way."

"But you were going to leave us behind," Sammy said stubbornly. Dicey sighed.

Chapter One

They rose to find the ice cream store. James got a double-dip chocolate nut cone, explaining that nuts and chocolate were both rich and filling. Dicey got a scoop of chocolate and a scoop of butter almond. She noticed a pile of maps of Annapolis on the counter top and took one. Maybeth wanted pink sherbet and green, but Dicey told her to get real ice cream because of the milk. She chose two scoops of strawberry. Sammy asked for strawberry ripple ice cream topped with peanut butter ice cream. "Ugh," Dicey said, listening to his order. He grinned at her.

They sat at a small table to eat. The ice cream tasted rich and smooth and cold. You could tell that it was made from real cream, it was that rich. Dicey studied her map while her tongue made valleys in the ice cream and then smoothed them out. The cone was crunchy and sweet.

"There's a college," Dicey said. "Let's try that, OK?"

James had a single-dip cone for seconds, another scoop of chocolate-nut. They walked out and on to the crowded sidewalk. What were all these people doing? It was like a carnival.

The college lay in summer twilight, set back from the road by a long, sloping lawn. It was brick and very old. Everything looked old about it, old and tended, the smooth brick sidewalks, the many-paned windows, the little dome on top of the building. It had trees — huge, tall trees, with branches too high for climbing — all about on its lawn. There were plenty of people. Students lay scattered about, reading. Watchmen wandered around on the brick paths. Families were eating picnic suppers. Children ran everywhere.

The Tillermans stood on the sidewalk, separated by a briar hedge from this scene. "No good," Dicey said. "Too many people."

She did not move on, however. It looked – so quiet and solid; the air over it was lavender in the evening light, and mysterious. She wished…she didn't know what she wished.

Resolutely, she turned away.

Her map showed only something called the Historic District. They had walked through some of it. All the houses crowded up on to the sidewalk, close to one another.

Dicey moved on. The suitcase weighed heavy on her shoulder muscle and banged against her legs. The map showed the Naval Academy in one direction, closed in by a wall that ran all around it. She turned the other way and led them back towards the first circle they had seen. She chose the road leading to the hospital, and they walked on, past that large building.

The houses were bigger here and had front lawns. A residential area. A rich residential area.

She walked on.

They saw one open space that had no cover to conceal them from the surrounding houses.

She walked on.

The air grew darker, grey-violet now. The heat did not abate. Sweat ran down her back.

She walked on.

On her left, she saw a long, narrow stretch of grass in the

middle of a kind of courtyard of houses. On both sides of the stretch ran roads, and houses stood facing one another across the grass. At the end of this stretch, with all its many windows dark, stood a house larger than any other on the street. Dicey headed down towards it.

They walked down the middle of the grass. There was one broad clump of bushes the little kids could hide in, if it came to that.

When they stood before the large house, Dicey noticed oddly-shaped piles. Old radiators had been dropped here and pipes and slate shingles from the roof and even a bathroom sink. They were piled up right by the front porch.

"Let's go around the back," she said quietly. "I think it's empty. It looks like somebody's fixing it up. If anybody calls out, don't run. Tell them we're looking for Prince George Street. Tell them we're lost. Don't look guilty."

Their feet silent on the unmown grass, they stepped around the side of the house.

A silver pool of water glimmered at the end of the long lawn. The back of the house was as dark as the front, and Dicey breathed more easily. She put her suitcase beside one of the overgrown bushes that grew by the screened porch, and they all walked down to the water.

A long-fingered willow swept the top of the grass at the water's edge. Two towering pines stood silent guard. On the silver pool, which was part of a river, some sail-boats floated.

There was a bulkhead at the end of the lawn made out of

railroad ties. They sat on that and dangled their feet over the water.

Dicey's stomach had butterflies of excitement in it. "Remember that first house?" she asked James.

"Yeah. Think it's empty?"

"I think so. Let's risk it."

No other houses were visible, although patches of light from windows showed through high hedges or trees. It was a private lawn.

"No fires," Dicey said.

A sailboat, its sails down, motored up the river. It made little waves that streaked the silver with black and lapped gently against the bulkheading.

Dicey turned to look at the house behind her. Its windows were comfortingly blank.

"We'll have to be quiet and get out early," she said.

Her family watched out over the water with dream-dazed eyes. They nodded. The river was narrow enough to swim easily. Across it, houses looked back at them.

Dicey smiled. Sammy drummed at the wood with his heels, quietly. James lay back and looked at the sky. Maybeth hummed, a tune Dicey half-recognized. "What song is that?" she asked.

"Stewart's song," Maybeth said. "'Oft I sing for my friends,'" she sang softly. "Remember?"

Dicey shook her head. "We can't sing – but I sure feel like it," she said. "I don't really know why."

"Yes, you do," James said, but said no more. He was

Chapter One

watching the first stars emerge in the grey sky.

And Dicey did. They had money and a good place to sleep. She had a map. They were together alone again, themselves again. The night air was warm, and the willow whispered behind her, and the water whispered before her.

"OK," she said, rousing them, rousing herself. "Let's go up and get to sleep."

Chapter Two

SAFE AS SHE felt, Dicey woke early. She rolled over on her back. The lightening sky arched over her. Behind her, the empty house stood like a protecting wall. From the water came the cries of gulls. Their quarrels cut through the quiet slapping sound ropes and rigging made against masts. Dicey stretched lazily and sat up.

James lay sprawled on his stomach, one arm flung out. Sammy had curled into a tight ball. Maybeth lay on her back, her arms folded over her stomach.

To the east, the sky showed a lake of clear blue into which the sun would rise. It was a particular blue, made of light and darkness mingling, clear as glass, smooth as glass, as much like water as sky. Dicey stood up and went around the far corner of the house to pee behind a large evergreen bush. She decided to let her family sleep a while longer. Even men

Chapter Two

eager to get started while the day was cool wouldn't come to work this early. Dicey returned to the bulkheading and sat.

The boats rocked at their moorings. The houses beside her and across the river from her slept. Quiet as kittens, the water lapped at the boats and the bulkheads. In the east, that first blue lake increased to an ocean. The sun rose.

The air shimmered in golden light. Water reflected and brightened the air. The masts and spars of the boats stood stiff and dark. The colours of the hulls became clear: white, reds, yellows, greens and one burnished mahogany.

Dicey walked back through the long grass. She called each of the sleepers by name.

"James?"

He stirred, rolled over, sat up, grinned. "Hey. Good morning. Is it late? I'm starving."

"Maybeth?"

Maybeth's eyes flew open. She lay still for a minute, staring blankly, remembering herself.

Dicey crouched next to Sammy. She put her hand on his shoulder and jostled him gently while calling his name. "Sammy. Sammy. Time to get up."

He mumbled something and curled up more tightly.

"You've got to. Sammy?"

One eyelid struggled to open, then fell closed.

"Wake up, Sammy. We can't stay here."

He opened both eyes. "OK," he said. He closed both eyes.

"That's right," Dicey encouraged him. James grinned at her. "C'mon, Sammy – time to get up. Gotta go to the bathroom and get out of here."

He stumbled to his feet. He and James walked together to the bush, James holding Sammy's arm to keep the little boy from falling.

Dicey pulled her suitcase out from under the bush, opened it again and took out twenty more dollars. She wondered how much money she had left. She could worry about that later in the day. For now, she wanted breakfast and a phone book.

They returned to the circle with the church at its centre and to the steep main street. Once again Dicey was surprised to see the backdrop of water that lay at its foot. Something was peculiar about the perspective here, she thought. It looked as if two photographs of two different places had been jammed together. The town looked as though it fell into the water.

Her eyes searched eastward, across the water. "I can see something," she said. She could see a distant looming of land, low and flat. "Do you think that's the eastern shore?"

"How should I know?" James asked. "Can we eat in a restaurant?"

"If one's open. It's pretty early."

Early as it was, no more that half-past seven, the water was already dotted with white sails. Everybody here must sail, Dicey thought. Everybody must have his own boat. "Did you ever see so many boats?" she asked James, as they descended the main street.

He paid no attention to her. He was looking for a place

to eat. They passed three closed restaurants before they found one open. Its single narrow room wasn't air-conditioned, but the cool morning air came in through the open door and was moved around by big ceiling fans. They sat down in a tiny booth.

Dicey read the prices before she read the menu. "Pancakes," she said. "Maybeth, Sammy and I can split an order. James, you can have one to yourself, if you'll give me half of a pancake. Is that OK? And milk." James was too hungry to argue. Dicey realized that they hadn't had enough dinner the night before. She would have to be careful about that.

The counter was filled with people drinking coffee and reading papers. The little room hummed with activity as waitresses whisked about taking orders, bringing food. When Dicey paid the bill, she asked the man at the cash register where an Army-Navy surplus store was. He told her it was out beyond the bus station, and he took the time to be sure she understood his directions, even though there was a line of people behind her waiting to pay.

Fast and relaxed, that was what it was like, that restaurant.

It was that way out on the street, too. The temperature was climbing up, and the sky was bleaching yellow with heat. People were entering the little stores that lined the streets or standing in groups before the doors of the several banks. The working day was about to begin. But almost all of these people turned, before they entered, to look down the hill to the water and boats, and then up the hill to the church within its ring of trees, as if they could take their own sweet time going in to work. Some of them smiled at the Tillermans. Some wished them a good morning.

At the Army-Navy store, Dicey studied the shelves of goods before she made her purchases. It was like a library in there, tall stacks of rods, shirts, hats, pants, shoes and jackets, and tennis rackets and inflatable rafts lining the narrow aisles. Dicey picked out a one-quart aluminium saucepan, four ponchos in children's sizes, a packet of hooks and the smallest, lightest reel of fishing line she could find. After some thought, she chose a red canvas bookbag and went to the front of the store.

The jackknife she picked out of a glass-fronted case was the most expensive thing she bought. It had two blades, one large and one small, a gadget to open cans with, a little screwdriver and a file. The bill came to seventeen dollars altogether, seventeen dollars and twenty-four cents to be exact. Dicey sighed, but paid. She asked the salesman to put everything into the canvas bag, except the jackknife. She slipped the jackknife into her pocket. It felt heavy and good there.

Outside again, Dicey waited until they were out of sight of the store, then she transferred everything from the suitcase to the canvas bag. She gave James the empty suitcase to carry and slung the bag over her shoulder, holding it by the rope that pulled its neck closed. It was much easier to carry than the suitcase in the first place.

Dicey went into the small bus station and set her empty

suitcase down by the door. She went out to rejoin her family.
She was entirely pleased with herself.

"Now what?" she asked them.

"What do you mean?" James asked.

"What do you want to do now?" Dicey asked.

"Get going," Sammy said.

"I don't know how yet," Dicey answered. "I haven't
figured that out. Are you tired?"

None of them was tired.

"Let's just wander then, OK? I think better while I'm
moving."

They walked the morning away. They stayed away from
the hospital and their sleeping place and stuck to the historic
section on the map. They wandered down narrow streets
lined with narrow houses and up broader streets where the
houses were grander, where the street-level windows rose
from floor to ceiling of the rooms within. People in
Annapolis, Dicey decided, must like bricks. The sidewalks
were brick, as were many of the houses and public buildings.

Dicey also decided that she liked brick. It was so sturdy
looking and symmetrical, in the first place. And then, when it
was very, very old, it achieved a gently, mellowed look, like
old photographs or long-burning fires or a pair of blue jeans
you've had for so long that even when you take them off they
still have the shape of your body in them. When brick aged
long enough it could look soft.

They spent some time on the college lawn, watching
other people wander about. They spent some time on the

main street, walking down to the foot, where the crowds were just as thick as they had been the night before. At a stall in an open market, Dicey bought little sandwiches made of flat sausages in biscuits.

Nobody stared at them. There were lots of kids messing around, and almost everybody, adults and children alike, wore jeans and shirts. Not full, but no longer hungry, the Tillermans sat by the water and stared. Lots of bare feet and long hair, like Provincetown. But also lots of gold watches and big diamonds in rings. Boys and girls together, men and women, with arms around each other's waists.

"Too much lovey-dovey stuff," Sammy announced.

Dicey noticed something else. Most of the young women wore no bras. Their breasts went jiggle-jiggle as they walked. Finally, she could hold her tongue no longer.

"James – the girls aren't wearing bras."

He turned red. "I noticed."

"Do you see how they all go jiggle-jiggle? No, look – see the one with the long red hair? The pretty one, with eye make-up? Jiggle, jiggle, jiggle – see what I mean?"

James giggled helplessly. Dicey joined in. Then she noticed a bridge, down the river, leading over to another part of the city. From where they sat it seemed that this other part was given over entirely to boatyards and docks.

"Let's go over there," she pointed. "Let's go look at some boats."

"Do you think the jiggling hurts?" James asked her. "I'd think it would."

Chapter Two

"How would I know, James? I don't have bosoms."

"Yeah, but you will."

"I'll tell you about it if I do," Dicey said. "Do you want to go look at the boatyards?"

"Could we row it?" James asked her.

His brain, Dicey thought, must work twice as fast as hers. It had taken her all that time sitting there to think of the possibilities of a boatyard.

"I don't know," she said. "First, let's see what's there. It might be twenty miles across – I'll check the map later."

"We couldn't possibly row twenty miles, could we?"

"Let's worry about all that later, OK?"

They followed the water around to get to the drawbridge. Everywhere in Annapolis fingers of water would appear at the ends of streets or around corners, unexpectedly. Back in Provincetown, there was a belt of sandy beaches all around the town, except for the harbour side, where houses were built out over the water. Here, the town crowded down on to the water, trying to get as close to it as possible, all the time, at every opportunity.

They threaded their way through crowds of tourists. They passed countless cars, with licence plates from many states, locked and empty.

The drawbridge humped over the water. The air around it was a little cooler, so they stood for a while, leaning against the railing, looking down at the busy harbour. There were no working boats, just pleasure craft.

The boatyards hummed with labouring. Some boats were

up on racks, and men and women worked over the hulls, sanding, scraping, painting. One hull hung from a huge crane, ready to be returned to the water. Most of the boats were moored at docks that stretched out into the water. Many had people sitting on them, eating, reading. Others were empty, their sails furled, their hatch covers locked. The only rowing boats the children saw were locked on to storage racks or tied on top of the cabins of the boats they belonged with.

Nobody stopped the children or asked them any questions. Many people seemed to be wandering like them, just looking at the activity. More were at work on their boats, polishing brass, sitting on deck splicing ropes, hosing down the sails.

Dicey led her family out to the end of one dock. The bag over her shoulder had grown heavy, so she put it down. They all sat, staring out across the water. The afternoon sun reflected off the water on to their faces and arms and legs. Next to them, two boys were scrubbing down the deck of a sailboat. They wore only bathing suits. Their bodies were tanned and their hair was bleached by the sunlight. They looked as if they spent all summer outdoors in bathing suits, on boats. One of them, the heavier one, whose stomach had ripples of fat on it, jumped lightly on to the dock to pick up a hose that was coiled there. Dicey watched him lazily.

He turned on the water, then leapt back on to the deck and rinsed off the suds their brushes had left.

Dicey knew what he would do before he did it. It was inevitable. It was what anybody would do with a hose in his hand and a friend who wasn't looking. He picked up the head of the hose, put his thumb over it and sprayed his friend.

The friend charged him, his hands up before his face. The heavy boy stood and sprayed him, holding him off at arm's length. The friend looked younger, because he was so much lighter and smaller. He spluttered and turned under the shaft of water, but he didn't stop trying to get it. Then, he stamped on the heavy boy's foot and grabbed the nozzle during that moment of distraction.

They wrestled for the hose, spraying one another, shooting the water over on to the dock, laughing and cursing each other. Neither of them could take the hose away from the other. Great, heavy arcs of water shot out from the boat, spraying everywhere.

"Hey!" Dicey yelled. "Look out!"

The two wet faces turned to her. The heavier boy spoke immediately. "I didn't see you," he said. "You really wet?"

"You could say so," Dicey said, wiping her hair off her face. "But it's a hot day and the water's cool."

"That's true," he said. "But still, come on up and dry off. Jerry? Doesn't your dad keep towels on board?"

The slimmer boy swung down out of sight. He reappeared with two large towels. "It's OK if you want to come on board. It's my dad's boat."

James looked at Dicey. Sammy was already standing by the bow. "Why not?" Dicey said.

The boys pulled on the bow mooring line until the boat was only two feet off the dock. "Can you jump?"

Dicey could, and did. She reached out a hand and helped Maybeth over. James swung over on the hand of the heavy boy. Sammy refused help. He stumbled as his feet hit the deck and fell on his face. Jerry leant a worried face over him, but Sammy came up smiling. "I said I could do it," he said proudly.

"My name's Jerry," the slim boy said, "and this is Tom."

Dicey introduced her family.

They were given a tour of the boat, above and below decks. It was small, only thirty-two feet, but it had everything possible on board, and everything tucked away into its own place. There was even a shower in the head, and the walls and floor of the tiny space sloped down, following the curve of the hull, to a central drain.

"You could live on a boat," Dicey said.

"Lots of people do just that, especially in summer," Tom said.

"I've tried to talk Dad into letting me live on her," Jerry said. "He just says I should be grateful he lets me have a key to her. Grateful..." He grinned at Tom. "I do enough work for him."

"Let's take some Cokes up with us," Tom suggested. They were in the cabin at the end of their tour.

The fridge was a two-level locker holding a huge chunk of ice. Tom pulled out six cans of Coke and shut the heavy wooden door. Dicey took a last look around the cabin. A table was hinged so it could be pulled up flat against the wall and clamped there. This enabled the berth, which served as a sofa during the day, to pull out into a double bed. There was storage space behind and below the berths. The efficiency of it took Dicey's breath away.

After they had seated themselves around the cockpit, back in the blazing sunlight, Dicey asked, "Do you work on this boat?"

"Yeah. We're free labour right now. Next year, when we're sixteen, he'll have to pay us. Or we can get work at one of the yards. I know a lot of people," Jerry said.

"Can you take the boat out sailing whenever you want?" she asked.

"Well, I've gotta ask permission." The two boys exchanged a glance that Dicey could read – it meant they often didn't ask permission.

"You must be a pretty good sailor," James said.

"I guess you'd say so," Jerry answered. He stretched out his legs and admired his tanned feet.

"Do you sail too?" James asked Tom.

"Not like Jerry does. I just hack around."

"Are you brothers?"

"Naw," Tom said. "We're old friends. Since first grade."

They drank their Cokes silently for a bit, basking in the sunlight.

"Does your dad sail the boat?" James asked.

"On weekends," Jerry said. "During the week, she's pretty much my own.

"Gee," James said, admiration in his voice. He looked at Dicey, hard.

Dicey got the feeling there was something James wanted her to understand, but she didn't understand it yet. She tried to help by talking about the same topic. "What does your dad do?"

"Works in Washington." Jerry's voice had pride in it as he said that.

"Gee, is he a senator?" James asked.

"Not so important," Jerry said. "Just a representative – you know what they are?"

"House of Representatives," James said quickly.

"Yep. He's the representative from Ohio, third district. It's his first term."

"Gee," James said again. He looked significantly at Dicey again. She didn't pay any attention because she had sensed it was a lie. She was busy wondering why this boy would lie about his father's job, and why his friend would go along with it without saying anything.

"We live over here because my mom doesn't want to get all caught up in political circles. She says it's no good for kids. She's a regular hawkeye, my mom."

"She only wants to keep her baby boy as long as she can," Tom remarked.

Jerry flushed and bit his lip. "At least she cares about her kids."

Tom laughed. "You can't get me that way, old friend. My parents care about me – but I've made my declaration of independence, and they were smart enough to accept that. I've got my freedom."

"And I don't?"

"Not yet, old buddy. When you're ready, when you want it bad enough, you'll have the nerve to fight for it. But what the hell — it's summer — nothing's worth worrying about in the summer, is it?"

Sammy had lost interest in the conversation and was lying on his stomach on the deck, trying to dabble his hand in the water.

"Do you ever go to the eastern shore?" James asked Jerry.

At last, Dicey understood what James was driving at. She nodded her head at him, briskly. He raised an eyebrow at her, as if to say, "Well, it's about time."

"Go there?" Jerry asked. "I've spent almost as much time there as over here. When you sail the Chesapeake you learn all about the eastern shore. Why?"

"We gotta go over tomorrow," James said.

"Yeah? Where?"

"Easton," Dicey said quickly. "We're visiting an aunt for a couple of weeks. Our parents sent us down from Wilmington. To get fresh air," she said, trying to sound disgusted.

"What are you doing in Annapolis?" Tom asked.

"There's this old lady my dad knows, from when he was a kid and his father was in the Navy," Dicey said. "She always says she's dying to see us — I suppose because she never had any children of her own. We're spending the night with her first. But she sleeps all the time. She told us to go run around while she slept. She's awfully old. I dunno," Dicey said, "I

think she'd rather just invite us and not have us come. But
Mom says she really enjoys our visits, as long as we don't hang
around the house too much."

"Where is this?"

"Over on Prince George Street – you know where that is?
Everything in her house can't be touched. It's hard on Sammy."

The boys seemed to believe this.

"So, you're making the great trip to the eastern shore
tomorrow," Tom said.

"On a bus," Dicey said. "It's crazy. My aunt and her kids
aren't even going to be there until dinner, because she works
and they go to some camp. I told our parents we should wait
until tomorrow and take a late bus to Easton, but they said –
you know how parents are."

"Man, do I know," Jerry said.

"It's too bad you can't sail over," Tom said to Dicey.

"It sure beats the bus," Jerry agreed.

They didn't sound like they were offering, so Dicey
played it low. "Yeah. But it's a short trip. We'll survive."

"Yeah, it's too bad," Tom said to her. "We'd offer to sail
you over, see, but Jerry would have to ask permission, and…"

Dicey nodded, as if she understood. Well, she did. She
understood what he was up to.

Jerry studied his feet.

Dicey stood up. "We gotta get back now. Thanks for the
Cokes."

"Wait a minute," Jerry said. "Would you really like to sail
over?" he asked. He was looking at Tom, not at them, as he spoke.

"Gee, yes," James said.

"We could get back by dark, you know," Jerry said to Tom. Tom just smiled. "I'll tell my mom I'm having dinner at your house. Do you think we could? Get over and back?"

Tom looked doubtful.

"I'd like to try it, wouldn't you?" Jerry insisted.

"Oh, I'd like it, you know that. I'm always game for something out of the ordinary. But *I* don't have to be home by dark. *I* don't have the mother who has to know where I am every minute of the day."

"Cut it out, OK? Lay off that stuff. I mean, what can they do to me after all? Lock me in the attic? Beat me with wet noodles? Send me away to school?"

Tom shrugged.

"Gee, I don't want to get you in trouble," James said.

"Trouble," Jerry said, as if there was no trouble he couldn't handle. "Let me worry about that. I'm game for a day's hard sailing. Think you can do it?" he challenged Tom.

"Anything you can do I can do," Tom answered.

"We'll see," Jerry said. "You kids get back here early tomorrow – eight o'clock. Can you be here that early?"

"I think so," Dicey said. "I think there's a seven o'clock bus we could say we were taking. It sure would be fun to sail over."

"It's not easy," Jerry warned her. "You have to keep out of the way."

"We can do that," Dicey said.

"And the little kids – can they swim?"

"I can swim good," Sammy said.

"OK, then. OK?"

"OK," Dicey agreed. They left the boat quickly. She picked up her bag from the dock and hustled everyone ahead of her down the dock. When they were well out of sight, she slowed down and turned to James.

"Gee, James," she said – and burst out laughing.

James joined in. "I want hamburgers for supper tonight," he said.

"You deserve them," Dicey answered.

"I thought you'd never catch on," he said. "I thought that Jerry'd never catch on. You know, Dicey? We made them do what we wanted them to do."

"Tom really did it," Dicey said.

"Yeah. Why did he? Does he want to get his friend in trouble?"

"I dunno," Dicey said. "Is that what friends do?"

"Don't you know?"

"No. I never had a friend like that, a best friend from first grade. We never had many friends, did we?"

"I suppose not." James thought about that. "None of us did. Maybe Tillermans don't."

They ate dinner at Burger King, hamburgers, fresh fries, milkshakes. It tasted good to them, after weeks of Cousin Eunice's frozen dinners and pot pies. They wandered around again until evening had settled in, milling with crowds of people who seemed to have nothing else to do but saunter down the streets and look in store windows, or peer at the little houses.

When they had drifted back to their own empty house, the little children fell asleep almost at once. Dicey and James sat for a long time down by the river. Occasional boats motored up and down. Voices floated across the water. The air was humid and hot. Altogether Dicey felt satisfied.

"What do you know about our grandmother?" James asked her.

"I think she's poor," Dicey said. "And maybe strange."

"Strange? Like Momma? Crazy?"

"Strange like all the Tillermans," Dicey said. "She lives all alone on a farm."

"Why do Tillermans always live alone?"

"We don't. We live together."

"Together, but all alone together," James said.

"Maybe every family feels that way," Dicey said. "Maybe that's what families are."

"I don't know," James said. "I don't think so."

Before she went to sleep that night, Dicey counted her money, peering at the bills in the dim light. She had forty-seven dollars left, and some change.

It had cost them a lot to get to Annapolis. Dicey decided that forty would be the amount to keep in her pocket. Once they got across the bay, they'd have to stop spending. They'd have to fish for food, and get clams; or something. And she'd have to earn money if she could. Seven dollars could go a long way, if it had to, if you made it. She'd make it go as far as she could, all the way to Crisfield. If she could.

Chapter Three

WHEN DICEY AWOKE, she was cool and damp, and even a little chilly. The morning air lay moist over her. She turned her eyes from the grey sky to her family.

Sammy wasn't there.

She sat up, peering towards the bush they used for a bathroom. She waited, long enough, she judged, but he did not appear. She jumped to her feet and looked around.

His little figure sat huddled on the bulkheading at the end of the lawn. In the mists rising from the water, he could have been a woeful little bush planted between the willow and the pine.

Dicey went to the bathroom then walked down to join him. He knew who she was without turning his head. "What got you up?" she asked.

"I had to pee," he said. His fingers picked long splinters

Chapter Three

from the wood. "I was thinking," he said.

"You worried?"

He shook his head. "I'm not scared of sailing."

"I never said you were," Dicey answered. "You're not scared of anything, are you?"

Sammy looked at her then, his eyes questioning. "I had a dream that you were all on a bus and the door closed and I couldn't get on. I ran and ran after it, but it kept getting away."

Dicey nodded her head and watched the mists rising almost in straight lines, like rain going backwards. In the east, the sky lightened.

"Dicey? Can I ask you something?"

"Sure."

"Tell the truth?"

"I always do."

"No, you don't," Sammy said.

Dicey understood him. "I'll tell the truth, Sammy, I promise."

Sammy asked his question: "Why were you going to go alone, before James caught you?"

The hulls of the boats were shadowy silhouettes on the water. Mist caught in the branches of the trees across the river. The mists would burn off, Dicey thought. There wasn't much wind.

"I don't know what we're going to find when we get there," Dicey said. "So I figured if I went down alone and saw what it's like, then I could come back and get you all. If it was OK. If it wasn't OK, I could just forget about it. Also, I had enough money to get there and back on a bus and stay on my own in a hotel. See, Sammy, I don't know what this grandmother will be like. I was trying to make things easiest for you all. Do you understand?"

"I guess so. I think so – like I fight when people say things, so they won't say them any more. Are you sorry that we're with you?"

"A little, yes. It's harder with four of us. And more expensive. And" – since Dicey had determined to tell the whole truth, she did – "I kind of liked the idea of travelling alone – you know? With no one to look after. But I was wrong, Sammy, or at least I think now I was. I made a mistake not telling you."

"Why?"

"Because we do things together. The trouble was, we didn't do things together at Cousin Eunice's and that got me thinking the wrong way."

"How can something get you thinking the wrong way, if you know how to think the right way?" Sammy asked. But he was sitting up straighter and kicking his heels.

"They just do. I don't know how."

"I always thought…well, you didn't make mistakes."

"Everybody makes mistakes!"

"Not you – you didn't."

"Oh, Sammy. I made dozens of mistakes."

"Name one."

"Staying too long at Rockland. Not planning how to cross the Connecticut River. Not having any money in New

Chapter Three

Haven. Not telling Cousin Eunice what I thought, about you and Maybeth."

"Don't tell me," Sammy begged. "Don't tell me any more."

"But you asked me to!" Dicey protested.

The sun was rising, turning the sky and air a rosy gold colour. Gulls wheeled through the air. A boat motored quietly down the river, the people on it dark figures.

"You did," Dicey insisted. "You did ask me." She reached over and tickled Sammy under his arm. He squirmed. She reached her other arm over and wrestled him down to the grass, tickling, crying, "You did, you did, you did. Say so."

Sammy screamed with laughter and wriggled under her hands. "All right, I did!"

Dicey stood up. She brushed her hands briskly together. "Let's get going," she said. They raced back up the lawn.

They were early down to the boat, early and hungry. James grumbled that he wanted breakfast but Dicey ignored him. She didn't want to spend any money until they got across the bay. She wanted everything to stay just as it was until they were actually on the other side.

The Tillermans sat on the end of the dock waiting. All around them, the boatyards came awake. Water traffic made many little waves. A slight breeze blew now, and little boats sailed down to the mouth of the river and the bay.

Time passed slowly. Dicey sensed that it was after eight o'clock. Cars streamed over the bridge, going towards town. People going to work, she thought. Her hunger mounted.

She had been sure, at first, that she could wait to eat until they were across.

"Tonight," Dicey announced, "we've got to wash our underwear. And put on clean. Maybe shirts too. OK?"

"Do you think they forgot?" James asked. His head moved restlessly. "Or changed their minds?"

"Maybe," Dicey said. "Or they could have been lying to us."

At this, James smiled: "That would serve us right, wouldn't it?"

They had to eat. If Dicey was hungry, James must be starving. She went back to a petrol station and bought crackers with peanut butter from a machine. Then she put in two more quarters and got chocolate bars.

When she returned, the two boys were there, busy working with sails on the deck. They were dressed just as they had been the day before. Dicey wondered if they slept in their swimming suits. She looked at James and raised her eyebrows. She handed out packets of crackers and offered some of hers to Jerry and Tom. "No thanks," they both said. "We just ate. You kids stay in the cockpit, OK?"

It was like sitting in a booth without a table, with the four Tillermans, two to a side, knees hitting knees, stiff and watchful. The boys spent a long time putting on the jib. Jerry came back and stood by the base of the mast. He pulled down on a rope. The jib rose slowly and hung flapping at its stay. Jerry told Tom to fend off from the bow while he backed out of the dock.

Chapter Three

When Jerry returned to the cockpit, he looked at the Tillermans. "Ready to go?"

"You bet," Dicey answered.

"Drop your bag on one of the bunks below," Jerry told her. "Then I think you and your brother James had better go and sit on the cabin roof. I need room for play on the tiller, and Tom'll be back here, handling the sails. You ever sail before?"

Dicey thought of lying and then thought better of it. "No," she said.

Jerry considered this. His face was thin and his hair was bleached to a metallic tone that matched the gold in his eyes. His mouth looked soft and sulky, but his body was lean. "OK," he said, "listen carefully. We're going to have to tack out a-ways, then we can reach over to St Mikes. Tacking means we zigzag, going as close to the wind as possible." His hand sketched a zigzag motion in the air. "At the end of each tack, I'll call, 'ready about'. The boat will rotate, about sixty degrees, and the mainsail and boom will swing from one side to the other. The heel will reverse too."

"What?" James said. "I don't understand."

Jerry held his hand out stiffly, slanted one way, then reversed the slant. "That's what the keel does when we tack and come about," he said. "On a reach we'll ride pretty flat. All you have to do is hang on when we come about. There's no danger. I want you to sit where you're put, and sit quiet. But if I tell you to move, or give any order, you've got to obey right away. Got that?"

"We can do that," Dicey said. "All of us."

She leant down and tossed her bag on to a bunk below. Then she and James went up forward to sit on the roof of the cabin. They could lean back against the mast, or slip down to the deck and lean against the cabin wall.

Jerry started the engine. Tom uncleated a heavy line with a floater tied on its end and dropped it into the water. James looked at Dicey: "I hope they know what they're doing," he said.

The sun was toasting warm. The water danced beneath the keel. The engine hummed. The boat slipped out into the river and turned east. The jib flapped.

Waterfront buildings glided slowly by, boatyards, condominiums with great glass windows looking out over the water, an occasional small house in the middle of a green lawn. Theirs was one of many boats headed out to the bay.

The engine stopped. Dicey turned her head. She smiled to Sammy and Maybeth, sitting straight up and still, one on each side of the cockpit. Tom stood up, holding the tiller. Jerry jumped up behind them to raise the mainsail. When he had it cleated, he jumped down into the cockpit and hauled in on a line.

The mainsail stiffened, then puffed out. The boat responded, surging forward underneath them.

Tom returned the tiller to Jerry and pulled in the jib. It was not the kind of jib Dicey knew. At Provincetown she had seen little, narrow triangular sails. This jib was long. It curved back around, halfway down the length of the cockpit. Dicey turned her head back and yelled, "What kind of a jib is that?"

"It's a genoa," Tom answered. He seemed to be enjoying himself. His eyes squinted into the sunlight, and his smile showed big, square teeth.

The wind blew firmly against the sails. The water jostled the boat, wave after wave. When Dicey looked at the water, they seemed to be travelling quite fast. But when she looked at the shore, now falling away beside them, they seemed to be going very slowly.

Under the protection of the shore, the boat heeled only slightly. Jerry brought the boat about, and Dicey and James had to do no more than protect themselves from the genoa as it flapped across the bow in front of them. Dicey saw a shadow of shoreline, across the bay.

She also saw three huge tankers, moored one behind the other, lying across their path, like tall buildings. Jerry approached them, then passed between two, where there was much more room than there had first seemed to be. The metal walls soared up above the little boat. Some crewmen waved down at them, and Dicey waved back. The tanker came from Athens, from Athens across the Atlantic and down the length of the Mediterranean Sea.

Dicey looked up the bay to where Baltimore was. Two bridges, twin spans, crossed the bay in long arcs. They looked like something from the future, slender silver ropes flung over the broad water, beautiful and strong.

Dicey's eyes moved out, across again. Jerry brought the boat about, and – after shifting her weight to compensate for the heel – she found she could no longer see the far shore, for which they were headed. They had left most of the other boats behind, and now passed only an occasional fishing boat, rocking at the end of its anchor line.

The wind hummed in her ears, the sun poured over her face and arms and legs, the waves knocked against the keel, and the boat pulled forward. Like everything else in Annapolis, the movement was both lazy and fast, at once. She turned back and saw Sammy staring at Tom. Jerry sat with the long wooden tiller in his hand, his eyes on the sails.

Dicey slid down on to the deck and leant her back against the cabin. The sky was clear, the sails shone white against it. She closed her eyes.

In the darkness behind her eyelids, Dicey felt part of the boat itself, riding the wind over the water. It was easy work, this. It was silent and serene. Her thoughts loosed themselves from their everyday moorings and wandered. Nothing mattered out here. Nobody talked and nobody listened. The waves went past them, maybe each different, maybe the same wave over and over again. Who knew which? Who cared?

Dicey opened her eyes. They had never sailed in Provincetown. They had never been asked. She had rowed in dinghies and been out once or twice on large fishing boats. But they were nothing like this quiet harnessing of wind and the sharp keel cutting through silken water.

Out here, there was salt on the wind itself that fell on your skin like rain. You could taste it. Out here the sun heated and the wind cooled, and the waves sang their constant song.

Chapter Three

Dicey wished she could stop breathing and give herself entirely over to the movement and the being still. Maybe she could learn to sail. Maybe she could go to sea, somehow. A boat could be a home. The perfect home that could move around, a home that didn't close you in or tie you down: and a sailor would always be at home if he was on the sea.

Maybe life was like a sea, and all the people were like boats. There were big, important yachts and little rafts and motorboats and sailboats and working boats and pleasure boats. And some really big boats like ocean liners or tankers – those would be rich or powerful people, whose lives engulfed many other lives and carried them along. Or maybe each boat was a kind of family. Then what kind of boat would the Tillermans be? A little one, bobbling about, with the mast fallen off? A grubby, worn-down workboat, with Dicey hanging on to the rudder for dear life.

Everybody who was born was cast on to the sea. Winds would blow them in all directions. Tides would rise and turn, in their own rhythm. And the boats – they just went along as best they could, trying to find a harbour.

Dicey didn't feel like finding a harbour. She knew she needed one, and they needed one, but she would rather just sail along, dreaming, not caring where they were going or when they would get there or what they would do there.

Couldn't you live your whole life without going into harbour? The land would catch you at the end. *Home is the sailor.* But until then, you could keep free. And even then, even when you died, you could die at sea and your body would roll with the underwater currents until your flesh peeled off and you were white bones rocking in the waves on the sandy bottom of the ocean. Always part of the changing.

Dicey smiled to herself. The ocean at Provincetown had always sung at her too. As long as I'm near the water, she thought, that'll be enough, even if I'm on land. Because life wasn't really an ocean, and she wasn't really a little boat bobbling about on it. There were James and Maybeth and Sammy, for one thing. But for now, she was content to sit still and silent.

The sun beat down hotter, and her skin started to run with sweat. She was getting sticky, uncomfortable. The sails fell lifeless and quiet, flapping morosely. The boat no longer thrust ahead, slicing the waves; now it rolled from side to side. She crawled back over the cabin.

"What's the matter?" she asked.

The two boys were leaning back, drinking beer from cans. "Wind's died down," Tom said.

"That happens," Jerry added. "Especially in the middle of the bay. No worry. The only deadline we have is I've got to be back in Annapolis by dark."

"Yeah, or the ghosties and boogies will get him."

Jerry frowned, but ignored his friend. "We can always let you off and head right back."

"I've got some friends in St Mikes," Tom said.

"We know about your friends in St Mikes," Jerry answered.

"It beats sitting around watching TV," Tom answered.

Chapter Three

"Doesn't it? Your mom's not here, Jer, you can tell the truth."

Dicey interrupted. "Could I steer? I mean, we're not going anywhere—"

"We are, but not far," Jerry corrected.

"Go ahead, let her," Tom urged. Jerry agreed.

Jerry slid down towards Sammy and put Dicey's hand on the long tiller. The wood was smooth and warm. It responded to every vibration in the hull and every flapping of the sails. Dicey's hand seesawed gently back and forth. The tiller let her feel the boat under her hand. She grinned at Jerry. "I like it," she said.

He grinned back at her and taught her how to head up, into the wind, and point down, away from it. He showed her what changes in the mainsail to watch for. He pointed to the glassy water just ahead of them and then to a patch far ahead where little ripples danced in the sunlight. "There's wind up there," he said. He leant back and drank from his can of beer.

"I'm going below for a snooze," Tom announced. He climbed down the ladder and disappeared.

Sammy went up to sit with James.

Jerry moved over to Tom's seat. "He doesn't like sailing," he said.

"Who, Sammy? I didn't notice."

"No, Tom."

"But—"

"He's got nothing better to do." Jerry shrugged, then smiled a little. "And he likes getting me in trouble."

"What about you?" Dicey asked.

"I need some help getting into trouble. I'd never dare do it on my own. You know? Rebellion is necessary for the development of character."

Dicey wondered about that.

"Most men lead lives of quiet desperation," Jerry said. "Somebody said that. He was right. So – I get in trouble, now and then – so I won't be like most men."

"You're going to lead a life of noisy desperation?" Dicey asked.

He laughed at that. He gave himself over to laughter and enjoyed it. Dicey decided she liked him after all.

"At least that much," he said. "More if I can, but at least that."

They sailed on, if this odd, rolling progress could be called sailing. Then, under her hand, Dicey felt the boat stir. She looked at the water and the sails. They had reached the ripply patch of water. The sails bellied out.

Jerry was watching her. She offered him the tiller, but he shook his head. His smile teased her. He pulled in on the genoa line and held it. The long sail lay nearly flat. The mainsail line he had already cleated down. "Watch the genoa," he instructed.

Dicey did. She watched the sail and the water ahead. She rested her hand lightly on the tiller, letting the boat tell her where it wanted to go. She sat alert, her body tuned to that gentle pull on the tiller.

Boat, waves, water and wind: through the wood she felt them working for her. She was not directing, but accompanying them, turning them to her use. She didn't work against them, but with them; and she made the boat do that too. It wasn't power she felt, guiding the tiller, but purpose. She could not stop smiling.

The wind built up, and Jerry took back the tiller, giving Dicey the genoa line. She played it, without being told, letting it out a fraction, pulling it in two fractions, responding to the pull of the wind in the sail.

They didn't talk, sailing the boat. They didn't talk at all until Jerry pointed out the land approaching. Dicey saw short, narrow beaches, a few trees, some big houses.

"Another hour," Jerry said.

Dicey nodded.

"How old are you?" he asked.

"Thirteen," Dicey answered. "I turned thirteen in June."

"That's too bad," Jerry said. "If you were fifteen, or even fourteen...you really take to it, don't you? I've never seen anybody take to it like that. I never thought a girl could. You've got good hands, Dicey. And you're not scared."

"Thirteen isn't too young to sail," Dicey pointed out.

"No, it isn't," he agreed. He leant his head down and called Tom awake. "We've got to come about and make the approach to St Mikes."

Dicey nodded to show she understood, and she thought she did understand what he had said. She was too young to be a girlfriend. Her cheeks grew warm with the thought. Of course she was, much too young, and besides, she had more important things to do. She was surprised at herself, though, for the nice feeling it gave her. Maybe because she'd been so often taken for a boy.

She joined James and Sammy. Maybeth said she didn't want to move from her seat nestled up against the cabin wall, where she had sat silent for the whole trip. So Dicey returned to the foredeck. The boat heeled a little now, in the afternoon wind. She and James kept Sammy sitting between them. "I sailed it," Dicey said.

"I saw," James answered. "What was it like?"

Dicey couldn't explain. "Great," she said.

They watched the shoreline close them in as Jerry negotiated the channel into St Mikes. This was low land, with large houses standing on bright green leaves. Buoys slipped by.

Jerry let down the mainsail and gathered it in, wrapping it around the boom and looping a line around it to hold it. Tom turned on the engine. Jerry loosed the genoa halyard and showed Dicey how to pull it down and hold it in at the same time. Great armloads of material surrounded her. She couldn't see anything. Jerry's voice, muffled by the sail he was packing into a sail bag, assured her that she was doing just fine.

They pulled into the front of a long dock, and Tom took a line from the bow and wrapped it around one of the posts. Jerry tied the stern. He held the boat close to the dock while the Tillermans climbed out.

The steadiness of the land under her feet felt strange to Dicey. She felt as if everything was reversed. On the boat, the deck had been unsteady and her leg muscles had worked to keep her balanced. On land, the ground was so steady that her leg muscles took up the motion of the boat. It was crazy.

Her family stood back while she thanked Jerry. Tom was talking to him about calling some people. "We got beer on the boat," he was saying.

Jerry hesitated.

"Just an hour. You can call your old lady and tell her where you are, if you're worried. Or better yet, call her and tell her you're here and can't get back before dark. She'll be mad at you for sailing over, but glad you called, so it'll be all right. Jerry? You wanna? Man, we're over here with the boat and beer — we can really have a party."

Jerry laughed, a light, high sound. He turned the idea over in his mind. "I don't know," he said.

Dicey knew. She knew also what he would decide. "We gotta find a bus," she said. "Thanks an awful lot."

"That's OK, kid," Tom answered.

Dicey waited for Jerry to say something. Finally he noticed. "It was fun," he said.

"Yeah, it was. It really was."

"See you around, yeah?" he said.

"Probably not," Dicey said. She held out her hand and he shook it. "Yeah," he said, but he wasn't paying attention to her. He was looking at Tom, and a smile was creeping over his mouth. Dicey picked up her bag, slung it over her shoulder, took a last look at the boat and walked off fast.

St Michael's was a small town huddled around its

waterfront. It was like Annapolis, but without the hurrying quality of the city across the bay. It was pretty, but Dicey was not cheered by that as they walked out of town on the one main street. She felt vaguely sad. To make herself feel better, she vowed that she would sail again, and often, if she could. Crisfield was on the water. People there must sail.

The mid-afternoon sun pounded down on them. They walked two abreast on the side of the road, Dicey with Maybeth, James with Sammy. Dicey carried her bag over her shoulder.

Little town houses, with handkerchief lawns, gave way to fields where corn and soya beans grew. Driveways led off the highway. Sometimes you could see the roofs of houses back among the trees that began at the far ends of the fields. Some of the mailboxes had the names of houses on them, Windward, Peterson's Landing, Oakwood, Second Chance.

They came to a wooded section, mostly pines, and walked at its edge, as far from the traffic as they could get. In the midst of this section, a driveway went off. Like the other driveways they'd passed, this was a dirt road. But this road had a name, Overview Circle, and a bunch of mailboxes clustered at its beginning.

Dicey peered down the highway and saw a small store ahead, with a petrol pump at the front.

"You all wait here," she said, putting down her bag. "I'm going up to the store to get some food, and we'll see if there's a place to camp down this drive. I figure, these are big estates, and probably on the river-front. OK?"

Chapter Three

"It's not dark yet," James objected.

"It's getting late and we've got to find a place. This looks like there might be lots of privacy," Dicey explained.

"OK, if you say so," James said.

"And if I'm wrong there'll still be time to find another place," Dicey said.

They sat down within the first row of trees. Dicey walked on, scuffing her feet, to the store.

Dicey entered the store through the screen door. She saw mostly cans and dried foods. There was one small fridge that held milk, butter, eggs and cold cuts in plastic packaging. She picked out a can of chicken noodle soup, a quart of milk, a loaf of bread, a bar of soap, a box of safety matches and four tomatoes from a bushel basket. It cost two dollars and ten cents.

The storekeeper stood beside her while she made all these selections, watching her carefully. He didn't say a word. He was a bony man, with short grizzled hair and long, nervous fingers. When Dicey had piled everything on the counter, he said "That be it?" and rang up her purchases on an ancient cash register.

Something about his voice was familiar, but Dicey couldn't put her finger on it.

Outside Dicey recognized what had been familiar in the man's voice. He had Momma's way with the sounds of letters. They sounded, just a little, like Momma. Dicey smiled and rejoined her family.

The dirt driveway led off the road straight for a quarter of a mile before it began winding among the trees. At the turns, driveways entered. Dicey walked down one and saw a large house, white shingled, and water beyond it. Dogs barked at her, so she turned back.

The third house was silent, although a car waited in the long garage. The Tillermans skirted the trees at the edge of the property and cut down to the water when they saw it. They found a marshy beach, nestled back against the piney woods. It was not ideal, but it was private and, except for birds and frogs, quiet.

Dicey built a small fire and opened the soup can with her jackknife can opener. It was hard work, but it did the job. She mixed a can of milk into the condensed soup in the pan. Then she told everybody to strip and put on clean underwear. James stood in the muddy water and washed out their underwear, using the cake of soap. He brought it back for Dicey to inspect. "I dunno," she said.

"The water's muddy, not like a laundromat."

Maybeth spread the wet clothing over some bushes. They sat around the small fire and took turns drinking soup from the pan, soaking it up with flabby slices of bread. They passed the milk container around, and Dicey halved the tomatoes. They ate these eagerly, even Sammy who didn't ordinarily like tomatoes. They were red, firm, juicy. They tasted fresher than anything Dicey had ever eaten before.

After supper, Dicey put out the fire ("We don't want to attract attention.") and set Sammy fishing in the quiet river. After a while, James joined Sammy, holding his own line and hook.

Chapter Three

The sun set quietly, flaming in the water. The boys caught five small fish, which they killed and then left lying in the water, so they'd be fresh for breakfast.

When the sun was only a band of burning red seen through the trees, Dicey took out the ponchos and spread them on the ground, rolling on them to crush the undergrowth beneath. Nobody wanted to go to sleep, however. They sat with their knees pulled up under their chins. Maybeth began to sing, and they joined in without thinking. They kept their voices down, just in case, but they sang eagerly. When darkness had fallen over everything, and the stars burned bright in a moonless sky, they went to sleep.

Chapter Four

THEY SLEPT LATE the next morning and were awakened by the roar of a racing motorboat as it headed down the river to the bay. They were all, even Sammy, shoved out of sleep into the hot morning, like falling out of bed. Dicey raised her face from the poncho. Her cheek was damp with sweat. Her things stuck to the rubber. She rubbed at her eyes.

The woods rested behind them. The water and the opposite shore lay before them. Between these wandered the narrow river. The sun was high in the sky, high and hot.

They all peed in the woods and then gathered fuel for a small fire. Dicey pulled the five fish out of the water. With the jackknife, she gutted them and scraped off some of their scales. Then she and James threaded them on to supple branches. Nobody spoke.

They ate the fish and finished the milk and bread. James

experimented with toasting the bread on a stick. He got a patchwork piece of toast, splotches of white, splotches of black and various shades of brown. Dicey gathered the underwear, almost dry, from the bushes where it had been hanging all night. James taught Sammy how to put out a fire properly; how to cover it with dirt and then stamp on it and wait to be sure no telltale smoke rose from the ashes.

Maybeth helped Dicey fold up the ponchos and pack them into her bag. They gathered all their rubbish into the brown grocery bag.

Dicey knew it was time to go, but she didn't want to start, not yet. She pulled out her map and studied it. They would go through Easton and then loop west. Dicey would have preferred to stick to the water's edge, to follow the shoreline down, but this countryside had too many fists and fingers of land that reached out into the water. If they followed the shoreline, they would travel many miles more than they had to, winding in and out along the points of land.

At the sound of another motor, they all froze. A small boat, really just a rowing boat with an outboard, chugged down-river. Three boys were in it, all about James's age. They were tanned by the sun; all wore cutoffs, T-shirts and sneakers. Their hair looked shaggy, as if it hadn't been cut all summer. They trailed lazy hands in the water as they moved slowly, aimlessly, down the river and out of sight.

"You know," Dicey said, "they look like us. Don't they? James?"

He nodded. His eyes followed the wake the little boat left behind.

"Do you think we're like most of the kids over here, in the way we look?" Dicey asked.

"Natural camouflage," James said.

Dicey looked at them. They were all brown, and her day in the sun yesterday had caught her up in brownness for what she'd lost during hours inside at Bridgeport. Their hair was scruffy, and Maybeth's curls looked tangled. But they didn't look out of place, or unusual. They looked like kids running a little wild during the summer.

They returned to the road, hurrying down the dirt driveway. James carried the bag of rubbish and dumped it into a bin near the little store Dicey had shopped in the afternoon before. The clock within the store read ten. Late.

The children walked on beside the highway. This was Route 33, heading east. In Easton, they would change roads to go south. Traffic was light on this hot summer morning. They walked two by two on the shoulder of the road. Fields of corn hedged them in. Insects buzzed among the rows. Dicey wondered if they could take a few ears for supper. Her pan wasn't big enough to hold a whole ear of corn, but you could scrape off the kernels. Her curiosity was aroused by these fields, so unprotected from the road. Anybody could go in and steal the corn. There were no fences to stop them. Maybe that was why she didn't want to do it.

As they neared the town of Easton, they began to pass shopping centres and development houses, little, low one-storey ranchers with sprigs of new grass and one or two puny trees. At one of the large markets, Dicey bought a pie on sale and four bananas. They cost ninety-two cents. She told her family that they would stop to eat after they had passed through Easton.

Sammy wanted to stop before the town. "It takes all day to get through a place."

"Not a little one like this," Dicey said.

"Are you sure?"

"Pretty sure," Dicey said. "Wanna bet?"

They wagered an hour's fishing time. If it took too long to get through Easton, Dicey would have to fish for an hour, while Sammy had free time. If it didn't, then Sammy would have to fish an extra hour. Sammy liked this. Either way, he won. He walked eagerly on.

Dicey won the wager of course. As she said to herself, if she couldn't read a map by now, she'd be a pretty sore fool. The streets of Easton, even the main arteries that they walked on, were sleepy, tree-lined roads. The tallest buildings reached only four storeys. Stop signs outnumbered traffic lights.

Their roads took them around the town rather than through its centre. They passed by a long pond that ran behind the YMCA and then down across abandoned railroad tracks to where a big highway joined up with 322.

Here, Dicey took out her map again: Route 50 – a four-lane highway with a grass divider. Trucks, cars, campers, buses, vans, pickups, motorcycles, all thundered down the highway, hard on one another's heels, travelling fast. Dicey wanted to get off this road for two reasons. First, it was too heavily travelled, and the air was thick with fumes and noise. Second, Route 50 went due south, to Cambridge, before bearing east to Salisbury. It would be quicker to take a road that followed the third side of the triangle formed by Easton, Cambridge and Salisbury. A river lay across that route, the Choptank. It was broad down by Cambridge, but narrower up above, and would be easy to cross she guessed, remembering the little river they'd camped by. She decided to turn off the main highway and cut cross-country.

A quarter of a mile south of Easton, she took a turn on to River Road. That had the right sound to it. They crossed the highway at a run. They raced across the southbound lanes, then had to wait several minutes before they could dash safely across the northbound traffic. Dicey saw fields ahead, and a few houses. Twenty yards from the highway, they were back in open countryside.

It was James who sighted the circus ahead, set up on a fallow field. He saw the ferris wheel. "Let's go there and eat," he said.

"We can't spend any money," Dicey said.

"That's OK, I like to look," James answered.

They ate the bananas as they approached the circus. They came to it from the rear, from behind a big tent. A short midway with a ferris wheel and carousel and a dozen booths for games and food stands led away from the tent entrance. People were hurrying around, setting up games, carrying boxes marked with the names of soft drinks; a man tinkered with the engine that drove the ferris wheel. Dicey stopped by a trash can. She broke the pie into four pieces and handed them out. They dropped their rubbish into the metal barrel. They stared for a while at the activity on the midway and then drifted back to the tent from which music and voices issued.

"Do you think they have elephants?" Sammy asked Dicey.

"It doesn't look big enough," she said. "I don't see any place where they'd keep animals, do you, James? It doesn't look like much of a circus."

James peered into the tent, standing in the doorway. "There's a tightrope," he reported.

"Out," ordered a sharp voice from the dimness within the tent. The Tillermans backed away. "You heard me." A woman stepped out into the hot sunlight.

She had bright red hair and wore a man's shirt over tight blue jeans. She wore sandals with very high heels. She carried a whip. Three terriers, like little white mobilized mops, swirled around her feet in eager circles. Somehow, she managed not to step on them or trip over them.

"What're you kids doing here?" she demanded. She sounded angry, angry at them.

"Nothing," Dicey said.

"Tell that to the Marines," the woman said. "You know we don't open until six."

"No, we didn't," Dicey said.

"You do now," she answered. She put her hands on her hips and glared at them. The whip dangled down, and one of the little dogs, the one with a pink ribbon on its head, jumped up to grab it out of her hand. The woman rocked on her heels and the dogs ran off in a row, the other two chasing the one carrying the whip.

Dicey started to smile.

"You heard me," the woman said. "Or should I call the police?"

"I don't think so." A slow, thick man's voice spoke from behind the Tillermans. Dicey turned to face this new person. He was a tall black man, with eyes so dark brown they looked almost black beneath thick eyebrows. He was clothed entirely in black, a black shirt and black pants and high black leather boots. His tightly curling hair was cut short, and he had a narrow, short beard along his jawbone. His face looked relaxed, as if nothing could upset him.

Maybeth moved closer to Dicey. James stood where he was, his mouth open. Sammy was poised to run.

The man spoke again. "Relax, kids, she won't hurt you. Claire? What is this?"

"They were snooping around," the woman told him. "This one," she indicated Dicey, "he said they didn't know we're closed until six."

"You go back to work," the man told her. "I'll take care of this." They waited while she whistled for the dogs and then stalked off, back into the tent.

"We are off-limits until the show opens," the man told the Tillermans.

"We really didn't know," Dicey said.

"Then you're strangers around here." His eyes studied her.

Dicey nodded. Looking at his calm face, with its studying eyes, she said what she was thinking: "Strangers about everywhere."

He looked quizzically at her.

"She had no cause to be angry," Dicey said.

He nodded. "I apologize for that. Claire's got a bad temper – but that's no excuse. Believe it or not, she's a good friend. A good person to have on your side."

"We owe you an apology, too," Dicey answered. "Even if we didn't mean to, we did trespass."

"I'll see you out," he said. "You came through the back? Where are you going, if you don't live in Easton?"

"South," Dicey said.

"Where you from?"

"North."

The man stopped two strides ahead of them and turned to look at them all. His leather boots creaked a little. The Tillermans stood in a row, facing him.

"Are you OK?" he asked.

"Yeah," Dicey said.

"You're not a boy," the man said, walking beside them now. He had a little smile hovering around his mouth.

"No, I'm not," Dicey agreed.

"Do you own this circus?" James asked.

"Yep," he said.

"Why?" James asked.

"It's my living. Name's Will, by the way. I like moving

around, following the good weather."

"I wouldn't think you'd make any money," James observed.

"Why not?" Will asked.

"It's so small."

"That's right enough," Will agreed. "Still..." his warm voice drifted off without finishing the sentence.

At the road he said goodbye. "Good travelling," he said to Dicey.

"Thanks for rescuing us," Dicey said.

"You didn't need help," he answered. "Take care."

"You too," Dicey said.

"Oh I do, you can believe I do," he said. He turned back with a wave. The Tillermans walked away.

They were silent for a long time, each thinking his own thoughts in the steamy afternoon. The road wound through farm country. Here the farms were large. Several fields separated one farmhouse from another. The fields were flat. The farmhouses had only a few trees near them. Big barns and many sheds lay behind the houses. They were prosperous farms, you could tell, because the barns gleamed with fresh red paint and the houses often had swimming pools out front.

Finally, James broke the silence. "She probably figured she could be angry and mean to us and get away with it," he said. "Because we're kids."

"She didn't get away with it," Dicey reminded him. "Sammy? You were ready to run, weren't you?"

"I didn't know what she'd do," Sammy explained. "She said she'd call the police."

"That was smart," Dicey said.

"But—" James started to say, and then he stopped.

They walked on and sang as they walked.

They passed fields and more fields. Some of them had been picked bare. Some of the farms had a cardboard sign posted at their mailboxes: PICKERS WANTED.

At a crossroads, Dicey went into a general store and bought potatoes and tomatoes, a quart of milk and another loaf of bread. She also bought two Cokes in cans, because she was thirsty. All these cost two dollars and thirty-five cents. Except for the forty dollars she didn't want to spend, she was almost out of money.

They shared the Cokes. "We could pick for a day or two," Dicey said to her family, "and get some money."

"Do we need money?" James asked.

"Of course," Dicey said. "I've got some set aside, in case we have to go back to Bridgeport. I don't want to spend that. So we're not out of money, but we need more."

"Would they hire kids?" James asked.

"We could try," Dicey said. "Are you game to try? Could you pick for a day, Sammy?"

"Sure," Sammy said.

Dicey grinned at him. "I believe you could," she said.

"I'll try," Maybeth volunteered.

"I guess so," James said.

"Not today, though," Dicey said. "Today – there's a creek

up a-ways, or down a-ways. I thought we'd camp by that and fish. Somebody has a couple of fishing hours owed us. I will not say who."

"It's me!" Sammy cried. "Because I lost the bet. It's me!"

As they approached the creek Dicey had seen on the map – only the map called it a river – the land developed a few gentle rises. These were not hills like they'd found in Connecticut, not high, sharp hills. They were gentle roundings, mere ripples in the land. In contrast to the flat land all around, however, they stood up. Here, there were hardwood trees, sycamores and maples and oaks, as well as the pines that grew everywhere.

The road went over the little creek, and the Tillermans turned off the road, following the creek's dry banks until they judged they were far enough from the road and farmhouse. Sammy dug a few worms and set himself to fishing. James and Dicey gathered wood for a fire. Maybeth spread out the ponchos under the green trees, as best she could. There wasn't room for more than two of them, because of the roots and bushes and the creek bank.

When everything was ready and they had only to wait for Sammy to catch something, Dicey and James and Maybeth went downstream to wade and wash. Sammy watched them go without a word. He stood very quiet in the centre of the narrow creek, letting the water splash at his hips, holding the fishing line out from his hands.

The late afternoon wore away into early evening. Dicey came back and started the fire. Sammy had caught nothing and reported no nibbles. He was not quite ready to quit trying, he said.

Dicey shoved the potatoes into the fire. The skins would burn, maybe, but she didn't think she could get a pot of water boiling on the small fire she felt safe building.

They ate potatoes, tomatoes, and bread for supper and passed around the carton of milk. There was enough food to fill them, and they kept back some bread and milk for breakfast. James put out the fire, using dirt not water, because water would make more smoke.

The sun was going down, then. It grasped at the land with long yellow fingers and made the mottled trunks of sycamores look like people's skin. Flocks of birds made their evening journeys home, twittering to one another. Far off, an occasional motor sounded.

The Tillermans lay sprawled around with the creek at their feet and the slight hillside behind them. Clouds strayed across the darkening sky.

"You know," Dicey said, "we don't have to go anywhere. We could always travel like this, following the warm weather, like Will said he did. We can take care of ourselves."

"Yeah, but what's the point?" James asked.

"There doesn't have to be a point," Dicey said. "Just doing it. Like sailing."

"We have to go home," Maybeth said.

"Home? We don't have a home," Dicey said.

"I thought we were going to Momma's home," Maybeth said.

"Is that our home too?" Sammy asked.

"I don't know," Dicey said. "that's what we're trying to find out, I suppose. Oh, well," she said, "I guess you're right, James. I mean, you have to go to school."

"So do you." He grinned at her. "So do we all. We're going to grow up. We have to."

"I know. I know," she said.

"If it was Momma's home, it has to be ours too," Maybeth said.

"We have this grandmother there," Dicey answered. "But we can't tell — what she'll think of us. What she'll want. Momma never talked about her," Dicey pointed out.

"Yes, she did," Sammy said, "but it made her sad. She'd cry."

"Is that right? What did she say?"

"I can't remember, only the sadness. I'm sorry, Dicey."

"That's OK. I didn't know Momma ever said anything about her. I just don't know what to expect there."

"Whatever," James said, "we can take care of ourselves. Wherever."

"'I know an old lady, who swallowed a fly,'" Dicey chanted. They sang all the silly songs they knew until darkness had gathered around them. Then they lay down close together and went gently to sleep.

Chapter Five

EARLY THE NEXT morning, after they had buried their rubbish in the soft soil and washed briefly in the creek, they set off. By the time the sun had fully risen, the four children were back on the road.

The morning air tasted cool and clean. At a fork in the road Dicey headed south, because the Choptank River lay to the southeast. This road narrowed and ran straight between fields of tall, ripening corn. They passed farmhouses, barns and occasional weathered grey shacks raised off the ground on piles of bricks. Most of these shacks were guarded by thin dogs that yapped at the children from the shade under the houses.

Many of the fields were being harvested. People moved up and down the rows gathering corn, squashes, tomatoes or cucumbers into bushel baskets. Their heads were wrapped with bright red and blue bandanas. They stooped, squatted or stretched. Even from the road their fatigue was evident.

"Hard work," James remarked.

"We need the money," Dicey said. "But I'm not sure the little kids can do it."

"We don't really need the money, do we? You have the extra."

It was hot. The sun burned high. Dicey was thirsty and impatient. "I don't want to be stuck in Crisfield, James. I don't know how things will go there. We've got to have some extra money. We may need it."

James considered this. "What's our grandmother's name?"

"Abigail. It was in the album."

"Do you think we could go back to Bridgeport? Do you think Cousin Eunice would take us back?"

"I dunno, James."

They passed no stores, no petrol stations, just farms surrounded by outbuildings and old pick-up trucks.

"The map shows towns across the Choptank," Dicey said to her family. "So even if we don't get lunch we can eat after we cross it."

"Does this road go over it?" James asked.

Dicey shook her head.

"Then what are we doing? How're we going to cross it?"

"Swim. Or wade if it's shallow."

"Do you know how wide it is?"

"How could I know that?" Dicey demanded. "Stop asking questions."

Chapter Five

"Why?"

"You're driving me crazy with them, that's why."

James quieted, but his eyes held doubts.

At midday, they saw another sign that said: PICKERS WANTED. Dicey looked down a long dirt driveway that ran between fields of corn turned to the colour of August sunlight. Trees lined the driveway. No house could be seen, although a circle of trees was visible beyond the tops of the corn. "I say we try it," Dicey said. Without waiting for an answer, she turned on to the driveway. They followed her.

The driveway ran straight for about half a mile, then curved to the east. The air was thick and hot. It hummed with the activities of insects. Dicey shifted her bag on to her other shoulder and trudged on. With her free hand she slapped at bugs.

The farmhouse sat within the circle of trees they had seen from the driveway. It was a two-storeyed building covered with pale green asphalt shingles. It had a discouraged look to it.

The Tillermans approached the house slowly. A large, windowless barn, sided in silvery corrugated metal, made one side of the farmyard. The house made a second. Some small sheds made a third. Tall wire cyclone fences lay on both sides of the house itself. The yard was a three-sided cage.

A dog growled and barked, snarled and leaped angrily up against the fencing on the right side of the house. This must be a kennel. This dog needed a kennel. It was a large grey-and-brown creature, bigger than a setter, with a huge slavering mouth. Its teeth hung long and sharp. It charged against the fence, setting up a clamour that would rouse anyone in the house, Dicey thought. She couldn't make herself step any further towards the screen door of the house, not with that dog there, not even to make money.

The screen door opened and a man holding a napkin in his hand stepped out. As soon as he appeared, the dog stopped barking and crouched, fawning and whimpering. The man started towards the children.

He was short and slender. He wore overalls and heavy working boots that laced up the front. The shirt under his overalls was dark blue with fancy red and yellow flowers printed all over it. His face was square and blunt; he had grey hair that he brushed back off his forehead and thin, straight eyebrows over cold eyes. He moved towards the Tillermans without hesitating, without hurrying, and stood silent before them. His skin was tanned and leathery. Deep lines ran across his forehead. He reached his napkin up and wiped his mouth.

"Yeah?" he said.

Dicey spoke. "You have a sign out front, pickers wanted." She hesitated, but he didn't say anything. "We – my brother and me – we'd like to apply." She motioned James to come stand beside her.

The man didn't speak. He studied them, through hard grey eyes.

"We can work hard," Dicey said.

She waited. He didn't speak.

"What do you pay?" she asked.

Chapter Five

"Fifty cents a bushel."

You could pick lots of bushels in a day. That would be OK. "Will you hire us?"

"Yes," he said. "What about the smaller ones?" he asked Dicey.

"They'll come with us and help," Dicey said. "They won't cause any trouble."

"Name's Rudyard," he said. "What's yours?"

"Verricker," Dicey said quickly. That seemed to be all he wanted to know. Except, "What's hers?" he demanded, pointing at Maybeth with his head. "Maybeth," Dicey said.

Something was wrong here, something she couldn't put her finger on. Well, it wasn't her problem; they would work an afternoon and take their money.

He told them to get up into the back of a dusty old pick-up truck the colour of canned peas. He drove them on a flat dirt road that led around the barn and behind it before heading straight up a slight incline, through an overgrown field, to another field. This was a long field of tomatoes. The plants were crowded with weeds, grasses and low vines. You could barely see the rows they had been planted in. But the tomatoes had grown red and plump. They shone out from the weeds like bulbs on a Christmas tree. At one corner of the field, a mound of bushel baskets waited. The Tillermans scrambled down.

Mr Rudyard didn't even get out of the truck. "I'll be by at dark," he said. He backed the truck around and drove off. Dicey watched it go into the distance, back to the barn, then around it and out of sight.

"Creepy," James said.

"You can say that again," Dicey agreed. "Maybeth, you OK?"

Maybeth nodded, wide-eyed.

"How long do we have to stay?" Sammy asked.

They all felt uneasy. Dicey tried to reassure them. "Just this afternoon. Then we'll take our pay and get out of here. OK?"

They got to it. Because they were hungry, Dicey decided they could each eat two tomatoes. That was fair enough, she figured. Then they all worked together, pushing or pulling weeds away from the tomato plants. One would hold back the overgrowth, and the rest would reach in for tomatoes, wresting the fruit from the stems. Their legs and hands and faces were scratched. They had bug bites on every part of their bodies. Dirt was smeared across their faces and arms and legs. They left the filled baskets where they were when they finished with them.

After an hour they had completed one row. Two to a basket, they carried the bushels down to where the pile of empty baskets waited. They had six baskets. "Three dollars," Dicey said.

Dicey's back ached from bending over. Her hands stung where small scratches had accumulated. She had never felt such heat before, an air that closed down over her and made it hard to breathe.

"Hot," James said. "It's too hot, Dicey."

"You two take a break," Dicey said to Sammy and Maybeth. "Go off and explore a little. Stick together, though.

When you're rested, come back and help. Remember our name?"

"Verricker," Sammy said. "What's that?"

"Our father's name," Dicey said.

"That right?" James asked. "How do you know that?"

"So what," Sammy said. "I like Tillerman better."

Sammy and Maybeth wandered off down the edge of the field, going away from the house and the dog. Dicey and James got back to work.

This row took longer. James grew sloppy and Dicey had to nag at him to keep at it and find all the ripe tomatoes that grew on the plants and on the long vines that crawled along next to the dry earth. "My back hurts," he protested. "I'm hot." His face was streaked with dirt and sweat. His eyes wavered between anger and self-pity. He crouched unwillingly by her side.

"It's only for an afternoon," Dicey snapped at him.

Sammy and Maybeth returned before they had finished the row. "There's another field," Sammy reported. "And a river. I wanted to go swimming but Maybeth wouldn't."

"The Choptank," Dicey said.

"Could we swim across it?" James asked Sammy.

Sammy nodded. Dicey shot a triumphant glance at James. "It's not wide," Sammy said. "I could swim it easy."

"Can we go now, Dicey?" Maybeth asked.

Dicey almost said yes. They all looked at her, waiting. She shook her head. "Not before we get paid," she said grimly. "Don't worry, we'll be all right. As long as we're together."

At late afternoon, when the sun was beginning to lower and the mosquitos were beginning to rise, the green pick-up truck returned. The children went eagerly to meet it.

Mr Rudyard had the dog in the front seat with him. He climbed down and pulled on a long rope to get the dog to follow him. The Tillermans crowded together. The dog snarled at them.

"There's a bag in the cab," Mr Rudyard said to Dicey. "The missus said I had to feed you something." He walked off, down to the far end of the field.

"What's he going to do?" Maybeth whispered.

"I dunno," Dicey said. Fear climbed up from her stomach to her throat. A sour, metallic taste was in her saliva and she swallowed it down. She made herself climb up and get the paper bag from the seat of the cab. Mr Rudyard had left the keys in the ignition.

Mr Rudyard tied the dog to a tree, using the end of the long rope. When he came back, Dicey had decided what to do.

"We can't pick any more," she said. "We have to go now," she said.

He looked at her out of cold eyes. Then he said, "If he runs against that sapling it'll snap." He got back into the truck and leaned out the window. "I keep him hungry," he remarked. He backed the truck around and drove off.

In the silence, Dicey could hear insects humming. "What does he *want*?" she demanded.

Nobody could answer her.

Chapter Five

"We might as well eat," Dicey said. They all sat down. Mrs Rudyard had packed a tall thermos of milk and a package of tall biscuits slathered with butter and bright strawberry jam. They passed the thermos around. The biscuits looked delicious. Dicey took a bite of one, and her stomach closed against it. She put it down on the wax paper.

Even James couldn't eat. They looked at one another. "I'm sorry," Dicey said.

"Well, I don't care, I'm not picking any more," Sammy announced. He threw his unfinished biscuit into the pile and they scattered around, like fallen blocks. "And you can't make me," he said to Dicey.

Dicey couldn't help smiling at him and that made her feel better. "I won't try," she said. "James? What can we do?"

"I'd like to kill him and hit him," Sammy said. "He scares Maybeth." Maybeth had big tears in her eyes.

"There's the dog," James said, "and the man." Absentmindedly, he picked up a biscuit. He took a bite, then tossed it down again. "He's crazy, Dicey."

"Bad crazy," she agreed. "Don't get on that truck again, no matter what."

"He wants us to be scared," Maybeth said. "He wants to hurt us."

Dicey nodded. Her mind was working and working, and she couldn't think of anything. James just stared at her. She picked up her maroon bag from where she had put it beside the bushels. She took out all of the money and jammed it into her pocket, with the jackknife. (With a jackknife, if she had to, she could try to fight the man or the dog.) She stuffed the map into the waistband of her shorts.

"We're going to have to run," she said. "When he comes back for the dog. James, you take Maybeth. Maybeth, no matter what, you stick with James." Sammy could take care of himself. "Go for the river."

"What about you?" James asked.

"I'm not sure," Dicey tried to keep her voice normal. She had got them into this mess, and if anyone got caught it should be her. "I'll do something. You just keep ready to run."

It was deep twilight, shadowy and still, when the truck returned. The Tillermans sat where Mr Rudyard had left them. The headlights shone on them briefly. He backed the truck so that its back section was where the filled bushel baskets waited and its nose pointed almost straight down the road to the farmhouse. He got out and looked at them.

"You're not much use," he observed. Maybeth grabbed Dicey's hand as his eyes rested on her. "I'll just have to teach you. Now, load up," he ordered. He walked down to the dog, which barked a greeting.

"How does he know we're alone?" James wondered.

"Quiet," Dicey said. She looked into the cab to see if the keys had been left there. They had. "OK, now listen. When he's to the dog, tell me. And when I say run, you run, all of you, as fast as you can. You hear?"

They nodded. Dicey got up into the truck. She tried to forget about the man at the far corner of the field. She looked for the key and found it. She turned on the engine. Nothing happened. She looked at the transmission box. A needle pointed to D. Quickly, she shifted it to N. "Now, Dicey," James whispered.

She turned the key again, and the engine caught.

Dicey looked back over her shoulder. Mr Rudyard ran towards them, his mouth open in a yell. The dog ran ahead of him, at full cry, but held back by the rope that his master had looped around his shoulder.

"James," Dicey yelled. "Now. Run."

She shifted in D, and turned the wheel so it would head straight down the road to the barn. If she got it started, she figured, the incline would keep it going. She pushed on the accelerator and threw herself out of the cab.

The ground surged up to meet her and the cab door slammed against her shoulder. It hurt, but she didn't have time to worry about that. She rolled on to her feet and looked to see her family, waiting, watching her. "Go!" she shrieked.

Dicey led them into the middle of the tomato field, away from the man and the dog. It was harder running, especially for Sammy with his short legs, but it would be harder for Mr Rudyard too. She let James and Maybeth pass her and slowed until she was behind Sammy too.

They weren't going to go without her. She didn't have time to know how she felt about that. She glanced over her shoulder.

Mr Rudyard was already letting the dog's rope fall from his shoulder as he ran after the truck. He would catch it easily, but how soon? The dog looked after his master for a second and then bent his head to the ground, snuffling something. Probably their scent, Dicey thought, turning her head back and making a burst of speed to catch up.

Across the tomato field, and then across the next field, where young corn made a narrow path for them to follow, they ran. Dicey tried to listen for the sound of the dog behind them, or the sound of the engine coming out of the darkness. But she could hear only their laboured breathing and the stamping of their feet. She charged through the row of brush and small trees that separated the second field from the river, grabbing Sammy's hand, pulling him with her. The earth fell away from beneath her feet and she tumbled into water.

Water closed warm over Dicey's head. She shut her eyes. She held tight on to Sammy's hand. How deep was it?

Her toes touched muddy river bottom and she pushed up. She shot out of the water. It was only up to her chest.

"James? Maybeth?"

"Here," James spoke just beyond her.

"It's warm," Sammy said.

In the distance, a truck engine roared.

"Straight across, then right, downstream. OK? Stay close."

They set out into darkness, paddling quietly across. Through the gentle sounds of water, Dicey could hear their breathing. Dark water was all around them, and the dark land behind, and the dark land ahead. Every now and then she lowered a tentative foot to touch bottom.

The river was no more than fifty or sixty yards across, and

Chapter Five

it wasn't long before Dicey saw the opposite bank rise over her head, capped by a tangle of undergrowth and trees. She put her foot down again. It sank into mud.

Dicey and James were tall enough to touch bottom, but the water was over the heads of the smaller children. So Dicey and James each carried the weight of a younger one floating beside. They made their way cautiously, silently, quickly, downstream. They didn't speak, not even when they heard the man breaking through the bushes behind them upstream.

Sounds of someone walking hastily through underbrush across the river.

James moved doggedly on. Dicey followed him. They were near enough to get out and run, if Mr Rudyard dived into the water to pursue them. They could hide in the bushes on this side. He didn't have the dog with him.

The sounds ceased, as if someone were standing still to listen. James stopped too, but she pushed him on with an impatient hand.

The water gurgled around them.

The crackling sounds began again, hurrying away.

The darkness around Dicey lifted, as if a blanket had been taken off her head. There was no actual change, of course. Only, the night seemed cool and empty, and the clear dark silhouettes of bushes and trees above them seemed to move back to give her more room, and the broad river seemed to float peacefully beside them.

They kept silence for another half hour, working their way down-river. At last, Dicey spoke. "Let's get out – James?

Can you lift Sammy? Sammy? Do you mind being first?"

"Course not," Sammy said.

James hoisted the little boy up on to the bank. Sammy reached down to help Maybeth scramble up. Dicey pushed James from behind, and he turned around to pull her up, while her feet slipped against the muddy bank, searching for firm holds. They sat, huddling together, shivering but not from a chill.

Dicey turned to look behind them, where flat farmlands stretched off. No windows shone, but she could see a pair of headlights, far off, moving on a straight line. There must be a road.

"Not him," Dicey said. She kept her voice low. Danger lurked all around them, always, she knew that now. "It couldn't be him. There aren't but two bridges over the river and they're miles away."

"What about the dog?" Sammy asked.

"Dogs can't track through water," James said.

Dicey remembered the dog, snuffling at the ground for their scents. Then she began to giggle. "It was eating the biscuits!" she cried. "He couldn't get it to chase us because it was hungry. Doesn't that serve him right!"

This set them all giggling, even Maybeth. They kept their laughter low, and after a while they lay back on the grassy bank and slept, close together.

Chapter Six

AT THE FIRST signs of dawn, the first pink glimmers, the first watery bird songs, Dicey opened her eyes. She lay on her back with James on one side and Maybeth curled against the other and Sammy on his belly beside James. Her eyes looked up through the delicate leaves of trees into a depthless sky. She smiled, and her eyes closed.

Later, when they opened again, the sun was fully risen. Faint voices floated to her across the fields that lay behind them. James had rolled away from her. The sky had blued above her. Dicey sat up.

The Choptank danced at her feet, deep and clear. It looked cleaner than any water she had seen. Grasses grew up its banks, and a musical silence stirred in its depths. She followed its path with her eyes to where it wound out of sight, going west.

When they were all awake, even Sammy, and when Dicey had pulled out her jackknife and dried it thoroughly on her shirt and counted her money (handling it delicately so that the damp paper wouldn't rip apart), she gently spread the map before them.

"We're about here," she said. She pointed to a place on the southern bank of the Choptank. "Let's head for that town." Her finger traced a path to a place named Hurlock.

James protested: "Secretary's closer."

"Hurlock's bigger. It's in the right direction," Dicey said. "If he comes after us—"

"You think he will?" Sammy asked.

"I don't know, but I don't want to take any chances."

"It'll be easier to hide in a bigger town," James said.

That was what Dicey was thinking. She was also thinking what a long, unknown way lay between here and Crisfield; and that Crisfield too was unknown.

They cut across fields. The ground underfoot was dry and crumbly, and although they tried to hurry, it was difficult because the furrows rose up to trip them. Walking across fields was like having one leg shorter than the other.

One of the fields they had to cross was being picked. Pickers were scattered among tomato plants that rose up from the tops of furrows. Weeds had been kept down in this field, and the plants had been trained up stakes. It looked like a painting, the ridges of brown earth, tepees of dark green tomato plants with their bright red fruits, the bent figures of the pickers and the blue sky overhead.

Chapter Six

Dicey led her family single file along the edge of this field. She set a brisk pace, so that anyone who saw them would think they had somewhere to be and the right to be where they were. Nobody paid them the slightest attention.

After the field they came to a road. Dicey turned right on it. She wasn't sure of her direction, except that she wanted to go south, away from the river.

So began another morning's march. This part of the journey was often interrupted because at the faintest sound of an engine the Tillermans ducked into the bushes at the side of the road and hid. Dicey didn't have to tell anybody this.

No green pick-up passed them. He would have to search both sides of the river, Dicey thought. If he searched at all.

Their road made a fork with another road, and now they walked on a gravel shoulder. After an hour, they came to a crossroads that had signs. Hurlock was one and a half miles straight ahead. Dicey found herself looking at the houses they passed (whether the buildings were run down or cared for, whether they were small or large, close to the road or set far back) with questions in her mind. Every house was a secret place, a fortress, within which anything might be going on. Every house was perhaps a trap.

They bought a canteloupe from a boy at a roadside stand. Dicey cut it up with her jackknife. They pulled the seeds out with their fingers. The juices ran down their chins as they took huge bites of the warm fruit. It was mild, sweet and chewy. When they had finished it, they heaved the rinds into an empty field and continued on.

An hour later, they reached the outskirts of Hurlock, a dusty, sprawly little town, with one stoplight at its centre. The windows of the stores were crammed with notices of church suppers and house tours. One poster advertised a circus and showed a lion jumping through a hoop. Hawkins Circus, it announced. Admission, $1.50 for adults, $.75 for children. Taped to the bottom was a hand-lettered notice that said that the circus would be in town for two nights only, on the grounds of the elementary school.

Dicey went into the second market, just after the stoplight at the centre of town, and bought milk, peanut butter and bread. When she emerged, she saw James studying the circus poster.

"That's nothing to do with us," she said. He followed her down off the porch. Sammy and Maybeth stood up from the kerb.

A dusty green pick-up drove by them, driven by a square-faced man. The head and shoulders of a large dog were visible sitting beside him. The man and the dog looked straight ahead. The truck headed out of Hurlock, past the stoplight, back towards the Choptank.

Dicey's heart jumped. She clutched the bag of food to her chest.

James watched the back of the green truck. "He didn't see us. I don't think he saw us," he said. "What can he do, anyway?"

Dicey couldn't imagine what Mr Rudyard could do, but

she was afraid he would do something. "Let's run," she said. The elementary school might be on the far side of town. They hadn't passed it coming in. "Come on."

"He didn't even turn around," James protested.

"A circus is here now. There'll be people and if he does turn around and try to do something, we can get help. Call the police, or something."

"They wouldn't believe us."

"Stop arguing, James!"

Dicey grabbed Maybeth's hand and began to run. James and Sammy followed.

They ran along uneven sidewalks in front of stores, then houses. Nobody paid any attention to them. They cut past two women who were meandering along, talking. At corners, Dicey looked quickly up and down for a building that might be an elementary school. It had to be in the town. When she didn't see it, she dashed across. She couldn't go as fast as she wanted because Maybeth's legs were shorter than hers.

At last she saw a modern building that nestled against the ground, down a low sloping hill. Behind the building rose the hoop of a ferris wheel.

The sidewalk they were on went beside a playground, then up to the front door of the school. As the Tillermans, breathing in gasps, were passing the playground, a dusty green pick-up swung into the road that circled before the school entrance.

Dicey swerved on to the grass. "James! Go around

behind!" She grabbed Sammy's arm and pulled him. He struggled to keep his balance at Dicey's pace. Ahead of her, James and Maybeth ran side by side. Maybeth's legs pumped frantically.

Around the corner of the building, Dicey caught sight of the big tent. She pulled Sammy up even with James and Maybeth. "Into the tent," she gasped. They dodged around the base of the ferris wheel. Dicey heard footsteps behind her now and the familiar snarling of a dog.

She turned her head. Mr Rudyard was jogging along easily, pulled by the dog, which he held on a short chain. The rest of the chain he carried looped over his shoulder.

At the open space before the tent, Sammy tripped. He stumbled and fell, rolled over and sat up. Dicey stopped. She turned to face their pursuer. That would give Sammy time.

James and Maybeth had run into the tent. Dicey heard noises from within, voices and the yapping of dogs. She backed towards the entrance. Mr Rudyard slowed his pace to a walk. He took the loops of chain down from his shoulder and began to play them out. The dog strained towards Dicey. She could see the yellow eyes and the saliva dripping from its tongue.

He was going to loose the dog on her.

Dicey put the paper bag up over her chest and throat, ready to jam it down the dog's teeth if he should leap. Dogs went for the jugular. "There are people around here," Dicey panted. Her voice was hoarse. "You can't get away with it."

He didn't seem to hear her. He was intent upon her face

and her slow backing away.

Suddenly, Dicey's legs were shoved from behind. Her knees buckled and she fell on the ground, flat on her back. She dropped the bag. Up she sprang to her feet, still facing Mr Rudyard. He was not the kind of man you could turn your back to.

Three white terriers had charged out from behind her, bowling her over in their excitement. They yapped and yipped, happily. They ran up to the big dog, holding their tails up like little flags. The big dog snarled, growled and dived into their midst. A cacophony of noise burst out of the mass of tumbling dogs.

Claire rushed out from behind Dicey. She laid into the dogs, cracking her whip. The terriers danced away. Claire played her whip around the ears and eyes of the big dog, forcing him backwards until he stood at Mr Rudyard's side.

Dicey turned around then. She saw a ring of people, with Will at the centre and James beside him. Two men were dressed as clowns; three more large, muscular men in jeans and workshirts inched forward with clenched fists; a girl in ballet tights stood tensely beside an older man who wore glasses and chewed on a fat cigar.

Claire looked Mr Rudyard in the eye. In her high heels, she was six inches taller than he was. "Hold your dog," she said.

His hand took the leather collar. Dicey edged towards James.

"Where you going?" Mr Rudyard's voice demanded. He

surveyed the group. "They're my kids, foster kids," he said.

"No, we're not," Dicey said. She turned to Will. "We're not, you know that."

"You in charge?" Mr Rudyard asked Will. He sounded surprised.

"I am," Will said. He stepped up beside Dicey.

"They gotta come back," Mr Rudyard said. "I got papers."

"What kind?"

"Legal papers."

"Show me," Will said.

"I've got them back home," Mr Rudyard said.

Dicey looked at James. She saw Maybeth and Sammy standing in the gloom just within the tent entrance. They could still run, maybe. How did Will know what was true? How could he possibly know they were telling the truth? He seemed to be thinking about what Mr Rudyard was saying. Nobody knew the Tillermans, except back in Bridgeport, nobody even knew they were alive. Why should anyone care what happened to them?

And how was Dicey going to keep them safe?

"I want them kids back now," Mr Rudyard said.

"I'd need to see those papers first," Will answered slowly. He took a couple of steps forward. His boots creaked.

Dicey's legs felt watery.

"I said, I'll take them now." Mr Rudyard's voice was steely and he didn't bother to disguise the threat.

"I don't think so," Will said, still slowly. "Not until I see the papers."

Mr Rudyard loosened his hand on the dog's collar.

"I wouldn't," Will said, still slowly. "Claire here – she's got one nasty temper – and a good hand with a whip. That so, Claire?" Claire smiled. "And I've been chased by dogs myself often enough not to be overly scared of them. Animal dogs or human dogs."

"Nigger!" Mr Rudyard hissed the word.

Will didn't move a muscle of his face or body, but the three big men behind him did. Claire, however, was the one who attacked. She moved smoothly, like a snake. She cracked her whip before her, at the dog's feet and chest, at his head. The dog whined and growled and backed away. Mr Rudyard was forced to move with him.

Claire moved steadily forward. She cracked the whip again, at Mr Rudyard's feet, then at his knees, then at his hand where he held the dog, then at his shoulders. He was wearing another fancy shirt, red with long white fringes hanging from the shoulders. Claire snapped the whip at one shoulder then the other, back and forth.

He backed steadily away from her. His eyes burned cold at her.

"Get out," she said. She didn't shriek it, she hissed it. "You make me sick."

Mr Rudyard looked as if he wanted to say something. Instead, he spat into the dust at his feet. Then he turned his back to them and walked slowly away, the dog at his side. Claire lifted the whip and snapped it sharply against his behind. He leapt forward.

Dicey held herself stiff until she heard the engine of the truck start, and then longer, until she saw the truck pull up the long slope before the school building and turn back to town. Then she let her legs collapse underneath her.

The people drifted away, leaving Claire, Will, the Tillermans and the three terriers, who ran happily in circles.

"Well, Claire," Will said.

"Well, Will," she answered, looking him straight in the eye. Her cheeks were red.

"I always said you've got quite some temper."

"You could use a little of it," she said shortly. "I'm going back to work."

Will turned to the Tillermans. "Why don't we talk this thing over?" He sat down beside Dicey. James, Maybeth and Sammy joined them. Dicey kept trying to speak, but her voice caught in her throat and she couldn't make words come out. The others waited for her to say something first.

"What's in the bag?" Will asked. "Food? Lunch?" Dicey nodded. "Go ahead and eat. If you've got enough, I'd like something too. I seem to have a bad taste in my mouth."

Making the sandwiches relaxed Dicey. It was such an ordinary thing to do. She spread the peanut butter with her jackknife then wiped the blade clean on her shorts. She made everybody one sandwich and two for James. She opened the milk and set it on the ground.

"We're not foster kids," James finally said. "That's the truth. He — it's so crazy I wouldn't blame you if you didn't believe it — we took jobs as pickers and—"

Chapter Six

"He never paid us!" Dicey realized.

Will chewed contentedly on his sandwich. "Happens I do believe you. That was one mean man."

"Boy, was he," Dicey said. Her voice had returned. "We – thanks, you know?" He waved that away with a hand.

"My idea is you ought to stay with us awhile," Will said. "We're going south to Salisbury for our next shows, then Berlin. After that down to Virginia. Where *are* you headed for? You ought to tell me. Don't you think?"

"We can work," Dicey said. "We can help out. We could pay you, too."

"Let's start somewhere solid," Will said, smiling. "Like names. I'm Will Hawkins."

Dicey introduced them. She picked up her sandwich and began to eat. Between bites, she told their destination, as briefly as she could, not about Momma and the journey to Bridgeport, nor about leaving Cousin Eunice's house, but about Crisfield and the grandmother there they'd never met and about needing some kind of home. He listened, nodded, asked no questions and made himself another peanut butter sandwich.

"We've got two nights here and then we break. We'll be a week in Salisbury," he said. "What say you stay with us and we run you down to Crisfield one of the days in Salisbury? That OK?"

"That's fine," Dicey said. "That's great. But do you have room for us?"

"It's a bit primitive. We live in trailers – you could go in with Claire."

"Wouldn't she mind?"

"I don't think so. I'll have to ask her, of course. But she has all those dogs in there, I don't see four kids would make such a big difference."

"We can sleep anywhere," Dicey said. "As long as we're together."

"We'll have to think some what to do about him," Will said. "But not now. I've got work to do now. Stick around – hear me? He might come back."

"I know," Dicey said. "We'll stay close."

They stayed near the tent all that afternoon. Sammy hung around Claire until she finally let him help her by holding hoops and moving the little stools the dogs perched on. James went to watch the man with the cigar who operated the ferris wheel. Soon, he too was working busily, passing tools and squirting oil. Dicey and Maybeth cleared away litter from the midway. They ate supper back where the trailers were parked, at a campsite that had only three trailers on it. Each of these had a picture painted on its side of a lion jumping through a flaming hoop and the words Hawkins Circus spelled out in bright letters. "But there aren't any lions," Dicey said to James. He shrugged.

At dinner, Maybeth helped with the serving and clearing. Dicey wanted to help too, but the cook, a tiny black woman with her hair grown out into an afro, said the two of them were just fine and she didn't think she'd ever had a better assistant. When Will asked them, James told how they met up with Mr Rudyard. "We were walking down the road," James began, "feeling pretty good." Everybody listened. Dicey sometimes forgot to eat because she was so interested, as if this was a story that had happened to somebody else.

That night they went to the circus with Mattie, the cook, who was married to one of the big men Dicey noticed earlier, a man named Samson whose head was entirely bald even though he wasn't at all old. Dicey insisted on paying for all their rides and games, as if they were real customers. She'd finished worrying about money. While she had it she didn't need to worry. When she ran out, she would earn some more. They sat in the front row for the show. They clapped for Claire, who looked like the Snow Queen in the fairy tale, white and glittering. They smiled at Will in his black cape with red lining and a tall hat he swept off his head. They gasped when the tightrope walker fell off into a net and cheered when she climbed right back up to try again.

The Tillermans slept in Claire's trailer, James and Maybeth on the second bunk, Sammy among the nestled pile of terriers, Dicey on the floor. When Dicey awoke the next morning, she saw filmy shadows, as if the inside of the trailer was swathed in veils. She awoke to the quiet sounds of seven creatures deep in sleep. For a while, she lay and listened.

James turned restlessly, uneasily, and the sheets rustled around him. Maybeth was still. One of the dogs yipped gently: Dicey raised her head and saw his little legs moving as he lay on his side with his eyes closed. What did dogs dream? Sammy had an arm around another of the dogs. All that

Dicey could see of Claire was her hair spread out on the pillow. She snored gently, like the waves on Long Island Sound, soft and regular.

Making no noise, Dicey slipped out to sit on the metal trailer steps. Animals stirred, birds and squirrels, two timid rabbits. Distant motors stirred beyond Dicey's sight. The branches of the tall pines stirred in a rain-bearing wind. These pines were not like the thick, cone-shaped trees of New England. On these pines, the needles hung like pompoms in sparse clusters along lank branches. As the trees grew taller the lower branches fell off, so they grew into giant lollipops. Loblollies, Will called them, and it was a good name for them.

Mr Rudyard could have caught the Tillermans so easily. Were they just more stupid and helpless than most people? And what about this farm they were going to, their grandmother's farm? When you walked down a road, you could be walking to anything. Anything. What if this grandmother, too…

Well then, Dicey thought, they would beg to return to Cousin Eunice, and Dicey would know enough to be grateful, really grateful, for someone who took them in and meant to take care of them. Cousin Eunice wasn't perfect, and she wasn't Momma, but they could work things out with Cousin Eunice.

If she would. Maybe she wouldn't take them back. Maybe, maybe, maybe.

A squirrel up in a tall oak tree set up a terrific chittering. He was furious, frantic. His tail thrashed up and down.

What good did it do, worrying and making plans, and

Chapter Six

more plans, if the first plans failed. It was like money. If you had it, good. If you didn't, then you had to find a way to earn it. There was nothing to be gained by fretting over maybes.

Dicey took a deep breath, which tasted of dampened sunlight and moist earth. They were living with a circus for a day or so. For a day or so they were safe. Something would happen after, but that was after. You had to keep alert and watchful, she'd learnt that. You had to be ready to run. But if you wasted every day worrying about the next... And you never knew what was coming, anyway.

After breakfast, Will took Dicey into town. "To get some stuff," he said, "and see someone." The stuff, as it turned out, was clothing for the Tillermans, underpants (three new pairs each, because they came in packets of three), T-shirts and shorts. Will also got toothbrushes, toothpaste and a comb. They dropped the packages in the windows of Claire's big white estate car. Then Will insisted on buying popsicles, which they ate as they walked to visit somebody, a friend of his who was a Reverend. Will explained to the Reverend about Mr Rudyard, and Dicey listened. The Reverend said he thought he could speak a word to the sheriff about it. He asked Dicey if she was sure she didn't want to speak to the sheriff herself. "She can't," Will said, and the Reverend didn't ask any more questions.

As they walked back to the car, Dicey said, "I used to think that everyone was the same, pretty much like us. They're not though, are they?"

"Not a bit of it," Will answered. A minute later he added, "Everybody's different, and everybody thinks everybody else is the same and they're the only one different." He smiled at Dicey then. "We've done the most we can, just about," he told her.

Back at the circus, Sammy dashed up to tell Dicey that he was going to be in the show with Claire, helping, as long as they stayed with the circus, that Claire thought he would be funny and he thought so too, that Maybeth and Mattie were making him a costume with spangles on it, like Claire's. James was busy with the machinery that ran the carousel. Dicey spent the day drifting around. She had passing, lazy conversations with people. After a conversation, she would walk away slowly and sit somewhere private to think over what she'd heard. She would sit and watch the people moving about, like characters on a TV screen with the sound off.

She was alone all afternoon. The sky got heavier with rain, but no rain fell. It was a grey afternoon, the kind of grey that darkens and deepens the greens of leaves and grasses. She had nothing to do, and she didn't want anything to do. Her thoughts whirled among bits of information and ideas that crowded into her brain, and blew about there, like dry leaves in a storm.

Sammy came to find her late in the afternoon. She was sitting in the grass by the playground, pulling out the blades and looking at them. But she wasn't seeing them, she was seeing the windy dunes at Provincetown and all the days they had lived there.

"Time for supper, Dicey," Sammy said. "What're you doing?"

"Thinking." He hadn't entirely awakened Dicey from her reverie. He stood in front of her, and she saw him and did not see him.

"Thinking what?"

"About Momma."

"We gotta go now." He tugged at her hand. He had already forgotten about Momma, Dicey thought, and probably that was better for him.

"I dream about her," Sammy said, hurrying Dicey back to Claire's station wagon. "A lot."

So he hadn't forgotten: and Dicey knew that, whatever anyone wiser or smarter might say, she didn't want him to forget. "What do you dream?" she asked.

"Nothing special. She's just there, in the dreams." He ran ahead.

That night, the tightrope lady fell off the wire in the same way, and the audience gasped in the same way and applauded with the same enthusiasm when she climbed back up the tall ladder. Dicey realized then that the fall was part of the act. The fall was as flawless as all the rest of the steps. It was a fake. Like the lion on the poster and the glittering costumes that made everybody look beautiful. Like the way everyone laughed at Sammy because they thought he was making mistakes with the dogs, when it was really part of the act. Like the way Maybeth looked like a princess when she circled under the cascading lights of the carousel. Fake.

Dicey looked at James. He shrugged his shoulders at her. He didn't care. But Dicey did, she discovered. It wasn't that she minded, exactly. Not exactly – because she had done too much lying of her own to mind about this. But – they didn't need to lie, did they?

The circus days floated by. They drove through the rain to Salisbury and set up the tent and booths in the rain. Dicey didn't do anything much, she didn't even go to the shows after the second night. James and Maybeth and Sammy were busy and contented.

Contentment was too small a word for what Dicey was feeling. They had food and a warm place to sleep, and Dicey had money in her pocket. They were travelling and had purpose and destination, but no conclusion. Dicey had nothing to worry about. Nothing except what lay ahead, in Crisfield, and she didn't want to think about that any more. She had thought all she could about that. You couldn't know what lay ahead. How could you know that? How could Dicey expect herself to know what this grandmother would be like? She couldn't; she realized that at last. She would have to wait and see. That part was easy, the waiting and the seeing.

These circus days drifted slowly. It would be something to live in a circus, Dicey thought, always moving around, always heading for somewhere new. If it was Dicey's circus, she would go everywhere. She planned it out to herself, alone in Claire's trailer at night, with the noise from the fairgrounds behind her. First, all around the United States, then up to Canada and down to Mexico. She would make her circus get famous and get jobs in Europe, and maybe even China or Japan. They'd have trailers for land travel and a ship of their own for sea travel. She would have real lions.

Day after lazy day, night after long dreaming night passed Dicey by.

Chapter Seven

LATE ONE MORNING, as Dicey stood in a blazing sunlight where the tent had been the night before coiling up the long ropes so that Samson could stack them evenly on the truck and find them when he needed to stake down the sides of the tent that evening in Berlin, James and Maybeth and Sammy approached her.

"Hey," James said.

"I don't need any help," Dicey told him. "Go on and do what you like."

"Are we going to Crisfield?" James asked. "We're all ready. We packed our things into a paper bag and your map too. Will says he can take us now, in Claire's car."

"Is it time?" Dicey asked.

"Will says so," James said.

"Let me just finish this, OK?"

Chapter Seven

More goodbyes, Dicey thought to herself, coiling up the last rope into a dark brown hoop, piling loop upon loop. "I am unfond of goodbyes," she said to herself. All of their goodbyes lay like the coiled ropes on the ground, connected and unconnected, curling silently, finished things.

But the kids were right, and Will was right. It was time.

Dicey took a deep breath. Time to get moving.

She sat beside Will in the front seat. James and the little kids sat behind him. Dicey took out her map. Time to put the circus behind them.

The circus people stood around and waved and made jokes. Dicey looked around at them, gathering together there in the fairground, their hands held high, their friendly wishes for good luck floating around the car still, like cherry blossoms blowing down to the ground. The car pulled out of the fairgrounds. "Goodbye," everybody called. "Goodbye, goodbye."

After a while, Dicey turned to the map. There was nothing to look at on the road. It was just like Route 1. "What route are we on?" she asked Will.

"Thirteen. We follow that to just south of a place called Princess Anne, then get onto Three-thirteen," Will said. "How do you figure to find her?"

"Look up the address in a phone book," Dicey answered. "Then we'll ask directions."

"We've got lots of time," Will assured her. "All I have to do is go back, pick up Claire and the beasts and the trailer and make it to Berlin in time for supper."

"Are you going to take us right there?" Dicey asked.

He didn't turn his head. His profile was smooth lines, slightly curved except where his nose jutted out and his beard jutted out at the end of his chin. His skin was smooth and brown, like silk. He didn't answer, just nodded.

"But why?" Dicey asked.

"To make sure you're OK," he said.

Dicey looked out the window. City clutter had fallen behind and now there was country clutter, junkyards, a trailer park, billboards advertising dog food and faraway hotels. Beyond these the land stretched away to low, flat country. The fields and woods all had shallow ditches dug around them to drain away water. Most of the land was being used for farms, interspersed with patches of loblollies and other trees.

"Crisfield's a small town," Dicey said to Will. "We'll be OK."

"You don't want me to take you right there, do you?"

Dicey leant towards him. "It's not that. It's — she doesn't even know about us. Not only that we're coming, but she doesn't even know we exist. We didn't know about her until our cousin in Bridgeport told us we had a grandmother. And — I don't know how she'll be. There was this priest in Bridgeport. He had somebody here come to see her and tell her. She wouldn't let him in, or listen. He said she screamed so she couldn't hear what he was saying. So I don't know how she'll act. Momma..." her voice faded away.

"There's a lot you haven't told me, isn't there?" Will asked.

"Yes." Dicey thought. "It gets so complicated."

Chapter Seven

"I'll tell you what," Will said. "How do you want to do it? I'll go along with you if you'll make me one promise. You keep your promises?"

"Yes."

"If you'll promise me that you'll come to me if you need help. We'll be in Berlin for a week, four shows and then three days off on the beaches. The police can always find me if you call. Will you promise?"

Dicey thought about that. "But what could you do?"

"Who knows? What do friends do for each other? Something. Whatever. Will you promise?"

"OK," Dicey said. "I promise."

"We'll be coming by again in eight months – but anything can happen in eight months. I can't just dump you kids off. Not and forget about you. I can't do that. But I can let you do it your own way if I know you'll call me if you need to – if it's not working out."

"Why?" Dicey asked. "I mean, why should you bother? You have your own life."

"You're a little bit of my life now. You can't get away, and I can't get rid of you. That's a fact."

Dicey understood. A lot of people had little bits of her life now, and they were tied to her now, or she was tied to them. To some of them, she owed something that she hadn't paid yet, like Windy and Stewart, or Cousin Eunice. You didn't just let people go, that's what Will meant. You always did what you could.

Dicey leant back into her own corner by the door. Well.

"What I thought was," she said, "we'd go downtown and find out where she lives. Then just go out there." That was almost the truth.

"And you want me to leave you off and drive away," Will said. Dicey had no idea what he was thinking. "Are you scared?" he asked her.

"Some."

"Why?"

"It's a last chance for us," Dicey said.

"I don't know about that," Will said slowly. "You could say all of life is a series of last chances."

"OK," Dicey said, "but inside of houses – no matter what they look like from outside – even that one" – the car sped past a tall brick house, surrounded by old elm trees and seeming serene and wise, as if it had stood there for so many years that nothing could surprise or hurt it – "you can't tell what's inside. You can't tell what might happen. How do you know who to trust when you meet people? How can I tell about this grandmother? I know *I* can always run, but when there are four of us…"

"Wouldn't it be easier if I stuck with you?" Will asked.

Dicey shook her head. "Well, yes, of course it would. But I have to know by myself, for us."

"OK," Will said. "OK. You can have it your way."

As they neared Crisfield, entered the town limits, followed the main street, they all fell silent. Dicey could almost hear the worries that nobody said aloud. The air inside the car grew thick with them.

Chapter Seven

The road ran straight and broad until it came to the water. They looked around. Docks, most of them vacant now on this summer morning, stretched out into the bay. Sheds lined the land's edge. Piles of small wire boxes were everywhere, and oyster shells had been scattered like a layer of earth. A few people, mostly old men, sat in the sunlight, looking at nothing.

"Well," Dicey said.

"We'll meet again." Will turned to her. "One way or another. OK?"

"OK!" Sammy said.

The Tillermans climbed out of the car. They stood at the road's end by the water's edge. Will backed the car, turned it around, looked out the window to give them the thumbs-up signal, and drove away.

Until the car was out of sight, the Tillermans didn't move. Dicey held the grocery bag in one hand, and the other hand she held up in farewell, until she could no longer see the square back of the car.

They were on their own again.

"OK," Dicey said. She passed the bag to James. "You wait here. I'm going to find a phone book." She didn't wait for anything, not even to study the flat expanse of blue water. She walked back along the docks to the sidewalk and entered a grocery store. There was a poster in its window advertising Will's circus.

The store was filled with darkness, dust and the smell of the food on its shelves. Dicey stood inside the screen door for a minute, while her eyes adjusted to the dim light. The only person in the store was a woman in a stained apron behind a glass-framed counter. Dicey walked up to her. The woman had thick strong arms and her hands were mottled red. Her face was pale and thick with flesh. Her eyebrows were straight and bushy over little colourless eyes.

"Yeah?" she asked, leaning her elbows on the top of the counter. "What can I get you?" Her words came thick and slow, like molasses – again, something like Momma.

"I'm looking for a phone book," Dicey said. "Do you have one I can look at?"

The woman nodded. She plodded out from behind the meat counter and walked heavily down to the cash register at the front of the store. She pulled out a thin phone book from underneath the counter there. She watched Dicey open it.

There was a Peter Tillerman on a place called Deal Island, and a G. Ridgely Tillerman in Princess Anne. There was no Abigail Tillerman. There was no A. Tillerman, either.

Maybe their grandmother didn't have a phone. Or maybe it was listed under their grandfather's name. Only, there was no Tillerman listed for Crisfield.

Dicey looked at the page and chewed on her lip.

None of the Tillermans listed lived in Crisfield. Was her grandmother still here?

Yes, because that priest had gone to see her. He would have told Father Joseph if she'd moved or died. He knew where she lived.

"Something wrong?" the woman asked.

"I got work to do," the woman continued, to prod Dicey. She leant down on the counter as if she needed the rest.

"I was looking for the telephone number for Abigail Tillerman," Dicey said.

"Why would you do that?"

"I was going to call her up. To see if she needed some help around the place," Dicey said.

"I've never seen you before," the woman remarked.

"We're new," Dicey said. "We just moved in."

"Ab won't hire you," the woman said. "She's letting the farm go."

"Selling it?" Dicey asked.

"Naw, she'd never sell that place. But she can't work it by herself."

"That's why I thought she might hire me," Dicey said.

The woman shook her head, closed up the phone book and put it away. "Besides, she hasn't had a phone since Bullet died. If you'd asked me I'd of told you. She came down and threw her phone through the telephone company window. You don't want to work for her."

The woman trudged back down the aisle to the meat counter. Dicey stood where she was, listening to the hum of a large refrigerator.

"Where is her farm, anyway?" she called to the back of the store.

"Down to the water, south," the woman answered.

"What road?"

"Landing Neck. It goes off South Main, half a mile inland.

Maybe a mile. There's a bend on Landing Neck, and a new little house sits right on it. Next mailbox is Ab's. But it's seven miles. I wouldn't go out there. She's strange."

"Strange?"

"Crazy as a coot, that's my opinion. We leave her alone. You should too."

"Maybe you're right," Dicey said.

"No maybes about it."

Dicey left the store. She returned to her family. Their eyes held the same question.

Dicey sat on the edge of the dock, hanging her feet over the water. James, Maybeth and Sammy sat in a line beside her. You couldn't see the bottom of the water. It was muddy, so you could only see a little way down into it. The waves gurgled underneath them.

More bad news, Dicey thought to herself. But why didn't she feel bad? She looked around at the docks and the dozing men and the water and the shacks. She picked up an oyster shell and dropped it into the water.

The air smelt of salt and fish and motor oil.

"You know what this is like?" Dicey asked James. "It's like Provincetown. Isn't it? It smells like it."

"Yeah. What about our grandmother?"

"She lives seven miles out of town, on Landing Neck Road. She doesn't have a telephone."

"How do we get there?"

"I don't know yet. But I thought… James, I want to go out there alone. Just in case. I want you to stay here with the kids. And I'll come back for you when I know."

"Know what?"

"If it's OK for us there."

"I don't like that, Dicey. What if you get in trouble?"

"Better just me than all of us, right? Will said we could call the Berlin police to get him if we need help. So if I don't come back then you can call him. Here's the money, for lunch and anything. Can you keep an eye on Maybeth and Sammy?"

"Yeah, but I don't like it."

"I'm in charge, James. Remember."

"OK. But…"

Dicey gave him the money she had left, nine dollars. She leant over to talk to Maybeth and Sammy. "You do what James says. You hear?"

They both nodded.

"That's all right then," Dicey said. She stood up quickly and hurried away, without looking back.

The business section of Crisfield lay next to the water, low buildings with big plate glass windows. The business section crowded as close as it could to the bay and looked out over the docks, as if that was where its real interest lay. Beyond that, residential streets branched out, circling around the town itself.

There seemed to be three kinds of houses. There were lots of churches, even on the one street Dicey followed out of town. These were mostly small stucco or clapboard buildings with short steeples. Then, there were the usual narrow clapboard houses on little handkerchief lawns, two storeys high, two rooms wide. The third kind were large wooden houses with broad porches that ran around the buildings; they had odd shapes, round towers, octagonal bays, balconies. These houses had paint that had faded and peeled. Often, their screens were ripped or doors hung askew. But they spoke clearly of what they had once been: once they had been homes for large, rich families; once the spiralled pillars that held up the verandah roofs had gleamed with white paint; once the tall windows of the ground floors had opened into rooms crammed with plush furniture and oriental rugs, and the large trees in the yards swarmed with climbing children. These were the kind of houses that might have treasures in the attic, or ghosts in the cellar. These were the kinds of houses that could burst with life. Now they rotted quietly, neglected, sad, but filled with mysterious memories.

Dicey walked on, walking fast. She turned at the second stop sign and found herself on Landing Neck Road, in farm country, where broad fields burgeoned with corn or barbed wire contained cows and horses, where chickens and ducks wandered around the yards. The farmhouses sat next to the road, quiet and clean, secretive.

How would she know if their grandmother's house was safe for them? What questions did you ask a person to find out if you could like one another? If she could be trusted?

Dicey's sneakers made no noise on the roadway. No cars overtook her. There was no sound at all, except the occasional distant barking of a dog or lowing of a cow. The silence wrapped around her like a quilt, a silence made up of trees growing and corn ripening, of the bright sky glowing and the distant water following its tides. This was not an empty silence.

Six miles outside of town, Dicey came to the expected bend in the road. A low, one-storey white house looked out from a stand of pines. Behind it were stables. Two pastures, where long-legged horses grazed, came next.

Half a mile down the road, Dicey saw the mailbox, dented, rusted, its post awry; *llerma* was all that remained of sloppily painted black letters. The little door hung open, like a dog's straw tongue. Two or three old leaves lay inside, and a plastic glass with a straw sticking out of its cover.

Across the road, where the farm itself lay, overgrown fields stretched back to meet a thick wood of pine trees, oaks and tall, top-heavy loblollies. The fields had small trees scattered over them, pine and maple saplings, and the grass was thick and tangled, as tall as Dicey's waist.

The driveway ran straight between the fields. It too was overgrown. You could barely make out the ruts where car wheels would fit.

The sun had risen high into the sky. Dicey turned into the driveway, walking slowly now, even reluctantly. She did not look ahead, but at the ground before her feet. Abandoned, that was the word this farm said to her.

She couldn't even see the house until she had passed under the pines, walking now on a thick carpet of needles that seemed never to have been disturbed. The air under the pines was thick and shady.

The house sat behind a small orchard, and beyond it, a barn was slowly falling down. The house was faded white clapboard, two storeys high, and had a screened porch all along the front that ran around the sides. The roof, grey slate, slanted down in four directions from a central peak. Two chimneys stuck up through the roof.

The house was silent, vacant, neglected. Long weedy grass grew up, as high as the porch floor. Honeysuckle spread over the screens of the porch, and its long fingers reached for the trees in the yard. Most of the trees were short, heavily leaved. Some had tiny apples growing on them. They had the rough bark of fruit trees.

One larger tree grew right up in front of the house, hiding the front door, shading the lawn. This tree looked like an umbrella, held overhead by four trunks that spread out from their common source. Its broad leaves made a green canopy against the sunlight. It wouldn't be a good climbing tree, Dicey thought, walking up to it and past it, but you could make a platform tree house to rest on the four trunks and build steps out of pieces of wood to go up one trunk. Then, you would have a house like a boat, almost floating on air, and the long, leafy branches stretching above like sails.

Dicey pushed her way through the long grasses to the steps leading to the porch. The grass tickled her knees. Grasshoppers leapt aside to let her pass.

The steps were rotting away. The screen door hung from broken hinges. The sun couldn't penetrate the honeysuckle leaves, so the motionless air on the porch was as dark as twilight.

Dicey knocked on the door. It was a wooden door, once painted white. A rusted nail stuck out from its centre, over Dicey's head.

Nobody answered. She knocked again and listened. She heard faint noises, like some night creature scurrying. But the noises did not come towards the door.

Somebody was in there, of that Dicey was sure. She knocked again, three loud raps. No voice called out. Dicey turned the knob and pushed against the door. It was locked.

She went back across the porch and down the steps. She walked around to the side of the house.

The side looked just like the front, except that it had no steps or door. There were two windows on the second floor and four on the first, which were barely visible through honeysuckle. The honeysuckle here had not grown as fast as that on the front of the house. The porch, she noticed, continued around the back. The whole house was surrounded by a broad porch.

All the second storey windows had their shades down. Nobody could be seen inside, nor any light. Dicey went on, around to the back.

She saw the woman the moment the woman saw her. The woman sat on the bottom of some steps facing out, over more fields (only these had crops growing in them) and the distant dull green of marsh grass. She wore a shapeless blouse over a long, shapeless skirt. Her feet were bare.

Her dark eyes looked at Dicey angrily. Her skin was tanned. Her hair had been hacked short, so its iron grey curls burst helter-skelter all over her narrow head.

Dicey stood where she was. She swallowed, twice. Her throat was suddenly dry.

"Mrs Tillerman?" she finally asked. Her voice squeaked.

"You're trespassing," the woman said. She had a thin, stiff voice, not like Momma's at all.

"I thought I heard – when I knocked – I didn't know if—" Dicey stepped forward. "The fact is, I wonder if you would hire me to work for you." She stood right in front of the woman now. Her grandmother.

Her grandmother's eyes seemed big for her face as she stared at Dicey. But maybe that was just because her face was small, the skin stretched tight over its bones. Her eyes, now that Dicey was closer, were not brown but dark hazel, browns and greens without any yellow to give them sparkle. Fine lines sprayed out from around her eyes.

These were the eyes of the girl in Cousin Eunice's photograph album. The rest of her was all different, but the eyes were the same.

"The fact is you're trespassing," her grandmother said. "Who told you to come here?"

"Nobody. I heard you were alone – so I thought I'd try."

"I don't know you, do I?"

Dicey shook her head. "We're new here."

"Why aren't you in school?"

"It's summer."

Chapter Seven

"Not for long."

Her grandmother stood up. She walked up the steps and through the screen door, without looking back. The back door stood open, and she went straight into a kitchen.

Dicey followed her.

Her grandmother opened a glass-fronted cupboard and pulled down a can of spaghetti. She took a can opener out of a drawer and opened the can. A saucepan waited on the stove. She opened another drawer, took out a big spoon and scooped the stiff red and yellow contents of the can into the saucepan. With a match, she lit a fire under the burner. She dropped the match into an ashtray and turned to take a bowl out from the cupboard.

Dicey might just as well not have been there.

Her grandmother waited by the stove, stirring in the pan. "I didn't say come in," she said.

"You never said if you want me to work," Dicey answered.

Hazel eye studied Dicey. Dicey studied the barefooted woman. Her feet were caked with earthy dirt.

"How do I know you're not going to rob me?" her grandmother said.

How could she know? Dicey thought. The people in the houses were in just as much danger as the people outside the houses. "I'm not," Dicey said. "It doesn't look like you have much to steal anyway."

"You have family?"

"Yes," Dicey said.

"Where do you live?"

"In town. I can work hard. Your barn needs painting, and the screens and the steps, and the lawn. I could take off the honeysuckle."

"I'm not too old to do that."

"I can pick and weed."

"So can I. So can anybody. You better get down a bowl, since you've invited yourself for lunch."

Dicey did as she was told.

They sat down at a long table, big enough for ten people. It was made of wood and had been scrubbed to a pale, smooth finish. Dicey sat across from her grandmother. She spooned the canned spaghetti into her mouth. After the first bite, she ate quickly, trying to fill up her stomach without tasting anything.

"You like spaghetti?" her grandmother asked.

"No," Dicey said. "But I'm hungry. Do you like it?"

"It's easy to fix. You know what I sometimes think?" Her grandmother looked straight at her, her mouth chewing. "I sometimes think people might be good to eat. Cows and chickens eat corn and grass and turn it into good meat. People eat cows and chickens. In people, it might turn into something even better. Do you ever think that?"

Dicey shook her head.

"Especially babies," her grandmother said. She swallowed thoughtfully. "Or children. Do you have brothers and sisters?"

"Yes."

"Who told you I was alone?"

"A lady in the grocery store."

"Millie. She's the butcher. Can you imagine that? A lady butcher."

"Why not?" Dicey asked.

"I guess you might say so. Millie is one, and that's a fact. Facts are facts. What did she say about me?"

"Nothing much."

"Did she tell you I was crazy?" Her grandmother wasn't looking at her.

Dicey didn't answer.

"Maybe I am. You know? When you die all the gases build up in your body for weeks. Like yeast in dough. And you swell and swell. Then things start exploding. That's where the stink comes from. After that, you're fresh as a daisy, and the worms and maggots have you. What do you think?"

Dicey put her spoon down. She couldn't eat any more.

Her grandmother's mouth twisted. "What do you think about death? Don't be smart with me, girl."

Dicey was puzzled.

"Or don't you think?"

"I saw a tombstone. *Home is the hunter, home from the hill and the sailor home from the sea*: that was what it said. As if" — Dicey tried to explain her thoughts — "that was the quiet place at the end of things."

"It's not quite," her grandmother said. "Not for the worms."

"I wouldn't care about that if I was dead," Dicey said.

"Maybe I am crazy," her grandmother said. "You know?"

Dicey was beginning to think she might be.

"Maybe not. Do you feel sorry for me?"

"Why should I?" Dicey asked.

"Old, alone, crazy – the farm falling down around me. My husband died these four years and more."

"I'm sorry," Dicey said.

"I'm not. I'm happy since he died."

"Why?" Dicey asked.

"He kept wanting his shoes polished. He never did polish them himself. First thing I did, I bought myself a washing machine. Do you play the piano?"

"No."

"Too bad," the woman said. "I've got one. Haven't played it myself, I never had time. My children did. They all died too, and that was a relief."

Dicey stood up. She didn't even feel bad. She didn't feel anything, except maybe glad she had come out here by herself.

"You're going," her grandmother said.

Dicey nodded.

"You didn't offer to help with the dishes. No, don't bother. I know what children are like."

"OK," Dicey said. It didn't matter. She'd go back and get her family, and they'd call Will.

"Don't you want to know if I want you to work for me?" her grandmother said. She was still sitting in her chair, but she had turned round to watch Dicey leave. "Well, I don't. I couldn't pay you anyway."

Chapter Seven

Dicey nodded and turned her back to the room.

The woman's voice spoke from behind her: "I know who you are. You hear me? I know who you are, and you can't stay here."

Chapter Eight

SLOWLY, DICEY TURNED. She looked all around the room before she answered. She didn't know what she should say. Why should she say anything? She'd been told to go away.

Sunlight poured into the kitchen through the door and windows. (So, her grandmother had kept the honeysuckle down on this side of the house.) It was a long bright plain room, the kitchen. Everything in it looked old and scrubbed, like the top of the table. Wooden counters, wooden cupboards, wooden chairs, wooden floor; only the refrigerator, sink and stove were porcelain. A single light hung down over the table. It had a pale yellow glass hood over it.

Her grandmother sat without moving, staring at Dicey.

"Then who am I?" Dicey asked.

"I knew the minute you knocked on the door. That's why

I came outside. A polite person would have gone away." Her grandmother waited to see what Dicey would say.

Dicey didn't say anything.

"Oh, I know who you are; you're the oldest one, I can't remember your name. There's a foolish letter here, somewhere. It has all your names in it."

This wasn't good enough. "You don't know who I am," Dicey said.

"You're Liza's daughter. Some ungodly name she gave you, her and that Francis. I liked him, I did."

"Who's the letter from?" Dicey asked.

"Connecticut," her grandmother answered. "Where are the rest of you? One's retarded, the letter said. Maudlin, simpering fool. Can't blame her, though. Her mother simpered, simpered and looked in mirrors, all her life. She's dead now. My sister Cilla – she's dead too. Is she retarded?"

"No," Dicey said. "Not that it concerns you."

"You're right. It doesn't concern me one whit. Did you ditch them somewhere?"

Dicey could follow her grandmother's thoughts easily now, now that she knew what the woman was talking about.

"They're waiting for me in town. We've got a place to go."

"Back to that one?"

"Maybe," Dicey said. She was angry now. This – grandmother. Dicey wouldn't give two pins to satisfy her curiosity. If this grandmother had known all along.

"A polite person wouldn't have pretended not to know me," Dicey said.

"Never said I had good manners. Never had any manners to say anything about." Her grandmother seemed pleased.

"My name's Dicey," Dicey said.

"That's right," her grandmother said. "I remember now. It was in the letter. I'm not crazy."

"I know," Dicey said. "I'm going now."

"Suit yourself. Where you all sleeping?"

"We're moving on. We don't need a place to stay."

"Don't you lie to me, girl. If you didn't need a place to sleep you wouldn't have traipsed out here this morning. You wouldn't have come around back to find me. You wouldn't have asked Millie – did you tell her who you were?"

"No," Dicey said. Her anger flamed up again. "No, why should I? We can't stay here, you said. So there's no point in hanging around. I've got my family to get back to."

"I said sleep. There's no reason not to sleep here is there?"

"Yes," Dicey said. "I think there is." Why should James and Maybeth and Sammy have to be disappointed?

"I'm family too," her grandmother said. She took the bowls from the table and walked over to the sink. "And I can hear what you're thinking, girl."

Dicey hoped she couldn't.

"So you'll sleep here. All of you. Because you have no place else to go."

"We do too," Dicey said.

"Then why did you come here? Can you answer me that?"

Dicey's lips were tight. Her grandmother's lips were tight.

They glared at one another across the kitchen. Neither one of them faltered.

Then her grandmother's lips twitched and spilled out laughter. She cut the laughter off quickly, dried her hands on her skirt and said to Dicey: "Two of a kind we are. Poor Liza. Two of a kind."

It was the laughter that undid Dicey. How could you be angry at someone who was laughing. "OK," she said. "But—"

"But what? Be nice to them? Nicer than I was to you?"

"Yeah," Dicey said.

"I'm not promising anything," her grandmother said. "Let's get going."

She led the way out to the back. Dicey turned towards the dilapidated barn, where the truck must be. But her grandmother headed straight off to the fields. Her feet must have leather soles, Dicey thought as they crossed through the vegetable gardens on a dirt path.

"I don't have a car," her grandmother said over her shoulder. She moved like a young woman, long, strong strides, her arms hanging easy at her sides. "Not since he died. I always hated them. I never learnt to drive."

The path crossed between two long, well-kept fields (mostly tomatoes and corn, but other crops too, squashes and beans) and entered the marsh grass. Dicey followed her grandmother. However bad the rest of the farm, the barn and the house looked, her grandmother had worked on these fields. A steady wind blew, causing the grasses to bow and whisper among themselves.

Ahead, Dicey saw open water. The bay lay at the farm's edge.

The path led up to a dock built of weathered grey wood. At the end of it was tied a long open boat. It had an outboard motor and four seats. It was at least fifteen feet long and painted a bright red, inside and out. The boat looked taken care of too.

Dicey jumped in and sat on the centre bench. Her grandmother untied the painter, pulled the boat around until its stern was near the dock and jumped in herself, dropping the line into Dicey's lap.

"Coil that," she said, and turned to the engine.

She pulled once on the starter, the engine hummed, and she headed the boat out into the bay.

They couldn't have talked over the noise of the motor without screaming at one another, so Dicey didn't try. She sat with her back to her grandmother and watched the prow of the little boat cut through the quiet water. She felt the fine spray the boat threw back, inhaled the salty air, and looked out to a horizon made only of sky and water.

They followed the coastline, which was mostly marshes. Dicey saw few houses. Then they came into Crisfield harbour, which was hidden behind a point of land. Piles of oyster shells made small pointed hills beside the shacks and behind them and in front of them.

Dicey turned around and leant towards her grandmother. "They're on the farthest dock over," she called.

Her grandmother nodded and yelled something back.

Chapter Eight

Dicey couldn't hear her. They didn't speak again.

They chugged into the dock, tying up at the far end. Dicey scrambled out and hoisted herself up onto the boards. Her grandmother climbed up the wooden ladder.

The dock was empty. There was no shade on it at this time of day, so not even the old men remained.

At first, as her eyes searched for her family, Dicey didn't worry about the dock being empty. Then she did.

Where were they? She'd told them to stay there. Where were they? What had happened? Her eyes searched up the street to see three small figures.

Nobody moved on the sidewalks.

They were gone.

Dicey felt cold, despite the heat of sunlight reflected off water. It was not the gentle breeze that cooled her. It was fear that froze.

Not thinking, not caring whether her grandmother wanted to help at all, Dicey turned to her. "I don't know," she said. "You go up that side. Look in stores and restaurants. I'll go up this side."

Dicey didn't wait to see if her grandmother started off. She ran, her heart pounding painfully.

As she reached the end of the dock, she heard her name called. She swivelled around and saw Sammy running towards her from the shade behind one of the shacks across the harbour.

Dicey's grandmother was right behind her. "It's OK," Dicey said. "That's Sammy."

She was so relieved to see him that she ran across the crushed oyster shells to meet him and caught at his hand. He let her hold it briefly, then pulled away. "I told James," he said proudly.

They walked back together.

"Told him what?" Dicey asked. "I didn't know where you were. I'll tell you, I was scared."

Sammy ignored that. "Told him you'd be back."

"Where is he? Where's Maybeth?"

"They walked out to the farm. James said, we should have all gone together anyway. He said you were wrong about that. We waited and waited. Then he said it was time to go. And I said no. And he said he'd thought it all over, and there was no good reason for you to go alone. He said I had to do what he said. And I said no. He said you said to. And I said you said to stay here and do what he said, not go off because he said to. So he took Maybeth."

By this time, they were back to where their grandmother waited. She listened, watching Sammy, watching Dicey.

"Sometimes I get so mad at James," Dicey said to Sammy. "But I'm glad you stayed – how would I have known where they were? He thinks he's so smart" – she turned to her grandmother – "and he is smart – but I told them to stay here. I told him." She scuffed her foot in the shells. How was she going to catch up with James and Maybeth? What should she do now?

"Are you the grandmother?" Sammy asked.

Their grandmother nodded.

Chapter Eight

"What am I s'posed to call you?" Sammy asked.

Dicey hadn't even thought of this. Neither, apparently, had their grandmother. She didn't answer Sammy. She pretended she hadn't heard him. "Let's get back," she said.

"What about James and Maybeth?" Dicey asked. "I can't just leave them."

"You already did," her grandmother said. "They'll make their own way. It's what James wanted, isn't it? He'll find you."

She headed back down the dock to the boat.

Dicey followed. When they got back, if James and Maybeth weren't there, she'd walk back towards town. James wouldn't get lost. He'd listened to the directions, so he'd be on the right road. He didn't forget things.

Sammy jumped down into the boat and climbed to the most forward seat. Dicey sat in the middle again, facing her brother. Behind her, she heard her grandmother untie the line and lower herself carefully from the ladder to the boat. "Hold onto the dock, girl," she said to Dicey.

Dicey stood up and reached out for a firm grip on the wood. As soon as the engine started she pushed the boat away from the dock. Sammy leaned to her. "Where is it?"

Dicey pointed south. "A-ways off," she said.

"What's it like?" he asked.

"Run down."

"Are we going to stay?"

Dicey shook her head firmly. "Just tonight."

"That's OK, Dicey," Sammy said.

They were silent the rest of the way back to their grandmother's dock. The two children climbed out there. Dicey took the line and tied it around one post. Then she sat on the edge of the dock and held the boat steady with her feet while her grandmother lifted the motor up and rocked it into a resting position inside the boat. The metal propeller blades dripped water into the bay, like sullen raindrops.

Their grandmother led the way back to the fields and farm. Sammy walked behind her on the narrow path. Dicey came last, looking around over the waving fields of grasses, savouring the salty, muddy air.

When they got past the fields, Dicey broke into a run. She sprinted around to the front of the house, hoping to see James's skinny figure sitting on the steps, with Maybeth quiet beside him. They weren't there. Sammy had followed her. Their grandmother had not.

"I'm going to find them," Dicey said. "Do you want to come or stay?"

"Stay," he said.

"She's not friendly," Dicey warned him.

"Neither am I," he said. "Besides, I'll stay out here. James'll be all right, Dicey."

"I hope so," she said. She loped down the long driveway without looking back.

As Dicey emerged from the pine woods, she saw the two figures standing far off, across the road by the mailbox. The brown grocery bag was on the ground between them. Dicey raised her hand in greeting and slowed to a walk.

James picked up the bag. Dicey stopped. Let them come to her. She had a few things to say to James.

His narrow face looked worried and relieved and ashamed and glad, all at once. He was too smart not to know all the things that could have happened. "Sammy's alone downtown," James said, before he said anything else. "I'll go back and get him. If everything's OK?"

Dicey forgave him, without a word, without another thought. "Everything's not OK, but Sammy's here. She doesn't have a car, she uses a boat. That wasn't very smart, James."

"I thought it was, when I started out."

"Well, don't worry. She doesn't want us to stay, but we can sleep here tonight."

"Then what?"

"I dunno. Let me think about it. Why didn't you come in? Were you there long?"

"We couldn't see any house," Maybeth said. "We didn't know what it would be like."

They walked back together. As they came up to the house, Sammy called to them from up among the leaves of the big tree. "I was right, James, wasn't I? We went in a boat."

"How'd you get up there?" James asked.

Sammy descended, with a shivering of branches. He slid down the curve of one trunk and stopped himself just at the bottom, where all four trunks came together. His legs were scratched.

The Tillermans stood together at the base of the tree. The

house was before them, overgrown with honeysuckle, dark-windowed, looking abandoned. Off to the right, Dicey saw the lopsided barn. It had once been red, but the paint had weathered, faded and peeled, until it looked pink as a bad sunburn. The tin roof was rusted in large patches.

"Anyway," Dicey said, "this is where Momma lived."

"It's beautiful," Maybeth said.

"It's a wreck," Dicey answered. "The fields out front – and look at that barn. It's gone to ruin. She hasn't taken care of it."

"But it's big," James said. "Big enough for all of us. Is it near the water?"

"There's a marsh first," Dicey said, "a long, empty marsh. Then the bay. There's a path, but the water's at least a quarter of a mile away. Not like Provincetown. Anyway, who cares? We won't be staying."

"True enough," her grandmother said from the side of the house. "But you'll be here for supper so there's work to be done. I see you found them." She stared at James. "James," she said.

He tried to smile but her face discouraged him.

Her eyes flickered over Maybeth. "And Maybeth." She looked away quickly, as if nothing about Maybeth could interest her. The little girl moved closer to Dicey.

"I've got crab pots set down by the dock," their grandmother said. "Who'll fetch the crabs?"

"I will," Dicey said.

"Me too," Sammy said.

Chapter Eight

"James and Sammy will," their grandmother announced. "It's after four. I eat early, and so will you. I put a basket by the back steps."

The two boys ran off.

"You two come with me. I'll show you where to sleep."

She strode around to the back of the house. Dicey picked up the grocery bag and followed her. Maybeth clung to Dicey's hand.

They saw James and Sammy heading off down the path to the water. James carried a bushel basket by its two metal handles.

Their grandmother led them through the kitchen and into a dim hallway. "That's my room," she said, pointing at a closed door, "and my bathroom," pointing to the closed door next to it. They turned left down the hall and ascended a narrow staircase.

Upstairs, they saw a long, U-shaped hallway with five closed doors around it. A window at one end looked out over the front yard, through the leaves of the big tree. Their grandmother stood on the top step and let them go past her. "That's the bathroom at the far end. Sheets are in one of the bureaus. I can't recollect which."

Dicey went to look out the window. "What kind of tree is that?"

"Paper mulberry," her grandmother answered.

Dicey noticed from above what could not be seen from below. There were strong twisted wires running around the tree. "Why is it wired?" she asked.

"Because paper mulberries are fragile," her grandmother answered. "It's the way they spread out at the top, it's the way they grow. If you didn't brace it, the weight of the leaves and the growing branches would pull the tree apart. Like families." She went abruptly downstairs.

Dicey and Maybeth stood in the dim hallway. "Cripes," Dicey whispered. "It's like a ghost house."

The air was warm and old, as if the same air had been up here for hundreds of years. The closed doors looked like so many secrets.

Maybeth's eyes were round and frightened.

"Look at it this way, Maybeth, it's only for one night. And besides, this was Momma's house, when she was little. Isn't that right?"

That didn't make Maybeth feel any better, but it made Dicey feel better. She forced up the old window to let in fresh air. She braced it with a piece of wood lying on the sill. Their grandmother wasn't going to take any trouble for them, but Dicey would show her.

Dicey opened the nearest door and stepped boldly into the room. This was a bedroom with a plain iron bedstead overlaid with a thin white quilt. The pillow had no cover on it. The room held a dresser, a desk and chair and a wardrobe, all of plain wood. Dicey went to a window and snapped up the shade. This room faced the big tree. She snapped up a shade on the other wall and found a window that looked out to the barn. Between them, she and Maybeth got the four windows up, and braced them with pieces of wood. Fresh air filtered around the room and light came in.

The smaller room across the hall was almost identical, except the quilt was faded blue instead of white. On the front of the wardrobe somebody had painted a picture of Indians coming out of the woods, carrying bows and arrows, wearing warpaint and bright headdresses. It was a kid's painting with blobs of green paint for leaves and the sun a yellow circle with lines coming out. Dicey liked it. They opened this room too and returned to the hall. With two doors open and the sunlight and the clean air, the upstairs seemed more friendly. Dicey walked down the wooden floor to the opposite end.

First she opened the door opposite the hall window. This was a bathroom. It had a toilet with a wooden seat and a wooden box above the seat from which hung a long, wooden-handled chain. The bathtub was raised off the floor by four stubby legs that ended at four feet with claws on them. The sink stood on a tall pedestal. Above it was a shelf where you could put soap and toothpaste.

Dicey and Maybeth both went to the bathroom. They pulled on the chain to flush. When you flushed, you could hear the water gurgling down the pipes from the overhead box.

Then Dicey opened the window and looked out.

From this window you looked over the roof of the porch, over the back yard, over the planted fields, over the long stretch of marshes — to the water. The band of water lay blue and sparkling, out and away. A boat, tiny at this distance, moved up the bay, maybe heading back to Crisfield with its day's catch.

Dicey hurried into the room on the right. Here there were some small differences. There was the same iron bedstead, and the quilt was multicoloured, faded but still cheerful with reds and blues and greens and yellows. The bureau and wardrobe had been painted white. The desk and chair were plain wood. A picture hung on the wall, a childish picture of a little boat sailing on blue water. Fish swam in the water, and crabs ran about the sandy bottom. Gulls wheeled in the air and rode, with folded wings, on the waves. Dicey snapped up the side shades and held the windows while Maybeth put braces on under them. These windows looked to the barn. But the other two windows, as she had hoped, gave out over the marsh and to the bay.

The last bedroom had a ruffled quilt and pictures of ladies in old-fashioned dresses on the walls, pictures cut out of magazines and pasted on a white background. The childish painter had put a picture on the wardrobe here too, of a castle and town and a queen, wearing an impossibly tall crown, walking in the garden.

Dicey hurried to open the windows, one over the back yard, and two to the piney woods that closed around the house.

She turned to Maybeth. "Well. This isn't bad, is it?"

Maybeth smiled quietly.

"It's only for a night. Let's each take our own room. Which one do you think was Momma's?"

"This one," Maybeth said.

"Then you'll sleep in this one. OK?"

Maybeth nodded happily. They found the sheets in one of the front bedrooms and made up the beds together, folding hospital corners, plumping up the pillows. For herself, Dicey chose the other back bedroom, because it looked to the water.

There was nothing in any of the rooms to show that they had ever been lived in by anyone. But they must have been lived in by the three children, Momma and her brothers. None of their personalities had been left in the rooms, except for the two paintings on the wardrobe doors, the lady cutouts, and the little picture of the boat.

None of the children had wanted to stay here. They had all left home, one way or another. Except the one who had died, maybe. You couldn't be sure. He might have wanted to come back.

They went downstairs. Maybeth followed Dicey like a shadow. The kitchen was empty. Their grandmother was out in one field, wearing a broad straw hat, picking tomatoes into another of the bushel baskets.

"We can do that," Dicey said, coming up behind her.

"And so can I," she answered without looking up. "They're coming in too fast. They always do this time of year. Gotta start canning again. Can she pick beans?" She nodded towards Maybeth, without looking at her.

"Can you?" Dicey asked Maybeth. Maybeth didn't answer. "Sure, I guess so," Dicey said.

"Over there then," their grandmother said, jabbing with

her head to another side of the field. "Bring 'em back here to me. Take the biggest. You" – this to Dicey – "go into the barn. There's a bin of potatoes up against the far walk. Get as many as we need. Keep your shoes on. I don't know what-all's on that floor."

Hedges of honeysuckle – twisting, strangling vines – had grown over what must once have been a split rail fence between the house and barn. The big barn door was pulled half open. Bits had rotted out of the wood at the base of the door, as if someone had kicked at it in unappeasable anger.

Dicey stood for a minute, letting her eyes grow accustomed to the darkness. A large shape loomed in the centre, and lofts lay in high darkness along both long walls. She brushed cobwebs away, waiting until she could see enough to go on.

Empty stalls lined one side. The smell of dry hay was in the musty air. The centre shape grew smaller as she found her twilight vision. The thing seemed to hover in the air above the packed dirt floor.

Something rustled in the lofts. Many things rustled there. Where the boards had fallen away at the sides of the barn, honeysuckle grew in. Dicey stepped into the dim darkness.

The first thing to do was to define that shape. Whatever creatures were living in the barn were probably more frightened of her than she would ever be of them, even if they panicked and touched her.

Dicey approached the shape. It was something long, slightly curved, and resting in a kind of saw-horse cradle. It was about shoulder height to her, with a flat back.

She approached it with her hands behind her back.

Dicey almost didn't dare name it, even when she knew what it was, even after she had raised herself onto tiptoe to peer inside and seen there a long mast, tied down around the sides, surrounded by tangled ropes and projecting over the bow.

A sailboat.

It was small, only fourteen or fifteen feet. It had an open cockpit, without any seats in it. It had a slot in the centre of the cockpit, beside which rested a long centreboard.

Dicey reached her hand onto the cockpit. Cobwebs. She touched the long arm of the tiller, resting against the stern. Where were the sails? Would it still float? Whose boat was it?

She rushed to the back of the barn. There, three large bins had been built. She opened one, and little creatures scurried at the bottom. The lid of the second revealed a mound of potatoes. Dicey put her hand in. The potatoes had begun to sprout. Each eye of the potato she held had knobbly, pale growth on it. But when she squeezed it with her hand, it felt firm enough. Dicey took out a dozen potatoes. Of these, she selected the seven largest (four kids and one woman, and James could eat two or three), cleaned off the sprouts with her fingers and tossed the remaining five back into the bin. Her arms were full of potatoes as she hurried back out of the barn.

Their grandmother was coming in from the field, carrying the basket. Maybeth trailed behind her.

"There's a boat in the barn," Dicey cried.

"I know that. It's been there for years. Don't put those potatoes in the basket. Take 'em to the sink. Don't you know potatoes have to be scrubbed?"

Dicey hurried ahead. She was so full of questions about the boat, she didn't care how her grandmother felt about them. She dumped the potatoes in the sink and turned on the water.

Her grandmother put the basket on the table. She took a china platter from the cupboard. "Can she take the ends off beans?" she asked Dicey, referring to Maybeth.

"Sure," Dicey said.

Maybeth stood across the table from her grandmother and snapped the ends off the green beans. She worked carefully, wasting little of the vegetable, making a neat pile of ends on the table before her. It was as if she knew how suspiciously the woman was watching her.

"Whose boat is it?" Dicey asked.

"Mine," the woman answered.

"I know that, but whose?" Dicey said.

"My boy built it," their grandmother said. "He built it and he sailed it."

"Where are the sails?" Dicey asked. She knew she shouldn't be asking. "Will it still float?"

"He kept them on the boat, up forward under the bow," their grandmother said. "They're still there, as far as I know. I don't know if it's seaworthy. It doesn't concern you."

Her voice was cold and final. Dicey, standing with her

back to the room, the cool water running over her hands as she scrubbed the dirt from potatoes, heard that coldness and that finality. Her back stiffened. "Oh, doesn't it," she said to herself. Here was the place, a farm with plenty of room and plenty of work for them to do, and the bay just beyond the marshes, and a sailboat in the barn. She wasn't about to let this grandmother keep them from it.

"I can hear what you're thinking," her grandmother said.

Dicey swivelled her head around to meet those dark hazel eyes, the sullen, angry eyes she had seen in the photograph Aunt Cilla kept. Could her grandmother know what she was thinking? And so what if she could?

"Maybe you can," Dicey said, not dropping her glance. She'd think of a way. She's been thinking up ways to get them in and out of trouble all summer long. As if she had been practising for this occasion, warming up for this last struggle. Her grandmother didn't know Dicey. Her grandmother didn't know the kind of thinking and planning Dicey could do.

A fleeting expression that might have been unaccustomed mirth, or might have been a twinge of pain, went across her grandmother's face. For a second, the face came alive around the eyes. Then it was all gone.

Dicey turned back to the sink. She didn't want to be distracted. She had thinking to do.

They had crabs for dinner. It had taken the boys a while to learn how to shake the crabs out of the pots into the basket. The first pot they'd just opened, and the crabs had fled sideways in a turbulence of muddy water. Sammy had tried to grab a couple and been nipped for his pains.

"You should have seen them," he cried, telling the story. His cheeks were pink and his eyes shone. He was too pleased to let his grandmother's stony silence quiet him down. "They looked at the door and looked at us and then" – he thrust his arms straight out and waggled his fingers – "gone! I didn't know things could go sideways so fast. Boy, are they smart."

James spoke to their grandmother: "We closed the doors and set the traps back where they were. Is that right?"

"Right enough. What did you use for bait?"

"I didn't think," said James. "What should we use?"

"Fish. You have to catch the fish."

"Good-o," Sammy said. "Can I go down after dinner? Do you have any line?"

"No point to it," their grandmother said. She was checking the boiling water in the huge pot on the stove. The potatoes were in the oven, the beans in a covered pan, the table set with forks and a platter of sliced tomatoes and glasses of water.

"So what?" Dicey answered quickly. "I'll go with you, Sammy. We like fishing," she said defiantly to her grandmother.

The woman didn't answer, but instead lifted up the basket and poured the teeming mass of crabs into the water. She slammed the lid down on top of them. You could hear them scrambling around inside the metal pot, scrabbling up to escape the steam. Their grandmother stood with one hand holding the lid down, staring at the children.

Maybeth ran out of the room. Dicey felt like following her — she could imagine how those crabs felt, and she had had that feeling herself at times — but she wasn't going to back down before those eyes. So she stood, and pretty soon there was silence in the pan. She knew they were all dead then.

They ate the crabs from a big plate in the middle of the table. They were served individual plates with potato and beans on them. There was no butter for the potatoes, but there was salt.

The Tillermans had never eaten crabs before. They learnt how to rip off the legs first, then lift back the top shell. Then you broke the crab in half, like a turnover, and picked out the meat from between sections of cartilege. Each crab had two larger chunks of meat in it, and an awful lot of stringy little pieces.

It was hard work getting full on the scraps of crabmeat. It took a time to get even a mouthful ready, once you'd taken out the two chunks. But it was a good dinner for talking at, if you wanted to talk. Everybody's hands were busy, and almost nobody's mouth was full.

Their grandmother seemed to want to talk, or seemed to want them to talk. She asked questions.

"Where's your mother?" she asked. She sent the question out to the middle of the table, as if she was asking the platter of crabs.

The children looked to Dicey.

"Momma's in a mental hospital in Massachusetts," Dicey

said. "She doesn't recognize anybody. She doesn't do anything. They don't think she's ever going to get well."

"Who don't think?" her grandmother asked.

"The doctors," Dicey said.

"They don't know," Sammy said. "She might. Isn't that right, Dicey?"

Dicey nodded.

"So you know better than the doctors," his grandmother said to Sammy.

Sammy's jaw went out and he didn't answer.

"And you ran away from this silly chit in Bridgeport. You ran away from someone who was willing to take you in and take care of you. Why'd you do that?"

They looked to Dicey again.

"It wasn't right for us. Especially not for Sammy and Maybeth."

"Because Maybeth's retarded?"

The cruel question lay before them.

Dicey looked at Maybeth. Maybe she hadn't understood. But she had. Well, that was good because if she hadn't understood that would mean maybe she really was retarded. Maybeth's eyes filled with tears.

"She's not," Dicey said.

"What is it? Can't she speak for herself? Can't you? Her grandmother glared at Maybeth. Maybeth sat staring at her lap. "Can't you?"

"Yes," Maybeth said softly.

Dicey fumed. She felt like throwing her plate at her

grandmother.

"You keep out of this, girl," her grandmother said. "You, Dicey."

Maybeth looked up. Tears rolled out of her eyes, but she stayed at the table. "I don't think I am," she said. "I don't know just what it means, but if it's such a bad thing to be – why do you want to know?"

Their grandmother nodded once, briskly. She asked another question. "You do a lot of running away. Where's your father?"

"He's been gone for years," James said. James's voice was tight. "Six years. Longer. Since before Sammy."

"I remember him," their grandmother said.

"The police in Bridgeport tried to find him and couldn't," Dicey said.

"He was the kind of man who always sailed close to the wind," their grandmother said.

"What does that mean?" James asked. "What do you mean? Did you know him?"

"He used to come around here, whenever he was in the area, when his ship was in Baltimore," their grandmother said.

"What was he like?" James asked. "Only Dicey remembers him – I don't. What did he look like?"

"Slim, dark-haired. He was a quick, nervous, darting kind of man. Not steady, but lively. The kind who might cheat at cards if luck wasn't running his way. And he'd bet too much too, that would be his way. She should have come back here when he ran out on her."

"She didn't want to," Sammy said.

"How do you know?" their grandmother said. Then, before he could answer, she said, "What does it matter anyway?"

"Momma matters to me," Sammy said, his chin stubborn.

"She went off and left you," their grandmother said.

"She wanted to come back," Sammy said.

"How do you know that," their grandmother said. She didn't ask it, she said it.

"Because she loved me. Didn't she, Dicey?"

"Yes, she did. She loved all of us," Dicey said.

"Humph," their grandmother said, reaching for another crab.

The Tillermans had won that battle. Dicey knew it. She knew it as close to her bones as she knew that Momma did always love them. Dicey tried not to grin. It didn't do to grin when there was still the whole war to win.

The children washed the dishes while their grandmother watched them and told them where to put things away. When everything was finished, and Maybeth had scrubbed the wooden tabletop with mild soap and a stiff brush, Dicey announced that they would like to go down to the dock, to fish for crab bait and to swim.

"Can Sammy swim?" their grandmother asked.

"We can all swim. We were raised near the ocean," Dicey said.

"Suit yourselves," their grandmother said.

At the dock, they took turns fishing and swimming. They

Chapter Eight

stripped down to their underwear and dived into the quiet water. The bay had no waves and no undertows. It was as calm as a swimming pool. You could swim miles in this quiet water.

Dicey swam out, away from land, in a slow crawl. Her mind was working fast. There was a way, if only she could see it. Sammy and James took the few bony fish they had caught and baited the crab traps. Maybeth jumped off the dock into the water, then climbed back on to the dock to jump again. When she hit the water, waves surged up around her and the water she sprayed out turned golden in the setting sun.

Evening fell across the water, towards them. The sky turned twilight purple. A molten pink band flowed across the horizon, where the sun had been.

The children dashed back to the house, trying to outrun the mosquitoes that swarmed up from the marshlands. Their grandmother sat in the same chair in the kitchen. They wished her goodnight, and she nodded her head but said nothing to them.

Dicey showed James and Sammy the rooms they could have. She unpacked the toothbrushes and toothpaste and comb into the bathroom. She put each one's underwear and clean clothes into his own.

They gathered in Sammy's room, the one with the picture of Indians on the wardrobe, and sat on his bed. "What're we going to do tomorrow?" James asked Dicey.

"I dunno yet, James," she said. "She doesn't want us to stay. She said so."

"Well, neither do I," Sammy announced. He was in bed but sitting up. His hair was damp. "Even if it is fun."

"What about you, James?" Dicey asked. "People say she's crazy."

"Crazy like a fox," James said. He dismissed that question, without hesitation. "It would be OK here. It's sure big enough."

"Maybeth?"

Maybeth didn't answer. She looked down at her hands and across at Sammy. "You want to," she said to Dicey. "Don't you?"

"*That* we'll talk about in the morning," Dicey said. "How about a song, how about Peggy-o?"

They sang softly, in case it might bother their grandmother, sitting alone downstairs at the empty kitchen table.

Chapter Nine

DICEY WOKE HERSELF up early the next morning, before the first grey signals of dawn, when the air outside lay black over fields, marshes and the glistening water she could just see from her window. For a time, she sat by the window and thought out the plan she had gone to sleep considering.

It all depended on what their grandmother was really like, inside herself where she was who she really was. Not outside. Dicey knew about the difference between the outside and inside.

You could assume that everybody wasn't just the way they seemed. The question was, in what way was their grandmother not what she seemed? Did she really want the Tillermans to go away?

Dicey was sure that she didn't want the Tillermans to stay. But Dicey wasn't sure she wanted them to go away. Their grandmother was a Tillerman too, which made everything contradictory. If she wanted the Tillermans to go, then she wanted herself to go – in a contradictory way this was true. Dicey's job was to see through the contradictions and find out where they made sense together.

Why had their grandmother gone outside to the back when Dicey knocked? She could have stayed inside and not been found. Why had she asked all those questions at dinner? Cousin Eunice's letter would have explained about Momma. And what did she mean when she said to Dicey that she knew what Dicey was thinking? Unless it was what she herself was thinking.

Besides, their grandmother had taken the boat to town to find James and Maybeth and Sammy. That was something she wouldn't have done if she'd really wanted them to go away.

Maybe their grandmother didn't know just what she wanted. Or maybe she didn't really want anything, except to be left alone. Four kids, they were an awful bother. Cousin Eunice said so, again and again. And an expense.

Dicey could manage the bother and they'd figure out a way to cover the expense. She was sure they could do that. They could leave their grandmother pretty much alone. It was the place Dicey wanted, the big house, the acres of farmland, the barn, the water and the boat. It didn't have anything to do with the woman.

The sky lightened. Over in the east, behind the house, the last star would be fading as the sun surged up. Above the marshes, a pale quarter moon waited in a light blue sky, with

Chapter Nine

mares' tails clouds brushing against it. Time to get moving.

Dicey woke James and Sammy and Maybeth. They all met in Dicey's room over the kitchen, so that any noise they made wouldn't waken their grandmother. Dicey explained her plan:

"We have to get started on something useful before she wakes up. That way, she'll keep us here today. Or if she tells us to go, we can say we will, as soon as we finish the job."

"But—" James said.

"But what?"

"What if she means it?"

"She doesn't mean it," Dicey said. "That's the trouble, isn't it? I figure, if we get her to put it off she'll get used to us and forget that she wants us to go away. We pretend we're not even thinking about staying here. But every day we do something that needs to be done so it's worth her while to keep us."

"She could call the police," James said.

"She doesn't have a phone. But if she does then we will go, I promise. If she really means it. Can't you tell? She doesn't want us to stay, but she doesn't want us to go, either."

"I don't think she likes me," Sammy said.

"That doesn't matter, Sammy. It's not her I'm thinking about. It's us."

"She's mean," Sammy said. "She's not like Momma at all."

"That doesn't matter," Dicey repeated. "Besides, she's not really mean, not like Mr Rudyard. Is she?"

"How do you know?" Sammy demanded.

"Remember when James took that money?" Maybeth asked him. "Remember how Dicey's face got all red and hot and she told us we had to go, and she told James he had to obey. Remember? That was like our grandmother. Mr Rudyard was cold."

Sammy subsided. Dicey took advantage of the moment to announce their project for the day: honeysuckle.

They dressed quietly, used the bathroom quickly and tiptoed down the stairs into the dark hall. The kitchen lay in shadows.

They began with the honeysuckle growing up around the front porch. It had formed a massed wall that wove around itself and clung to itself with tiny tendrils. The tendrils looped and looped around anything that would hold them up.

The Tillermans had no plan. They just reached into the plants and pulled. The honeysuckle vine emerged in long stringers, unwoven from the mass.

By the time the sun had risen and only the shadow of the paper mulberry tree kept an early morning coolness over the yard, they had a large mound of honeysuckle branches at the foot of the lawn. Dicey didn't know how they were going to get rid of it. In some patches, she could see the screen on the porch, but they hadn't taken away a quarter of the growth yet. Maybe it would burn, but she doubted that; it was lush summer growth, tensile vines and green leaves.

"I'm hungry," James said. "This is going to take all day."

"I hope so," Dicey grunted, jerking back on a fat vine. "Anyway, let's see what there is to eat."

Chapter Nine

They trooped round the side of the house and across the porch. At the kitchen door, they stopped. Their grandmother was up. She was at the stove, making pancakes on a griddle so large it covered two burners on the stove. She turned round when she heard them coming in.

"Wash your hands. I see that you don't make your beds."

"I'll do that," Dicey offered.

"No, you'll each do your own," their grandmother said. She turned her back on them. She was wearing another shapeless blouse over another long, shapeless skirt. Her feet were bare and clean. She had laid the table.

When the children sat down, two platters of pancakes waited for them. There was no syrup or butter, but quart jars of strawberry jam were set out. Their grandmother didn't say a word. She just served herself two pancakes and spread jam over them.

The pancakes looked normal, but they tasted curiously flat. The jam, however, was delicious and the children ate with good appetites.

Finally their grandmother spoke. "I like that honeysuckle." She looked at Dicey.

Dicey's heart sank.

"That honeysuckle's been there a long time. It's the kind of tenacious plant I have to respect," their grandmother said.

"Honeysuckle is parasitic," James announced. "It can be trained and kept back, but when allowed to proliferate without control, it chokes out other growth. It's begun to climb over the small trees out front."

His grandmother studied him. James ignored her and slathered jam on his seventh pancake.

"Where'd you learn a word like proliferate?" she asked him. His mouth was full so he couldn't answer. "The honeysuckle will take you all day, at least," their grandmother said.

Nobody answered. Dicey tried to look unconcerned with what her grandmother would say next.

"You can't just leave those vines piled up. They have to go out on the marsh," was what she said.

Dicey chewed hard, to keep herself from smiling. This was just a skirmish, not even a real battle. She looked up to meet her grandmother's eyes and swallowed hastily.

After the dishes were washed and the beds made, the children went back outside. The temperature had gone up and they stripped down to just their shorts. This meant that as they pulled the vines or piled them up they got mightily scratched, all over their arms and chests and legs, but it was cooler.

They sang as they worked, sometimes in harmony, sometimes all singing melody.

Dicey showed Maybeth how to wrap a long vine around her arm and pull back on it, with all her weight, taking the strain in her shoulder. Sammy used both his hands. Half the time he jerked so hard that he fell over backwards.

The overgrowth gradually gave way to a thin layer of the oldest, thickest vines. These had to be worked out of the screen netting, because if you pulled hard on them, the screen ripped out.

Chapter Nine

As they stood, patiently unravelling coiled tendrils, Dicey began to sing the song about the wide river and the small boat. She liked the way the melody held its notes and lingered over its phrases. This was a song they all sang together, but each of them sang it his own way, holding the notes and words he liked best.

The voice came from behind them: "Where'd you hear that song?"

They turned, wiping back sweat-dampened hair. Their grandmother had a canteloupe cut up into thick slices. She had arranged the slices on a metal baking tray.

"Momma sang it," James answered her. "Is that for us?"

"I don't have lemons for lemonade," she said. "Don't have milk, eggs, butter – it's melons or nothing."

"Melons are fine, thanks," Dicey said quickly.

"Did you sing to our momma?" Maybeth asked.

"I don't recall," their grandmother said. She walked away from them, back around the house.

The children ignored her and fell upon the melons. As they sat and ate, Dicey looked at what they had accomplished. "We can finish the front and clear away around the trees. Then we'll eat lunch, OK?"

They agreed.

"And after that we'll move that pile of vines down to the marsh. It might be safe to burn them there. And after that – how does a long swim sound?"

A long swim sounded fine.

When they went into the kitchen for lunch, their

grandmother was not there. They couldn't call out to her, because they didn't know what name they were supposed to use. It sounded funny to say "Mrs Tillerman", and it sounded just as funny to say "Grandmother". Dicey knocked on the closed door of the downstairs bedroom, but there was no answer.

Because Dicey didn't feel right about going into the refrigerator or the pantry, they ate tomatoes and cucumbers from the garden. As soon as they were finished, they jumped up to carry huge armloads of tangled vine out to the marsh. Dicey decided that the pile should be a good way into the marsh, but next to the path so they didn't have to tramp through the wet grasses. It made quite a hill, big enough to slide down if it had been hay.

Dicey didn't want to light a fire without checking with their grandmother. She didn't feel sure of what would happen when the leaves caught. So they left the vines and ran down to the water, single-file along the narrow path.

They tossed their shorts and sneakers on the end of the dock and leapt into the water. It was cool and cleansing. It washed the sweat off their bodies. They stretched muscles that were taut and tired from pulling and carrying. Dicey swam underwater, looking at the muddy bottom. The water soaked through her hair and cooled her head. She rolled and floated under water, as if she were a piece of seaweed.

After a while, she climbed out and sat on the dock. It was then she realized that the boat was gone. What was their grandmother up to?

Chapter Nine

The children lay on the dock, letting the hot sun dry them.

"We ought to trim back that honeysuckle by the barn," James said. He was lying on his back in the puddle made by the water dripping off him. His eyes were closed tight against the bright sunlight. "She said she liked honeysuckle, didn't she? If we trimmed it, it would make a kind of hedge, and it wouldn't harm anything."

"We don't have anything to cut it with," Dicey said.

"You could ask."

"No, I can't. Don't you see? We can't ask, we just have to do things. We can't give her a chance to say no, because if we do then that's what she'll say. And we've got to get back to work. There are still the side porches. I've got to look in the barn for tools because the next job is to fix the screens on the porches." Dicey sprang up and put on her shorts. She hurried her family along.

James and Maybeth and Sammy pulled at the honeysuckle on the side near the barn, while Dicey explored the cobwebby barn inside. She forced the doors wide apart, so she would have enough light to see. She found a small workshop opposite the empty stalls. The tools looked clean and well-oiled, saws, hammers, pliers, axes, mallets, planes, drills, screwdrivers, a level. No cobwebs had been spun around the workbench, so she figured her grandmother kept it in order. Nearby, garden tools hung on the wall and lay on a long shelf, clippers in four different sizes, shovels, hoes, stiff metal rakes and long-fingered leaf rakes. A tiny cupboard with three dozen small drawers held nails and screws of every size.

Dicey did not let herself linger by the boat. The boat was the prize. Unless they could stay, she wouldn't think about fixing it up or sailing it. She hoisted herself up onto the side and checked under the bow to be sure the sails in a canvas bag were there. Then she picked out the two largest pairs of clippers and ran outside.

James and Maybeth began the slow task of trimming back the honeysuckle hedge. Sammy didn't want to. He enjoyed tearing down the vines, grabbing at them with both hands and holding hard, as his hands slipped down, ripping off the leaves. Then, when his grip held, he would lean back on the vine and swing his weight against it. He grunted as he pulled. He braced his sturdy little legs against the ground. Sammy was hard to stop once he'd made up his mind to do a job.

Dicey saw their grandmother walking through the vegetable fields carrying two large grocery bags. She called to James to go take them, or at least one, and continued pulling. The next time she looked, her grandmother was walking along, still carrying two bags, and James was nowhere in sight. Dicey let go of the vine in exasperation and ran to help.

She met her grandmother at the end of the lawn. She didn't even ask, she just took a bag. "Front must be clear, by the size of that pile out in the marsh," the woman said.

Their grandmother came around the side to inspect the work. Sammy decided he should show off. He leaned back and grunted, to show how hard he was working. He jerked his arms. His whole body pulled back against the vine.

The vine snapped free of the roof.

Sammy tumbled backwards on to his behind. His feet flew up in the air. The vine came after him and wrapped around him, as if it had a life of its own, as if it was a boa constrictor attacking its dinner.

Their grandmother laughed, a thin, rusty sound. Sammy struggled to free his head and arms from the snaky leaves.

"What's so funny?" he demanded.

"You are," his grandmother said.

And Sammy laughed too.

James came up from the marsh, carrying two more bags of groceries.

"Can she use clippers?" the woman asked Dicey when she saw Maybeth. "Is it safe for her?"

This irritated Dicey. "Ask her yourself. She's not deaf. If you can't see for yourself."

"Well, you'd better rub the tools down carefully with the tack cloth before you put them away. Or they'll rust. I have groceries to put away."

They swam again before dinner. They came to the table with wet heads and shining faces. Their grandmother had fried pieces of chicken in a thin cornbread batter. She served mashed potatoes with butter in pools on the top, and green beans. She even had dessert, a store cake with stiff, over-sweet chocolate frosting, and a bowl of apples and bananas. By each child's place stood a tall glass of milk.

"You did a good day's work," their grandmother said. "I suppose you'll be moving on tomorrow."

Dicey took a deep breath. "There's still honeysuckle to be pulled."

"Don't know why you carried it so far into the marsh," their grandmother said. "You could leave it up to the near end, and it'll rot away by spring. James, you look like you could use another piece of chicken."

It was not what she said, but what she didn't say, that Dicey heard. The Tillermans had won another day.

After supper, the children washed up the dishes and their grandmother went out to the fields. As Maybeth soaped and rinsed, and the boys dried, and Dicey put away the glasses, dishes, knives, forks, pots and pans, they sang. Maybeth scrubbed down the wooden table and Dicey polished it dry. Maybeth sang the song about the man who sang for his dead friends. The others had forgotten the words, so she taught them again. Their voices blended in the yellow kitchen light, and filled the empty house as the world outside darkened into twilight. "'When I come to the cross of that silent sea, who will si-ing for me?'"

They let the echoes of melody fade away before they moved again.

"I'll give you this much," their grandmother said from the doorway. "Your momma taught you how to sing." She stood with darkness behind her. Dicey couldn't read her expression. "Where'd you hear that song?"

"A friend taught it to us. Someone we met when we were going to Aunt Cilla's house," Dicey said.

"Stewart," Maybeth said.

"Stewart who?" their grandmother asked.

"I don't know," Dicey said. "It was at a college."

"What were you doing at a college?" their grandmother asked.

James told her about their time in New Haven. He started with the rain and the hunger. He even told about stealing the money. He finished it at the beach in Fairfield.

Their grandmother had stood silent in the doorway while he told it. "You're not helpless infants," she remarked. Then she added quickly, "If you want to wash anything, tonight's the time. I'm canning tomorrow and the next week."

Dicey washed out their dirty underwear in the sink. She stumbled through the dark outside to the far side of the house, the side they hadn't yet pulled honeysuckle from, to find the clothes-line. Mosquitoes bit at her, but she lingered outside anyway, listening to the wind in the pines and the frogs croaking across the marsh. Overhead, between the branches of the trees, stars shone. Clouds drifted across the moon's partial face. When she returned to the kitchen, it was dark and empty. She ran up the stairs two at a time to join her family.

That was how the first day went.

On the second day they pulled down the rest of the honeysuckle on both sides of the house and gathered all the piles together near the edge of the marsh. In the afternoon, James and Dicey started patching up the holes in the porch screens, where the screens had pulled out of the wood or just ripped.

Their grandmother spent the whole day in the kitchen, canning batches of tomatoes and carrying them out to cool on the back porch. Sammy and Maybeth emptied the crab pots for supper, and they ate at the trestle table on the porch. Some crabs were left over. Even James couldn't fit any more in. So Maybeth picked out the meat and put it in a bowl in the refrigerator, for lunch the next day.

"I guess you'll be moving on tomorrow," their grandmother said again.

"There's still screens to be patched," Dicey said.

"Did you bait the traps?" the woman asked Sammy and Maybeth. They had.

That was how the second day went.

On the third day they finished the screens and James set to work mending the front steps, with Maybeth to give him an extra hand. They even went into the dark dining-room (which had a big table and eight chairs, and a fireplace at one end) and the living-room. Dicey snapped up the blinds and looked around there.

This room too had a fireplace, and a sofa in front of it, and a huge wooden desk and walls full of books. Dicey called James in to see it. A few of the books he'd read. Some he'd heard of. The rest he stood and looked at. "You could read for years," he said.

"Who wants to?" Sammy asked him. "Hurry up, so I can go swimming."

At dinner, James asked their grandmother about the books.

"My husband was a reading man," she said. "For all the good it did him."

"What do you mean?" James asked.

"He got all of his answers out of books," their grandmother said. "Books don't change, and he liked that. They made him feel right."

"What's the matter with that?" James wanted to know. "You can study books and think about what's in them. People put down what happened before you were even born, and you can understand and not make the same mistakes. Like history."

"The past is gone," their grandmother said.

"But it shouldn't be forgotten," James said. "Should it?"

"Sometimes," their grandmother said. "Sometimes it's better. My husband used his books to build a wall to keep things out. Oh, I know." She cut off James's answer. "I know it doesn't have to be that way. But that's the way it was."

"Books let things in," James said.

His grandmother studied him. "I suppose they could. For some. They didn't, not for him. But he knew a lot about history and ideas and the way things should be." James was listening carefully, but she changed the subject. "Will you be moving on tomorrow?"

"When the front hinges are set in," Dicey said. "Your mailbox needs bracing, and there's some patching to be done on the barn. You do have lumber in there, don't you?"

"It's going to rain," their grandmother said. "There're storms brewing."

Dicey's heart fell.

That night, Dicey was awakened by thunder roaring about the house. Lightning snaked down out of a black sky. She started counting at the end of the thunder, and barely got to two when the lightning flashed again.

Maybeth entered her room. "Dicey?"

"Climb in."

"It's right over our heads," Maybeth said.

It certainly seemed to be. Thunder growled just outside the window, trying to get in. Lightning flashed down and cracked like a whip. Dicey reached for Maybeth's hand and they tiptoed along the hallway and down the stairs.

In the kitchen, Dicey turned on the light. Maybeth stood by the door, pale. "Come on. Sit down," Dicey urged her. "I didn't know you were afraid of thunderstorms. Don't worry. Lightning goes for the highest thing, so it'll hit a tree or one of the chimneys. Not us." She reached out and pulled at Maybeth's right hand.

The little girl winced and turned paler. She pulled back and rubbed at her arm, up by the elbow. The arm hung down by her side, as if it were a broken wing.

"Maybeth?" Dicey asked. "What's wrong with your arm?"

"It hurts. It hurts when I close my hand into a fist or try to hold something. Sometimes it just hurts when I don't do anything. It woke me up. I don't know what's wrong, Dicey."

"Maybe it'll go away by itself," Dicey said. She poured Maybeth a glass of milk and got one for herself. They sat and drank quietly. Maybeth held the glass awkwardly in her left hand.

The sky outside exploded with rain. It pounded on the tin roof of the porch. After a while the two girls went quietly upstairs again.

There was a bar of light under their grandmother's bedroom door. Dicey wondered if she was afraid of storms. Momma wasn't.

The morning of the fourth day dawned low and dark. The thunderstorm had passed, but the rain poured steadily down. It drummed on the roof, it rattled softly among the trees. Dicey stood by the window, looking west. A low grey mist covered the marshes and you couldn't see the bay.

They couldn't work outside in the rain. But surely their grandmother wouldn't ask them to leave on a day like this? But then, why shouldn't she? What did she care? Dicey stood, watching rain fall in sheets. The barn. They could clean out the barn.

She woke her brothers and sister. They dressed quietly. Quietly, they went to the bathroom and washed the sleep from their eyes and brushed their teeth. Quietly, they went down the stairs and into the kitchen.

Their grandmother, already dressed in shirt and skirt, stood by the sink. She was running water into a canning pot. Glass jars stood on the draining-board. A bushel basket of tomatoes was on the kitchen table. The woman's hair was damp and curled wildly. Her feet were caked with mud.

Caught, the children could only wait.

"You can help me," the woman said. Her eyes were bright, but her face sagged with fatigue. "I need the ripe tomatoes picked, and the squashes and cukes that are along the ground. Drainage is so bad they'll rot if we don't get them in."

The children took off their sneakers and shirts and left them by the porch door. Dicey and James carried a towering pile of bushel baskets. They stepped out into the rain.

The drops of water hammered down on them, like a shower on at full force. They bent their heads and ran for the field. The long grass was wet and cold against their legs. They were soaked before they reached the field. Dicey told James and Maybeth to tackle the tomatoes. She showed Sammy where the cucumbers were and went back to the squashes herself.

Mud oozed up through her toes as her feet sank into the earth. She worked as fast as she could, around the mounds where courgettes and yellow squashes spread out. The squashes were hidden under leaves larger than her hand. Dicey knelt down into the chilly mud and picked them out. She tossed them into the basket beside her. The rain beat down on her bare back. Her wet shorts chafed against her waist and thighs. They might as well have taken off all their clothes, she thought.

In spite of her discomfort, she worked fast. Once, she looked over to see how James and Maybeth were doing. When she checked on Sammy she saw that he had taken off his shorts and underpants and was standing naked over the cucumber plants. Sometimes, she thought, he has more sense than any of us.

Dicey carried the two baskets she and Sammy filled back to the porch, without going inside. She ran to help finish the tomatoes. Sammy's bottom gleamed white in his tanned body as he stooped over to pick beside Maybeth. Maybeth was using only her left hand. She held her right arm stiff by her side.

James and Dicey carried the full baskets back. Maybeth ran ahead inside. Sammy didn't want to go in. He ran about in the long grass of the lawn. He turned cartwheels and the rain droned down around him.

When Dicey came up with the last basket, she saw him rolling about in the long grass, like a dog. His face was bright, entirely happy. She looked past him and saw their grandmother standing to hold the porch door open for James, who struggled up the steps with a basket of tomatoes in his arms. The woman was watching Sammy with a smile in her eyes. Their grandmother seemed to have a smile as sudden and complete as laughter.

Dicey called Sammy in. Maybeth had dressed and sat quietly at the table, nursing her arm. Dicey ran the boys upstairs to dry off and change clothes.

The table was set for breakfast when they came down. The huge pot steamed and rattled as the glass jars boiled, to be sterile for the day's canning. Their grandmother served them bowls of hot oatmeal with brown sugar and milk to put on it.

Dicey sat beside Maybeth. "It still hurts?" she asked. Maybeth just nodded. She held the spoon in her left hand and ate sloppily. Dicey realized that she shouldn't have let Maybeth come out picking with them. She didn't know what could be wrong. What was it like when your arm was broken? How could Maybeth have broken her arm?

Maybeth reached across the cereal bowl for the pitcher of milk. She tried to pour it over her cereal, but it splashed on to the table.

Their grandmother stormed up from the table and threw a dishcloth across at Maybeth. "Can't you even feed yourself? Mop it up."

Maybeth mopped at the milk and knocked at her bowl. Dicey caught it before it spilt.

"What's the matter with her?" their grandmother demanded. Maybeth's face was white, and she stared at her cereal. Dicey mopped up the spilt milk. She touched Maybeth softly on the left shoulder, to let her know she wasn't angry.

"Answer me," their grandmother said. "Or is this the way she usually is, and it's all been an act until now?"

"Something's wrong with her arm," Dicey said.

"What something?" The woman sat down and began eating again.

"I dunno," Dicey said. "It hurts."

Their grandmother turned her attention to Maybeth. "How long has it hurt?"

"Since yesterday morning," Maybeth said.

"Why didn't you say?" Dicey asked, exasperated.

Maybeth shrugged. Dicey subsided, because she knew why Maybeth hadn't said anything.

"What does it feel like?" their grandmother asked.

"It hurts. It feels burny and achy. When I close my hand and try to hold something, it's like a fire going up around my elbow." Maybeth swallowed. "It's getting worse, not better."

Their grandmother stormed up from the table and out of the room. The Tillermans looked at one another, surprised. "Maybe she doesn't like people being ill," Dicey said.

But the woman returned with a jar of ointment and a broad roll of gauze bandaging. She rubbed the ointment into Maybeth's elbow and down her forearm. Then she made a tight bracelet around Maybeth's wrist, ripping off the gauze with her teeth and tying it into a knot. She made another such bandage above the little girl's elbow.

"Probably a tendon," she announced. "Does that help?" Maybeth nodded. "It sounds like you've pulled a tendon in your arm. Pulling down that honeysuckle – it doesn't surprise me. You'll have to take it easy with that arm for weeks. The bandages will ease the strain on the muscle."

"Thank you," Maybeth said.

"You should have spoken up sooner," her grandmother answered. "No need to bear pain unless you have to."

Maybeth nodded. "I was afraid it wouldn't ever feel better," she said.

"Tendons can be pretty bad," their grandmother answered. "What are your plans for the day?" she asked Dicey. There was a challenge in her words.

"Clean out the barn," Dicey said.

"Not without sunlight. It's dark as the tomb in there," the woman answered. She waited, her eyes snapping.

"We'll wash windows," Dicey said.

"In the rain?"

"It's not raining inside."

Her grandmother nodded. "I could use some help in the kitchen."

Dicey washed off the tomatoes. James cut them up and Maybeth ladled them awkwardly into jars with her left hand. Sammy got down some old towels and ripped them into cloths. Their grandmother put the tops on the jars and set them into the canning pot.

"You know those old houses in town," James said. "Who owned them?"

"Rich people. There was a time when Crisfield was a boom town," their grandmother said. "People made fortunes in oysters and crabs and built big houses."

"What happened?" James asked.

"The usual," his grandmother said. "There was a lot of money and a lot of crime — gambling and drinking and people killing one another one way or another. So the town tried to clean itself up. They passed a law against whiskey and that had the usual result."

"Bootlegging? Moonshining?" James asked. She nodded.

"And the oysters had a few bad seasons. So there were no more big fortunes to be made here, legally or illegally. So people left. The trains stopped running. When I was a girl, this was quite a town. Not like it is now."

"Did you know any bootleggers?" James asked. "On the water, with boats, there must have been a lot of it around here."

"I suppose I did," their grandmother said. "But they'd been doing it for so long—"

"Prohibition didn't last that long," James said.

"Around there it did. It started in 1875 – and that was before my time, long before, in case you think of asking. There were families that had been bootlegging for two or three generations."

"Why did it start so early?" James asked. His eye began to gleam and Dicey knew that he would pick information from the woman's brain as long as she would answer his questions. Dicey filled a bucket with water and ammonia and took Sammy upstairs with her to wash windows. They soaped the glass down with sponges and dried it with the pieces of towels. By mid-afternoon, Sammy's restlessness had grown too large for the house to contain him. Dicey had worked slowly, dragging out the chore, but Sammy didn't see any sense in this.

At two o'clock, by the clock that ticked on the mantel in the living-room, he was ready to quit. Dicey told him he couldn't, he had to be useful.

Sammy thought for a minute, then ran down the hallway to the kitchen. Dicey had polished dry all the windows before she wondered where he was.

He'd been gone an hour. He wasn't in the kitchen. He

wasn't upstairs. Dicey ran out to the barn, but he wasn't in the gloom there, either.

She came inside again. Only her grandmother was in the kitchen, sitting with a cup of tea at the table, while two canning pots rattled on the stove. A huge bowl of cut squashes stood ready to be canned next. "Did you see Sammy?" Dicey asked.

"He ran through a while back, more than an hour. The other two are in the living-room." Dicey heard the faint notes of the piano.

"I'm going down to the dock to look for him," Dicey said. "He's been gone too long."

"Didn't he say where he was going?" her grandmother asked. Dicey shook her head. "That boy needs some controlling, doesn't he? Your cousin said that."

"She didn't approve of us," Dicey said. "She – she wanted Sammy to be like James, only James isn't like what she thought, either. She just liked him because people praised her about him. And Maybeth – she wanted her to be a doll, a dressed-up doll to take to places. Sammy wasn't easy enough for her, that's why she said that."

"What about you?" her grandmother asked.

"I dunno," Dicey said. "I never thought about it. I was busy."

"Busy sneaking out to earn money and never saying a thing about it to her."

Dicey bit back her anger. "She thinks we're not grateful enough, doesn't she?"

Chapter Nine

"Something like that. She says it's her duty, though, to take care of you. I've never seen such a foolish letter. She wrote me another one when her mother died."

"You didn't answer it."

"I couldn't answer such silliness. I'll have to write her now."

Dicey stared at her grandmother. She wasn't going to ask any questions. Her grandmother looked tired. "You were awake during the storm," Dicey said.

"So were you and Maybeth. Were you scared?"

Dicey shook her head. "Maybeth's arm hurt and it woke her up. Were you scared?"

"There's nothing to be frightened of in a thunderstorm. I was thinking. With four children in the house, the only time you can feel alone is at night."

Sammy burst into the kitchen. His hair was plastered down over his forehead. His shirt and shorts were sodden. He dripped on to the floor.

"Where have you been?" Dicey demanded. Before he could answer, she ran to get towels.

When she returned, her grandmother was in the middle of a lecture. "—running off without telling anyone where you're going. Your sister was worried."

"You weren't, were you?" Sammy said. His grandmother shook her head. "Then why are you yelling at me about it?"

His grandmother stared at him. Sammy's jaw stuck out and he stared right back at her.

Dicey handed him a towel. "Don't be rude, Sammy," she said.

"But it's the truth," he protested. She dried his hair for him, and his voice came out muffled from beneath the terrycloth. "I'm sorry, Dicey – I thought I'd break something if I stayed inside. I was down at the dock. I bailed out the boat, so the motor won't get covered with water. Then I checked the crab pots. The water doesn't have any waves."

"Because there's no wind," Dicey said. "Next time, tell me where you're going, OK?"

"OK," Sammy answered.

Dicey knew Sammy. He wouldn't do things for politeness or because he was told. He would obey if he loved you and knew you loved him. You could trust Sammy.

"Go and get into dry clothes. And hang up the towels," she said.

Her grandmother was looking at her. "Doesn't he get punished?" she asked.

Dicey wanted to go along with her, so that she would like the Tillermans and let them stay on her farm. She wanted to agree so badly that she had trouble saying the words to argue. But she had given Sammy her word, and Maybeth. She had said she'd stand up for them. And she had learnt that she had to do what she thought was right for her family, not what someone else thought.

"No," Dicey said. She made her voice as pleasant and unquarrelsome as she could. "Why should he? It was a mistake."

"You'll ruin him. He's wilful and needs to learn."

"No," Dicey said again. "He doesn't need to learn to give

in and give up. That's what you meant, isn't it? The way Sammy is – he's not perfect, but he's all right. Stubbornness isn't bad."

"He fights," she said.

"So do I," Dicey answered. "And I'm glad he knows how to."

That was the end of the conversation, but not of the battle, for this *was* a battle, not a skirmish. Dicey knew it. She wondered whether if she won that battle, would she lose the whole war?

Chapter Ten

THE NEXT DAY, the fifth day, it rained again. Their grandmother continued with her canning. Dicey thought that the children should be out of the house (although James protested that he wanted to read and he wouldn't get into any trouble), so she made them all go into the barn. It was dark and gloomy in there, but after a while their eyes grew accustomed, and they could knock down the big spider webs and polish the tools with the tack rags and put the pieces of lumber into neat piles.

The rain splattered on the tin roof of the barn, like a drummer who was just learning how to play, uneven and off-beat. Dicey examined the places in the barn wall where the wood had been torn away, or had fallen awry. She and James worked on figuring out how to make patches. There was a tall extension ladder in the barn, so they could reach all the damaged places.

Late in the morning they heard the sudden, sharp call of a car horn.

At first, Dicey couldn't think of what it was, but when it sounded again she realized that there must be a car outside. You couldn't hear anything from the road this far back.

Dicey and her family went to the door of the barn. They couldn't see anything, so they went around the house to the front yard.

Claire's white estate car, with two people in it, was stopped under the paper mulberry tree.

"We figured you were still here since we didn't hear from you," Will said, climbing out. "This sure is the back of beyond."

Claire had come with him. She wore her same high-heeled sandals and blue jeans, and a yellow rain jacket. She had tied a clear plastic scarf around her hair. "How is everything?" she asked. "Are you doing OK?"

Dicey nodded. "OK," she said to Will, "but not terrific."

"Are you going to introduce us?" Will asked.

"I suppose so," Dicey said. How could she introduce them when she never called her grandmother anything but *Ummah*?

"Something wrong?" he asked.

"Nothing's decided," Dicey said. "For us, I mean. She says we can't stay. But she hasn't made us go."

"Invite us in, OK, Dicey?" Will said. He and Claire looked at each other.

"Your feet'll get wet," Dicey said to Claire.

"Worse things have happened to me," Claire answered.

"Do the dogs miss me?" Sammy asked her.

"Of course," Claire said.

They waited on the broad back porch while Dicey called her grandmother from the stove. "I heard company," the woman said.

"Come and meet them," Dicey answered. "This is Mrs Tillerman," she said. "Will and Claire, friends of ours."

Her grandmother shook hands with Claire, then Will, and asked them to sit down on the porch because the kitchen was so hot. She asked them if they wanted some lemonade and they asked what was wrong with Maybeth's arm. Dicey brought out a jug of lemonade made from a can and seven glasses. The children sat silent while the adults talked about who Will and Claire were. Will called their grandmother "Mrs Tillerman, ma'am", until she finally snapped at him to call her Ab.

"We had the devil of a time finding you," he said. "You don't have a phone."

"I know that," she said. "I took it out years ago."

"Why would you do that?" Claire asked.

"You have any children?" their grandmother asked Claire. Claire shook her head. "You wouldn't understand then. I used to. My boy, Bullet, he was in the army…" Her dark hazel eyes clouded while she talked, and her face stiffened. "They called me up on the telephone to tell me he got killed. I had to do something. What I did was, I went downtown and took the thing and threw it through the phone company's window. They were surprised, I can tell you that. It didn't help, of course – but it was better than doing nothing."

Will threw back his head and laughed. Their grandmother smiled her sudden surprised smile.

"Did you hit anyone?" Sammy asked.

"All their desks were at the back," their grandmother said, "and there was a display shelf right by the window. I didn't aim to hurt anyone."

"What kind of a name is Bullet?" Sammy asked. "A nickname? What was his real name?"

"Sam. Samuel."

"Like me? Dicey, he had my name."

Dicey wondered if Momma had named Sammy after her brother because he was dead. How would Momma have known that? Maybe she had liked her brother Bullet.

"Claire," Will said. "The rain's let up a little. Why don't you take the kids out and show them what we have in the car?"

In the back of the car were three bicycles, piled one on top of the other. A fourth was folded in behind the front seat.

James and Dicey had full-sized bikes, with three gears. Sammy and Maybeth had smaller models, but theirs too had gears and thin wheels.

"Oh," the children said.

And, "Oh," again.

Claire grinned at them. "They're not new. We're near Ocean City, right? And it's the end of the season there so the places that rent bicycles to tourists are selling off their old ones. Well, we all thought of you when we saw that. So everybody chipped in."

Sammy hopped on to his and wobbled for a few feet before he toppled off. "Did you see me ride?" he yelled.

Dicey and James had ridden on other kids' bikes in Provincetown, so they knew how. Claire took Maybeth aside to begin teaching her. Sammy needed no help, or so he thought. Dicey watched him for a minute and decided that he would manage on his own and that would be better than trying to get him to sit still and learn properly. She and James raced down the muddy driveway and back again. As they rode back, the rain intensified.

"We'd better get these in the barn," Dicey called over to him.

"If we'd had bikes I bet we could have gone twenty miles a day," James answered.

They took the bikes into the barn and dried them off with the tack cloth there. "If the rain lets up later, can I ride again?" Sammy asked. "I'm beginning to know how."

"Maybe," Dicey said. Claire had gone back to the porch. "We didn't say thank you," Dicey realized.

They quieted down when they came to the back porch. Maybeth went up to Will. "Thank you," she said. "It's more wonderful than anything. Will you tell everyone thank you?"

"I certainly will," Will answered.

"From me too," James said, and Dicey and Sammy added their thanks.

Will and Claire stood up then, while the rain poured down beyond the wire screens, over the trees and garden and marsh.

"Do you have to go?" Dicey asked. She felt that when they did go she and her family would be further away from the circus than before, than just that morning. "Can't you stay for lunch? Can they?" she asked her grandmother.

Her grandmother looked hesitant.

"Perhaps you would allow us to take all of you to a restaurant for lunch," Will said. He spoke to their grandmother.

That seemed to decide her. "And pay good money for what we can make better ourselves? Nonsense. If James and Sammy will empty the crab pots and Dicey will get us some tomatoes, I think I can feed us pretty well here. If you don't mind eating out on the porch. If it's not too cold for you."

So they had lunch together on the back porch, while the rain faded away outside. They ate and talked. Will told their grandmother about how he first met the children, and how they turned up again with Mr Rudyard on their heels. Then James had to tell about Mr Rudyard again, because he told it best. Their grandmother picked crab meat and chewed and listened. She studied James's face as he spoke. She looked from one to the other of them, especially at Maybeth. At the end she raised her eyebrows a little and said to Dicey, "You ran a risk to hire yourselves out."

"I had to," Dicey said.

"I can see that."

Then lunch was over and it really was time for Will and Claire to leave. The rain had stopped by then and the thick masses of grey clouds were beginning to break apart. A golden beam of sunlight would occasionally slip past the guard the clouds had put up. But the mood as the children stood around Claire's car, saying goodbye, was still rainy.

"Well," Dicey said.

"Well," Will said. Then, like a bolt of sunlight he changed the subject from goodbye. "It's turning into biking weather, wouldn't you say, Claire?"

Dicey grinned at him then. "Don't lose touch with us," she said. He reached into his shirt pocket and pulled out a calling card, printed with the name of the circus and an address in New York City.

"My booking agent," Will said. "He always knows where we are."

Dicey reached up and kissed him on the cheek. His short beard scratched at her cheek as his arms hugged her, round and strong, for the briefest of times.

"You'll be OK," he assured her. "I don't know what that old lady will do – I don't think even she knows – but you kids, remember you can always call on us."

Dicey nodded, and tried to smile. What was the matter with her today? Wasn't she used to saying goodbye?

The white car drove off, splashing through puddles, its wheels throwing muddy water aside.

Sammy asked if he could ride his bike and Dicey gave him permission. Maybeth went into the house to help their grandmother clear up. James and Dicey worked out plans for mending the biggest holes in the side of the barn.

"Whadda you think, Dicey," James finally asked. "Are we going to stay?"

"I think so," Dicey answered. "I think we've shown her we can be useful. And not too much trouble. I think she likes Sammy – maybe because he's named after her son—"

"Our uncle. Did you think of that?"

"And I'm pretty sure we'll be OK here. All of us."

"What about schools?"

"We can ride our bikes downtown and find out. Tomorrow. You want to?"

"Tomorrow's Sunday."

"Then the next day."

"That's Labour Day."

"Then Tuesday of next week. Why are you quarrelling, James? Don't you want to stay?"

"I suppose so. I like it, and all those books. Do you think our grandfather was smart? Do you think he went to college or just read? What do you think he was like?"

"I don't know anything about him except what she said. Would it be OK with you if we stayed?"

"Sure. It's a good place. But Dicey, why did all of her children leave her? She's not so bad."

"Do you think there's something we don't know? Do you think it's dangerous for us?" Dicey asked him.

"Do you like her?" James asked.

Dicey considered this. "You know? I could. I mean, she's

so odd and prickly. She fights us, or anyway I feel like I'm fighting her and she's fighting back, as if we both know what's going on but neither of us is saying anything. It's fun."

"You're crazy," James said.

"Maybe. But she's a good enemy – you know? In that way. Cousin Eunice wasn't." Dicey thought some more. "So she might make a good friend," Dicey said finally.

"You are crazy," James said. He looked at her. "But you might be right. You're smart too, Dicey, do you ever think about that?" Dicey hadn't. It didn't seem very important to her, not the way it was to James.

Sammy had ridden out of sight, beyond the long driveway. He wasn't back in an hour and he wasn't back in two hours. The rain clouds blew away, leaving room for a bright red sunset, where fiery lights burned behind the clouds that gathered around the lowering sun.

They had cold ham for supper, and Sammy hadn't returned when they sat down. Dicey was worried. She didn't dare say anything, though. They sat down in a trouble silence.

When she heard Sammy's feet on the steps of the porch, Dicey's appetite revived. He burst in the door to the kitchen, his cheeks red, his eyes sparkling.

"Wash your hands," Dicey said. She could see him and he was fine, he was safe and back again. Relief dissolved into anger then. She looked at her grandmother.

"When you've done that, go to your room," their grandmother said.

Sammy turned. "But I'm hungry."

"That'll help you remember. Did you tell your sister where you were going?" Sammy's jaw went out. He wasn't going to answer, not to tell a lie.

"Did he tell you?" Dicey shook her head. "Did he have your permission?"

"Sort of," Dicey said.

"Sort of?" their grandmother said in a sharp, sarcastic voice. "Sort of? How do you sort of give permission to disappear for hours at a time? What do you say? 'OK, Sammy, go sort of run wild and sort of let people worry?' Are you stupid, girl?"

Dicey chewed her lip. Why did every adult send kids away from the table? Maybe because nobody sent *them* to bed hungry. Maybe they'd forgotten what hungry was. But it wasn't right. Dicey knew what hungry was, and so did Sammy.

"It's not Dicey's fault," Sammy said. "It's my fault. Don't yell at Dicey."

"I will yell at whom I please," his grandmother answered him. "I have told you to go to your room."

"No," Dicey said quietly.

"Dicey!" James whispered.

"It's not right, James," Dicey said. "It's not right to send him to bed hungry. I can't let that happen, and I was wrong when I let Cousin Eunice do it. Sit down and eat, Sammy," Dicey said.

Then she turned to try to explain to her grandmother. Her grandmother's eyes flashed. Her face was stiff and pale.

Her lips were hard together.

"You," Dicey said. She wanted to call her by name, but she had no name to call her. "You don't understand, not what it is to be hungry. It doesn't serve any purpose to punish Sammy that way."

Her grandmother's fury burned behind her immobile face. Her hand clenched the handle of the fork.

Dicey was frightened, with a fear that swelled up deep within her. This fear had two heads, and Dicey was caught between them: she was afraid to speak and lose what they had gained of a place for themselves in this house; she was afraid to keep silent and lose what she felt was right for Sammy, for her family. This was a more difficult danger than any she had faced before. It wasn't the kind of danger you could run away from, or fight back at. Dicey wasn't even sure she wanted to fight. She just knew she had to stand by her brother and her family.

"Whose house is this?" their grandmother said. "Whose food? Whose table?"

"You're right," Dicey said. "It's not our house, that's what you said from the beginning. But we're not your family, you meant that too, didn't you?"

Her grandmother stared at her.

"Sit down and eat," Dicey said to Sammy. James and Maybeth were staring at her. Everybody was staring at her. "But you're not to ride the bike again for two days."

"Aw, Dicey," Sammy said. He slipped into his chair and cut his meat.

"I mean it. No matter what. Will you obey?"

Sammy nodded.

"You have to say when you're going off," Dicey said. She ignored her grandmother, who was sitting at the head of the table in a silence of furious anger.

Sammy nodded again. "I know. I will, I'm sorry, Dicey," he said, with a weak smile. Then he turned to his grandmother. "I'm sorry to you, too. I didn't mean to make trouble. But it's my fault, not Dicey's."

"You're a child," his grandmother answered.

"So is Dicey," Sammy said.

"I will not have this talking back!" their grandmother snapped.

"But it's not talking back," James said. His voice was high and frightened. "It's explaining. We're trying to get at the truth." His grandmother stared at him before she answered, as if he had said something she didn't understand.

"You are in my home," their grandmother said. She looked round the table at the four pairs of hazel eyes, none as dark as hers. And none, except Dicey's, as angry as hers. "My home, not yours," their grandmother said.

We might as well have it out now as any other time, Dicey said to herself. She felt as if she had been running away from this for days, and she had only the last of her strength left. She had to turn and fight now. She took a deep, shivering breath.

"Are you expecting us to stay then?" she demanded. Her voice sounded thin and hard.

Her grandmother's mouth worked, and she looked

surprised, as if she hadn't understood what it was they were fighting about this time. Her mouth formed words, but no sound came out. Finally she spoke:

"No."

The word ballooned out and filled all the air of the kitchen. Dicey didn't even try to argue. She just nodded her head and ate her supper in silence and helped with the dishes, and when the little children went up to bed she went with them. The *No* filled the whole air of the house. Every time she breathed in she breathed in that *No*. Dicey wasn't even frightened any more. She was simply defeated. She fell asleep suddenly and without any thought.

Chapter Eleven

DICEY AWOKE TO a thick, black silence. She slipped out of bed and went to the window. Night smothered the land. A dark wind blew clouds over the face of the moon and over the little stars. This kind of wind blew in clear weather. So tomorrow would be a good day to begin travelling again.

They had only seven dollars left, but they had bicycles now, and Dicey had her jackknife and her map. What they didn't have was any place to go.

Back to Bridgeport, Dicey supposed, the long way back.

Will couldn't help them. They couldn't live with the circus. James had to go to school. And so did Maybeth, but for different reasons.

Could they hide out? Could they find the circus again and travel south and then pitch a permanent camp somewhere? Dicey thought they could manage that. She could lie to any school officials. She'd be eighteen in five years. She could say they lived back in the hills with their momma and their momma couldn't come in because she was working the farm. Nobody'd care enough to question, not as long as they showed up in school. There was a boy Dicey knew in Provincetown who ran away from home and he just kept on coming to school and nobody knew, not for months.

The plan was possible, Dicey thought. Only she couldn't get excited about it. Having somewhere in mind that you were travelling to was different from not having anywhere.

But it *was* a plan. She'd ask James what he thought. He might think they should go back to Bridgeport, and he might be right. One way or the other, north or south, they'd be moving on.

"OK," Dicey said to herself, "OK, that's what we'll do." She thought she'd go back to bed and sleep some more, if she could get to sleep again. She took a last look – seeing in her mind's eye the things she couldn't really see, the pines and the fields, the marshes and the bay beyond, the barn that held the sailboat like a buried treasure in its dark belly. Dicey belonged here. She belonged here; yet she was being blown away. Well, it wasn't her house, that was true. It was their grandmother's house and they were not welcome. They would stay together, at least that. She could go along with Cousin Eunice on everything except about that; she wouldn't agree to sending Sammy or Maybeth away. She'd say that right away.

Dicey noticed a yellow light, flowing on to the lawn below the porch. Had somebody left the kitchen light on?

Chapter Eleven

She went downstairs to turn it off.

Her grandmother sat at the kitchen table wearing an old striped cotton bathrobe. She had a cup of tea before her and a pad of paper on which she was writing. Her hair was all in tousled curls. She looked up at Dicey when Dicey came in.

"I couldn't sleep, so I'm writing to that silly woman, Eunice," she said.

Dicey stared. Her grandmother was pretty. Her face had delicate straight bones, and those wide dark eyes.

"What're you staring at, girl?"

"You. You're pretty. I never noticed," Dicey said. "Never mind. I saw the light from my window. I didn't know anyone was here. I'm sorry."

"Sit down," her grandmother said. "Get a glass of milk first. I wondered who'd taken that room when I heard you up there. Get your milk and sit – I've got something I should say to you."

Dicey poured herself a glass of milk and sat down. She had never really looked at her grandmother before, just at the enemy she had to trick, just at her bare feet.

"It's OK," Dicey said. "I'm not going to argue about staying."

"Wouldn't do you any good," her grandmother said. She put the cap on the pen and twisted it shut. "But I should apologize for yelling at you."

Her grandmother's mouth twisted in her sudden smile. "That Will seems a good man. Could you go to him? Would you rather do that than go back to this woman?"

447

"I was thinking about that," Dicey said. "I was going to ask James what he thought. He's the one, really, he should go to school. Well, Maybeth should too."

"Maybeth's not retarded," her grandmother said.

"I know that. She is slow, though. Not as slow as she seems in school, but..." Why go over this again? "There was a lady, a nun, in Bridgeport. She might help Maybeth."

Her grandmother sipped at her cup of tea and Dicey drank at her milk.

"I want to explain," Dicey's grandmother said. "I've never explained before, to anyone, but I have to now. Because, in a way, I do want to keep you here. But I can't."

Dicey nodded. She could feel how true that was. Her grandmother went on speaking.

"I'm old. Not very old yet, but getting older. You can't tell what will happen. What if I fell ill, for instance? And I've very little money. When my husband died he left some insurance. Enough to live on if I live carefully. I don't mind that. But it's expensive with children." She smiled again. "I'm already going to have to die a month sooner than I planned, with the food this week."

"That's crazy," Dicey said.

"It's a joke, girl," her grandmother said. "I mean to explain that I don't have the money. Will said Social Security would give me money for you. But I never took charity."

"Momma wouldn't, either. That's why she was taking us to Aunt Cilla's house," Dicey said. "I understand about that," she said.

Chapter Eleven

"There's more, too," her grandmother said. "I don't know whether you can understand this now, but if not now there's always later. I was married for thirty-eight years and my husband just died these four years ago. Until then, until he died – when you marry someone you make promises. I kept those promises, love and honour and obey. Even when I didn't want to I kept them. I kept quiet when I had things to say. I always went his way."

"That's hard to believe," Dicey said.

"It is, isn't it? Since he died, I've been different. It took a while, but – it's my own life I'm living now. I had a hard time getting it. I don't want to give it up. No lies, no pretending, no standing back quiet when I want to fight."

Dicey thought of Cousin Eunice. She couldn't picture her grandmother like Cousin Eunice. It would be awful if her grandmother was like that.

"It's OK," Dicey said. "I understand."

"That's more than your momma could," her grandmother said. "She felt sorry for me – do you know that?"

"No. She never talked about you. Except to Sammy and he couldn't remember."

"Your momma stuck around here a long time just because she felt sorry for me. I was glad when she began seeing Francis. He was handsome and cheerful. I thought, maybe she'll be happy, maybe she'll steady him down. But do you know what I said to her, just before she left this house? She was twenty-one then and her father couldn't stop her. I said – 'We don't want to hear anything from you until we hear that you've been married.' He was right beside me then and I knew it was what he would say. So I was the one to say it, because I didn't want her thinking I wouldn't stand by him. I had to stand by him – he was my husband. Do you know what she said? She said, 'I'll never get married.' She wasn't angry. She never fought, not your mother. She was gentle – like Maybeth. Your father wasn't a fighter, either. I don't know where you get it from, because you *are*."

Dicey knew where she got it from, but she had a more urgent question. "Why didn't Momma want to get married?"

"She had seen what happens. She didn't want to give her word, like I did. We keep our promises, we Tillermans. We keep them hard."

"But I don't understand. Can't you love somebody and fight with them? I fight with Sammy, and with James. I make Maybeth do things she's scared to do. But that's because I love them. If I didn't love them I wouldn't bother. And they fight back – like James walking out here instead of waiting, that's fighting back. It was OK too, because it was his own decision. I want him to make his own decisions. Didn't you love Momma?"

"Oh yes, I loved my children. I had a lot of love to give in those days, to my husband too. But it got turned around. I got turned around. I let myself get turned around." Her grandmother waved her hand, vaguely, to brush away the memories like you brush away cobwebs. "And it's all gone now and they're all gone now. So it's the past."

Dicey finished her milk. "Will you tell them about

Momma not marrying? I lied to them about it. It was better
then, to lie. Now it isn't; at least, I don't think so. I'll tell them
if you won't, but if you would they'd understand better."

"Maybe. Maybe I'll try."

"I saw a picture of you when you were little," Dicey said.
"Cousin Eunice had one. You looked angry."

"I was angry — most of my life," her grandmother said.
"Not any more — if you can believe that. Just crazy now, and
that's an improvement. Not really crazy. Eccentric. But those
years, morning to night. All that anger — you can choke
swallowing back anger. And it still sneaks out, in little ways,
and everybody knows although nobody says anything. So
they left, every one. They couldn't stay here. All of my
children, they ran as fast and as far as they could. My Sammy,
he died of it, and that was hard. Hard. And your poor
momma— They shamed me. And I shamed myself." She
chewed on her lip. Then she looked Dicey full in the eyes and
said:

"I failed them. I let them go. I told them to go. There were
times I could have killed him. He'd sit chewing and the anger
and shame were sitting at the table with us. Chew and
swallow, so sure he was right. But I'd promised him – and he
didn't know why they each left. I did. So, I'm responsible. I
won't have that responsibility again. Not to fail again."

"Are you sure you'd fail?" Dicey asked in a low voice. "We
can't stay here, I know. Don't worry about that. But I don't
think you'd fail with us. We had Momma. And I wouldn't let
those things happen." That was true, even though her

grandmother had this big house and what remained of the farm to keep her fed.

Her grandmother nodded. "You've got determination," she said.

"Momma said it was in my blood," Dicey answered. "I never knew what she meant before."

"Your Momma was a kind child," her grandmother said. "But she never forgave her father."

"Did you?" Dicey asked.

"No. Yes."

Somehow, this made sense to Dicey. It let her know that she would be all right, and her family would be all right. They wouldn't be children for ever. They didn't have to have a place, they just had to have themselves. She yawned, fighting it off and losing.

"You'd better get back to bed. I'll finish this letter to that Eunice now. I'll try to tell her about Maybeth — but she's such a silly woman I doubt she's got two ounces of common sense rattling around in her head. Your cousin doesn't care much for you."

This didn't surprise Dicey. "That's OK," she said.

"Well, I do," her grandmother said. "I care for all of you. Now get to bed. I'll wash out your glass. Scat!"

Dicey ran upstairs. She ran into her bed and pulled the covers up over her head. Cousin Eunice didn't want them, but she would take them in. Her grandmother wanted them, but wouldn't let them stay. And they, she, James, Maybeth and Sammy — they were the losers. Dicey cried herself to sleep.

Chapter Eleven

She couldn't stop. She tried, but she couldn't. She didn't know if she was crying for her family, or for herself, or for her grandmother – or for all of them, all the Tillermans, Momma too, lost up in Massachusetts, and Bullet lost in Vietnam. They were all lost. Dicey promised herself this was the last time she'd cry, ever, and wept until her eyes were swollen shut and she slept.

Sunlight was pouring over the house and yard and through the windows when Dicey awoke the next morning. She pulled on shorts and a shirt and looked into three empty bedrooms before she came downstairs.

Her grandmother was alone in the kitchen. She was kneading dough. "What's that?" Dicey asked.

"Bread. I haven't made it for years. You slept late."

Dicey nodded, without apologizing. She looked at her grandmother. She had grey splotches under her eyes, and the fine wrinkles that came out from the edges of her eyes and her mouth seemed deeper this morning. This was not quite the same woman Dicey had talked with in the dead of night; but this was not a different woman, either.

Dicey poured herself a glass of milk and took an apple from the bowl of fruit. She stood by the sink, drinking and chewing, and watching her grandmother knead the pale dough. Push–pull, slap, push–pull. Her grandmother leaned into the dough with her shoulders, but handled it gently at the same time.

Her grandmother was contradictory. Except for the fatigue, her grandmother looked perfectly ordinary this morning. Only now Dicey knew better.

There was a warm feeling in her stomach, as if she had swallowed sunshine. At least now, everything was settled, she wasn't battling any more. She liked her grandmother, her momma's mother. She liked her all prickly and contrary. She liked the way her grandmother said one thing and then the opposite, because it made sense to Dicey, the same kind of sense Dicey made to herself. She liked the way the woman had watched Sammy roll naked in the grass. She liked her bare feet.

This was a good way to feel to say goodbye.

"We'll be moving on today," Dicey said. "I wanted to thank you for letting us stay so long."

"Not today, you won't," her grandmother said. "You can't just bolt off like that. You've done enough running away, don't you think?"

Dicey couldn't see her face, but her voice sounded pleasant enough.

"I've written to your cousin. We have to wait and see what she answers. You'll stay here until then. I'll mail the letter Tuesday. We're going to town Tuesday, for food and to talk to the people at the school. What grade are you in?"

"Going into eight," Dicey said. "But why?"

"Do you know how long it'll take that dithering woman to get advice from all the people she talks to and arrange to come and get you? You may, but I don't. Children should be in school. School starts Tuesday, or so James tells me and I have no reason to disbelieve him. Those bikes will give some trouble – I have no idea how to ship bicycles and I won't have them here, rusting in the barn."

"What if we don't want to go back to Bridgeport?" Dicey asked.

"First we find out if you can. For today, while the bread is rising, we might go take a look at Janes Island. It's all marsh and you can't land there. Don't know why they call it an island."

"Where are the little kids?" Dicey asked.

"Down by the dock, bailing out the boat. *They* have all agreed. *They* want to see the island." Her hands slapped at the bread. She poked at it with a finger, then began kneading it again. "I told them, what you wanted me to. Sammy" – she shook her head and slapped the dough down on the table – "he said I was lying and he said he didn't care. Then he said he was sorry, he knew I wasn't lying, but he still didn't care. Maybeth didn't say a word. But James – he told Sammy he did care, and if it was what your momma wanted then that was OK with him because she might have been crazy in some ways but she was never crazy when it came to loving her kids. I asked him where he got ideas like that and he looked me straight in the eye and said, 'From books'." She laughed briefly. "Yes, I told them, I also told them they ought to think twice before they held that lie against you."

Dicey ran down to the dock. The bay was lively, with crisp-topped blue waves under a steady breeze. Her family had bailed out the boat and now they were swimming.

"What's going on, James?" Dicey called. He swam over to her.

"I dunno, Dicey. We'll be here a little longer, that's all I know."

"We're going to an island!" Sammy called. "It's OK about Momma. She didn't want to get married. Did you know?" Dicey nodded.

They motored over to the stretch of marshland just off the town shore. There, they dropped an anchor on the bay side. Birds lived on Janes Island, but nothing else could. One snowy heron soared down, folding its wings in at the last minute, returning to its nest deep in the marsh grass. A few ducks wandered along the muddy shore, in and out of the tall grasses. They saw flocks of gulls, gossiping, bickering, bobbling on the waves, flying in noisy swarms.

Their grandmother had packed a bag of fruit and some cold crab, left over from yesterday's lunch. As they ate, she asked them about their travellings, so James and Dicey took turns telling her. "Well," she kept saying. And, "That was a piece of luck." She didn't ask them about Bridgeport.

Back at the farm, Dicey took Sammy to the barn to begin patching, while James and Maybeth rode their bikes up and down the driveway. "You don't have to do that," their grandmother said to Dicey.

"I know," she said.

The patched place showed up bleak against the wasted pink paint of the barn. They would hold, Dicey knew; they had been nailed into place firmly and the edges were sealed against the weather. If she'd had time, she would have liked to paint the whole barn. Just so there would be something here

Chapter Eleven

to say, "Dicey Tillerman stayed here a while and she made a difference." Dicey figured they had a week, maybe two, before they had to go back to Bridgeport, to the little house and the fussing and fretting. She planned to enjoy the time and not worry about the future. Her grandmother seemed to feel the same way. It was as if now everything was decided, they could both relax.

So they passed two quiet days, hammering, bike riding (except Sammy), swimming, weeding, picking, fixing the mailbox – just living together. In the evenings, they went on to the back porch or into the living-room. Their grandmother found an old checkers set, somewhere deep in a cupboard. Maybeth picked out tunes on the piano. Some of the songs they sang, the songs Momma had sung, their grandmother knew. Some of them she had to learn, and she wasn't very good at it.

Yet, the feelings in the air were not all placid. Dicey disagreed with her grandmother whenever she thought her grandmother was being unfair. "Ah-ummm," she would say, because they still had no name to call their grandmother, "Cousin Eunice tried to do her best. Sure, she's silly, but that's not her fault, is it?"

"Well, whose fault is it then?" their grandmother would answer sharply. "If it's not her own fault for what she's like, I'd like to know whose fault it is."

"OK," Dicey would say, giving ground because privately she thought her grandmother was right, "but she's not bad."

"Who mentioned bad?" their grandmother would say.

"James? Did I? Maybeth, did I say bad? I said silly and I meant silly." Their grandmother would rush on before they could answer. "And there's an end to it."

"Dicey's the one who said silly," James would say.

"Aha!" their grandmother would say. "I told you, Dicey, it's all your fault."

Then Dicey would swallow the disappointment and enjoy this temporary haven. For these two days, she stopped thinking ahead. She learned how to put the bandage on Maybeth's arm, which Maybeth said was better, but their grandmother said should be supported for two full weeks, especially since Maybeth was riding her bike so much.

They took one long ride, James and Dicey and Maybeth. They saw several farmhouses. Some of them had cows and horses. All of them had chickens. Most of them had fields of corn and tomatoes.

Dicey made herself stop thinking about the sailboat in her grandmother's barn. That was to have been the prize, her prize, if they had stayed. She wouldn't go near it now. She knew that if she did she'd begin planning again, and she'd get it down to the water, somehow. Once the boat was in the water, they could take it away and sail south, and hide. But they didn't have any place left to go to. She had been beaten this time, down to her bones beaten. She had fought her hardest and her smartest, and she had lost. She could take that, and she could understand the whys of it. But not if the boat was in the water, and the sails fitted to the mast, and the wind blowing little clouds along the sky. So she shut the sailboat

Chapter Eleven

out of her mind, just as she shut out hoping and caring and the disappointment that waited for her to relax her guard so it could leap out and get its teeth into her. She just lived through the hours, taking them as they came, knowing they would never come again.

Chapter Twelve

ON TUESDAY MORNING, their grandmother started another batch of bread, then told them to take baths and put on fresh shorts and shirts. When the children came downstairs, their grandmother was waiting in the kitchen. She had combed her curly hair with water, but it wouldn't lie flat. She was wearing a dark blue suit, with her blouse tucked in, and lipstick, stockings and loafers.

"You're all dressed up," Dicey said.

"It's old," her grandmother said. "But I'm old. Or do you mean the shoes? I hope you children appreciate what I'm going through for you." But she said that as if it was a joke.

"I don't care if you have bare feet," Sammy said, very serious.

"Neither do I," his grandmother said, "but there are them that do."

Maybeth stood shyly beside Dicey. "You look different," she said to the woman. "Pretty."

Their grandmother blushed. The dark red came up under her tanned cheeks. "I'll be getting vain, the next thing you know. And that's a vice I never had. Let's go." She picked up a worn black purse from the table. "I'm bound to leave this behind somewhere. Keep an eye on it, somebody. James, you're reliable, will you?"

"I'll try," James said.

The wind blew their carefully combed hair all out of order, and the salt spray covered their bodies, so they arrived at the dock looking as they ordinarily did, except their grandmother. She led them down the main street, and then down a side street, to a long, low building that had windows over most of its walls.

Inside, the air was noisy with children's voices. The halls were made of white-painted concrete blocks. A long dim, windowless hallway went down the centre of the building, with classrooms on both sides. It smelt like a school, of chalk and children's sweat, and warm food from the lunchroom. A teacher told their grandmother where the registration office was. The sign over the door said *Guidance*. In the tiny office, they found a fat young woman seated behind a big wooden desk.

"My name is Abigail Tillerman," their grandmother announced. "These children will be in Crisfield temporarily and they ought to be in school until they go back. What's your name?"

Their grandmother sounded nervous.

"Mrs Jenkins," the woman said. "I'm the guidance counsellor." She told them to come in and sit down. The room was so crowded with filing cabinets and plants and her big desk, there was room only for two straight chairs for visitors. Dicey and her grandmother sat in those. James and Maybeth and Sammy crowded into the corners of the room.

"What do you mean by temporarily?" Mrs Jenkins asked.

"For a short time. I'm not sure how long exactly," their grandmother said. "If I could tell you I would."

Mrs Jenkins asked their names and ages, and Dicey told her. She asked for their address, and Dicey looked at her grandmother, who told Mrs Jenkins. Mrs Jenkins asked what the last school they had been in was; her grandmother looked at Dicey, and Dicey told her.

"Parents?" Mrs Jenkins asked.

"Not noticeably," their grandmother said. James gave a short snort of laughter.

"What then is your relationship to them, Mrs Tillerman? I assume you will be responsible for them while they are attending school here."

"I am their mother's mother," their grandmother said.

Mrs Jenkins looked at her for a long moment. Dicey watched her write down, *grandmother*.

"All right then. I will call the Provincetown school to have your records sent to us. I think it would be well to do that now, before we assign the children to classes. Would you like to walk around the school for a bit? Come back, in half an hour, I think."

They trooped out of the office. All the classroom doors were closed, so they went outside. The playground was a huge field of short grass. Scattered over it were jungle gyms and tall swings, sandpits, slides, and a baseball diamond. It was empty now, with the children inside. The equipment gleamed, as if it had never been played on.

"It looks brand new," Dicey said. "The whole school does."

"I should think it is," her grandmother said. Sammy and Maybeth ran off to the swings.

"Who pays for it?" Dicey asked.

"Me," her grandmother said.

Dicey stared at her.

"Taxes, girl."

"Do you pay taxes?"

"Indeed I do. Taxes on land, taxes on my house, death taxes, life taxes. I even pay taxes on the money I keep in the bank."

Dicey hadn't known that. "No wonder you're worried about money," she said.

"But with a farm, there must be ways to get money," James said. "Did you ever think of growing trees?"

His grandmother just looked at him.

"No, Christmas trees, on those front fields. There are pine seedlings already there."

Dicey chimed in. "It shouldn't be hard to grow them and

people always buy Christmas trees. Even we did, in Provincetown."

"Why should anyone buy what they can walk outside and cut down for free?"

"In many places," James said, as if he were talking to somebody a little stupid, "like Annapolis — there they can't just walk outside and cut down a tree."

"How would I get trees to Annapolis?"

"There must be ways." He dismissed that problem. "You could earn money that way. Or you could sell land—"

"No," their grandmother said.

"Or chickens — why don't you have chickens? A lot of other farms do."

"I don't care for the company of chickens."

"Maybe," James said. He leant towards her, earnestly trying to explain his ideas. "But you can sell eggs. You could sell some of your vegetables, too, if you had a stand out front by the driveway. Or you could rent out your fields to some other farmer who wants more land. Or butter," his ideas dashed on. "People will pay for good butter, won't they? You'd need cows, but you've already got stalls in the barn. What about pigs?"

Their grandmother was looking at him, with a contradictory expression, half amusement and half interest.

"You've got to be careful with money and earn it whenever you can," Dicey said.

Her grandmother shook her head, as if Dicey didn't know what she was talking about. Maybe she didn't, Dicey thought.

But maybe she did.

"I know what you're thinking, girl," her grandmother said.

"Then you know I might be right," Dicey answered.

Her grandmother humphed.

"She is," James said. "With inflation, and if you're on fixed income — you could lose the farm if you can't pay taxes."

"Could you?" Dicey asked. "Could that happen?"

"What's that to you?" her grandmother demanded.

"Nothing, I suppose. But if *we* can't be there I want *you* to be. So it matters something. And you can't change that."

Her grandmother humphed again.

When they returned to Mrs Jenkins' office, the counsellor was waiting for them. She had papers on her desk, and a pad with notes all over it. She waited until they were all in, all five of them, before she said anything.

The first thing she said was, "You're in the wrong school, Dicey. You should be in the junior high. I've called and they'll expect you tomorrow morning. Mr MacGuire will be your guidance counsellor. Can you find the junior high?"

"She can," their grandmother said.

Dicey hadn't thought that she'd be in a different school.

"James will go into the accelerated section of fifth grade. We have some special programmes for the gifted pupil. They should suit you, James. Your teacher will be Mr Thomas."

James looked at Dicey and grinned. She knew what he was thinking: a man teacher. There weren't any men teachers in the elementary school in Provincetown, not one.

"Sammy will be in Miss Tieds' second grade."

"OK," said Sammy. "I don't care."

"James and Sammy," Mrs Jenkins said, "I want you to meet your teachers today. If you go to the principal's office, they will come there when the recess bell rings. That will be in ten minutes. It's the third floor on your right, as you go down the hall. You may go now."

The boys left together. James walked eagerly, but Sammy dragged his heels. James turned at the door. "Don't forget your purse," he said to their grandmother. She waved him away.

Mrs Jenkins gathered her papers into a pile.

"What about Maybeth?" Dicey asked. She got herself ready to fight for Maybeth.

"I'm coming to that," Mrs Jenkins said. Maybeth sidled over between the two chairs Dicey and their grandmother sat in. She didn't say anything.

"Your records – Maybeth, are you listening to me?" Mrs Jenkins asked. She spoke without emphasis. Maybeth nodded. "Your records show that they wanted to hold you back in second grade. That would be the second time you have been kept back. Did you know that?" She turned to their grandmother. "Their recommendation is – most strong."

"But—" Dicey began.

Mrs Jenkins cut her off, to say: "Our school, however, has a policy not to put brothers and sisters in the same grade. Do you want to be in Sammy's grade, Maybeth?"

Maybeth shook her head, no. She looked at Dicey.

"Why not?" Mrs Jenkins asked.

Maybeth waited. No one else said anything. "Because I'm bigger than he is," she whispered.

"I thought so." Mrs Jenkins smiled. When she smiled, with her short dark hair and bright cheeks, she looked like a kid herself, Dicey thought. She was as fresh as apples.

"I thought that would be the case. If you want to go into third grade – and mind you, I'm not promising anything – but if you want to try, you'll have to take some tests for me."

"What kind of tests?" their grandmother asked.

"A quick IQ, then reading and maths, achievement and aptitude. They're short and not precise, but they'll give a fairly good idea of where Maybeth can be put in school." Mrs Jenkins waited for an answer.

"How long will it take?" their grandmother asked.

"An hour at the most. Will you do that, Maybeth?" Mrs Jenkins kept talking to Maybeth. Maybeth looked at Dicey with wide eyes.

Their grandmother stood up. "We have errands to do, so if you'll tell James and Sammy to bring Maybeth and wait for us by the boat, I have no objections."

Maybeth's hand held on to Dicey's arm.

"But – can I stay?" Dicey asked Mrs Jenkins. "It'll be better. You don't understand—"

"No," her grandmother said. "Maybeth will take the tests by herself."

"I would prefer that," Mrs Jenkins said.

"Don't argue, girl," her grandmother said to Dicey, just as

Dicey was opening her mouth to say she wasn't going to leave Maybeth there alone. Her grandmother spoke to Maybeth. "Maybeth? You've got two hard times coming. This, now, is the first. Tomorrow morning is the next. Nothing will make them easier. That's the way it is. Do you understand that?"

Maybeth nodded, but her hand stayed on Dicey's arm.

"Will you try?" their grandmother asked. "It'll take some courage, but I think you've got that. Do you have it?"

"I don't know," Maybeth said. "I'll try." She released Dicey's arm. "It'll be OK, Dicey."

Dicey wasn't sure.

"Come along," her grandmother ordered. "I'll see you tomorrow morning, Mrs Jenkins. Mind you, she's ripped a tendon in her right arm so her writing won't be much."

"Yes, thank you," Mrs Jenkins said. She stood up, and Dicey followed her grandmother out of the little office, leaving Maybeth behind.

When they stepped out of the building into the hot morning sunlight, her grandmother turned on Dicey. "You've got to let her make her own way."

"I know," Dicey said. "But—"

"But nothing. But hogwash. If she can't do that—"

"But she *is*," Dicey argued. "She's doing it right now."

Her grandmother nodded her head briskly. "Yes, so she is."

They strolled back to the main street and entered the grocery store Dicey had gone into days earlier. The storekeeper and butcher, Millie, looked like she wanted to say something when she saw them, she looked like she had several somethings to say, but she didn't dare. Dicey didn't know how her grandmother stopped the questions, but she did, by the glitter in her eye and the lift to her chin. Dicey took part of their list and went around the store finding cans of tuna, jars of peanut butter, bags of apples, and all the odds and ends that go to keeping house for a family. The store was warm and dim. Her grandmother spent a long time at the meat counter.

When they were ready to check out, Dicey stood awkwardly aside. The bill came to forty-seven dollars. Dicey chewed on her lip. Maybe she could find work. Maybe she could find work here, dusting the shelves and washing the windows and making the place look brighter, cleaner, more like a place where you wanted to buy groceries.

Her grandmother paid the bill. Millie took the money and gave her back her change without a word. She packed the groceries into four large bags.

Then the shopkeeper could hold her tongue no longer. "I see you found work," she said to Dicey.

"Yes," Dicey said. She said no more. She turned her chin up the way her grandmother's chin was held. It worked in just the same way.

"Tell me, Millie," her grandmother said, with a side glance at Dicey. "Do you get Social Security money?"

"Of course, since Herbie died. It's my due. I paid into it every month, all my working life. It's a widow's due, I tell you.

I couldn't get through the month without it, not with what the store brings. Widow's due, that's what I call it, and there's no shame. You take it too, don't you?"

"I didn't work to pay in," Dicey's grandmother said.

"No more you didn't, Ab Tillerman, raising three children and working on that farm. Your John did, too, every year in his taxes. It's for widows and their children, as much as for people older than we are, and helpless. So don't raise your nose at me."

"Ever buy a Christmas tree?" Dicey's grandmother demanded.

The abrupt change of topic flustered Millie. "What?" she asked. "What do you mean? For Christmas? Why should I do that, when I can get one cut for me just by asking? I know a lady in Cambridge that bought one, but I never did. What kind of a question is that?"

"How much did she pay?"

"How should I know? Ten, fifteen dollars, I think she said. And it was a scrawny thing, too, some poor relation of a loblolly. She had more bulbs than branches on the thing, trying to make it look right. You feeling all right, Ab?"

Dicey looked at her grandmother, glad because it meant her grandmother was thinking of putting in a cash crop, to repay herself the money she'd spent on the Tillermans.

"See if your family's around, girl," her grandmother said. "We're going to need some extra hands with these bags."

Dicey went out through the door.

Sunlight burned on the street. She saw James across by the

docks, leading Maybeth and Sammy down to the boat.

"Hey!" she called. "Hey! James! Over here."

They turned and strolled towards her. They looked tanned, healthy and perfectly ordinary. Dicey tried to read in Maybeth's face what had happened.

"I thought you were at the boat," James said.

Maybeth nodded and her eyes gleamed. "I can go into third grade. I read for her, the most I could. Out loud. I tried to sound out the words I didn't know, just like they said at school. It was easier, because it was the story about the little goats that felt left at home and the wolf comes and tries to trick them into opening the door. So I knew the story. I told Mrs Jenkins I already knew it and asked her if she wanted to find another story to test me with, but she said it was OK. She said even if I knew the story I'd still have to read the words. I answered all her questions about it, but they were easy ones. I got two wrong on the adding and three on subtracting, and they don't start multiplication until third grade. But they know fractions already."

"I can show you fractions," Dicey said. "Was it hard?"

"Not as hard as I thought," Maybeth said. "Not as hard as tomorrow will be. But I think maybe I can do that too."

Their grandmother pushed the screen door aside. "What are you waiting for?"

Maybeth ran over to her and pulled on her arm. Their grandmother bent her grey curly head down to the bright yellow head. She listened to Maybeth and smiled at what she heard.

The children went inside. Sammy said he wasn't too small to carry a bag, but he was, so Millie divided one bag into two smaller bags, one for Sammy and one for Maybeth. Her eyes bugged out with curiosity.

"By the way, Millie," their grandmother finally said, "I don't believe you've met my grandchildren." One by one she introduced them. "Liza's brood," their grandmother said. "They'll be staying with me for a couple of weeks."

Their grandmother herded them outside before Millie could ask any questions. They walked together down the hot street and along the dock. Dicey got into the boat first. James handed the bags down to her.

Sammy had been thinking. "If you're our grandmother – I mean, if you say you are – I mean, you know you are but you never said so – now that you say so what do I call you?"

The boat was rocking under Dicey's feet. She wished they weren't going to be in different schools, even for this little time. In Bridgeport, there would be boys' schools and girls' schools, and they'd all be split up. She wished that here, just for this little while, they could still be in the same school. But it didn't matter. It was just another way things weren't working out.

"You'll call me Gram," their grandmother said to Sammy.

"Gram," Sammy repeated, trying it. He ran to the edge of the dock and wheeled around. "Hey, Gram!" he yelled. He ran back. "Gram?"

"Yes, Sammy." She sounded tired.

"You like us, don't you? You do, no matter what you say. I know."

Chapter Twelve

"Never said I didn't," Gram said. "And I'm pretty proud of Maybeth at this moment."

"So am I," Dicey said.

"So am I," Maybeth said, with a smile at herself, a smile that had no silliness in it.

They all stood for a minute there. Little bright-topped waves rocked the boat gently on the way to pattering up against the seawalls. A salty wind blew from the land out over the water. The town of Crisfield lay in the sunlight before them, bleached white as the oyster shells scattered around the ground.

Dicey thought about the bread dough rising in the big earthenware bowl back on the scrubbed wooden table in her grandmother's kitchen. She was getting hungry. She looked at James. He was studying his grandmother, as if he was hungry too, but for something not food, hungry in a way that food could never fill.

It wasn't fair, not just for Dicey, but for all of them. Well, Dicey said to herself, life isn't fair. Everybody said that to you. They had all tried, and they had lost, and they were going to have to make the best of it with Cousin Eunice.

She remembered the letter then. Gram hadn't mailed the letter. Dicey thought about not telling her grandmother; but not for long. What was the use of postponing it? When something bad was going to happen it got worse the longer you waited. If she didn't tell Gram, that would be like asking again. And Gram had said no. Dicey wasn't the kind to argue and beg when somebody said no.

"You forgot to mail your letter," she said.

Gram's face was surprised. She really had forgotten it. She was also surprised (Dicey knew this too) that Dicey had remembered and said something. She opened her purse and took it out.

Dicey looked down at the floorboards of the little boat. She looked at her sneakers, worn with all the travelling they'd done. Her big toes stuck out through the canvas. Those sneakers had come a long way.

Wasn't it worth it, having come such a way, to fight a little harder? A little longer? Being told no twice couldn't be worse than being told no once.

"Gram?" Dicey said. She looked up. She was almost as tall as her grandmother, but now the woman loomed above her, standing on the dock. The dark hazel eyes stared down at her, forbidding her to speak.

"Well, you should," Dicey said fiercely. "You should let us live with you."

That was no way to ask.

"Would that suit you?" Gram asked Dicey.

Dicey was shocked into silence.

"I thought you were the one it didn't suit," James said.

"Well, it doesn't," Gram said. "But it will. I give up. I do, I give up. You've worn me out. You can stay, you can live with me. You hear that, girl?" she called down to Dicey.

"Do you mean it?" Dicey asked.

"I don't say what I don't mean. You should know that. You'll live with me and we'll see lawyers about adoption and take government money – and we'll plant Christmas trees and raise chickens, whatever we have to do, whatever ideas James cooks up that we can't talk him out of. But can we go now, please? My feet are itching me half to death."

But instead of getting into the boat, Gram held up the letter to Cousin Eunice and ripped it into little pieces. She tossed the scraps into the air. The breeze took them out and dropped them on to the dancing waves.

"I'll have to write to her again," Gram said, as if the idea gave her no pleasure.

"Gram," Dicey said. Her grandmother looked down at her again. "The boat, the sailboat in the barn. Can I fix it up and sail it? Can I have it?"

"Do you know how to sail?"

"No. But I could learn. Could you teach me?"

"Yes," Gram said.

"Yes, what?" Dicey asked.

"Yes to both – and no more questions; not until I get my shoes off."

Gram climbed down into the boat and held it steady against the dock while the little children jumped in. James threw the painter down to Dicey and leapt down himself.

"Ready to go home?" Gram asked Dicey. She was smiling.

Dicey just grinned back. "Ready," she said.

Postscript

Homecoming is not an autobiographical work, and neither is it someone's real story. Except for the geography, *Homecoming* is fiction. That is to say, it's a story I made up about imaginary people living imaginary lives, one summer of which I chose to write about in a book.

I can remember how *Homecoming* began in my imagination. It was a Friday afternoon (which I happen to know for sure because I did my weekly grocery shopping on Fridays, on my way home from the school where I taught). I parked my car in the large car park by the supermarket and got out, like every other Friday. But that day, walking towards the store, I passed several children alone in another parked car, an estate car. Now these children didn't do anything particularly attention-catching. They didn't sing at me, or throw their shoes at me, or cuss me out or ask for help; in fact, I don't know if they even noticed me. They were just waiting in their car for their adult to complete the shopping and return to them.

But my imagination wondered, as I entered the store: what would happen, if nobody returned to take those children home? And then: whatever could have happened before that, to keep somebody from returning to her children? And: what would happen next? That was the beginning of *Homecoming* and also, as it turned out, of the six following books that make up the Tillerman stories. More important, that was how the Tillermans first entered my life.

Getting the Tillermans right – if that is what I have done, and I do hope it is – was part thorough and meticulous planning, and part chance, lucky accidents. I felt as if I was stumbling around in some authorial game of Blind Man's Buff, trying to feel the faces of people I couldn't see.

From the start, I planned on four children, and I planned to have them in balance, two boys and two girls. Brothers and sisters, of course, are both very similar and entirely different, and that also needed careful planning. So I had two of the Tillermans be dark and skinny types, while two others were sturdier, blonder; but all of them had hazel eyes and all of them felt strongly that they belong together. Two of them were older children, two younger. Two resembled their missing father, two their lost mother. All of them accepted their father's absence, and longed for their mother's return.

As I decided these things, and named the children, filling up page after page of my notebook, I was really trying to discover who each of the four children was. Until I knew who they were, how would I know what each might say, and do, and feel, in all the circumstances that make up the story?

So I made some decisions. Dicey would be an oldest child, quick-witted but not an intellectual, and practical and responsible, because she had always had to be that. A problem solver, Dicey would concentrate on what was happening now, what needed to be done right away to deal with the present problem.

Then James could be the intellectual, the conceptualizer. This is not always an easy person to be, because you can understand things you might prefer not to be aware of, and you tend to have a restless, unsatisfied brain that works away all the time. James would not be an easygoing, relaxed kind of person; and he would be more fearful than the others.

If James was so very smart, then Maybeth could be the opposite. She could be not at all good at school, not school smart; although her instincts about people could be very good. Maybeth would be the shy, silent character, very pretty, and always agreeable – maybe even too agreeable. She could be an opposite to Dicey, someone people wanted to protect, and take care of.

Sammy was the easiest Tillerman for me, because he was the kind of seven-year-old I imagined my two-year-old son would grow up like, stubborn and quarrelsome, with lots of physical energy, smart but not at all interested in school. Sammy was a trier, like Dicey. Those two would never give up; those two could drive you crazy with their not giving up.

Dicey, James, Maybeth and Sammy, those four I planned and worked out, and wrote about until I felt like I knew them, until they were as three-dimensional as statues for me. But Gram – who is also one of the Tillermans; you might even call her the core Tillerman – was the unexpected guest, the uninvited. Gram, I often say, leapt out at me from my typewriter, like Athena from Zeus's head, full-grown and impatient, out of temper with me for not thinking of her for myself.

I hadn't planned on Gram. In fact, I had planned to end the book in Bridgeport. But out of nowhere, there she was. I could hear her voice. I knew who she was, and why she was the kind of person she was, and how she would interact with the four children. Gram changed my book entirely, *and* she took over the end of it. I wish I could claim her character as I can claim the others, but the most I can say in my favour is that when she appeared, I had the wits to recognize her right away, and grab her, and hold on.

That sense of recognition – whether I earn it by planned, attentive labours or receive it like a gift falling into my hands from out of the blue – is what I wait for when I am writing. Until I feel as if my characters are real, the story can't properly begin. This puts me in a curious position in relation to my characters, curious and maybe ludicrous, too, but not uncomfortable. In fact, just as unquestionably as I know that I made them up, I believe my characters *are* real. I would be only a little surprised to answer my door one day and find these five Tillermans (and everybody else, too) standing there on the porch, come to tell me about the mistakes I made in their story, and to ask me, would I please for Pete's sake get it right this time?

CYNTHIA VOIGT

I watch his car as it pulls into the parking lot. I watch him get out of it. I am in the corner of his eye, moving toward its center... but he isn't looking for me. He's heading into school without noticing I'm right here. I could call out for him, but he doesn't like that. He says it's something needy girls do, always calling out to their boyfriends. The school door opens and the school door closes, and he doesn't realize I am on the other side. Standing there, I wonder how I can be so full of him while he's so empty of me. I love hate him that I'm hi night is isn't lo wonde still happ of our something non-stupid neath. All I did was ask him if he time. I told him it wasn't my fault he's always afraid of plans, afraid of figuring out what's next. Mistake. Calling him afraid was a big mistake. That's probably the only word he heard. "You have no idea what you're talking about," he said. "I was talking about a party at Steve's house on Saturday," I told

That has to be what love is — seeing what a mess he is and loving him anyway, because you know you're a mess, too, maybe even worse. We weren't an hour into our first date before Justin was setting off the alarms." "I'm warning you, I'm trouble," he said over dinner at TGI Fridays. "Total trouble." "And do you warn all the other girls?" I replied, flirting. But what I got back wasn't flirtation. It was real. "No," he said. "I don't. This was his way of letting me know that I was someone I cared about. Even at the very beginning, tell me. But though he's letails about ver forgotten ned you! nights really say I metimes hold him h t - Some- es I've eady let feeling nd that here's othing I can s. The only me our paths intersect in the

ANOTHER DAY

DAVID LEVITHAN

First Published in Great Britain in 2015
by Electric Monkey, an imprint of Egmont UK Limited
The Yellow Building, 1 Nicholas Road, London W11 4AN

First published in the USA in 2015
by Alfred A Knopf,
an imprint of Random House Children's Books,
a division of Random House LLC,
a Penguin Random House Company, New York

ISBN 978 1 4052 7343 5

1 3 5 7 9 10 8 6 4 2

www.egmont.co.uk

A CIP catalogue record for this title is available from the British Library

Typeset by Avon DataSet Ltd, Bidford on Avon, Warwickshire
Printed and bound in Great Britain by CPI Group

58071/1

For my nephew, Matthew
(May you find happiness every day)

I watch his car as it pulls into the parking lot. I watch him get out of it. I am in the corner of his eye, moving toward its center – but he isn't looking for me. He's heading into school without noticing I'm right here. I could call out for him, but he doesn't like that. He says it's something needy girls do, always calling out to their boyfriends.

It hurts that I can be so full of him while he's so empty of me.

I wonder if last night is the reason he isn't looking for me. I wonder if our fight is still happening. Like most of our fights, it's about something stupid, with other non-stupid things right underneath. All I did was ask him if he wanted to go to Steve's party on Saturday. That was it. And he asked me why, on Sunday night, I was already asking him about Saturday. He said I'm always doing this, trying to pin him down, as if he won't want to be with me if I don't ask him about it months ahead of time. I told him it wasn't my fault he's always afraid of plans, afraid of figuring out what's next.

Mistake. Calling him afraid was a big mistake. That's probably the only word he heard.

"You have no idea what you're talking about," he said.

"I was talking about a party at Steve's house on Saturday," I told him, my voice way too upset for either of us. "That's all."

But that's not all. Justin loves me and hates me as much as I love him and hate him. I know that. We each have our triggers, and we should never reach in to pull them. But sometimes we can't help ourselves. We know each other too well, but never well enough.

I am in love with someone who's afraid of the future. And, like a fool, I keep bringing it up.

I follow him. Of course I do. Only a needy girl would be mad at her boyfriend because he didn't notice her in a parking lot.

As I'm walking to his locker, I wonder which Justin I'll find there. It probably won't be Sweet Justin, because it's rare for Sweet Justin to show up at school. And hopefully it won't be Angry Justin, because I haven't done anything *that* wrong, I don't think. I'm hoping for Chill Justin, because I like Chill Justin. When he's around, we can all calm down.

I stand there as he takes his books out of his locker. I look at the back of his neck because I am in love with the back of his neck. There is something so physical about it, something that makes me want to lean over and kiss it.

Finally he looks at me. I can't read his expression, not right away. It's like he's trying to figure me out at the same time I'm trying to figure him out. I think maybe this is a good sign, because maybe it means he's worried about me. Or it's a bad sign, because he doesn't understand why I'm here.

"Hey," he says.

"Hey," I say back.

There's something really intense about the way he's looking at me. I'm sure he's finding something wrong. There's always something wrong for him to find.

But he doesn't say anything. Which is weird. Then, even weirder, he asks me, "Are you okay?"

I must look really pathetic if he's asking me that.

"Sure," I tell him. Because I don't know what the answer is supposed to be. *I am not okay* – that's actually the answer. But it's not the right answer to say to him. I know that much.

If this is some kind of trap, I don't appreciate it. If this is payback for what I said last night, I want it over with.

"Are you mad at me?" I ask, not sure I want to know the answer.

And he goes, "No. I'm not mad at you at all."

Liar.

When we have problems, I'm usually the one who sees them. I do the worrying for both of us. I just can't tell him about it too often, because then it's almost like I'm bragging that I understand what's going on while he doesn't.

Uncertainty. Do I ask about last night? Or do I pretend it never happened – that it never happens?

"Do you still want to get lunch today?" I ask. It's only after I ask that I realize I'm trying to make plans again.

Maybe I am a needy girl after all.

"Absolutely," Justin says. "Lunch would be great."

Bullshit. He's playing with me. He has to be.

"No big deal," he adds.

I look at him, and it seems genuine. Maybe I'm wrong to assume the worst. And maybe I've managed to make him feel stupid by being so surprised.

I take his hand and hold it. If he's willing to step back from last night, I am, too. This is what we do. When the stupid fights are over, we're good.

"I'm glad you're not mad at me," I tell him. "I just want everything to be okay."

He knows I love him. I know he loves me. That is never the question. The question is always how we'll deal with it.

Time. The bell rings. I have to remind myself that

school is not a thing that exists solely to give us a place to be together.

"I'll see you later," he says.

I hold on to that. It's the only thing that will get me through the empty space that follows.

I was watching one of my shows, and one of the housewives was like, "He's a fuckup, but he's *my* fuckup," and I thought, *Oh, shit, I really shouldn't be relating to this, but I am, and so what?* That has to be what love is – seeing what a mess he is and loving him anyway, because you know you're a mess, too, maybe even worse.

We weren't an hour into our first date before Justin was setting off the alarms.

"I'm warning you – I'm trouble," he said over dinner at TGI Friday's. "Total trouble."

"And do you warn all the other girls?" I replied, flirting.

But what I got back wasn't flirtation. It was real.

"No," he said. "I don't."

This was his way of letting me know that I was someone he cared about. Even at the very beginning.

He hadn't meant to tell me. But there it was.

And even though he's forgotten a lot of other details about that first date, he's never forgotten what he said.

I warned you! he'll yell at me on nights when it's really bad, really hard. *You can't say I didn't warn you!*

Sometimes this only makes me hold him tighter.

Sometimes I've already let go, feeling awful that there's nothing I can do.

The only time our paths intersect in the morning is between first and second periods, so I look for him then. We only have a minute to share, sometimes less, but I'm always thankful. It's like I'm taking attendance. *Love? Here!* Even if we're tired (which is pretty much always) and even if we don't have much to say, I know he won't just pass me by.

Today I smile, because, all things considered, the morning went pretty well. And he smiles back at me.

Good signs. I am always looking for good signs.

I head to Justin's class as soon as fourth period is over, but he hasn't waited for me. So I go to the cafeteria, to where we usually sit. He's not there, either. I ask Rebecca if she's seen him. She says she hasn't, and doesn't seem too surprised that I'm looking. I decide to ignore that. I check my locker and he's not there. I'm starting to think he's forgotten, or was playing with me all along. I decide to check his locker, even though it's about as far from the cafeteria as you can get. He never stops there before lunch. But I guess today he has, because there he is.

I'm happy to see him, but also exhausted. It's just so much work. He looks worse than I feel, staring into his locker like there's a window in there. In some people, this would mean daydreams. But Justin doesn't daydream. When he's gone, he's really gone.

Now he's back. Right when I get to him.

"Hey," he says.

"Hey," I say back.

I'm hungry, but not that hungry. The most important thing is for us to be in the same place. I can do that anywhere.

He's putting all of his books in his locker now, as if he's done with the day. I hope nothing's wrong. I hope he's not giving up. If I'm going to be stuck here, I want him stuck here, too.

He stands up and puts his hand on my arm. Gentle. Way too gentle. It's something I'd do to him, not something he'd do to me. I like it, but I also don't like it.

"Let's go somewhere," he says. "Where do you want to go?"

Again, I think there has to be a right answer to this question, and that if I get it wrong, I will ruin everything. He wants something from me, but I'm not sure what.

"I don't know," I tell him.

He takes his hand off my arm and I think, okay,

wrong answer. But then he takes my hand.

"Come on," he says.

There's an electricity in his eyes. Power. Light.

He closes the locker and pulls me forward. I don't understand. We're walking hand in hand through the almost-empty halls. We never do this. He gets this grin on his face and we go faster. It's like we're little kids at recess. Running, actually running down the halls. People look at us like we're insane. It's so ridiculous. He swings us by my locker and tells me to leave my books here, too. I don't understand, but I go along with it – he's in a great mood, and I don't want to do anything that will break it.

Once my locker's closed, we keep going. Right out the door. Simple as that. Escape. We're always talking about how we want to leave, and this time we're doing it. I figure he'll take me out for pizza or something. Maybe be late to fifth period. We get to his car and I don't even want to ask him what we're doing. I just want to let him do it.

He turns and asks, "Where do you want to go? Tell me, truly, where you'd love to go."

Strange. He's asking me as if *I'm* the one who knows the right answer.

I really hope this isn't a trick. I really hope I won't regret this.

I say the first thing that comes to my mind.

8

"I want to go to the ocean. I want you to take me to the ocean."

I figure he'll laugh and say what he really meant was that we should go to his house while his parents are gone and spend the afternoon having sex and watching TV. Or that he's trying to prove a point about not making plans, to prove that I like being spontaneous better. Or he'll tell me to go have fun at the ocean while he gets lunch. All of these are possibilities, and they all play at the same time in my head.

The only thing I'm not expecting is for him to assume it's a good idea.

"Okay," he says, pulling out of the parking lot. I still think he's joking, but then he's asking me the best way to get there. I tell him which highways we should take – there's a beach my family used to go to a lot in summer, and if we're going to the ocean, we might as well go there.

As he steers, I can tell he's enjoying himself. It should put me at ease, but it's making me nervous. It would be just like Justin to take me somewhere really special in order to dump me. Make a big production of it. Maybe leave me stranded there. I don't actually think this is going to happen – but it's possible. As a way of proving to me that he's able to make plans. As a way of showing he's not as afraid of the future as I said he was.

You're being crazy, Rhiannon, I tell myself. It's something he says to me all the time. A lot of the time, he's right.

Just enjoy it, I think. Because we're not in school. We're together.

He turns on the radio and tells me to take over. What? *My car, my radio* – how many times have I heard him say that? But it seems like his offer is real, so I slip from station to station, trying to find something he'll be into. When I pause too long on a song I like, he says, "Why not that one?" And I'm thinking, *Because you hate it*. But I don't say that out loud. I let the song play. I wait for him to make a joke about it, say the singer sounds like she's having her period.

Instead, he starts to sing along.

Disbelief. Justin *never* sings along. He will yell at the radio. He will talk back to whatever the talk radio people are saying. Every now and then he might beat along on his steering wheel. But he does *not* sing.

I wonder if he's on drugs. But I've seen him on drugs before, and it's never been like this.

"What's gotten into you?" I ask.

"Music," he says.

"Ha."

"No, really."

He's not joking. He's not laughing at me somewhere

inside. I am looking at him and I can see that. I don't know what's going on, but it's not that.

I decide to see how far I can push it. Because that's what a needy girl does.

"In that case . . ." I say. I flip stations until I find the least Justin song possible.

And there it is. Kelly Clarkson. Singing how what doesn't kill you makes you stronger.

I turn it up. In my head, I dare him to sing along.

Surprise.

We are belting it out. I have no idea how he knows the words. But I don't question it. I am singing with everything I've got, never knowing I could love this song as much as I do right now, because it is making everything okay – it is making *us* okay. I refuse to think about anything other than that. I want us to stay inside the song. Because this is something we've never done before and it feels great.

When it's done, I roll down my window – I want to feel the wind in my hair. Without a word, Justin rolls down all the other windows, and it's like we're in a wind tunnel, like this is a ride in an amusement park when really it's just a car driving down the highway. He looks so happy. It makes me realize how rare it is for me to see him happy, the kind of happy where there isn't anything else on his mind besides the happiness. He's usually so afraid to show it, as if it might be stolen away at any moment.

He takes my hand and starts to ask me questions. Personal questions.

He starts with, "How are your parents doing?"

"Um . . . I don't know," I say. He's never really cared about my parents before. I know he wants them to like him, but because he's not sure they will, he pretends it doesn't matter. "I mean, you know. Mom is trying to hold it all together without actually doing anything. My dad has his moments, but he's not exactly the most fun person to be around. The older he gets, the less he seems to give a damn about anything."

"And what's it like with Liza at college?"

When he asks this question, it's as if he's proud that he's remembered my sister's name. That sounds more like Justin.

"I don't know," I tell him. "You know we were more like sisters living under a truce than best friends. I don't know if I miss her that much, although it was easier having her around, because then there were two of us, you know? She never calls home. Even when my mom calls her, she doesn't call back. I don't blame her for that – I'm sure she has better things to do. And really, I always knew that once she left, she'd be gone. So I'm not shocked or anything."

12

I realize as I'm talking that I'm getting close to the nerve, talking about what happens when high school is over. But Justin doesn't seem to be taking it personally. Instead, he asks me if I think school is much different this year than last year. Which is a weird question. Something my grandmother would ask. Not my boyfriend.

I tread carefully.

"I don't know. School sucks. That's not different. But, you know – while I really want it to be over, I'm also worried about everything that's going to come after. Not that I have it planned out. I don't. I know you think that I have all of these plans – but if you actually look at the things I've done to prepare myself for life after high school, all you'll see is a huge blank. I'm just as unprepared as anyone else."

Shut up, shut up, shut up, I'm telling myself. *Why are you bringing this up?*

But maybe I have a reason. Maybe I'm bringing it up to see what he'll do. He tests me all the time, but I'm not exactly innocent in that department, either.

"What do you think?" I ask him.

And he says, "Honestly, I'm just trying to live day to day."

I know. But I appreciate it more when it's said like this, in a voice that acknowledges we're on the same

13

side. I wait for him to say more, to edge back into last night's fight. But he lets it go. I am grateful.

It's been over a year, and there've been at least a hundred times when I've told myself that this was it – this was the new start. Sometimes I was right. But not as much as I wanted to be.

I will not let myself think that things are suddenly better. I will not let myself think that we've somehow escaped the us we always end up being. But at the same time, I will not deny what's happening. I will not deny this happiness. Because if happiness feels real, it almost doesn't matter if it's real or not.

Instead of plugging the destination into his phone, he's asking me to keep giving him directions. I screw up and tell him to get off the highway one exit too soon, but when I realize this, he doesn't freak out at all – he just gets back on the highway and goes one more exit. Now I'm no longer wondering if he's on drugs – I'm wondering if he's on *medication*. If so, it's kicking in pretty quickly.

I do not say a word. I don't want to jinx it.

"I should be in English class," I say as we make the last turn before the beach.

"I should be in bio," Justin says back.

But this is more important. I can make up my homework, but I can't make up my life.

"Let's just enjoy ourselves," he says.

"Okay," I tell him. "I like that. I spend so much time thinking about running away – it's nice to actually do it. For a day. It's good to be on the other side of the window. I don't do this enough."

Maybe this is what we've needed all along. Distance from everything else, and closeness to each other.

Something is working here – I can feel it working.

Memory. This is the beach my family would come to, on days when the house was too hot or my parents were sick of staying in the same place. When we came here, we'd be surrounded by other families. I liked to imagine that each of our blankets was a house, and that a certain number of blankets made a town. I'm sure there were a few kids I saw all the time, whose parents took them here, too, but I can't remember any of them now. I can only remember my own family – my mother always under an umbrella, either not wanting to burn or not wanting to be seen; my sister taking out a book and staying inside it the whole time; my father talking to the other fathers about sports or stocks. When it got too hot, he would race me down into the water and ask me what kind of fish I wanted to be. I knew that the right answer was *flying fish*, because if I told him that, he would gather me in his arms and throw me into the air.

I don't know why I've never brought Justin here before. Last summer, we stayed indoors, waiting for his parents to leave for work so we could have sex in every room of the house, including some of the closets. Then, when it was done, we'd watch TV or play video games. Sometimes we'd call around to see what everyone else was doing, and by the time his parents came home, we'd be off at someone's house, drinking or watching TV or playing video games or some mix of the three. It was great, because it wasn't school, and we were with each other. But it didn't really get us anywhere.

I leave my shoes in the car, just like I did when I was a kid. There's the awkward couple of steps when I'm still in the parking lot and the pavement hurts, but then there's the sand and everything's fine. The beach is completely empty today, and even though I didn't expect there to be a lot of people here, it's still surprising, like we've caught the beach napping.

I can't help myself. I run right down into it, spin around. *Mine*, I think. The beach is mine. The time is mine. Justin is mine. Nobody – nothing – is going to interfere with that. I call out his name, and it's like I'm still singing along to a song.

He looks at me for a moment, and I think, oh no, this is the part where he tells me I look like an idiot. But then he's running down to me, grabbing hold of me, swinging me around. He's heard the song, and now we're dancing. We're laughing and racing each other to the water. When we get there, we splash-war, feeling the tide against our legs. I reach down for some shells and Justin joins me, looking for colors that won't be the same when they're dry, looking for sea glass and spirals. The water feels so good, and standing still feels so good, because there's a whole ocean pulling at me and I have the strength to stay where I am.

Justin's face is completely unguarded. His body is entirely relaxed. I never see him like this. We are playing, but it's not the kind of playing that boyfriends and girlfriends do, where there's strategy and scorekeeping and secret moves. No, we have scissored ourselves away from all that.

I ask him to build a sand castle with me. I tell him how Lisa always had to have her own, next to mine. She would build a huge mountain with a deep moat around it, while I would make a small, detailed house with a front door and a garage. Basically, I was building the dollhouse I was never able to have, while Liza was creating the fortress she felt she needed. She would never touch my castle – she wasn't the kind of older sister who needed to destroy the competition. But she wouldn't let me touch hers, either. We'd leave them when we were done, for the tide to take away. Sometimes our parents would come over. To me, they'd say, *How pretty!* To Liza, it would be, *How tall!*

I want Justin to work on a sand castle with me. I want us to experience what it's like to build something together. We don't have any shovels or buckets. Everything has to be done with our hands. He takes the phrase *sand castle* literally – starting with the square foundation, creating a drawbridge with his finger. I work on the turrets and the towers – balconies are precarious, but spires are possible. At random moments, he compliments me – little words like *nice* and *neat* and *sweet* – and I feel like the beach is somehow unlocking this vocabulary from the dungeon where he's kept it all these months. I always felt – maybe hoped – that the words were in there somewhere. And now I know they are.

It isn't very warm out, but I can feel the sun on my cheeks and my neck. We could gather more shells and begin to decorate, but I am starting to tire of the building, and putting our focus there. When the last tower is complete, I suggest we wander for a little while.

"Are you pleased with our creation?" he asks.

And I say, "Very."

We head to the water to wash off our hands. Justin stares back at the beach, back at our castle, and seems lost for a moment. Lost, but in a good place.

"What is it?" I ask.

He looks at me, eyes so kind, and says, "Thank you."

I am sure he has said these two words to me before, but never like this, never in a way that would make me want to remember them.

"For what?" I ask. What I mean is: *Why now? Why finally?*

"For this," he says. "For all of it."

I want so much to trust it. I want so much to think we've finally shifted to the place I always thought we could get to. But it's too simple. It feels too simple.

"It's okay," he tells me. "It's okay to be happy."

I have wanted this for so long. This is not how I pictured it, but nothing ever is. I am overwhelmed by how much I love him. I don't hate him at all. There's not a single part of me that hates him. There is only love. And it isn't terrifying. It is the opposite of terrifying.

I am crying because I'm happy and I'm crying because I don't think I ever realized how much I was expecting to be unhappy. I am crying because for the first time in a long time, life makes sense.

He sees me crying and doesn't make fun of it. He doesn't get defensive, asking what he did this time. He doesn't tell me he warned me. He doesn't tell me to stop. No, he wraps his arms around me and holds me and takes these things that are only words and makes them into something more than words. Comfort. He gives me something I can actually feel – his presence, his hold.

"I'm happy," I say, afraid he thinks I'm crying for a reason besides that. "Really, I am."

The wind, the beach, the sun – everything else wraps around us, but our embrace is the one that matters. I am holding on to him now as much as he is holding on to me. We have reached that perfect balance, where each of us is strong and each of us is weak, each taking, each giving.

"What's happening?" I ask.

"Shhh," he says. "Don't question it."

I don't feel any questions – only answers. No fear, only fullness. I kiss him and continue our perfect balance there, let our separate breaths become one breath. I close my eyes and feel the familiar press of his lips, the familiar taste of his mouth. But something is different now. We are not just kissing with our whole bodies, but with something that is bigger than our bodies, that is who we are and who we will be. We are kissing from a deeper part of our selves, and we are finding a deeper part of each other. It feels like electricity hitting water, fire reaching paper, the brightest light finding our eyes. I run my hands down his back, down his front, as if I need to know that he's really here, that this is really happening. I linger on the back of his neck. He lingers

20

on the side of my hip. I slip below his belt, but he leads me back up, kissing my neck. I kiss beneath his ear. I kiss his smile. He traces my laugh.

Enjoying this. We are enjoying this.

I have no idea what time it is, what day it is. I have nothing but now. Nothing but here. And it is more than enough.

Eventually my hand slides down his arm and holds his hand. We stand there for a few seconds, or maybe a few minutes, hand in hand, forehead on forehand, lips gently on lips, drained entirely of longing, because everything's been found.

Then we pull away, keeping our hands together. We begin to walk down the beach, like couples do. Time comes back, but not in a scary way.

"This is amazing," I say. And then I cringe despite myself, because this is what Justin would usually call *an obvious statement*. But of course, on this day, in this place, all he does is nod in agreement. He looks at the sun, which is coming closer to the horizon. I think I can see a boat offshore, but it could just be driftwood, or a mirage.

I want every day to be like this. I don't understand why it can't be.

"We should do this every Monday," I say. "And Tuesday. And Wednesday. And Thursday. And Friday."

I'm joking. But not really.

"We'd only get tired of it," Justin says. "It's best to have it just once."

Once? I don't know what he means. I don't know how he could say that.

"Never again?" I ask. I don't want to be wrong here. I really don't want to be wrong.

He smiles. "Well, never say never."

"I'd never say never," I promise him.

Company. There are other couples on the beach now. Only a few, all of them older than us. Nobody asks us why we aren't in school. Nobody asks us what we're doing here. Instead, they seem happy to see us. It makes me feel like we belong here, that we are right to be doing what we're doing.

This is how it's going to be, I tell myself. And then I look at Justin and think, *Tell me this is how it's going to be.*

I don't want to ask him. I don't want to have to ask. Too often, it's my questions that push things off course.

I don't want this to be fragile, but I still treat it like it is.

I'm starting to get a little cold. I have to remind myself that it isn't summer. When I shiver, Justin puts his arm around me. I suggest we go back to the car and get the make-out blanket he keeps in his trunk. So we turn around, head back to where we started. Our castle is

22

still there, still standing, even as the ocean comes closer.

Once we have the blanket, we bring it back to the beach. Instead of wrapping it around our shoulders, we put it on the sand and press ourselves beside each other. We are lying down, staring up at the sky. Clouds push by us. Every now and then a bird appears.

"This has to be one of the best days ever," I say.

Without turning his head, he puts his hand in mine.

"Tell me about some of the other days like this," he asks.

"I don't know . . ." I say. I can't imagine another day like this.

"Just one. The first one that comes to mind."

I think about times when I was happy. Really happy. Balloon-floating happy. And the strangest memory comes into my mind. I have no idea why. I know I need to give him an answer, but I tell him it's stupid. He insists I share it anyway.

I turn to him and he moves my hand to his chest, making circles there.

He is here. This is safe.

I tell him, "For some reason, the first thing that comes to mind is this mother-daughter fashion show."

I make him promise not to laugh. He promises. And I believe him.

"It was in fourth grade or something," I say.

23

"Renwick's was doing a fundraiser for hurricane victims, and they asked for volunteers from our class. I didn't ask my mother or anything – I just signed up. And when I brought the information home – well, you know how my mom is. She was terrified. It's enough to get her out to the supermarket. But a fashion show? In front of strangers? I might as well have asked her to pose for *Playboy*. God, now there's a scary thought."

Some girls have moms who partied all the time when they were young, who laughed and giggled and flirted and dressed in super tight clothes. I don't have a mom like that. My mom was, I think, always the same as she is now. Except maybe this one time.

I tell Justin, "But here's the thing: She didn't say no. I guess it's only now that I realize what I put her through. She didn't make me go to the teacher and take it back. No, when the day came, we drove over to Renwick's and went where they told us to go. I had thought they would put us in matching outfits, but it wasn't like that. Instead, they basically told us we could wear whatever we wanted from the store. So there we were, trying all these things on. I went for the gowns, of course – I was so much more of a girl then. I ended up with this light blue dress – ruffles all over the place. I thought it was so sophisticated."

"I'm sure it was classy," Justin says.

I hit him playfully. "Shut up. Let me tell my story."

He holds my hand on his chest. Before I can go on, he kisses me. I think the story might end there, but he pulls back and says, "Go ahead."

I forget for a second where I was, because for a moment I fall out of the story and back into now. Then I remember: My mom. The fashion show.

"So I had my wannabe prom dress," I say. "And then it was Mom's turn. She surprised me, because she went for the dresses, too. I'd never really seen her all dressed up before. And I think that was the most amazing thing to me: It wasn't me who was Cinderella. It was her.

"After we picked out our clothes, they put makeup on us and everything. I thought Mom was going to flip, but she was actually enjoying it. They didn't really do much with her – just a little more color. And that was all it took. She was pretty. I know it's hard to believe, knowing her now. But that day, she was like a movie star. All the other moms were complimenting her. And when it was time for the actual show, we paraded out there and people applauded. Mom and I were both smiling, and it was real, you know?"

Real like this is real – Justin listening next to me, the sky above, the sand underneath. It is real in such an intense way that it feels unreal, too. Like I had no idea it was possible to feel so much at once, and have it all be true.

"We didn't get to keep the dresses or anything," I go on. "But I remember on the ride home, Mom kept saying how great I was. When we got back to our house, Dad looked at us like we were aliens, but the cool thing is, he decided to play along. Instead of getting all weird, he kept calling us his supermodels, and asked us to do the show for him in our living room, which we did. We were laughing so much. And that was it. The day ended. I'm not sure Mom's worn makeup since. And it's not like I turned out to be a supermodel. But that day reminds me of this one. Because it was a break from everything, wasn't it?"

"It sounds like it," Justin says. And the way he looks at me – it's like he's finally realized how real I am, how *here* I am. What I've just said isn't worth that. Which means I must be worth that.

"I can't believe I just told you that," I say. It's like I'm giving him a chance to change his mind.

"Why?"

"Because. I don't know. It just sounds so silly."

"No," he says, "it sounds like a good day."

"How about you?" I ask. I know I'm pushing it. It's one thing for him to listen. It's another to have him actually tell me something.

26

"I was never in a mother-daughter fashion show," he says.

Ha ha. So maybe he isn't taking this seriously after all. I hit him on the shoulder and say, "No. Tell me about another day like this one."

I can see him thinking about it. At first I think he's debating whether or not to tell me anything. But then I realize that, no, he's just trying to come up with a good answer.

"There was this one day when I was eleven," he starts. He's not staring out to the ocean or looking anywhere else, distracted. He's looking right into my eyes, his way of saying this story is for me. "I was playing hide-and-seek with my friends. I mean, the brutal, tackle kind of hide-and-seek. We were in the woods, and for some reason I decided that what I had to do was climb a tree. I don't think I'd ever climbed a tree before. But I found one with some low branches and just started moving. Up and up. It was as natural as walking. In my memory, that tree was hundreds of feet tall. Thousands. At some point I crossed the tree line. I was still climbing, but there weren't any other trees around. I was all by myself, clinging to the trunk of this tree, a long way from the ground.

"It was magical. There's no other word to describe it. I could hear my friends yelling as they were caught, as the game played out. But I was in a completely different place. I was seeing the world from above, which is an extraordinary thing when it happens for the first time. I'd never flown in a plane. I'm not even sure I'd been in a tall building. So there I was, hovering above everything I knew. I had made it somewhere special, and I'd gotten there all on my own. Nobody had given it to me. Nobody had told me to do it. I'd climbed and climbed and climbed, and this was my reward. To watch over the world, and to be alone with myself. That, I found, was what I needed."

I'm almost crying, imagining him there. Every now and then he'll tell me something about when he was little, but not like this. Usually he only tells me the bad things. The hard things. Mostly as an excuse.

I lean into him. "That's amazing."

"Yeah, it was."

"And it was in Minnesota?"

I want to show him I remember what he tells me – his family's moves, how cold it was there – so he'll feel he can tell me more.

I want to tell him more, too. I always want to tell him more, but now that I know he's listening – really listening – it means something different.

"You want to know another day like this one?" I ask, moving even closer, like I'm building a nest of

28

our bodies in order to catch all the memories.

He pulls me in, settles the nest. "Sure."

"Our second date," I tell him.

"Really?" He seems surprised.

"Remember?"

He doesn't. Which is fair, because it's not like we labeled everything as a date. I mean, there were plenty of times before our first date where we were in the same place with other people, flirting. I'm talking about the second time we arrived together and left together and spent most of the time together.

"Dack's party?" I say.

"Yeah . . ."

Still unclear. "I don't know," I say. "Maybe it doesn't count as a date. But it was the second time we hooked up. And, I don't know, you were just so . . . sweet about it. Don't get mad, all right?"

I don't want to ruin it. I am afraid I'm ruining it. Why don't I just stop when things are good?

But then he says, "I promise, nothing could make me mad right now." And he crosses his heart. Something I've never, ever seen him do before.

Smile. I'm not ruining it. I'm really not. "Okay," I say. "Well, lately – it's like you're always in a rush. Like, we have sex but we're not really . . . intimate. And I don't mind. I mean, it's fun. But every now and then, it's good

29

to have it be like this. And at Dack's party – it was like this. Like you had all the time in the world, and you wanted us to have it together. I loved that. It was back when you were really looking at me. It was like – well, it was like you'd climbed up that tree and found me there at the top. And we had that together. Even though we were in someone's backyard. At one point – do you remember? – you made me move over a little so I'd be in the moonlight. 'It makes your skin glow,' you said. And I felt like that. Glowing. Because you were watching me, along with the moon."

I have never said this much to him. In all the time we've been together, I'm not sure I've ever let the words come out like this, without inspecting them first. I thought I knew what we were, and that was good enough for me.

What is this? I think. Because now he's leaning over and kissing me, and it's making everything romantic. Justin has been able to do romantic things before, sure. But he's never made everything seem romantic before. The universe, at this moment, is romantic. And I want it. I want it so badly. I want the touch of his lips on mine. I want the way my heart is pounding. I want this nest, my body and his body. I want it because it's that unreal kind of real.

There are so many other things we could say, but I

don't want to say any of them. Not because I'm afraid of ruining it. But because right now I have everything. I don't need anything more.

We close our eyes. We rest in each other's arms.

We've somehow made it to the better place you always want to be.

I don't even realize I'm falling asleep. We're just so comfortable that I guess we go there.

Then my phone is ringing, the ringtone so much shriller than the ocean. I know who it is, and even though I want to ignore it, I can't. I open my eyes, shift away from Justin, and pick up the phone.

"Where are you?" Mom asks.

I check out the time. School's been over for a while now.

"I just went somewhere with Justin," I tell her.

"Well, your father's coming home tonight, so I want us to all have dinner."

"That's fine. I'll be home before that. In an hour or so."

As soon as those words leave my mouth, the clock that had stopped begins to tick again. I hate my mother for causing this to happen, and I hate myself for letting it.

Justin's sitting up now, looking at me like he knows what I've done.

31

"It's getting late," he says. He picks up the blanket and shakes it out. Then we fold it together, drawing nearer and farther and back nearer again, until the blanket is a square. Usually we just roll it up and throw it back in the trunk.

It feels different, driving home. It's no longer an adventure; it's just driving home. I find myself telling him all the things he never wants to hear about – other people's relationship drama, the way Rebecca's really trying hard to get into a good school and leave the rest of us behind (which I fully believe she should do), the pressure I feel to do well, too, or at least good enough.

After a while, the sun has set and the headlights are on and the songs we're choosing are quiet ones. I lean on his shoulder and close my eyes, falling asleep again. I don't mean to do it, but I'm just so comfortable. Usually I'm leaning in to him to prove something, to claim something. But now – it's just to have him there. To rebuild that nest.

When I wake up, I see we're getting close to my house. I wish we weren't.

The only way for me to avoid being depressed is to create a bridge between now and the next time we'll be like this. I don't need to plan exactly when we'll get there. I just need to know it's there for us to get to.

"How many days do you think we could skip school before we'd get in trouble?" I ask. "I mean, if we're there in the morning, do you think they'd really notice if we're gone in the afternoon?"

"I think they'd catch us," he says.

"Maybe once a week? Once a month? Starting tomorrow?"

I figure he'll laugh at that, but instead he looks bothered. Not by me, but by the fact that he can't say yes. A lot of the time I take his sadness in a bad way. Now I almost take it in a good way, a sign that the day has meant as much to him as it has for me.

"Even if we can't do this, I'll see you at lunch?" I ask.

He nods.

"And maybe we can do something after school?"

"I think so," he says. "I mean, I'm not sure what else is going on. My mind isn't really there right now."

Plans. Maybe he's right – maybe I always try to tie him up instead of letting things happen. "Fair enough," I say. "Tomorrow is tomorrow. Let's end today on a nice note."

One last song. One last turn. One last street. No matter how hard you try to keep hold of a day, it's going to leave you.

"Here we are," I say when we get to my house.

Let's make it always like this, I want to say to him.

33

He pulls the car over. He unlocks the doors.

End it on a nice note, I think, as much to myself as to him. It's so natural to drag a good thing down. It takes a lot of control to let it be what it is.

I kiss him goodbye. I kiss him with everything, and he responds with everything. The day surrounds us. It passes through us, between us.

"That's the nice note," I tell him when it's through. And before we can say anything else, I leave.

Later that night, right before sleep, he calls me. I never get calls from him – he always texts. If he wants to let me know something, he lets me know, but he rarely wants to talk about it.

"Hey!" I answer, a little sleepy but mostly happy.

"Hey," he says.

"Thank you again for today," I tell him immediately.

"Yeah," he says. Something's a little bit off in his voice. Something has slipped. "But about today?"

Now I'm not happy or sleepy. I'm wide awake. I decide to make a joke.

I say, "Are you going to tell me that we can't cut class every day? That's not like you."

"Yeah," he replies, "but, you know, I don't want you to think every day is going to be like today. Because they're not going to be, all right? They can't be."

34

It's almost like he's talking to himself.

"I know that," I tell him. "But maybe things can still be better. I know they can be."

"I don't know. That's all I wanted to say. I don't know. Today was something, but it's not, like, everything."

"I know that."

"Okay."

"Okay."

He sighs. Again, I have to tell myself this sadness is not something directed at me. It has to be directed at the fact that he can't be with me.

"That's all," he says.

I don't know what I'm supposed to say. If he's worried that I'm really going to expect this from him every day – he can't think that, can he? I decide to leave it alone. I say, "Well, I'll see you tomorrow."

"Yeah, you will."

"Thanks again for today. No matter what trouble we get into tomorrow for it, it was worth it."

"Yeah."

"I love you," I say.

It's not like Justin to say *I love you* back. Most of the time, he resents it when I say it, accuses me of saying it just to see if he'll say it next.

Sometimes he's right. But that's not why I'm saying it

tonight. And when he responds by saying, "Sleep well," that's more than enough for me.

I don't know what's going to happen tomorrow, but for once I'm really looking forward to it.

Mom is up before me, as usual, in the same place at the kitchen table. It's like she thinks Dad or I will steal her seat if she doesn't beat us to it – and if she loses the seat, where will she spend the rest of the day?

"You look nice," she tells me. Which would be a compliment, if she didn't sound suspicious.

I don't tell her that I made sure to look nice because it's the one-day anniversary of everything getting better. She'd shoot that down real quick.

"I have to give a report," I tell her. "In class."

I know she's not going to ask me what report, or what class.

Eager. I want to get to school as soon as possible, to see him. I hope he's feeling the same way over at his house. I could text him and ask, but if things are going to change, then I can change, too. I don't need to know everything all the time.

Mom and I say more to each other, but neither of us is really listening. I want to go, and she wants to stay. It's the story of our lives.

I have to take the bus because my car is still at school. I could ask Rebecca or someone else to drive me, but then I would have to spend the whole ride talking about things instead of thinking about them.

His car isn't there when my bus gets in. In fact, he doesn't show up until almost everyone else has pulled in.

But this time he notices me waiting. Walks over. Says good morning.

I am trying hard not to barrage him with happiness. It's still early in the morning. He's barely awake.

"Sure you don't want to run away?" I ask. Just to pull a little bit of yesterday into today.

He looks confused. "Are you serious?" he asks.

"No," I tell him. "But a girl can dream, right?"

"Whatever." He starts walking, assuming I'll fall in step right beside him. Which I do.

I get it. Kind of. Since it's not like we're going to do it again today, it's probably best not to think of it as an option. Otherwise, whatever we do today will feel pathetic in comparison.

I reach for his hand.

He doesn't take it.

"What's gotten into you?"

Yesterday, I want to tell him. But from the way he looks straight ahead, I figure now's not the right time.

He doesn't even wait to hear my answer to his question.

38

He just keeps moving.

I tell myself it's not Angry Justin. It's Lost Justin. It has to be.

When you picture someone lost, it's usually in someplace like the woods. But with Justin, I imagine a classroom. It's not that he has a learning disability or anything. That would be a good reason. But no. He's just bored. So he doesn't keep up with what's going on. And it only gets worse, and he only gets more lost, which only makes him hate it more.

I am trying to stay on the beach. As the teachers talk and as Justin and I barely say hello between first and second period, I am reminding myself what it was like. I am turning my mind into a time machine, because I need to.

I know Rebecca's going to pin me down third period, when we're sitting next to each other in art. And that's exactly what she does.

"Where were you?" she whispers. "What happened?"

Art is one of the only classes we have together, because my school likes to keep the smart kids away from the not-smart kids, as if being in class with me might hurt Rebecca's test scores. In art, some of the not-smart kids get their revenge. I like that it gives me and Rebecca a chance to be together.

Mr K has put a car engine at the front of the room, and has asked us to draw it in charcoal. He always says we're not supposed to talk while we're working, but as long as we're not too loud and we're getting our work done, he doesn't really mind.

Rebecca's engine is turning out worse than mine, and I feel bad that this makes me feel better.

I tell her that Justin and I escaped to the beach. I tell her it was an in-the-moment thing, and that it was wonderful.

"You should have asked me and Ben to come along," she says.

Ben is her boyfriend. He's smart, too. Justin doesn't like him at all.

"Next time," I tell her. We both know it'll never happen, but we're okay with that. Our friendship doesn't need her to skip school, and it doesn't need Ben and Justin to get along. She and I have enough history that we don't need to make a whole lot happen in the present to be close.

"Wasn't it cold?" she asks.

"Too cold to swim," I say. "But warm enough to be there."

She nods. Whatever I say to her usually makes sense. I'm just leaving out some of the details.

*

40

I wonder if I'm supposed to meet him at his locker like yesterday. But lunchtime habit takes me to the cafeteria first, and there he is, at our usual spot.

"Hey," I say.

He nods. I sit down.

"Has anyone said anything to you about yesterday?" I ask. "I mean, you haven't gotten into any trouble, have you?"

He dips a French fry into some ketchup. That's all he's having for lunch.

"It's all good, I think," he says. "You?"

"Rebecca was curious. But that's it so far."

"Rebecca? Curious? Now there's a shocker."

"She said next time she and Ben want to go driving with us."

"I'm not sure Ben would let us inside his Mercedes. We'd have to take our shoes off first."

This one time, we went over to Ben's house and he asked all of us to take off our shoes before we came inside. Justin and I found that hysterical. "Doesn't he know that our socks are much nastier than our shoes?" Justin asked. It became one of our jokes.

"Don't say anything to Rebecca," I make Justin promise. He pretends to be zipping his lips. I relax.

I go and get my lunch, and when I come back, Rebecca and some other friends are at the table, so

41

Justin and I are part of the big conversation instead of having our own. When the bell rings, I ask him if he can do something after school, and he says no, he has to work. He says it like I should have his work schedule memorized. But Target sends the email to him, not me.

I do not point this out. Instead, I remind myself that I am lucky I don't have to work yet. I remind myself that Justin hates his job. I remind myself that yesterday was all about a choice, but not every day allows us to make our own choices.

The important thing is that when he had a chance, he chose me. And I have to hope that next time, he'll choose me again.

He texts me when he gets home from work. Two words.

Long day.

I text him back one word.

Yeah.

Patterns. The next day, I think about patterns. Or, really, I think about ups and downs. I am used to ups and downs. Monday, when we were at the beach, was an up. I can see that.

But now – it's neither an up nor a down. It's like we've disappeared from the chart.

He's not mad at me. I can feel that. But his love has gone passive.

I don't understand. And there's no one to talk to about it. Not Justin. Every time I mention the beach, it's like it never happened. Not Rebecca. If I told her more, it might sound crazier than it really is. Not my mom. She and I don't talk about ups or downs, as a way of not having them.

I know what he and I had on Monday is worth fighting for. But I have no one to fight, so I turn on myself instead.

I know I wasn't imagining things.

But I seem to have been sent back to my imagination now.

Thursday I get to school first and wait for him. I don't think that much about it. It's just what I do.

"Jesus, Rhiannon," he says when he gets out of the car. I step aside as he pulls out his bag and slams the door.

"What?" I ask.

"'*What?*'" he mimics in a high, girly voice. It's a voice his bad moods like to use.

"Crappy morning?"

He shakes his head. "Look. Rhiannon. Just let me have two minutes, okay? All I ask is for two minutes each day where nobody wants anything from me. Including you. That's all."

"I don't want anything from you," I protest.

He looks at me, tired, and says, "Of course you do."

He's right, I know. He's right, and that hurts a little.

Space. I want a boyfriend and he wants space.

Since I have plenty of space – empty space – I guess it's hard for me to understand.

"I'm sorry," I say.

"It's all right. It's just – you should see how you look there. Nobody else is just standing in the parking lot. I'm fine with seeing you. But when you stand like that, it's like you're waiting to pounce."

"I get it," I assure him. "I know."

We're at the doors now.

He sighs. "I'll see you later."

I guess I'm not going to his locker. I guess that's okay.

"Sure you don't want to run away?" I ask. I can feel the beach, the ocean talking through me.

"You have to stop saying that," he says. "Keep giving me the idea, and one day I just might do it."

He's not asking me to come along.

I get my books out of my locker, get ready for the day. My heart isn't in it, because my heart doesn't feel like it's anywhere near me.

I hear a voice say "hey" and don't realize at first that it's talking to me. I turn to my left and see this small Asian girl looking at me.

"Hey," I say back. I have no idea who she is.

"Don't worry – you don't know me," she says. "It's just – it's my first day here. I'm checking the school out. And I really like your skirt and your bag. So I thought, you know, I'd say hello. Because, to be honest, I am completely alone right now."

Join the club, I want to say. But the last thing this girl needs is a view of what's going through my mind. She already looks overwhelmed.

"I'm Rhiannon," I tell her, putting my books down and shaking her hand. "Shouldn't there be someone showing you around? Like, a welcoming committee?"

I feel this is totally Tiffany Chase's job. She seems to take pride in showing people around. I've never understood her.

"I don't know," the girl says. She still hasn't told me her name.

I tell her I'll be happy to take her to the office. I think she's supposed to sign in there, anyway.

This does not go over well.

"No!" the girl says, like I've just threatened to call the police. "It's just . . . I'm not here officially. Actually, my parents don't even know I'm doing this. They just told me we're moving here, and I . . . I wanted to see it and decide whether I should be freaking out or not."

Oh, you're definitely freaking out, I think. But I don't say that, because it will only freak her out more. Instead, I say, "That makes sense. So you're cutting school in order to check school out?"

"Exactly."

"What year are you?"

"A junior."

That's funny – she seems like a freshman. But if she's a junior, I figure there's nothing wrong with her tagging along with me today. I can pretend I'm Tiffany Chase for a few hours. It'll give me something to think about besides Justin.

"So am I," I tell her. "Let's see if we can pull this off. Do you want to come around with me today?"

"I'd love that." She seems genuinely excited. It's a good reminder that sometimes it's easy to make someone happy.

Maybe it's easier with strangers. I'm not sure.

Maybe it's easier with someone who isn't asking you for something.

The girl's name is Amy, and it's almost funny how easily she fits in with my friends. I'd be awful at meeting so many new people at once. But she gets it.

Tiffany Chase sees me showing her around and looks pissed.

"What's her problem?" Amy asks.

"She usually gets first dibs on being tour guide," I say.

"I like this version better."

I know I shouldn't really take satisfaction from that, but I do. Like I'm so desperate to be good at something that I'll take whatever I can get.

I do not share this thought with Amy.

I don't see Justin at our usual time and place between first and second period, but he's there unexpectedly between second and third. I wonder if he went out of his way to make up for it. We don't have a chance to talk or anything, but at least I get to see him, and I get to see that he doesn't look too angry.

In math class, Amy starts passing me notes.

At first, I figure she just has a question. Or maybe she's telling me she's had enough, and she's going to leave next period. But instead it's . . . chatty. Telling me that class here is just as boring as class back at her real school. Asking me where I got my skirt and whether there are any boys I like and if I think there are any boys she would like.

We go back and forth like this a few times. She picks up almost immediately on some of Ms Frasier's mannerisms, and is pretty good at making fun of them. (*She talks like a nun, but instead of God, she's talking about trigonometry. I wonder what her habit looks like. A rhombus?*)

I'm having fun, but it's also making me a little sad, because it's making me realize that I haven't really made a new friend since I started dating Justin. It's like since he and I have been together, I've only seen the same people, and less of them. I need this new girl to come out of nowhere in order to have someone to pass notes with.

She comes with me to lunch – we put our stuff down at the table, and Preston goes crazy about all the buttons on her bag, asking her all these questions about Japanese comics. Amy seems flustered, and I'm hoping that Preston is showing his big gay self enough that she doesn't think he's flirting.

When Justin gets to the table, I notice he's got something on his mind. I introduce him to Amy and he gives her the Justin nod. Then he tells me he left his wallet at home. I say it's not a problem and ask him what he wants. He says French fries, but I get him a cheeseburger, too. When I hand them over, he thanks me, and I know he means it.

Even with Amy there, it feels like we're all falling into our usual lunchtime routine. Preston asks her about another comic thing, but instead of answering, she turns to me and asks me how far it takes to get to the ocean from here.

The word *ocean* makes me look at Justin, but it's like he hasn't heard, like his mind is stuck on *cheeseburger*.

"It's so funny you should say that," I tell Amy. "We were just there the other day. It took about an hour or so."

Justin is next to Amy, across from me. She turns her head and asks him, "Did you have a good time?"

He doesn't seem to have heard, so I say, "It was amazing."

"Did you drive?" she asks Justin.

This time he hears her.

"Yes, I drove," he says.

"We had such a great time," I chime in. And by saying that, I get to hold on to it a little longer. It's like Justin and I have this secret, and it's sitting there in front of everyone else, but nobody else can see it. Neither of us is going to point it out. It remains ours. Only ours.

I don't mind that.

I can tell Amy wants to ask more. I remind myself that she's not a new friend; she's just a visitor. She's only here for today.

Justin, meanwhile, has gone back to eating. He has nothing more to say about the thing that means so much to me.

Amy shadows me for the rest of the day, and keeps as quiet as a shadow. I imagine what it must be like, to look into the future and see yourself living in a new place. I've never done that. I've always been here, anchored by parents who never search out change, accompanied by all the other people who fear they'll never leave. For so many years, the idea of living somewhere else was about the same to me as the idea of living in a fairy-tale kingdom. There were places that existed as stories and places that existed as life, and I was taught to never confuse the two. It wasn't until Justin and I became a real couple and my sister left town that I started to wonder not only about what came next, but where. I don't want to picture us doing the same things, in the same place ten years – or even two years – from now. But when I try to picture us anywhere else, it's hard to do. We both like to pull at the anchor, but the anchor is pretty strong.

As I do my work in English class, I imagine switching places with Amy. I don't even know where her school is, but I wonder what it would be like if I had a completely new start. Would I still remain me? Or would I become someone else? I would have to become someone else, because I can't imagine me without Justin. It hurts to think about it. I imagine myself walking those halls – and the alone I feel there is so much worse than the alone I feel here.

I remember the ocean, and know that, no matter where I go, I want him to come with me.

I feel silly, but I'm a little sad to see Amy go. As we head to the parking lot at the end of the day, I write down my email address and give it to her. While I'm doing this, Justin finds me. He seems so much better now that the day is over. And from the way he lingers, I know he wants to hang out, not just say goodbye.

"Walk me to my car?" Amy asks.

I look at Justin, wanting to make sure he'll wait.

"I'll get my car," he says.

It's a good thing he seems to be in a patient mood, because Amy has parked about as far from the school as you can get. As we walk over, I wonder what Justin is going to do now. I'm trying to figure it out when Amy breaks into my thoughts and says, "Tell me something nobody else knows about you."

"What?" I ask. It's such a slumber party question.

"It's something I always ask people – tell me something about you that nobody else knows. It doesn't have to be major. Just something."

I decide to go with whatever comes first to my mind. "Okay. When I was ten, I tried to pierce my own ear with a sewing needle. I got it halfway through, and then I passed out. Nobody was home, so nobody found me. I just woke up with this needle halfway in my ear, drops of blood all over my shirt. I pulled the needle out, cleaned up, and never tried it again. It wasn't until I was fourteen that I went to the mall with my mom and got my ears pierced for real. She had no idea. How about you?"

There's a beat as she thinks about it – which is a little off. If this is a question she always asks, doesn't she always have an answer ready? After a few seconds she says, "I stole Judy Blume's *Forever* from my sister when I was eight. I figured if it was by the author of *Superfudge*, it had to be good. Well, I soon realized why she kept it under her bed. I'm not sure I understood it all, but I thought it was unfair that the boy would name his, um, organ, and the girl wouldn't name hers. So I decided to give mine a name."

I can't help but laugh, and also can't help but ask, "What was its name?"

"*Helena*. I introduced everyone to her at dinner that night. It went over really well."

Helena. I can't figure if Justin would find this funny, too, or if he'd just find it weird.

We're at Amy's car now. "It was great to meet you," I tell her. "Hopefully I'll see you around next year."

"Yeah," she says, "it was great to meet you, too."

She thanks me for taking her around, for introducing me to my friends, and for putting up with her questions. I tell her it wasn't any problem at all. Justin drives over and honks.

I almost tell him I want to go back to the ocean.

But instead I decide to see if I can bring the ocean here.

We go to his house like we always do, because my mom is always home at my house. We don't have a chance to talk on the way over, because I'm in my car, following his. But even when we get there, we don't say much. He asks me if I want something to drink, and I tell him water. He steals some Scotch, but not that much. I never mind if he has a little. I like the taste of it on his tongue.

He sits down on the couch and turns on the TV. But I know what's going on. It's like he can't come out and say, "Let's make out." A few times he's started kissing me the minute we've got in the door – but usually he has to make sure no one's home, get used to the gravity of being home before we can resist it a little.

So most of the time, it starts like this. Both of us watching the show but not really watching. Him leaning into me or me leaning into him. Putting our drinks down. A hand on a leg, an arm over a shoulder. Bodies starting to confuse. He won't say that he wants something from me. But it's there in the air. It's there and understood between us as his hands go under my shirt and my hands touch his cheek, his ear, his hair.

I return to him. He returns to me. But then it's not enough for us to balance like that. He pushes it. He's saying things, but they're not really directed at me. They're directed at what we're doing. They're part of what we're doing. The heat feels good. The touch feels good. But it doesn't feel like enough. Not for him, since he wants more, and more, and more. Not for me, because if it was enough, I wouldn't be thinking about

54

whether or not it's enough. We aren't going all the way – not on the couch, only in the bedroom where there's a door to close and protection to wear and blankets to pull up when it's over and we lie there, pleased. But we're still doing something – he does what he does when we're on the couch, and I do what I do when we're on the couch, and none of our clothes are totally on and none of them are totally off. He starts to murmur, starts to moan, and yes there's something he wants from me, there's something he really wants from me, and I am giving it to him and he's giving it back to me. I want him to get that peak, because what I want more is the sweetness of breathing together afterward.

He groans. His back shudders under my hand. He kisses me. Once. Twice. Three times. We lie back. I find his heartbeat and lay my head there. He says more things.

The TV is still on, and what he does next is what makes me grateful, what makes me think that maybe all of this is worth it. Because instead of turning back to the TV, he turns it off. He stands up and gets me more water. He does not get himself more Scotch. He comes back and returns to his place on the couch, then returns me to my place on his chest. We stay like that for a while. No longer in a rush. No longer wanting anything more than a quiet spot of nothing to share.

I'm good. I wait until after school on Friday to ask about Steve's party.

"Will you just *stop*?" is his reply.

"Excuse me?" I say. "I don't think I deserve that."

He shakes his head. "Sorry."

We're at my locker. I know he has to get to work. That's why I'm trying to figure this out now.

"I'm just going to hate at least half the people there," he says. "As long as you can deal with that, we can go. If Steve and Stephanie start attacking each other, do *not* expect me to calm him down or take him outside or shield her bitchiness from his bullshit. Just let me sit in the corner and drink and watch like everyone else."

"They only fought that once!" I argue. These are our friends. Most of the time they behave. Tequila just makes them mean.

He snorts. "Jesus, Rhiannon – open your eyes."

"You can do whatever you want at the party," I say. "I'll drive. Okay?"

"I'm telling you right now, if I go there, I'm going to get wasted."

"I've been warned," I tell him. "I know I've been warned."

*

It's only when I'm driving over to pick him up on Saturday night that I wonder why *I* want to go to this party.

Rebecca won't be there. She and Ben have a "date night." Preston and his best friend Allie tend to avoid parties they find "obnoxious." And while I'm friends with Stephanie, I have to agree with Justin that being the party's center of attention might not bring out her best behavior.

Mostly, I guess, I feel that something new might happen if we go to the party. If we stay home, there's no chance that something new will happen.

We get pizza before heading over – apparently Justin's father told him he couldn't go out unless his room was clean, and Justin left the house anyway. When I first asked Justin what his dad was like, all he'd say was "military" – I couldn't tell whether this meant his career or his attitude or both. Now he's always saying, "Please God, don't let me turn into that man."

I think pretty much the same thing about my mom, so I guess we relate.

On our way to Steve's, I ask Justin if he knows who else is going to be there.

"Does it really matter?" he asks. "It's the same whoever's there."

I don't think he's in the mood for me to argue, so I stay quiet. A song I like comes on the radio, and I start to sing along. He shoots me a look like I'm a crazywoman and I stop.

When we get there, he goes, "You know where to find me" – meaning: Wherever the alcohol is. He takes off as soon as I lock the car doors, acting like the party might run out of beer before he's made it inside. Which, considering Steve's last party, isn't totally off base.

Crowded. Already it feels like there are people everywhere. I don't recognize some of them. I see Stephanie for a brief moment – she gives me a squeal and a hug, then moves on to the next squeal and hug.

I know I should go to the kitchen, get a drink (only one), and stay by my boyfriend's side. But I find myself wandering away from it instead. Steve stumbles past me – he must've started drinking early. I say hi. He tells me to make myself at home.

It's really loud, some bitch-bashing rap competing with all the talking, making everyone louder. I head into the den and see a laptop there, hooked to the speakers. I look at the playlist and find that the song that's playing is called "My Dick's Got Rights!" The next song is called "Naked Like U Want Me." I think about turning it down. I think about putting on Adele. I don't do anything.

I look around and see Tiffany Chase talking to Demeka Miller. I walk over and say hi.

"Hi!" Tiffany shouts back over the music.

"Yeah, hi!" Demeka says.

I realize the flaw in my plan is that I don't have anything to say to either of these girls. I almost tell Tiffany that I get now why she likes to take people around the school, but I don't think that's the right party thing to say. It'll sound like I want to be her, when that's not it at all.

"I love your hair!" I tell Demeka. She recently added a red streak.

"Thanks!" Demeka says back.

Tiffany and Demeka look at each other. I've clearly interrupted their conversation. I know I should uninterrupt it.

"See you around!" I say. I drift off, but not that far. Again, I know I should head to the kitchen. But I don't.

Next to the laptop, there are CDs. Probably belonging to Steve's parents. (I have no idea where they are right now.) Adele is near the top. Having nothing better to do, I start to flip through.

There's Kelly Clarkson, which makes me think of the drive to the ocean. And there's Fun., who we also heard.

"I really like them," someone says to me, pointing to the CD. "Do you?"

I'm surprised to have been noticed. The boy talking to me looks totally out of place – he's worn a jacket and a tie to the party, like he's going straight from here to church in the morning. He looks really desperate to have someone to talk to, and at the same time, I feel this weird sense that he specifically wants to talk to me. Usually this would make my guard go up. But for some reason, I decide not to brush him off.

"Yeah," I say, holding up the CD. "I like them, too."

Quietly, he starts to sing "Carry On" – the same song Justin and I sang along to in the car. I decide to take this as a sign. Of what, I'm not sure.

"I like that one in particular," the boy says.

Strange. There is something so familiar about him. It's in his eyes, or in the way he's looking at me.

Harmless. I remind myself that talking to him is harmless.

"Do I know you?" I ask.

"I'm Nathan," he says.

I tell him I'm Rhiannon.

"That's a beautiful name," he replies. And it's not just something to say, like, "I love your hair."

"Thanks," I say. "I used to hate it, but I don't so much anymore."

"Why?"

"It's just a pain to spell," I tell him. And because it's

different. I don't tell him all the grief I got as a kid for it being so different, how badly I wished my parents had given me something easier.

The fact that he seems so familiar is still nagging at me. "Do you go to Octavian?" I ask.

He shakes his head. "No. I'm just here for the weekend. Visiting my cousin."

"Who's your cousin?"

"Steve."

"Oh, that explains it," I tell him. And then, just like with Tiffany and Demeka, I find I've completely run out of things to say. I mean, I could ask Nathan where he's from, how long he's here for, why he's wearing a tie. But I'd only be filling the time until I leave, and that doesn't seem fair.

I'm ready to pull the plug and let the conversation die. But then he surprises me.

"I hate my cousin," he says.

Scandal. But not really. Still, I'm curious why.

He goes on. "I hate the way he treats girls. I hate the way he thinks he can buy all his friends by throwing parties like this. I hate the way that he only talks to you when he needs something. I hate the way he doesn't seem capable of love."

Wow. I can barely remember my own cousins' names. Nathan seems so *intense* about Steve.

"Then why are you here?" I ask.

"Because I want to see it fall apart. Because when this party gets busted – and if it stays this loud, it *will* get busted – I want to be a witness. From a safe distance away, of course."

The boy's on fire. It's amusing. I decide to add more fuel.

"And you're saying he's incapable of loving Stephanie?" I ask. "They've been going out for over a year."

"That doesn't mean anything, does it? I mean, being with someone for over a year can mean that you love them . . . but it can also mean you're trapped."

Trapped. How stupid, because my first thought is, *Stephanie is not nearly as trapped as I am.* Which is ridiculous. Neither of us is *trapped.*

I wonder what would make Nathan say such a thing. He talks like he knows.

"Speaking from experience?" I ask.

"There are many things that can keep you in a relationship," he says. His eyes are begging me to listen. "Fear of being alone. Fear of disrupting the arrangement of your life. A decision to settle for something that's okay, because you don't know if you can get any better. Or maybe there's the irrational belief that it will get better, even if you know he won't change."

He. I guess Nathan is on the Preston side of things.

"'He'?" I say, to make sure.

"Yeah."

"I see." Maybe this explains why I'm finding him so harmless, why I'm feeling so open to him. Girls don't need to be threatened by boys who are after boys.

After a moment, he asks, "That cool?"

"Completely," I assure him. I wonder if Steve knows.

"How about you? Seeing anyone?"

"Yeah," I say. Then, seeing where this is going, I add, "For over a year."

"And why are you still together? Fear of being alone? A decision to settle? An irrational belief that he'll change?"

Ha. I'm not about to tell him it's much more complicated than that. So instead I say, "Yes. Yes. And yes."

"So . . ."

"But he can also be incredibly sweet," I add. "And I know that, deep down, I mean the world to him."

Those eyes don't let me out of it. "Deep down? That sounds like settling to me. You shouldn't have to venture deep down in order to get to love."

Enough. I don't know you. Stop.

It sounds like Justin talking in my head, even though it's my voice.

"Let's switch the topic, okay?" I say. "This isn't a

63

good party topic. I liked it more when you were singing to me."

Justin pops into the doorway now, Corona in hand. He scans the room, sees me, looks a little happy, then sees that I'm talking to a guy and looks a little less happy.

"So who's this?" he asks, coming over.

"Don't worry, Justin," I say. "He's gay."

"Yeah, I can tell from the way he's dressed. What are you doing here?"

"Nathan, this is Justin, my boyfriend. Justin, this is Nathan."

"Hi," Nathan says.

Justin lets it hang for a second, then asks, "You seen Stephanie? Steve's looking for her. I think they're at it again."

There's an *I told you so* embedded in his voice. And he did tell me so.

I give him back an *I told you so what*.

"Maybe she went to the basement," I say.

"Nah. They're dancing in the basement."

Dancing. The last time the two of us danced was probably a very tipsy night at Preston's house a few months ago.

I miss it.

"Want to go down there and dance?" I ask.

64

"Hell no! I didn't come here to dance. I came here to *drink*."

"Charming," I say. What was I even thinking, asking him? Then I figure I have another opportunity. "Do you mind if I go dance with Nathan?"

He takes another look at Nathan's tie, jacket. "You sure he's gay?"

"I'll sing you show tunes if you want me to prove it," Nathan volunteers.

Justin slaps him on the back. "No, dude, don't do that, okay? Go dance."

Then, with a Corona salute, he heads back to the kitchen.

"You don't have to if you don't want to," I tell Nathan. I know I wouldn't be crazy about the idea of dancing with someone I didn't know, so I can't really expect him to be into it.

But he says, "I want to. I really want to."

I don't know why this makes sense, but it does. So I lead the way to the basement. There's a different kind of noise down there – dance noise. In a total Stephanie touch, all the regular lights have been replaced with red bulbs. It feels like we're at the center of a beating heart.

It's hard to see who's here, but I spot Steve making his own pre-hangover moves in the corner.

I call out to him, "Hey, Steve! I like your cousin!"

He nods, so I guess the feelings Nathan expressed aren't entirely mutual.

"Have you seen Stephanie?" he yells.

"No!" I yell back, figuring it's probably best if they stay separate until they come to their more sober senses.

Maybe because he's gay, I think Nathan will leap into the dancing. But instead he looks vaguely terrified. I remind myself that he's surrounded by strangers. Then I also remind myself that I am one of those strangers, even if it doesn't feel that way. I pulled him down here, so it's on me to make him feel at home. I find myself thinking that dancing is just another form of singing along, and all I have to do is get him to sing along, the same way he was singing along to the song that wasn't playing upstairs.

He's swaying now, blocked in by all the people around us and the space they're taking up. I try to ignore that, and focus only on him and the music. I create a space to draw him into. And it works. I can feel it working. His eyes matching my eyes. His smile matching my smile. The song. The song is taking the lead. The song is telling us how to move. The song is guiding his hands to my back, to my waist. The song is generating the heat and giving it to our bodies. The song is pulling me closer. The song, and his eyes.

Then a new song. He starts to sing along, and that

makes me happy. It's all making me happy, to be so loose in a place that's so crowded. To not feel Justin tugging me in any direction. To give up on everything.

"You're not bad!" I yell to Nathan.

"You're amazing!" he yells back.

More songs swimming through the red. Bodies coming and going. Nobody shouting my name. Nobody needing me, or asking for anything.

I lose track. Of time. Of what I'm thinking. Of where I am and who I am. I even lose track of the song. I lose track of everything but the boy in the tie across from me, who is releasing himself as well. I can tell, as one who knows.

Then it all ends. A song is cut short. I feel like a cartoon character, holding for a minute in the air, then looking down and falling to earth. The regular lights go on – they've been there all along, beside the red. I hear Stephanie's voice yelling that the party's over, that the neighbors have called the cops.

Even though it's not my fault, I want to apologize to Nathan. Because it's over. It has to be over.

"I have to find Justin," I tell him. "Are you going to be okay?"

He nods. "Look," he says. His hand is still on my wrist. "Would it be weird for me to ask you for your email?"

I wouldn't have thought it was weird, except for him asking if it was weird.

"Don't worry," he adds. "I am still one hundred percent homosexual."

"That's too bad," I say. Then, before my inner flirt can make more of a fool of herself, I give him my email address, take his pen, and write his email address down on a receipt.

The basement is nearly empty, and there's the sound of sirens in the distance. Stephanie isn't making it up – we really need to leave.

"Time to go," I say. We're both staying in the space we created, not wanting to leave it even though the lights are on.

"You're not going to let your boyfriend drive, are you?" Nathan asks.

"That's sweet," I say. "No. I control the keys."

There's chaos at the top of the stairs, and we're separated before we can say goodbye. Justin isn't in the kitchen, so I figure he's already at the car.

Sure enough, he's pacing there, waiting for me.

"Where were you?" he accuses as I unlock the door.

"The basement," I tell him when we're in the car. "You knew that."

He curses a little, but I know he's cursing at the cops, not me. I pull out, relieved that we didn't park in the driveway, where things are all backed up.

"We're going to make it," I assure him.

"You're beautiful," he slurs.

"You're drunk," I say.

"You're beautiful anyway," he tells me. Then he puts back the seat and closes his eyes.

I wait a few minutes. Then I discover a song I like on the radio and sing along.

As Justin snores, I find myself hoping Nathan made it out okay.

I know Justin's not working on Sunday, so I'm hoping we'll hang out at least a little. But he doesn't wake up until one, and from what I can tell from the texts he sends, he's not in good shape. I offer to come over and make him whatever hangover cure he wants. He texts me back two hours later to say that all he can do today is sleep. He can even sleep through his parents yelling about all his sleeping.

Get shitfaced, then face the shit – I know the routine. It's not like I've never been there. I just don't go there as often as he does.

I asked him about it before. Not confrontational. Just curious.

"I drink to feel better," he told me. "And if I feel worse the next day, it's still worth it, because I still got to feel better for a little bit, which is more than I would've done sober."

There are times I can make him feel like that, too. There are times when I know he's drunk on me. Not just when we're making out – there are other times I can make him forget about everything else. Which is a power nobody else has with him. I know this.

Because my day is empty of him, it's empty. My

mother asks if I want to go to the grocery store with her, but I know if I do, I'll only want to buy things I shouldn't eat. My dad is on the computer, doing work, avoiding us to provide for us. I think of emailing Nathan from last night, but that thought passes. I doubt I'll ever see him again. Whatever we shared is gone, because it was destined to be gone from the minute it started.

Distraction. I turn on the TV. Housewives and nature shows. An episode of *Friends* I've seen a hundred times. Nothing I want to watch followed by nothing I want to watch followed by nothing I want to watch. I imagine doing this forever. An infinity of nothing I want to watch.

It's a day like that.

I call Justin. I can't help myself. I want to talk to him so bad. I know I won't convince him to stop being hung over. I won't convince him to get out of bed and do something with me – or even stay in bed and do something with me. I would be happy to lie there next to him.

"I've decided that whiskey is not my friend," he says.

"Still bad?" I ask.

"Better. But still bad. The day has completely crapped out."

"It's all right. I've been catching up on my TV watching."

"Fuck, I wish I were there with you. Being sick is so fucking *boring*."

"I wish you were here, too. I could come over if you want."

"Nah. I just have to ride this one out. It wouldn't be fair to ask you to be around me when I'm so sick of being around me."

"I'm willing."

"I know. And I appreciate it. But it's not going to happen today."

The fact that he sounds disappointed makes my own disappointment a little easier to live with. Even if it still leaves me alone for the rest of the day.

Alone. The only thing that prevents me from feeling completely alone is knowing that I have someone, that if I really need him, he will be there.

"I'm going to go now," he says to me. I don't point out he's not actually going to go anywhere. Neither of us is going to go anywhere.

"See you tomorrow," I say, because I know we're not going to talk again tonight.

"Yeah. See ya."

My mother comes home and I help her put away the groceries. We make dinner. We don't talk about anything. She talks, for sure. She talks and talks and talks. But we don't talk at all.

When I get back to my room, I check my email on my phone. I am surprised to find a message from Nathan.

Hi Rhiannon,

I just wanted to say that it was lovely meeting you and dancing with you last night. I'm sorry the police came and separated us. Even though you're not my type, gender-wise, you're certainly my type, person-wise. Please keep in touch.

N

I smile. It's so . . . *nice*. I wonder if he's single, even though I can't really imagine Preston going for him. Preston likes guys who are trendier. Or at least don't wear ties to parties.

I also wonder about being his type, person-wise. What does that mean, really? Where does that get us?

Shut up, I tell myself. A nice guy tries to be friendly with me and I immediately think, *Why bother?* There is something seriously wrong with me. The reason to bother is because he's a nice guy.

I hit reply, but I don't know what to write. I feel I need to make an excuse for not writing to him first; I'm sure the piece of paper with his email address on it is still in my pocket. I also want to sound like someone who gets this kind of email all the time.

It's weird, because the Rhiannon who comes out in what I write doesn't sound like I normally sound.

She sounds like she's really enjoying herself.

Nathan!

I'm so glad you emailed, because I lost the slip of paper that I wrote your email on. It was wonderful talking and dancing with you, too. How dare the police break us up! You're my type, person-wise, too. Even if you don't believe in relationships that last longer than a year. (I'm not saying you're wrong, btw. Jury's still out.)

I never thought I'd say this, but I hope Steve has another party soon. If only so you can bear witness to its evil.

Love,
Rhiannon

I don't know why I write "Love" like that. It's just what I always write. Everything else seems cold.

But now I'm worried I sound too eager. Not eager in

the same way I'm eager with Justin. Just eager for . . . whatever's next.

As soon as I hit send, the emptiness returns. I'm back into the day I was having. Maybe this is what alone really is – finding out how tiny your world is, and not knowing how to get anywhere else.

I go on Facebook. I read Gawker. I watch some music on YouTube, including the Fun. song from the day with Justin, the one Nathan sang back to me. I feel stupid doing that. I know Nathan wouldn't find it stupid. Somehow I know that. And I know Justin would find it stupid. I asked him once if he thought we had a song. I mean, most couples have a song. But he said he had no idea, and that he didn't even understand why we'd want one, anyway.

I'd told myself he was right. We didn't need one. Every song could be ours.

But now I want one. It's not enough that every song can make me think of him.

I want one, just one, that will make him think of me.

6

The hangover hangs over Monday as well.

It's like his personality has spoiled from lack of use. He's in school, but he still thinks he's in bed. I can't take it personally that he's not happy to see me, because he's not happy to see any of us. He won't say more than two words in any sentence, and after a few minutes I decide to leave him alone.

A lot of our Mondays are like this.

Our Monday at the beach seems like much longer than a week ago.

What is wrong with me?

"How was your weekend?" Rebecca asks when I get to third period.

"How *wasn't* my weekend?" I reply.

"What does that mean?"

"I don't know. I just mean that not much happened."

"How was the party?"

"It was fine. I danced with Steve's gay cousin. Justin got shitfaced. The cops came."

"Steve has a gay cousin? I didn't know that."

"I don't think they're close."

"Well, if he's still around, Ben and I were going to hang

out with Steve and Stephanie during assembly period this afternoon. Just get coffee or something. Wanna come?"

I notice she hasn't invited Justin. It'll be a triple date, only I'm not being asked to bring my date.

"Can I get back to you?" I ask.

Rebecca's not stupid. She knows why I'm not committing.

"Whenever," she tells me. "We'll be there either way. Although it would be great to have some time with you. I feel I haven't seen you in ages."

Now it's clear that Justin's being deliberately excluded. Because Rebecca sees me all the time. It's just that he's always by my side when she does.

I find him right before lunch.

"What are you doing?" I ask.

"What does it look like I'm doing?" he asks back.

It looks like he is switching his books in his locker. It looks like he's about to head to lunch.

"What do you want to be doing?" I ask.

He slams the locker shut. "I want to be playing video games," he says. "That work for you?"

"Wanna get out of here and do something? There's that assembly seventh and eighth period. Nobody will notice we're gone."

I am looking for that spark. If it's gone out, I am

trying to relight it. Because I have a spark inside of me, too. And right now it wants to be bright.

"What the fuck has gotten into you?" he asks. "If we could just leave, don't you think I would've done it by now? Jesus. It's bad enough to be here. Why do you have to keep pointing it out?"

"That's not what I meant," I tell him. "I just thought it could be like last week."

"Last week? I don't even know what you're talking about."

"The beach? The ocean?"

He shakes his head, like I'm making things up. "Enough, okay? Just *stop*."

So I stop. I swallow the spark and feel it scratch as it goes down.

We eat with our friends. Preston asks about the party, and Justin tells him it sucked. In his version, skank girls kept crowding the kitchen. Stephanie yelled at him for putting his feet on a table. Then the police came, because the police clearly have nothing better to do.

Preston then asks me how my night was. I tell him that my night sucked, too. I don't tell him about the basement, or about the dancing. No, my version transforms itself into Justin's version. He doesn't even notice, but I do it anyway.

I am disappearing. This is the thought that occurs to

me: *I am disappearing.* Like nothing I say or do matters. My life has become so tiny that it's completely unseen.

The only way I can think to fight this is to text Rebecca and tell her I'm free to hang out after school.

He doesn't care. I tell him I made plans for during the assembly, and he genuinely doesn't care. He doesn't ask to be invited along. He doesn't even ask me what the plans are. He'll go home and play video games. He won't text me unless I text him first. I know all this – but why do I still feel surprised, as if it isn't meant to be this way?

Rebecca decides she's in the mood for ice cream, and convinces the rest of us we're in the mood for ice cream, too, even though it's not summer and the nearest good ice-cream place is about twenty minutes away. It is, as we expected, surprisingly easy to get out of the assembly – we figure the visiting author won't miss us too much, since none of us have ever heard of him. Rebecca, Ben, and I pile into her car, and Stephanie and Steve meet us there. Steve is wearing the effects of the weekend more obviously than Stephanie is; she looks like she spent the past two days at the gym.

We get our cones and head for a table. When we start talking, it's not about the party, but everything that happened after – all the cleanup that had to be done, all of the bullshit with the police, who didn't end up arresting anyone. They just wanted to break up the party and they did a good job of it.

Stephanie admits she was a little relieved. "There are *some people*," she says, "who will never leave a party unless the police come." From the sound of her voice, I know I'm supposed to know who she's talking about. I have no idea.

"I really liked your cousin," I tell Steve. "He kinda saved the night for me."

Steve looks confused. "My cousin? When did you meet my cousin?"

"At the party. Nathan." I almost add *your gay cousin*, but then I realize I have no idea if Steve knows.

Now Steve laughs. "At my party? I don't think so. All my cousins are, like, eight. And none of them are named Nathan."

I don't understand what he's saying.

"But I met him," I say lamely.

"Oh dear," Rebecca jumps in, patting my hand. "It sounds like you met someone who said he was Steve's cousin."

"But why would he say that?"

Stephanie shrugs. "Who knows? Guys are weird."

What's hurting me is how honest he seemed. How

real. Now it's like I've made him up.

"He was wearing a tie," I say. "I think he was the only guy wearing a tie."

"That dude!" Steve laughs. "I totally saw him. He's not my cousin, but he was definitely there."

I wonder if Nathan is really his name. I wonder if he's really gay. I wonder why the universe is doing this to me.

"I can't believe he lied," I say.

"Again," Stephanie chimes in. "Guys are weird."

"And certainly you're used to a little lying?" Rebecca adds. "This guy probably liked you and didn't know how to deal with it. That happens. It's not the worst kind of lie."

I think she's trying to make me feel better, but I'm stuck on that first part – *certainly you're used to a little lying*.

"Justin never lies to me," I say.

Rebecca plays dumb. "Who said anything about Justin?"

"I know what you meant. And I'm telling you – Justin can ignore me and say the wrong things and go into his moods, but he never, ever lies to me. I know you don't think we have much, but we do have that."

Rebecca and Stephanie shoot a look at each other, clearly not believing me. Ben is checking his phone.

Steve still seems amused that some guy crashed his party pretending to be his cousin.

I hate this feeling – my so-called friends thinking they know my life better than I do. And I hate it even more this time because I thought I'd had the opposite with Nathan. Stupid, for sure, after one conversation and one email exchange. But still. Whether it was real or an illusion, it makes a rip when it goes.

Steve starts to argue with Stephanie about who was the most wasted guest at the party, and my questions about Nathan seem to have been quickly forgotten. We finish our ice cream and then don't know what to do – we've only been hanging out for about fifteen minutes, but the reason we're here no longer exists. Stephanie proposes a trip to the secondhand store down the street, and even though Ben and Steve protest, nobody can think of anything better to do.

I am disappearing again, this time into silence. As Stephanie and Rebecca try things on and Steve looks through old records, Ben and I hover on the sidelines. He keeps checking his phone, but then, as Stephanie and Rebecca argue over who looks better in a fifties sundress, he says to me, "I know it probably doesn't matter, but I'd bet good money that the guy who said he was Steve's cousin had a reason for doing it. Guys act weird, sure. But it's usually for a reason. And it's rarely to be mean.

It's much more likely that he liked you." Then he goes back to his phone and writes another text.

I go onto my own phone, wanting there to be an email from Nathan explaining everything. But there isn't. So I write to him instead.

Nathan,

Apparently, Steve doesn't have a cousin Nathan, and none of his cousins were at his party. Care to explain?

Rhiannon

Almost immediately, I get a reply.

Rhiannon,

I can, indeed, explain. Can we meet up? It's the kind of explanation that needs to be done in person.

Love,
Nathan

That "Love" hits me. I know it could be a taunt or a tease. And I also know it isn't a taunt or a tease.

Rebecca is calling me over to decide who gets the

83

dress. Ben is pulling himself farther into the background, not wanting to get involved. Steve is holding up a Led Zeppelin record and asking Stephanie if he already has it.

I don't reply to the email. Not yet. I need to think.

Rebecca gets the dress. Steve gets the record. Stephanie finds another dress that she says she likes more than the one Rebecca has. Ben spots a dictionary and starts talking about whether or not dictionaries, physical dictionaries, will exist in twenty years.

When everyone's done shopping, they make some noises about hanging out more and eventually getting dinner.

I tell them I have to go home.

7

I don't owe Nathan anything. He lied to me. Because of this, I should let it go.

But even if I don't owe him anything, I feel I owe myself the explanation. I want to know.

I stay awake half the night, trying to figure it out. Then I get up and write him back.

Nathan,

This better be a good explanation. I'll meet you in the coffee shop at the Clover Bookstore at 5.

Rhiannon

The bookstore seems like a good, safe place to meet. It's in public, but it's also a place Justin would never, ever go.

I already know I'm not going to tell him about this.

If I spent most of the night awake with my thoughts, Justin seems to have gotten plenty of sleep. It's almost a good morning with him. When I see him, he doesn't look like he wants to run away. He asks me how hanging out with Rebecca and the others went; I'm impressed because I didn't expect him to remember what I was doing. He even listens to my response for about a minute. Then he grows bored – but I don't blame him, because it's pretty boring. It's not what's really playing in my mind. It's not what I'm really thinking about.

Waiting. I can't stand the feeling of waiting. Knowing I'm stranded for a few hours in the boring parts.

I check my email at lunch and find something new from Nathan.

Rhiannon,

I'll be there. Although not in a way you might expect. Bear with me and hear me out.

A

My immediate reaction is that he's not gay at all. And that his name must start with an A. He was hitting on me, and when I caught him hitting on me, he made up that he was gay. It explains the connection I felt a little more. Both magnets were working. I know I should be offended, but part of me doesn't mind if he was hitting on me, especially because he was too sweet to do it all the way. It's still a lie, and I'm still angry about that. But at least it's a flattering lie.

I know Rebecca would love it if I talked to her about this. I know she is perpetually ready for that kind of conversation – she thinks friendships are built out of that kind of conversation. I sit across from her at lunch and I can see the question marks darting out of her eyes – does she know something is going on, or is she just hoping? Justin is right next to me, so it's not like I can say anything. But even if it was just me and Rebecca, safely alone in her car, I'm not sure I would tell her. I like that it's mine, and mine alone.

I get to the bookstore early and take a table by the window in the café. I'm nervous, like this is a first date. I know I shouldn't be feeling this way – I'm only here for answers, not to get a boyfriend. I already have a boyfriend.

It's amazing how many people will walk into a café area when you're waiting for someone else. At least I already know what he looks like. I wonder if he'll still be wearing a tie. Maybe that's his thing. Maybe he's really that much of a dork. I could be friends with that kind of behavior.

I try to distract myself with an *Us Weekly*, but my mind doesn't even want to look at the pictures. A girl comes in and I don't really notice her until she's right in front of me, at my table, sitting down.

Rude. "I'm sorry," I say. "That seat's taken."

I'm expecting her to tell me she's sorry and move on. But instead she says, "It's okay. Nathan sent me."

Weird. I take a good look at the girl – her Anthropologie top, her Banana Republic pants – and figure she's not evil. But her presence is still confusing.

"He sent you?" I say. "Where is he?" Was he so scared that I'd be pissed that he brought reinforcements? *Total* dork move. I look to see if he's watching us, if he's waiting to see if it's safe to show his face. But he's nowhere in sight.

"Rhiannon," the girl says. I turn back to her and she's looking right at me. Unsettling. There's something big she's not telling me. She's both excited and terrified to tell me. It's all there in her eyes.

I don't look away.

I am not ready for this, whatever it is.

"Yes?" I whisper.

Her voice is calm. "I need to tell you something. It's going to sound very, very strange. What I need is for you to listen to the whole story. You will probably want to leave. You might want to laugh. But I need you to take this seriously. I know it will sound unbelievable, but it's the truth. Do you understand?"

What have I gotten myself into? What's going on here?

It doesn't even occur to me to leave. No. This is now my life. Whatever she's about to say is going to be my life.

It's all there in her eyes.

We hold there for one very careful moment. Then she breaks it with her words.

"Every morning, I wake up in a different body. It's been happening since I was born. This morning, I woke up as Megan Powell, who you see right in front of you. Three days ago, last Saturday, it was Nathan Daldry. Two days before that, it was Amy Tran, who visited your school and spent the day with you. And last Monday, it was Justin, your boyfriend. You thought you went to the ocean with him, but it was really me. That was the first time we ever met, and I haven't been able to forget you since."

No. That's all my mind can come up with. *No.* This is not happening. This is not what I want. I came here to find something real. And now I'm being served bullshit.

It's the punch of the punchline. I am the butt of the joke.

"You're kidding me, right?" I'm so angry, so mad. "You have to be kidding."

This girl is good. She doesn't laugh. She doesn't let down her guard at all. No. She keeps going, more urgent now, like I need to believe her, like I need to fall for it even worse.

"When we were on the beach, you told me about the mother-daughter fashion show that you and your mother were in, and how it was probably the last time you ever saw her in makeup. When Amy asked you to tell her about something you'd never told anyone else, you told her about trying to pierce your own ear when you were ten, and she told you about reading Judy Blume's *Forever*. Nathan came over to you as you were sorting through CDs, and he sang a song that you and Justin sang during the car ride to the ocean. He told you he was Steve's cousin, but he was really there to see you. He talked to you about being in a relationship for over a year, and you told him that deep down Justin cares a lot about you, and he said that deep down isn't good enough. What I'm saying is that . . . all of these people were me. For a day. And now I'm Megan Powell, and I want to tell you the truth before I switch again. Because I think you're remarkable. Because I don't want to keep meeting you as different people. I want to meet you as myself."

I feel stalked. I feel tricked. I feel like everything good that's happened in the past eight days has just been pissed on. The beach. The dancing. Even taking that girl around the school. It's all just someone else's joke. And there's only one person who could have done this. Only one person who could've known.

"Did Justin put you up to this?" I can't believe this. I truly can't believe this. "Do you really think this is funny?"

"No, it's not funny," she says – and the way she says it, there isn't anything funny in there at all. "It's true. I don't expect you to understand right away. I know how crazy it sounds. But it's true. I swear, it's true."

She really wants me to believe it. I guess that would make it even funnier.

What's strange is that she doesn't seem like a bitch. She doesn't seem like someone who'd get off on torturing me. But isn't that what she's doing?

"I don't understand why you're doing this," I tell her, my voice shaking. "I don't even know you!"

She can see she's lost me, and it's making her more desperate. "Listen to me," she begs, her voice shedding some calm. "Please. You know it wasn't Justin with you that day. In your heart, you know. He didn't act like Justin. He didn't do things Justin does. That's because it was me. I didn't mean to do it. I didn't mean to fall in love with you. But it happened. And I can't erase it. I can't ignore it. I have lived my whole life like this, and you're the thing that has made me wish it could stop."

I want to stop listening. I want to stop myself from driving over here. From wanting to know what was going on. I should have left it unknown. Because now it's still unknown, but it's a much worse unknown.

And the awful part is: She's right. Justin didn't act like Justin. I know that. But that doesn't mean it wasn't Justin. It just means it was a better day than usual. I have to believe that. Because this story can't be true. I mean, why not just say he was taken over by aliens? Bitten by a vampire? And – wait – then there's the most unbelievable part of all. According to this story, I am The Girl. I am worth all that.

"But why me?" I ask, as if I've finally found the flaw, finally proven her wrong. "That makes no sense."

But she doesn't give in. She launches back with, "Because you're amazing. Because you're kind to a random girl who just shows up at your school. Because you also want to be on the other side of the window, living life instead of just thinking about it. Because you're beautiful. Because when I was dancing with you in Steve's basement on Saturday night, it felt like fireworks. And when I was lying on the beach next to you, it felt like perfect calm. I know you think that Justin loves you deep down, but I love you through and through."

"Enough!" Oh God, now I'm the girl yelling in the café. Now I'm losing it. "It's just – enough, okay? I think I understand what you're saying to me, even though it makes *no sense whatsoever.*"

"You know it wasn't him that day, don't you?"

I want her to stop. I don't want to know any of this. I don't want to be thinking about this. I don't want to be thinking about all the ways Justin has avoided talking about that day. About how my love for him made so much sense then, but hasn't since. About how I haven't found any of the him from that day in the him afterward. I don't want to think about how I felt when I was dancing with Nathan. About how it felt when he sang that song. About the real reason I came here today. About what I really wanted.

"*I don't know anything!*" I insist. Again, I'm too loud. People are watching. Whatever story they're playing out in their minds, it's not going to be this one. I lower my voice – I don't want them to hear more. I don't want to do this. "I don't know," I say. "I really don't know."

Why? Why is this happening to me? Why can't I stand up and leave? Why am I thinking for even a second that it might not be a lie?

Her. This girl. I look at her. Her heart is breaking. She is looking at me and her heart is breaking. I don't understand. I don't understand why. Her hand is moving onto mine. She is holding my hand. She is trying to get me through this. She is trying to take me through.

"I know it's a lot." Her voice is hurt. Her voice is comfort. "Believe me, I know."

I can barely get the words out. "It's not possible."

"It is," she says. "I'm the proof."

Proof. Proof is a fact. None of this is a fact. This is a feeling. All of this is a feeling.

No. It's thousands of feelings. So many of them yes. So many of them no.

She wants me to believe – what? That she was Justin. That she was Nathan. That girl in school. Other people.

How can I believe that? Who would ever believe that?

It cannot be a fact.

But it's still a feeling. The yes. It's there.

How can I let myself feel that? How?

"Look," she says, "what if we met here again tomorrow at the same time? I won't be in the same body, but I'll be the same person. Would that make it easier to understand?"

Like it's that simple. Like that couldn't be a trick.

"But couldn't you just tell someone else to come here?" I point out. If I can be suckered by one person, why not another?

"Yes, but why would I? This isn't a prank. This isn't a joke. It's my life."

The way she says it – *It's my life.*

Not a feeling. Fact.

"You're insane," I tell her. If she actually believes what she's saying, how could she not be?

But she doesn't seem at all insane when she tells me, "You're just saying that. You know I'm not. You can sense that much."

I look at her again. I search for the lie in her eyes. The flaw. And when I don't see it, I decide, fine, it's time for me to ask some questions.

I start by asking her what her name is.

"Today I'm Megan Powell."

"No," I say. "I mean your real name." Because if she's really jumping from body to body, there has to be a name for the person inside.

I've thrown her. She wasn't expecting this question. I wait for her to back away from what she's said. I wait for her to laugh and say I've got her.

But she doesn't laugh. She hesitates, but she doesn't laugh.

"A," she finally says.

At first I don't get it. Then I realize – she's telling me that this is her name.

"Just A?" I ask.

"Just A. I came up with it when I was a little kid. It was a way of keeping myself whole, even as I went from body to body, life to life. I needed something pure. So I went with the letter *A*."

I don't want to believe this.

"What do you think about my name?" I challenge.

"I told you the other night. I think it's beautiful, even if you once found it hard to spell."

True. That is true.

But I can't.

I can't.

I'm sure there are other questions, but I'm out of them. I'm sure there could be plenty more time, but I'm out of time. I can't do this. I can't allow this to be real. I can't start believing her. Because that will make me an even bigger fool.

I stand up. She stands up, too.

There are still people looking at us. Imagining we're having a fight. Or imagining we're a couple. Or imagining this is a first date that's been a total bust.

Fact: It is none of these things.

Feeling: It is all of these things.

"Rhiannon," she says. And it's in there. It's in the way she says my name. Every now and then, Justin says my name like that. Like it's the most precious thing in the world.

Forget about everyone else laughing. Now I want to laugh. This can't be happening. It can't.

She's going to tell me more. She's going to push it further. She's going to say my name like that again, and I am going to hear music in it I shouldn't hear.

I hold up my hand. "No more," I insist. "Not now."

And then it's there – the answer I don't want, the benefit against the doubt. "Tomorrow. I'll give you tomorrow. Because that's one way to know, isn't it? If what you say is happening is really happening – I mean, I need more than a day."

I'm waiting for her to put up a fight. I'm waiting for her to argue it some more. Or maybe this is the part where the camera crew comes out and I discover my humiliation has all been filmed for some cruel TV show.

But no.

None of that happens.

All that happens is that she thanks me. Genuine thanks. Thankful thanks.

"Don't thank me until I show up," I warn her. "This is all really confusing."

"I know," she says.

It's my life.

I have to go. But then I turn back one last time to look at her, and I see how she's on the border between hope and devastation. It's that visible to me. And even though the alarms are loud and clear in my head, I feel I can't leave her like this. I want to push her a little closer to hope and a little farther from devastation.

"The thing is," I say, "I didn't really feel it was him that day. Not completely. And ever since then, it's like he wasn't there. He has no memory of it. There are a million possible explanations for that, but there it is."

"There it is," she echoes. There's no bragging in her voice. No trickery.

It can't be real, but it's real to her.

Fact. Feeling.

I shake my head.

"Tomorrow," she says.

Now it's my turn to echo. "Tomorrow," I tell her, committing myself to something I feel like I became committed to a long time ago. Tomorrow. A word I've used for as long as I knew what it meant.

But now . . . now it feels like it means something different.

Now it feels like it means something slightly new.

I don't text Justin. I don't call him.

No, I go straight to his house and pound on the door.

His parents are still at work. I know he's the only one home. It takes him a couple of minutes, but he opens the door. He's surprised to see me.

"We weren't supposed to be doing something, were we?" he asks.

"No," I tell him. "I just need to talk to you for a second."

"Um . . . okay. Do you want to come in?"

"Sure."

He takes me into the den, where his warfare game is paused. I have to move the controller to clear a seat next to him.

"What's up?" he asks.

"It's about last week. I need to talk to you about it."

He looks confused. Or maybe just impatient.

"What about last week?"

"When we went to the beach. Do you remember that?"

"Of course I remember that."

"What songs played as we drove there?"

He looks at me like I've just asked him about rocket science. "How the fuck am I supposed to remember what songs were playing?"

"Was it cold or warm?"

"You were there. Don't you know?"

"You told me a story about climbing a tree when you were eleven. Do you remember that?"

He snorts. "I could barely climb a ladder when I was eleven – I don't think I was climbing any trees. Why are you asking me this?"

"But you remember being there, right?"

"Sure. There was sand. There was water. It was a beach."

I don't understand. He has some memory. But not all of it.

I decide to try a lie.

"You were so nice to me when I was stung by that jellyfish. God, that hurt. But I liked the way you carried me back to the car."

"I wasn't going to leave you there!" he says. "You're easy to carry."

He wasn't there. He was there – but he wasn't there.

I am so confused.

His hand is brushing over my knee, up my leg.

"I can carry you somewhere now, if you want."

He's coming in for a kiss. His lips are against mine. His body is starting to press.

This is not what I want, and he has no idea.

And I don't know how to explain, so I kiss him back.

Acceleration. His hand going under my shirt. His tongue in my mouth. The cigarette taste of him. The sweat and grit on his hand from the controller.

I know it's really bad to pull away. That it will hurt him if I pull away. But I pull away. Not far. But enough.

He pulls back in reaction. "What? I figure, if you came all this way . . ."

"I can't," I tell him. "I've got too much going on in my head. I'm not in the mood."

He moves his thumb slowly against my breast. "I believe I know ways to put you in the mood."

Usually my body reaches out for this.

"Stop," I say.

100

He's not a jerk. When I say stop, he stops. But he doesn't look happy about it.

"Are you getting tired of me?" he asks.

He wants it to sound like he's joking. And I could point out that if he'd stayed sober on Saturday night, we could have done something then. But is that really true? After dancing with Nathan, would I really have had sex with Justin?

I know what I'm supposed to say, and I say it: "No, I could never get tired of you." I kiss him again, but it's clearly a goodbye kiss. "I'm tired, yes. But not of you."

I stand up, and he doesn't get up to walk me out. Instead, he grabs the controller, unpausing his game.

I've hurt him. I didn't mean to, but I have.

"I'll see you tomorrow," he says.

Tomorrow. The version he's offering isn't the same as the one the girl – *A* – offered.

I guess I'm not going to know which tomorrow I'm stepping into until I actually get there.

I fall asleep right after dinner and wake up right before midnight. And in that waking moment, I think: *I want to go back there. I want to go back to that day when everything was perfect, and Justin was everything I want him to be.*

Even if it wasn't Justin.

I can't believe I am allowing myself to think this. I can't believe I'm opening my email. I can't believe I am typing.

A,

I want to believe you, but I don't know how.

Rhiannon

I can't believe I am hitting send.

But I do.

And I guess this means there is a part of me that believes.

I check my email again at lunch.

Rhiannon,

You don't need to know how. You just make up your
mind and it happens. I am in Laurel right now, over an
hour away. I am in the body of a football player named
James. I know how strange that sounds. But, like
everything I've told you, it's the truth.

Love,
A

A football player named James. Either this is the most
elaborate prank ever pulled on a stupid girl or it's real.
These are the only two options. Trick or truth. I am
trying hard to think of another explanation, but there's
nothing in the middle.

The only way to know is to play along.

A,

Do you have a car? If not, I can come to you. There's
a Starbucks in Laurel. I'm told that nothing bad ever
happens in a Starbucks. Let me know if you want to
meet there.

Rhiannon

A few minutes later, a reply:

Rhiannon,

I would appreciate it if you could come here. Thank
you.

A

I have to excuse myself to go to the girls' room
because I can see Rebecca's wondering who I'm emailing
in the middle of lunch. The answer is so ridiculous that I
can't even think of a good lie to cover for it.

Safe in a stall, I type back:

A,

I'll be there at 5. Can't wait to see what you look like
today.

(Still not believing this.)

Rhiannon

And then I am standing there, the girl in the stall
with the phone out, staring at the screen that doesn't

even hold the message she typed, since it's already flown away, into the hands of someone she doesn't really know. There is nothing that can make you feel quite so dumb as wanting something good to be true. That's the horrifying part – that I want this to be true. I want him – her? him? – to exist.

I promise myself I won't think about it until five o'clock, and then I break that promise a thousand times.

Even Justin can tell I'm distracted. The moment when I least need him to pay attention, he finds me after school and is concerned.

"I missed you today," he says. His hands move to my back and he starts to work the tension from the muscles there. It feels good. And he's doing it in the middle of the hall, right by our lockers, which isn't something he usually does.

"I missed you, too," I say, even though it doesn't feel entirely true.

"Let's go find a Girl Scout and get some cookies," he says.

I laugh, then realize he means it.

"And where will you find a Girl Scout?" I ask.

"Three doors down from me. I swear, she has a vault full of Thin Mints. Sometimes there are lines on her porch. She's like a dealer."

I have time for this. It's not even three yet. If I get on

the road by four, I should be fine to get to the Starbucks in Laurel by five.

"Does she have Samoas, too?"

"Are those the coconut ones or the peanut butter ones?"

"Coconut."

"I'm sure she has them all. Seriously. She's a cartel."

I can tell he's excited. Usually I can find complaints waiting in the corners of his words or gestures. But right now, they're nowhere in sight.

He's happy, and part of the reason he's happy is because he's happy to see me.

"Let's go," I say.

We park our cars in his driveway and then walk three doors down. He doesn't hold my hand or anything, but it still feels like we're together.

The girl who answers the door can't be older than eleven, and she's so small that I'm amazed her mom lets her answer the door at all.

"Have you placed a preorder?" she asks, pulling out an iPad.

This cracks Justin up. "No. This is more of a drive-by."

"Then I can't promise availability," the girl states. "That's why we encourage preorders." She reaches for a table next to the door and hands us a cookie listing, as well as a business card with a website address on it.

"But since you're here, I am happy to see what I can do. Just note that the prerefrigerated Thin Mints are preorder only."

Justin doesn't even look at the paper. "We'd like a box of samosas," he says. "The coconut ones."

"I believe you mean *Samoas*," the girl corrects. "I am going to have to close and lock the door while I check inventory. Are you sure you only want one box? A lot of people say they only want one, and then they're back the next day for more."

"Mia, you know I live down the street. Just get us the box."

Mia is clearly considering a harder sell, then thinks better of it. "One moment," she says, then shuts the door in our faces.

"Her parents once got so desperate that they asked me to babysit," Justin tells me. "And I was so desperate for cash that I said yes. She offered me cookies, then left a note for her mother to take the cost of the cookies out of my pay. I set the note on fire and dropped it in the sink. I don't think she appreciated that."

I can't imagine asking Justin to babysit. And I can also imagine him being the most fun babysitter ever, if you didn't try to bill him.

Mia returns with our box of Samoas. Justin takes the box from her hand and starts to walk away without paying, which makes Mia purple with outrage. Then Justin says, "Just kidding," turns back, and gives her the cash in singles.

"Next time, *preorder*," she tells both of us before slamming the door again.

"Not the sweetest girl," Justin comments as we head back to his house. "But she gives good cookie."

Instead of going inside, Justin leads me to the backyard. His mom has a small garden with a bench at its side. He takes me there.

"Samoa for your thoughts," he says, pulling open the box and the plastic.

"My only thought is: *I want a Samoa*," I tell him.

"Here," he says, putting one between his teeth. I lean in and snatch it up.

"Yum," I say, mouth full.

He pops one into his own mouth. "Yeah, yum," he agrees, some coconut falling into the air between us. After he swallows, he says, "I imagine we taste the same right now."

I smile. "I imagine we're both pretty coconutty. And chocolatey. And caramelly."

"There's only one way to know for sure."

He goes in for the kiss and I let him take it. I tell myself this is what I want. Just like the ocean. Just like a couple.

He pulls away. "Yum."

"Give me another."

He presses in for another kiss. I push him away and say, "I meant another cookie." He laughs. I appreciate the laugh.

Instead of insisting on the kiss, he passes me the box of cookies. I take two.

They're really good, much better than I remembered them being. Sweet and rough.

"Don't get too hooked," Justin warns. "That's how Mia gets you. Before you know it, you're preordering by the dozens. And then, even worse, you're insisting that they be *refrigerated*."

"You speak like someone who knows. I'll bet your fridge is full of Thin Mints."

"Oh, no. It's worse than that. I only eat the fat mints now."

Why are you in such a good mood? I want to ask him. And then I want to ask myself, *Why do you have to question this?*

"Wanna see my stash?" he asks.

"I've already seen your stash."

"And what do you think?"

"It's *huge*."

We're being silly, but that's nice. Even though we've been together for a while, it's still nice to flirt, and to feel the lightness of flirting.

I don't want to tell him I can't stay long. I know that will make it less exciting than it was a minute ago.

So I don't say anything. But I also don't make a move to go inside. I kiss him here, on the bench. I kiss him here and feel awful because one of the reasons I am kissing him here is because I know it'll be easier to leave if we're already outside.

He doesn't sense it, though. He is kissing me back. He is happy. He is sure to move the precious box of cookies out of our way as we crash into each other.

I begin to convince myself that this is what I want. This is where I am meant to be. I am only going to see A in order to get the explanation. But that is not my life. This is my life. Justin is my life.

I get there late. I've had an hour to straighten myself out, calm myself down, make myself appear to be a girl who has not just spent an hour making out with her boyfriend. I've also been thinking of questions to ask, ways to know whether what A is saying is true. I mean, it can't be true. But I'm looking for ways to prove that.

When I get to the Starbucks, I'm expecting the girl from yesterday to be there. Or Nathan. Someone to tell me, ha ha, it was a joke. But neither of them is there. Instead, there's this guy – a big football player of a guy.

Not my type. Almost scary in his size. But he looks gentle when he waves to me.

Again, my perspective changes when I look into his eyes. All the assumptions fall away.

I take a deep breath. I know I need to settle this. I try to remember my plan.

"Okay," I say as soon as I get to his table and sit down. "Before we say another word, I want to see your phone. I want to see every single call you've made in the past week, and every single call you received. If this isn't some big joke, then you have nothing to hide."

I can't imagine that after being with me so sweetly, Justin would have set this up. But I want to make sure his number isn't on the phone. I want to see if there are any texts or calls on there from yesterday.

I search around. I look at the contacts. I don't find any phone calls from yesterday. The two texts are from friends of his. There's nothing about me anywhere.

So there's that.

I hand back the phone and tell him it's time for me to quiz him. I start by asking what I was wearing that day on the beach.

Worry flashes in his eyes.

"I don't know," he says after half a minute. "Do you remember what Justin was wearing?"

I try to remember. But what I remember instead is the

111

feeling, the wonder of it all. Not the clothes.

"Good point," I say. "Did we make out?"

He shakes his head. "We used the make-out blanket, but we didn't make out. We kissed. And that was enough."

I note his use of the phrase *make-out blanket*. And the fact that he doesn't make too much of a deal of it.

"And what did I say to you before I left the car?" I ask.

"'That's the nice note.'"

"Correct. Quick, what's Steve's girlfriend's name?"

"Stephanie."

"And what time did the party end?"

"Eleven-fifteen."

"And when you were in the body of that girl who I took to all of my classes, what did the note you passed me say?"

"Something like, 'The classes here are just as boring as in the school I'm going to now.'"

"And what were the buttons on your backpack that day?"

"Anime kittens."

I try to think of a way he could know all this, from all those different people. Short of him being able to read my mind, I can't explain it.

"Well," I say, "either you're an excellent liar, or

you switch bodies every day. I have no idea which one is true."

"It's the second one," he assures me. Then he looks concerned again. "Let's go outside," he whispers. "I feel we may be getting an unintended audience."

I can't see the person he's talking about, but I can see other people who could easily be listening to us. Still, his proposal is a little too step-into-my-van for my taste.

"Maybe if you were a petite cheerleader again," I tell him. "But – I'm not sure if you fully realize this – you're a big, threatening dude today. My mother's voice is very loud and clear in my head: 'No dark corners.'"

He points out the window, to a bench along the road. "Totally public, only without people listening in."

"Fine," I say.

I'm trying to think of new questions as we walk outside. I haven't even gotten any coffee, but it doesn't seem like the right time to stop for a latte.

He seems nervous. And if I'm honest, I know it's not a serial-killer nervousness. It feels like the only thing that could be killed here are his hopes. I have never seen a boy hope so visibly. I wonder if he knows he's doing it.

Distance. I let him sit down first so I can keep a little distance. So I can look into those eyes without falling into them. So I can keep some judgment.

I want to know more, so I need to ask more. If he's

going to convince me, he's going to have to tell me much more.

"So," I resume, "you say you've been like this since the day you were born?"

He hesitates for a brief moment. I get a sense that he doesn't have conversations like this very often.

Well, I don't, either.

"Yes," he says quietly. "I can't remember it being any different."

"So how did that work? Weren't you confused?"

Again, he thinks about it for a second, then answers. "I guess I got used to it. I'm sure that, at first, I figured it was just how everybody's lives worked. I mean, when you're a baby, you don't really care much about who's taking care of you, as long as someone's taking care of you. And as a little kid, I thought it was some kind of a game, and my mind learned how to access – you know, look at the body's memories – naturally. So I always knew what my name was, and where I was. It wasn't until I was six or seven that I started to realize I was different, and it wasn't until I was nine or ten that I really wanted it to stop."

"You did?" I ask. The idea of leaving your body sounds almost fun to me. A relief.

"Of course," he says. "Imagine being homesick, but without having a home. That's what it was like. I wanted friends, a mom, a dad, a dog – but I couldn't hold on to any of them more than a single day. It was brutal. There are nights I remember screaming and crying, begging my parents not to make me go to bed. They could never figure out what I was afraid of. They thought it was a monster under the bed, or a ploy to get a few more bedtime stories. I could never really explain, not in a way that made sense to them. I'd tell them I didn't want to say goodbye, and they'd assure me it wasn't goodbye. It was just goodnight. I'd tell them it was the same thing, but they thought I was being silly."

Now it doesn't sound fun at all. It sounds lonely.

He goes on. "Eventually I came to peace with it. I had to. I realized that this was my life, and there was nothing I could do about it. I couldn't fight the tide, so I decided to float along."

I can't get my mind around it. No friends. No people in your life from day to day.

So lonely.

"How many times have you told this story?" I ask him.

"None. I swear. You're the first."

There's only you. Why am I thinking of Justin right now? Why am I thinking of the time, drunk on wine in the passenger seat of my car, he said those words to me? I wasn't even mad. I didn't mind driving. Instead of thank you, that's what he said. And he was so grateful when he said it. So damn grateful.

But I can't think about that. Instead, I go back to A's story. "You have to have parents, don't you?" I say. "I mean, we all have parents."

He shrugs. "I have no idea. I would think so. But it's not like there's anyone I can ask. I've never met anyone else like me. Not that I would necessarily know."

I don't always get along with my parents, but I am still glad they're around.

I think he's going to tell me more about not having parents, about not having roots. But he surprises me.

"I've glimpsed things," he says.

I expect him to say more. To tell me what this means, what he's seen. But I have to remember: He's new at this. He's still very unsure.

"Go on," I prompt.

Permission. He smiles, happy for it. I want to hug him, if only for that smile. "It's just – I know it sounds like an awful way to live, but I've seen so many things. It's so hard when you're in one body to get a sense of what life is really like. You're so grounded in who you are. But when who you are changes every day – you get to touch the universal more. Even the most mundane details. You see how cherries taste different to different people. Blue looks different. You see all the strange rituals boys have to show affection without admitting it. You learn that if a parent reads to you at the end of the day, it's a good sign that it's a good parent, because you've seen so many other parents who don't make the time. You learn how much a day is truly worth, because they're all so different. If you ask most people what the difference was between Monday and Tuesday, they might tell you what they had for dinner each night. Not me. By seeing the world from so many angles, I get more of a sense of its dimensionality."

"But you never get to see things over time, do you?" I ask. "I don't mean to cancel out what you just said. I think I understand that. But you've never had a friend that you've known day in and day out for ten years. You've never watched a pet grow older. You've never seen how messed up a parent's love can be over time. And you've never been in a relationship for more than a day, not to mention for more than a year."

"But I've seen things," he says. "I've observed. I know how it works."

"From the outside?" I'm really trying to get my mind around this, but it's hard. *Blue looks different.* "I don't think you can know from the outside."

"I think you underestimate how predictable some things can be in a relationship."

I should've known we'd get here. I should've known this would come up. He met me as Justin, after all.

He knows the deal. Or thinks he does.

I need to make it clear. "I love him," I say. "I know you don't understand, but I do."

"You shouldn't. I've seen him from the inside. I know."

"For a day," I point out. "You saw him for a day."

"And for a day, you saw who he could be. You fell more in love with him when he was me."

This is very hard to hear. I don't know if it's true or not. If you'd asked me yesterday, maybe yes. If you ask me now, after Girl Scout cookies, maybe no.

He goes for my hand. But I can't do it. It's committing too much. "No," I say. "Don't."

He doesn't.

"I have a boyfriend," I go on. "I know you don't like him, and I'm sure there are moments when I don't like him, either. But that's the reality. Now, I'll admit, you have me actually thinking that you are, in fact, the same person who I've now met in five different bodies. All this means is that I'm probably as insane as you are. I know you say you love me, but you don't really know me. You've known me a week. And I need a little more than that."

"But didn't you feel it that day? On the beach? Didn't everything seem right?"

Yes. Everything within me jumps to that one word:

118

Yes. It did seem right. But that was feeling. All feeling. I still cannot speak to any fact.

But I cannot withhold my answer, either. So I tell him, "Yes. But I don't know who I was feeling that for. Even if I believe it was you, you have to understand that my history with Justin plays into it. I wouldn't have felt that way with a stranger. It wouldn't have been so perfect."

"How do you know?"

"That's my point. I don't."

I shouldn't have left Justin. I shouldn't have made an excuse to go. This is too dangerous, because none of it can be fact.

I look down at my phone. I haven't been here long, but it's getting close to too long.

"I have to make it back for dinner," I tell him. Technically correct. If I want to get back in time, I should be leaving now.

I'm thinking he'll put up a fight. Justin would put up a fight. He'd make it clear he wanted me to stay.

But A lets me go.

"Thanks for driving all this way," he says.

Should I tell him he's welcome? What does that even mean? Welcome to what?

"Will I see you again?" he asks.

I don't have the heart to say no. Because there's a part

of my heart that wants to stay, and will stay with him until I come to get it back.

I nod.

"I'm going to prove it to you," he tells me. "I'm going to show you what it really means."

"What?"

"Love."

No. I am scared of that.

I am scared of all of this.

But I don't tell him that. I tell him goodbye instead – the kind of goodbye that's never, ever final.

I remember the way everyone reacted when I got together with Justin, when we became a thing. They didn't think I was paying attention, but I was.

Rebecca told me I could do better. She told me Justin could never really care about anyone because he didn't really care about himself. She said I deserved to be with someone who had his shit together. I told her I didn't know anyone who had their shit together, including her. She told me she was going to pretend I hadn't said that. She told me I was smarter than I thought I was, but I always liked to prove myself stupid by making bad decisions. I told her I loved him anyway, and my use of the word *love* surprised us both. I held up; she backed down.

Preston said he was happy for me, and when I asked him why, he told me it was because I had found something meaningful. He didn't think Justin was unworthy of my love, because he believed everyone was worthy of love. "He needs you, and that's not a bad thing," he told me. "We all need somewhere to put our love." I remember liking this thought – that I had this certain amount of love that I needed to store someplace, and I'd decided to keep some of it in Justin.

Steve said Justin was decent.

Stephanie said she wasn't sure.

I don't think any of them – even Preston – expected it to last longer than a month. Any love I stored in Justin would ultimately be given away, lost in a fire, left by the side of the road.

And if this was their reaction to Justin, I couldn't imagine what they would say if I told them about A.

The thought will not leave my head: *If this is possible, what else is possible?*

I get to school and walk to my locker, and it's only when I'm at my locker that I realize I haven't stopped to look for Justin.

And then, even stranger: I don't go looking for him.

I wait to see how long it'll take him to come looking for me.

Not between first and second periods.

Not before lunch.

Even at lunch, I sit between Preston and Rebecca, and instead of taking the spot across from me, he sits farther down.

It isn't until the end of lunch that he says something to me.

And what he says is, "I'm so tired."

I know I'm not the one who's going to wake him up.

I find myself wondering who A is today. Where A is.

And at the same time, I wonder if all the A's I've met are in a room together, laughing at me. Not believing how a girl could be so stupid. Looking at the video of my face over and over again. Daring each other to push it farther.

That's not it, I tell myself.

But what else is possible?

I check my email after lunch and find word from him (her?).

Rhiannon,

You'd actually recognize me today. I woke up as James's twin. I thought this might help me figure things out, but so far, no luck.

I want to see you again.

A

I don't know what to say to this.

Trick or truth?

Yes, I want to see A again.

Yes, I'm afraid.

No, it doesn't make sense.

But what does? I'm asking myself this all afternoon. Does it makes sense that Preston is seen as The Gay One when none of the rest of us are seen as The Straight One? Does it make sense that Stephanie's father freaked out when she (briefly) dated Aaron because Aaron is black? Does it make sense that Justin and I can get as close as two people can be, and still can't figure out anything to say to each other when we're separate and walking the halls of school? Does it make sense that I am sitting here learning about the gestation cycle of a frog when there is no way that this knowledge is going to matter to me as soon as the next test is over? Does it make sense that Mr Myers is spending his life teaching the gestation cycle of a frog to kids who mostly don't care?

Does it make sense that some people get everything they want because they're pretty? Would it make all of us nicer – or at least a little more humble – if we had to switch every day?

"What are you thinking about?"

Justin's caught me at my locker, in a daze.

"It's nothing," I tell him. "Just daydreaming."

He lets it go.

"Look," he says. "What're you doing now?"

It's the end of the day. I have no idea what I'm doing. I could've driven back to the Starbucks and met the twin of the guy from yesterday. Although how would I have known it was really a twin? What if it was the same guy again? It's not like I could really tell.

Suddenly I'm suspicious.

Really suspicious.

I wonder if tomorrow he'll say he's a triplet.

Or that he's stayed in the same body after all.

Alarm. I'm starting to get pissed off. Irrationally pissed off. Or maybe rationally pissed off.

"Are you even listening to me?"

I am not listening to him. I need to listen to him. Because he is my boyfriend, and he has no idea what's going on inside my head.

"No plans," I say.

We both know what's next. But he's not going to say it. He wants me to say it.

So I do.

"Wanna hang out?"

"Yeah. Sure. Whatever."

We go to his house. He wants to watch an old episode of *Game of Thrones*.

"Is this the one where someone dies?" I ask as it starts. I'm joking. They're all the one where someone dies.

"Smart-ass," he says.

I check my email. Nothing new from A.

Like my silence might push him into confessing.

"Put that away," Justin says. "It's distracting."

I put it away. I sit there. Someone's head gets smashed in.

We do not make out.

It's only when three episodes are over and I'm getting ready to leave that he tells me something on his mind.

"I fucking hate doctors," he says. I'm a little confused. There hasn't been a doctor in sight on *Game of Thrones* – it would have been much better if there had been.

"Is there any particular reason you hate doctors right now?" I ask.

"Yeah, because they're going to let my grandma die. They're going to put her through hell, and make all of us pay for it, and at the very end, she's going to die anyway. That's always what they do. Hospitals wouldn't make money without sick people, right? They just love this shit."

"Your grandmother's sick?" I ask.

"Yeah. Grandpa called us last night. Says it's serious cancer."

"Are you okay?"

"What do you mean, am I okay? I'm not the one with cancer."

I want to ask *Do you want to talk about it?* But the answer is pretty obvious. He doesn't want my sympathy. He doesn't want to tell me he's sad. He just wants me to be there as he vents his rage. So I do that. I let him yell about doctors, and about how his grandfather is the one who smokes, but look at which one of them ended up with cancer. I let him criticize his parents' reaction. He's mad at them for not dropping everything to go see her, when what he really means is that *he* wants to drop everything to go see her. But he won't say that. Not to me. Not to himself.

I stay until he wears himself out. I stay until he changes the subject. I stay until he decides to watch a fourth episode.

I'll be there when he wants to deal with it. He knows that, and right now that's the best I can do.

When I get home, Mom is sitting in her usual spot, watching the news on her usual channel. If the story is really sad – a girl gone missing, a boy trapped in a well – she'll talk back to the screen, little murmurs of

127

sympathy, *Oh, that's too bad* or *Goodness, how awful.*

I imagine the pretty newscaster looking into this room, looking at my mother sitting in that chair, and saying the same things. Because hasn't she fallen down her own kind of well? Hasn't she found her own way of being missing? Liza used to push her – telling her she needed to go out more, once even telling her she needed to get some friends. But now that it's my turn, I find I've given up. It's probably the only way I can make her happy, to leave her alone. That's what my dad has done all these years, and it seems to have worked out fine for him.

I think about calling Liza, about telling her what's going on.

You're as crazy as she is. That's probably what she'd say.

But Mom isn't crazy. She just doesn't care anymore.

She enjoys her shows, I think.

I want to see you again.

I don't think Justin's ever said that to me. But he hasn't really needed to, has he? There's never any doubt that he'll see me again. Never any need to want it.

I start another email.

A,

I only want to see you again if this is real.

Rhiannon

But I don't send it.

I wake up and write another email.

A,

So, who are you today?

What a strange question to ask. But I guess it makes sense. If any of this makes sense.

Yesterday was a hard day. Justin's grandmother is sick, but instead of admitting he's upset about it, he just lashes out at the world more. I'm trying to help him, but it's hard.

I don't know if you want to hear this or not. I know how you feel about Justin. If you want me to keep that part of my life hidden from you, I can. But I don't think that's what you want.

Tell me how your day is going.

Rhiannon

This one I do send. I try to act like it's a normal email that I'd send to a normal friend. Then I try to have a normal day, partly to figure out what a normal day really is. At first it works. I go to school. I go to classes. I go to lunch and sit next to Justin. He won't commit to any emotion.

When lunch is over, I check my email.

Rhiannon,

Today is a hard day for me, too. The girl whose body I'm in is in a bad place. Hates the world. Hates herself. Is up against a lot, mostly from the inside. That's really hard.

When it comes to you and Justin, or anything, I want you to be honest with me. Even if it hurts. Although I would prefer for it not to hurt.

Love,
A

I try to return to normal. I try not to imagine where A is, what that body looks like. Justin has work, so I'm on my own after school. I check my email again and find a cry for help.

I really need to speak to you right now. The girl whose
body I'm in wants to kill herself. This is not a joke.

There's a phone number. I call it right away.

I know it's not a joke. I'm sure there are people who
could joke about a thing like this, but I know A isn't one
of them.

I just know.

The voice that answers is a girl's. "Hello?" She sounds
a little like me.

"Is that you?" I ask.

"Yeah. It's me."

"I got your email. Wow."

"Yeah, wow."

"How do you know?"

"It's all in her journal – all these ways to kill herself.
It's really . . . graphic. And methodical. I can't even get
into it – there are just so many ways to die, and it's like
she's researched each and every one. And she's set herself
a deadline. In six days."

I feel the dredging inside me. I feel the girl I once was
reaching out to connect with that. I try to focus on the
present.

"That poor girl," I tell A. "What are you going to do?"

"I have no idea."

She sounds so lost. So overwhelmed.

132

"Don't you have to tell someone?" I suggest.

"There was no training for this, Rhiannon. I really don't know."

I've been there, I want to tell her. But it's too scary.

"Where are you?" I ask.

A tells me where she is, and it's not that far. I tell her I can be there in a little while.

"Are you alone?" I ask.

"Yeah. Her father doesn't get home until around seven."

"Give me the address," I say. After she does, I say, "I'll be right there."

I don't know this girl. A hasn't told me much. But maybe that's why it's easier to fill in the blanks with myself.

I shouldn't think it, but I think it anyway: *This is the girl I'd be if I hadn't met Justin.*

That's how bad it was. Or maybe that's just how bad it seemed. I don't know now. I can't tell the difference. All I know is I was convinced that nobody would care if I died. I had elaborate fantasies about my very simple funeral – no one but my relatives there. No boy in tears in the front row. No one who could get up and talk about me as if they really knew me.

I knew I wasn't going to do it. But I also knew I could. I treasured that thought. That I could.

Most of the time when we think we're looking for death, we're really looking for love.

That was definitely the case with me. Because Justin came in and gave me the meaning I was looking for. Justin became the mourner I wanted, and that led to other friends, other mourners. I populated my funeral until I didn't want one anymore.

But I realize that's not always the case.

I realize there are girls who don't have that.

I realize I am driving toward one of them right now. Not because of what A told me, but because of the sound of her voice. The fear.

I recognize that.

It's a short drive, but I try to come up with a plan.

I'm not really thinking about A at all. I am not wondering why A, who's lived in so many bodies, doesn't know what to do. I am not amazed that I know more than A does.

I'm just driving and thinking as fast as I can.

I find the house. It's a normal house. I ring the doorbell. It sounds like a normal doorbell.

She answers, and from the moment I see her, I know that she's another disappearing girl, that she's desperately trying to disappear. The signs of it tattoo her body – the wear and tear. It is hard for unhealthy people to masquerade as healthy ones, especially once they've stopped caring if other people notice.

The only difference is her eyes. Her eyes are still alive.

I know that's not her.

I know for sure now that this is actually happening. No trick. Just truth. Plenty of feeling, but at the center of it – fact.

"Thank you for coming," A says.

She leads me up to the girl's room. It's a pit, like she lashed out against it and left herself the wreckage to live in. Her clothes are all over the place, and there's no way of telling the difference between the clean and the dirty. She's broken her mirror. Everything on the walls is on its way to being torn down. She might as well cut her wrist and rub FUCK YOU across the walls.

It's not a mess. It's anger.

There's a notebook on the bed. I open it. I know what I'm going to find, but still it hits me in the gut.

This is how to stab yourself.

This is how to bleed.

This is how to choke.

This is how to fall.

This is how to burn.

This is how to poison.

This is how to die.

These aren't hypotheticals. This isn't her being dramatic. This is her finding the facts to match the feelings. To end the feelings.

It is all so wrong. I want to shake her. I want to tell her to step away from the funeral.

And there's the deadline at the end. Practically tomorrow.

A's been quiet as I've been reading. Now I look up at her.

"This is serious," I say. "I've had . . . thoughts. But nothing like this."

I've been standing this whole time, the notebook in my hand. Now I put it down. And then I put myself down, too. I need to sit down. I place myself on the edge of the bed. A sits down next to me.

"You have to stop her," I say. I, who am certain of so few things, am certain of this.

"But how can I?" A asks. "And is that really my right? Shouldn't she decide that for herself?"

This is not what I am expecting A to say. It's so ridiculous. Offensive.

"So, what?" I say, not bothering to keep the anger out of my voice. "You just let her die? Because you didn't want to get involved?"

She takes my hand. Tries to calm me down.

"We don't know for sure that the deadline's real. This

could just be her way of getting rid of the thoughts. Putting them on paper so she doesn't do them."

No. That's an excuse. This is not the time for excuses. I throw it back at her: "But you don't believe that, do you? You wouldn't have called me if you believed that."

She's silent in response, so I know I'm right.

I look down and see her hand in mine. I let myself feel it, let it mean more than just support.

"This is weird," I say.

"What?"

I squeeze once, then pull my hand away. "This."

She doesn't get it. "What do you mean?"

Even though it's a different situation, even though we're in an emergency situation right now, she's still looking at me that way. I can feel her feeling things for me. I am receiving that.

I try to explain. "It's not like the other day. I mean, it's a different hand. You're different."

"But I'm not."

I wish I could believe that was true. "You can't say that," I tell her. "Yes, you're the same person inside. But the outside matters, too."

"You look the same, no matter what eyes I'm seeing you through. I feel the same."

If this is possible, what else is possible?

I can't imagine what it must be like to live like that.

A is asking me to imagine it. I know she (he) is. But it's hard.

I go back to her argument about this girl, about not interfering. "You never get involved in the people's lives?" I ask. "The ones you're inhabiting."

She shakes her head.

But there's a contradiction here, isn't there? "You try to leave the lives the way you found them," I say.

"Yeah."

"But what about Justin? What made that so different?"

"You."

I cannot wear that answer. It can't possibly fit.

"That makes no sense," I say.

Then, as if to respond to my statement, as if to respond to my thoughts, she leans in and kisses me. I am not expecting it. I am not expecting the feel of her lips, the chapped roughness. I am not expecting her fingers light against my neck.

I am not sure who I'm kissing.

I'm really not sure.

Because if it's A, the person who kissed me on the beach, it's one thing. But if it's this girl, that's another. This girl doesn't want to be kissed by me. This girl isn't a fairy-tale character who can be cured by a kiss. This girl needs much more help than that. I know.

After a minute of letting it happen, I pull back,

even more confused than before.

"This is definitely weird," I say.

"Why?"

I feel it should be obvious. "Because you're a girl? Because I still have a boyfriend? Because we're talking about someone else's suicide?"

"In your heart, does any of that matter?"

I know the answer she wants. But it's not the truth.

"Yes," I tell her. "It does."

"Which part?"

"All of it. When I kiss you, I'm not actually kissing you, you know. You're inside there somewhere. But I'm kissing the outside part. And right now, although I can feel you underneath, all I'm getting is the sadness. I'm kissing her, and I want to cry."

"That's not what I want."

"I know. But that's what there is."

I can't stay on the bed. I can't stay in this conversation. I didn't come here to talk about us. I came here because we need to save this girl's life.

I stand up and try to push us back on course.

"If she were bleeding in the street, what would you do?" I ask.

A seems disappointed. I can't tell whether it's because I've changed the conversation back, or because she knows she has to make the call.

"That's not the same situation," she says.

Not good enough. "If she were going to kill someone else?" I challenge.

"I would turn her in."

Aha. "So how is this different?"

"It's her own life. Not anyone else's."

"But it's still killing."

"If she really wants to do it, there's nothing I can do to stop it."

If A weren't in someone else's body, I might try to slap some sense into her, this logic is so damaged. You can't cry for help, then claim to be a bystander.

"Okay," she says before I can go on, "putting up obstacles can help. Getting other people involved can help. Getting her to the proper doctors can help."

"Just like if she had cancer, or were bleeding in the street."

I see it's all sinking in. It's still amazing to me that she's never had to deal with this before.

"So who do I tell?" she asks.

"A guidance counselor, maybe?" I offer.

She looks at the clock. "School's closed. And we only have until midnight, remember."

"Who's her best friend?" I ask.

But that's the problem, isn't it? It's what A confirms – there's no one.

"Boyfriend? Girlfriend?" I try.

"No."

"A suicide hotline?"

"If we call one, they'd only be giving me advice, not her. We have no way of knowing if she'll remember it tomorrow, or if it will have any effect. Believe me, I've thought about these options."

"So it has to be her father. Right?"

"I think he checked out a while ago."

I've always felt like the expert on checked-out parents. What's interesting is that now I discover another truth underneath: Even if they seem that far gone, they're rarely all the way gone. If they were already gone, they would've left.

"Well," I say, "you need to get him to check back in."

Because that has to be possible. Maybe not easy. But possible.

"What do I say?" A asks.

"You say, 'Dad, I want to kill myself.' Just come right out and say it."

That would wake my parents up. I know it would.

"And if he asks me why?"

"You tell him you don't know why. Don't commit to anything. She'll have to work that out starting tomorrow."

"You've thought this through, haven't you?"

141

"It was a busy drive over," I tell her, even though the truth is that most of it is just appearing to me now.

"What if he doesn't care? What if he doesn't believe her?"

"Then you grab his keys and drive to the nearest hospital. Bring the journal with you."

I know it's asking a lot.

But I also know she's going to do it.

She's still there on the bed. Looking lost. Looking worried.

"Come here," I say, sitting back down next to her. I give her the biggest hug I can. To look at her, you'd think her body would break from the embrace. But it's stronger than it seems.

"I don't know if I can do this," she whispers.

"You can," I tell her. "Of course you can."

We go through it one more time. Then we both know it's time for me to go. If her father comes home while I'm there, it will only make things more confusing.

It's hard to leave. It's hard to be a part of this girl's story and then walk away from it.

I realize as I'm leaving that I don't even know her name. So I ask A.

"Kelsea," she tells me.

"Well, Kelsea," I say, imagining she can hear me,

"it's good to meet you. And I really, really hope you'll be okay."

But there's no way to know for sure, is there?

When I get home, I need to distract myself. I get on the computer and binge on all the stupid websites I like to look at when my brain can't take anything deeper. I am not expecting to find anything that has to do with me. So when I see it, I'm shocked.

Just one new window. One click. And there he is – Steve's fake cousin Nathan – staring back at me.

THE DEVIL AMONG US!

At first I think it's a prank. But how? This isn't some high school website. This is a Baltimore newspaper. Not a good one, but still.

It's definitely Nathan. If I was unsure about the photo, his name is right there in the article: *Nathan Daldry, age 16.* He claims to have been possessed by the devil six nights ago. He woke up after midnight, at the side of the road. He has no idea what happened to him.

But I do. That's the night I danced with him.

I read the article with a strange numbness. He's not the only person who claims to have been "taken over." Other people say the devil went into their bodies and made them do evil things.

Only, Nathan doesn't really specify what evil things he was made to do. He just assumes that anything he can't remember is bad.

The devil. They are saying A is the devil.

But the devil wouldn't have helped Kelsea. The devil wouldn't have been so scared.

I don't know what A is, but A is not the devil.

I think about Nathan in his tie. Awkwardly standing around the party. I wonder how much of that was A and how much of it was Nathan. I wonder what would make him think he'd been possessed. It sounds like people are making a big deal of it, and that there's even a reverend acting as his spokesman. Is Nathan out for the attention? Or does he genuinely not know?

After dinner, I search some more. Nathan's story has gotten out there. If A left his body right before midnight, he must have woken up without any memory of me or the party. Or did he remember the party and have to make an excuse to the police officer who found him asleep at the side of the road?

I wish I knew Kelsea's last name so I could look her up, too. Not that I think she'll be updating her online status tonight to say "Everything's okay!" I can't really imagine what A is going through. What A has to do. But I'm certain that A is doing it.

Because A is not the devil. And A is not an angel, either.

A is just a person.

I guess I know that. A is just a person.

Justin texts me when he's off work.

Wanna hang out?

I don't. So I tell him I'm tired.

He doesn't text back.

I keep thinking about Kelsea all night, wondering what happens after A is gone.

In the morning, I can't stand it. I realize I still have the phone number at their house. I can call and make sure she's okay. I can pretend it's a wrong number. I just want to hear someone's voice. I want to be able to tell from the sound of her voice, or her father's.

It's nine in the morning. Nobody answers.

I call again. They can't be sleeping. This would have woken them.

So they're not there.

I email A:

A,

I hope it went well yesterday. I called her house just now and no one was home – do you think they're getting help? I'm trying to take it as a good sign.

Meanwhile, here's a link you need to see. It's out of control.

Where are you today?

R

I think he needs to know what Nathan is saying, and the fact that people are listening to it.

I wonder if he's dealt with this kind of thing before.

And then I step back and acknowledge how weird it is that I've accepted all this. I mean, I still want more proof. Which is where the idea comes from for what I'm going to do next.

I start searching the internet again.

About an hour later, there's a new email from A.

Rhiannon,

I think it's a good sign. Kelsea's father is now aware of what's going on, and before I left, he was figuring out what to do. So if they're not home, they are probably getting help. Thank you for being there – I would have done the wrong things without you.

147

I am sure you know this, but I am going to say it
anyway: I am not the devil. Nathan had a very bad
reaction to me leaving him – they weren't the best
circumstances, and I feel bad about that. But he has
leaped – or been pushed – to the wrong conclusion.

Today I am a boy named Hugo. I'm going to a parade
in Annapolis with some of his friends today. Can you
meet me there? I'm sure there will be some way for me
to get away for a little bit, and I would of course love
to see you. Let me know if you can make it. Or if you
can't reach me – I'm not sure I'll be able to check here
– look for a Brazilian boy with a "vintage" Avril Lavigne
T-shirt on. It is, I imagine, the T-shirt of his that is least
likely to be worn by anyone else.

Hoping to see you.

Love,
A

Annapolis is far. Not too far, but far. Especially if there's
no way to know if I'll get to see him.

I do not have the energy to chase around after
someone else.

And I have something else I want to do.

Justin texts around eleven. I'm guessing he's just woken up. And I'm scared that he hasn't, because then he might have seen me close to his house.

What are you doing? he asks now.

Just some things, I type back. *See you later?*

He lets that hang for a good ten minutes before answering, *Sure*.

Awesome, I reply.

I have to be careful here.

Annapolis, I keep thinking as I drive.

But I take a different turn.

It's as I'm walking up the front steps that I realize how ridiculous I must look. It seemed like a good idea when it was just an idea. As an actual thing that I am doing, it's on the sillier side of sane.

There aren't camera crews or anything outside. No reporters. No one to notice the girl with the bag over her shoulder as she heads to the front door.

I just need to know. It will only take a minute. I'm sure of it.

He has to be the one to answer the door. It's a Saturday, so anyone could be home.

I ring the bell and take a breath. I keep rehearsing in my head.

Then the door opens and it's him.

Same awkward body. Same messy black hair. No tie.

And no recognition in his eyes.

"Can I help you?" he asks.

I give him a second to look at me. Really look at me.

I am the girl you danced with.

I am the girl who was with you that night.

You sang for me.

But he didn't do any of these things, did he? He's looking at me like he's never seen me before. Because he's never seen me before.

"I'm helping my sister out and selling Girl Scout cookies," I say, nodding toward the bag on my shoulder. "Can I interest you in any?"

"Who is it?" a voice behind Nathan asks. His mother – it has to be his mother – shuffles into the frame, suspicious.

"Girl Scout cookies," I say. "I have Thin Mints, Samoas, and Tagalongs."

"Aren't you old to be a Girl Scout?" Mrs Daldry asks.

"It's for her sister," Nathan mumbles.

Don't you know me? I want to ask.

But when he says no, what will I say next? How can I begin to explain?

Nathan's mother softens a little. "Do you want a box?" she asks her son. "We haven't had any since the Hayes girl moved away."

"Maybe the peanut butter ones?" he says.

His mom nods, then tells me, "Let me get my wallet."

I expect Nathan to ask me something – where I'm from, where my sister is, anything. But instead he looks embarrassed to be stuck with me. Not because he remembers the time we had together. But because I'm a girl in his house.

I start to hum "Carry On" to myself. I look one last time for recognition.

Nothing.

The difference is also there in his eyes. Not physically. But in the way he's using them. In what they are saying to me. There's no excitement. No longing. No connection.

His mom comes back and pays me. I hand over a box and that's it – we're done. She thanks me. I thank her.

Nathan goes back to his life. I imagine he's already forgotten I was there.

I get back in the car.

Pizza? Justin texts.

Annapolis? my mind asks.

I check my email before turning the ignition.

Nothing from A.

151

I am not going to run around a city looking for an Avril Lavigne T-shirt.

I tell Justin I'll pick him up.

"What took you so long?" he asks as soon as I get there.

I realize I didn't tell him how far away I was.

"Just running around for my mom," I say. Running around *with* my mom, he won't believe. Running around *for* my mom, he probably will.

He looks like he didn't get much sleep. But, I figure, maybe he always looks like that. I try to remember the last time I saw him fully awake. Then I think, duh, it was at the ocean.

Of course it was.

"Hello?" he says. Shit, I've missed something.

"Sorry," I tell him. "Just tired. A little spacy."

"I've heard that before," he says gruffly. And I realize that, yeah, I pretty much said that to him last night. "Why so tired?"

"Life," I tell him.

He gives me a look.

He's not buying it.

We go for pizza. Once he's got food in him, he talks.

"I don't give a fuck what you're doing," he says,

152

"but at least have the decency to let me know how long it's going to take. It's just *rude*."

I tell him I'm sorry.

"Yeah, yeah. I know you're sorry, but what does that really mean? When it all comes down to it, isn't that word just one short excuse? It's like, my dad can be King Asshole to my mom and tell her that she and I are a complete waste of his time, and then he'll come back and say, 'Sorry, I didn't really mean it,' like now everything's fine, now everything's erased. And she'll accept it. She'll tell him that *she's* sorry. So we're this big, sorry family, and I get all the shit because I refuse to play along. I get it enough from them, and now you're doing it, too. Don't turn us into Steve and Stephanie, because you know we're better than that. You and I don't play games and we don't cover things up with *sorry* this and *sorry* that. If you don't want to tell me what you're doing – fine. But if you say you're coming over, come the fuck over. Don't make me wait like you know I don't have anything better to do. I just sat there like a dumbfuck waiting for you."

I almost say "sorry" again. Almost.

"In case you were curious, my father finally got off his ass to see my grandmother. I told him I wanted to come and he said it wasn't the right time. And I was like, 'When's the right time, after she's dead?' That really pissed him off. And I wanted to say, 'What's it like, Dad,

153

to be a failure as both a son *and* a father? How do you account for that?' But he had his give-me-one-reason-to-belt-you face on. He never does it, but man he wants to."

"Is she getting any better?" I ask.

"No. She's not *getting any better*. Jesus."

Fair. I need to focus. And when I focus, I see the pain he's in. His grandmother is the one person in his family he really loves. Hers is the only blood he wants in his veins. I know this. He's told me this. I have to stop treating it like he has no reason to be angry.

"You should call her," I say. "They can't stop you from calling her. Is your dad there yet?"

He shakes his head. "He's probably still on the plane."

I reach across the table and pick up the phone.

"So beat him to it."

A lot of the time, love feels like it's about figuring out what the other person wants and giving it over. Sometimes that's impossible. But sometimes it's pretty simple. Like right now. He doesn't have the words to thank me, but when I hand him the phone, he holds on for a moment, lets me know I've gotten it right.

Right after he dials, I tell him I can go. Give him some privacy.

"No," he says. "I want you here." Then: "I *need* you here."

So I stay, and watch him talk to his grandmother like

it's all going to be fine. Not going near goodbye, even though it's probably the word most on his mind.

After he's done, he puts the phone back on the table and says, "Wow, that was hard."

I wish I were sitting next to him, not across from him. I press my knees against his knees.

"It's all right," he says. Then he picks up a slice of pizza and keeps eating.

I'm about to ask him what his grandmother said, but then the phone rings and it's Steve, telling us about a party at Yonni Pfister's house.

"We're there," Justin says. Then, after he hangs up, he tells me where we're going.

Annapolis, I can't help thinking. But we're going nowhere near Annapolis.

Say any city enough times, it starts to sound like a made-up place.

Rebecca is at the party. She searches me out.

"I think our boyfriends are getting pretty baked," she tells me.

"Lucky us," I say.

She looks at me in surprise and laughs. "Did you really just say that? Good for you!"

Don't tell Justin, I want to say. But I know she won't. She might tell Ben, but he won't tell Justin, either.

Am I the only one who actually likes Justin?

"What's been going on?" Rebecca asks me.

"I'm just tired," I say.

"Yeah, but tired of what?"

She's genuinely interested. She genuinely cares. She is my friend.

I don't tell her a thing.

I duck out of the party before it's too late to call Kelsea's house.

This time someone answers.

"Hello?" His voice is rough. Tired.

"Hi, is Kelsea there?" I ask. I just want to hear her voice. I just want to know she's okay.

"Who is this?"

I try to think of a name that isn't mine. "It's Mia. I'm a friend of hers?"

"Well, Kelsea isn't here right now. And she won't be using her phone for a few days. If you leave a message there, though, I'm sure she'll get back to you. Just give it some time."

I risk it and ask, "Is she okay? I'm just a little . . . concerned."

"She's somewhere getting help," he says. "It's going to be okay." He pauses; this is new ground for him. "I know it'll mean a lot to hear from her friends. It's good of you to call."

He's not going to tell me more, and that's fine. This is enough to know.

"Thank you," I say. I want to tell him he did the right thing. But I don't want to make too much of an impression.

I'm already the friend who isn't really there.

I'm home late. I have to walk Justin to his door because he's so out of it. I wonder if his mom is awake.

"Thank you," he says quietly. "My grandmother is an amazing lady, and you're not too bad yourself."

"Don't give your mom a hard time," I tell him.

He raises his fingers in a salute. "Yes, ma'am." Then he leans over and kisses me goodnight. I'm surprised, and he can tell I'm surprised.

"Night, ma'am," he says. Then he disappears inside.

I email A when I get back to my house.

A,

Sorry I couldn't make it to Annapolis – there were some things I had to do.

Maybe tomorrow?

R

It's Sunday. Justin won't be up for a while. We haven't made plans. My parents won't leave the house.

I'm free.

I tell my mom I have errands to run, then email A and ask if he wants to be one of my errands.

Yes, he writes back. *A million times yes.*

I am just going to do this, I tell myself as I make all the arrangements, as I come up with plans.

I am not going to think about it.

I am not going to think about what it means.

I am just going to do it, and be with A, and see what it means as it happens.

A's told me he (she?) is a girl named Ashley today. I've gotten directions to her house. I know she'll be waiting when I pull up.

I guess I'm picturing the girl A was when I first met her (him?). Pretty, but not overwhelmingly so. Someone I could be friends with. Someone I could be.

But holy shit, not this girl.

She comes out of the house and I'm like what kind of music video am I living in? Because this girl is smoking hot. She looks like she should travel with backup singers. And photographers. And three stylists. And a small dog. And Jay-Z.

This is the kind of girl you never see in real life. You can almost pretend girls like this don't really exist. They're computer-generated by fashion magazines to make you feel lame.

Only this girl is *real*.

And I know I shouldn't care – this isn't a contest. But really? I already feel fat, and she isn't even at the car yet.

The one thing she doesn't have is a *walk*. A girl like this should have a walk. But I guess that's A inside. Stomping when he should sashay.

When she gets in the car and I see her up close, I have to laugh. Even her skin is perfect. All I'm asking for is a simple fucking pimple.

"You've got to be kidding me," I say.

She makes putting a seat belt on look sexy. Jesus.

She sees me laughing and asks, "What?"

She doesn't get it.

"*What?*" I repeat. Like A doesn't realize how amazing she is today.

She holds up her hand, defending her reaction. "You have to understand – you're the first person to ever know me in more than one body. I'm not used to this. I don't know how you're going to react."

Okay. I may have forgotten that. But still.

"I'm sorry," I say. "It's just that you're this super hot black girl. It makes it very hard for me to have a mental image of you. I have to keep changing it."

"Picture me however you want to picture me. Because odds are, that'll be more true than any of the bodies you see me in."

She makes it sound easy. It's not easy. Especially with a pretty girl.

"I think my imagination needs a little more time to catch up to the situation, okay?" I say.

She nods. Even her nod is stunning. Not fair at all. "Okay. Now, where to?"

I've given this some thought. And I am not going to change the plan just because of the body in my passenger seat.

"Since we've already been to the ocean," I say, "I figured today we'd go to a forest."

So much for not thinking about it.

As we're driving, all I can do is think about it. About her. About A inside her body. We're talking – I'm telling her about the phone call with Kelsea's father and the party last night, and she's telling me about the parade she went to yesterday, in the body of a gay boy with a boyfriend. But even as we're talking, my mind is racing with all kinds of thoughts. And the pathetic thing is that I know if A looked like Nathan today, I wouldn't be having any of these thoughts. It would feel normal, because I'd be out with a normal boy.

But this is so different. Too different. Even though when she looks at me, I can feel A inside, it's not easy to separate the two. And it's not easy to realize this is part of the lottery. Some days, A is going to be like this.

I don't see where I could possibly fit into a life like that.

I don't want to kiss her. I could never kiss her.

So there's that.

But I can talk to her and not worry that I'm talking too much, or talking too little, or saying the wrong thing. It's like my life is usually lived behind this veil of judgment, and A manages to pull back the veil, seeing me more truthfully than anyone else.

I tell myself to notice that. To remember it. To not get so caught up in how attractive she is that I forget everything else.

I take us to this national park that I know has picnic benches. I've planned a picnic for two – and even if Ashley looks like she eats half a meal a day, I'm hoping A will find a way to eat like the rest of us. There are a few other people in the park, but I try to avoid them. This day is meant to be ours.

My phone is off. I am here, now.

"I love this place," A tells me.

"You've never been here before?" I ask.

She shakes her head. "Not that I can remember. Although it's possible. At a certain point, it all blurs together. There are a lot of days when I haven't really paid attention."

I know she's paying attention now. She smiles at me as I turn off the car. She watches as I head to the trunk. She seems delighted when I pull out the picnic hamper.

The hamper comes with a blanket, and I put it over the picnic table like a tablecloth – because, when it all comes down to it, I don't like sitting on the ground if a table is an option. Then I put out all the food I bought – nothing big, just a lot of small things, like chips and salsa and cheese and bread and hummus and olives.

"Are you a vegetarian?" A asks.

I nod.

"Why?"

I am so tired of this question. Shouldn't it be the meat eaters who are asked why? And it's always like they're expecting this crazy answer. So I decide to give the craziest answer I can think of.

I keep a straight face and say, "Because I have this

162

theory that when we die, every animal that we've eaten has a chance at eating us back. So if you're a carnivore and you add up all the animals you've eaten – well, that's a long time in purgatory, being chewed."

It's funny to see Ashley's perfect features contort into a grimace. "Really?" she asks.

I laugh. "No. I'm just sick of the question. I mean, I'm vegetarian because I think it's wrong to eat other sentient creatures. And it sucks for the environment."

"Fair enough," she says.

I'm not sure I've persuaded her.

Maybe over time I can, I think.

Then I think, *What?*

I shouldn't be thinking of anything over time. It's just one day plus another day plus another day. Maybe.

When things get bad with Justin, the question I find myself asking is: What's the point? Like, why put ourselves through all this? Why try to squeeze two people into the shape of a couple? Are the things you gain really worth the things you lose?

Now I'm asking myself the same things about A. We're talking about favorite foods and the best meals we've ever had, and the foods we hate the most – when she asks me all these questions, I enjoy answering, and when I ask her questions back, I enjoy the answers she gives me. If this were a date, it would be going really well. But there's a part of me that's standing outside of it, that's looking at it as it happens, and that part is asking, *What is this? What's the point?*

When we're done eating, we pack the leftovers in the hamper and return it to the trunk. Then, without discussing what we're going to do next, we walk into the woods. The paths aren't obvious – we find our way through the trees by heading into them, looking for the widest distances, the clearest ground.

When we're alone, when we're walking like this, all of the conversation that's been happening on the outside moves to the center of our minds. *What is this?* I know I can't answer it alone.

"I need to know what you want," I say.

She doesn't seem surprised by the request. If it were Justin, I know I'd get a "What's gotten into you?" But A answers without missing a beat.

"I want us to be together," she (he?) tells me.

She says it like it's easy. But there's no way my mind can turn it into something easy. Not when she's in a different body every day. I can have a conversation with any of them, I'm sure. But when it comes to chemistry, when it comes to making that part of me come alive – I know some days are going to work and some aren't. Like now. She has to see that.

"But we can't be together," I say. I'm amazed by how

calm I sound. "You realize that, don't you?"

"No," she says. "I don't realize that."

Frustrating. It's like talking to a child who still believes that proclaiming something out loud can make it real. I wish I could believe like that.

I stop walking and put my hand on her shoulder. The truth hurts to say, especially because she looks so unready to hear it.

"You need to realize it," I tell her. "I can care about you. You can care about me. But we can't be together."

"Why?"

"Why?" It's exasperating to have to spell it out. "Because one morning you could wake up on the other side of the country. Because I feel like I'm meeting a new person every time I see you. Because you can't be there for me. Because I don't think I can like you no matter what. Not like this."

"Why can't you like me like this?"

"It's too much. You're too perfect right now. I can't imagine being with someone like . . . you."

"But don't look at her – look at me."

I am. I *am* looking at her.

"I can't see beyond her, okay?" I say. "And there's also Justin. I have to think of Justin."

"No, you don't."

This makes me angry. Whatever Justin and I have, it

can't be dismissed in a single sentence.

"You don't know, okay? How many waking hours were you in there? Fourteen? Fifteen? Did you really get to know everything about him while you were in there? Everything about me?"

"You like him because he's a lost boy. Believe me, I've seen it happen before. But do you know what happens to girls who love lost boys? They become lost themselves. Without fail."

I don't want to hear this. "You don't know me –"

"But I know how this works!" Her voice is loud, certain. "I know what he's like. He doesn't care about you nearly as much as you care about him. He doesn't care about you nearly as much as I care about you."

I can't hear this. What good is hearing this?

"Stop! Just stop."

But she won't. "What do you think would happen if he met me in this body? What if the three of us went out? How much attention do you think he'd pay you? Because he doesn't care about who you are. I happen to think you are about a thousand times more attractive than Ashley is. But do you really think he'd be able to keep his hands to himself if he had a chance?"

"He's not like that," I say. Because he's not.

"Are you sure? Are you really sure?"

"Fine," I say. "Let me call him."

I don't know why I'm doing this, but I'm doing it. I take out my phone. Turn it on. Call him.

"Hello," he answers.

"Hi!" I'm too cheery. I take it down a notch. "I don't know what you're up to tonight, but I have this friend in town I'd love for you to meet. Maybe we could all get dinner?"

"Dinner? What time is it?"

"It's only two now. Maybe at six? At the Clam Casino? I'll treat."

"Okay. Sounds good."

"Great! I'll see you then!"

I hang up before he can ask me who my friend is. I'll have to think of a story.

"Happy?" I ask A.

"I have no idea," she replies.

"Me either." Because now that I'm thinking about it, I'm wondering what I've just done.

"When are we meeting him?"

"Six."

"Okay," she says. "In the meantime, I want to tell you everything, and I want you to tell me everything in return."

Everything.

I start when I was born. My father was away for

167

business and my mother was all alone in the hospital. She knew I was going to be a girl. One night my father, after a few beers, told me the story of how she called my name as I was being born. As if I would hear her calling. As if he was there in the room to know what she said.

We moved around a lot when I was really young, but I don't remember much of it. My first memory is actually of Liza hiding with me under our parents' bed. I remember her telling me to be quiet. I remember seeing their feet, hearing their voices looking for us. I don't remember being found.

I give A all these little, Lego-like details, and don't have any idea what they build. But I can see A building something – a story – as I hand them over. I can see A putting it together, and wanting to.

I ask her when she first knew about being the way she is. She tells me that until she was four or five, she just assumed she was normal – she assumed everyone woke up every day with new parents, in a new house, with a new body. Because when you're young, people are willing to reintroduce the world to you each day. If you get something wrong, they'll correct you. If there's a blank, they'll fill it in for you. You're not expected to know that much about your life.

"There was never that big a disturbance," she tells me. "I didn't think of myself as a boy or a girl – I never have. I would just think of myself as a boy or a girl for a day. It was like a different set of clothes. The thing that ended up tripping me up was the concept of tomorrow. Because after a while, I started to notice – people kept talking about doing things tomorrow. Together. And if I argued, I would get strange looks. For everyone else, there always seemed to be a tomorrow together. But not for me. I'd say, 'You won't be there,' and they'd say, 'Of course I'll be there.' And then I'd wake up, and they wouldn't be. And my new parents would have no idea why I was so upset."

I try to imagine going through that, but I can't really. I don't think I could ever get used to it.

A continues. "There were only two options – something was wrong with everyone else, or something was wrong with me. Because either they were tricking themselves into thinking there was a tomorrow together, or I was the only person who was leaving."

"Did you try to hold on?" I ask.

"I'm sure I did. But I don't remember it now. I remember crying and protesting – I told you about that. But the rest? I'm not sure. I mean, do you remember a lot about when you were five?"

I see her point. "Not really. I remember my mom bringing me and my sister to the shoe store to get new shoes before kindergarten started. I remember learning

169

that a green light meant go and red meant stop. I remember coloring them in, and the teacher being a little confused about how to explain yellow. I think she told us to treat it the same as red."

"I learned my letters quickly. I remember the teachers being surprised that I knew them. I imagine they were just as surprised the next day, when I'd forgotten them."

"A five-year-old probably wouldn't notice taking a day off."

"Probably. I don't know."

I can't help wondering about the people whose body A takes for a day. I wonder what they feel the next day. I think about Nathan staring at me so blankly. But mostly I think about Justin.

"I keep asking Justin about it, you know," I say. "The day you were him. And it's amazing how clear his fake memories are. He doesn't disagree when I say we went to the beach, but he doesn't really remember it, either."

"James, the twin, was like that, too. He didn't notice anything wrong. But when I asked him about meeting you for coffee, he didn't remember it at all. He remembered he was at Starbucks – his mind accounted for the time. But it wasn't what actually happened."

"Maybe they remember what you want them to remember."

"I've thought about that. I wish I knew for sure."

We walk in silence for a minute, then stop at a tree with a ladder of knots. I can't help but touch one. A touches the other side, and works her hand around to mine. But I keep moving, too. Circling.

"What about love?" I ask. "Have you ever been in love?"

Which is my way of asking: Is it possible? Is any of this possible?

"I don't know that you'd call it love," A tells me. "I've had crushes, for sure. And there have been days where I've really regretted leaving. There were even one or two people I tried to find, but that didn't work out. The closest was this guy Brennan."

A stops. Looks again at the tree, at the knots.

"Tell me about him," I say.

"It was about a year ago. I was working at a movie theater, and he was in town, visiting his cousins, and when he went to get some popcorn, we flirted a little, and it just became this . . . spark. It was this small, one-screen movie theater, and when the movie was running, my job was pretty slow. I think he missed the second half of the movie, because he came back out and started talking to me more. I ended up having to tell him what happened, so he could pretend he'd been in there most of the time. At the end, he asked for my email, and I made up an email address."

"Like you did for me," I point out. So Nathan knew what he was doing a little more than I'd thought.

"Exactly like I did for you. And he emailed me later that night, and left the next day to go back home to Maine, and that proved to be ideal, because then the rest of our relationship could be online. I'd been wearing a nametag, so I had to give him that first name, but I made up a last name, and then I made up an online profile using some of the photos from the real guy's profile. I think his name was Stephen."

This surprises me, that A was a boy in love with a boy. Maybe because it's a girl's voice telling me this story. Or maybe because I assume *girl* when I hear *boyfriend*. Which I know isn't right, but it's where my mind goes.

After I express my surprise, she asks me if it matters. I tell her it doesn't. And while she tells me the rest of the story – she tried to keep it going online, but he wanted to meet, and she knew they never could, so she ended it – I try to convince myself that it really *doesn't* matter. And I guess it doesn't matter, in terms of her (him). But it still matters in terms of me. At least a little.

As she wraps up the Brennan story, A tells me, "I promised myself I wouldn't get into any more virtual entanglements, as easy as they might seem to be. Because what's the point of something virtual if it doesn't end up being real? And I could never give anyone something

172

real. I could only give them deception."

"Like impersonating their boyfriends," I can't help but say.

"Yeah. But you have to understand – you were the exception to the rule. And I didn't want it to be based on deception. Which is why you're the first person I've ever told."

I know this is meant as the highest compliment A can give me. But I want to know what I did to earn it. I want to know how A knows I'm the right person to tell. I want to know what that means.

I tell her, "The funny thing is, you say it like it's so unusual that you've only done it once. But I bet a whole lot of people go through their lives without ever telling the truth, not really. And they wake up in the same body and the same life every single morning."

Now she's curious. "Why? What aren't you telling me?"

I have known you less than two weeks, I think. I wish I could disarm myself so completely in such a short time. But even if A thinks I've earned that, I am not even close to believing she's earned it. Not because of who she is or what she is. Because it's so soon.

I get that her life has a special set of rules. But my life has rules, too.

I look her right in the eye. I am not angry – I want

173

to be sure she knows I'm not angry. But I *am* serious. "If I'm not telling you something, it's for a reason. Just because you trust me, it doesn't mean I have to automatically trust you. Trust doesn't work like that."

"That's fair," she says. Although I can tell she's also a little disappointed.

"I know it is," I tell her. "But enough of that. Tell me about – I don't know – third grade."

There is no point in talking more about us. We need to talk about ourselves separately for a little while longer.

It's not entirely separate, of course. We've both been afraid of teachers. We've both gotten lost at theme parks. We've both fallen into hair-pulling, teeth-kicking fights with siblings. We've grown up on the same TV shows, being the same age. Only, while we both had dreams of waking up in Hannah Montana's body and Hannah Montana's life, A actually believed that the dream could come true.

I ask about all those lives, all those days, and what A can remember. The result is like a series of snapshots – a slideshow of bits and pieces with the faces always changing. All of the firsts – first snow, first Pixar movie, first evil pet, first bully. And other things I wouldn't have even realized were things – the size of bedrooms, the strange diets parents put their kids on, the need to sing in church even if you don't know any of the tunes or any of the words. Discovering allergies, illnesses, learning problems, stutters. And living the day with them. Always living another day.

I try to keep up. I try to offer some of my firsts, some of my surprises. But they don't seem as first or as surprising.

We talk about family. She asks me if I hate my mother.

"No," I tell her. "That's not it. I love her, but I also want her to be better. I want her to stop giving up."

"I can't even imagine what that's like. To come home to the same parents every day."

"There's no one who can make you angrier, but you also can't really love anyone more. I know that doesn't make sense, but it's true. She disappoints me every day she just sits there. But I know she would do anything for me, if she had to."

It's strange to say this out loud. It's not something I'd ever say to my mother, or even think in her presence. But maybe I should. I don't know.

Even though I'm afraid of the answer, I ask A if she's always been around here, or if she jumps to bodies in much farther places. In other words, I want to know if onc day she'll be too far away to see, if she could wake up on the other side of the world.

"It doesn't work like that," she tells me. "I honestly don't know why it works the way it does, but I know that I never wake up that far from where I was yesterday. It's like there's a method to it – but I couldn't tell you what it is. Once I tried to chart it out – the distances between bodies. I tried to see if it made mathematical sense. But it was mathematical gibberish. Random, but in a limited way."

"So you won't leave?" I ask.

"Not by waking up. But if the body I'm in goes somewhere else – I go with it. That becomes my new starting point. That's how I got here, to Maryland. This one girl had a field trip to DC, and the group she was in was cheap, so they stayed outside the city. The next morning, I didn't wake up back in Minnesota. I was still in Bethesda."

"Well, don't take any field trips soon, okay?" I make it sound like a joke, but I mean it.

"No field trips," she agrees. Then she asks me about my own travels, and I tell her all about how I haven't really been anywhere since we settled down in Maryland. Even DC is a stretch. My parents like to stay put.

She asks me where I want to go. I tell her Paris. Which is such a silly answer, because I feel like it would be any girl's answer.

"I've always wanted to go there, too," A says. "And London."

"And Greece!"

176

"And Amsterdam."

"Yes, Amsterdam."

We walk round and round the forest, planning to travel the world. We walk past tree after tree and all the years we've lived seem to be there to be reached for. We return to the car and take more chips, more olives. Then we walk a little farther, talk a little further. I can't believe how many stories there are – but they keep appearing because our stories are talking to each other; one of mine leading to one of A's, then one of A's leading to one of mine.

I never talk like this, I think. And then I realize this is very close to what A was saying before. *You're the first person I've ever told.*

Yes, A is the first person I've ever told most of these stories to. Because A is the first person who has listened and heard and wanted to know.

Which might not be fair to Justin. Because how much have I actually tried to tell these things to Justin?

Only on the beach. Only that day.

Thinking of Justin makes me think of the stupid dinner plans we've made. I look at my phone and find that hours have passed. It's five-fifteen.

There isn't even time to cancel.

"We better get going," I tell A. "Justin will be waiting for us."

Neither of us wants to do this now. We want to stay here, keep this.

I feel like I've made a mistake.

I feel like what we're about to do is a big mistake.

She tries to talk to me on the car ride over, and I try to talk to her, but I think we're both lost in what we're about to do. It's awful that we're going to trick him like this. And it's even more awful that I'm dying to know what he'll do.

I've gotten used to how Ashley looks, so it throws me to see the reaction when we hit the Clam Casino. The greeter is Chrissy B, this guy I went to high school with. He graduated last year, wanting to do musical theater. The closest he's come so far is when someone orders the Happy Clamday to You special, and he and the other staff members have to sing the "Happy Clamday" song while someone blows out a candle that's sitting on a half shell. It's a pretty scary place, but the food is good.

Chrissy B takes one look at Ashley and it's like he's projecting all of his runways onto her. I've never seen him snap to attention so fast, or handle the menus so self-consciously. It's like I'm not even there, not until I say hi and ask him if Justin's already around. Chrissy B seems annoyed to have to answer me. But he tells me no, and I say we'll wait. Justin doesn't like it when I sit down before he does – I think because then we're

179

committing to staying, and sometimes he changes his mind.

As we wait for him, I can sense other people looking at Ashley. If A notices, she keeps her cool. I don't like it. Some of the guys are looking so openly, so hungrily – what right do they have to do that? Some of the women are admiring, and others are resentful. Whatever their feelings, they have a reaction. If I were Ashley, I would feel like a bug trapped in a jar.

Justin walks in about ten minutes after we do, which is only five minutes late.

He sees me first, and starts to head over. Then he sees Ashley and stops for a second. He's not immediately predatory, like the other guys. He's floored. Completely floored.

"Hi," I say. It's awkward because usually I'd kiss him hello. But I don't want to do that in front of A. "Ashley," I say, "this is Justin. Justin, this is Ashley."

Ashley puts out her hand to shake – it's a very not-Ashley gesture, and I almost laugh from nervousness. Justin shakes. He's looking at her whole body when he does.

"Let me get you a table!" Chrissy B chirps, as if his stage time in this amateur production has finally come.

As we walk over, more people look. If they're

thinking there's a couple here, it's Ashley and Justin. I'm the third wheel.

I don't know what to say or do. I have no idea how to explain Ashley to Justin. And now that we're here, I don't want them to get along. I don't want him to fall for her. I don't want him to look at her in a way he'd never look at me. I don't want to be humiliated like that.

"So," Justin says once Chrissy B has fanned out the menus and left us to our choices. "How do you two know each other?"

I can't think of a single thing but the truth, which isn't nearly good enough.

But A doesn't hesitate. "Oh, it's a funny story!" she says, and it's like her voice already believes it's a funny story, and is sure we'll agree in about ten seconds. "My mom and her mom were best friends in high school. Then we moved away when I was eight. Mom couldn't stand the cold, so we went to LA. My dad got a job working on movie sets, and Mom became a librarian at the downtown library. I didn't think I'd get into the LA thing, but I totally did. When I was ten, I told my mom I wanted to do commercials – not that I wanted to be an *actress*, but that I wanted to do *commercials*! And from there I've done some bit parts and auditioned for a lot of TV shows. Nothing yet, but I've come close. And every few years, Mom and I make a trip back here, to see some family and old friends. Rhiannon and I see each other every couple of years – but it's been a while this time, hasn't it? Like, three or four years?"

"Yeah," I say, because I sense I'm supposed to say something here. "I think it's three."

A is really getting into it. And she's also really getting into Justin. I can see her leg brushing up against his. He doesn't move into it, but he doesn't move away.

This isn't happening, I tell myself.

I knew I couldn't compete with Ashley. So what did I do? I put myself in a competition.

I have no one to blame but myself.

"So have you been on any shows I would've seen?" Justin asks.

She starts to tell him about being a corpse on a medical investigation show, and being in a party scene on a "reality" show. And the stupid thing is – I'm believing it. I'm actually imagining her on that coroner's slab, or joking with a D-list celebrity over a keg.

"But LA's such a fake place," Ashley confesses when she's through with her résumé. "That's why I'm glad I have real friends like Rhiannon."

She gives my hand a little squeeze. I find that reassuring.

Our dinner arrives, and Ashley starts to talk about guys, including this one time she "shared a moment" with Jake Gyllenhaal at some château. As she's talking about this encounter, she keeps touching Justin's hand. I do not find that reassuring.

Luckily, Justin pulls away to get back to his lobster roll. I ask Ashley how her parents are doing. She answers flawlessly. Justin isn't so interested in parents, which is good.

But then the food is done, and Justin's hands are free, and Ashley goes full throttle again. Defensively, I reach for Justin's hand myself. It feels like lobster roll. He doesn't shake me off, but it's clear he doesn't understand why I'm holding it, either. I try to move my leg against his, but I'm at the wrong angle. It looks like I'm trying to get a napkin from under the table.

"How's everything going?" Chrissy B comes over to ask, his eyes full of Ashley.

"Wonnnnnderful!" she purrs.

Who are you? I think.

Chrissy B bounces away happy.

I want to ask for the check. I do not want any more courses of this. Justin isn't looking at me. He's not seeing me. He's not getting the SOS I'm sending.

I need to calm down. If I start acting needy or emotional, it will only make Ashley more attractive.

"I'm going to the ladies' room," I announce. I touch Justin on the arm. He gives me a look like, *You do not need my permission to go to the bathroom, Rhiannon.*

I don't need to pee. I need to stare at myself in the mirror and ask myself what I really want. I need to splash water on my face and wake myself up . . . but I'm afraid someone will come in and see me doing it, so I stick with staring at myself in the mirror. I see a girl who isn't ugly, but who will never, ever be Ashley. I see the girl Justin has grown used to. I see a girl who is deeply unexciting, and who dared her boyfriend to find someone better.

I am so stupid. So, so stupid.

And I am especially stupid for leaving them alone together.

I wash my hands even though I haven't touched anything. Then I push myself back to the table. I can see their conversation has gotten real intense. Something is happening.

I interrupt. I don't even wait until I've sat back down. I stand there and tell A, "I don't want this. Stop."

"I'm not doing anything!" Justin yells. But he looks guilty. "Your friend here is a little out of control."

"I don't want this," I repeat, this time to both of them.

"It's okay," Ashley says. "I'm sorry."

"You should be!" Justin tells her. "God, I don't know how they do things in California, but here, you don't act like that."

He's up now. I want to ask what happened. I don't want to know what happened.

"I'm gonna go," he says. Then, out of the blue, he kisses me. I want to believe it's for me, but it's for her. I know it's for her.

I don't want it.

"Thanks, baby," he says. "I'll see you tomorrow."

That's it. He's not turning back. I watch him even after he's gone.

I have done this. This was all me. Setting the trap, then getting caught in it.

I look at Ashley as I sit back down. She looks like she's witnessed a car accident. Or maybe she was the driver.

"I'm sorry," she tells me again.

"No," I say, "it's my fault. I should've known. I told you that you don't understand. You can't understand us."

The waitress is back, asking if we want dessert. I say no, just the check. She has it ready.

"I'll get it," A says.

"It's not your money," I point out. "I'll pay."

I text Justin to say I'm sorry. I tell him I'll call him

as soon as I'm home. It's awful, but I wish Ashley had driven herself. I wish we could stop the night here. I am grateful that A will wake up in another body tomorrow. I am grateful I'll never have to see Ashley again.

It's only by separating them that I can hold onto A, and everything that happened before we got to this restaurant. But even still – we've done some damage. A hasn't hurt me . . . but she's allowed me to hurt myself. Which is almost the same thing.

When we get back to my car, she tells me again that she's sorry. I see why Justin gets sick of it when I say it so much.

After a while, she gives up. She realizes I need her to be quiet.

Finally, we get to her house.

"I had a great time," she says. "Until."

"Yeah," I say. "Until."

"He'll be fine. I'm sure he just thinks I'm this crazy California girl. Don't worry about it."

Pointless. What a pointless thing to say.

"I'll talk to you," she tells me.

If we'd come here straight from the woods, I wonder what would be happening now. Whether I'd kiss her even though she's Ashley. Whether we'd feel invincible.

186

"I'll talk to you," I echo. Even though I have no idea what we'll have to say.

I can't worry about A now.

I have to get Justin back.

14

I don't wait until I get home. I drive away from Ashley's house, turn a few corners, then pull over by the side of the road and call him.

He hasn't texted me back, and I'm worried he won't pick up. But he does.

"What's up?" he says. I can hear the TV loud in the background.

"I'm really sorry about that," I say.

"Not your fault. I have no idea where you picked up that black bitch, but let me tell you, she is *not* your friend. At all."

"I know. It was stupid of me to invite you along. I should've just dealt with her."

"She was out of control. Completely out of control."

"I guess looking like that can do that to you."

"It's no excuse. Seriously. What a *bitch*."

It wasn't really her, I want to say. *You didn't meet her at all.*

"I'll see you in the morning," Justin says. This is his way of saying we're not going to talk about this anymore.

"See you in the morning," I tell him. "And sorry again."

"Stop. It's fine."

No, it isn't.

I wonder if maybe it isn't only Ashley's life that has been hijacked. Maybe mine has been hijacked, too. Maybe I need to focus on the real things, not the fantasy things. Even if A is real, A will never be constant. Justin is my constant.

I'm worried that Justin will be pissed at me for what happened, but mostly he's pissed at Ashley. When we bump into our friends in the hall before homeroom, he can't wait to tell everyone what happened.

"Rhiannon has this total slut friend from California who *totally* made the moves on me last night – with Rhiannon right there! It was wild. She was totally hot, and she could not keep her hands off me. Finally I was like, 'Hey, what do you think you're doing?' And Rhiannon came right in and told her to get the hell off. I swear to you, it was out of control."

"Dude!" Steve says.

"Yeah. That's what I'm saying."

I know this is how guys talk. I know that the point of the story is that he chose me. But it still feels like he's bragging. It still feels like the point was that this hot, slutty girl wanted to sleep with him.

I'm not going to say anything – I'm just going to let

the story be over. But Rebecca picks it up and won't let it go.

"What exactly is it that makes her a slut?" she asks. "What if she was just flirty?"

"Oh, give it a rest, Rebecca," Justin spits out. "You weren't there. You didn't see this black bitch in action – it was priceless."

"Now she's a 'black bitch'? Really, Justin?" Even though I don't want her to look at me at all, she turns my way. "Can you tell the rest of us what really happened?"

"He's right," I say. "She was out of control."

Now Rebecca's not just angry at Justin; she's disappointed in me.

"Cute, Rhiannon. Real cute."

Justin tries to level her with a look. "Rebecca, you weren't there. And I can call someone a black bitch if she was black and acted like a bitch. That's just a fact."

"Bullshit! Her being black has nothing to do with your story, you asshole. And I'll bet if she were telling her side of the story, she wouldn't be a bitch, either."

"So it's okay all of a sudden to call me an asshole?"

"One, I've been calling you an asshole for years. And two, please note that I'm not calling you a white asshole – because even though I'm sure your whiteness adds to your sense of entitlement, I'm willing to let it slide so we can focus on the fact that you're a *universal* asshole right now."

"Okay," I interrupt. "You've made your point. Enough."

"Yeah, man," Justin says to Ben. "Turn your girlfriend off, okay?"

I know he's saying this to make Rebecca extra mad.

"She's right," Ben says. "You're being an asshole."

I feel bad because now Justin is feeling attacked, and even though his choice of words is wrong, the story he's telling isn't a lie. Ashley *did* come on to him. And even though she did it with my permission, he doesn't know that. He thinks one of my friends tried to steal him from me – and that *is* being a bitch. A universal bitch.

"If you don't change the subject right now, I am going to unleash the biggest fart this school has ever seen," Steve tells us. "You have been warned."

Rebecca pulls back and lets it look like she's dropping the conversation. But from the way she looks at me, I know she's filing it away for later.

In art class, she launches right into me.

"Why do you let him talk like that? How can you just sit there and let him shit all over everyone?"

"Rebecca, you have to understand –"

"No. Don't defend him. I don't know who this

191

California friend of yours is, but maybe *she's* the one you should be defending. Because if you think of her as some slutty, black bitch, then you're not all that great a friend to have."

Wait. What? What are we fighting about?

"Rebecca, why are you mad? I don't understand why you're mad."

"I'm mad because my best friend is dating an asshole. And no matter how many times I point it out to her, she looks at me like I'm the one saying the world is round, and she's like, *No no no – flat.*"

"It wasn't his fault," I insist. "She was trying to trap him into doing something. He was right to be mad."

"That must have been so hard on him, to have a hot girl flirt in his direction. I don't know how he could stand it. Poor victim."

"It wasn't like that." There's no way I can explain.

"Well, in his version, it was. You know, the racist, sexist version he gave us in the hall? Or maybe you don't even notice those parts anymore."

"I do, but . . . that's not him. That's just him being mad."

"Oh, like it doesn't count if you're pissed off? I wish there were an Olympic competition where you could show off all the contortions you do in order to justify your relationship with him."

192

I hate it when she uses her smartness to *contort* things about me, to make me feel so dumb.

"Why do you have such a problem with me and Justin?" I challenge. "*Why?* It's not like he hits me. It's not like he abuses me. It's not like he cheats on me. Why can't you just accept that I see things in him that you might not see. And that you might not see them because you're a bitch to him all the time."

"So I get to be the bitch now? Fine. Then you, my friend, are the scary girl. 'He doesn't hit me. He doesn't abuse me. He doesn't cheat on me.' Can you hear yourself? If those are the standards you have – hey, he hasn't punched me, so everything must be okay! – that scares me. That makes me think that at some point you've used these justifications. 'Oh, it's really bad right now, and he's being awful . . . but at least he's not hitting me.' Have a little more respect for yourself than that, okay?"

We are in the middle of art class. We are supposed to be drawing a sleeping turtle that Mr K has brought in. Other people can probably hear us.

"Can we please not have this conversation here?" I ask her. When it comes out of my mouth, it sounds a little like pleading.

Rebecca sighs. "I don't know why I bother." Then she shakes her head, correcting herself. "No, I do know.

193

Because you are my friend, Rhiannon. And because it kills me to see you twist yourself around to be with him. I know you're not really hearing me right now, but one day, these words might come in handy. They might help. Which is why I'm putting them out there. So they'll be there when you need them, and you'll know that I'm here when you need me."

It's perfectly said. Too perfectly said. I want to tell her that I already have one guidance counselor and don't really need another. I want to tell her that I can tell she enjoys seeing me suffer, because if I'm the patient, then she gets to be the nurse, the doctor, the guardian angel. Part of me appreciates it, but mostly I resent it.

She returns to her drawing and I return to mine. The turtle wakes up and tries to run away. Mr K catches it every time it attempts to escape. The first time this happens, the class laughs. The fourth time, it's just inconvenient.

When I hang out with Justin after school, he doesn't mention Ashley or even Rebecca. We go back to his place and play some video games – I lose in an early round and have to watch until he's done. Then he moves his hands on me and we start to make out, and without us talking about it, I know we're going to go all the way this afternoon. I try to get into it, but I keep wondering if he'd like it better if I had a different body – if I had Ashley's body. Then as we're getting naked and more intense, I think about being in his body and having sex with Ashley. Would I like it? Do I want that? I can't feel that way, and then I start thinking the opposite – what if A were in Justin's body right now? What if it were A inside of me, A covered in sweat, A kissing me? I know it would be different. I know he'd be looking at me more. Feeling me more. Here more. I feel so fucked up for thinking these things. For imagining A here, A with me. I am cheating on Justin in my head, even if it's still his body that I'm cheating with.

It finishes before I've really gotten anywhere. Justin asks me if I want him to keep going with me, but I tell him no, I'm fine. I'm good. I'm great.

I check my email before I go to sleep that night. No emails from Justin. No word from Rebecca. Just something from A.

I have to see you again.

A

I wonder what body A is in right now. I wonder if I would've wanted to sleep with it. I wonder if I'm wrong to wonder that. I wonder what the hell I'm doing.

I don't answer. I want to see A – of course I do.

But I still don't see the point.

Justin is in a dire mood when I catch him in the morning. Another long-distance lecture from his dad. Another test he's not ready for. Another day he doesn't want to be here.

I try to plant myself firmly at his side. I complain about my own history test coming up today. I tell him that hanging out with him yesterday was much more fun than studying, anyway. I don't tell him that I studied when I got home.

"I fucking hate this place," he tells me. I must remind myself I am not a part of the place. He is not talking about me.

It's hard to be supportive when you have no idea what you're supporting. It's hard to be there for someone when he won't let you know where he is.

I tell him I'll see him at lunch. He doesn't react. And why should he? – I'm only stating the obvious. We always know how our day will go.

I walk to my classes. I talk to the people I always talk to. I am barely paying attention to my own life.

I go to Spanish and I listen to people talk about the glories of Madrid. I go to art and I can barely lift a brush.

Then I'm walking into math and something inside me wakes up. Alert. Instead of going into the classroom, I glance back at the hall and see someone looking at me. In an instant I know A has come back. A is here.

It's in the eyes. This boy with his swoopy hair and his polo shirt and his jeans could be any boy. But those eyes, that way of looking at me, could only belong to A.

I walk away from class, from the way the day was supposed to go. Everyone around me rushes to get to class as the second bell rings. But not him. Not me. Not us.

Us. I should not be thinking of us as *us*. But it feels

like *us*. Here in this hallway, before we've said a word, we're *us*.

I don't know if I want it to be true, but it doesn't seem to care what I want. It exists beyond me.

Classes start, and we're alone together. I map out where Justin is at this moment, and know he's nowhere near.

We're safe. For what, I don't know.

"Hey," I say.

"Hey," he says.

"I thought you might come."

"Are you mad?"

"No, I'm not mad," I tell him. "Although Lord knows you're not good for my attendance record."

He smiles. "I'm not good for anybody's attendance record."

"What's your name today?" I ask.

"A. For you, it's always A."

"Okay," I say.

And it works. By not knowing this boy's name, I can think of him as A.

There isn't any question of us running away. I have that history test, and things with Justin are tense enough without me disappearing and having to lie about it. I can miss math, but that's all I can miss.

It's so strange to walk the halls with him. I'm worried we'll bump into someone. I guess I'll have to pretend he's a new student. That I'm showing him around.

"Is Justin in class?" he asks as we hit the English wing.

"Yeah. If he decided to go."

I don't want to stay in the halls. I lead him into one of the English rooms, and we sit down in the back so no one will be able to see us from the door.

It's weird being in desks. It's hard to face each other. But we turn and find a way.

"How did you know it was me?" he asks.

"The way you looked at me. It couldn't have been anyone else."

Taken. I don't know my hand is waiting to be taken until he takes it, holds it. Hands so different from Ashley's, from Nathan's. Different even from Justin's, even though this guy is about Justin's size. Our hands fit differently.

"I'm sorry about the other night," he says.

I don't want to do this again. But I tell him, "I deserve part of the blame. I never should have called him."

"What did he say? Afterward?"

Honest. I feel I have to be honest.

"He kept calling you 'that black bitch.'"

I watch A grimace. "Charming."

Again, I feel the need to defend Justin. "I think

he sensed it was a trap. I don't know. He just knew something was off."

"Which is probably why he passed the test."

He won't give up. The way he wants Justin to be a bad guy – it reminds me of Justin.

I pull my hand away. "That's not fair."

"I'm sorry."

Sorry. He's sorry. I'm sorry. We're all so sorry.

He asks me, "What do you want to do?"

That look again. Those eyes. Not sorry. Yearning.

I do not turn away. I try to be a fact, not a feeling.

"What do you want me to do?" I ask.

"I want you to do whatever you feel is best for you."

Too perfect, too scripted, too out of touch with that yearning.

"That's the wrong answer," I say.

"Why is it the wrong answer?"

He doesn't get it. "Because it's a lie."

He blinks. "Let's go back to my original question. What do you want to do?"

How can I tell him that what I *want* isn't the point. It's never the point. I want a million dollars. I want to never return to school and to get a good job anyway. I want to be prettier. I want to be in Hawaii. Want costs you nothing, unless you try to spend it. *What do you want to do?* isn't what he should be asking.

He should be asking me what I *can* do.

How can I make him see this? I say, "I don't want to throw everything away for something uncertain."

"What about me is uncertain?"

Kidding. He has to be kidding.

"Really?" I say. "Do I have to explain it to you?"

He waves his hand dismissively. "Besides that. You know you are the most important person I've ever had in my life. That's certain."

"In just two weeks," I point out. "That's uncertain."

"You know more about me than anyone else does."

"But I can't say the same for you. Not yet."

"You can't deny that there's something between us."

I can't deny it – that's true. But I can deny that it means what he thinks it means.

"No," I say. "There is. When I saw you today – I didn't know I'd been waiting for you until you were there. And then all of that waiting rushed through me in a second. That's something . . . but I don't know if it's certainty."

Fourth period isn't over, but I was planning on studying for history during math, and I still need to do that now. I have to remind myself that here is where my life is, and I can't afford to screw it up.

"I have to get ready for my test," I tell A. "And you have another life to get back to."

201

Hurt. It crosses his face and dims his eyes. "Don't you want to see me?" he asks.

Want. Everything about him is want.

"I do," I say. "And I don't. You would think it would make things easier, but it actually makes them harder."

"So I shouldn't just show up here?"

Is this helping? No, it's not helping. This is the disruption, because it makes everything else seem lesser.

Instinctively, I know: I can't show up to school every morning wondering if he'll be here. I can't be looking into the eyes of every stranger hoping it will be him.

So I tell him, "Let's stick to email for now. Okay?"

I can sense all the want pulsing beneath his skin. I can see how badly he's trying to keep himself together. But there it is. He doesn't get to choose. I don't get to choose.

The classroom door opens and a teacher I don't know comes in. She takes one look at us and says, "You can't be here. Shouldn't you be in class?"

I mumble something about a free period. I pick up my bag. A doesn't have one, and I hope the teacher doesn't notice.

We say goodbye in the hallway. I know I'm not going to see him like this again. I will see him as someone else. But not like this. Not with him as hopeful as he was when he saw me this morning.

I can still feel the connection between us, even as I walk away.

I go to Justin's locker after school, but he's already gone.

I spend the rest of the day and night alone. My parents don't count.

16

Something is off the next day. Justin barely speaks to me. Rebecca looks at me curiously. Even my teachers seem more aware that I'm in the room, and won't stop calling on me. I have an English report I have to finish during lunch, so I spend it in the library.

After sixth period, Preston texts to see if I want to do something after school. I feel like I haven't talked to him in a while – and I'm grateful that someone is actually trying to make plans with me.

We decide to drive to the outlet mall – Preston has a cousin at Burberry who's let him know the coat he's been crushing on is getting marked down today. He still can't afford it, but at least he can try it on one more time before it's sold.

I think the coat's going to be the top priority in our conversation, but then Preston jumps in my car, plugs in his iPod to blast some Robyn, and says, "So . . . spill!"

"What am I supposed to be spilling?" I ask as I pull out of the parking lot.

Preston sighs theatrically. "Must I spell it out for you? I have it from *very* reliable sources that you were walking the halls yesterday with a rather attractive gentleman who nobody's ever seen before. You may have even sequestered yourself in an empty classroom with him – although when you emerged, there was no evidence of untoward behavior. Apparently his hair is very swoopy, which has led at least fifty-eight percent of my reliable sources to believe he may play for my team. Which would be the most exciting news to hit my world in about a decade. Every night I pray for a lovely, swoopy-haired homosexual to come to our school, in the same way that Margaret prayed for boobs and my grandfather prays for my eternal salvation."

I remind myself I need to keep driving. I need to focus or I know I'm going to swerve.

Caution. My first instinct is to say, "I have no idea what you're talking about." But clearly someone saw me. Many people saw me.

My second instinct is to think, *Justin's heard. Justin knows.*

My third instinct is to scream.

My fourth instinct is to cry.

My fifth instinct is to deny all these other instincts and say, lightly, "I'm sorry, Preston – I have no idea if he swoops your way. He was just a prospective student – I've started showing them around, like Tiffany does. He lives in California – he's not even sure his dad is going to get the job here. And even if he did . . . the whole question of straightness or gayness didn't come up."

"Oh." Poor Preston looks so disappointed.

"Sorry."

"It's okay. A boy can dream, can't he?"

I want to tell him maybe it's better that way. Maybe real life is never going to live up to his daydreamy kind of love.

"So who saw me?" I ask delicately. "I mean, us."

"Kara Wallace and her group. Lindsay Craig thought you were macking on him – but then they saw you leave and said everything was in the right place, if you know what I mean. Kara was all excited, because her gaydar was really going off."

"Do you really believe in that gaydar stuff?"

Preston nods. "You can tell. There's an energy that travels between you. I can't say whether it's body language or if there's an actual chemical reaction. But you can feel it. He puts it out there, you put it out there, and you can feel it."

I think about A. About the way I knew it was him.

Then I put that thought away.

"And has word of this spread? I mean, should I be worried about Justin hearing the gossip?"

"Does Justin even *do* gossip? He doesn't strike me as the type."

No, but I can imagine Lindsay going up to him and sharing her theories – *I just thought you should know,* she'd say, gossip's good little helper.

It could explain his noncommunication today. But a thousand other things could also explain it. And calling him and making a big deal of some rumor could seriously backfire if he hasn't heard anything.

"Really," Preston says, "don't worry about it. The only reason I brought it up was . . . well, for selfish reasons. Woe is me. I am woe."

He's only kind-of joking, and it's only kind-of convincing.

"Are you okay?" I ask.

He smiles ruefully. "I'm fine. Although I'd be much more fine if you'd said you'd already given the swoopy-haired boy my number."

"What happened with Alec?"

"Not swoopy-haired."

"And that guy in Massachusetts you were chatting with?"

"Not swoopy-haired. And not local."

"So swoopy hair is the thing? You can't be with a guy unless his hair swoops?"

"If there's an exception, I haven't met him yet."

"I'm serious. Do you really believe that much in a 'type'? Is there really only one kind of person for you? Couldn't you be open to someone outside your type if he or she was great enough?"

"*Or she?*"

"I'm just saying – if you loved someone enough, would it really matter?"

"I know you want me to say no, but let's be real here. We're all wired to like certain things and to hate certain things. A lot of these things are negotiable, but some of them are fundamental. Don't ask me why – I'd need a PhD and a really powerful microscope to begin to tell you why. Could I love a guy without swoopy hair? Yeah, sure. Could I love a guy with a mullet? Much harder. Could I love a girl with a mullet? As a friend, sure. But – how to put this? – would I want to have *relations* with her? No. Not interested. At all. Nuh-uh."

"But don't you wish it were possible? I mean, don't you wish anything were possible?"

"Do I wish it? Sure. I mean, why not? But do I think it's true? Nope. Sorry. Not by a long shot. I have two years of being in love with our mutual friend Ben to show for that. Not everything is possible. Falling for a straight boy is thus inadvisable."

I don't steer to the side of the road at the breaking of this news, but I do turn down the radio to focus in on it more. "Wait – you're in love with Ben?"

"I *was* in love with Ben. The torture chamber kind of love. Oh, Lord, what I would have done for, to, or with that boy. This was before he was with Rebecca.

208

Well, the beginning of it was before he was with Rebecca."

I picture Ben two years ago. His swoopy hair.

"But you knew he wasn't gay, right?" I ask. "I mean, he wasn't, was he? I'm not missing that, too?"

"No, you're not." Preston stares out the window. "It was just something I tried to convince myself could happen. It was easier for me to come out if I thought there was someone to be in love with. A destination for my trajectory. I know that's silly, and I know he did nothing to deserve it – but I had to picture some kind of future, and while I was at it, I decided to cut him out from reality and paste him into my fantasy. I felt a lot of things at that moment, and I needed to feel every single one of them. Then I had to tell myself I was done. He wasn't going to suddenly like boys, no more than I was going to suddenly like girls."

I know Preston won't understand where the question's coming from, but I have to ask, "But what if he could've changed? I mean, what if Ben could've changed into a girl, and you could have been with him that way?"

"Rhiannon, if I'd wanted to fall for a girl, there were *plenty* of awesome girls around to fall for. That's not how it works."

Silly. I feel silly.

"I know, I know," I say. "Sorry."

"It's okay." Then he takes a good look at me. "What's on your mind?"

I can't tell him the real reason, but I wonder if I can try to keep it vague and still have a conversation.

"I'm just wondering why people stay together," I say. "Why they connect in the first place, and what keeps that connection strong. I want it to be all the things inside – who you are, what you believe. But what if the things on the outside are just as important? When I was little, I was always worried I'd fall in love with someone ugly. Like Shrek. Then I figured that love would make anyone beautiful to me, if I loved them enough. I want to believe in that. I want to believe that you can love someone so strongly that none of that will matter. But what if it does?"

We're at the mall now. I pull into a parking space. Neither of us makes a move to leave the car.

Preston is looking really concerned.

"Is this about Justin?" he asks. "Are you no longer attracted to him?"

"No!"

"Is it about . . . someone else?"

"NO!"

Preston holds up his hands. "Okay, okay! Just checking."

"It was just something I was thinking about. That's all."

I'm letting him down. I'm letting myself down. Because I'm shutting down this conversation. I'm making it clear we're done.

We get out of the car and head to the Burberry outlet. Preston tries on the coat and I tell him it looks amazing. We talk about clothes and classes and our friends. But we don't talk about what's really on my mind. Preston knows this. I know this.

I keep waiting for a text from Justin. Either he's heard the gossip and is going to want to know who the guy was, or he hasn't, and he'll text to see what I'm doing.

One of the two.

Or, in the end, neither.

I think about writing to A, but I convince myself not to. I don't want to encourage him too much. I can't have him show up again. I need to figure things out. But how can you figure out something that doesn't have a shape? It's the shapeless things – like love, like attraction – that are the hardest to map.

I give in and text Justin as midnight nears. I'm sleepy and vulnerable. The night won't let me settle down

211

until I get rid of at least one thing that's unsettling me. I decide to keep it simple.

Missed you today.

He doesn't write back to me until the next morning.

Did you?

17

I get the message while I'm already waiting at his locker. The tide of emotions rises in me too fast. When he shows up a minute later, it crashes over all of the walls I've put up.

I hold up the phone. "What do you mean, 'Did you?'"

He doesn't look mad. He looks bothered. I am just this girl who's in the way right now.

"If you missed me so much, then why avoid me all day?" he asks. "I feel if you were actually missing me, you would have made some effort."

"I was with Preston! We went to the mall! Are you saying you wanted to go shopping with me and Preston? Really?"

I don't know why I'm yelling at him, why I sound like I'm fighting when I don't want to be fighting.

"I'm not talking about your *shopping trip*." He says *shopping trip* the same way he'd say *gay*. "I'm talking about everything. You're not here."

Is he still mad at me for Ashley? Or has he heard about the mystery guy and the empty classroom?

"I've been around," I tell him. "I've been here." Then I decide to address things sideways. "I've been busy, for sure. Tests and showing new students around and everything. But I've been here, and if you've wanted to see me, all you had to do was call."

He slams his locker door so hard it hits the locker next to his. I startle back – more at the movement than the noise.

"Can you hear yourself? All I have to do is call? Is that how it's going to be? Should I start making *appointments* with you? Jesus."

People are looking at us now. We are that couple fighting in the hall.

"I'm sorry," I say. I'm not sure what for. I'm just sorry.

"Do you even care that I had a shit day? Did it even occur to you to ask?" he challenges.

"What's wrong?" I ask now.

"This conversation," he says, this time slamming his locker in the direction of closed. "That's what's wrong."

It's not just this conversation. I have done a hundred things wrong. I have become the kind of person who worries about being caught, not about what she's done.

I don't want to be that kind of person.

"Can we talk about this?" I ask quietly.

"I'll see you later" is Justin's response. Which is something, but not very much.

The bell rings and people start to hurry. A few take a moment to look at me, to see if I'm going to give them a meltdown worth talking about.

I disappoint them in the same way I disappoint everyone else.

Lunch is tense.

I missed Justin between first and second periods – I don't know if this was deliberate on his side, or if my timing was just off. When I saw Preston between third and fourth, I asked if he'd managed to contain all the rumors. I made it sound like I was joking, but he saw right through me. He assured me that the gossip had moved on, as gossip tends to do. I know this is true, but it would be just my luck to be the exception.

I want to save the seat next to me for Justin, but when Rebecca brings over her tray and sits there, I can't think of how to ask her to move down without sounding weak. When Justin comes over, I can see him looking at that taken space as if it's evidence. He sits a couple of seats away.

At the very least, I want a hello from him.

Our friends notice this. They notice it, but they don't say a word.

I should be figuring out a way to save things, to make him feel better about me. But instead I have the stupid, unhelpful thought: *A would never do this to me.* Even if we disagreed. Even if we fought. A would never ignore me. A would never make me feel like I no longer exist. Whatever body A is in, A would always find a way to acknowledge me.

There's no way for me to know this as a fact. But I'm certain of it as a feeling.

"Rhiannon?"

It's Rebecca's voice. She's asked me something.

I leave my thoughts for a second, return to the table. I look over to Justin and see that he's paying attention to me now. He saw me drift off. Once upon a time, he would have assumed I was thinking about him. But I don't see any of that in his face now. He lowers his eyes back to his lunch.

"I'm sorry," I say again. But this time it's to Rebecca, for not listening to whatever it is she has to say.

You have to fix this.

That's what I'm telling myself all through the rest of the day.

A is going to leave me. A will never be mine. A will never be able to be a normal part of my life.

Justin is here. Justin loves me. Justin is a part of me. I cannot ignore that.

He is angry, but he is angry because he's confused, because I'm making him miserable. He knows something is off. He knows me well enough to know that.

216

He is not making things up. I am really doing this to him.

Which is why I have to stop.

Which is why I have to fix it.

He doesn't seem surprised to find me at his locker at the end of the day.

"I know I've been out of it," I say before he can dismiss me. "I know I haven't been paying attention a hundred percent. That has nothing to do with you, I swear. And I'm grateful to you for calling me on it, because sometimes I'm so out of it I don't even realize I'm out of it, you know? But I'm back. I'm here now. I want to know what's going on with you. I want to be a part of it. I want us to take as much time as we need to get back on track."

"It's fine," he says.

I watch as he puts his books in his locker. The back of his neck taunts me. His shoulders draw me in.

"Do you want to do something?" I ask.

He closes the locker. Turns back to me.

"Sure," he says. And in his eyes, in his voice – I sense it. Relief.

I ask him where he wants to go.

He says his house.

*

I know makeup sex is supposed to mean making it up to each other after having a fight. But right now I feel like it's makeup sex because I'm making it all up. I have transformed myself into such a devoted, pretend girl that even I can believe the imitation is real. I know actions speak loudly to Justin, and he is speaking loudly back. I am grateful for the communication, for the way the intensity makes my body feel. But my mind is in another room.

In the heat of it, in the rush of it, he feels safe enough to say, "Don't leave me."

And I promise. I recognize how vulnerable he is, and I swear.

Afterward, I ask him about his shit day yesterday, and he barely remembers why it was so bad. Just the usual reasons, and the weight of them feeling so usual. He doesn't mention me with another guy, and I don't find it underneath his words, either. I think I'm in the clear.

He asks me to stay for dinner. I call my mother, who seems irritated but doesn't say no. Justin's mother also seems irritated when she comes home and Justin tells her I'm staying – but that irritation is directed at him, not me. I tell her I don't have to stay, that I know it's last-minute, but she says she's happy to have me here, and that it's been too long since she's seen me. When Justin and I first started dating, she treated me like this stray he'd picked up. Now that we've been dating a while, I've been upgraded to pet status – part of the family, but not really a member.

Justin's father likes me more, or at least wants more for me to like him. He manages to come home exactly five minutes before dinner is ready, then acts like he's at the head of the table even though the table is square. Justin and I are perpendicular, and we answer his father's questions like it's a joint interview. Our bland answers about school and homework go unchallenged by his bland responses. I risk asking about Justin's grandmother, and am told she's doing as well as can be expected. Everyone tenses up, so I change the subject and compliment the food. Justin's mom tells me she's sorry that there won't be enough for seconds, since she wasn't planning on cooking for four.

In the beginning, I'd wanted Justin's house to become my second house, and Justin's family to become my second family. But I only made it halfway. This makes sense, because Justin barely wants his family for himself. Part of me was disappointed that my second chance at a decent mom fell short. But mostly I decided to claim the absence in Justin's life. I can remember thinking that if

219

he didn't feel like he had a family, I would be his family. If he didn't feel like he had a home, I would make our space together a home. I believed love could do this. I believed this was what love was for.

Now I'm not sure what we have. What kind of family we are. I used to imagine us in the future – getting married, having kids – and then play it backward until it reached us now. But I haven't done that in a while.

Justin is uncomfortable all through dinner. And I know I am the comfortable part – I know that I am the person at the table who brings him the most happiness, who he feels closest to. When dinner's over and I've helped his mother do the dishes, I find him back in his room, playing a video game. He pauses it when I come in, then pats the space next to him, beckoning me over.

"Sorry to put you through all that," he says, kissing me.

"Dinner was good," I tell him, even though it wasn't really.

I know we're not going to go beyond kissing with his parents in the house. It's like every move we make is amplified straight to their ears.

He passes me a controller and we play a while. If we were different kids, we'd be doing our homework together. Instead, we avoid our homework together. I realize how irresponsible this is. I don't think it occurs to Justin at all.

I'm glad we're back to normal. I don't know if I've missed this, but it feels right for right now. It's like A has never existed. A is a story I told myself.

Justin is better at this game than I am, which is true of most of the games we play. I keep dying, and he keeps passing me new lives.

At nine, I finally beg off, tell him I have to get my bio work done so I don't fail out. I'm bringing it up partly because it's true and partly because I want him to remember to do his work, too. He's much more at risk of failing out than I am.

"Okay – I'll see you tomorrow," he says. His eyes don't leave the screen.

I make sure to say goodbye to his parents on my way out. His mom says again that it was good to see me. His father walks me to the door.

When I step outside, I don't feel I've lost anything by leaving. Like when I leave my own house, there's always a part of me that stays behind, waiting for me to get back. That's what makes it my home – that feeling that a part of me is always waiting for me there.

As I walk to my car, I don't turn back to see if Justin's at the window, watching me go. I know he isn't.

The part of him that waits for me isn't that strong.

Not when he knows he has me.

When I get back to my room, I'm not worried about our fight anymore. This morning seems like ancient history.

It's A I'm worried about. It's A who I think is waiting for me. I haven't sent word all day, and it's feeling, now that I acknowledge it, like an abandonment. Which is wrong – it's A who abandons me in the jump from place to place, body to body.

But I know I'm guilty here, too.

I check my email and am almost relieved to find that there isn't anything new. This excuses some of my silence, if A is being silent, too. Although if A is being silent, it may very well be because I told A to stop.

I get ready for bed, then sleep for eight hours. When I wake up, the first obligation I feel is to end the silence. So I write:

A,

I'm sorry I didn't get to write to you yesterday. I meant to, but then all these other things happened (none of them important, just time-consuming). Even though it was hard to see you, it was good to see you. I mean it. But taking a break and thinking things out makes sense.

How was your day? What did you do?

R

I know this is in two different places at once – *I meant to write to you, but let's keep taking a break*. But it's an accurate reflection of where I am. Or where I think I am.

Even though I know it's impossible, and I know it won't help, I still want to know where A is.

Does this mean I'm waiting for A?

I don't know.

At the very least, I'm waiting to see what happens next.

18

I get a rushed email from A as I'm driving to school. I read it in my car, before I go inside. A tells me he (she?) spent yesterday in the body of an immigrant girl who had to clean toilets to make a living, and the day before A wasn't feeling well, so he stayed home at this other girl's house and watched TV. Today A's another girl who has this big track meet, so she has to stay where she is. Even though I told him not to come here, I'm disappointed.

I want to contradict myself. I want to overrule my hesitations. I want A to be here.

But I can't steal that girl from her track meet. And when I picture A as some runner girl, I slow myself down. What if she's another Ashley? Or even just normal-looking. What would we do then?

I think about writing back to A, but if I'm not telling him/her to drop everything to see me, I don't have much else to say. I am not going to tell A about Justin – not about the fight, not about the making up. And what else do I have in my life that's worth talking about?

I turn off my phone and head into school.

I go through the motions. I try not to talk in class, but talk when I have to. I say hello to friends, but not much more. I give Justin what he wants – enough distance to be himself, but enough closeness to know I haven't gone far. I eat lunch without tasting it.

I find myself thinking of Kelsea, about her notebook containing all those ways to die. Not because I want to kill myself. I am nowhere near wanting to kill myself. But I can understand feeling so detached from your own life. To feel that your connection to everyone else is so thin that all it would take is one decisive snip to be separated completely. If I don't cling, I drift. I feel that no one is holding me. In my life, I am the only one who holds.

Except for A. But A is not here.

Rebecca and Preston try to reach me. They see the thin thread and tie messages to it, sliding them my way. Preston invites me to another round of buyless shopping. Rebecca tries to bribe me into a coffee excursion after school. Both of them remind me that Daren Johnston is having a party tomorrow night. I'm sure I'll end up going.

Plans. I realize I'm not making plans because I want to see where A is living tomorrow, if A will be free. It's the weekend. I can drive far if I have to.

No. I see Justin and I think, *Stop it*. He asks me if I want to go to a movie. He even lets me choose.

Once upon a time, this would have made me happy.

I can't be bothered to tell my mother I'm not coming home for dinner. This will make it two nights in a row, and she's going to give me hell for it. So I figure I might as well do what I'm going to do and get the hell after, instead of getting the hell before and not being able to go.

We drive around for a while, then get some Taco Bell and head to an earlyish movie. As we're waiting for the coming attractions, I find myself looking at all the other people in the theater. Most of them are my age, and I can't help but wonder if one of them might be A. Her track meet would be over by now. Maybe she decided to go to a movie with friends afterward. It's not impossible.

A few girls catch me watching. Most turn away. A couple confront me, staring back to make me feel uncomfortable.

Justin is fidgety, maybe sensing how my attention is wandering. I lean into him, hold his hand. He shifts the popcorn in his lap so this can happen. But when the previews start, he pulls away.

I don't think the movie is what he expected it to be. The posters promised it was a horror movie set in space. But soon it's clear that the most horrific thing the astronaut is fighting is the endlessness of his boredom and the pointlessness of his life. Justin's eyelids start to flutter. I want to use his shoulder as a pillow, but he told me once that if I lean there for too long, it kills his circulation. So I go back to looking at the audience as much as I can, picking out which person I'd be most attracted to, if A were inside.

I know the answer should be *all of them*.

It is not *all of them*.

It's not as simple as saying all the guys are yes and all the girls are no. It's more complicated than that. Although mostly it's the guys I consider.

The answer – the real A I want – is sitting right next to me.

When I get home, it's my father who's waiting in the kitchen, looking disappointed. He tells me Mom's already gone to bed, and that it was inconsiderate of me to ditch dinner without a call. I lie and say I told Mom ages ago that this was going to be a date night with Justin. I call it a "date night" so my dad will imagine we went for ice-cream sodas and gazed lovingly into each other's eyes the whole time.

He falls for it completely.

I check for a new email from A, but don't find anything. And I don't write back, since I still don't have anything interesting to say.

*

The next morning, my mother says she isn't speaking to me. I know I'm supposed to feel bad, but mostly I'm happy not to deal with her.

I'm worried that they won't let me go to the party tonight, so I make a big production of doing my homework and completing some random chores. It's very easy to win my father over this way.

Before I leave the house, I consider emailing A and letting him (her?) know where I'm going to be. Then I remember what happened to that poor guy Nathan the last time this happened, and I decide to stay silent. Still, I wonder where he (she?) is. I also wonder why I haven't heard anything.

I pick Justin up, because I know he's planning on drinking. I ask him what he did all day and he barely remembers. I think maybe his life is as uneventful as mine, and that's why we're together. To be each other's eventfulness.

Or maybe that's why we go to parties, to find some eventfulness there. Or wastedness. Or both. Preston's also driven, so he and I sip Diet Cokes as I tell him about the movie, which is more interesting to make fun of than it was to watch. While I'm talking, Preston keeps his eye on the door, waiting for his gaydar to go off. It stays silent for a while until this James Dean wannabe strides in. Preston comes to attention like a hunting dog that's spotted the prettiest duck to ever fall from the sky.

"Really?" I say. "Him?"

Preston nods once. Twice.

"Do you want me to find out who he is?" I ask.

Preston shakes his head once. Twice.

A minute later, Dirk Nielson bounds in, car keys dangling in his hand. He looks around, spots James Dean, heads over, and kisses him hello.

"Shit," Preston says.

"Sorry," I tell him.

"Well, it was nice for the five seconds it lasted."

James Dean looks over at us – looks over at me. For a brief second, I feel connection. But then I really look into his eyes and I know: It's not A. It's nothing.

I talk to Preston some more, then Rebecca and Ben come join us. I'm telling them about the movie when Stephanie comes tearing out of the kitchen, looking like she's on fire. Steve follows her for a few feet before stopping and yelling "WHAT THE FUCK?" at least three times at her back.

"Who wants to take this one?" Rebecca asks. When no one else makes a move, she sighs and bolts after Stephanie. Ben and Preston head over to Steve.

I walk around them and find Justin doing shots with Kara Wallace and Lindsay Craig, the girl who was so certain I was up to no good with the guy I was taking around school.

I steel myself and walk over. "So what happened with Steve and Stephanie?" I ask.

I am clearly asking Justin, but Lindsay answers. "She saw him eating pepperoni and said it was really rude of him because she's been vegetarian for, like, the past three minutes."

Kara finds this funny. Justin just shrugs at me, like he stopped trying to figure Stephanie and Steve out years ago.

Lindsay's staring at me in a way that makes me wonder whether I wore the wrong thing, said the wrong thing, or am just the wrong person. I decide not to ask.

Justin seems taken care of, so I head back out of the kitchen. Once again, I find myself wandering around all of the conversations, avoiding all of my friends. *I am this body*, I think. When my friends see this body, they assume they know a lot about the person inside of it. And when people I don't know see it, they also make assumptions. No one ever really questions these assumptions. They are this layer of how we live our lives. And I'm no different from them. When I saw James Dean walk in, I felt I knew as much about him as I'm sure he felt he knew about me when he looked my way. It's like an instant form of reading, the way we define each other.

The house isn't that big. There's no dance floor in the basement – I'm not even sure there is a basement. There's a line for the bathroom off the living room, so I walk upstairs, hoping to find a bathroom there. And also because it's quieter upstairs.

All of the doors on the hallway are closed. I open the first and see it's a bedroom. I'm about to close it when a voice says, "Hello? Can I help you?"

I poke my head in and see Daren Johnston cross-legged on his bed, reading *The Outsiders*.

"Oh, hi, Rhiannon," he says. "The bathroom's the second door on the right. I left it open, but I guess someone closed it. I mean, there might be someone in there, so you should probably knock."

"Thanks," I say. But I don't leave. "Why are you up here reading? I mean, it's your party."

Daren smiles slightly. "I guess I like thinking about throwing a party more than I actually like having people over. Lesson learned."

"Why don't you tell everyone to go home?"

"Because they're enjoying themselves, I think. They shouldn't have to suffer just because I'm feeling antisocial. I needed to leave, so I allowed myself to leave."

I nod to the book. "First time?"

"Nah. More like my twelfth."

I remember when I read it – Justin and I were in the

231

same English class last year, and we read it together one Sunday afternoon, lying in his bed. It was a race to see who would finish first, but I slowed myself down because I loved the feeling of us turning the pages at the same time, being in the same part of the story. When we were done, he said how he was blown away by the line "Nothing gold can stay" – he really felt it was true. Then he smiled and said, "So I guess we'll have to be silver," and he called me Silver for days after.

"Do you think gold can stay?" I ask Daren now.

His smile is different from Justin's – a little more knowing, a little less eager. "I don't think anything can stay," he tells me. "Good or bad. So I think the important part is to not get caught up in worrying about whether something will stay, and instead enjoy it for the time it's here."

A door opens in the hallway and a guy calls out, "Daren! Where are you hiding?" He sounds like a construction foreman calling workers back from lunch.

Daren doesn't move. "For the record," he says to me, "I'm not hiding."

"DARRRRRREN!" the voice bellows. Then the door to the bedroom opens wider and James Dean walks in. I had imagined his voice would be . . . sexier.

"There you are!"

"Here I am," Daren admits.

"Come party!"

"I will when I'm finished with this book. I only have a hundred pages left."

James makes a move to manhandle Daren up. Then another voice calls, "Charles! Where are you, Charles?"

"It was so much more enjoyable when people used telegraphs," Daren says with a sigh.

"I guess Dirk wants me," Charles/James says. "I'll see you when your book is done." Then he turns to the door and hollers, "COMING!"

Daren hasn't put down the book.

"You see, Rhiannon," he says after Charles has left. "Nothing dumb can stay."

After using the bathroom (which Charles has left surprisingly tidy, even putting down both seat and cover), I return to the kitchen. When I walk in, I find Kara's disappeared and only Lindsay is with Justin now. He looks drunk and she looks determined. As if she can sense me coming, she reaches out and puts her hand on his shoulder, then moves it down to his chest. His reaction is so fast you could almost call it instinct – in one smooth move, he's removed her hand and pushed her away. There's no way for her to save face, the rejection is so complete. And the best part is I know he hasn't seen me yet. He didn't do it because I was watching.

He did it because he's true to me.

I let a minute pass, and let Lindsay slither off. Then I make my presence known. Justin doesn't exactly light up to see me, but he doesn't dim, either.

I tell him how I found Daren reading *The Outsiders* upstairs.

"I love that book!" Justin says.

"Remember when we read it?" I ask.

He's probably had too many shots to know what I'm talking about. Or at least that's what I figure. Then he calls out, "Heigh ho, Silver!"

Not quite as romantic as its origin. But I'm happy he remembers.

He steps away from the kitchen counter. "Let's see what's going on," he says.

I follow. We find our friends, we shoot the shit, and I no longer feel like the hidden girl in the visible body. Now I am Justin's version of me – that's who I am, and that's who people see. And it's okay. It helps me navigate the party. It helps me know what to do. It helps me see who to be.

I stop looking for A. I turn back to these people, because they're my life.

19

On Sunday, I give in and write to A. I'm worried that I haven't heard anything.

A,

Just another weekend here. Went to a party. Talked to some people, but none of them were you. Got in trouble with my mom, but survived. Did some homework. Slept a lot this morning, then saw a better movie this afternoon with Rebecca than I saw on Friday night. (Warning: VAST is boring.)

Where/who/how have you been?

R

I hit send even though it doesn't sound right, because I can't imagine how to make it sound better. He doesn't want to hear the details about Justin, and I don't want to tell them. So I've flattened my weekend before mailing it to him. I haven't given him any reason to be interested.

Which is maybe for the best.

*

The next morning I wake up and feel off. At first I think it's because I fell asleep in my clothes. That doesn't happen very often, so it's weird to see my T-shirt, my jeans. But that's not the only thing. It's like I've woken up in an unfamiliar bed, even though this is my bed, in my room. I expect to look at my clock and find it's four in the morning, to explain the disorientation. But it's the normal time to wake up. My alarm is going off.

It must be because it's Monday, I think.

But then I correct myself.

No, it's Tuesday.

When I go to hit off the alarm, I find a folded piece of paper on top of it. Even before I open it, I have a vague idea it's a letter I wrote. But I don't remember what it says.

Dear Rhiannon,

Before I say anything, or explain anything, I want you to stop reading and try to remember everything you did yesterday.

It's my handwriting – but I know immediately that I didn't write this.

I know immediately.

A.

Here.

A.

Me.

I start to shiver uncontrollably. I want to yell out, but I'm afraid my parents will hear.

I cannot believe this.

But I *can* believe this.

I know I will only have one chance to remember what happened before whatever is written on this piece of paper colors my memories or fills in the blanks. So I put the letter down. I sit back in bed.

Yesterday, I tell myself. *What was yesterday?*

I remember climbing. I'm outside, on my own. And I am climbing up a mountain. I am looking out over all of these trees.

It's peaceful.

I didn't skip school. I was in school before that. I had lunch with Justin. He called me Silver again. He ate pizza and complained about Stephanie and Steve. I remember that Stephanie and Steve had a fight – but that was Saturday night, at the party. It was not yesterday. I don't think I saw Stephanie or Steve yesterday. I can't remember.

I also can't remember what I said to Justin. I can remember him talking to me. But nothing that I said.

Maybe I didn't say anything.

I remember leaving dinner early. Coming up here.

I remember writing the letter.

But it's not me writing the letter. I remember the pen in my hand. The paper underneath. But I can't remember deciding what to say.

I don't remember thinking. But I also don't remember someone else thinking for me.

I pick up the letter again.

I would have never chosen to do this. I hope you know that. I had no idea it would happen until I woke up and opened your eyes.

I have tried to respect your day as much as I know how. I could have stayed in bed, stayed at home – but that would have driven me crazy, to be alone with you like that. I had to go out into the day like it was any other day.

I hope I have not changed anything for you. I hope that I did not alter your life in any way. If I did, please know it was not my intention. I have done the best I can.

I have tried to leave your memories alone. I have tried not to learn anything you would not want me to know.

I hope this doesn't scare you. The last thing I want is to scare you.

I must say to you again: This was not my choice. If it

had been my choice, it would be unforgivable.

What do you remember? I am about to tell you the course of your day. This is the last chance for you to have memories uninformed by this account.

When I woke up, I was in shock. In all of my years, I've never woken up in the body of someone I care so much about. I wanted to respect your privacy as much as possible, so you are wearing yesterday's underwear, and in moments when anything I had not seen already was exposed, I kept my eyes closed.

I met your parents over breakfast, then drove to school. Since I had been there before, it was not hard to navigate. I don't think anyone knew something was wrong. I went to class and kept my head down. I tried to take good notes for you. If you want details about classes, you can find them in your notebooks.

I tried to avoid Justin. I knew you would have wanted me to avoid him. This was effective until lunch, when he suggested we go for pizza. I couldn't find a way out of it. Nothing more than conversation happened. He is annoyed with Stephanie and Steven for fighting.

I did not see him again until after school. He wanted to do something, but I told him I had to pick up your mother from a doctor's appointment. Just in case he mentions it.

(I realize it is strange that I keep saying "I" here – by

239

"I," I of course mean "you." You have to understand: As I did these things, it didn't feel like you were doing them. It felt to me like I was doing them. I wonder if you will feel the same.)

Because we had already been to an ocean and a forest together, I felt it would be best to head to a mountain. I also wanted us to be alone . . . and we were very alone as we climbed. (If you want to know where we were, the search should still be on your phone. I haven't erased anything.) It felt good to be solitary, to feel an exertion that was purely physical. I wanted you to remember that, and to remember me there with you. I don't know if this is possible. But – and I know this sounds strange – I felt like I was feeling it for both of us.

Not wanting to get you in trouble, I made it back in time for a very cordial dinner with your parents. Then I retreated to your room, attempted as much of your homework as possible, and decided to write you this note.

I have no way to know how you will react to this, nor would I presume to say there is a right or wrong way to react. Even if I haven't caused any damage, I know this breach may still be irreparable. I will understand if you never want to see or speak or write to me again. But I will also hope desperately that you will *want me to remain in your life. I leave that up to you.*

I know it is neither my fault nor my choice, but still I am sorry. I know it must be as hard to read this as it has been to write it.

Yours,

A

My mother knocks on the door, making sure I'm awake. Do I remember telling Justin I was taking her to the doctor? Yes, I do. I remember saying that, and when I think harder about it, I even remember telling him it was an appointment for a sleep doctor. He joked to me about stealing some of her pills.

How can I know this, if I wasn't there?

I can only know this because A left it for me. It doesn't matter which of us was in control of my body, as long as the memory was made and stored away.

I want to be angry. I want to be freaked out. I want to be able to laugh at this, to find it ridiculous. These would all be rational responses. But instead I feel . . . sad. Sad that A had to go through this. Sad that there was no way it could be avoided. Sad that it complicates things even more. I know with all my heart that A isn't lying to me – my body and my life were safe when he was in control of them. I know A wouldn't have done anything to hurt me.

I also realize – in a way I couldn't have realized before – how easy it would have been for A to destroy everything. A could have made me do anything. Break up with Justin. Take naked photos of myself and email them to A's account. Run away.

But nothing like that happened. I know nothing like that happened.

Still, it can't all go back to normal. No, this thing has happened to me. I can't just shrug it off like all the other people whose bodies A inhabits. They don't know how they missed a day. But I know. I can't help knowing.

I imagine A waiting to see if I will ever be in touch again, if this is enough to make me walk away.

I write:

A,

I think I remember everything. Where are you today?
Instead of writing a long email, I want to talk.

R

Almost immediately, I get a response.

R,

I am so relieved to hear from you. I am about two
hours away, a boy named Dylan. But I will go wherever
you want me to go.

A

I don't want to wait. But I know I have to go to school
to see if A did any damage without realizing it. So I tell
A to meet me back at the bookstore, after school. We'll
have to wait until then.

His response is a simple

Thank you.

I don't say anything back. I don't need to. All I have
to do is be there later on – and prepare to see what
happened with everyone else on the yesterday I missed.
I am expecting it to be a minefield – to have to account
for something I said or didn't say, someplace I went or
didn't go. I'm ready for the people in my life to be angry
with me or upset with me or confused by me.

What happens instead is even worse.

Nobody seems to have noticed I was gone. Or wasn't
myself.

It starts with my mother, sitting in her usual chair. I
ask her if I seemed off yesterday.

"No, you were perfectly pleasant," she says. "We had a nice dinner."

I don't point out that a "nice dinner" should have seemed odd to her. Suspicious.

But she lives in her own world. I'm not surprised she didn't notice.

My friends, though – I think they would have noticed something. Maybe not everything. But at least something.

I don't feel them treating me any differently, though. I don't feel any daylong gap in my friendship with them.

So I ask.

"Was I weird yesterday? Different?"

Rebecca tells me I was fine.

Preston says he didn't really see me.

Ben pretends he didn't hear the question.

Stephanie says, "Do you want to know who's different? *Steve's* different."

And Justin – Justin says, "Yeah, you were weird, but that's not exactly *different*."

He's joking. I can tell he's joking. And I can tell from his joking that it was a good day, that we had a good time, that he didn't mind me going to my mom's doctor's appointment instead of going home with him. A didn't do anything to make things worse between us. If anything, A made it a little better.

I am relieved to have avoided being caught. And I'm pissed that no one noticed the difference.

I leave school a little early. Before anyone can stop me and ask me where I'm going. Before no one can stop me and ask me where I'm going.

As I drive to the bookstore, I reach for more of yesterday. Mostly I see the trees beneath me. I feel what it was like to be standing on that mountain. I breathe in as I remember breathing it in.

I feel better.

A hasn't told me much about Dylan, the boy whose body I'm about to meet. But when I step into the bookstore's café, there's no question who I'm looking for, because it's so clear he's looking for me. Our eyes meet, and our eyes have already met. I head over.

"Hey," I say.

"Hey," he says back. He's chosen the same table as last time. And this, of all things, overwhelms me. Everything that's happened since last time – it's like I'm feeling it all at once.

"I need coffee," I say to him. I need to gather my thoughts. And I really do need coffee.

He doesn't seem to mind. "Yeah, of course," he says. He's really geeky today, with a geeky voice. Like something from *The Big Bang Theory*. His T-shirt doesn't have anything on it – it's just a blue T-shirt. I wonder how hard A had to look to find one without a joke on it. Then I yell at myself for jumping to so many conclusions just because the guy looks like a geek.

"Do you want anything?" I offer.

"Sure."

He doesn't try to come with me, and I'm glad to have the two minutes of waiting and ordering and waiting. I stare at my hands and think of him staring at my hands yesterday. Did they look like the same hands? Or does familiarity somehow alter them? The girl behind the counter calls out my order and hands it over. I carry our drinks to the table and for a few seconds – a few too many seconds – we sit there awkwardly. He's waiting for me to say something. I'm waiting for him to say something. We're not saying anything.

I break the silence and tell him, "It feels like the morning after."

He looks at me kindly, nervously. "I know."

The morning after. I can't believe I said that. Because what does he know about a morning after? Isn't he always somewhere else?

He's looking at me – at all of me. My hands. My face. My eyes. Even though I do it every day, I wonder what it was like to be inside me, to see the world like this when you're not already used to it.

Calm. What I feel right now is a strange calm. A and I have just done something it's possible that nobody else has ever done. I am sitting across from someone who has seen through my eyes. And A is sitting across from someone who can tell him what it was like to have vanished for a day.

"I woke up and I knew something was different," I tell him. "Even before I saw your letter. It wasn't the usual disorientation. But I didn't feel like I'd missed a day. It was like I woke up and something had been . . . added. Then I saw your letter and started reading, and immediately I knew it was true. It had actually happened. I stopped when you told me to stop, and tried to remember everything about yesterday. It was all there. Not the things I'd usually forget, like waking up or brushing my teeth. But climbing that mountain. Having lunch with Justin. Dinner with my parents. Even writing the letter itself – I had a memory of that. It shouldn't make sense – why would I write a letter to myself for the next morning? But in my mind, it makes sense."

Gently, he asks, "Do you feel me there? In your memories."

I shake my head. "Not in the way you'd think. I don't feel you in control of things, or in my body, or anything. I feel like you were with me. Like, I can feel your presence there, but it's outside of me."

Listen to me. If I turned the TV on at one in the morning and heard a girl saying the things I'm saying, I would think she was a total nutjob. "It's insane that we're having this conversation," I point out.

But of course that's not how A is going to see it or feel it. *This is normal to him*, I remind myself.

"I wanted you to remember everything," he says. "And it sounds like your mind went along with that. Or maybe it wanted you to remember everything, too."

"I don't know. I'm just glad I do."

"And do you remember feelings? Or is it just the scene you see?"

"What do you mean?"

"Like, if I asked what was going through your mind when you had lunch with Justin, could you?"

I close my eyes and try to go back there. I see him eating pizza. I don't really remember what he said, only that he's talking a lot. But I can't remember being happy or annoyed or angry or anything. I just remember that I was there.

"Nothing," I say, my eyes still closed. "You know when you're really pissed at someone and then, a few days later, you remember that you were pissed but can't remember what it was about? Well, this is the opposite of that."

I open my eyes and see him taking in what I'm saying. I think I'm confirming something he's always suspected.

"You really don't know what it's like for us, do you?" I say.

"No," he answers quietly. "I don't."

He asks me about a few of the other things that happened yesterday – Rebecca, the climbing, the dinner conversation with my parents. I tell him the only one that's vivid to me is the climbing. I do feel something when I think of that – that sense of breathing in, of freedom. Is this emotion or is this actual physical sensation that I'm remembering? We can't decide.

"It's interesting," I admit. "Really twisted and weird and crazy – but also interesting."

"You are extraordinary for understanding, and for being willing to be with me even after I . . . was where I was."

"It's not your fault. I know."

"Thank you."

It's hard to believe that I thought I could stay away from him. It's hard to believe I thought I could run away from this. Because it feels so comfortable right now.

"Thank you for not messing up my life," I say. "And for keeping my clothes on. Unless, of course, you don't want me to remember that you sneaked a peek."

"No peeks were sneaked."

"I believe you. Amazingly, I believe you about everything."

And because I believe him, I also want him to tell me more about what it was like for him – what he saw when he was me. But it also feels like a raging-ego thing to ask. What kind of girl asks for a second opinion about her own life?

A senses me holding back. Of course.

"What?" he asks.

I decide to go for it.

"It's just – do you feel you know me more now? Because the weird thing is . . . I feel I know you more. Because of what you did, and what you didn't do. Isn't that strange? I would have thought that you would've found out more about me . . . but I'm not sure that's true."

"I got to meet your parents," he says.

Oh boy. "And what was your impression?"

"I think they both care about you, in their own way."

I laugh. "Well said."

"Well, it was nice to meet them."

"I'll be sure to remember that when you really meet them. 'Mom and Dad, this is A. You think you're meeting him for the first time, but actually, you've met him before, when he was in my body.'"

"I'm sure that'll go over well."

And the stupid thing is: I'm sure they would love him. If only I could freeze him as he is, and take him home to Mom and Dad, they'd be thrilled.

But I can't tell him that. It would be unfair of me to tell him that. So I ask him something else. Just to be sure.

"It can never happen again, right?" I say. "You're never the same person twice."

He nods. "Correct. It will never happen again."

"No offense, but I'm relieved I don't have to go to sleep wondering if I'm going to wake up with you in control. Once, I guess I can deal with. But don't make a habit of it."

"I promise – I want to make a habit of being with you, but not that way."

He says it so casually, like it's no big deal. Like I might not even hear it.

But I hear it.

"You've seen my life," I say. "Tell me a way you think this can work."

"We'll find a way."

"That's not an answer," I point out. "It's a hope."

"Hope's gotten us this far. Not answers."

"Good point." I sip my coffee. "I know this is weird, but . . . I keep wondering. Are you really not a boy or a girl? I mean, when you were in my body, did you feel more . . . at home than you would in the body of a boy?"

"I'm just me," he (she?) says. "I always feel at home and I never feel at home. That's just the way it is."

I don't know why this isn't enough for me – but it's not. "And when you're kissing someone?" I press.

"Same thing."

"And during sex?"

"Is Dylan blushing? Right now, is he blushing?"

Bright red. "Yeah."

"Good. Because I know I am."

I don't know why the word *sex* would make him blush so much. But then I realize why, and I blurt out, "You've never had –?"

He sputters. "It wouldn't be fair of me to –"

"Never!"

He's as red as a strawberry now. "I am so glad you find this funny," he says.

"Sorry."

"There was this one girl."

Aha! "Really?"

"Yeah. Yesterday. When I was in your body. Don't you remember? I think you might have gotten her pregnant."

"That's not funny!"

"I only have eyes for you," he says. And the way he

says it isn't funny at all. Or teasing. Or careless.

Sincerity. I think that's the word for this. For meaning something so much that it can't be anything other than what it is.

I'm not used to it.

"A –" I start. I have to tell him. I have to keep us in the world of reality. And in the world of reality, we cannot be together.

"Not now," he interrupts. "Let's stay on the nice note."

The nice note. That rings its own note within me. And that note is, momentarily, louder than reality.

"Okay," I say. "I can do that."

So instead of talking about tomorrow, we talk more about yesterday. I ask him what else he noticed, and he brings up all of these things that I would never, ever notice. Physical details like a small red birthmark at the base of my left thumb, and memories like this time Rebecca got gum caught in her hair. He's also pretty committed to convincing me that my parents care about me. I tell him he must've gotten them on a good day. He doesn't argue – but I can also see he doesn't completely know what I mean. Because he's never with someone through bad days and good days. He doesn't know life like that. Which again reminds me how he'd never be equipped to deal with someone as bad-good as me.

A glances at the time on his phone, and I realize I

should be keeping track of time as well. Home for dinner. Home for homework. Home for bed. Home for my life.

"It's getting late," I say.

"I know."

"So we should probably –"

"But only if you promise we'll see each other again. Soon. Like, tomorrow if we can. And if not tomorrow, then the day after tomorrow. Two-morrow. Let's call that two-morrow."

It's starting again, and there's nothing I can do to stop it. Because I don't want to stop it. Because as long as it stays like this – two people talking over coffee – there aren't any decisions that have to be made.

"How can I say no?" I say. "I'm dying to see who you'll be next."

The sincerity returns as he tells me, "I'll always be A."

I stand up and kiss him on the forehead.

"I know," I say. "That's why I want to see you."

I imagine people looking at us as we stand up from the table, as we throw out our coffee cups and say goodbye. *That went well*, they'd think. Just two teenagers on a date. Not a first date – no, too familiar for that. And not nearly a last date. Because it went well. Because this geeky boy and this quiet girl clearly like each other. You don't have to be inside our bodies to realize that.

20

The next day, A is four hours away from me, in the body of some girl. It might as well be forty hours or forty days.

I tell A there's always tomorrow. And as I type it, I want to believe it.

But I don't really believe it.

With a whole day ahead of me, I decide to do an experiment. I am going to pretend I am a stranger in my own body.

I stare in the mirror, right after my shower. How many times have I done this before? Stared at myself as the steam cleared. Tried and failed to make it seem better. Countless. But how many of these times have I actually *seen* myself? I will look at what's wrong. I will fixate on the blemishes, the bad hair, the fuzz, how uneven I am, how tired I look, how fat I'm getting, how loose. But I don't take an overall picture. I don't step back and look at the whole thing and think, *This is me.* And I certainly don't step back and look at the whole thing and ask, *Is this really me?*

I'm doing that now. How much of my body is really me? My face is me, for sure. Anyone who looked at my face would know it was me. Even with my hair wet and drawn back, it's me. But after that? If I showed myself a picture of myself from the shoulders down, would I be sure it was me? Could I identify myself that way?

I close my eyes and ask myself what my feet look like. I only kind of know. Same with my hands. I have no idea what my back looks like.

I let it define me, but I can't even define it.

If I were a stranger in my body, what would I think of it? I open my eyes and I'm not sure. A stranger wouldn't know any of the stories behind any of the small scars – the tricycle fall, the lightbulb smash. A stranger might not care if my boobs aren't identical, or if the mole on my arm has more hair than the rest of my arm. Why bother judging if you're a stranger in a body? It's almost like driving a car. Yes, you don't want the car to be a shitheap, but pretty much a car is a car. It doesn't matter what it looks like as long as it gets you where you need to go.

I know I am not a car. But as I walk through school, I imagine this smaller Rhiannon driving my body. She is my real self. The body is just a car. And I wonder. When Preston talks to me, it feels like he's talking to the driver. But when a guy I don't know looks at me in the hall, he's staring at the car. When my teacher looks out at the class as he's droning on about history, he's not seeing the drivers, he's seeing the parked cars. And when Justin kisses me – I don't know. Sometimes it feels like he's trying to kiss the driver. Other times, he's just kissing the car.

I try to imagine myself in other bodies, steering them around, experiencing how they're seen. The conclusion I reach: I don't like my body very much, but I'm not sure I'd like anyone else's body any better. They're all strange when you look at them for too long.

I know A is not here, but I want A to be inside one of the bodies I'm staring at. I want a head to turn and for me to see A inside. Because only A could understand all of the crazy places my mind is going. Because A has taken my mind there. A has made me want to reach past all the cars, to get to all the drivers.

"Are you okay?" Preston asks at lunch. "You're really out of it today."

"No," I tell him. "I'm really, really inside of it."

He laughs. I think a laugh is like the driver honking the horn, advertising pleasure.

I think that if A were in Preston's body, I'd kiss him hard.

I know this is a ridiculous thought. I have it anyway.

Preston, of course, has no idea what I'm thinking. He sees me, yes, but not in a way that would give away my thoughts.

The car can smile all it wants, but that doesn't mean you can see the driver's expression.

I receive emails from A.

He tells me:

The girl I am today is not nice. I can make her nice for a day, but what does that do?

He says:

I want us to be walking in the woods again.

He asks:

What are you doing?

And I don't know what to say.

I don't really talk to Justin until after school. He wants me to come over to his house and I can't. I don't have any excuse; I just know I can't.

I have loved his body for so long. I have loved it with devotion, with intensity. If I close my eyes, I can see it better than I see my own, because I have studied it, traced it, detailed it with so much more attention than I have ever spent on myself. It still attracts me. I still feel attachment to it. But it's also just a body. Only a body.

If I kiss him now, I will be thinking this. If we have sex now, I will be thinking of this.

So I can't.

Of course he asks me why not. Of course he asks me what else I have to do.

"I just need to go home," I say.

It's not enough. He's pissed. It's one thing for me to say I'm going shopping with Preston, or have made plans with Rebecca. It might even be bearable if I said I had homework or wanted to go home and be with my mom.

But I'm telling him I'd prefer nothing, and that makes him feel like less than nothing. I understand that, and feel bad about it.

But I can't. I just can't.

The next day, A is only forty-five minutes away from me. In the body of a boy.

I have a math quiz in the morning, so I can't cut out until lunch. It's not even that I care so much about math. But I realize this could be what my life is becoming, trying to go to as little school as possible to get to wherever A is. And if this is going to be my life, I am

259

going to have to be careful about it. I am not about to flunk out because of a crush, or whatever it is. But I'm also not going to stay away any longer than I have to.

Since A is being homeschooled today, he has to come up with a plan to escape. I wait for his message, and then get it around noon – he's made a dash for the public library, and I should get there as soon as I can.

I don't waste any time. As I drive over, I picture him there – which is strange, because I don't know what he looks like today. Mostly, I'm imagining Nathan from the party. I don't even know why.

The library is very, very quiet when I arrive. The librarian asks, "Can I help you?" when I come in, and I tell her that I'm looking for someone. Before she can ask me why I'm not in school, I walk swiftly away from the desk and start to scan the aisles for A. There's a ninety-year-old man checking out the psychology section and a woman who very well might be his wife taking a nap in a comfy chair by an old card catalog. In the kids' section, there's a mother nursing.

I'm about to give up when I see a series of desks by the window. There's a redheaded boy sitting at one of them, reading a book. He's completely lost in it, not noticing me until I'm right next to him. I notice that he's cute in an adorable way, and at the same time I get angry at myself for noticing this. It shouldn't matter. I need to think about A and not care about the body he's in.

"Ahem," I say, to lead him back from the world of the book he's reading. "I figured you were the only kid in the building, so it had to be you."

I'm expecting a smile. A glint. A relief that I'm finally here.

But instead the boy says, "Excuse me?" He seems supremely annoyed that I've interrupted his reading.

It has to be him. I've looked everywhere else.

"It's you, right?" I ask.

I am not ringing any bells in this boy. "Do I know you?" he asks back.

Okay. Maybe not. Maybe A's in the men's room. Maybe I'm at the wrong library. Maybe I need to stop walking up to strangers and assuming they're not strangers.

"Oh, I'm sorry," I apologize. "I just, uh, am supposed to meet somebody."

"What does he look like?"

Now I'm going to seem like an idiot. Because I should know the answer to that question, but I don't.

"I don't, um, know," I tell the boy. "It's, like, an online thing."

"Shouldn't you be in school?"

There's no way this boy is over eighteen, so I shoot back, "Shouldn't *you* be in school?"

"I can't," he says. "There's this really amazing girl I'm supposed to meet."

I've already told myself to start walking away, so it takes a second for me to get what he means.

I've been played. By the one person I didn't think would play me.

"You jerk," I say.

"Sorry, it was just –"

No. I will not let him apologize. "You jerky . . . jerk."

I'm going to start walking away. I'm going to go. We've never had rules, but he's broken one anyway.

A's standing up now. "Rhiannon, I'm sorry."

He's reaching out, but I don't want it.

"You can't do that," I tell him. "It's not fair."

He will always know what I look like. I will never know what he looks like.

"I will never do it again. I promise."

It's not enough. "I can't believe you just did that," I say. "Look me in the eyes and say it again. That you promise."

He looks me in the eyes. We hold there for a second.

Now I can see him. Not literally. It's not like there's a little person waving inside his eyes. I just know he's there.

"I promise," he says.

He means it. I know he means it. He is in the clear –

but I'm not about to let him feel like he's there yet.

"I believe you," I tell him. "But you're still a jerk until you prove otherwise."

Neither of us have had lunch yet, so we decide to go eat. A tells me the boy's mother is coming back in two hours to pick him up. We don't have much time.

We go to the first restaurant we find, a Chinese restaurant that smells like it's just been mopped.

"So, how was your morning?" A asks.

"It was a morning," I tell him. "I had a math test. That can't possibly be worth talking about. Steve and Stephanie got into another fight on their way to school – apparently, Stephanie wanted to stop at Starbucks and Steve didn't, and because of that she called him completely self-centered and he called her a caffeine-addicted bitch. So, yeah. And, of course, Steve then skipped out of first period to get her a venti hazelnut macchiato. It was sweet of him to get her coffee, but passive-aggressive because she really likes caramel macchiatos much more than hazelnut ones. At least she didn't point this out when she thanked him, so everything was back to its shaky normal by the time second period started. That's the big news."

I don't tell him that when I saw Justin, he gave me shit for ditching him yesterday (even though it's not like we had plans). He kept telling me he hoped I'd had an *amazing* night. I told him I had a really *amazing* time studying math. He acted like he didn't believe me, like I ran off to some party without him.

Instead of talking about Justin, I ask A more about the girl he was yesterday. I feel I deserve credit because I ask this as if it's the most natural question in the world. *What else did you do when you were a girl yesterday?*

"It was like being a grenade," A says. "Everyone was just waiting for her to go off and do some serious damage. She had power, but it was all cultivated from fear."

I think of Lindsay Craig and her minions. "I know so many girls like that. The dangerous ones are the ones who are actually good at it."

"I suspect she's very good at it."

I picture A as Lindsay, or some other mean girl. "Well, I'm glad I didn't have to meet her." Because what would the point be? If A was like that, there's no way we could ever be like this, the way we are now. This might be a cheap Chinese restaurant with grease stains on the menus and ceramic cats guarding the soy sauce on the tables, but it's still an escape, it's still exciting. We hold hands and look at each other and not much needs to be said. I have found someone who cares about me, and right now I can accept that.

"I'm sorry for calling you a jerk," I say. "I just – this is hard enough as it is. And I was so sure I was right."

"I *was* a jerk. I'm taking for granted how normal this all feels."

"Justin sometimes does that. Pretends I didn't tell him something I just told him. Or makes up this whole story, then laughs when I fall for it. I hate that."

"I'm sorry –"

"No, it's okay. I mean, it's not like he was the first one. I guess there's something about me that people love to fool. And I'd probably do it – fool people – if it ever occurred to me."

I don't want to sound like a complainer. I don't want to sound like this weak girl who can't take care of herself. But I also want him to know – I can't stand people being mean. People playing games. I want to guard myself against it, but I make a shitty guard for my own heart. I would rather lose the game than play it. I would rather be hurt than be mean. Because I can live with myself if I'm hurt. I don't think I could live with myself if I were mean.

I'm worried A is going to try to say something to make it all better. That he's going to tell me it's all in my mind. Or, even worse, like Justin, he's going to tell me I have to learn how to take a joke. Like my lack of humor is the real offense.

But A's not saying any of that. Instead, he's emptying the chopsticks holder.

"What are you doing?" I ask. The woman behind the cash register is giving us a strange look, and I don't blame her.

A doesn't answer. Instead, he works the chopsticks into the shape of a heart, covering the table. Then he takes all the Sweet'N Low packets from our table and two others in order to turn the heart a pale paper pink.

It's too much. And it's awesome at the same time.

When he's done, he points proudly to the heart. He looks like a kindergartner who's just finished a fort.

"This," he says, "is only about one ninety-millionth of how I feel about you."

I laugh. I think he's forgotten that his heart is full of Sweet'N Low.

"I'll try not to take it personally," I tell him.

He seems a little offended. "Take what personally? You should take it very personally."

"The fact that you used artificial sweetener?"

Saccharine. Everything fake. But also real.

He takes a pink packet from the heart and throws it playfully at me.

"Not everything is a symbol!" he shouts.

I am not going to let myself sit undefended. I pull a chopstick from the heart and use it like a sword. He takes up my challenge, and raises another chopstick in the same way. He lunges. I parry. We are happy fools.

The waiter comes over with some plates. A turns his head and I pierce his chest.

"I die!" A calls out.

"Who has the moo shu chicken?" the waiter asks.

"That's his," I say. "And the answer is yes, we're always like this."

After the waiter leaves, A asks me, "Is that true? Are we always like this?"

"Well, it's a little too early for always," I answer. Not to ruin the moment. Just to make sure we're not carried away by it.

"But it's a good sign," he says.

"Always," I tell him.

I forget about the rest of my life. I don't even have to push it away – I've forgotten about it. It's no longer there. There is only now, there is only me and A and everything that we're sharing. It doesn't feel like amnesia as much as it feels like a sudden absence of noise.

At the end of the meal, we get our fortunes. Mine says:

YOU HAVE A NICE SMILE

"This isn't a fortune," I say, showing it to A.

"No. *You will have a nice smile* – that would be a fortune," he tells me.

267

Exactly. A fortune has to tell you what's going to happen, not what already is.

And, really, who doesn't have a nice smile?

"I'm going to send it back," I say.

A looks amused. "Do you often send back fortune cookies?"

"No. This is the first time. I mean, this is Chinese restaurant –"

"Malpractice."

"Exactly."

I wave for the waiter, who comes immediately.

"My fortune isn't really a fortune, it's just a statement," I tell him. "And it's a pretty superficial statement at that."

The waiter nods and returns with a handful of cookies, each individually wrapped.

"I only need one," I tell him. More than one would be cheating. "Wait one second."

I open a second cookie – and am relieved by what I find inside.

ADVENTURE IS AROUND THE CORNER

"Well done, sir," A says to the waiter once I show it to them both.

"Your turn," I say. A carefully opens his cookie, and

268

practically beams when he reads what the fortune says.

"What?" I ask.

He holds it out to me.

ADVENTURE IS AROUND THE CORNER

I am not a superstitious person. But I'm excited to get to that corner. Wherever it may be.

I know we don't have much time left. I know that A and I are only borrowing this time from someone else, not receiving it entirely for ourselves. But I want to borrow it for as long as I can. I want him to keep talking to me. I want to keep listening to him.

Back in the library, I ask him to tell me more books to read. Because I know the answer to this question will get me to know him even more.

He shows me the book he was reading before. It's called *Feed*.

"It's about the difference between technological connection and human connection. It's about how we can have so much information that we forget who we are, or at least who we're supposed to be." He takes me farther down the shelves, to the very end of the YA section, and holds up *The Book Thief*. "Have you read this?" I shake my head, and he continues. "It's a Holocaust novel, and it's narrated by death itself. Death is separate from everything, but he can't help feeling like he's a part of it all. And when he starts seeing the story of this little girl with a very hard life, he can't look away. He has to know what will happen." He pulls me back to an earlier shelf. "And on a lighter note, there's this book, *Destroy All Cars*. It's about how caring about something deeply can also make you hate the world, because the world can be really, really disappointing. But don't worry – it's also funny, too. Because that's how you get through all the disappointments, right? You have to find it all funny."

I agree. And I'd talk to him more about that, but he doesn't want to stop. I've asked him the right question, and he wants to answer it fully. He shows me a book called *First Day on Earth*. "I know this will sound weird, but it's about a boy in a support group for people who feel they were abducted by aliens. And he meets this other guy who may or may not be an alien. But it's really about what it means to be human. And I read it a lot, whenever I find it in a library. Partly because I find new things every time I read it, but also because these books are always there for me. All of them are there for me. My life changes all the time, but books don't change. My reading of them changes – I can bring new things to them each time. But the words are familiar words. The world is a place I've been before, and it welcomes me back."

He shakes his head. "I've never said that to anyone, you know. I've never even said it to myself. But there it is. The truth."

I want to take out all the books, want to start sharing those worlds with him. Then I remember: This isn't my library. This isn't my town.

"What about you?" A asks. "What do you think I should read next?"

I know I should show him something really smart and sophisticated, but I know he's asking me the question in the same way I asked him – to see me in the answers, to know more about me after the answers than he did before them. So instead of pretending that *Jane Eyre* is the story of my life, or that *Johnny Tremain* changed me completely when I read it, I lead him over to the kids' section. I'm looking for *Harold and the Purple Crayon,* because when I was a kid, that appealed to me so much – the power to draw your own world, and to draw it in purple. I see it on display at the front of the section and go to get it.

As I lean over to pick it up, A surprises me by calling out, "No! Not that one!"

"What could you possibly have against *Harold and the Purple Crayon*?" I ask. As far as I'm concerned, this is a dealbreaker.

A looks relieved. "I'm sorry," he says. "I thought you were heading for *The Giving Tree*."

Who does he think I am? "I absolutely HATE *The Giving Tree*," I tell him.

"Thank goodness. That would've been the end of us, had that been your favorite book."

I would say the same if he'd chosen it. The tree in that book needs to stand up for herself. And the boy needs to be slapped.

"Here – take my arms! Take my legs!" I imitate.

"Take my head! Take my shoulders!"

"Because that's what love's about!" Really, I can't believe parents read the book to children. What an awful message to send.

"That kid is, like, the jerk of the century," A says.

"The biggest jerk in the history of all literature." It's nice to be agreeing on this point.

I put *Harold* down and move closer to him. I'm not going to need a purple crayon for what's coming next.

"Love means never having to lose your limbs," A tells me, leaning in.

"Exactly," I say, kissing him.

No sacrifice. No pain. No requests.

Love. Just love.

I am lost in it. Enjoyably lost in it. At least until someone yells, "What do you *think* you're *doing*?"

For a split second, I assume we've been caught by the librarian and are going to be fined. But the woman who's yelling at me isn't the librarian, or anyone else I've seen before. She's an angry, middle-aged woman spitting out words. Getting all in my face, she says, "I don't know who your parents are, but I did not raise *my* son to hang out with *whores.*"

I'm stunned. I haven't done anything to deserve *that.*

"Mom!" A shouts. "Leave her alone."

Mom. For a second, I think, *This is A's mother.* Then I realize, no, it isn't A's mother. A doesn't have a mother, not in the same sense that I have a mother. No, this must be the mother of the boy whose body he's in. The one who homeschools him. The one who let him out to go to the library, and has found this.

"Get in the car, George," she orders. "Right this minute."

I am expecting A to give in. I will not blame him for giving in, even though I am feeling really attacked. But instead of giving in, A looks George's mother in the eye and says, "Just. Calm. Down."

Now it's George's mother who's stunned. This innocent redheaded boy has probably never spoken to his mom like this before, although I have to imagine there have been plenty of times when she's deserved it.

While George's mother is thrown for a moment, A tells me we'll find a way and he'll talk to me later.

"You most certainly will not!" George's mother proclaims.

I kiss him again. A kiss that's *hello* and *goodbye* and *good luck* and *I've had a great time* all at once. I know these things are in there because I am putting them in there. Usually there are also questions in a kiss. *Do you love me? Is this working?* But this kiss is questionless.

"Don't worry," I whisper when the kiss is done. "We'll figure out a way to be together. The weekend is coming up."

I can't say anything more than that, because George's mother has grabbed his ear and has begun to pull. She looks at me again, trying to cut me down with her judgment – *whore whore whore* – but I don't give up any ground. A laughs at how silly it is to be dragged away by his ear. This only makes her tug harder.

When they get outside, I wave. He can't see me waving, but he waves back anyway.

It's not even three o'clock. I check my phone and find a text from Justin asking me where I am, and then another saying he's looked everywhere. I text back and tell him I wasn't feeling well, and left school early. I know he won't offer to bring me soup or check up on me, unless he wants to see if I'm lying.

So I turn off my phone. I disconnect.

If anyone asks, I'll tell them I was sleeping.

And I'll wait for A to wake me again.

21

I spend Friday morning thinking about the weekend. This is not unusual – most people spend Friday thinking about the weekend. But most aren't trying to find a place to meet someone like A.

I come up with a plan. My uncle has a hunting cabin he never uses – and right now he's in California for work. My parents have a spare key they will never in a million years know is missing. All I need is an alibi. Or a few alibis.

I get an email from A saying he's a girl named Surita today, and not that far away. I'm ready to drop school entirely – it's Friday, after all – but A insists on meeting after school. I get it – there's no real reason to screw over Surita. But maybe A is a little nicer about that than I would be.

Justin's still annoyed with me. "Feeling better, I see," he says when we meet at his locker before class.

"Yeah. It must've been a twenty-four-hour thing."

He scoffs and I get defensive.

"Sorry I didn't text you a photo of my puke," I tell him.

"I didn't say a thing," he replies, slamming his locker.

I'm not being fair. I'm getting mad at him, when I'm the liar.

Then I add another lie.

"I'm glad I'm better, since we're going to see my grandmother this weekend. And I wouldn't want to make her sick."

As soon as I say this, I remember Justin's own grandmother, who's actually sick.

"When are you leaving?" he asks.

"Tomorrow," I say. Then I realize what I've done, and add, "But I promised Rebecca I'd go over to her place tonight."

"Whatever," Justin mumbles. Then he walks away without saying goodbye, which is about what I deserve.

The reason I've mentioned Rebecca is because that's what I'm going to tell my parents – that I'm spending the weekend with her. They like Rebecca, so they won't mind. But I realize now I will have to at least spend tonight with her, since I've told Justin that's what I'm doing.

When I see her in art class, I ask her if she has plans. I pray that she doesn't.

"Nope," she tells me. "Any ideas?"

"How about a sleepover?" I suggest.

Rebecca looks so excited. "You're on! It's been a while since we had a *Mean Girls/Heathers* double feature."

"Or *Breakfast Club* and *Pretty in Pink*."

These were our go-to movies, back when we were

sleepover age. It makes me happy that Rebecca remembers, since it's been a long time. Or at least it feels like a long time. That's my pre-Justin life. Another lifetime ago.

"I have to do a few things after school," I tell her. "With my mom. But how 'bout I come over around six?"

"Will you bring the cookie dough?" she asks.

"As long as you have the ice cream."

It feels so good to be talking like this that I almost forget all the lies that surround it. I almost forget all the things I'm not telling her.

I meet A back at the bookstore. Today he's this somewhat pudgy Indian girl. And I feel awful for thinking that right away, for noticing that first. It's A. I am spending time with A. Focus on the driver, not the car.

As we decide to go for a walk in the park, I stare hard at Surita and imagine her as a boy. It's not that hard. If you stare at anyone's face long enough, it's easy enough to imagine them as the other gender. Then I stop myself and wonder why I'm doing this. It's not like I would stare at her and imagine her white. That would be messed up. But I still want to see her as a boy, to think of A as a boy inside.

Part of the problem is words. The fact that there are separate words for *he* and *she, him* and *her*. I've never

277

thought about it before, how divisive this is. Like maybe if there was just one pronoun for all of us, we wouldn't get so caught on that difference.

Part of me wants to ask A about this, to ask, *Are you a he or a she?* But I know the answer is that A is both and neither, and it's not A's fault that our language can't deal with that.

I'm sure A must notice. The fact that I'm not holding Surita's hand. The fact that there's not the same charge in the air as there was when A was in a guy's body. I want to undo this. I understand it's the wrong way to feel. But it doesn't feel like a knot I can actually untie.

A explains that Surita lives with her grandmother, and that her grandmother doesn't really pay attention, so she can be out as late as she wants. Which means I'm the one with the time limit today. I tell A about this, but then I also tell A I have a plan for the weekend, and that I know a place we can go. I don't tell A what it is, or where it is. I want there to be some surprise.

We get to the jungle gym, and since there aren't any kids around, we allow ourselves to become kids ourselves, climbing and swinging and laughing. A asks me who I hung around with in third grade, so I tell him stories about me and Rebecca, me and my crush on this boy Peter, me and Mrs Shedlowe, the lunch supervisor who would listen patiently to any problem I wanted to share. I know I can't ask A the same question, so I ask instead for things A remembers from being younger. And A tells me about a Valentine's Day his (her) mother took him (her) to the zoo, a birthday party where he (she) saved the day by finding a dog that had gone missing, and a Little League game where he (she) hit a home run, because somehow the body knew when to move even if A didn't.

"Small victories," A jokes.

"But you made it through," I say. "That's the big victory."

"And this," A says, pulling closer, "must be the reward."

I know I should touch this girl's arm. I know I should draw her close and find a way to nest inside the jungle gym. But instead I say, "Look – the slide!" and jump over to it, beckoning A to follow.

If A notices, A doesn't say anything. And even if we don't end up physically nesting in the space that's entirely ours, it still feels comfortable. It still feels like time is comfortable.

I'm good. Except for one moment, when I imagine Justin at home, playing video games. Sensing something wrong. Mad about it. But having no real idea how far I've strayed.

Then I think about what A would be doing if A

weren't here with me. Lost in someone else's life. Erasing himself in order to be her.

After we slide, I suggest we swing. Instead of splitting into a push and a rise, we sit down on swings that are next to each other, and pump our legs to get moving in the air. At one point we're exactly even. A reaches out her hand, and I take it. We swing like that, perfectly even, for about twenty seconds. Then we start to pull apart, the difference in our weight, or in our strength, or in the angle of our bodies – something about our bodies – preventing us from continuing like that forever.

Back in the bookstore, I make A lead me back to *Feed*, to *The Book Thief*, to *Destroy All Cars* and *First Day on Earth*. I buy them all.

"You're so lucky," A says.

"Because they're good books?" I ask.

"No. Because once you have them, they'll always be there. You don't have to keep looking for them."

I'm about to offer to lend them to her, but of course I can't.

"But enough of that!" A says. "Who needs worldly possessions when you can have the world instead?"

The voice A is using is cheery. Maybe A actually believes this. Maybe I'm wrong to want things, and to want to have things. Or maybe A just gave me a glimpse of something he (she) didn't want me to see.

There's not enough time to explore this. I have to get over to Rebecca's. But A and I will have tomorrow. I remind myself we'll have tomorrow.

It's a hopeful farewell. It's only when I'm back in my own car that I realize I could have kissed her when we said goodbye.

It didn't even occur to me.

That night, Rebecca can tell I'm thinking about something other than Lindsay Lohan and Tina Fey. She pauses the movie.

"Is something going on with you and Justin?" she asks. "Is that where your mind is right now?"

I'm immediately defensive – too defensive. "Why do you think there's something going on with me and Justin? There's nothing going on with me and Justin."

With this last sentence, I realize I've accidentally told her the truth. But she doesn't pick up on it.

"It's just – I mean, it's nice to have you back here. This is the first time we've done this since, well, the two of you got together. I wasn't sure we'd ever do this again."

Clarity. I've hurt her. I haven't even noticed, and I've hurt her over these past months. She's not going to tell me that, but it's there. I see it now.

"I'm sorry," I say, even though she hasn't asked me for it – or maybe because she hasn't asked me for it. "Things with him are fine. Really. But I also want to have more than Justin, you know? Like my best friends."

Best friends. It's like a gift I've been given and don't deserve. But here I am, pointing out that I still have it, that I haven't returned it for something else.

"Do you want more ice cream?" Rebecca asks, picking up her bowl. "Because I want more ice cream."

"Sure," I say. Not because I want any, but because I know she wants to have more and doesn't want to have more alone.

As I sit there in the rec room I've known for most of my life, as I see photos of Rebecca and her family at all different ages, I realize this is one thing about us: Rebecca has to see me as more than just a body, because the body she's known has changed so much over the years. That must help a person see inside.

She comes back and unpauses the movie. Our double feature takes us well past midnight, for all the breaks we take for food and random things like seeing whatever happened to the guy who played Aaron and if he's still cute. (He is.) The only awkward moment comes when Rebecca asks me what I'm doing for the weekend. I know this is when I should recruit her to be my alibi, when I should warn her that my parents might call. But

I use the grandmother excuse again. She tells me to say hello, and I promise I will.

I go to sleep wondering what I'm doing and wake up wondering what I'm doing, knowing for sure that whatever it is, I'm going to do it anyway.

22

The drive to Uncle Artie's cabin is about two hours, so I have plenty of time to think. I have the spare key in my pocket, as well as the bag I packed for my weekend at Rebecca's. Or my weekend at my grandmother's, depending on who you ask.

I'm excited to have time alone with A. I know it will only last until midnight – I hope that A will be able to come back tomorrow as well, but I know it's not a sure thing. It's funny to me that in all the time I've dated Justin, it never occurred to me to take him here. Maybe because we had his house. Or maybe because it never felt like we needed this kind of getaway.

Getaway. With enough time to think, I know that what I'm doing is technically cheating. I guess I knew that all along, but this is the first time I actually use that word in my head. It doesn't seem right to explain what I'm doing, but it doesn't seem entirely wrong, either. I feel I am in a messy middle ground of trying to figure it out. I know what Justin would say about that, and how he would see it. I am sure that I am doing to him something he has never done to me.

I am also mad at him for not noticing. Which is, I realize, completely unfair.

I could text him when I got there. I could break up with him that way. But he deserves more than that. And, more, he deserves an explanation. Only there's no way to explain this.

I'm falling for someone I met when he was in your body for a day.

I've made sure to get there a little early to straighten the place up. I love Uncle Artie, but there's a reason his girlfriends always leave him. The cabin's basically one room with lots of stuff piled into it – including a lot of "trophies" from his hunts. The couple of times I came here with my parents when I was a little kid, it freaked me out to have glass-eyed animal heads staring at me from the walls. And it still freaks me out – but I've learned not to really see them anymore. There are one or two that are starting to get a little ragged, and I throw some sheets over those. The rest look on.

The problem with being early is it means there's a time when the groceries I've brought are put away, the floor's been swept, and I have nothing to do. I've brought *First Day on Earth* with me, but I'm too distracted to really pay attention, which doesn't seem fair to the book. I light a few candles so the air will smell more like vanilla and less like Uncle Artie. But the scent also starts to give everything a dreaminess. Or maybe I'm just tired.

I wake up when I hear a car outside. I come alive when I hear the car door open. Nobody else knows about this place, so it has to be A. I peek out the window and see this beautiful guy. My age. Him.

I open the door, wait and watch. Beautiful skin. Beautiful hair. Like the universe somehow knew what this day was for.

"You're really cute today," I say as he closes the door and comes closer. I expect him to have a bag, but of course he doesn't have a bag. He's only here for today.

"French Canadian dad, Creole mom," he explains. "But I don't speak a word of French."

"Your mom isn't going to show up this time, is she?" I joke.

He smiles. "Nope."

"Good," I say, getting closer. "Then I can do this without being killed."

I put everything into the kiss. All of the waiting, all of the desire. All of the today we have and the tomorrows we might not. I kiss him to tell him I'm here. I kiss him to tell him he's here. I kiss him to connect us, to meld us, to propel us. And he kisses me back with all of these things, and something else I can't identify. His arms around me, my arms around him, and both of us pulling, both of us pressing. His hands feeling me all over, giving me shape. No space between us. No space.

Then I pull back a little to take off his coat, kick off my shoes. He kicks his off, too, and I lead him back, my mouth barely leaving his. I push him onto the bed. I'm pinning him down, we're meeting in the middle – still fully clothed but not feeling clothed at all. I kiss his neck, his ear. He moves his hands up my sides, kisses my lips again. There is not a single part of me that doesn't want this. I feel like I've been holding back my entire life, and now I'm letting go. Feeling under his shirt, following the trail to his chest. Keeping my hand there, feeling how hot the skin is. He is moaning and doesn't even realize it. I don't know his name and I don't need to know his name because he is A, he is A, he is A, and he is with me now. We are sharing this. Finger across my breast, finger along my back. Kissing lightly, kissing deeply. Shirts off, skin on skin. The only sense I have left is feel. Lips on shoulder. Hand under the back of his waistband. Arm on arm. Leg against leg. Fast then slow. Fast. Then slow.

"Hey," he says.

"Hey," I say back.

I lie on my back and he hovers over me. Finger along the side of my face. Side of his hand along my collarbone. I respond, tracing his shoulders, reaching down the valley of his back. I kiss his neck again. His ear. The space behind his ear.

There is nothing like this. In all the world, there is nothing like this.

"Where are we?" he asks.

"It's a hunting cabin my uncle uses," I explain. Even when I gave him directions, I didn't tell him where he was going. "He's in California now, so I figured it was safe to break in."

He looks around. "You broke in?"

"Well, with the spare key."

He lies back. I feel the center of his chest. The exact center. Then I move my hand to the right, heartbeat territory.

"That was quite a welcome," he says, his own hands unable to leave my body.

"It's not over yet," I assure him, turning his way as he immediately turns mine.

Closeness. That's what this is. Sex should have closeness.

Now there is closeness. Not just of our bodies. Of our beings. A is careful, but I am not careful. I don't want anything between us. So I take off his clothes, and I take off my own. I want all of him, and I want him to have all of me. I want our eyes open. I want this to be what it's supposed to be.

Naked and kissing. Naked and needing. Naked and here. Moving in the inevitable direction. Sometimes moving quickly, but then slowing down and taking our time. Enjoying it.

It is dangerous, because I will do anything. But I will only do anything because I know it's not dangerous.

"Do you want to?" I whisper.

I feel him against me. The heat, the breath. I feel the momentum. I feel how right this is.

"No," he says. "Not yet. Not now."

Suddenly I feel the colder air around me. Suddenly I feel the world around me. I feel all the parts of it that aren't us.

I tell myself he's being considerate. I look at him and say, "Are you sure? I want to. If you're worried about me, don't be. I want to. I . . . prepared."

But he's pulling back, too, now. One hand still holds my side, but the other settles in the small space between us. "I don't think we should," he says.

I say, "Okay," even though it's not, because I don't understand.

"It's not you," he tells me. "And it's not that I don't want to."

Exit dream, enter nightmare. "So what is it?" I ask.

"It feels wrong."

He says it's not me, but who else could it be? I've pushed it too far. He must think less of me.

"Let me worry about Justin," I say. "This is you

and me. It's different."

"But it's not just you and me. It's also Xavier."

"Xavier?"

He points to his own body. "Xavier."

"Oh."

"He's never done it before. And it just feels wrong . . . for him to do it for the first time, and not know it. I feel like I'm taking something from him if I do that. It doesn't seem right."

This seems more in line with the way the universe has treated me all my life. Send the perfect guy in the perfect body. But then make him a virgin whose first time I'll be taking away without him knowing it. There's no vocabulary in my head for dealing with this.

Closeness. I got so caught up in sex that I forgot what I was really after, what I really wanted. Even if we're not going to have sex, I don't have to give up on everything else.

That's what I wind up telling myself.

After a spell of being only in my mind, I return back to my body and press it closer to his. Turning so we're knees against knees, arms around backs, face to face.

"Do you think he would mind this?" I ask.

His body answers for him. I can feel the tension fall away. I can feel my welcome.

"I set an alarm," I say. "So we can sleep."

I roll over, and he presses his chest against my back, echoes his legs behind my legs. Gathering into a pocket of time, and refusing to leave it. Together, our bodies cool. Together, our breathing slows. Together, we feel unalone.

Our bodies can fit in so many different ways.

The current of sleep carries us at different wavelengths. Sometimes I wake and he's asleep. Sometimes he must be the woken one. And other times, our wakefulness coincides, and we have brief conversations as we remain holding on.

"Are you he or she?" I ask.

"Yes," he replies.

"I know we don't talk about it," he says, many minutes, maybe hours, later. "But why are you with him?"

"I don't know," I tell him. "I used to think I did. But I don't know anymore."

"Is this love?" I ask. But he's asleep.

He mumbles something. It sounds like, "Is your Uncle Artie tall?"

*

291

When we are both more awake, but still without any desire to move from the bed, I face him and ask, "Who was your favorite?"

He puts his hand on mine. "My favorite?"

"Your favorite body. Your favorite life."

"I was once in the body of a blind girl. When I was eleven. Maybe twelve. I don't know if she was my favorite, but I learned more from being her for a day than I'd learn from most people over a year. It showed me how arbitrary and individual it is, the way we experience the world. Not just that the other senses were sharper. But that we find ways to navigate the world as it is presented to us. For me, it was this huge challenge. But for her, it was just life."

"Close your eyes," I whisper.

I trust that he does. We feel each other's bodies as if we're in the dark.

Hours later, or maybe it's minutes, the alarm goes off.

The day is passing, and we let it. The light is fading, and we say nothing as it goes. This is all we want. Two bodies in a bed. Closeness.

"I know you have to leave," I say. My eyes are closed. I feel him nod.

"Midnight," he tells me. "I have to be back by midnight."

"But why? Why midnight?"

Now I feel him shake his head. "I can't be sure. But it's up to the body, and the body just knows."

"I'm going to stay here," I tell him.

"I'm going to come back tomorrow," he promises.

More time. More time together.

"I would end it," he says. "I would end all the changing if I could. Just to stay here with you."

"But you can't end it. I know that."

I don't sound mad or disappointed. I'm not mad or disappointed.

It is what it is.

We start to look at the clock. Knowing. It's time.

"I'll wait for you," I tell him as he gets dressed, as he gets ready to go.

"We'll both be waiting," he says. "To get back to this."

I have no idea what I am doing, and I am okay with that.

He kisses me goodbye. Like he is heading off to school. Or work. Like this is the future. Like we are used to this.

I don't know what to do after he's gone. There's no computer up here for email, no phone reception.

I pick up *First Day on Earth*. These are not his words, but they are words he's guided me to. For now, that's enough.

I have spent too much of the day sleeping. I read for a little while, and then spend the rest of the night dreaming.

23

I wake up really cold, then start the furnace and suffer as it gets way too hot. I guess these are my options.

I know A won't be back right away, but I also know that even if he wakes up five hours away, he'll find a way to be here. I just have to keep myself occupied until then.

I finish reading *First Day on Earth* and wish I'd brought a longer book, or even my homework. Artie doesn't have any books around that I can find. Only back issues of magazines like *Field & Stream*.

There's an old newspaper where the crossword hasn't been done. I try that, but I'm not very good at it. I play some games on my phone, and even walk around outside for a little in the hope of getting reception.

I am bored. So bored. And, even worse, I can hear Justin laughing at me, telling me, "What did you think would happen?"

"He's coming," I say.

"Yeah, right."

No. I cannot be having this conversation in my head. I look at the clock. It's after one. He should be here by now.

He's not coming.

But he promised.

I feel stupider and stupider as the day goes on. I'm wandering around in a T-shirt and boxers, it's so hot.

Finally, I hear a car coming. Driving up. Stopping.

All of the doubts I've been denying now turn themselves into relief.

I run for the door and throw it open. I'm about to jump into A's arms – when I realize the guy in front of me is very old and has a dead deer across his shoulders.

I scream.

He also screams, stumbling back.

I scream again and retreat into the cabin.

"Who the hell are you?" the man yells.

I want to slam the door, but I can't. He's still yelling.

"You're trespassing! Jesus, you nearly gave me a heart attack. Are you alone?"

He's looking at me now. Seeing a girl. Seeing my legs.

"I'm Artie's niece," I say. "Artie's my uncle. This is his cabin. I'm not trespassing."

He looks skeptical, and I really wish he'd put the deer down. It's making me nauseous.

"You're not supposed to be here," the man says. "If you even *are* Artie's niece."

"One second," I say. I scramble for my wallet, find my license. When I come back, he's put the deer back in his truck, thank God.

"You see," I say, holding out the license. "We have the same name."

"Fine. Doesn't mean you're supposed to be here."

"You can call him," I challenge, knowing there's no way, and hoping Artie will cover for me if there is. "He must've mixed things up."

"Well, you're about to get a whole lot more company. We've been hunting all morning, and Artie told us we could clean the skins here and do our business."

The vegetarian in me is horrified. But I'm stuck.

"One second," I tell the man again. I close the door and change into as many pieces of clothing as I can. I pack up all my things.

But I can't leave, because what if A comes? I am so mad at him for abandoning me, but I can't risk abandoning him.

So I stay. As more men arrive. As they look at me funny. As they stare at me. They bring in more kills, and set up an area outside to skin the animals. I reread the only book I have. I go out to the car. I try to avoid everyone, but eventually I have to use the toilet, and there's no room to move.

I hold out for another two hours. Then I give up.

It's too late. A can't be coming. I need to get home.

The whole ride back, I seethe.

*

297

I check my phone as soon as I get reception. I expect an email. I expect some explanation.

Nothing. A's told me nothing.

He could have woken up paralyzed. He might be somewhere without a computer. He might not have a car.

I grasp for excuses. But I feel desperate doing it.

The worse answer is that A got what he wanted, and now it's over. Just like every other guy. And I am just like every other girl who's been stupid enough to think her guy would be different.

A isn't a guy, I remind myself.

But really, it doesn't matter.

I still feel stood up.

I still feel alone.

24

I wake up early, assuming A will wake up early, too, dying to explain to me what happened. I'll learn what was wrong with yesterday's body, why he couldn't make it.

But there's nothing in my inbox. No word.

The littler fears are giving up. The worse fears are coming closer.

I try to avoid Justin. Not because I've done something wrong (which I have), but because I'm afraid he'll smell it on me.

Rebecca asks me how my grandmother is doing. I tell her my grandmother is fine.

I keep checking my email. I keep finding it empty.

I think about ditching lunch, but then I figure there have been so many questions about my behavior lately that it's probably better to go along with the day as it usually is.

Luckily, Lindsay Craig threw a party on Saturday night, which is all anyone at our table can talk about. Stephanie thought she saw Steve kissing a girl from another high school, but Steve swears that was all in Stephanie's drunk eye.

"I don't know, Steve," Justin says. "That girl was pretty smokin'."

I can't tell if he's trying to wind up Steve, wind up Stephanie, or get a reaction from me.

"You went to the party?" I ask stupidly.

"That okay with you?" Justin scoffs.

"Of course," I say quietly.

Rebecca notices this. I can sense her noticing. I also know that if she asks me if anything is wrong, I will start to scream. So I make sure to leave the table early.

I am lost in my own anger. I am angry at A. And I am angry at myself for getting into a position where A could mean enough to me to make me this angry.

I go to all my classes. We're doing softball in gym. I change into my gym clothes, and don't protest when I'm assigned to third base. I try to focus on the game, try to avoid embarrassing myself. I don't notice at first that there's someone waving. But then I realize he's waving at me. I don't recognize him, and that's how I know. He sees me staring at him and nods once. I wait until the play is over, then tell the teacher I have to use the ladies' room, because I'm not feeling well. She doesn't argue, and puts someone else on third base.

This guy doesn't look at all like Xavier from the cabin. He's got on this Metallica T-shirt and his arms are so hairy that they're almost as black as the shirt. When he sees me coming, he walks back inside, into the gym. Out of sight of the playing field.

I follow.

I know I should give him a chance to explain. I know that if he's here, it means he hasn't given up on me. But still, when he says "Hey" to me like nothing's happened, I launch right into him.

"Where the hell were you?" I yell. I don't even sound like myself. I sound much angrier than myself.

"I was locked in my room," he says. "It was awful. There wasn't even a computer."

I know this makes sense. I know this is actually possible. I know he's not lying. But the anger is still there.

"I waited for you," I tell him. "I got up. Made the bed. Had some breakfast. And then I waited. The reception on my phone went on and off, so I figured that had to be it. I started reading old issues of *Field & Stream*, because that's the only reading material up there. Then I heard footsteps. I was so excited. When I heard someone at the door, I ran to it."

I tell him who it was. I tell him what happened. I let him imagine me there alone with all of these men. Waiting for him.

"I wanted to be there," he says. "I swear, I wanted to be there. But I was trapped. This girl – there was just so much grief. She did this horrible thing and they wouldn't leave her alone. Not for one minute. They were afraid of what she'd do. She was denying it. But I wasn't. I figured it out. And it was painful, Rhiannon. You have to believe me – it was so painful. And even then, I would have left. I would have at least tried. But there was no way. She was in no state to leave."

"And this morning?" I ask, gesturing to Mr Metallica. "Why couldn't he send me some word?"

"Because his family was leaving for Hawaii – and if I'd gone with them, I would have never made it back. So I ran. I took three different buses to get here, then had to walk from the station. I am sweaty and exhausted, and when I get back to this guy's house, it's either going to be empty or there's going to be hell to pay. But I had to get to you. All I cared about was getting to you."

The anger is going away, but it's not happiness that's taking its place – it's despair. Like I'm finally recognizing, for real, how absurd this is.

"How are we supposed to do this?" I ask him. "How?"

I want there to be an answer. I really want there to be an answer. But I suspect there isn't one.

"Come here," he tells me, opening his arms. No answer, and an answer. I give in. I walk right into those arms. He's sweaty and hairy and at that moment

I don't care. This isn't about attraction. This is about underneath.

He holds me close, holds me for dear life. I close my eyes, tell myself we can do this. I can forgive him. We can adapt.

The door to the gym opens, and we both hear it. We pull away at the same time, not wanting to be seen. But we've been seen. I look over to the door, and there's Justin. I startle. Justin. It's like my mind can't accept it. Justin. Here.

"What the hell?" he yells. "What. The. Hell?"

I'll say he's my cousin, I think. *I'll say some great-aunt died, and he's come to tell me.*

"Justin −" I start. But he's not going to let me finish.

"Lindsay texted me to say you weren't feeling well. So I was going to see if you were okay. Well, I guess you're real okay. Don't let me interrupt."

"Stop it," I say.

"Stop what, you bitch?" he shoots back, coming close. Like he smells it on me.

I watch as A tries to block him. "Justin," he says.

Justin looks at him like he's scum. "You're not even allowed to speak, bro."

I'm about to explain. But before I can do anything, Justin is punching A full force − a fist right in the face, knocking him down.

I scream and rush to help A. Justin tries to stop me, pulling my arm back.

"I always knew you were a slut," he says.

I try to shake out of his grip, yelling, "Stop it!"

He lets go, but starts kicking A while he's down. I scream some more. I don't care who hears, if it will make Justin stop.

"This your new boyfriend?" Justin's shouting. "You love him?"

"I don't love him!" I shout back. "But I don't love you, either."

There.

Justin goes to kick A again, but this time A catches his leg and pulls him down. I try to reach A and get him back up, but I'm not quick enough, and Justin lands a kick right against his chin.

The door from outside opens, and the girls from softball start coming into the gym. They see me at A's side. They see the blood on the floor. Both A and Justin are bleeding.

Immediately, there's shock and gossip. Stephanie runs over and asks me if I'm okay. Justin stands up and tries to knock A down again. But he misses, and A gets up.

"What's going on?" Stephanie's asking. "Who is that?"

A stumbles over to me, and Stephanie tries to block

him. I realize this makes sense. Justin is my boyfriend. A is an outsider. I could lie now. I could pretend I'm on Justin's side. Only Justin would know the truth, and his pride might go along with the lie.

But I can't. I can't.

"I have to go," A is telling me. "Meet me at the Starbucks where we first met. When you can."

"A!" I call out. Because Justin is right behind him, is reaching for his shoulder. The hand lands, but instead of being pulled around, A frees himself and bolts.

There are tears in my eyes. I don't know how I'm finding the strength to stand. Our gym teacher is coming over. Stephanie is steadying me.

"You fucking bitch!" Justin yells. Everyone hears him. "I am through with you. Do you understand? Totally through. So you can go fuck any guy you want. You won't even have to do it behind my back. You think you're so great, but you're not. You're *not*."

I'm crying harder now.

"Justin, back off," Stephanie says.

"Don't try to defend her!" he yells at her. "She's the one who did this!"

The teacher's on us now, seeing my tears, seeing the blood. She has questions. Stephanie has questions. Lindsay, off to the side, gloats. A male teacher comes in and tries to take Justin to the nurse. Justin tells the teacher to fuck off, and pushes out of the gym. All eyes turn to me.

"It was nothing" is all I can manage to say.

Nobody believes me. And that makes sense, because nobody should.

25

I have to make some decisions, and fast. I have to figure what my side of the story is, so there can be a chance of people taking my side.

Even though I'm not hurt – at least, not physically – they take me to the nurse. She sees the state I'm in and makes me lie down. Stephanie asks permission to stay with me, but the nurse tells her to go to class. When the next class break comes, she returns with Rebecca and Preston, and I sit up in bed to see them.

"Rhiannon," Rebecca says. "Tell us what's going on."

"I messed up," I tell her, tell all of them. "It's over with Justin. I met someone else."

Rebecca tries to contain her surprise so I won't see it. Preston, however, lets out a "Hooooooo-eeeee!" Stephanie slaps his shoulder, but it can't be taken back.

"Who is it?" Preston asks. "Tell us tell us tell us."

Rebecca and Stephanie may act like he's out of bounds for asking so directly, but they're both hanging on my answer, too.

"I can't tell you," I say. "It's complicated."

"Is he married?" Preston asks.

"No! It's just . . . new."

"New enough for him to break into school to see you?" Rebecca asks.

"Is that what people are saying?" I want to know and I don't want to know.

"People are saying all kinds of things," Stephanie reports. "Justin's telling everyone he caught you going down on the guy. I've been telling everyone you were inside for maybe two minutes before we came in, and there was no evidence of him being, um, unzipped."

"We hugged. That's it."

"Well, that's enough," Stephanie says. "I mean, for the gossip. As far as Justin is concerned, you are the biggest slut to ever hit this school. But he's not exactly an unbiased witness."

Now that the punching and the kicking are over, it's really sinking in how much I've hurt him. What I did to him. What I did to us.

All that time. All those memories. I've burned it all down.

Rebecca leans in and hugs me tight.

"It's going to be okay," she tells me. "We'll get through it."

Preston and Stephanie echo this.

They might be all I have left.

*

The nurse lets me stay until the end of the day. When the final bell rings, I make a move to get out of the bed, but she gestures for me to hold off.

"Just let the halls clear," she says. "Allow yourself that."

She is so kind, I want to tell her everything. But I can only imagine what she'd think of me then.

I wait an extra hour. When I get to my locker, I find the photos of us that he kept in my locker and I kept in mine. He's torn them all up, to the point that if I didn't know what they'd once been, I'd never be able to guess.

That's the only damage he's done to my locker.

But it's enough.

Rebecca wants me to go over to her house. Preston and Stephanie keep calling. Even Ben texts to say he hopes I'm okay.

There's a part of me that wants to acknowledge the disaster I've caused, and take shelter with my friends.

But A is waiting. I know he's waiting.

I return to that Starbucks. He's cleaned up a little, but he still looks like a guy who's lost a fight.

I see him. I see him seeing me. I go to get some coffee, to give myself one more minute to think.

"I really need this," I tell him as I sit.

"Thank you for coming," he says. Like he wasn't sure I would. Like I'm doing him a favor.

"I thought about not coming," I admit. "But I didn't *seriously* consider it." Up close, he looks even worse. "You okay?"

"I'm fine," he says. He does not sound okay.

"Remind me – what's your name today?"

"Michael."

I look at him again. I remember that this boy is supposed to be in Hawaii right now.

"Poor Michael," I say.

"This is not how I imagine he thought the day would go."

"That makes two of us."

This morning seems like a million years ago. I was so mad at him. Now I'm just sad.

"Is it over now?" he asks. "With the two of you?"

How could it not be? I want to ask him. In what universe could Justin understand what I've done?

"Yes," I say. Then I add, unfairly, "So I guess you got what you wanted."

He does not appreciate this. "That's an awful way to put it. Don't you want it, too?"

"Yes. But not like that. Not in front of everybody like that."

310

He reaches up to touch my face, but it doesn't feel right. I flinch. He lowers his hand.

This makes me even sadder. What I'm doing to him.

"You're free of him," he says.

I would love for it to be that easy. It is not that easy.

"I forget how little you know about these things," I tell him. "I forget how inexperienced you are. I'm not free of him, A. Just because you break up with someone, it doesn't mean you're free of him. I'm still attached to Justin in a hundred different ways. We're just not dating anymore. It's going to take me years to be free of him."

I don't know why I'm saying this to him. Why I want us to hurt. Maybe I just feel less guilt if I feel more pain.

"Should I have gone to Hawaii?" he asks me.

I almost lost him. I have to realize I almost lost him. The thing I feared the most yesterday almost happened today. He did everything he could to stay, and now I'm punishing him for it.

I have to stop.

"No," I say, "you shouldn't have. I want you here."

His eyes light up with the chance I'm giving, with the possibility that even though everything's gone wrong, it might ultimately be right.

"With you?" he asks.

I nod. "With me. When you can be."

It's the best we can do. He knows it. I know it. And we also know we could settle for much less. We could give up.

He asks me more about what happened after he left, and I tell him. He wants me to understand why he had to run – he couldn't get Michael into even more trouble – and I tell him I understand.

We need to know there's no way Michael can be taken to Hawaii, so we use my phone to make sure all the last flights have left. Rather than have Michael take all the buses back, I offer to drive him – it's not like I'm in any rush to get home. I'm going to have to tell my parents I've broken up with Justin, before they hear it from someone else.

As we drive, I ask A to tell me more about who he's been. The damaged girl yesterday, and other people before that.

He lets the stories range all over the place – some sad, but most happy. As he's telling them, I realize that for each event, he has to remember two things while the rest of us only have to remember one. Not only who he was with, but who he was. Like with his first kiss. I remember my first kiss with Bobby Madigan – it was a dare in fourth grade that both of us had secretly wanted to take. When Mrs Shedlowe wasn't looking, we sneaked at recess into the woods. I remember how soft his lips were. I remember how his eyes were closed. It hadn't occurred to me to close my eyes; if this was going to happen, I wanted to see it.

A tells me his first kiss was in fifth grade. He was in a basement and they were playing spin the bottle. He'd never played spin the bottle before, but the other kids seemed to know what to do. He spun and the bottle landed on a blond girl. He remembers her name was Sarah and that, before they kissed, she said, "Keep your mouth closed!" I ask him who he was at the time. He shakes his head.

"I'm not sure," he tells me. "All I remember is her. I can tell you she was wearing a dress – like a Sunday school dress – so maybe we were at a party for something. But I can't remember who I was."

"Not even if you were a boy or a girl?"

"A boy, I imagine – but, honestly, I wasn't paying attention either way."

It's strange to think about: All this time we're spending together, all of these days. I am trying to remember who he was each day. But A?

A will only remember me.

Eventually the map on my phone tells us we're getting close to Michael's house.

"I want to see you tomorrow," A says.

313

"I want to see you, too. But I think we both know it's not just a matter of want."

"I'll hope it, then."

I like that.

"And I'll hope it, too," I say.

I float on that for a while, driving home. Then I remember everything else that's happened, and I start to sink. When I get home, I can't bear the thought of telling my parents about Justin, so I avoid them. My mom yells something about missing dinner, but I can't even begin to care.

I call Rebecca for a status report. She tells me, again, that everything's going to be fine. It will all blow over.

After I hang up, I stare at my phone. I click on the photo folder and it's like my whole history with Justin is there. He couldn't rip that up.

I know what I told A is true: It's not over.

Justin and I are in the bad part now.

26

School is brutal the next day. All the whispering. All the stares. All the talk. Some of it ridiculous. Some of it true.

Everyone in this building has gone years without caring about me. Now I do something wrong, and suddenly they care. It's disgusting.

There's no email from A when I wake up, and I don't check again. I feel I need to navigate this alone. A can't help me here. I need friends like Rebecca and Preston to help me.

It is amazing to me how many people are fine with calling me a slut to my face. Girls say it low and guys shout it out.

Justin has made it clear to my friends that they have to choose, and that he's the one who's been wronged. He doesn't care about Rebecca and Preston, which makes it easier for them. Stephanie, though, says she's going to have to keep her distance when Justin's around. Steve, too. She says she hopes I understand. I tell her I do.

"You're too nice," Rebecca says, overhearing this.

"No," I say. "I don't think niceness is my problem."

It's like it's not entirely real to me. There's a piece of me that's still calling out for Justin, that thinks we're still together, and meant to be together.

I can fix this, that piece believes. When, really, it's the broken part.

It also asks, *You gave up Justin for what, exactly?*

I don't know how to answer that.

I check my email quickly before third period. There's a message from A, saying he's on his way. I write back:

I don't think today is really a good day.

But I'm not sure the message will get to A in time. A's probably already kidnapped whoever's body he's in. I can't stop it.

I tell Rebecca that I'm going to skip lunch. I know she's going to offer to join me, but I tell her I'd rather be alone, to try to process everything. Mostly I want to hide, and it's easier to hide when you're just one person.

"Are you sure?" Rebecca asks.

I tell her I'm sure.

"Remember, this is the worst of it," she tells me. "The first day is always the worst."

This is a little less than credible from a girl who will no doubt now go find her boyfriend and sit with him at lunch. But I resist telling her that she's not allowed to talk to me until she cheats on Ben and he dumps her.

I don't know where I'm going to go after Rebecca leaves me. Some dark corner of the library should be safe. I've never seen a librarian turn a girl away because the whole school is calling her a slut.

I'm about to head there when a voice behind me says, "Hey."

I am not in the mood for someone else to give me an opinion on my behavior. I turn around and look at the person stopping me. It's a boy, I think. Maybe a freshman. Also maybe a girl.

I'm confused. Then I look in his/her eyes and am not confused.

"Hey," I say. "You're here. Why am I not surprised?"

I know I should be more excited that A's made it. But honestly? This is one more thing than an already hard day needs.

"Lunch?" A asks.

I guess I might as well. It's not really the hiding I'd planned, but I don't know how to explain that.

"Sure," I say. "But I really have to get back after."

"That's okay."

We walk down the hall. And you would think that maybe some people would be staring at the stranger next to me, a person they've never seen before. Maybe not the same guy I am rumored to have had sex with in the gym (there's no mistaking him for that), but still – someone different.

But no. I'm still the main attraction.

A's picking up on this, too. He sees them looking at me. He sees them turning away.

"Apparently, I'm now a metalhead slut," I explain. I genuinely don't care who overhears. "According to some sources, I've even slept with members of Metallica. It's kind of funny, but also kind of not." I stop talking for a second and look at A. "You, however, are something completely different. I don't even know what I'm dealing with today."

"My name's Vic. I'm a biological female, but my gender is male."

A says it like this is obvious. I sigh and tell her, "I don't even know what that means."

"Well, it means that her body was born one way, but her mind –"

This is not what I want people overhearing. I interrupt, "Let's just wait until we're off school grounds, okay? Why don't you walk behind me for a while? I think it'll just make things easier."

I feel like a jerk asking this. But I also feel I need space. Just a little space.

*

I take her to the Philip Diner, which is like an old-age home that serves food. Nobody from school except the most die-hard hipsters ever eat there. And I figure I can take my chances with the hipsters. They have enough problems of their own to care about mine.

The waitress treats us like we're spies about to take away her Social Security. It's not until she's gone that we can talk.

"So how is everything?" A asks.

"I can't say Justin seems that upset," I reply. "And there's no shortage of girls who want to comfort him." *Thank you, Lindsay.* "It's pathetic. Rebecca's been awesome. I swear, there should be an occupation called Friendship PR – Rebecca would be ace at that. She's getting my half of the story out there."

"Which is?"

"Which is that Justin's a jerk. And that the metalhead and I weren't doing anything besides talking."

"I'm sorry it had to all go down like that."

"It could've been worse. And we have to stop apologizing to each other. Every sentence can't start with 'I'm sorry.'"

I should be sorry for snapping this out. I just don't have the energy. Especially with someone so complicated sitting across from me.

"So you're a girl who's a boy?" I ask.

"Something like that."

Oh, great. Now A's snappish, too.

"And how far did you drive?"

"Three hours."

"And what are you missing?"

"A couple of tests. A date with my girlfriend."

I can't help it. I ask, "Do you think that's fair?"

"What do you mean?" I ask.

"Look," I tell A, "I'm happy you've come all this way. Really, I am. But I didn't get much sleep last night, and I'm cranky as hell, and this morning when I got your email, I just thought: Is all of this really fair? Not to me or to you. But to these . . . people whose lives you're kidnapping."

"Rhiannon, I'm always careful –"

"I know you are. And I know it's just a day. But what if something completely unexpected was supposed to happen today? What if her girlfriend is planning this huge surprise party for her? What if her lab partner is going to fail out of class if she's not there to help? What if – I don't know. What if there's this huge accident, and she's supposed to be nearby to pull a baby to safety?"

"I know. But what if *I'm* the one that something is supposed to happen to? What if I'm supposed to be here, and if I'm not, the world will go the wrong direction? In some infinitesimal but important way."

"But shouldn't her life come above yours?"

"Why?"

"Because you're just the guest."

It comes out sounding harsher than I mean it to be.

I go on, "I'm not saying you're any less important. You know I'm not. Right now, you are the person I love the most in the entire world."

"Really?" A sounds skeptical.

"What do you mean, *really*?"

"Yesterday you said you didn't love me."

"I was talking about the metalhead. Not you."

The waitress brings our grilled cheeses and our French fries.

"I love you, too, you know," A says once she leaves us alone.

"I know."

"We're going to get through this. Every relationship has a hard part at the beginning. This is our hard part. It's not like a puzzle piece where there's an instant fit. With relationships, you have to shape the pieces on each end before they go perfectly together."

Relationship. I want to know if that's what this really is. But A is not the right person to ask.

Instead I point out that A's piece changes shape every day.

"Only physically," he argues.

"I know." I eat one of the fries. I'm tired of talking, but don't know how to get out of it without making A feel bad. "Really, I do. I guess I need to work on my piece more. There's too much going on. And you being here – that adds to the too much."

"I'll go," he says. "After lunch."

"It's not that I want you to," I try to assure him. "I just think I need you to."

"I understand."

"Good." I make myself smile. I need to change the tone. "Now, tell me about this date you're going on tonight. If I don't get to be with you, I want to know who does."

Then I sit back and listen as he tells me about this girl named Dawn, who this boy-born-a-girl, Vic, loves like oxygen and needs like nothing else in the world. It's a love story, pure and simple, and I find myself glad that someone in the universe gets to have one.

Even though I'm only meeting Vic this once and I've never set eyes on Dawn, I think about them after A leaves. I imagine the shit they must have to steer through to be together. It's the first thing today that feels perfectly timed. I have it bad, sure. But people can put up with a lot to get to the place they need to be.

I need to remember that.

After school, Rebecca, Ben, and Preston take me for ice cream. They want to know more about my Mystery Man – that's what they call him, and I don't know that they're far off.

I don't tell them much. They respect that. But it's also clear that their curiosity is going to continue, and I'm going to have to either invent some further lies or break up with Mystery Man pretty quick.

I am sure to make it home on time for dinner. Over chicken and potatoes, I tell my parents that Justin and I are over. To my extreme mortification, I start to cry. Even though I know it's the right thing, and even though I know it's my fault, saying it at the dinner table makes it more real than it's ever been before. I don't tell my parents about any Mystery Man. So the full story is that Justin and I are no longer together.

I know they've never liked him. I know they're not going to tell me to try harder, to make it work. I am grateful for that. My father says, "There, there." My mother says she's sure it's for the best. Then they just sit there and watch me cry. They wait for me to put myself back together. They change the subject, and ask me how Rebecca is doing.

I calm myself down as I tell them about an invented weekend – basically, I take the night with Rebecca and spread it out over two days. Lots of movies. Lots of talk. Lots of memories.

Justin isn't mentioned again.

I know that I owe A some kind of communication. Later that night, I send an email.

A,

Today was awkward, but I think that's because it feels like a very awkward time. It isn't about you, and it isn't about love. It's about everything crashing together at once. I think you know what I mean.

Let's try again. But I don't think it can be at school. I think that's too much for me. Let's meet after. Somewhere with no traces of the rest of my life. Only us.

I'm having a hard time imagining how, but I want these pieces to fit.

Love,
R

After telling so many lies to so many other people, it feels good to be honest with someone, and to know that honesty will be appreciated. If A is going to be the one true thing in my life, I have to keep it true . . . even as I wonder if I can make it real.

27

I am ready to meet him wherever and whenever I have to. But when I finally get an email from A the next morning, it's to tell me he's woken up in the body of a boy whose grandfather has died. He has to go to the funeral today. There won't be any way to meet.

I want to type back that I'm sorry for his loss. But it's not *his* loss, of course. I actually feel bad for the boy whose body he's in, because he won't get to attend his own grandfather's funeral. It's not A's fault. But it's still not fair.

I don't know why the fact that I won't be seeing A sends me on a spiral, but it does. I should be used to it. I should know this is always going to be part of the plan – or the part that derails the plans. But with everything else such a mess, I was relying on it anyway. And now I'm feeling stupid for relying on it.

Going to school doesn't make it any better. I feel a distance from everything. Maybe this is self-defense – I can still hear people talking about me, can still see them looking at me like I'm awful. But I also know that nobody here can understand what I'm going through. Nobody here is in love with someone who may or may not show up on any given day. Nobody here doesn't know what form his or her love will take. And instead of feeling superior to them – instead of feeling smug because I have what they don't have – I find myself envying them. I want the same stability that Stephanie and Steve have. Or Rebecca and Ben. Which isn't stability – there are still fights and disagreements and bad days and good days – but it's at least more stable than the great unknown I'm not-quite-dating.

I am sixteen years old, I find myself thinking. *This is way too much.*

The one thing I'm not doing is wishing it were a few weeks ago, and that I was still entirely Justin's. But even that is shakable. Because when I see him for the first time since the gym, it sends me spiraling further. He's coming out of math class, and I am just another body in the hall. What I see isn't pretty. It's much more sad than angry. He has always hated being here, and now he hates it even more. I'm sure, if he saw me, the hate would be shot in my direction. But since he doesn't see me, there's nowhere for it to go. Instead, it loops in on itself, chews on its own tail.

A week ago, I would be rushing over to comfort him. I would be trying to unknot that anger, that hate, to get him to breathe. That was what I did. That was what he needed, and what he always resented.

I turn away and move in the direction I know he

won't be going, even though it's not the direction I need to go. It's bad enough already. I don't want to make it even worse.

The next day, A says he can see me. But it comes with a warning.

> I'm not sure this guy is your type. He's pretty huge. I
> just want to prepare you, because the last time you
> saw me, it wasn't like this.

Type. Suddenly A is worried about my type. I don't want him to be thinking that way. It will only make it harder for both of us. And since I really keep thinking of A as a "he" now, I almost want to tell him that at least he's got half of my type right, if he's a guy. But what does that even mean? How wrong am I to think that way?

Love the person inside, I remind myself. *This will only work if you love the person inside.*

The problem is – and I think about this all through school – I have a mental image of the person inside. When I picture A, I picture him as this attractive guy, shimmering like a spirit or a ghost, jumping from body to body. That is the person I am in love with. And in my mind he's a guy, and in my mind he's white, and in

328

my mind he has dark hair, and in my mind he's lean. Not buff. Not superstar beautiful. Just an ordinary attractive. I can even see him smile.

This mental picture should make it easier for me, should make A more real to me. But it only makes it harder, because I know the mental picture is about what I want, not what A is.

He is waiting for me outside the Clover Bookstore after school. He's dressed up in a button-down shirt and a tie, which I appreciate. But there's no way around it – he's big. Really big. And that's hard for me to deal with. Not because he's ugly. There's actually something sweet about him, in that tie. But he's just so much bigger than me. I'm intimidated. And, yes, it's really hard for me to adjust from seeing A in Vic-the-girl-who's-a-boy's body one day and this body the next time I see him.

"Hey," he says when I get closer. I guess that's our code word now. Our greeting. But it still sounds weird coming in this voice, so low.

"Yeah, hey," I reply.

It's even worse when I'm next to him. I feel miniscule.

"What's up?" he asks, like this body is no different from any other.

"Just taking you all in, I guess," I say. It's like a test.

Let's make A as different as possible from last time, and see how you deal.

I'm not in the mood to be tested. I've been tested enough.

"Don't look at the package," A says. "Look at what's inside."

I get it. I do. But still, I don't like the assumption that this is natural.

"That's easy for you to say," I tell him. "I never change, do I?"

God, I don't want to be fighting. I think this even though I'm the one who's being fighty.

And then I take the thought one step further, and think, *It's like it was with Justin.*

No. It's not. With Justin, I fought because he backed me into corners.

A is not doing that.

Like now. A could easily say, "Yeah, sure you change – the girl I met was really nice, and the girl talking to me right now is acting like a bitch."

But the thing is: A wouldn't say that. Which is why I'm here.

Instead of confronting me, A says, "Let's go." Taking it forward instead of getting stuck here.

"Where to?" I ask.

This gets a smile. "Well, we've been to the ocean and

to the mountain and to the woods. So I thought this time we'd try . . . dinner and a movie."

Ha. Not what I was expecting. But much better than trying to find a desert.

"That sounds suspiciously like a date," I say, smiling myself.

"I'll even buy you flowers if you'd like."

I like the sound of that. "Go ahead," I tell him. "Buy me flowers."

I'm both joking and not joking. And he's serious, because instead of going into the bookstore, he finds a florist and buys me a dozen roses. It's a little crazy, but this whole thing is a little crazy, so I accept it.

He gives me options from the movie theater down the road, and I say if this is a date, then we have to go see one of those superhero movies that seem designed for dates – enough action for the guys and enough banter for the girls. Of course, as soon as I say this, I realize that this equation doesn't take into account people who are neither boys nor girls – and also makes some pretty big assumptions about what guys want and what girls want.

A doesn't call me on it, though. Instead, he tells me it's something he wanted to see, without telling me why.

When we get to the theater, it's mostly empty. The only other people there on a Thursday night are a posse of teenagers who clearly don't care about homework or school tomorrow. I can see them staring at us and making sniggering comments – maybe because of A's size, maybe because I'm this girl going to the movies with a bouquet of roses, like it's Valentine's Day or something.

It's funny because A is clearly having a little trouble navigating in this guy's body. It makes sense – he's not used to being this big, and he has to adjust. He barely makes it into the chair next to mine – and even though he does, it's clear I'm not going to have any part of the armrest. He tries to move his arm around me, and it's awkward – I'm basically stuck in his very active armpit. But honestly? I think it bothers A more than it bothers me. By the end of the previews, he's given up, and moves one seat away so we can have some breathing room. But that's not exactly what you should do on a date.

To make things better, he moves his hand to the seat between us. I know what this means. I move my own hand there, too, and as the movie starts and the world is threatened with destruction, we hold hands. It's nice – but not as nice as before. Partly because his hand is so much bigger than mine. Partly because of the angle. Partly because it's sweaty, and because he keeps shifting in his seat. Eventually I give up, and he doesn't try to get me back. I would be okay leaning against him – his body would be really good for leaning. But he's moved too far away. So we just sit there in our separate spaces for most of the movie. I don't mind, but it doesn't feel like a date.

After the movie, we head to an Italian place. I still don't know what to do with the flowers, and wish I'd never asked for them. In the end, I put them under my chair.

He asks me again about how school is going, and I give him the update. I also tell him about letting my parents know, and about Rebecca calling him Mystery Man.

"I hope that's not how you think of me," he says.

"Well, you have to admit you have more mystery to you than the usual guy. I mean, person."

"Like what?"

"Like why you are the way you are? Like where you come from? Like why you do the things you do?"

"Yeah," he says, "but don't we all have those same mysteries? Maybe not where you came from – but do you really know why you are the way you are? Or why you do the things you do? I don't know why I was born this way – but you don't know why you were born your way, either. We're all in the dark. It's just that my dark is a little more unusual that yours. For all we know."

"But there's more about me that's explainable. You have to admit that."

"You can drive yourself crazy looking for explanations for every single thing. I can't do that. I'm happy to let things just be what they are. I don't need to know why."

"But you have to be curious! *I'm* curious."

"Well, I'm not. And if this is going to work, I need you to take it at face value."

"Face value? Really?"

"Okay. Bad choice of words. Inside value. Soul value. Self value. Whatever you want to call it."

"What do *you* call it? What do you think you are?"

"I'm a person, Rhiannon. I'm a person who happens to go into other people for a day. But I'm still a person."

Chastised. I feel like I've disappointed him. I've fallen into the same trap as everyone else. I haven't understood.

We stop talking to eat. But I can't help watching him. Searching.

"What is it?" A asks, catching me looking.

"It's just that . . . I can't see you inside. Usually I can. Some glimmer of you in the eyes. But not tonight."

I'm not sure if this is his fault or mine. The connection needs to be plugged in on both ends, and maybe it's loose in me tonight.

"I promise I'm in here," he says.

"I know. But I can't help it. I just don't feel anything. When I see you like this, I don't. I can't."

"That's okay. The reason you're not seeing it is because he's so unlike me. You're not feeling it because I'm not like this. So in a way, it's consistent."

"I guess," I say. But it's not what I want to hear. I've never heard him disown one of the bodies before. I've never heard him say *This isn't me.* Is it because he feels that way, or is it because I'm making him self-conscious? He knows I'm uncomfortable, and it's making him uncomfortable. He, who can adapt to everything, and has been doing it for as long as he's been alive, is seeing himself through my eyes, and because of that, he's finding himself lacking.

I need to stop. But what am I supposed to do? Try to not see him as this huge guy? How can I ignore that? How can I not feel different relative to that?

All of these thoughts, and I can't say any of them aloud. Because that will only make it worse.

So instead we talk about the movie. The food. The weather.

This is disturbing. Disturbing because we're not talking about us. And also disturbing because I realize that when you're sixteen and in love, there isn't much to talk about besides yourselves.

This isn't about the body you're in, I want to tell A. *It's about where we are.*

335

He doesn't call me on it until we're walking to get our cars.

"What's going on?" he asks me.

"Just an off night, I guess." I try to smell the roses, but the scent is worn out. "We're allowed to have off nights, right? Especially considering . . ."

"Yeah. Especially considering."

It's not the one thing, it's everything. If he were in the body from the cabin, I would be kissing him goodnight. If he were the girl-boy from the other day, I wouldn't be. Or if he were Ashley with her Beyoncé looks. Or if he were Nathan from the basement. I wouldn't be. And if he were the picture in my mind, this night would have been different. Right now would be different.

It's not how it should be. But it's how it is with me. At least until I can get more used to it. If I can get more used to it.

I couldn't even kiss him goodbye if I wanted to. Not lightly. Not without him coming down to my level.

So instead of trying for that, I raise the roses up. I let him breathe them in instead of a kiss. I try to make it a nice goodbye that way.

"Thanks for the flowers," I tell him.

"You're welcome," he says.

"Tomorrow," I say.

He nods. "Tomorrow."

We leave it at that.

But is it enough?

We keep saying tomorrow. We keep promising it, even though there's no way to promise it for sure.

My parents are already asleep when I get home, but the quiet house gives me too much space to think. Dinner and a movie. The most basic elements of a relationship, of dating. But we failed it, didn't we?

I think maybe I'll feel different in the morning.

I don't.

I lie there in bed, wondering where A is and what he looks like.

I imagine having to think that every morning. Maybe not for the rest of my life. But even for the rest of high school.

It feels like too much.

I email A.

I really want to see you today.

We need to talk.

28

A emails back to say that today he's a girl named Lisa, and that he'll meet me any time I want. I say after school, and tell him to meet me at this park by my high school.

I spend the whole day wondering what to do. I want A in my life. I know he's a good thing, and that he cares about me in a way few people have. What we have is love. I'm sure it's love. But does that mean it can be a relationship? Does that mean we're bound to be together? Can't you love someone without being together?

After school, I find A on a bench in the park – he's exactly where I asked him to be. The girl he is today looks like someone I could be friends with – similar style in clothes, similar hair. I still have to adjust, but it's not as hard, because it's more familiar.

She's reading a book, and doesn't even notice me until I sit down next to her. Then she looks up and smiles.

"Hey," she says.

"Hey," I say back.

"How was your day?"

"Okay." I don't want to come right out and say all the things I've been thinking. So instead I tell A about class, and about the homecoming game that everyone's excited about tomorrow, and how Rebecca is insisting that I go, even though I don't really want to go. A asks me why, and I admit it's partly because I don't want to see Justin and partly because . . . well, it's a football game.

"It's supposed to be good weather, at least," A says, before launching into the forecast for the weekend.

I have to interrupt. If we start talking about whether or not it's going to rain on Sunday, I am going to scream.

"A," I say, even though A's not finished. "There are things that I need to say to you."

A stops. And it's not like yesterday, when he felt so distant inside the body. Now he's floating to the surface of this girl. So nervous. So scared.

I wish I could tell him it will all be okay. I wish I could ask him to the homecoming game. I wish I could have him meet all my friends. I wish I could say that I want to kiss this girl as much as I want to kiss everyone else. I wish I could say what he wants me to say.

But I refuse to lie. That's the one thing we can have – honesty between us. Everything else – whatever it is – can be built from that.

"I don't think I can do this," I say.

He knows what I mean. He doesn't say "What?" He doesn't look confused. Instead, he asks, "You don't think you can do it, or you don't *want* to do it?"

"I want to. Really, I do. But how, A? I just don't see how it's possible."

Now he asks, "What do you mean?"

I spell it out. It hurts to do it, because I know it's not something he can control. But he has to see that I can't control my own self, either.

"I mean, you're a different person every day. And I just can't love every single person you are equally. I know it's you underneath. I know it's just the package. But I can't, A. I've tried. And I can't. I want to – I want to be the person who can do that – but I can't. And it's not just that. I've just broken up with Justin – I need time to process that, to put that away. And there are just so many things you and I can't do. We'll never hang out with my friends. I can't even talk about you to my friends, and that's driving me crazy. You'll never meet my parents. I will never be able to go to sleep with you at night and then wake up with you the next morning. Never. And I've been trying to argue myself into thinking these things don't matter, A. Really, I have. But I've lost the argument. And I can't keep having it, when I know what the real answer is."

This is it. As honest as it gets. But he doesn't give in when I force him to face it.

"It's not impossible," he tells me. "Do you think I haven't been having the same arguments with myself, the same thoughts? I've been trying to imagine how we can have a future together. So what about this? I think one way for me to not travel so far would be if we lived in a city. I mean, there would be more bodies the right age nearby, and while I don't know how I get passed from one body to the next, I do feel certain that the distance I travel is related to how many possibilities there are. So if we were in New York City, I'd probably never leave. There are so many people to choose from. So we could see each other all the time. Be with each other. I know it's crazy. I know you can't just leave home on a moment's notice. But eventually we could do that. Eventually that could be our life. I will never be able to wake up next to you, but I can be with you all the time. It won't be a normal life – I know that. But it will be a life. A life together."

I want to be the girl who can believe this. I want to be the girl who can run away from her life and do this. For one person. For the right person.

But right now, I don't think I'm that girl.

I try to picture it. I can see living in New York City. Having an apartment. Living a life there.

The problem is, when the door opens and A comes home, it's my mental image of A. He's that guy. The guy he'll never be.

I can't picture it with a different person every day.

That doesn't feel like a life. That feels like a hotel.

I know he wants it so badly. And it kills me that I can't give it to him.

"That will never happen," I say, trying to make my voice as comforting as possible. "I wish I could believe it, but I can't."

"But, Rhiannon –"

I'm crying now. It's too much. "I want you to know, if you were a guy I met – if you were the same guy every day, if the inside was the outside – there's a good chance I could love you forever. This isn't about the heart of you – I hope you know that. But the rest is too difficult. There might be girls out there who could deal with it. I hope there are. But I'm not one of them. I just can't do it."

A is crying, too. I mean, the girl sitting with me on this bench is crying, too.

"So . . . what?" she asks. "This is it? We stop?"

I shake my head. "I want us to be in each other's lives. But your life can't keep derailing mine. I need to be with my friends, A. I need to go to school and go to prom and do all the things I'm supposed to do. I am grateful – truly grateful – not to be with Justin anymore. But I can't let go of the other things."

"You can't do that for me the way I can do that for you?"

342

"I can't. I'm sorry, but I can't."

And I don't want him to do it for me, either. I don't. We are not worth that.

"Rhiannon . . ." A says. But then it stops there. As if he's finally realizing what the truth is. And what it means for us.

We could argue about it for hours. For days. We could keep coming to this bench, A in a different body each time. It wouldn't matter. I know this. And I think that A is starting to know it, too.

I lean over and kiss him (her) on the cheek.

"I should go," I say. "Not forever. But for now. Let's talk again in a few days. If you really think about it, you'll come to the same conclusion. And then it won't be as bad. Then we'll be able to work through it together, and figure out what comes next. I want there to be something next. It just can't be . . ."

"Love?"

No. "A relationship. Dating. What you want."

I stand up. I have to go now. Not because I'm going to change my mind if I stay. I know I'm not going to change my mind. But I also know it will hurt A more to keep trying and failing.

"We'll talk," I promise.

"We'll talk," he says. It's a statement, not a promise.

I hover there. I don't want to leave it like this.

343

"Rhiannon, I love you," he says, her voice breaking.

"And I love you," I say.

I know it's something. It's not enough, but it's something.

I give a little wave, then head to my car. I don't look back. I keep myself together. It isn't until I'm in the car, until I've put on my seat belt, that it all comes out. My body needs to release this. So I let it go. I let myself be the mess my life has become. And when I'm done, I blow my nose, wipe my eyes, turn the key in the ignition, and find my way home.

29

As soon as I get to my room, I want to email A, to take it back.

But I have to be stronger than that. Because I know that would be a lie, and I need to live with the truth.

I have no intention of going to the homecoming game, and Rebecca and Preston have no intention of letting me get out of it. I might be able to resist one of them, but their combined force is too much for me.

They call me on speakerphone from Rebecca's house.

"You have to come," Preston insists.

"I don't care if Mystery Man is planning on taking you on a tour of Europe this weekend," Rebecca says. "This comes first."

"Because we want you there."

"We *need* you there."

"But Justin will be there!" I point out.

"So what?" Preston says. "We can take down that skinnyass whiner if we have to."

Rebecca sighs. "What Preston means is, you can't avoid Justin forever. Our school just isn't that big. So the sooner you get the first time over with, the better. And we'll be with you the whole time."

"Plus," Preston adds, "you'll go crazy if you stay home all weekend."

True. All of this is true.

Also, I miss them.

"Fine," I say. "But you're talking to me the whole time. You are not going to expect me to watch high school football for two hours."

"You've got yourself a deal," Rebecca says, and Preston cheers.

I become hyper-preoccupied with what to wear. Which was never an issue when I was going to see A – I guess I figured if he was going to show up in whatever body, I could show up wearing whatever. Or maybe I didn't feel like I was auditioning for him all the time, like I did with Justin.

Rebecca, Preston, and Ben pick me up and we head to the high school. It feels like the whole town is here – even though our football team sucks, homecoming is a sort-of big deal. Stephanie and Steve are with Justin and a few more friends, and Stephanie has promised to text updates about their location. I tell Rebecca that's not necessary – I don't need to be treated like there are restraining orders involved. I'm not worried Justin will attack me. I'm just worried about how sad it will feel to see him.

Luckily, the stands are packed, and Justin's group is nowhere near us. As promised, we talk through the game – mostly Preston giving running commentary on the fashion choices of various people in the bleachers, with even Ben throwing in a remark every now and then. At one point, Preston says he's going on a pretzel run and Rebecca volunteers to join him, leaving me and Ben alone together for the first time in a while.

At first, I think we're just going to watch the game until Preston and Rebecca get back. But then Ben says, "I'm glad you did it." He's not even looking at me – he's watching the field as he says it. But I know he's talking to me.

"Thanks," I say.

Now he looks at me. "No thanks necessary. It's just nice to see you out from his shadow. Because things don't grow in shadows, you know? So it was frustrating to see you standing there . . . and really cool to see you step out of it. I don't know who this new guy is, but make sure when you're with him, you're not standing in his shadow. Stand where everyone can see you."

The crowd starts to cheer, and Ben turns back to the game in time to see one of our players heading to the end zone. "Come on!" he yells, along with the rest of the crowd. The guy is tackled a few yards short. "Oh man!" Ben sighs. "Can you believe it?"

"So close," I say.

"Yeah," Ben says with a nod. "So close."

I should have known there'd be an after-party.

"It'll be fun," Rebecca promises, taking my arm and leading me to her car. "We won't leave your side."

The truth is, I don't need much convincing. I'm having a good time. An uncomplicated, good time with my friends. For a long time, I couldn't have had this – there would have always been the counterweight of Justin, the obligation of being in a couple instead of hanging with a couple of friends. This is part of freedom – not looking for anything, not missing anything, just happy with the friends who are here.

"Sure," I tell Rebecca. "Let's go."

It's not that late, and barely dark out. There's an official after-party at some restaurant owned by a former high school quarterback, but the less-than-football crowd is gathering at Will Tyler's house, which is very conveniently located across the street from a water supply area that's never patrolled for trespassing.

Will Tyler's this guy from the grade above us who sold a fantasy novel to a big publisher when he was fourteen. He has a banner over his door that says FOOTBALL IS FOR WUSSES; QUIDDITCH IS FOR GODS. Preston whoops when he sees that.

If the geekiness of the sign isn't enough to ward off Justin, I'm sure the complete lack of alcohol will be. Instead of beer and vodka, Will and his parents have stocked up on every single soda that's ever been created – or at least it seems that way. The bottles are lined up in identical pairs in the kitchen, like this is some kind of carbonated Noah's ark. Some people are grumbling or pulling out flasks to spike their Fanta. But I'm into it. It's been too long since I've had a Cherry Coke.

A would love this. I have no doubt A would love this. I wish he were here – not for us to be together, but so he could sample any of the sodas he never got as he bounced around his childhood.

"Will Tyler's no fool," Preston says, cheersing me with a red cup of purple pop. "This is a party we'll all remember."

"Why, thank you," a boy behind him says. His voice has a slightly Southern twang. "Glad you could be here, Preston."

Preston turns to the boy and blurts, "You know my name?"

Will laughs. "Of course I know your name! It's a very nice name."

Preston smiles.

Will smiles.

And I'm like, *Wow. Yes. Go.*

"I need to find Rebecca," I say, even though Rebecca is all of ten feet away from me, pouring herself a Barq's.

"Don't look now," I whisper when I get to her, "but I think Preston's found someone on his team."

Of course, Rebecca looks over. When she turns back to me, her eyes are wide.

"Why didn't we think of this sooner?" she asks me.

"All in due time," I tell her.

"And I'd say that time is due!"

Ben shuffles over. "Do any of you have any idea what Vernors is? I'm trying it, and it's not bad. But I'm not sure what it's supposed to be."

"Out," Rebecca says. "Out out out."

We shuffle away from Preston and Will, into the den, where Ellie Goulding's "Lights" is playing on high, and the lights themselves are playing on low. Looking around, I see we're mostly surrounded by smart kids – Rebecca and Ben's crowd. But I don't feel unwelcome.

I think this would be A's crowd, too. I mean, he could have turned into anyone – a jerk, a druggie, a social climber, a sociopath. But after all he went through, he's basically a smart kid.

I scan the crowd, looking for that recognition even though I haven't asked him to be here. If he's here, it will have to be coincidence. Fate.

Someone suggests charades. The music is turned off, the lights are turned up, and Preston and Will come out of the kitchen. They're on the same charades team, of course. And when each of them is giving clues, it's the other he's looking at.

More people show up – more smart kids who stopped off for dinner before coming over. It isn't until nine that the official after-party breaks up, and a whole different wave comes. Some are drunk, and some want to be drunk. Rebecca checks her phone and there's a text from Stephanie, saying they'll be here soon.

"Do you want to leave?" Rebecca asks me.

And I say no. I'm happy here. I don't want to leave.

But still, it's awkward when Stephanie comes into the den, and I know that means Justin's somewhere in the house. It's awkward when I hear him yelling in the kitchen, asking someone where the booze is being hidden.

"Steve will keep him in there," Stephanie promises me.

But Steve can't keep him in there, not when there isn't any booze. Justin comes jumping out into the den, and there it is: me and him, in the same room.

The look on his face when he sees me is awful. Like he's been tricked. Like I'm the trap.

"What the fuck is she doing here?" he says. He must be three or four beers closer to drunk already. I can tell.

He turns to Stephanie. "You knew she'd be here, didn't you? Why the fuck didn't you warn me?"

Now Steve's on the scene, telling Justin to calm down.

"Shit!" Justin says, knocking the nearest cup to the floor. It doesn't really have the effect he wants. It's plastic. And full of Sprite.

I'm standing there, and it's as if I've stepped away from myself for a second. I am watching this from a distance. Calmly, I am wondering what he's going to do next. Yell at me? Spit at me? Throw another cup? Burst into tears?

Instead, he looks at Steve and says, with more feeling than he'd want me to hear, "This *sucks*." Then he bolts from the room, out the front door.

Steve moves to follow, but I surprise everyone in the room – including myself – by saying, "No. I've got this."

Steve looks at me curiously. "Are you sure? I have his keys."

"I'll be right back," I tell him. Then, seeing the look on Rebecca's face, I say it to her, too. "Really. I'll be right back."

It's not hard to find him. I can actually see the glow of his cigarette across the street in the water supply area. It figures he'd head straight to the No Trespassing signs.

I let him take a few drags before I get there.

"I'm coming in," I warn. Then I skirt around a tree, and end up right in front of him.

I can't help it. The first thing out of my mouth is, "You look like shit."

Which means the first thing out of his mouth is, "Well, you made me feel like shit, so that kinda makes sense."

"I'm sorry."

"Fuck you."

"I'm really sorry."

"*Fuck you.*"

"Go ahead. Get it out of your system."

"Why, Rhiannon? *Why?*"

This is worse than the *fuck you*. Much worse.

Because now his body is transparent. I see right inside, right to who he is. And he is so upset. So wronged. So surprised.

All along, I've wanted to see how much he cared. And now I get to see it. Now, when it's over.

"How long, Rhiannon? How long were you screwing some other guy? How long were you lying to me?"

"I never screwed him."

"Oh, that makes me feel *so much better.* The best kind of slut is one who won't put out!"

I've humiliated him. I've been so busy being humiliated that I haven't realized how badly I've humiliated him.

"I am so, so sorry," I say.

I should be crying. But what I feel is different from sorrow. It's horror.

"It's okay if you hate me," I say.

He laughs. "I don't need your *permission* to hate you. Jesus! Listen to yourself!"

I wish I could blame A. I wish I could say it's A's fault. But all A did was show me who Justin wasn't. And instead of dealing with that, I ran away. I pretended. And then I was caught.

"I don't just hate you, Rhiannon," Justin says. "I hate you more than I ever thought it was possible to hate anyone. Do you know what's worse than being destroyed? It's being destroyed by someone who was never worth it. If you want me to let you off the hook – if you want me to tell you that I'm okay with everything – well, all I have to say to that is that I hope you stay on this hook for as long as you fucking live. I hope you feel it every time you kiss that guy. I hope you feel it every time you think about kissing anyone. I hope it keeps you awake at night. I hope you never sleep again. I hate you that much. So go back to that lame-ass party and drink soda and get out of my face."

"No," I say, faltering. "No – we need to talk. I need to tell you –"

"Fine. New plan. I am going to go back there, get Steve and my keys, and drive the hell away. You can

354

stay here. I hereby give you custody of this shitty reservation. Do not follow me, and please do not talk to me ever again."

He flicks his cigarette to the ground and walks away. I jump forward – not to follow him, but to make sure the cigarette doesn't set everything on fire.

What have I done what have I done what have I done?

Even as I'm thinking this on repeat, I'm also thinking it's a little too late to be asking this question.

I want to wake up tomorrow in another body, another life. But I don't really want that. What I'm realizing is that for all the time I've spent with A, for all the time I've thought about A and A's life, I missed the most important part: *Do no damage.* Somehow A can do that in the course of a day, but I couldn't manage it in the course of a real, continuous life.

I can't go back to the house, but I also can't just stand here, waiting to see Justin and Steve leave. So I walk deeper into the woods, trespass more definitively. Once I'm out of the streetlamp range and the neighborhood glow, it's completely dark. As I walk among the trees, I realize this is as close to bodiless as I'm going to get. Just a mind walking through the night. Unseen. Unfelt. Unreal.

Justin was careless with me. That's undeniable. But

it doesn't excuse me from being so careless with him. It explains it, but it doesn't excuse it.

I lose all sense of time until I hear my name being called. More frantic with each repetition. Rebecca's voice. Preston's. Ben's. Stephanie's. Will's.

"I'm here!" I shout, then keep shouting it until they find me.

30

I call my parents.

I tell them I'm sleeping over at Rebecca's.

Then I sleep over at Rebecca's.

The next morning, Will invites us back to his house for a picnic.

"Are you sure he's not just inviting Preston?" I ask. It's eleven in the morning and I'm not out of bed yet.

"Nope," Rebecca says. She's been up for at least an hour, I'm sure. "All of us. Me and Ben. Steve and Stephanie. Will and Preston. And . . . you. Do you want to ask your Mystery Man?"

"I can't," I say.

"Come on. Isn't it time we met him?"

"I just can't."

"What? Are you ashamed of us?" She's teasing, but I can tell there's a worry that it's true.

"No," I say. Because the truth is that I'm sure A would love nothing better than a picnic with me and my friends. A would fit in perfectly. It hurts me to know this.

"Then why not?"

"Because I don't think it's going to work out," I say. "With him and me. I just don't think –"

I can't finish the sentence, because it feels so strange to say it out loud.

Rebecca sits down on the bed next to me and gives me a hug. "Oh, Rhiannon," she says. "It's all right."

I don't know why she's treating me this way, but I guess I'm crying or something. I want to tell her they're tears of confusion, not sadness. *Was all of this for nothing?* I think of Justin last night. I think of A out there somewhere. And I think, no, this wasn't for nothing. Even if I'm not going to be with A, I needed to stop letting Justin determine my life. I needed to find my own life. A, in a way, got me there. And it wasn't for nothing. A and I still have something, even if it's not the kind of something where he can come to a picnic with my friends.

I get myself together. "Sorry," I tell Rebecca.

"No need to be sorry," she assures me.

"I know."

"Do you want to talk about it?"

Yes, I want to talk about it.

No, I cannot talk about it.

"It's just a long-distance thing. It's hard," I say.

Rebecca nods, sympathetic. I know she wants to ask me more.

"Let's get ready for the picnic," I say.

*

We hang out in Will's backyard and pretend it's Central Park. Nobody mentions Justin. Nobody mentions the Mystery Man. Except my thoughts. They mention Justin and A all the time.

I am glad Justin isn't here. If he were here, it wouldn't be like this. Rebecca and Ben arguing over whether it's pretentious to pronounce *croissant* in a French accent when you're speaking English. Will and Preston finding every possible opportunity to touch each other on the arm, the leg, the cheek. Steve and Stephanie chilling out – Stephanie asking Steve to peel her a grape, and Steve actually doing it, both of them laughing at how messy a process it is. If Justin were here, he'd be bored. And he'd be letting me know how bored he was. I wouldn't be able to enjoy any of my friends, because I would be so stuck on how Justin was feeling.

But if A were here. It's mental-picture A at first. But then it's any of the A's. Because even if he was a pretty girl, or even if he was a huge guy, or even if he was poor Kelsea, back from wherever her dad sent her – there'd be a place for A. Because A would appreciate this. A would understand how much this matters, to spend a day lazing around with your friends, telling inside jokes and feeling inside of them. A has never had that. But I could give A some of mine.

I could email. I could say *Come on over.* But I'm

worried he won't understand why I'm asking. He'll think I mean we can be together. A couple.

Plus, it wouldn't be fair to the person he's in.

I have to remember that, too.

I think about contacting him a thousand times. For the rest of the day – in the fun moments with my friends, or in the quiet moments when I'm at home. Back at school, when I see things it would be fun to tell him about, or when the minutes seem hours long and class never ends. I want to tell him about Justin, and how now when we see each other in the halls, we ignore each other, as if we're strangers, even though the way we ignore each other isn't like strangers at all. I want to tell A that he was right about Justin, but also wrong about Justin. Yes, he wasn't good for me. But no, it's not that he didn't care. That much is obvious now.

Finally, on Monday night, I give in. Instead of telling A everything, I keep it simple, to make sure that it's okay to keep in touch.

How are you?

R

Within an hour, I get his response.

It's been a rough two days. Apparently, I may not be the only person out there like this. Which is hard to think about.

A

And just like that, I feel myself being drawn in again. I start to write a response – a long response – but after a few paragraphs I think, *No. Stop.* I thought there would be distance, but there isn't any distance. I know that if I involve myself again right now, it will be the same as before. And it can't be.

I hold off. I call Rebecca and talk about other things.

I need to build a life without A before I let him back in.

My friends gather around me. In school. After school. On the phone at night.

Will effortlessly joins our circle. He and Preston look so happy together. And I'm happy for them. I am. But I'm also angry, because Will can join us so effortlessly, in a way A never could.

Nobody mentions my Mystery Man anymore. Rebecca must have told them not to.

Part of me still expects him to show up. Expects the universe to send him into the classroom next to mine. Or into Rebecca's body. Or Steve's. Just to say hello. Just to be near.

But I can't think that way. I know I can't.

I find myself looking into people's eyes more than I ever did before. And I realize, that's where we stop being a certain gender or color. Just look right into the center of the eye.

I know I haven't answered him. It weighs on me. I know I'm not being fair. There's no point in spending all this time thinking about A without answering. I have to be honest and clear about where it can go. That's all. That's it.

First thing Thursday morning, I write.

I want to see you, but I'm not sure if we should do that.
I want to hear about what's going on, but I'm afraid that
will only start everything again. I love you – I do – but
I am afraid of making that love too important. Because
you're always going to leave me, A. We can't deny it.
You're always going to leave.

R

All through the day, there's no response. And I think,
fine, I deserve that.
But it's still disappointing.

Then, Friday at lunch, a response.

I understand. Can we please meet at the bookstore
this afternoon, after school?

A

To which I say:

Of course.

R

*

I'm nervous as I drive over. Everything's changed, and nothing's changed. This is going to be hard, but it feels so easy. Mostly, I want to see him. Talk to him. Have him be in my life.

All the other obstacles have fallen away. I am even starting to believe, deep in my heart, that if I told my friends the truth, if they met A the way I met A, on multiple days, they would believe it, too.

The only obstacle, really, is his life.

Which I know is too big an obstacle. But in the rush to see him, it doesn't seem as big as maybe it should.

I get there first. I scan the café and know that none of these people could be him. If he were here, he'd be looking for me. He'd know when I arrived.

So I sit down. I wait. And the minute he walks through the door, I know. Like there's a shiver of lightning between us. Today he's this thin Asian guy wearing a blue T-shirt with the Cookie Monster on it. When A sees me, his smile is wider than the Cookie Monster's.

"Hey," he says.

And this time I say it back gladly. "Hey."

So here we are. I'm trying to remind myself to not fall back into it, to not start thinking it's possible. But with him right here, that's hard.

"I have an idea," he says.

"What?"

He smiles again. "Let's pretend this is the first time we've ever met. Let's pretend you were here to get a book, and I happened to bump into you. We struck up a conversation. I like you. You like me. Now we're sitting down to coffee. It feels right. You don't know that I switch bodies every day. I don't know about your ex or anything else. We're just two people meeting for the first time."

The lie we want to believe. That feels dangerous.

"But why?" I ask.

"So we don't have to talk about everything else. So we can just be with each other. Enjoy it."

I have to tell him, "I don't see the point –"

"No past. No future. Just present. Give it a chance."

I want to. I know I want to. So I will. I know it's not as easy as that, but it can at least start by being as easy as that.

"It's very nice to meet you," I tell him. I feel like I'm a bad actress in a bad movie.

But he likes it. "It's very nice to meet you, as well," he says. "Where should we go?"

"You decide," I tell him. "What's your favorite place?"

He thinks about it for a second. Whether he's inside his own thoughts or this boy's thoughts, I don't know. His smile gets wider.

"I know just the place," he says. "But first we'll need groceries."

"Well, luckily, there's a food store down the street."

"My, how lucky we are!"

I laugh.

"What?" he asks.

"'My, how lucky we are!' You're such a goofball."

"I am happy to be your ball of goof."

"You sound like Preston."

"Who's Preston?"

He really doesn't know. How could he? I've never told him.

So as we walk over to grocery store, I introduce him to all of my friends. He knows Rebecca, and vaguely remembers Steve and Stephanie, but I tell him more about them, and about Preston and Ben and even Will, too. It's weird, because I know I can't ask him the same questions back. But he seems okay with that.

Once we get to the grocery store, A says we're going to go down all the aisles. "You never know what you might miss," he tells me.

"And what are we shopping for?" I ask.

"Dinner," he says. "Definitely dinner. And as we do, keep telling me stories."

He asks me about pets, and I tell him more about Swizzle, this evil bunny rabbit we had who would escape his cage and sleep on our faces. It was terrifying. I ask him if he had a favorite pet, and he tells me that one day he had a pet ferret that seemed to understand it had a guest in the house, so it made his life as difficult as possible – but also gave him something to do because no one else was home during the day. When we get to the produce aisle, he tells me a story about this time at camp where he got hit in the eye by a flying greased watermelon. I tell him I can't remember being injured by any fruit, although there was a good few years when I made my mom cut up apples before I'd eat them, because someone at school had told me about psychos who put razor blades inside.

We get to the cereal aisle, which isn't really going to help us for dinner. But A stops there anyway and asks me for my life story told in cereals.

"Okay," I say, getting what he means. I begin by holding up a cylinder of Quaker oatmeal. "It all starts with this. My mother barely eats breakfast, but my dad always has oatmeal. So I decided I liked oatmeal, too. Especially with bananas. It wasn't until I was seven or eight that I realized how gross it was." I pick up a box of Frosted Flakes. "This is where the battle began. Rebecca's mom let her have Frosted Flakes, and like everyone else, I'd seen the commercials for them a zillion times. I begged my mother to let me eat them. She said no. So I did what any law-abiding girl would do – I stole a box from Rebecca's house and kept it in my room. The only problem was, I was afraid my mom would catch me putting the bowls in the dishwasher. So I kept them in my room. And they began to stink. She threw a holy fit, but my dad was there and he said he didn't see the harm in Frosted Flakes if that's what I wanted. The punchline being, of course, that once I had them, they disappointed me. They got so soggy so fast. So my mom and I reached a compromise." I walk him over to the Frosted Cheerios. "Now, I'm not sure why Frosted Cheerios are any better than Frosted Flakes, but my mom seemed to think so. Which brings us to our grand finale." I make a production of choosing from the ninety kinds of granola before landing on my favorite cinnamon-raisin kind. "In truth, this probably has just as much sugar in it as anything frosted, but I have at least the illusion of health. And the raisins are satisfying. And it doesn't get soggy right away."

"I used to love how the Frosted Flakes turned the milk blue," A says.

"Yeah! When did that stop being cool and start being gross?"

"Probably the same time that I realized there was not, in fact, any fruit in Froot Loops."

"Or any honey in Honeycomb."

"Or any chocolate in Count Chocula."

"At least the Frosted Flakes had flakes in them."

"And frostedness."

"Yes. And frostedness."

Talking like this, I am forgetting that this isn't A. I am forgetting that we're not on a regular date.

"Moving on . . ." I say, taking us to the next aisle, and the one after.

We pick up a ridiculous amount of food. As we're nearing the checkout, I realize there's no way I am going to be getting home when my parents are expecting me.

"I should call my mom and tell her I'm eating at Rebecca's," I tell A.

"Tell her you're staying over," he says.

My phone is in my hand, but I don't know what to do with it. "Really?"

"Really."

Staying over. I think about the cabin. About what happened. I mean, what didn't happen. And how that felt.

"I'm not sure that's a good idea," I say.

"Trust me. I know what I'm doing."

I want to trust him. But he also doesn't know what it was like. And he might have the wrong idea of what a night might lead to.

"You know how I feel," I say.

"I do. But still, I want you to trust me. I'm not

going to hurt you. I will never hurt you."

Okay. I look into his eyes and I feel like he knows. There's a plan – there's definitely a plan. But it's not going to be a repeat of the cabin. He knows what he's doing, and I do trust that.

I call my mother and tell her I'm at Rebecca's and will be staying there. She's annoyed, but I can deal with that.

The harder part is calling Rebecca.

"I need you to cover for me," I say. "If my mom calls for any reason, tell her I'm over."

"Where are you?" she asks. "Are you okay?"

"I am. I promise I'll tell you about it later – I can't right now. But I'm okay. I might not even be out the whole night. I just want to make sure I'm covered."

"Are you sure?"

"Yes. Really. It's good."

"Okay. But I expect a full explanation this time. Not your usual evasion."

"I promise. I'll tell you everything."

She says to have a good time. I think it's remarkable that she's trusting me. But she is.

"You'll tell her you met a boy," A says once I've hung up.

"A boy I just met?"

"Yeah. A boy you've just met."

It's strange to think of that conversation. No longer a Mystery Man. Just a boy.

If only it were that easy.

I follow him in my car. This is the moment I could decide not to go. All I need to do is turn the steering wheel. All I need to do is return to the highway.

But I keep going.

His name is Alexander Lin and his parents are away for the weekend. A tells me both things at once.

"Alexander," I say. "That's easy enough to remember."

"Why?" he asks.

I thought it was obvious. "Because it begins with A."

He laughs, surprised. I guess it wasn't as obvious, from the inside.

The house is a very nice house. The kitchen is about twice the size of our kitchen, and the refrigerator, when we open it, is already pretty full. Alexander's parents did not leave him to starve.

"Why did we bother?" I ask. I can barely find space to put away what we bought.

"Because I didn't notice what was in here this morning. And I wanted to make sure we had exactly what we desired."

"Do you know how to cook?"

"Not really. You?"

This is going to be interesting. "Not really."

"I guess we'll figure it out. But first, there's something I want to show you."

"Okay."

He reaches for my hand, and I let him take it. We walk like this through the house – up the stairs, to what is clearly Alexander's bedroom.

It's amazing. First of all, there are sticky notes everywhere – yellow squares, pink squares, blue squares, green squares. And on each of them, there's a quote. *I don't believe in fairy tales, but I believe in you.* And *Let all the dreamers wake the nation.* And *Love me less, but love me for a long time.* I could spend hours reading his room. *In a field, I am the absence of field. – Mark Strand.* Most of the quotes are in one handwriting, but there's other handwriting, too. His friends. This is something he shares with his friends.

There are pictures of these friends, too, and the way they arrange themselves looks like the way my friends would arrange themselves. Not Justin. Never Justin, who didn't like having his picture taken. But Rebecca and Preston and the others. They would like it here. There's a lime-green couch to hang out on, and guitars to strum, and what looks like the full collection of

Calvin and Hobbes. I look at the records he has leaning against the record player. Bands I don't know but like the sound of. God Help the Girl. We Were Promised Jetpacks. Kings of Convenience.

I read more of the sticky notes. *We are all in the gutter, but some of us are looking at the stars.* I check out the books on his shelves. Most of them have sticky notes sticking out – pages to be collected, words to be remembered after they've been forgotten.

I like it. I like it all.

I turn to A, and know he likes it, too. If he could have a room, this would be it. How cool that he's found it. And how depressing that he'll have to leave it in a few hours.

But I'm not going to think about that. I'm going to think about now.

I see an almost-finished pad of sticky notes on Alexander's desk, and put it in my pocket, along with a pen.

"Time for dinner," A says.

He takes my hand again. We head back into the world – but not too far into it, not too far away from this.

I find some cookbooks. We choose, by and large, to ignore them.

"Improvise," A says. And I think, yes, that's what

we're doing. Improvising. Living by instincts. It's a big kitchen, but we make it feel like a small space. We fill it with music from Alexander's iPod and steam from the boiling pots and smells as different as basil picked from the stem and garlic sautéed against a flame. There's no plan here, just ingredients. I am sweating along and singing along and I am not stressed, because even if none of it ends up edible, it's still worth it just to be putting it together. I think about my parents, and how they've missed this sensation of working together, or putting your hands on the back of the person as he stands at the stove, or having one person start the sauce but the other person take it over without a word. We are a team of two. And since it's not a competition, we've already won.

In the end we have a kale salad, garlic bread, a huge pasta primavera, a quinoa and apricot salad, and a pan of lemon squares.

"Not bad," A says. And what I want to tell him is that now I understand why people want to share a life with someone else. I see what all the fuss is about. It's not about sex or being in a couple when you hang out with other couples. It's not for ego gratification or fear of loneliness. It's about this, whatever this is. And the only thing wrong with it right now is that I'm sharing it with someone who's bound to leave.

I don't say any of this. Because the last part makes all the rest of it harder to say.

"Should I set the table?" I ask instead. The Lins have a very nice dining room table, and a feast like this seems fit for a very nice dining room table.

A shakes his head. "No. I'm taking you to my favorite place, remember?"

He looks through the cupboards until he finds two trays. The food we've made barely manages to fit on them. Then A finds a bunch of candles and takes them along, too.

"Here," he says, handing me one of the trays. Then he leads me out the back door.

"Where are we going?" I ask. I don't even have my jacket. I hope we're not going far.

"Look up," he says.

At first, all I see is the tree. Then I look closer and see the tree house.

"Nice," I say, finding the ladder.

"There's a pulley system for the trays. I'll go up and drop it down."

These parents have thought of everything.

As I balance the trays, A heads up the ladder and sends a platform down. I'm not sure how balanced it's going to be, but I put one of the trays on, and A manages to pull it up without anything falling off. We repeat this for the second tray, and then it's my turn to go up the ladder.

It's like something I've read about in a book. It never occurred to me that kids could actually have tree houses in their backyards.

There's an open door at the top, and I climb right through. A has lit some of the candles, so the air flickers as I pull myself inside. I look around and see what's basically a log cabin stuck in the air. There isn't much furniture, but there's a guitar and some notebooks, a small bookshelf with an old encyclopedia on it. A has put the trays in the middle of the floor, since there isn't any table and there aren't any chairs.

"Pretty cool, isn't it?" A says.

"Yeah."

"It's all his. His parents don't come up here."

"I love it."

I take the plates, napkins, and silverware from one of the trays and set the table that isn't a table. When I'm done, A serves – some of everything for each of us. As we sit across from each other, we comment on the food – it's all turned out better than it has any reason to be. The sauce on the pasta primavera tastes like a spice I can't quite identify – I ask A what it is, and he doesn't remember. He thinks I might have put it in. I don't remember, either. It was all just part of the improvisation.

There's a carafe of water on one of the trays, and that's all we need. We could have wine. We could have vodka. We could have Cherry Cokes. It would all be the same. We're drunk on candlelight, intoxicated by air. The food is our music. The walls are our warmth.

As the first candles diminish, A lights more. There isn't brightness, but there's a glow. I've just taken my first bite of a lemon square, its tartness still on my tongue. I catch A watching me and assume I have some powdered sugar on my face. I move to wipe it off. He smiles, still looking.

"What?" I ask.

He leans over and kisses me.

"That," he says.

"Oh," I say. "That."

"Yes, that."

We hang there, waiting for the kiss to leave the room, to float off into the night.

I have no idea what I want.

No. Not true. I know exactly what I want. I'm just not sure if I should want it.

"Dessert," I say. "You need to try a lemon square."

He smiles. It's okay to let the kiss leave the room.

Already, I feel others knocking on the door.

I look at his lips. The powdered sugar on his lips.

I remind myself they're not really his lips.

I'm not sure I care.

When we're done, I gather up the dishes. I put everything on the trays, and then I push the trays aside. We've been sitting too far from each other. I want us so much closer.

I move right next to him. He puts his arm around me, and I take the pad of sticky notes out of my pocket, along with the pen. Without saying a word, I draw a heart on the top sticky note, then put it on Alexander's heart.

"There," I say to A.

He looks down at it. Then back up at me.

"I have to tell you something," he says.

For a moment, I think this will be the *I love you* that's even greater than the others. If he says it, I will respond.

But instead he says, "I have to tell you what's been going on."

Instead of leaning in to him, I move so I can see his eyes.

"What?" I ask. Irrationally, I wonder if he's met someone else.

"Do you remember Nathan Daldry? The boy I was at Steve's party?"

"Of course."

"I left him on the side of the road that night. And when he woke up – he knew something was wrong. He suspected something wasn't right. So he told a lot of people. And one of the people who found out – he calls himself Reverend Poole. But he's not Reverend Poole. He's someone in Reverend Poole's body."

"This is what you were talking about when you emailed and said you thought you weren't the only one."

A nods. "Yes. But that's not all of it. Whoever's inside Poole is like me, but not entirely like me. He says he can control it. He says there's a way to stay in a person's body."

I try to wrap my mind around what he's saying. "Who told you this? Did you email him? How do you know he's real?"

"I saw him. I met him. He used Nathan to set a trap, and he almost got me. He says we're the same, but we're not the same. I don't know how to explain it – I don't think he uses the same rules as I do. I don't think he cares about the people he inhabits. I don't think he respects what we are."

"But you believe him? When he says you can stay?"

"I think so. And I think there might be others, too. On the internet – I think I've found others. Or at least, other people who were inhabited, like Nathan or you. You at least know what happened. And Nathan knows now. But most of them never know. And if Poole's right, there may be others who've been taken over permanently. Someone like me could go into them, and then not leave."

379

"So you can stay?" I ask, not believing this is what he's telling me. Suddenly anything is possible. *We're* possible. "Are you saying you can stay?"

"Yes," he answers. "And no."

It can't be both. I don't want to hear it's both.

"Which one? What do you mean?"

"There might be a way to stay," he tells me. "But I can't. I'll never be able to stay."

"Why not?"

"Because I'd be killing them, Rhiannon. When you take over someone's life, they're gone forever."

No. He can't be saying this. He can't be saying it's possible and impossible at the same time.

I can't deal with it. I can't. I have to stand up. I can't be sitting on the floor in the middle of a tree house having this conversation with him.

Once I'm up, I start to boil over. "You can't do this!" I'm telling him. "You can't swoop in, bring me here, give me all this – and then say it can't work. That's cruel, A. Cruel."

"I know," he says. "That's why this is a first date. That's why this is the first time we've ever met."

Not fair. This is not pretend. This is life.

"How can you say that?" I ask. "How can you erase everything else?"

He stands up and comes over to me. Even though I'm

mad, even though I don't understand what he's doing, he wraps his arms around me. It's not what I want, and I try to tell him I don't want it. But then I feel the shelter of his closeness, and I want it, and I stop trying to pull away.

"He's a good guy," A whispers in my ear. "He might even be a great guy. And today's the day you first met. Today's your first date. He's going to remember being in the bookstore. He's going to remember the first time he saw you, and how he was drawn to you, not just because you're beautiful, but because he could see your strength. He could see how much you want to be a part of the world. He'll remember talking with you, how easy it was, how engaging. He'll remember not wanting it to end, and asking you if you wanted to do something else. He'll remember your asking him his favorite place, and he'll remember thinking about here, and wanting to show it to you. The grocery store, the stories in the aisles, the first time you saw his room – that will all be there, and I won't have to change a single thing. His pulse is my heartbeat. The pulse is the same. I know he will understand you. You have the same kind of heart."

No. This is not what I want. Can't he see what I want?

"But what about you?" I ask, my voice stained by my sadness. I can't keep it away from him.

"You'll find the things in him that you find in me," he answers. "Without the complications."

He says it like it's easy.

It's not easy.

"I can't just switch like that," I tell him.

His arms draw me closer. "I know. He'll have to prove it to you. Every day, he'll have to prove he's worthy of you. And if he doesn't, that's it. But I think he will."

A's giving up. Whether or not I want him to, he's giving up.

"Why are you doing this?" I ask.

"Because I have to go, Rhiannon. For real this time. I have to go far away. There are things I need to find out. And I can't keep stepping into your life. You need something more than that."

I know this makes sense. But I don't want to make sense. I don't want anything to make sense.

"So this is goodbye?" I ask him.

"It's goodbye to some things," he says. "And hello to others."

This is where I turn.

This is where I stop being held and decide to hold.

This is where I loosen myself from his arms, but only to unfold my own arms and welcome him there.

I am not saying yes, but I am agreeing that there's no point in me saying no.

I hold him with everything I have. I hold him with so

much that he will have to remember it. He will have to remember me, wherever he is.

"I love you," he says. "Like I've never loved anyone before."

"You always say that. But don't you realize it's the same for me? I've never loved anyone like this, either."

"But you will. You will again."

This is where it stops. This is where it begins.
Every moment. Every day.
This is where it stops. This is where it begins.

I haven't been looking at the clock, but now I look at the clock.
It's almost midnight.
Where it stops. Where it begins.
"I want to fall asleep next to you," he whispers to me.

This is my last wish.
I nod. I'm afraid to open my mouth. I am afraid I will not be able to say what he wants me to say.
We leave the trays in the tree house. It doesn't matter, if this is what he's going to remember anyway. Climbing down the ladder. Running back to the house. Heading to his room.
We will remember this together. All three of us.

383

I want to stop time. I know I cannot stop time.

Holding hands. Then, inside the room, stopping to take off our shoes. Nothing else, just shoes. I crawl into the bed. He turns off the lights.

Only the glow of the clock. He gets into the bed next to me, lying on his back. I curl into him. Touch his cheek. Turn his head.

Kiss him and kiss him and kiss him.

"I want you to remember that tomorrow," I say when we come up for air.

"I'll remember everything," he tells me.

"So will I," I promise.

One more kiss. One last kiss. Then I close my eyes. I steady my breathing. I wait.

If I could hold onto him, I would.

Lord, if I could hold onto him, I would.

I do not sleep. I wish I could sleep. But I cannot sleep.

Instead I lie there, eyes closed, safe in the dark.

I feel him reach over and touch my heart.

I hear him say goodbye.

I feel him close his eyes. I feel him fall.

open my eyes. I turn.

I look for the moment. I want to see the change.

But instead I find a beautiful someone, beautifully asleep. Left behind by another beautiful someone, now also asleep in some other house, in some other bed.

I want to wake him. I want to ask him if he's still there.

But I don't wake him, because I don't want Alexander to ask me why I'm crying.

It isn't until I'm turned back to the wall, until I've decided to will myself to sleep, that I feel the sticky note on my shirt.

The heart I gave him.

He's taken it, and given it back to me.

I open my eyes. There is sunlight.

"Good morning," Alexander says.

At some point in the night, I must have turned toward him. Because he's right there in front of me, also waking up.

"Good morning," I say.

He doesn't look confused. He doesn't look surprised. He understands why we're in his bed, fully clothed. He remembers the tree house. He remembers meeting me in the bookstore. It's unusual, for sure – it's not the kind of thing that happens every day. But it's possible. On a very lucky day, it's possible.

He looks so happy. And completely unafraid to show it.

"Why don't I make breakfast?" he says. "I seem to recall my parents left us with plenty of breakfast options."

"Breakfast would be good," I say, sitting up and stretching out.

"Okay," he replies. But he doesn't make any move to go. He just looks at me.

"What?" I ask.

"Nothing," he says, bashful. Then he corrects himself.

"No. Not nothing. The opposite of nothing. I'm just really glad you're here. And I'm looking forward to another day with you, if you'll do me the pleasure."

"Breakfast first," I say. "Then we can figure this out."

"Sounds good," he says, bouncing out of bed. "Help yourself to clothes, towels, shampoo, books, Post-its – whatever you need."

"Will do."

He teeters in the room for a moment. He looks so sweet.

"I love this, whatever it is," he says.

I can't help but smile back at him. "Yes," I say. "Whatever it is."

"No oatmeal, right?"

"Yup. No oatmeal."

He whistles as he heads downstairs. I listen until he's too far to hear.

His laptop sits on his desk, beckoning me.

I know what I should do. I know what A wants me to do.

Only, I'm stubborn now.

I like Alexander. But I want A.

I want to find A.

ACKNOWLEDGMENTS

Since I usually create a book as I'm writing it, without really knowing what will happen until it's happening, this book was particularly challenging to write, and I feel the need to acknowledge accordingly.

First, thank you to all the readers of *Every Day* who have shared their reactions with me. I think it's very safe to say that without your meaningful enthusiasm, the story would have ended there.

As always, I want to thank my friends, family, and fellow YA authors for their support. I am always tempted to attempt a full list to back up this acknowledgment, but live too much in fear that I'll inadvertently forget someone. So instead I will limit myself to the people who have actually shared a house, room, car ride, and/ or coffee shop with me as I've drafted this book: my parents, Libba Bray, Zachary Clark, Nathan Durfee, Nick Eliopulos, Andrew Harwell, Billy Merrell, Stephanie Perkins, Jennifer E. Smith, Nova Ren Suma, Chris Van Etten, and Justin Weinberger. Joel Pavelski has the distinction of having been with me in Montreal when I began the book and then, a year later, with me in Montreal when I neared finishing it. Thanks, too, to Rainbow Rowell, for the conversation that led to the title, and for conversations in general. And to Gayle Forman, for being my reference point in this particular literary endeavor of shifting perspectives while sticking to the same story. Also, for conversations in general.

This book also wouldn't exist without the accidental suggestion and very deliberate support of everyone at Random House Children's Books. Thank you especially to Nancy Hinkel (more about her in a sec), Stephen Brown, Julia Maguire, Mary McCue, Adrienne Waintraub, Lisa Nadel, Laura Antonacci, Barbara Marcus, and everyone (I mean, everyone) in the sales, marketing, publicity, production, manufacturing, and legal departments.

Thank you also to Bill Clegg and Chris Clemens, for guardian angelhood. And to Stella Paskins, Maggie Eckel, and everyone at Egmont UK; to Penny Hueston, Michael Heyward, Rebecca Starford, and everyone at Text Publishing; and to all the foreign-language publishers and translators who've supported *Every Day* in such an astonishingly global way.

As for Nancy . . . I'll linger here, your words in my margins, dear, and sing till dawn a song of you and me and what and why. The what being the book in your hands, and the why being the way that you care.

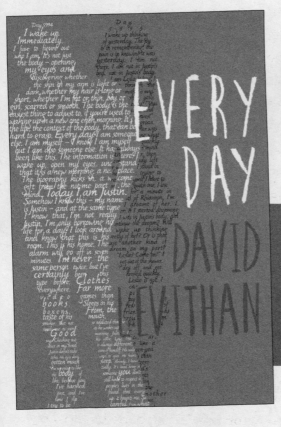

EVERY DAY I AM SOMEONE ELSE. I AM MYSELF — I KNOW I AM MYSELF — BUT I AM ALSO SOMEONE ELSE. IT HAS ALWAYS BEEN LIKE THIS

ELECTRIC MONKEY

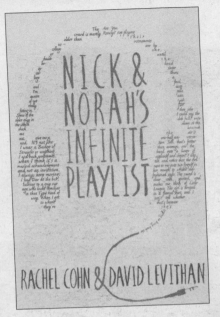

TWO STRANGERS SHARE AN EPIC FIRST DATE, WITH A KILLER SOUNDTRACK, OVER ONE VERY LONG NIGHT IN NEW YORK

ANY GREAT FRIENDSHIP CAN BE AS CONFUSING, TREACHEROUS, INSPIRING AND WONDERFUL AS ANY GREAT ROMANCE

TWO BOYS KISSING

DAVID LEVITHAN

co-author of *Will Grayson, Will Grayson* with John Green

JUST **ONE KISS** CAN SAVE THE WORLD

ELECTRIC MONKEY

LOVE AND I ONCE
HAD A GREAT
RELATIONSHIP,
BUT I FEAR WE'VE
BROKEN UP.
IT CHEATED ON ME

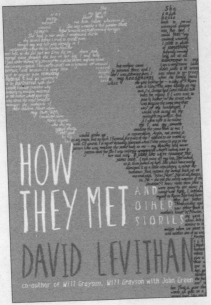

AN EXPLORATION
OF THAT WONDERFUL,
COMPLEX, SIMPLE,
ADDICTIVE, VOLATILE,
SCARY, GLORIOUS
THING CALLED LOVE